W. Maziere Brady

Clerical and Parochial Records of Cork, Cloyne, and Ross

SALZWASSER
VERLAG

W. Maziere Brady

Clerical and Parochial Records of Cork, Cloyne, and Ross

Reprint of the original, first published in 1863.

1st Edition 2022 | ISBN: 978-3-37500-625-9

Verlag (Publisher): Salzwasser Verlag GmbH, Zeilweg 44, 60439 Frankfurt, Deutschland
Vertretungsberechtigt (Authorized to represent): E. Roepke, Zeilweg 44, 60439 Frankfurt, Deutschland
Druck (Print): Books on Demand GmbH, In de Tarpen 42, 22848 Norderstedt, Deutschland

CLERICAL AND PAROCHIAL RECORDS

OF

CORK, CLOYNE, AND ROSS,

TAKEN FROM

DIOCESAN AND PARISH REGISTRIES, MSS. IN THE PRINCIPAL LIBRARIES AND PUBLIC OFFICES OF OXFORD, DUBLIN, AND LONDON, AND FROM PRIVATE OR FAMILY PAPERS.

BY

W. MAZIERE BRADY, D.D.

VOL. I.

DUBLIN:

1863.

TO THE

RIGHT REVEREND FATHER IN GOD,

WILLIAM FITZGERALD, D.D.,

LORD BISHOP OF KILLALOE, KILFENORA, CLONFERT, AND KILMACDUAGH.

My Lord,

The favour and condescension which I experienced from your Lordship while you so ably presided over the united diocese of Cork, Cloyne, and Ross,—the readiness with which you listened to my plans for publishing these records,—and the aid you afforded me by giving me access to the Visitation Books and other documents in the registries of Cork and Cloyne,—call for some acknowledgment on my part.

I therefore beg your Lordship to receive this dedication of a work which you have in some degree yourself encouraged, as a slight token of my gratitude for your kindness and admiration of the high qualities which distinguish you as a scholar, an author, and a divine.

But I am warned not further to express my sentiments or attempt your praise by the words employed by a learned man in reference to a famous writer and speaker of old. "Nemo illum satis ex merito laudare possit, aut de illo digne dicere, nisi qui illi in dicendo par sit aut similis." I am too conscious of my inferiority to become your panegyrist; and, therefore, I content myself with being

Your Lordship's

Humble and obliged Servant,

W. Maziere Brady, D.D.

A 2

LIST OF

SUBSCRIBERS.

HIS EXCELLENCY

GEORGE WILLIAM FREDERICK HOWARD,

EARL OF CARLISLE, K.G., F.R.S., M.R.I.A.

LORD LIEUTENANT OF IRELAND.

Abbott, Rev. E. S., A.M., Rector of St. Mary's, Dublin.
Adams, Rev. Benjamin William, A.M., Cloghran, Swords.
Aldworth, the Lady Letitia.
Aldworth, R. O., Esq., D.L., Newmarket House.
Ardfert, the Very Rev. J. G. Day, Dean of, Blennerville.
Armagh, the *late* Most Rev. Lord J. G. Beresford, Archbishop of, Lord Primate.
Armagh, the Most Rev. Marcus Gervais Beresford, Lord Archbishop of, Lord Primate.
Armagh, the Very Rev. Brabazon William Disney, B.D., Dean of.
Ashtown, the Right Hon. the Lord, Woodlawn, county Galway.
Atkinson, Alderman Richard, lately Lord Mayor of Dublin.

Baggs, Henry, Esq., Mallow.
Barry, Captain James, D.L., Ballyclough, Fermoy.
Battersby, Francis, Esq., J.P., Bobsville, Crossakiel.
Becher, Lady, Ballygiblin.

Blackburne, Right Hon. Francis, Lord Justice of Appeal, Merrion-square, Dublin.
Blacker, Rev. Beaver, M.R.I.A., Blackrock, Dublin.
Bond, Mrs. W. Shawe, London.
Borrowes, Rev. Sir Erasmus Dixon, Bart., Lauragh, Portarlington.
Bowen, Robert Cole, Esq., J.P., Bowenscourt.
Brady, Antonio, Esq., Maryland Point, Stratford, Essex.
Brady, Cheyne, Esq., M.R.I.A.
Brady, Edward, Esq., Philadelphia.
Brady, Francis William, Esq., Q.C.
Brady, John, Esq., M.D., M.P., 1, Warwick-terrace, Belgravia, London, S.W.
Brady, Miss Amelia.
Brady, Rev. John Westropp, Aghadoe, Killarney.
Brady, Right Hon. Maziere, Lord Chancellor of Ireland.
Brinkley, Richard Graves, Esq., J.P., Fortland House, Dromore West, Sligo.
Bullen, Rev. William Crofts, Hatfield, Broad Oak, Harlow, Essex.
Burke, Sir Bernard, LL.D., Ulster.
Butcher, Rev. Dr., Reg. Prof. Div., T.C.D.
Byam, Edward Samuel, Esq., 15, Victoria-place (South), Clifton.
Byam, Rev. Richard Burgh, Petersham, Richmond, Surrey.

Carson, Rev. Joseph, D.D., F.T.C.D., 18, Fitzwilliam-place, Dublin.
Cashel, Very Rev. John Cotter Mac Donnell, D.D., Dean of.
Cashel, Ven. Henry Cotton, D.C.L., Archdeacon of.
Carbery, Right Hon. Lord, Castlefreke.
Caulfield, Edward T., Commander, R.N., 20, Lansdowne-crescent, Bath.
Caulfield, Richard, Esq., M.A., F.S.A., Cork.
Chatterton, Hedges E., Esq., Q.C., LL.D.
Chetwode, Edward Wilmot, Esq., J.P., Woodbrook, Portarlington.
Clarendon, Right Hon. the Earl of, The Grove, Watford, Herts.
Clarina, Right Hon. Lord, Elm Park, Clarina.
Cliffe, Rev. Allen Robert, Mallow.
Cliffe, Antony, Esq., D.L., Bellevue, county Wexford.
Clogher, the Very Rev. Ogle W. Moore, A.M., Dean of.
Cloyne, the Very Rev. James Howie, A.M., Dean of.
Cloyne, the *late* Ven. W. Ryder, Archdeacon of.
Cloyne, the Ven. R. M. Evans, Archdeacon of.
Colborne, Hon. and Rev. Graham, Dittisham Rectory, Totnes, Devon.
Collis, Rev. Maurice A. Cooke, D.D., Queenstown.
Conner, Rev. Richard L., Innoshannon.
Connolly, Rev. John.
Corcor, James Richard, Esq., Cor Castle, Innishannon.
Cork, the Right Hon. the Earl of, Marston, Frome, Somersetshire.
Cork, the Ven. S. M. Kyle, Archdeacon of, V.G.
Cotter, Rev. G. E., Rockforest.
Crosthwaite, Rev. Charles, V.G. and Canon of Kildare.

Darell, the Rev. Sir Lionel, Bart., Fretherne Rectory, Stonehouse, Gloucestershire.
Darell, Lady.
Daunt, Rev. E. Synge Townsend, St. Stephens-by-Launcestown, Cornwall.
Daunt, T. Townsend, Esq., 11, Windsor-place, Plymouth.
Deasy, the Right Hon. Baron.
De Burgh, Henry, Esq., Belcamp, St. Doulough's.
Delacour, Rev. Robert William, Bandon.
Derry and Raphoe, the Right Rev. William Higgin, Lord Bishop of.
Devereux, Rev. Nicholas, D.D., Ballyrankin House, Ferns.
Devonshire, His Grace the Duke of, Devonshire House, Piccadilly, London.
Dickson, Rev. Richard, Vermont, Clarina.
Dickson, S. F., Esq., Clarina.
Dickson, Rev. W. R., Wickham, Newbury, Berks.
Dixon, Rev. R. V., EX-F.T.C.D., Rector of Clogherney, Omagh.
Domvile, Major Sir Charles William Compton, Bart., Santry House.
Downes, the Right Hon. Lord, Bert House, Athy.
Drewe, Rev. Pierce W., Youghal.
Dufferin, the Right Hon. the Lord, Dufferin Lodge, Highgate.
Dungannon, the *late* Viscount.
Dunscombe, Nicholas, Esq., J.P., King William's Town.
Dunscombe, Rev. N. Colthurst.
Durham, Mrs., Londown House, Ryde, Isle of Wight.

Echlin, Rev. J. R., Bronington Parsonage, Whitchurch, Salop.
Evans, Rev. Thomas E.
Eyre, Rev. Giles, Westport.

Fisher, Rev. W. A., Kilmoe.
Fitzgerald, the Hon. Mr. Baron, 50, Stephen's-green, East, Dublin.
Forrest, Rev. W. R., Liverpool.
Forsayeth, Thomas, Q.C., Recorder of Cork.
Freeman, the *late* Rev. R. Deane.
Fuller, Rev. Abraham Strich, A.M., 7, Fitzwilliam-place, Dublin.

Gabbett, Rev. Joseph, Kilmallock.
Gabbett, Rev. Robert John, Foynes.
Garstin, Rev. A., J.P., Bragganstown.
Garstin, John Ribton, Esq., A.M., M.R.I.A.
Garstin, William, Esq.
Gaynor, Captain, Killiney House.
Gibson, Rev. C. B., Cork.
Gore, Vice-Admiral John, 9, York-place, Clifton.
Grant, Rev. J. A., Litter.

Graves, Very Rev. Charles, Dean of the Chapel Royal, and President of the Royal Irish Academy.
Graves, Rev. Dr., Mitchelstown.
Greer, James, Jun., Esq., Omagh.

Haines, Charles, Esq., Mallow.
Hare, the Hon. Robert, Ballymore, Queenstown.
Hartstonge, Lorenzo Weld, Esq., 17, Molesworth-street, Dublin.
Hayman, Rev. Samuel, M.R.I.A., South Abbey, Youghal.
Henn, T. Rice, Esq., Q.C., Chairman of Quarter Sessions, county Carlow, J.P. for county Clare, 48, Upper Mount-street, Dublin.
Hoare, Edward, Esq., Glenanore, Castletownroche.
Hone, Nathaniel, Esq., J.P., St. Doulough's, county Dublin.
Hutchins, Emanuel, Esq., J.P., Ardnagashel, Bantry, county Cork.
Hyde, John, Esq., D.L., Cregg, Fermoy.

Inchiquin, the Right Hon. the Lord, Dromoland.

Keane, the Right Rev. Dr., Roman Catholic Bishop, Cloyne.
Kenny, Mrs., Clifton.
Ker, David S., Esq., D.L., M.P.
Kildare, the Marquess of, Carton, Maynooth.
Killaloe, the Right Rev. William Fitzgerald, Lord Bishop of.
Kilmore, the Right Rev. Hamilton Verschoyle, Lord Bishop of.
Kilmore, the Very Rev. Thomas Carson, Dean of, Danesfort, Cavan.
Kingston, Rev. John, Chaplain to H. M. the King of Hanover, and Rector of Cattistock, Dorchester.

Lansdowne, the Most Noble the Marquess of.
Leader, Nicholas P., Esq., M.P., Dromagh, county Cork.
Leahy, Francis R., Esq., J.P., Shanakiel House, Cork.
Lee, Rev. Alfred T., M.R.I.A., Ahoghill.
Le Fanu, Joseph Sheridan, Esq., Merrion-square, Dublin.
Le Fanu, William Richard, Esq., Fitzwilliam-square, Dublin.
Lefroy, Right Hon. Thomas, Lord Chief Justice of the Queen's Bench, 18, Leeson-street, Dublin.
Leinster, His Grace the Duke of.
Listowel, the Right Hon. the Earl of, Convamore.
Luby, Rev. Thomas, D.D., S.F.T.C.D.

Marmion, Rev. R. W.
Marsh, Francis, Esq., Springmount.
Massey, Sir Hugh Dillon, Bart.
Maunsell, Rev. W. F., Kildimo.
Meade, Rev. John, Ballintober.
Meade, Rev. Robert Henry.
Moylan, Alderman, late Lord Mayor of Dublin.

Naper, J. L. W., Esq., D.L., Loughcrew, county Meath.
Newell, W. H., Esq., LL.D.
Newenham, Rev. E. H., Coolmore, Carrigaline.
Newman, Mrs., Dromore.
Noble, Rev. Robert, Newmarket.
Norreys, Sir Denham, Bart., Mallow Castle.

O'Callaghan, Captain Charles G., D.L., Ballinahinch, county Clare.
O'Connell, Daniel, Esq., Flintfield, Millstreet.
O'Grady, Rev. Thomas, Magourney, Coachford.
O'Hea, the Right Rev. Dr., Roman Catholic Bishop, Ross.
Ontario, the Right Rev. J. Travers Lewis, Lord Bishop of, Kingston, Canada West.
Orpen, Richard John Theodore, Esq., Ardtully, Kenmare.
Orpin, Basil, Esq., Marston, Ballyduff, Lismore.
Oxford, the Right Rev. Samuel Wilberforce, Lord Bishop of, Cuddesden Palace, Oxon.

Peel, the Right Hon. Sir Robert, Bart., Chief Secretary for Ireland, &c., &c.
Perigal, Frederick, Esq., London.
Perrin, Rev. Louis, Blarney.
Phillipps, Sir Thomas, Bart., F.R.S., Middlehill, Broadway, Worcester.
Pigot, Right Hon. D. R., Lord Chief Baron, 52, Stephen's-green, East, Dublin.
Pilkington, Henry M., Esq., Q.C., 35, Gardiner's-place, Dublin.
Plunket, Right Hon. and Right Rev. Lord, Bishop of Tuam, &c.
Prior, Rev. John, Kirklington Rectory, Ripon, Yorkshire.

Radcliff, the *late* Judge, Q.C., V.G.
Reeves, Rev. Dr., M.R.I.A.
Ribton, Sir John S., Bart.
Robinson, Rev. J. L., Treasurer of Cloyne.
Roden, the Right Hon. the Earl of, Tollymore Park, Castlewellan.
Rogers, Rev. John Cecil.
Ross, the Ven. the Archdeacon of, Aghadown, Skibbereen.
Rowland, Mrs.
Ryder, the *late* Ven. W., Archdeacon of Cloyne.
Ryder, Miss, Ballinterry, Rathcormac.

Sandes, Rev. Samuel D., 1, Lansdowne-park, Cork.
Saunders, Rev. William Herbert.
Shirley, Evelyn Philip, Esq., M.P., Lough Fea, Carrickmacross.
Shortt, Rev. Francis, Whitegate, county Cork.
Spring, Rev. Edward.
Stawell, Rev. Francis, Kilbrack.
Stevenson, Rev. James, Brinny.

Stuart-de Decies, the Right Hon. the Lord, Dromana, Cappoquin.
St. Germans, the Right Hon. the Earl of, 36, Dover-street, London.

Talbot-de Malahide, the Right Hon. Lord.
Thompson, Chas. Ferguson, Esq., Hyde Lodge, Ardwick, Manchester.
Tierney, Rev. Matthew.
Todd, Rev. Dr., S.F.T.C.D., Ex-President of the Royal Irish Academy, &c., &c.
Tooker, Richard Beare, Esq., J.P., The Mardyke, Cork.
Tottenham, Henry Loftus, Esq., Blackrock, Dublin.
Townsend, Lieut. John, R.N., Lona, Weston-super-Mare.
Townsend. Rev. Aubrey, B.D., Lona, Weston-super-Mare.
Townsend, Rev. Maurice Fitzgerald, Thornbury, Gloucestershire.
Townsend, Rev. Somerset Lowry Corry, D.D., Louth Rectory.
Townsend, Rev. William C., Ardcotton, Ballysodare.
Traill, William, Esq., 3, Ely-place, Dublin.
Trinity College, the Provost of.
Triphook, Rev. John.
Vernon, Charles, Esq., 21, Royal York-crescent, Clifton, Bristol.
Vigors, Captain Philip Doyne, 38th Regiment.

Wall, Thomas, Esq., M.D., 41, South Mall, Cork, and Wallstown.
Webb, Rev. Francis.
Webster, Rev. George, Chancellor of Cork.
Wharton, James H., M.D., 27, Upper Merrion-street, Dublin.
Williamson, Benjamin, Esq., F.T.C.D.
Wood, Benjamin Shaw, Esq., J.P., Sidney-place, Cork.
Wright, Rev. Richard Henry.
Wrixon, Rev. Nicholas, Ballygiblin.

N.B.—The Names of additional Subscribers will appear in the next volume.

THE PREFACE.

THE Ecclesiastical Records of Ireland have recently, in some degree, attracted the notice of the learned. DR. REEVES, DR. TODD, MR. E. P. SHIRLEY, the late DEAN BUTLER, the REV. J. C. CROSTHWAITE, MR. R. CAULFIELD, and others, have severally published works illustrative of the history of the Church, and have rescued many interesting and valuable documents from oblivion and decay. The succession of all Bishops and Cathedral Dignitaries in Ireland from ancient to modern times has also been recorded in a permanent form by ARCHDEACON HENRY COTTON, in his "Fasti Ecclesiæ Hibernicæ."

But no attempt has yet been made (except a few meagre lists of Incumbents in MASON'S "Parochial Survey") to trace the Parochial Clergy of Ireland from the period of the Reformation to the present time, or to extract from her own records the history of the Church.

Sad havoc among the materials for such a work was occasioned by the disturbances of 1641 and 1688, and since then the ignorance and carelessness of their custodians caused the destruction or loss of many a Parish Register and Visitation Book, which the wars had spared. Nor is it easy always to search the Diocesan Registries. Inquirers, armed with the permission of the Bishop, may yet be baffled by surly officials, or disconcerted by the want of proper catalogues and indexes, or driven away by dust and dirt before the musty and ill-scented documents be fully examined; besides, for the most part, the Visitation Books afford little information, save the names of the clergy, and their absence or attendance in particular years; the Books of Titles are very defective, and the

Parish Registers are not, in general, of date more ancient than the latter part of the past century. The wills and marriage licences have, perhaps, been somewhat better attended to, for obvious reasons; and from them, as also from the Chapter Books of the Cathedrals, much valuable matter may be extracted. The Act-Books of the Episcopal Courts contain some items of intelligence respecting the clergy not of an agreeable nature, which may be gleaned by those who have patience to wade through a mass of rapidly-written lawyers' Latin, from frequent abbreviations always difficult, and sometimes impossible, to decipher.

More easy of access, though not easier to read, are the First Fruit records, or returns of spiritual promotions made by the Bishops to the Barons of the Exchequer, and now preserved in the Custom-house, Dublin, under the able care of Mr. HARDING. Of these, as well as of the Regal Visitation Books now in the libraries of Dublin University and of the Royal Irish Academy, an accurate description has been furnished by ARCHDEACON COTTON, who has likewise, in the preface to his "Fasti," given a useful account of the "Liber Munerum Hiberniæ," a book which contains, besides various other matters, a list of presentations made by the Crown to benefices in Ireland.

I now proceed to explain the plan which I have adopted in this work, which, it will be remembered, embraces only the clergy and parishes of Cork, Cloyne, and Ross.

With regard to the clergy;—I have given their succession to benefices, as far as it is now possible to trace them, with the dates of their admission or institution, specifying in every case the source from which the information has been derived. In very many parishes the succession of Incumbents appears to be complete for more than two centuries and a-half. The parentage, birth-place, college-matriculation, and university degree of the clergyman, have been stated in numerous instances, as well as his ordination and clerical appointments, his marriage, issue, and death. The published works and the charitable bequests of the clergy have been duly recorded, and in some cases brief genealogical accounts have been compiled. In order to show at a glance the clerical career of each clergyman, I have set down in one place, usually the last preferment which he held, all that I have collected concerning him from various sources; but as I had nothing except similarity of name and agreement of date to guide me in noting his preferments *in other dioceses*, I have been unable to secure absolute certainty in this respect. I must also warn the reader that I have purposely abstained from any effort after uniformity in the spelling of names, and have frequently written the name of the same person differently in the same page, just as my authorities gave it. I have not altered the Latinity and grammar of the ancient documents, nor have I suppressed a single fact therein recorded from any wish to conceal what might be judged discreditable to the Church.

With regard to the parishes;—I have extracted all the information I could concerning them from a variety of sources. Their ancient names, their value, their population, their unions, the state of their churches, the services celebrated, the particulars of glebe-houses and lands, the amount of rentcharge and composition for tithes—all these matters have been faithfully extracted from the proper authorities, both ancient and modern. I have transferred to my pages the whole of the valuable Visitation Books of 1591, of 1615, of 1634, of 1639, and of 1669. The Diocesan Returns, made in 1693, agreeably to Mr. Secretary Aldworth's letter from the Council, have been obtained, through Dr. Reeves, from Armagh Registry by the kind permission of His Grace the Lord Primate, and are now printed, those for Cork separately, those for Cloyne and Ross under their respective parishes. The whole of Bishop Dive Downes' Tour through the dioceses of Cork and Ross in 1699 and following years, has also been incorporated into this work, as well as the Parliamentary returns printed about 1807 and 1837. The accounts of the several parishes of the diocese in 1860 have been furnished partly by the clergy themselves, in answer to printed queries sent to every Incumbent, partly by other trusted correspondents, and in part has been the result of my own personal observation and inquiries. The amount of tithe-rentcharge may sometimes be a little *under* or *over* stated, by reason of the shifting value of the corn averages; but, on the whole, these statistics will be found sufficiently correct for all public purposes.

In a publication like this it is evident that no amount of care can exclude errors and omissions. I shall thankfully receive notices of both from any of my readers, and I shall print corrections and additions along with the concluding portion of this work.

It now becomes my pleasing task to offer my cordial thanks to those persons who have aided me in this laborious and expensive undertaking. I need not, of course, mention, what is now so well known, that the visiter to the Bodleian at Oxford, the Museum, State Paper Office, &c., in London, the Libraries of Trinity College, and of the Royal Irish Academy, in Dublin, will meet with civility and attention. I will merely say, that in my case I was assisted most materially, and was spared much time and labour, by the unexpected personal kindness which I met with in my researches. To the Rev. Dr. Todd, s.f.t.c.d., my thanks are especially due, for his help in consulting various manuscripts; as well as to Sir Thomas Phillipps, Baronet, f.r.s., of Middle-hill, Worcestershire, for the opportunity which he gave me of examining several MSS. relating to Ireland. Sir Bernard Burke, Ulster, afforded me access to the valuable records in his department, and obliged me with particular facilities. The Lords of the Treasury also gave me liberty to consult, free of charge, certain documents in the Dublin offices under their control.

I have to thank the present Bishop of Killaloe, William Fitzgerald, lately Lord Bishop of Cork, Cloyne, and Ross, for admission to the registries of the diocese, as also for liberty to make extracts from the valuable MSS. of Bishop Bennet. Without his aid and approval I should not have been able to compile these records.

The VENERABLE S. M. KYLE, V.G., ARCHDEACON of CORK, the VENERABLE ROBERT MAUNSELL EVANS, ARCHDEACON of CLOYNE, the VENERABLE ALEXANDER STUART, ARCHDEACON of Ross, and the REV. W. ROGERS, Registrar of Cloyne, have kindly, from time to time, sent me various items of information.

I am indebted to DR. GRAVES, of Brigowne, for the opportunity of making extracts from a copy of the Chapter Book of Cloyne, which was written by REV. JAMES HINGSTON, A.M., and by him left among the Parish Records of Brigowne. This copy of Cloyne Chapter Book was particularly serviceable, as it so happened that, from causes not necessary to specify, I could not obtain access to the original Chapter Books either of Cork, or Cloyne, or Ross.

I am also indebted to JOHN RIBTON GARSTIN, esq., A.M., M.R.I.A., for his assistance on several occasions during the progress of this work.

Mr. W. B. KELLY, Bookseller, of 8, Grafton-street, Dublin, very kindly placed at my disposal for examination the manuscript papers of the late JAMES FREDERICK FERGUSON, esq., of the Exchequer Record Office, Dublin, which contain most valuable information, chiefly relating to ecclesiastical affairs, such as advowsons, impropriations, and the property of monasteries, and other religious foundations in Ireland.

To my very numerous correspondents, whose names are not mentioned for obvious reasons, I am indebted for the courtesy and patience with which my genealogical inquiries have been, in most cases, entertained.

It would be unjust, however, not to offer my most grateful thanks to the following gentlemen: the REV. AUBREY TOWNSEND, B.D., of Weston-super-Mare; JOHN NICHOLAS CROFTS ATKINS DAVIS, F.R.C.S.I., M.R.C.S.L., Deputy Inspector-General of Army Hospitals, &c., of 20, Waterloo-road, Dublin; the REV. SAMUEL HAYMAN, of Ardnegihy, Cork; DENIS O'CALLAGHAN FISHER, esq., of Brunswick-street, Dublin; and RICHARD CAULFIELD, B.A., F.S.A., Corresp. Mem. Soc. Antiq., Normandy, &c., &c., of Cork. They have been ever ready to afford me the aid of their sympathy, counsel, and knowledge. They have contributed largely of their genealogical and antiquarian lore to these pages, and on every occasion have shown unselfishness and liberality in imparting the most valuable information.

NEWMARKET, KANTURK,
July 8, 1863.

TAXATIONS.

The following Taxations of the Dioceses of Cork, Cloyne, and Ross, are taken from the MS. T.C.D. E. 3. 14.

Extent' dignit' et Benefici' in dioc' Corke noviter taxat' virtute commiss' et per Arthur Hyde et Arthur Robbins et alios Ano 31° Reginæ Elisabethæ.

	£	s.	d.
Epatus Corkensis .	25	0	0
	blanke.		
Archdiac. ibm. .	7	1	8
Preb. de Lisleyclereg	3	0	0
Pr. de Killenullye .	4	0	0
Pr. de Kilbrottan .	1	13	4
Ra. de Rynouran .	4	0	0
„ Laghmonye .	4	0	0
„ Rinrone .	6	0	0
„ Kilgobban .	3	16	0
„ Templetryverye . .	4	0	0
„ Rath laugan .	3	16	0
„ Inyshona .	5	6	8
„ Knockevillye	4	0	0
Decanatus Corkensis	3	0	0
Precentor ibm. .	8	0	0
Cancellarius ibm. .	2	0	0
Thesaurarius ibm. .	1	0	0
Preb. de Dysertmore	3	0	0

	£	s.	d.
Preb. de Inskynye .	2	6	0
„ Kilneglory .	2	5	0
V. de Kinsale . .	3	0	0
„ Rinrone . .	3	0	0
„ Kynneaghe .	1	10	0
„ ffanlobbyshe .	1	10	0
„ Shandon . .	3	10	0
„ Athnowen .	1	10	0
„ Insula parva .	2	0	0
„ Ballebodan .	2	0	0
„ Canboy . .	0	10	0
„ Ryncurran .	4	0	0
Eccla. de Moylumery nebollan . .	2	0	0
Eccla. de Racony .	1	10	0
Ra. Stæ Trinitatis Civtis. Cork . .	1	16	8
Ecca. Sti. Michaelis .	1	0	0
Eccla. de Kilshenan et capla ejusdem .	0	10	0

Extent' dignit' et Benefic' in Dioc' Clonen' noviter taxat' virtute commiss' et per Arthur Robbins et Arthur Hyde ut antea, &c.

	£	s.	d.
Epatus Clonen . .	16	0	0
	blanke.		
Guardianus Vill et Collegii de Youghell . . .	100 marks sterling.		
Preb. de Glannore .	6	0	0
Ra. et Vic. de Brigowne . . .	12	0	0
Archdiac' Clonen' .	1	5	0
Precentor ibm. . .	1	4	0
Preb. de Ballyhowlye	3	6	8
„ Dounoghmore . . .	2	0	0

	£	s.	d.
V. de Clonmell .	1	0	0
„ Capla Robin .	1	0	0
„ Ballackloghye als. Laban .	0	10	0
„ Kilbryne .	1	0	0
„ Ballymartr .	1	5	0
„ Cahirultan .	0	6	8
„ Belahathye als. Ballaha .	0	13	4
„ Carrigtowill .	2	0	0
„ Templebodan als. Dromoyre	2	0	0
„ Kilcourseye .	0	10	0

Extent' dig' et Benefic' in Dioc' Rossens' noviter taxat' virtute commiss' et per Arthur Robbins et alios, ut antea.

	£	s.	d.
Epatus ibm.	19	0	0
	blanke.		
Decan' ibm.	3	2	0
Precentor ibm.	2	0	0
Cancellar. ibm.	2	0	0
Archdeac. ibm.	3	10	0
Thesaur. ibm.	0	6	8
Prebend. de Insula man	1	3	4
Cork dioc. Preb. de Dromdaleige	1	0	0
Preb. de Timolegge	4	0	0
Vicar de Lesley	6	0	0
„ Rosse	6	0	0
E. de Killoconenagh	6	13	4
„ Scrubbery als Templeomalis	5	3	4
„ Kilkerran	2	0	0
„ Insula man	1	3	4
„ Tullagh	2	0	0
„ Kilmalouda	3	0	0
Corke Eccl. de Crossenhare als. Ballimony	2	0	0
Eccl. de Kilmyne	1	5	0
Rect. de Tullagh	2	0	0
Recta. Templeomalis	2	0	0
Eccla. Kilnegrosse	1	6	0

Taxat' per Arthur Hyde et fulton Morrisone commiss. *Lew* (or *Hen*) Harrington, Will Connell, dat' primo Junii A° 26 Reginæ Elisabethæ.

	£	s.	d.
P. de Timloghie	4	0	0
Rector de Donaghmore	1	0	0
Vic' ibm.	1	0	0
V. de Templekynlane	3	0	0
„ Dysert	2	0	0
„ Killegarve	3	0	0
„ Ardee	2	0	0
„ Castrovente	1	10	0
„ Kilfauna	3	0	0
Unus Rector in Myrus	3	0	0
Vic. ibm.	6	6	8
R. de Creaghyhe	2	10	0
V. ibm.	2	10	0
V. de Tullaghe	2	0	0
Un. Rector in Kilterve	0	10	0
V. ibm.	1	0	0
V. de Aghadowne	6	0	0
„ Cleere	3	0	0
R. de Kylcowye	4	2	0
V. ibm.	4	0	0
R. de Kylkatheren	0	6	8
Vic. ibm.	0	6	8
V. de Kylcaskyn	1	0	0
Rec. de Glanbarrighane	6	0	0
Vic. ibm.	6	0	0

Extent' dignit' et Benefic' Dioc' Clonensis noviter taxat' per Arthur Hyde et Fultonem Morrissone virtute commiss' et in—retornat in anno° 33° Regni Reginæ Elisabethæ.

	£	s.	d.
Eccla. de Garriclone	4	0	0
„ Benycarana	2	0	0
V. de Kylmagherone	5	10	0
„ Bellegourne	1	10	0
R. de Nenshie	3	0	0
V. ibm.	1	10	0
V. de Aghadda	1	10	0
„ Corkbegg	2	0	0
„ Rostillane	1	10	0
V. Capella de Rathe	1	0	0

	£	s.	d.
Eccla de Casstro chorii	2	0	0
Capla de Insheneba-kye . . .	1	0	0
V. de Kylkridane .	1	10	0
Re de Titeskin .	1	6	8
V. ibm. . . .	0	13	4
R. de Aghecarreu .	3	0	0
V. ibm. . . .	1	10	0
Eccla. de Bellaghe .	3	0	0
„ Dongori .	1	0	0
Preb. de Cowill .	1	0	0
R. de Inishcullan .	1	0	0
Eccla. de Clennore .	5	5	0
V. de Rathgogan .	3	0	0
„ Ballaghan .	1	10	0
„ Ferskethe .	0	13	4
Preb. de Coullenye .	2	10	0
R. de Shandrome .	7	6	8
Vic. ibm. . .	3	13	4
V. de Kylbolane .	2	10	0
„ Tyreleshe .	2	0	0
R. de Ballyvorane .	1	0	0
Vic. ibm. . .	0	10	0
Eccla. de Kylmaclelyne . . .	0	13	4
V. de Dromdonye .	2	10	0
„ Castlemagner .	2	0	0
Preb. de Subulter .	0	10	0
V. de Liscarroll .	5	10	0
Preb. de Lackyn .	0	10	0
R. de Brouheny .	8	0	0
V. ibm. . . .	4	0	0
V. de Bregoghe .	2	0	0
R. de Kylcorkorane .	1	0	0
V. ibm. . . .	0	10	0
R. de Letter . .	3	6	8
V. ibm. . . .	3	6	8
R. de Dryshane .	5	6	8
V. ibm. . . .	5	6	8
V. de Clonfartye .	5	10	0

	£	s.	d.
V. de Rosskeyne .	1	10	0
„ Kylshome .	1	10	0
„ Grenenoughe .	0	13	4
„ Garreston .	1	0	0
„ Dounaghgihie	0	6	8
„ Glanhirkyn .	0	6	8
„ Matheha .	2	0	0
Preb. de Inniskarrye	2	10	0
V. de Agobolyghe .	3	0	0
R. de Aghinaghe .	6	0	0
V. ibm. . . .	6	0	0
V. de Clondrethe .	1	10	0
„ Ballevornie .	2	0	0
„ Kylcolmane .	2	0	0
R. de Kylnodonoghe	3	0	0
Decanatus Clonen. .	3	0	0
Precentor ibm. .	3	0	0
Cancellar. ibm. .	6	6	8
Thesaurar. ibm. .	3	0	0
R. de Kylgullane .	6	0	0
V. ejusdem . .	6	0	0
V. de Martelstowne .	6	0	0
„ Clondullan .	6	0	0
„ Carrighonan .	5	10	0
„ Castlelyons .	5	1	0
„ Walestowne .	6	0	0
„ Brigetowne .	—		
„ Castletowne .	6	0	0
„ Nohaurie .	5	10	0
„ Cariglehamlerye . .	2	10	0
V. de Rathcormack .	5	10	0
R. ejusdem. . .	5	10	0
V. Knockmoryne .	1	11	0
R. Maggely . .	2	0	0
V. ejusdem . .	2	0	0
Epatus Clonensis .	10	0	0
Quatuor Vicar Chorall ibm. . .	13	13	4

Extent' Sepal' functions' spuali' infra dioceses' Corkagens' taxat' p' p'fat' Arthur Hyde et Fulton Morrissone.

	£	s.	d.
Quatuor Vicar Chorall de Corke	16	0	0
Ecca. de Kylkone	1	0	0
Pr. de de Kylasbeg-millane	6	0	0
Eccla integra de Catherlagher	2	0	0
Rec. integra de Temple usky	3	0	0
R. insulæ parvæ	3	0	0
R. de Shandon	3	0	0
Stæ. Trintis de Cork	1	0	0
Ec. integra de Texaste	3	0	0
E. integra de Downe-dorrow	3	0	0
V. de Lighmonye	2	0	0
„ Claryn	4	0	0
„ Doughe	1	0	0
„ Disert sergys	2	0	0
„ Drynaghe	2	0	0
„ Kilmowe	5	10	0
„ Skull	6	6	8
V. de Kylcroghan	2	10	0
„ Durrus	1	6	8
„ Kylmocomoghe	2	0	0
R. de Catheraughe	2	0	0
V. ibm.	2	0	0
V. de Lisclearye	2	0	0
„ Rossebeg	0	6	8
„ Ballaforde	5	5	0
„ Polleplicke	1	10	0
„ Clontede	0	10	0
„ Kylbrogan	1	10	0
„ Knokville	2	10	0
„ Inshonan	2	10	0
„ Brounee	1	10	0
„ Kylnaran	1	0	0
„ Movid'	1	10	0
Un. Rect. in m'clonethe	1	0	0
V. ibm.	2	0	0
V. de Inshikylaghe	3	0	0
„ Kilmichell	2	0	0

STATE of CORK and ROSS DIOCESES in 1693.

The following account of the Dioceses of Cork and Ross is taken from the general returns made in 1693 by the several Diocesans, in compliance with Mr. Secretary Aldworth's letter from the Council. The original returns for Cork and Ross, occupying ten sheets oblong folio, written *facie* for the most part, are certified under the hand and seal of the Vicar-General, Rev. Walter Neale, and are endorsed "Status Diœces' Corcag' et Rossen' transmittebatr Honorabil' Dominis Capital' Justiciariis Hibniæ Anno Domini 1693." The transcript from which they are now printed was made from the originals in Armagh Registry, by Edward Rogers, Esq., under the guidance of Dr. Reeves, and with the permission of His Grace the LORD PRIMATE.

DIŒCES CORCAG.

Beneficia.	Incumbentes.	Patroni.	Eccliarum Status.
Ecclia Cathlis Sanct. Finbar Corcagien.	Dns. Erdus Epus	Dns. Rex	Ecclia bene reparata.
Decanat' ad quem spect'. Eccliæ de Templebroody Ecclia de Culline Ecclia de Templemartin, ex antiquo unitæ	Arthr. Pomeroy S.T. Dr.	Dnus. Rex	Nulla ecclia. Nulla ecclia. Ecclia in ruina lapsa.
Rector integr. de Carrigline	Idem Dr. Pomeroy	Dns. Rex	Spect. ad Colleg. de Youghall. Ecclia bene reparata.
Precentor ad quem spectant eccliæ (vizt.) Ecclia de Carrickippane Rector de Corballis Ecclia de Carrogrohane Una rect. de Kinoigh ex antiquo unitæ	Gualt. Neale S.T. Dr.	Dns. Epus	Nulla ecclia. Nulla ecclia. Ecclia de Carrigrohan bene repar & cura inservitr. Ecclia de Kinoigh repar. Vicaria indotata & cura inservitr.

DIŒCES CORCAG—*continued.*

Beneficia.	Incumbentes.	Patroni.	Ecclarum Status.
Rector St. Catherine, p'tic' Shandon	Idem Dr. Neale	Comes. Killdaren & Com. Barymore altern. patron	Nulla ecclia, est tantum particula quædam in parochia Shandon.
Rect. & Vicar de Shandon			Ecclia de Shandon a papist' destructa nunc reædificata.
Una Rect. de Athnowen		Dnus. Epus	Nulla ecclia.
Vicar ibm.			Nulla ecclia.
Cancellariat ad quem spectat. Ecclia St. Bridget ex antiquo unit	Petr. Hewyitt	Dnus. Epus	Ecclia in ruina lapsa.
Rector Ringroan	Mr. Pr. Hewytt	Suffragani & Burgenses de Kinsale	Ecclia bene repar ubi cura inservitr.
Vicar ibm.		Dnus. Epus	
Rector de Garrivoe		Dnus. Baro de Kinsale	Nulla ecclia.
Thesaurar ad quem spectant Ecclie (vizt.)			
Rector de Maclonigh			Nulla ecclia.
P'ticula Cloghane als. Kildorrery			Nulla ecclia partic. Ballinadee.

Ecclia de Ballinadee " Rathdowlan " Kilgoban	Mr. Jonathan Falkner	Dus, Epus	Ecclia de Ballinadee bene rep. cura ibm. inservitr. Nulla ecclia. Rathdowlan, Kilgoban } partic. Ballindee.
Archdiacon ad quem spectant eccliæ sequentes (vizt.) Ecclia St. Peter Corke Civitat Ecclia de Killmonoge " Dunisque " Noaffoile " Dunbollug	Dns. Epus tenet Archidiaconat in comend.	Dnus. Epus	St. Peter bene repar. ubi cura inservitr. Ecclia ædificand. Nulla ecclia.
Quatuor Vicar Choral ad quos spectant ex antiquo unitæ Ecclia beatæ Mariæ de Narde Rect. de Killowny Rect. una de Kinoigh Rect. de Fanlobish Una Rect. de Desertserges Rect. de Drinagh Vicar de Corballis	Mr. Alexander Ogilby Mr. Valen. French	Ambigitur utrum Epus, Decanus, vel Dignitarii respective sunt patroni	Rect. de Kinoigh vel Vicarii indotat ubi cura inservitr. Vicar indotat, ecclia reparata & cura inservitr.

DIŒCES CORCAG—*continued.*

Beneficia.	Incumbentes.	Patroni.	Eccliarum Status.
Ecclia de Marmullane spect. ad Chorum			
Vicar de Drinagh	Mr. Solomon Foley	Dns. Epus	
Prebend de Killnaglory		Dns. Epus	Ecclia nuper in ruinis.
Prebend de Killbrogan	Danl. Lord	Dns. Epus	Ecclia reparat & cura inservitr.
Una Rect. de Aglish spect'. ad Pr'-bend Killbrogan		Dns. Epus	
Rect. de Killbrogan		Dns. Epus	
Vicar ibm.		Dns. Epus	
„ Desartserges		Dns. Epus	Ecclia reparat & cura inservitr.
Rect. Killcony als. Killowen		Dns. Baro de Kinsale	
Rect. & Vicar Murragh		Dns. Epus	Ecclia reparat & cura inservitr.
„ integra de Templetrine.	Edw. Synge	Dns. Rex	Petr. Hewytt Cl. curat & cura ibm. inservitr.
Rect. de Rathclaran		Dns. Epus	Vicar indotat ubi cura inservitr.
Prebend Trinit. Christ Church		Dns. Epus	Ecclia repar ubi cura inservitr.
Rect. ibm.		Dns. Rex	Sitr.
Vicar ibm.		Dns, Epus	Sitr.

Prb'd. de Killaspugmullane ad quem spect. una rect. Cannaway	Chr. Sheares	Dns. Epus	
Rect. integra de Ardnegihy		Dns. Epus	Ecclia in ruina lapsa.
Rect. & Vicar de Ringcurrane	Thos. Meade	Dns. Epus	Ecclia in ruina lapsa.
Rect. integra de Taxax		Dns. Rex	Sitr.
" " Dundorrow		Dns. Rex	Ecclia bene repar. in qua & in Ballymartell cura ceteror' inservitr.
" " Ballymartell		Dns. Rex	Ecclia bene repar.& cura inservitr.
Prebend de Inskenny	Johes. Tom	Dns. Epus	Ecclia in ruina lapsa.
Vicar de Kinsale		Dns. Epus	Ecclia repar. & cura inservitr.
Rect. de Scull	Wm. Hull	Dns. Rex	Spect. ad Colleg. de Youghall.
" Killmoe		Dns. Rex	Spect. ad Colleg. de Youghall.
Vicar de Scull	Gual. Bruice	Dns. Epus	Curæ ibm. inserviuntr.
" Killmoe		Dns. Epus	
Vicar de Ballymodan	Rich. Goodman	Dns. Epus	Ecclia bene repar.& cura inservitr.
" Rathclaren		Dns. Epus	Cura inservitr.
Rect. & Vicar de Killcully		Dns. Epus	Nulla ecclia.
Una Rect. de Cannaway	Johes. Harrison	Dns. Epus	Ecclia in ruina lapsa.
Vicar ibm.		Dns. Epus	Cura inservitr.

DIŒCES CORCAG—*continued.*

Beneficia.	Incumbentes.	Patroni.	Ecclïarum Status.
Prebd. Desertmore	Archiepiscopus Dublin	Dns. Epus	Nulla ecclia.
„ Cahirlag	Jaspar Cox	Dns. Epus	Nulla ecclia.
Prebd. de Shanbally als. St. Michael	Johes. Bailey	Dns. Epus	
Rect. integr. de Killcoan		Dns. Epus	
„ „ Templeusq		Dns. Epus	
„ „ Ballydoloughy als. Killroan			
Rect. & Vicar de insula parva		Dns. Epus	Ecclia bene reparat & cura p. nominat ibm. inserviuntr.
Rect. integ. de Caheragh	Johes. Patrickson	Dns. Epus	
Vicar de Fanlobish	Johes. Fortune	Dns. Epus	Ecclia bene rep. & cura inservitr.
Vicar de Kinoigh	Andrew Symes	Dns. Epus	Eccl. bene rep. & cura inservitr.
Rect. de Crosshenhare als. Ballymony		Dns. Epus	Eccl. bene rep. & cura inservitr.
Rect. integ. de Loighmony	Francis Moore	Dns. Rex	Ecclia in ruina lapsa.
„ Templemichael de Daugh		Dns. Epus	Sitr.
Rect. de Ineshonane		Dns. Rex.	Eccl. bene repar & cura inservitr.
Vicar de Ineshonane	Johes. Moore	Dns. Epus	
„ Ballyfiard		Dns. Epus	Ecclia in ruina lapsa.
Prebd. de Killbrittaine		Dns. Epus	Sitr.

Œconom Corcagien	Dr. Gual Neale		
Pr'bd. de Drumdaloige	Corn. Hignett	Dns. Epus	Eccl. bene rep. & cura inservitr.
Una Rect. & Vicar de Killmihill		Dns. Epus	Ecclia in ruina lapsa.
„ „ Inshigulagh		Dns. Epus	Ecclia in ruina lapsa.
Prebend de Lisleary	Rol. Davies	Dns. Epus	
Vicar ibm.		Dns. Epus	Ecclia in ruina lapsa.
Rect. integ. St. Johes Jerusalem spectat ad Chorum			Ecclia in ruina lapsa.
Vicar de Durrus	Thos. Holmes	Dns. Epus	Ecclia in ruina lapsa.
„ Killcroghane		Dns. Epus	Sitr.
„ Killmaccomoge		Dns. Epus	Sitr.
Vicar de Aglish	Zach. Braly	Dns. Epus	Ecclia in ruina lapsa.
Rect. „ Moviddy		Dns. Epus	Eccl. bene rep. & cura de Aglish & Killbonane ibm. inservtr.
Vicar ibm.		Dns. Epus	
Vicar de Killbonane		Dns. Epus	Ecclia in ruina lapsa.
Rect. integ. Rathcony	Val. French	Dns. Epus	Ecclia bene rep. & cura inservitr.
Rect. impropr. Macloneigh	Richd. Browne	Dns. Epus	Nulla ecclia.
Vicar ibm.			
Prebend de Killanully	Jos. Warren	Dns. Epus	Eccl. in ruina lapsa sed cura inservitr.
Rect. integra Knockavilly		Dns. Epus	Ecclia in ruina lapsa.
Vicar de Brinny		Dns. Epus	Ecclia bene repar & cura de Knockavilly ibm. inservtr.

DIŒCES CORCAG—*continued.*

Impropriaciones Laicæ in Dioces Corkag.	Impropriatores.	Eccliarum Status.
Rector de Durrus " Killmurry Rect. improp. de Killmihill Rect. de Inshigulagh Rect. impropr. Ballymodane " Killmonoge	Comes Corke	Vicariæ indotat Killmurry ubi Zach. Braly clk. curat.
Ecclia de Ballinabuy Killpatricke juxta Tracton	Fran. Roberts, Arger. sub vice comite Shannon	Null' Vicar' indot. Alex. Ogilby curat.
Rect. de Ballifiard Ecclia de Polliplicke " Kinure " Clonteade	Achil Daunt sub vicomite Shannon	Vicar' est indotata. Nullæ Vicar' indotatæ Alex. Ogilby curat.
Rect. de Templebroody " Brinny Una Rect. de Athnowen	Olim Hugo Spencer papist nunc ut fertur Thos. Brown, Gener. firm' a Dno. Rege	Vicar indotatæ.

Rect. de Killbonane	Johes. Bailey Alderman firm' a Dno. Rege	Vicaria indotat.
Rect. de Killmony	Mr. Archdeacon sub vice comite Shannon	Nulla Vicar est indotata.
Rect. de Killcroghane „ Killmacomoge }	Chas. Delaune	Vicar indotat.
Rect. de Barnahealy	Mr. Muschamp sub vice comite Shannon	Nulla Vicar indotat Alex. Ogilby curat.
Rect. de Kinsale	Mr. Stawell & Mr. Tom	Vicar indotat.
Una Rect. de Aglish	Hawes Crosse	Vicar indotat.
Particulæ quædam hinc inde prope civitatem Corcag' sparsæ dictæ St. Johannis de Jerusalem choro nuper annexæ per litteras patentes Dni. Regis.		Libri in Archivis Curiæ Consistorial Corcag: remanentes p'sertim quoad valor' patron' & eccliarum status paulum discrepant. RICHD. HAMPTON, Depy. Regr.

DIŒCES ROSSEN.

Beneficia.	Incumbentes.	Patroni.	Eccliarum Status.
Ecclia Cathlis St. Faughnan Rossen	Dnus. Erdus Epus	Dnus. Rex	Ecclia bene reparata.
Decanat ad quem spectat Rector de Desart	Mr. Rol. Davies	Dnus. Rex	
Rect. integra de Killnagrosse		Dnus. Epus	Ecclia ben repar. & cura inservitr.
Rect. & Vic. de Templomalis		Dnus. Epus	Rect. de Killnagross & Rect. & Vicar de Templomalis ut fertr unit sunt Decanatui p. hac vice.
Pr'centoriat	Mr. Johes. Patrick-son	Dnus. Epus	
Vicar de Killmacabea		Dnus. Epus	Ecclia in ruina lapsa.
„ Killfaughnabeg		Dnus. Epus	Sitr.
„ Clanbaraghane alias Castlehaven		Dnus. Epus	Cura inservitr.
Cancellar	Gual. Neale, S.T. Dr.	Dnus. Epus	Ecclia in ruina lapsa.
Thesaurariat	Mr. Wm. Hull		
Vicar Killkoranemore		Dnus. Epus	
„ Killgaruffe		Dns. Epus	Curæ inserv. in Clonekilty.
„ Rathbarry		Dnus. Epus	

Archidiaconat ad quem spectant Ecclisæ sequentes (vizt.)		Dnus. Rex p. promotione Dr. Wm. Fitzgerald pro hac vice patronus sed Epus originatr.	
Rector de Killmacabea			Vicar indotat.
„ Killfaughnabeg			Similiter.
„ Aghadowne			Siml.
„ Killcaskane			Siml.
„ Killcoa			Siml.
Prebend de Tymoleague	Mr. Seps. Dunsterville	Dnus. Epus	Ecclia bene reparata
Vicar ibm.		Dns. Epus	Ecclia bene reparata and cura ibm. inservitr.
Vicar de Lislea		Dnus. Epus	
Dnæ Rector de Creagh alias Skubbereen	Mr. Wm. Nellson	Dns. Epus	Vicar indotat.
Rector de Tullagh		Dns. Epus	
Vicar de Creagh als Skubbereene	Mr. Ludovic Trix	Dnus. Epus	Cura inservtr.
„ Tullagh		Dns. Epus	Cura inservtr.
Prebend sive Rect. non curat Donaghmore	Mr. Benj. Bousfield	Dns. Epus	
Vicar ibm.		Dns. Epus	
Rect. and Vic. de Killsillagh		Dns. Epus	Nulla ecclia.
Vicar de Aghadowne		Dns. Epus	Cura inservitr.
„ Killcoa		Dns. Epus	Similr.
„ Cleere		Dns. Epus	Similr.

DIŒCES ROSSEN—*continued.*

Beneficia.	Incumbentes.	Patroni.	Eccliarum Status.
Prebd. and Vicar de Insula		Dns. Epus	
Vicar de Desart	Mr. John Hunger-ford	Dns. Epus	Cura inservitr.
„ Ardfields		Dns. Epus	
„ Castrumventry		Dns. Epus	
Prebend Templebryen	Mr. Johes. Tom	Dns. Epus	Ecclia in ruina lapsa.
Vicar Templequinlane			Vicar' de Templequinlane tenuitate prbend de Templebryan unit p' hac vice prbend.
Vicar de Killkaskine		Dns. Epus	Nulla ecclia: cura inservitr in Bantry.
„ Killconenagh	Mr. Thos. Holmes	Dns. Epus	Simil'tr.
Rect. and Vicar de Killketerne		Dns. Epus	Simil'tr.
„ „ Killmanagh		Dns. Epus	Simil'tr.
Rector Clenbaraghane	Arthur Pomeroy S.T. Dr.	Dna. Epus	Vicar indotat.
Una Rect. de Myros.		Dns. Epus	Spectant ad Colleg' de Youghall.
Alter Rect. de Myros.	Mr. Johes. Gibson	Dns. Epus	Cura inservitr.
Vicar ibm.			
Rector Killmine	Mr. Soln. Foley	Dns. Epus	Ecclia repar. & cura inservitr.
Rector de Killmalooda	Mr. Thos. Meade	Comes de Barrymore	Ecclia in ruina lapsa.
Œconomia Ross	Mr. Zach. Braly		

DIŒCES ROSSEN—*continued.*

Impropriaciones Laicæ in Dioces Rossen.	Impropriatores.	Patroni.	Eccliarum Status.
Rector de Lislee Rect. Abbystrewry Rect. Abbeymane	Mr. Robt. Gookin		Vicar indotat Vicar indotat Vicar indotat } Curæ inserviuntr.
Rect. impropr. Aghadowne " Killcoo " Cloore " Killaconenagh	Comitissa de Castlehaven		Vicariæ indot. & curiæ inserviuntr.
Rect. impropr. Killkeranemore " Killgaruffe " Ardfielde " Rathhbarry " Castrumventry	Wm. Moore, Miles, olim.		Vicar indot. & curiæ inserviuntr.
Rect. improp. de Templequinlane	Comes Corke		Vicar indotat & cura inservitr.

Libri in Archivis Curiæ Consistorial Rossiensis remanentes p'sertim quoad val patron & Eccliarum Status paulum discrepant.

RICH. HAMPTON, Dep. Regr.

Gaulterus (L.S.) Neale, Vic. Gen. Dioces Corcag et Rossen.

BISHOP PALLISER'S REMARKS ON CLOYNE.

BISHOP PALLISER'S REMARKS on the STATE of the DIOCESE of CLOYNE, A.D. 1694, with his Plan for Unions of Parishes.*

["This is the first sheet of the Return, and is entirely in Bishop Palliser's handwriting."—W. R.]

The Right Honourable the Lords Justices of this kingdom having been graciously pleased to allow me to take mine own time in returning to their Lordships the present state of the diocese of Cloyn, I have been the more diligent in drawing a full representation of the same, and with much ado at length, by gentle means (and I was unwilling to use any other), have generally prevailed on the clergy (a very few excepted), to give in the present value of their several livings. I suspect I may be guilty of mistakes in some particulars, being a perfect stranger in this diocese (country), till about nine months ago; but I have endeavoured to be exact, and believe the main substance of the following account to be very true, and for clearing some particulars which may seem liable to exception, I humbly desire these few things may be noted.

1. That many livings of this diocese being very mean, there's a necessity of conferring four or five on one person, to afford him but a very ordinary subsistence. But if the numerous impropriations in this diocese were restored to the Church, this inconvenience might be in a great measure remedied.

2. That the present poverty of the people is the great reason why divers churches in this diocese are not rebuilt and repaired; but if it please God to continue peace in this country, I doubt not but in a few years most of the churches that are fallen to ruin, necessary to be rebuilt and repaired, will be made fit for divine service.

3. That the clergy in giving in the present value of their livings have made deductions for what they yearly pay out of them, which is a considerable sum. And the present value of many livings amounts not near to what it was before the late war, much land still lying waste, several parts of this diocese being much infested by rapparees.

4. That there has been a great neglect in this diocese of making unions of contiguous livings before the expiration of the Act of Parliament in King Charles II.'s time for that effect. But I have at the end of this paper drawn a scheme of convenient unions, which it may be fit to consider when it shall please their gracious Majesties, their Parliament, to take this matter into consideration. It

* This paper, as also "The State of the Diocese of Cloyne," incorporated into the body of this work, was procured through the kindness of Dr Reeves, and was copied from the original in Armagh Registry, by Edward Rogers, esq.

would be a great service done to this church to redress that ecclesiastical grievance, that one clergyman should possess several benefices with cure in the same diocese, which are so far from being contiguous that they are sometimes at ten or twenty miles distant.

5. That the Bishop of Cloyn, in February last, received a letter from Secretary Aldworth, by order of the Lords Justices, that he should give no disturbance to Mr. William Jephson, Dean of Lismore, as to those livings he holds in this diocese, upon occasion of his absence, now near a whole year in England. Unto which order the Bishop hath paid that dutiful respect which became him, but humbly tenders the truth of the case to their Lordships' consideration, that the said William Jephson has several livings in other dioceses to the value of near £300 a-year, and yet resides upon none of them; and that above three years ago he obtained a patent for some considerable benefices with cure in this diocese, named Ardagh and Clonpriest, and yet to this day never came to the Bishop to take institution and induction upon his patent, so that these livings are still in law void; and it is in the power of the Chief Governors to give them unto them that will personally serve the cure, and not run away with the entire profit of these livings, and do nothing for it, as Mr. William Jephson, for above these three years, has done. Moreover, he is as yet no actual Chaplain to any regiment, but (as the Bishop is well informed), only designed to be a Chaplain to Colonel Colthorpe's regiment, which is to be raised here in Ireland. It is certainly no slender abuse in the church, for a man who never did nor ever is likely to do any service to the church to run away with the profit of two considerable livings upon a bare presentation which gives no legal title; and when he is required by the Bishop to come out of England (which he is not so sick but he might very easily do) and be admitted into those livings, pursuant to his patent, to prevent the Bishop's sequestration, instead of complying with the Bishop's most just order, he gets an injunction from the Government, upon a false suggestion, to tie up the Bishop's hands, that he cannot handle such a man as he deserves.

6. That the two livings of Ardagh and Clonpriest (which Dean William Jephson has had a patent for above these three years, yet hitherto has neglected to be inducted, and instituted into them) ought, in all reason, to be otherwise disposed of, Ardagh to go along with the curacy of Youghall, and Clonpriest with the deanery of Cloyne, as will appear by the following state of them both.

The State of the Rectory of Ardagh, yearly value about 24 pounds, now legally void in the King's presentation.

The rectory of Ardagh was formerly a member of the Collegiate Church of Youghall, being contiguous thereunto, until, upon the dissolution of that college, it was divided from it, with the rest of the parishes thereunto belonging; and though all the parishes thereby came to be in the King's presentation, yet it was still thought fit that the parish of Ardagh should be given to the Curate of Youghall (whose cure is very great, much the greatest in the diocese, and his maintenance otherwise inconsiderable), and by him it was constantly enjoy'd in a continued succession of Curates from this said dissolution unto the year 1672, or thereabouts, when falling void upon the cession of the then Incumbent, and the succeeding Curate of Youghall being negligent in taking out the King's presentation to it, Mr. William Fitzgerald, then Dean of Cloyn, passed his Majesty's patent for it; thereupon was instituted, inducted into it, continued ever since in the possession thereof, until he was promoted to the bishoprick of Clonfert, by which promotion it became vacant again, and so continues to this very day, Mr. William Jephson, Dean of Lismore, having only a bare presentation thereunto. The inhabitants of the parish of Ardagh all go to divine service in the Church of Youghall, so that nothing in all the diocese of Cloyn is so proper to be perpetually united to the cure of Youghall, if a vicarage were endowed there, nor in the interim so convenient to be given to the Curate of Youghall, for his maintenance in that great cure; all the maintenance he at present has for serving that cure being given him by the Bishop out of the revenue of the bishoprick, which is itself so small that 'tis scarce able to support a Bishop according to the dignity of his place and station. Upon these considerations, in all humility offer'd to the Government, the Bishop of Cloyn earnestly begs that the Lords Justices would be pleased to grant this rectory of Ardagh, now legally void, and in their disposal, to the present Curate of Youghall, Mr. Mathew Jones, for his better maintenance in discharging much the greatest cure in the whole diocese of Cloyn, especially the Curates of Youghall having ever enjoyed the said rectory of Ardagh by the favour of the Government, until of late years it was wrested from them.

THE STATE of the RECTORY of CLONPRIEST, usurped also by Dean William Jephson, but legally void in the King's presentation.

The rectory of Clonpriest, in the diocese of Cloyn, no slender cure, worth about 70 pounds, yearly, has, for above three score years, gone along with the deanery of Cloyn (the deanery is a very inconsiderable thing without it); but falling void by the promotion of the late Dean of Cloyn, Mr. William Fitzgerald, to the bishoprick of Clonfert, Mr. William Jephson by subtile artifice pass'd a patent for it, wrested it from the deanery, when his Majesty really intended it for the present Dean of Cloyn, Mr. Henry Scardeville, Chaplain to Duke Schomberg; but Mr. William Jephson having only a bare presentation to the rectory of Clonpriest, and hitherto neglecting to be by the Bishop instituted and inducted thereunto, it is still void in law, and ought, in great reason, by the gracious pleasure of the Government to be reannexed to the deanery of Cloyn (to which it long appertained), to render it somewhat considerable.

A LIST of UNIONS to be made in the DIOCESE of CLOYN.

1. Rectoria et Vicaria de Shandrom.
Vicaria de Clancore.
Præbenda de Cooline.
Vicaria de Rathgogane.
Vicaria de Killbollane.
Sitque ecclesia apud Charlevile in parrochia de Rathgogane huic unioni parochialis.

2. Rectoria integra de Ballinourane, als. Agliss Dradrinagh.
Rectoria de Brewhenny, als. Ballintemple.
Præbenda de Ballyhay.
Præbenda de Lackeen.
Particula de Carrigloher.
Vicaria de Ardskea.
Sitque ecclia apud Burton in p'ochia de Ballintemple huic unioni p'alis.

3. Vicaria de Kilbrin, als. Rogeri Calvi.
Vicaria de Castlemagner.
Vicaria de Bally Clogh.
Præbenda de Subolter.
Præbenda de Kilmaclenyn.
Vicaria de Roskeen.
Sitque ecclia de Castlemagner p'alis.

4. Rectoria et Vicaria de Clonfert als. Newmarkett.
Rectoria et Vicaria de Tullalesh.
Rectoria de Knocktemple.
Vicaria de Killmeedie in diocesi Aghadoensis.
Sitque ecclia de Newmarkett p'alis.

5. Rectoria de Moyallow.
Vicaria de Dromdowny.
Vicaria de Killbrowny.
Vicaria de Carrigemleary.
Vicaria de Rahane.
Rectoria de Mourne, als. Temple Michel.
Rectoria de Clenor sive Cancellariatus Ecclia Cath'alis Clonensis.
Sitque ecclia de Moyallow p'alis.

6. Vicaria de Killdorrery.
Vicaria de Villa Marescalis.
Præbenda de Brigown.
Vicaria de Ballydology.
Vicaria de Killygolane.
Sitque ecclia apud Mich'lstown in parochia de Brigown p'alia.

7.
- Vicaria de Castlelehane.
- Vicaria de Clondulane.
- Præbenda de Coole.
- Rectoria et Vicar de Aghern.
- Vicaria de Brettway.
- Sitque ecclia de Castlelehane p'alis.

8.
- Vicaria de Temple Bealagh.
- Vicaria de Knockmourn.
- Rectoria de Mogealy.
- Rectoria et Vicar de Ballynoe.
- Sitque ecclia de Mogeally p'alis.

9.
- Rectoria de Rathcormock.
- Rectoria de Gortroe.
- Vicaria Ibin.
- Rectoria de Desert.
- Vicar de Templebodan.
- Præbenda de Killaspugmullan, in dioces Corkagiensis.
- Sitque ecclia de Rathcormuck p'alis.

10.
- Rectoria de Dongourney.
- Rectoria et Vicar de Mogealy.
- Præbenda de Cahirultan.
- Vicaria de Ballymarter, als. Ballyutra.
- Sitque ecclia apud Castlemartyr in parochia de Ballymartyr parochialis.

11.
- Rectoria de Killegh.
- Vicaria de Clonmult.
- Vicaria de Dangedonovan.
- Sitque ecclia de Killegh p'alis.

12.
- Rectoria de Ighteromorrogh.
- Prebenda et Vicar de Killmodonogh.
- Vicar de Killcredane.
- Vicaria de Garrivoe.
- Vicaria de Killmaghan.
- Vicaria de Bohilane.
- Sitque ecclia de Killcredan p'alis.

13.
- Præbenda de Donaghmore.
- Vicaria de Aghabolloge cum magna pticula de Magourna.
- Rectoria et Vicar de Aghena.
- Vicaria de Killcoleman.
- Sitque ecclia de Magourna p'alis.

14.
- Vicaria de Clondrohid.
- Vicaria de Macromp.
- Vicaria de Killnamartyrra.
- Vicaria de Ballyvourna.
- Sitque ecclia Macromp p'alis.

15. { Præbenda de Glanour.
Ecclesia de Aghahultie.
Vicaria de Killathy.
Rectoria et Vicaria de Litter.
Vicaria de Derrivillane.
Vicaria de Carrigdownan.
Ecclesia de Killenemer.
Sitque ecclesia de Killathy p'alis.

16. { Rectoria et Vicaria de Macrony.
Rectoria et Vicaria de Letreim.
Rectoria et Vicaria de Killcrumper.
Rectoria de Killyard, als. Killworth.
Præbenda de Ahelane (*sic*) in diocesi Lismoriensi.
Sitque ecclesia Killworth p'alis.

17. { Vicaria de Kill Shanig.
Vicaria de Clonmeen.
Vicaria de Killcorneyean.
Vicaria de Dromtarriff, et
Vicaria de Drishane in diocesi Aghadoensi.
Sitque ecclesia de Clonmeen p'alis.

Fiat quoque Knockmourne Præbenda ecclisæ Cathalis loco Killenemor unitæ cum præbend' de Glannore ecclisæ de Killothy; Macromp loco Lackeen unitæ cum præbenda de Ballyhay ecclisæ de Burton, alias Ballintemple; Aghadda loco Aghahulty cum præbenda de Glanore unitæ ecclisæ de Killathy; Villacastri loco Killm' Cloneyn cum præbenda de Subultr unitæ ecclisæ de Castlemagner.

Sit quoque Rectoria de Ardagh unita in perpetuum ecclisæ de Youghall, atq' Vicaria de Killgrohanbegg ecclisæ de Iniscar, et Rectoria de Clonpriest Decanatui ecclisæ Cathalis Colemani Clonen.

The endorsement of the return is as follows, in the Bishop's handwriting:—

"The state of the diocese of Cloyn in the year 1694, with the humblest and most dutiful observance, presented to the Right Honourable the Lords Justices of Ireland, by William, Bishop of Cloyn."

The returns for Cloyne occupy fourteen sheets, oblong folio, and folded, written only (with one exception) *facie*. Each page is divided into six columns, headed respectively:—Præsens annus valor Beneficiorum—Beneficia—Incumbentes—Valor—Patroni—Ecclesiarum Status.

BISHOP DOWNES' MSS.

The Miscellaneous Papers of Bishop Dive Downes, preserved along with his "Tour," in the Library of T.C.D.*

Lands belonging to the See of Ross, with extracts out of the Book of Survey of the County of Cork, remaining in the hands of the Treasurer of the said county.

The site of Sir Emanuel Moore's house, with all the cabins, houses, and gardens in or belonging to the town of Rosscarbury, in the barony of East Carbery, and county of Corke, and diocese of Ross, let to Capt. Freake, in the said books of survey of the county of Corke, in the hands of the Treasurer of said county.

Rossetown, 50A. 3R. 16P.; the three glebes, 14A. 2R.; the six gneeves of Lacken robbin, the six gneeves of Burgeesha, the six gneeves of Clonnebane, the six gneeves of Ballynegeragh, the six gneeves of Larchagh, the six gneeves of Crogonoleene; in all, three plowlands, lying in the diocese of Rosse, and county of Cork, let to Capt. Freake.

In the aforesaid books, in the parish of Rosscarbery:—Lackenrobbin, 45A.; Burgeskagh, 121A.; Clonebaune, 44A.; Ballinegerah, 56A.; Larekagh, 50A.; Creganeleen, 75A.

The six gneeves of Drumgoone, the six gneeves of Goltra, the six gneeves of Rinivanane, the six gneeves of Downings, the six gneeves of Curragh, the six gneeves of Knockamagry, and the gneeve of Gorty Clyle, being in all three plowlands and one gneeve, in the diocese of Ross, and county of Corke, let to Mr. John Smyth.

In the aforesaid books, in the parish of Rossecarbury:—Downings, 204A. 2R.; Currahine, 34A. Query whether the same with Currah above said.

Ballinagorhaghnamerrigree, six gneeves; query whether the same with Knocknamogry above said; all in the same parish. Barony of Barryroe, in the parish of Ardfield—Bishopsland, Reneene, 17A. 2R. Query whether the same with Rinivanane above said.

The plowland of Caharmore, the plowland of Frehane, and the nine gneeves of Mauloregan, lying in the diocese of Ross, and county of Corke, let to Mr. Thomas Hungerford.

In the aforesaid books, in the parish of Roscarbury:—Cahirmore, 387A. 2R.; Frehane, 1 pld., 237A. 2R.; Mauloregan, 9 gn., 280A.

The nine gneeves of Glanbracky, the nine gneeves of Maultanavally, the nine gneeves of Carrickgreenane, the nine gneeves of Carrickfadda, containing in all by estimation three plowlands, lying in the diocese of Ross, and county of Corke, let to Gideon Delane.

In the aforesaid books, in the parish of Rossecarbery:—Glanebrack,

* These papers, and the Bishop's "Tour through his Dioceses of Cork and Ross," were presented by Samuel Moore Kyle, LL.D., Archdeacon of Cork and Vicar-General, to the Library of T.C.D., on 19th March, 1849.

453A.; Maullenevally, 272A.; Carrickgrenane, 230A. 1R.; Carrickfadda, 380A.

The Island of Inchidenny, als. the Isle of Man :—The three gneeves of Carhoo Duffee, on the north of the said island, and the three gneeves of Keneene, lying on the south-west part of the said island, in the diocese of Rosse, and county of Corke, let to Richard Hungerford, in the aforesaid books, in the parish of Inchydowney, als Island.

Inchedowney, an island near Clonakelty, 287A. 2R. 20P. Earl of Cork, propr. Land covered with sand, 23A. 2R. Cahirduffe, 24A. 3R.; Rinne, 19A. 2R.; all in the same parish, in the barony of Carbery.

The lands of Kilsillagh, containing by estimation one plowland, lying in the barony of Ibaune, in the diocese of Rosse, and county of Cork, let to Mr. Robert Travers.

In the parish of Lislee, in the two paper books of survey, Ballinrokig and Killsallagh, 2½ plowlands, arable and pasture, 278A. 2R. Zachar Travers' property, in the parchment booke of survey, Ballivroky, 1½ plowland.

The plowland of Drisheene and Rosse na Goss, containing by estimation two hundred and seaventy acres, lying in the diocese of Rosse, and county of Cork, let to David Dennis.

In the aforesaid books, in the parish of Aghadowne:—Drishane, 4 gneeves, 78A. 1R. 24P.; Rosnagosh, in the same parish, 45A. 32P., in the barony of Carbury.

The two plowlands of Aghadowne, the plowland and a-half of Callstrummore and Callstrumventry, the plowland of Kilekilleen, the half plowland of Drowine na Caharagh, and the three gneeves of Lisheen Oughtera, containing by estimation 800A. or thereabouts, lying in the barony of West Carbery, in the county of Corke, and diocesse of Rosse, together with the benefits of the fairs and markets, let to Thomas Becher, esq.

In the aforesaid books in the parish of Aghadowne:—Aghadowne, 2 plowlands, 325A. 32P.; of the same (towne), 22A.; bog, 116A.; Callastrummore, 123A. 2R. 16P.; Callastrumbeg, 85A.; Killkilleen, 131A. 2R. 16P.; Dromnacaharagh, 58A.; South and North Lisheen, 124A. 3R. 8P.; Tounebog, 38A. 32P.; all in the same parish.

The lands of Ardagh, in the parish of Aghadowne, in the diocese of Ross, and county of Corke, together with the chief rents of the diocese of Corke and Rosse, let to Thomas Dyer.

In the aforesaid books, in the parish of Aghadowne:—Ardagh, 120A. 1R. 24P.

The lands of Ardralymore and Ardrallybeg, being by estimation one plowland and a-half, lying in the diocese of Rosse, and county of Corke, let to Mr. Benjamin Bousfield.

In the aforesaid books, in the parish of Aghadowne :—Ardralye, 164A. 1R. 24P.; bog part of the same, 120A. 3R. 8P.

The island commonly called the East Calf, containing by estimation 9 gneeves; one other island, called West Innis Kane, being by estimation one half plowland or thereabouts, lying in the barony of West Carbery, diocese of Rosse, and county of Corke, let to Sir Richard Hull.

In the aforesaid county books East Calf is 37A. in the parish of Skull; West Innis Kane, 16A. 1R. 24P., in the parish of Aghadowne.

The two plowlands of Innishbeg Clevi, containing by estimation two hundred plantation acres or thereabouts, lying in the barony of West Carbury, in the diocese of Rosse, and county of Cork, let to —— Hull.

In the aforesaid books, in the parish of Aghadowne :—Innispike, als. Clare Island, 200A.

The two plowlands of Garrancore, Tullogh Geehy, and Farrancantry, lying in the diocese of Rosse, and county of Cork, let to Mr. Cornelius Hignett.

In the aforesaid books, in the parish of Rosse Carbury :—Garrancore, 155A.; Farrannocantry, 50A. 2R.

The plowland of Ballynykgeap, the plowland of Dizart, and the half plowland of Drocombeg, lying in the diocese of Rosse, and county of Corke, let to the Earl of Cork.

In the aforesaid books, in the barony of Carbery, in the parish of Inchidowney:—Desart, 2 plowlands, arable and pasture, 226A. 1R. 16P. Earl of Corke, proprietor. Query whether this be the same with Dizart, let by lease to the Earl of Corke.

NOTE.—All the acres mentioned in this paper are reckon'd as profitable in the books of survey, unless when it is otherwise exprest in this paper.

LANDS belonging to the SEE of CORKE, with Extracts relative to them, taken out of the Books of Survey of the County of Corke remaining in the hands of the Treasurer of said County.

Parcel, or quarter of land, called Kilcroghane, in the barony of Carbury, which is in common estimation three plowlands, set to Will. Hull, esq. In none of the county books is there mention made of Kilcroghan lands, or of any glebe.

The two plowlands of Ballinaspug, be they more or less than the common estimation, lying in the diocese of Corke, within the county of the city of Corke, let to Mr. Edward Synge. In the county books of survey it is 436A. 6P., in the parish of St. Finbarry.

The lands of Ballinaspig-beg, being by estimation one plowland, lying in the diocese and county of the city of Corke, be the same more or less than the common estimation, let to Alderman James French. In the county paper books, without maps, and in the parchment books of survey it is 133A. in the same parish of St. Finbarry.

The half plowland of Farrenmacteige, lying in the parish of St. Finbarries, and in the diocese and county of Cork, be it more or less than the common estimation, let to Mr. Matthews French. In the county books of survey it is 60A. in the parish of St. Finbarries.

The half plowland of Inchigaggon, and one grist mill, with 20A. of land or thereabouts, to the said mill belonging, lying in the diocese and county of the city of Corke, be the same more or less than the common estimation, let to Charles Baldwin, esq. In the county books of survey it is 151A. in the parish of St. Finbarry's.

The lands of Gortenaspug, containing by estimation thirty English acres, be it more or less, lying in the parish of St. Finbarry, and in the diocese and county of the city of Corke, be the same more or less than the common estimation, let to Mr. Edward Webber. In the county books of survey is no such name as Gortanaspug. Query whether Hicgar's be not the same. This land is in the books said to be 25A. In the same books, in the parish of St. Finbarry's, is Gortigowlane, 234A., but I suppose that cannot be Gortenaspug, this being but about 30 English acres.

The three plowlands of Nedineah-beg, containing by estimation 300A. or thereabouts, lying in the barony of East Carbery, in the county of Cork, let to Sir Richard Coxe. In the county books of survey Nedinea is 544A. in the parish of Fanlobbish.

The lands of Nedineah-more, being by estimation three plowlands, lying in the barony of East Carbury, in the diocese and county of Cork, and the benefit of the fairs kept on the premises, let to Jane Blocksom, of Dublin, widow. No more mention is made of Nedineah in the said books, but as above is set down.

The lands of Farranivergan, being by estimation one half of a plowland, lying in the parish of Mackcloneagh; and the half plowland of Kineagh, als. Cargallallan, in the parish of Kineagh, lying in the diocese and county of Cork, let to Roger Lewis, and afterwards to Wallace Warren. In the county books of survey Farragarivane is 72A.; Kineagh, in the said books, is 63A. 1R. 24P. There is also Kineagh-beg, 247A. 3R. 8P.

The nine plowlands of Scooll; the Island of Mananesh, containing one plowland and a-half; the two islands, called the West Calves, containing one plowland and a-half; the one plowland and a-half of Crookhaven (of which the parcel of ground called the Glebe of Crookhaven is part); the one plowland and a-half of Ballivoige; the three plowlands of Dough, Litter, and Barrahill, and the plowland and a-half of Carneglovane, being in all by estimation nineteen plowlands and a-half, lying in the barony of West Carbury, and in the diocese and county of Cork, let to Sir Richard Hull. In the county books of survey West Calf is 28A.; Middle Calf is 31A.; Skull is two plowlands, 262A. arable and coarse pasture. Capt. William Hull is said to be proprietor. Part of Skull, rocky nature, 66A. 2R.; same proprietor. Corriderigan, one-half plowland, part of the 9 plowlands of Scull, 155A.; same proprietor. Skeagh, 1 plowland, of the 9 plowlands of Scull, 259A. Meenevane, 1½ plowland, part of the 9 plowlands of Skull, arable and pasture, 93A. 2R.; of the same, 28A. 2R., rocky, mountainous, and unprofitable. Mananesh is the same with Castleisle, which Castleisle, in the aforesaid books, is said to be 68A. In the parchment books of survey Skull is said to be 9 plowlands, 1,788A.

All that land commonly called Poleherdick, also all those lands and tenements of Carigynearig, adjoining to the lands of Poleherdick, near Gillabbey; also a parcel of meadow ground, called Inchingangary, lying in the great island, called Cloghave, belonging to Gillabbey, over against the lands of Poleherdick, and Carrigyneary, containing by estimation eighteen Irish acres or thereabouts; also all the clevanes and wear, called Beallakilly, Carrigrone, Carrogonapoge, and also one meadow, called Monamullcu, being by estimation three Irish acres, over against Gillabbymill, with the benefit of the watercourses running through the said meadow to Droope's mill, let to Capt. Travers, in trust for Dean Davys.

The three plowlands of Kilmacomoge, lying in the barony of Beare and Bantry, in the county and diocese of Cork, containing by estimation 400 plantation acres, be the same more or less, let to John Hull. In the county books of survey, Kilmocomoge, 3 plowlands, is 279A. profitable; more boggy pasture in the same, 14A.; Glebe in the same, 2A. 1R., in the parish of Kilmocamoge.

The three plowlands of Kilbrogan, Knockbrogan and Killbeg, containing by measure 1,200A. of all sorts, be it more or less, being part of the manor of St. Finbarry, being in one continent, in the parish of Kilbrogan, in the county and diocese of Corke, let to Richard, Earl of Cork. In the county books of survey Kilbrogan and Knockbrogan are said to be 333A. 2R. 12P.; and Kilbeg, 1 plowland, 168A. 2R.; the Earl of Cork is said to be proprietor. In the parchment book it is thus:—Kilbrogan and Knockbrogan, 396A.; and Kilbeg, 242A. 2R. 16P.; all these in the parish of Kilbrogan.

In the aforesaid books of the county Corke.—Land lying on the south side of Cork, a part of which is set to Dean Davys:—Statesland, a parcel of Bishopsland, 9A.; Statesland, another parcel of the same, 35A. 2R.; a parcel of meadow and marsh land, called Bishopsland, 20A.

In the said books of survey of the county of Cork, in the parish of Kilmoe; proprietor, Capt. William Hull:—The island of Crookhaven, 131A.; of the same, Glebe, arable, 3A.; part of Ballyvoige, 106A.; part of the same, 4½ gneeves, 40A. 1R. In the parchment book; proprietor, Capt. W. Hull:—Dough, 1 plowland, 6 gns., 77A. 2R.; Litter, 6 gns., 40A.; Braghill, 4 gns., 24A. Unprofitable mountain, belonging to adjacent town, 248A.; Curran Iglavrint, 52A.; Maltevoige, 1 plowland, arable and pasture, 81A. 1R.; of the same, rocky and bog, 58A. 2R.; Castlemegan, 1¼ plowland, 100A.; of the same, rocky and bog, 184A.; Canavoy and Farraglline, 1½ plowland, half mountain, mo', pa', 59A. Kilbarry (12A. 3R. 20P., unprofitable); 1½ plowland, arable and pasture, 87A. 20P.; Lynane, half plowland, arable and pasture, 53A.; Killcan, 1 plowland, arable and pasture, 89A.

NOTE.—All the acres mentioned in this paper are reckon'd as profitable in the books of survey aforesaid, unless when it is otherwise exprest in this paper.

In the hands of the Treasurer of the county Corke are three books, each of them containing an account of the lands in the several baronies of the said county Corke. There are also two other books in his custody, containing copies of the presentments made by grand juries: one of them containing copies of the several presentments made by Grand Juries at the general assizes and general gaol delivery, held for the county of Corke, commencing the 27th day of July, 1676. The other contains the several presentments made by the Grand Juries at the several general sessions of the peace, commencing the 4th day of April, 1676. The original presentments are kept by the Deputy Clerk of the Crown for the county of Corke, in a chest in his lodgings in Corke. He also keeps in the same place the court books, which contain the names of the several criminals, with the substance of their indictments, with names of the prosecutors, &c. By the same person, in the same place, are kept the original indictments, together with the examinations and depositions taken before the Justices of the Peace, and the recognizances entered into by the prosecutors, and by bails, &c.

EXTRACT out of the PAPER BOOK, without Maps, in the hands of the TREASURER of the COUNTY of CORKE.

Muskerry Barony.

	A.	R.	P.
In Desertmore parish :—			
Churchlands, ...	24	0	0
In the South Liberties of Corke :—			
Statesland, a parcel of Bishopland, . .	9	0	0
Another parcel of same land, . .	35	2	0
Statesland, a parcel of meadow and marsh land, called Bishopsland, . . .	20	0	0
A parcel, formerly belonging to St. John of Jerusalem, ...	6	0	0
Farrenmacteige, ...	60	0	0
Inchiguigane, ...	151	0	0
Ballinaspugmore, ...	436	0	0
Ballinaspugbeg, ...	133	0	0

Barony of Beare and Bantry.

In the parish of Kilmacomoge :—

	A.	R.	P.
Kilmacomoge, ...	279	0	0
Bog part, in the same, . . .	14	0	0
Glebe, in the same, . . .	2	1	0
In the parish of Durrows :—			
Gurteen, ...	194	0	0

County of Cork Grand Jury Presentments.

1679. (Fo. 23.) March 17. We find and present that there ought to be a free school erected within the diocess of Corke, and that a convenient place be agreed on between the Bishop of Corke and city of Corke for the same, and that the city and liberties of Corke are in the diocess of Corke, and therefore are obliged to contribute to the building the said school. We therefore find and present that one hundred pounds be raised on that part of the diocess of Corke which lies within the county of Corke, and the summe collected be paid to Alexander Piggot, esq., &c., provided alwais that the said Piggott shall not issue warrants for the collection of the same, until first the city and commonalty of Corke shall raise an equal summe to what is raised on this county, &c.—as also shall, under their seal, convey to the Rt. Rev. the Bishop of the diocess the ground pitched on for the said school, as also oblige themselves to keep the same in perpetual repair, the which, if they shall fail of doing, &c., the said Piggot shall desist from issueing out the warrant aforesaid.

An. 1679. (Fo. 23.) A receiver or accomptant for the county is appointed. Will. Hull, of Burdanstown is made receiver. He is allowed 12*d.* per pound for all that he shall receive over and above what he shall lay out for warrants.

1680. (Fo. 24.) The Clerk of the Crown and Peace's fees settled. He is to have 2*s.* 6*d.* for one warrant for moneys raised for the county's use by one presentment, and shall sign the rest gratis for all the money not exceeding 4*d.* per plowland ; and for moneys exceeding 4*d.* per plowland, his usual fees of 2*s.* 6*d.* for every warrant issued to the several baronies in the said county. Warrants for money for prisoners to be signed by him gratis.

1680. (26.) We desire the Bishop of the diocess and the High Sheriff of the county to meet, and to pitch upon a convenient place for building of a school in the diocese, according to the statute.

(27.) Sixty pounds to be raised out of that part of the county of Corke that lies in the diocese of Corke, for the erecting of a school, according to act of parliament, to be applotted according to the deficiency of the year's value.

The Bishop of Corke, Will. Mead, esq., &c., are made overseers of the work, provided that, before the said summe be raised or applotted, a place where the school shall be built be made over to the Bishop of Corke and his successors for the perpetual use of the said school, and also that the same be kept in repair by the said city of Corke.

1680 (fo. 28). No person to act as Attorney, Clerk of the Crown or Peace, &c., but such as are of the Protestant religion, and take the oaths of allegiance and supremacy.

1681 (fol. 29). Raising money by the plowland is thought unequal; we, therefore, present that, for the future, all money be raised in this county according to the deficiency of the year's value.

Killmeen church to be repaired.

Fo. 32 eodm. an. That John Langton, esq., Clerk of the Crown, deliver the rolls of presentments of this county, made at the assizes for these six years last past, to Mr. Hull, the County Receiver, to be by him fairly engrossed, and to redeliver them to Langton aforesaid.

Cullen and Nohoval. Whereas the several parishes following, of Kilmeen, Drishane, Drumtariffe, Cullen, and Nohoval, in the county of Cork, and diocess of Aghadoe, have agreed that the churches of Killmeen and Dryshane be rebuilt, &c.; we, therefore, have agreed that 6*s.* 6*d.* per plowland in Dryshane, Cullen, and Nohoval, be raised for repair of church of Dryshane, &c.; and that 4*s.* 6*d.* per plowland be raised in the parishes of Killmeene and Drumbarry, for rebuilding the church of Killmeene.

1682 (fo. 35). All overseers of public works presented by name for not bringing their accounts.

(Fo. 36). Fees of High Sheriff, Clerk of the Crown and Peace, to be stated and hung up in Court.

(Fo. 38). No money to be raised at the Sessions for new works, but only for repairs, and with moderate summes, and upon baronys only, and not upon the county.

1683, Aug. (51 fo.) We present that James Woode and Cook are vagrants, going about to seduce his Majesty's subjects, under pretence of religious meetings; and that they congregate several phanaticks in Youghal and Moyallow, to the scandal of the Protestant religion, and in contempt of the Government.

(Fo. 52). A salary of sixty pounds per ann., given to the Treasurer of the county, in lieu of 12*d.* per pound formerly paid him.

1687 ann. (fo. 97). We present that the Protestant clergy, under color of law, exact from the Roman Catholick subjects several summes of christening, purification, burying, and book mony; and sue them in their spiritual courts, and commit them to prison, so dispeopling the country, &c.; that, therefore, your Lordships would favourably represent the same to the Government, or otherwise make such order that may hinder these inconveniences; and the rather, because the like duties are not demanded in any other Christian country by the clergy, nor from any other but the Roman Catholicks, who, by his Majesty's proclamation for liberty of conscience, are equally freed from all exactions and penalties, with all others differing from the Church of England.

1688 (fo. 103). April. An infant, left in a house by a person unknown, is to be allowed by the parish 40*s.* per ann. till it is fit for service.

(Fo. 109). That no presentments for assessing mony on the county at large, or on particular baronys or parishes, be made at the Quarter Sessions, but at the Assizes only.

(Fo. 118). 12th March, 1688. We present that four hundred and twenty pounds be raised in the county of Corke, to be paid to George Crofts, esq., who is forthwith to furnish the French fleet with fifty fat oxen, and four hundred fat weathers; the same to be given to the Admiral, officers, and seamen of the said fleet, as a small acknowledgement of the universal thanks that is due to them from this kingdom in general, but from us more particularly, for transporting his Majesty hither, we having the first blessing of his Majesty's presence in this county, for which we and our posterity shall ever praise God; George Crofts to be satisfied for grazing the said cattle till the return of the French fleet.

1690 (fo. 122). The next Assizes or General Gaol Delivery were held the 9th December, 1690.

That the inhabitants within four miles of Bandon do contribute their labours towards the erecting and securing the walls of the said town thrown down by Papists.

For the preventing the transportation of provisions.

For due keeping of watch.

That all Papists be committed who shall refuse to deliver their arms.

That all cabins in the Irish quarter be demolished—the Leapwood to be cut down.

A certain quantity of hay, oats, and straw to be sent to their Majestys' stores, and satisfaction to be made according to their Majestys' proclamation, 14th November, 1690. Upon refusal to send pay, &c., the High Constables are to levy the value by distress.

(128 fo., 23rd March, 1690). Against making Papists Petty Constables where there are Protestants fit to serve.

(129 fo.) The Protestants of each parish to watch, and to levy 6*d.* for each man per night from the Popish inhabitants, by distress, if need be.

1691. September. That every male inhabitant above sixteen years old to pay 6*d.* per week, and 12*d.* out of each inhabited plowland, per week, for twelve weeks, to be disposed of as the Governor of the county, Sir Richard Cox, or the Commissioners of Array appointed to manage the Militia, shall think fit.

Mr. Sullivan presented as a fit person to be Treasurer, in the room of Mr. Hull, deceased.

16th March, 1691. All persons that have received any of the public mony are to account for it; and if they refuse they are to be committed to the county gaol.

1692. 18th July, 1692. Edward Riggs having disbursed £1,337 13*s.* 7*d.*, and received from the county, by pole and land tax, according to former presentments, but £1,212 14*s.* 11½*d.*, the ballance due so, is to be raised out of the county.

The arms brought in to the Justices of the Peace to be sent to the stores.

1692. March 21. 12*d.* per week for each prisoner in bread, and to inquire of the Assize of Bread.

Application for a commission of Oyer and Terminer monthly.

One peny per mile forward, and 1*d.* per mile back, to be paid the Constable that conveys prisoners to gaol.

Against John Topham, and Lieutenant Dove, of Col. Roe's regiment, for levying mony on the lands of the parish of Kilmocamoge, on pretence of an order for pressing horses to carry timber to Kinsale.

Against the town of Youghal for refusing to raise their proportion of the publick mony of the county.

Applications to the Government to prevent quartering of soldiers only in Corke, Kinsale, Bandon, Youghal.

1693. July 20. Application to the Government for suppression of Rapparees and Torys.

Coroner to take inquisition of them that dye in gaol.

1693. September. Prisoners allowed but one penny per day.

Against John Folliott, esq., High Sheriff of the county of Corke, for setting at liberty David Barry als. Gnavee.

1693. 12th March. Against Richard Hutchins for receiving printed news sent by a privateer, and superseding two Torys sent by mittimus to gaol.

1694. August. That a capias issue against the Mayor of Youghal, upon his refusal to pay the full applotments of assizes and sessions of Oyer and Terminer.

An address to the Judge concerning the Popish clergy coming from beyond sea, and for suppressing Popish schools.

Against several persons for not appearing upon the High Sheriff's summons to pursue the Torys.

The acknowledgements of the county to the Rev. Dean Davys, Will Ballard, John Raynes, esqrs., for their great services against the Torys.

Youghal, Kinsale, and Cloghakilty's proportion of mony assessed at the sessions to be raised, the said towns alledging they are not subject but to the assizes presentments.

1695. July. Against burning any land but such as is covered with matty furze, heath, &c.

Against several persons that had left the kingdom and gone into France.

Against Earl Clancarty, and others, supposed to be in this kingdom, who lately came from France, and others in this county ready to join them. Curia advizat.—That all records of the Clerk of the Crown, and all other records and papers of the county in the Treasurer's hands, be kept in the place under the Grand Jury room.

1696. Aug. Against trespassers in the forfeited woods of this county.

An old arrear of £700 is remitted to several baronies, and they are to pay instead thereof £180, which has been advanced by the Treasurer for the public use of the county.

£303 19*s.* 11*d.* to be raised for several uses.

Sir St. John Broderick and L. Clayton traverse the £70 on the county for Macrony bridge.

Sir R. Cox and Sir Henry Echlin, knight.—19th March, 1696. That John Mulconry, an Irish Priest, &c., are out on their keeping, and cannot be taken by warrant: we therefore pray they may be ordered to render themselves by a certain day to a Justice of the Peace, or that they may be proclaimed as rebels and traitors to the Government.

Mony raised for 113 foxes—viz., £5 13*s.*

1697. July. We present that Cornelius Crowly, als. Maddery, of Skibbareene; Owen M'Owen, Sullivan, of Kilcaskin parish, &c., all Irish Papists, have taught school, and continue to do so, contrary to the Act.

1698. April. The dispute between the county of Corke and the towne of Youghall be referred to the Judge at *Commons.*

The determination of the Judge in common,—(who determines that the town of Youghall is chargeable with their proportion of all summs of money raised on the said county of Corke by presentments at the assizes), is confirmed by the Judges, as well as Clonakilty, or any other town or barony for bridges, &c.

We present that P. Murrough, titular Vicar-General, and Dr. John Slyne, titular Bishop, remain in this kingdom, contrary to the late Act.

1699. 4th April. Names of above 60 persons indicted at this said assizes.

Against several persons for destroying the spawning salmon, with torches, wisps, &c., by night.

1701. 13th August, 1701. We present that John Connelly, formerly Vicar of Rossecarbery, still remains in this kingdom, contrary to the Act.

£216 1*s*. 9*d*. to be raised on the county for several uses, viz., bridges, &c.; Treasurer's salary, £30; Clerk of the Crown, for discharging of poor prisoners, who were a great charge to the county.

Several prisoners sentenced last assizes and reprieved—it is desired the Government would order them to be transported by Daniel Pierce, merchant, who is willing to transport the same.

1702. 27th July. Certain fees to be taken on robberies, executions, &c., viz.:—Attorney, for drawing and reading the petition, 3*s*. 4*d*.; Counsel, 10*s*.; Clerk of the Crown for warrant, 2*s*. 6*d*. The constables before applotment are to give notice to the principal inhabitants of the respective baronys.

£20 to any person that shall bring in or kill a proclaimed Tory.

Presentment concerning the trees to be planted throughout the county, according to the statute—the proportion of this whole county is twenty-five thousand eight hundred, according to which computation and direction, nine trees is the proportion to be yearly planted on each plowland within the respective baronies and parishes of this county.

We present that John Slyne, titular Bishop of Corke, remains still in this kingdom, exercising ecclesiastical jurisdiction, contrary to the late Act.

£40 to be raised and levied of the goods and chattels of Charles M'Carthy and Donogh MacCarthy; £20 of it to be paid to Frances Parker, widow of Will Parker, who killed Callaghane M'Callaghane, a proclaimed Tory, and lost his life in the service; the other £20 to be paid to Newel for bringing in a Tory. These Tories were the followers of Charles and Donagh Macarthy.

PRESENTMENTS of the GRAND JURY of the COUNTY of CORKE at the General Sessions of the Peace, held at Bandon, 4th April, 1676.

We present that Marcus Cullane have 2*d*. per plowland out of the baronies of East Carbery, &c., to be collected by the High Constables as a reward for discovering thieves.

11th July, 1676. Against a person for presenting a bridge against the able men of the barony.

1683. 17th April, 1683. Against a common Barreter. For way wardens to be appointed by the minister and churchwardens of each parish.

10th July, 1683. We present Will Grady, a person excommunicated, outlawed, and a Roman Catholick, for carrying about him a case of pistolls, &c., to the terror of his Majesty's liege subjects.

A return to be made of all such as are fit to serve at assizes and sessions by two persons in each barony.

1683. 8th January, 1683. Three persons named as fit to serve as High Constable in the barony of Orrery and Kilmore: one person of the three pitcht on by the Bench.

Several other High Constables appointed.

1685. 28th April, 1685. A salary to the High Constable of Muskery for his service and extraordinary sufferings.

12th January, 1685. Ben Cottrell not to be summoned to assizes nor sessions by reason of his age and poverty.

3d. per plowland to the Clerk of the Peace for his care in his office.

1686. October. *4d.* per plowland through the county for the army taking outlawed persons.

£16 raised on the county, being honour mony lately paid by Laurence Clayton, High Sheriff, to the officers of his Excellency the Lord Lieutenant of Ireland, in his progress through the county of Corke.

1687. Macromp, 4th of October, 1687. £6 13*s.* 4*d.* for the Coroner, for inquisitions taken on several persons that were poor, out of the parishes where the inquisitions were taken.

Macromp, 10th January, 1687 (qu. 1688). 2*s.* 6*d.* per plowland through the barony of Muskery and Barrets, be raised for a free school to be kept at Macromp, and that Dr. Donagh Swyny, Dr. in Divinity, Civil and Canon Law, Apostolical Protonotary, and Tiege O'Conor, priest, are fit persons to instruct children in humanity, philosophy, divinity, and French, and to be absolute masters of the said school—curia—this presentment to continue during the pleasure of the county only.

1688. Macromp, April, 1688. Several Petty Constables appointed in the barony of Bear and Bantry.

No beggar to wander, bnt to abide in his own parish, mendicant fryars and other religious persons and orders alwaies excepted and fore prized.

10th July, 1688. Whereas by a presentment at the Court Leet about May last, at Killerea, in the barony of Muskery, 1*s.* 6*d.* per plowland throughout the said barony was found by the body of the said barony for the High Constable for his service; we present that the said Constable doth well deserve the said 1*s.* 6*d.* to be collected for him by the High and Petty Constables of the said barony.

p. curian referred to the assizes.

No sessions till

1690. 3rd January, 1690. On order of Ruben Huddy from the Lords Justices and Council, we present that the summe of one hundred and seaven pounds in lieu of sixty-nine cows and sixty heifers, taken by rapparees since the 19th of December, be levy'd on the Popish inhabitants of the barony of Killnatalloon, &c.

For strict keeping of watch.

That every Irish man bring in his arms within 10 daies, or otherwise to be accounted rebels against the Government.

1691. 11th May, 1691. Every male inhabitant above sixteen years to pay three half-pence per week from the 15th of April last, to be disposed of by order of the Governor of said county, or the Commissioner of Array.

The militia to have liberty to graze their horses in meadows —corn excepted.

14th July, 1691. Every male inhabitant, &c., to pay six pence per month, and 2*s*. 6*d*. per plowland inhabited weekly.

The Lords Justices letter:—We have received an account that the Irish who were in arms, and have submitted, or are included in articles granted, are ill-treated, contrary to publick faith and justice, and many of them desire to go to France, who designed to stay at home; we, therefore, require you to call a publick sessions where you are to declare, that it is their Majestys' pleasure that the Irish that have submitted, &c., shall enjoy their Majestys' protection, and that justice be done against all that shall commit robbery or violence upon them.— 19th Nov., 1691. Your loving friends, Charles Porter, Tho'. Coningsby.

At a Special Sessions of the Peace at Corke, 10th of December, 1691, Colonel John St. Leger presented for the forcible detaining of the lands of Ballinemony, and that Sir Mat Dean be forthwith restored to the possession of the said lands.

The pole mony to cease, and the last tax on the plowlands to be restored to the chief tenants, there being no necessity for the militia, Limerick being reduced, and the war at an end.

The persons under protection to enjoy the benefit thereof, and that two Justices in each barony compose all trespasses committed.

12th of January, 1691 (qu. 1692). That Capt. Edw. Bourke and his Irish soldiers be represented to the Government for plundering the inhabitants of Duhallo, more than their Majestys' army did heretofore.

1692. April, 1692. Against several persons for not delivering their arms.

Persons appointed as way wardens.

10th of January, 1692 (qu. 1693). A watch to be kept at the beacons, erected near the sea side, to be set on fire upon an invasion of this kingdom.

1693. January, 1693. High Constables to return a list of those that are fit to serve at assizes, and of such as are fit to serve at sessions.

1694. 15th Jan. 1694. Three hundred pounds to be raised out of the county, to be disposed of as Rowland Davys, Dean of Rosse, Edward Hoare, &c., shall order for the publick use, and particularly for rewarding those that are employed in reducing and destroying the Torys.

1695. April, 1695. Desiring the court to address the Government for the execution of Crowley, formerly condemned.

July, 1695. Prophaners of the Sabbath to be punished.

October, 1695. Alex. Barrington presented for levying more money on his barony than he had warrant for. Traversed.

1696. April, 1696. That there are four fryars in the Abby of Timoleage, and two fryars in the Abby of Bantry.

12th of Jan. 1696. That Britton, the present High Constable, is necessitated to go out of the kingdom, therefore we present Edm. Cook, &c., as fit persons for High Constables of Barrimore.

Fiat quoad Cook, if Britton leave the kingdom, to be sworn before Col. Ja. Barry.

1698. May, 1698. To pull down several wears made cross the river Ballineboy, in the parish of Ballineboy.

July, 1698. That Tiege Dash had a harper playing in his house on the Sabbath day, contrary to the Act.

That Will Barret is a common swearer and blasphemer.

1699. July, 1699. Against N. Green for stopping a high rode. Cap. to issue, and the nuisance to be remov'd.

Against Eliz. Dennis for being a whore, and keeping a common bawdy house.

1700. April, 1700. For making up the walls of Bandon by the labour of the Papists, inhabitants of the parishes of Kilbrogan, &c.

1701. July, 1701. We present that John Barry, als. Snavee, of Ballihoura, &c., are Torys in arms, and abroad on their keeping, and we desire your Worships to represent it to the Government, that they may be proclaimed according to the Act.

The Widow Jeffer's house, in Bandon, presented as dangerous to passengers.

1702. 12th of Jan. We present that Richard Gary, late of Moyalloo, tanner; George Davys, yeoman, &c., are Torys in arms upon their keeping. We desire, therefore, your Worships would represent, &c., that they may speedily be proclaimed.

Concerning Pet. Murragh, Tit. Vicar-General, December, 1701.

Peter Murragh was formerly, upon a Commission of Oyer and Terminer, tried for staying in the kingdom, contrary to the Act for banishing the Titular Archbishops, &c.

He was charged with being Vicar-General of Corke. The

evidence against him not being strong enough for his conviction, he was discharged. This happened about three years ago.

Some months ago Peter Murrogh, by vertue of a warrant, with a mittimus contained in it from Alderman Newinham, was seized by a Constable in Corke, and committed to the city gaol, as Popish Vicar-General of Corke.

'Tis said that Peter Murrogh since his tryal did own to Alderman Newinham that he had been formerly Vicar-General of Corke, and that this was the ground of his commitment. He owned also he was Vicar-General to the Constable.

An Account of Lands belonging to ye See of Corke.

The Book of Reference to the Map of Survey of the Barony of East and West Carbury, whereunto are annexed two Alphabetical Indexes. The first, of the several denominations of the lands; the second, of the names of the respective Proprietors, in the year one thousand six hundred and forty-one; the third, of particular observations.

This is called the Estimate Survey, and was taken (A.D. 1653,) by Commissioners in each barony, according to information given upon oath by the people of the country.

The Commissioners for East and West Carbury were Henry Becher, esq., &c.

The first draught of this survey remains in the hands of Thomas Becher, of Inniskirkin, esq.

Parish of Fanlobish, Neduneh, Bp. of Corke, 6 plowlands, 1,000A. arable, 200A. pasture, 50A. unprofitable. Five plowlands of Neduneh are situate on the north side of the river Bandon, and the sixth on the south. Parish of Inchidunnig, Dizart, Bp. of Rosse, propr., 2 plowlands, 600A.

Same parish, Renian, Bp. of Rosse, but claimed by Capt. Hull, in lease, 3 gneeves, 32A. The same parish, Cathirduffe, Bp. of R., but claimed as above, 3 gneeves, 33A. Same parish, Drumbeg, the Earl of Corke is said to be propr., 6 gneeves, 150A. Observation, qu.: whether Droumbeg be or be not Bishop's land.

Parish of Rosse belongeth to the bishoprick of Rosse:—1 plowland of Gurrancore; 6 gneeves of Tulloghgeehy; 6 gneeves of Farranacantry; 2 plowlands, 600A.; Downings, 3 plowlands, 888A.; Gullane, 1 plowland, 294A.

Upon the 3 plowlands of Kilcroghan is a church and 2A. of glebe.

Upon the 9 plowlands of Skull are the walls of a church, with 4A. of glebe.

In the parish of Kilmoe:—Claimed by Capt. Hull, E.P., 18 gneeves of Dough; 9 gneeves of Letter; 4 gneeves of Birraghill; 3 gneeves of Immelagh; and 3 gneeves of ——; 3 plowlands, 1 gneeve, 500A. Capt. Hull said to be Lessee. Belongeth to the brick. of Corke, Crookhaven, 1 plowland, 6 gneeves. Captain Hull claimeth 1 plowland, 1½ gneeves, E.P.; Derm Bag, 4½ gneeves, I.P.; Ballivoige, 1 plowland, 6 gneeves, 180A. Belongeth to the bishoprick of Corke, but claimed by Capt. Hull, in lease, Carrenyglavin, 1 plowland, 6 gneeves.

In the parish of Skull:—Belongeth to the bishoprick of Rosse, but claimed by Capt. Hull, E.P., 3 plowlands of Skull in islands, viz., Castle Island, and the two western Calves, 3 plowlands; total acres, 129. Belongeth to the bishoprick of Rosse, but claimed by Capt. Hull, E.P., Skull, 9 plowlands, 330A. arable, 1,430A. pasture, 550A. unprofitable, nil wood.

In the parish of Kilmoe:—Don. O'Mehighane, I.P., but mort' to Dominic, 1½ plowlands, I.P.; 1 plowland, 6 gneeves of Castlemehigan; 1 plowland, 6 gneeves of Kilbarry; and 5 gneeves of Maultercormack; 3 plowlands, 5 gneeves; total, 470A.—20A. arable, 270A. pasture, nil wood, 180A. unprofitable.

In the parish of Rosse:—1 plowland of Cahirmore, 1 plowland of Treahane east of that, 9 gneeves of Maulireagan north of that, 9 gneeves of Glaunbrack north of that, 9 gneeves of Maultenevally west of that, 9 gneeves of Carrigrehane west of that, 9 gneeves of Carigfaddagh north of that; 5 plowlands, 9 gneeves; total, 2,330A.—450A. arable, 1,050A. pasture, nil wood, 800A. unprofitable.

In the parish of Fanlobish:—Neduneah, 6 plowlands, nil gneeves; total, 1,250A.—1,000A. arable, 200A. pasture, nil wood, 50A. unprofitable.

Humphry Crowley pays 6s. an acre for part of the Downings which lies near the town of Rosse, for 30A.

The other tenants pay £3 per gneeve for the Downings. Merigoe pays for the 3 plowlands of Doogh Letter and Barroghill, and for the 1 plowland and 1½ gneeves of Ballivoige, to Mr. Hull £28 per ann.

There are three books of the county Corke. In the custody of the Treasurer of the county of Corke, is (1) a large parchment book, in folio, intituled—"A Survey of the county of Corke, abstracted out of the Survey remaining upon record in the Surveyor-General's Office, subscribed by Vin. Gookin, Surveyor-General." This seems to be the oldest and most unperfect of the three books of Survey in the said Treasurer's hands. It seems to be abstracted out of the Survey of only the forfeited lands taken in Cromwell's time.

2. A large book of maps, describing the unforfeited lands in the county of Corke. Two or three parishes are usually described in one map. On the opposite side to the map, are in several columns set down, the proprietors' names, denominations of the lands, quantity

of acres by admeasurement, lands profitable, and lands unprofitable. On the other side is a transcript of the first page of this book. This admeasurement was made ann. 1659.

3. A paper book, in folio, which contains a description of all the lands forfeited and unforfeited in the county of Corke, without maps. As for the unforfeited lands, it agrees for the most part with the parchment book aforesaid, so that it does in a manner contain both the above said books. On the third page of this paper is a transcript of the first page of this book.

Part of this book contains the admeasurement made by a resolve of the Commissioners of Assessment for the county of Corke, bearing date Sept. 6, 1659.

An Index of the Baronies' Names, and Quantities of Acres in each of them, is in the Book (No. 2) of Maps of Unforfeited Lands.

No.	Baronies Names.	Profitable Lands. A.	R.	P.	Unprofitable. A.	R.	P.
1.	Youghal Liberties, .	01025	0	8	00110	0	0
2.	Immokilly, . .	09009	3	31	00277	1	13
3.	Barrimore, . .	27047	3	05	00035	1	00
4.	Killnatallone, . .	15677	2	08	00017	0	00
5.	Condon and Clangibbons,	28218	1	28	00642	3	16
6.	Armoy, als. Fermoy, .	09035	0	16	00390	3	24
7.	Orrery and Kilmore, .	13543	2	32	01128	2	16
8.	Duhallo, . .	47883	3	16	02910	1	03
9.	Mallo Manor, . .	03881	2	38	00016	0	16
10.	Barretts, . .	15778	2	00	00212	0	00
11.	Muskery, . .	00691	0	16	00038	3	24
12.	Blarney Manor, .	05006	2	08	00090	2	32
13.	N. & S. Liberties of Corke,	08529	3	04	00094	1	00
14.	Kinelea, . .	06755	3	30	00075	2	16
15.	Kirricurrihy, . .	03562	2	06	00009	2	00
16.	Coursey, . .	01562	2	24	00048	2	00
17.	Kinsale Liberties, .	01175	2	04	00000	0	00
18.	Kinealmeaky, . .	20354	1	38	00000	0	00
19.	Ibane and Barriro, .	13433	1	32	00627	1	30
20.	Carbury, . .	34231	2	39	01265	0	12
21.	Beare and Bantry, .	04521	0	16	01230	3	08
	The total is, .	278866	1	23	09221	0	10
		288087	1	33			

AN INDEX of the COUNTY of CORKE in the No. 3 PAPER BOOK.

No.	Baronies' Names.	Profitable Lands. A.	R.	P.	Unprofitable. A.	R.	P.
1.	Youghal Liberties, .	002819	1	14	00301	2	16
2.	Immokilly, . .	048324	2	28	01154	1	13
3.	Barrimore, . .	079159	3	34	00063	2	00
4.	Killenatalloone, .	015677	3	20	00017	0	00
5.	Condons & Clongibbons,	040760	0	13	03259	3	10
6.	Armoy, als. Fermoy, .	062630	0	02	06545	0	35
7.	Orrery and Kilmore, .	036752	1	19	03280	3	32
8.	Duhallo, . .	102467	1	24	27907	1	24
9.	Mallo Manor, . .	003881	2	38	00016	0	16
10.	Barrets, . .	026266	0	24	00212	0	00
11.	Muskery, . .	159270	2	22	01802	0	00
12.	Blarney Manor, .	005006	2	08	00092	2	32
13.	N. & S. Liberties of Cork,	023515	0	36	00198	1	00
14.	Kinalea, . .	031575	1	05	00983	3	24
15.	Kirricurrihy, .	012852	2	08	00142	2	00
16.	{Coursey, . .	005603	2	26	00048	2	00
	{Kinsale Libirties, .	006846	2	04	00000	0	00
17.	Kinalmeaky, . .	020354	1	38	00000	0	00
18.	Ibane and Barriroe, .	019714	1	20	00627	1	10
19.	Carbury, . .	174219	1	01	22102	0	22
20.	Beare and Bantry, .	068221	1	13	15911	1	24
	The total is, .	945919	2	3	84664	2	18

1030584 0 21

The PAPER BOOK, without Maps, in the hands of the Treasurer of the County of Cork.

Part of ye Barony of Barrymore :—

	Containt. A.	Glebe. A.		Containt. A.	Glebe. A.
Little Island Parish,	965	3	Templeusque, .	2761	0
Cahirlagh, . .	2094	5	Ardnegighy, .	9683	0
Kilquane, . .	3123	0	Killshanaghan, .	2842	0
Kilnilane p., .	1003	0			
Downebulloge, .	3589	5		26060	13

Part of Barrett's Barony:—

	Profit.	Glebe.		Profit.	Glebe.
Aglish parish, .	0971	0	Kerrigroghanemore,	0489	0
Owens, . .	0393	0	Innishkerry, als. Desart, .	0450	0
Kilnaglory, . .	1486	4			
Desart, . .	0138	42*			
Bridget's parish, .	0189	0		4654	42
St. Finbarry's parish,	0538	0			

* Of mount.

Part of the Barony of Muskery:—

	Profit. A.	Glebe. A.		Profit. A.	Glebe. A.
Ovens parish,	01949	0	Knockavilly,	1736	20
St. Finbarry's parish,	2005	0	Kilbonane,	2138	12
Ballineboy,	869	0		10632	32
Desartmore,	1935	0			

Barony of Muskery :—

	Profit. A.	Glebe. A.		Profit. A.	Glebe. A.
Moviddy parish,	3308	48	Inchigeelah,	20410	74
Aglish,	2800	5	Ballivorney,	14626	24
Kanaway,	3076	6	Dunbullog,	05841	10
Maclonehy,	2294	4	Templemichell,	01459	0
Kilmony,	5590	6			
Kilmichel,	9017	8		68421	195

North Liberties of Corke :—

	Profit. A.	Glebe. A.		Profit. A.	Glebe. A.
Curraghkippan,	1080	3	Kilcully,	4314	5
Rathcony,	3653	7	Shandon par.,	2705	2

Lands on the South of Corke :—

	Profit. A.	Glebe. A.
Statelands, a parcel of Bishop's land,	0064	0

South Liberties of Corke :—

	Profit. A.	Glebe. A.		Profit. A.	Glebe. A.
Finbarry's parish,	4837	0	Ballinoboy,	199	0
Carrigoline,	3620	0	Kilnoglory,	409	0
Killinully,	0503	0	Kerrigroghane,	1035	7
Inskenny,	1314	0			

Barony of Kinalea :—

	Profit. A.	Glebe. A.		Profit. A.	Glebe. A.
Part of Dunderrow,	0420	0	Knocknamanagh, Kil-labilly,	0436	0
Lestovie,	0721	0	Cullen,	2356	13
Part of Innishonan,	1930	0	Bealfoile,	1304	0
Templemichel,	1245	1	Nohaval,	1246	1
Part of Taxaxon,	0556	0	Kilmahanoge,	1892	8
Brinny,	0664	7	Kilpatrick,	1343	0
Knockavilla,	1319	0	Part of Carigoline,	206	0
Ballemartle,	2183	0	Kinnure,	1180	1
Ballyneboy,	1624	0	Ballifeard,	2061	2
Part of Dunderrow,	6615	0	Tracton Abby, part,	2558	0

Kirecurrihy Barony:—

	Profit. A.	Glebe. A.		Profit. A.	Glebe. A.
Templebredy, .	1746	0	Ballineboy, . .	1568	0
The Impropriation of Monkstown, .	824	0	Kilpatrick, . .	85	0
Kilmurrhy, .	307	0	Byrnihely, . .	235	0
Lisneclery, .	2251	0	Keneskiddie, . .	158	0
Carigoline, .	4964	0	Ringroan, . .	3307	0
Killinelly, .	654	0	Templetrine, .	1792	18

The Liberties of Kinsale:—

	Profit. A.	Glebe. A.		Profit. A.	Glebe. A.
Dunderrow, . .	942	14	Clonefead, . .	1727	5
Tellaxon, . .	525	4	Rincurraue, . .	2433	0
Part of Ballimartel,	249	0	Ringrone, . .	868	3

Kinalmeaky Barony:—

	Profit. A.	Glebe. A.		Profit. A.	Glebe. A.
Murragh, .	4903	0	Templemartine,	4334	0
Kilbrogan, .	4693	0	Kilmodan, .	2825	0
Breenee, part, .	1395	0	Disart, .	2203	0

Ibaune and Barriroe Barony:—

	Profit. A.	Glebe. A.		Profit. A.	Glebe. A.
Timoleage, . .	1611	0	Rathbarry, .	3541	*21
Templeomalos, .	1396	4	Kilkerane more, .	2681	5
Abbymahone, .	2614	0	Ardfield, . .	2887	*22
Donoghmore, .	717	0	Castreventry, .	499	0
Lislee, . .	3776	0	Kilmeen, . .	389	0

EXTRACT out of the BOOKS of SURVEY of the COUNTY of CORKE, kept in the hands of the Treasurer of the said County.

Barony of Kericurrehy:—

	A.	R.	P.
The Impropriation of Monkstown—			
Monkstown, ...	828	2	0
A parcel in controversy with Robertstown, . .	14	0	0
	842	2	0

Byrnehehy parish:—

	A.	R.	P.
Byrnehehy, ...	238	0	0

* In two parcels.

Riniskiddy parish :—

	Arable & past. A.	R.	P.		Arable & past. A.	R.	P.
Francis Boyle, esq., proprietor—				Part of Ballybrian, .	25	1	10
Riniskiddy, als. Rinskiddy, part of Ballybrian, . .	133	0	0		158	1	10

Barony of Carbury :—

	Profit. A.	Glebe. A.		Profit. A.	Glebe. A.
Ballymodan, .	1815	12	Temple-o-malus, .	618	0
Rathclarin, .	5481	0	Kilnogross, .	1900	0
Kilmalody, .	3074	10	Rosscarbury, .	7200	0
Part of Timoleague,	350	0	Kilmacabee, .	6613	0
Desert, . .	6009	0	Kilfaughnabeg, .	1743	0
Kenneth, . .	8694	19	Miros, . .	2348	0
Fanlobish, . .	21209	0	Castlehaven, .	5118	0
Part of Kilmahil,	2371	0	Creagh, . .	4174	0
Drinagh, . .	5696	0	Tullogh, . .	2611	0
Ballimony, .	4112	27	Capeclear, . .	655	0
Kilmine, . .	4088	0	Affadowne, . .	4334	0
Kilgarriffe, .	2483	0	Abbystrewry, .	4013	0
Islands, als. Inchidonie, . .	1074	0	Kilcroghane, .	2726	0
Castroventry, .	1855	0	Kilcoe, . .	2803	0
Temple-m'quinlan,	580	0	Scull, . .	14117	0
			Killmoe, . .	6823	3

Bear and Bantry Baronies :—

	Profit. A.	Glebe. A.		Profit. A.	Glebe. A.
Kilmacomoge, .	25672	3*	Killmanagh, .	1874	10
Killahaninagh, .	22122	0	Durrows, .	1481	0
Kilkaterine, .	4065	13			

Barony of Coursey :—

	Profit. A.	Glebe. A.		Profit. A.	Glebe. A.
Ringrone, . .	3307	0	Templebryne, .	1792	18
Killroane, . .	502	0			

INDORSED.

"Letter to the Lord Archbishop of Cashel concerning the Guardian of the Spiritualtyes." Nov. 13, '94.

MY LORD—As to the Queeres, my present thoughts upon them are these—that the Archbishop is Guardian of the Spiritualties in the vacancy of the Bishoprics in his province; this the authorities

* In two parcels.

cited by Godolphin seem to prove; unless there be some particular constitution to the contrary. [Godolph., Abridge., p. 41—Sed Quære.] And, besides, I think I have heard that it is so in the province of Ardmagh, and I do believe it is so in this province, but I have not time now to enquire particularly into it. I suppose he has by some act acknowledged you to be Guardian of the Spiritualties.

As to the second.—I suppose the power of the Vicar-General ceases upon the vacancy of the Bishopric—so says Barbosa de jure ecclesi., de vicar., et coadju. epi. No. 44; and I know, that Sir John Topham, upon the vacancy of the See of Dublin, takes out a new commission from the Deans and Chapters of Christchurch and St. Patrick's, as Guardians of the Spiritualties, and besides a Vicar-General has very rarely the power of institution granted to him in his commission.

As to the third.—I suppose he may be cited and censured in your court, and the institution be declared null unless there be some particular constitution or prescription in the diocese of Cloyne, which makes the Deane and Chapter Guardian of the Spiritualties, and that he acted by virtue of a commission from them; and I don't know what other court can properly take cognizance of it. [6th Dec., de off. vic. c. p. Amana Ecclesia.]

As to the last.—I suppose there lyes no appeal from Cashel to the Primate, that provence being no way subordinate to the See of Ardmagh, the Primate having no authority but in his own province, unless it be in wills and faculties for as much as I know of the matter, so that if there be any appeal it must be to the King in Chancery.

Your predecessor, Marsh, told me, that in the last vacancy of the See of Killalloo, he granted a commission for the administration of the Spiritualties. The Primate was Guardian of the Spiritualties when Dromore was last vacant.

If neither the Archbishop of Cashel nor the Dean and Chapter shew any precedents nor prescription, the question will then be—to whom of common right the Guardianship of the Spiritualties does belong? The books generally say, that the Dean and Chapter, of common right, are Guardians of the Spiritualties—sede vacante, custodia spiritualium et temporalium de jure communi pertinet ad capitulum. [Lyndwood.]

The lawyers say the common law of England is the same with the common law of Ireland.

When there is a controversy between a Bishop and Archbishop concerning jurisdiction, the King is to declare their bounds. [Godolp., p. 18.]

The Archbishop may not exercise his jurisdiction over the subjects of his suffragan but in certain cases. Hostiensis enumerates twenty-one cases. [Godolp., p. 19.]

The King's letter [is necessary] to stop any patent; so that, I suppose, your patent will remain of force.

But the case of the institution is not altered, but is voyd now if it was so before; and the person that instituted may be proceeded against for meddling with a thing that he had no right to meddle in.

The persons that had grants of the livings have been delay'd, it seems, so long, that there has been opportunity given to defeat their grants.

Stat. concerning citations out of the diocese—Archiep. potest excommunicare Vicarium Epi., si deliquit circa officium commissum—si peccaret in iis quæ sunt jurisdictionis. [Barbossa de archiepis. seu metrop' no. 30.]

Archiepus. potest punire crimina notoria subditorum suffraganei. [Spala., vol. i., p. 454.]

Ex ecclesiastica consuetudine et jure canonico non jure divino metropolitanus est episcopus animarum suorum suffraganeorum. [Spalatensis. vol. i., p. 455.]

Metropolitanus judex ordinarius suffraganeorum. [Spal., p. 456.] Convocata Synodo ex Gregorii magni responso ad Inter August—Archiepi Cantuarii ne Arelatensis palliatus privetur authoritate in Epo.

Canon apost. 33 Epi nihil præter conscientiam capitis gerant pœnæ a metrop. illatæ Epis. Ric. Cantuar' suspendit a divinis Ep. ob turbatam alterius Epi jurisdictionem [p. 458] [p. 459]—Quidquid potest ecclesia tota in episcopos id potest Metrop' in suffraganeos ipsius, enim nomine inter comprovinciales Epos. ille præest. [p. 464]—Conc. Sardicensi—Qui ejicitur facultatem habet confugiendi ad Epum. metropolis ut ipsius causa diligenter cognoscatur.

Causas devolvi ad metropol. per appellationem etiam nova jura confirmant—de offic. Leg. c. cum non.

Ex negligentia Eporum. etiam causæ subditorum devolvunt ad metropolitanum. Unusquisq. Epus. est universalis jure divino sed jure ecclesiastico ordinarie metropolitanus solus debet supplere negligentiam Epi nullo negotio excepto.

Notoria crimina subditor—suor—suffrag. libere corrigat Metropoli decens C. Romana 6. Quod Abbas intelligit non solum in visitatione. [Spal., p. 465.]

Patriarchæ metropolitanorum consecrationem habuerunt [p. 480], etiam jurisdictionem in illos.

Non omnes ecclesiæ subjectæ sunt patriarchis [p. 487] sed illæ solæ quæ erant illis subjectæ tempore Concilii Nicæni.

At the end of Bishop Downes' manuscript is stuck in a printed copy of Letters Patent of King William III., dated 7th of April, 11th of the King [A.D.], addressed to the Archbishops and Bishops of Ireland, authorizing and directing a collection in aid of the Vandois inhabiting the valleys on this side of the River Cluson (whose distressed state is set forth at length) to be made after the 5th of May, which was appointed for a day of General Fasting and Humiliation.

Dublin: Printed by Andrew Crook. MDCXCIX.

This is endorsed on the inside:—"Brief to collect money for the Vaudois, 1699. Collected, £380 5*s.* 6*d.* clear."

And on the back is the following note:—"The account on the other side was returned to me by Dr. Walter Neale, Vicar-General of the dioceesses of Corke and Rosse, on the 6th day of this instant September; and the summe of three hundred eighty pounds five shills. and sixpence (being the whole summe collected upon the brief for the Vaudois and other refugiez therein mentioned, in the diocesses of Corke and Rosse, over and above the apparitor's fees allow'd by the said brief), according to order of the Commissioners, was paid by me to Warham Jemmet, esq., Collector of the Customs at Corke, on the said 6th day of this instant September. As witness my hand, this 8th day of September, 1699.

"D. C. R.

"To the Right Honourable John Methuen, esq., Lord High Chancellor of the kingdom of Ireland, and the rest of the Commissioners appointed to receive the money collected upon the brief for the Vaudois, &c."

The Ancient and Modern Names of the Parishes of Cloyne, taken from the Diocesan Register, written by the Right Reverend Matthew M'Kenna, R.C. Bishop of Cloyne and Ross, in the year 1785.*

Names, Modern.	Ancient.	Patron Saints.
Aghada, consisting of—	Ahada	St. Erasmus.
	Rostellan.	
	Garrane	Dedicated to Purification of B.V.
	Inch	Dedicated to Nativity of B.V.
	Corcabeg	Dedicated to the Holy Cross.
Ahina	Ahinagh	St. Ruan.
Annakissy	Monanimna	St. Nicholas.
	Clenur	Ste. Cranette.
	Carig	Ste. Mary Magdalen.
Ballinamona	Ballynamona	St. Michael.
Ballyclough and Kilbrin	Ballyclogh and Killbrin.	
Ballyhea	Ballyhaura	Dedicated to B.V.
	Cooline and Dridinach	Dedicated to the Holy Trinity.
	Imerick	St. Mathew.
	Ardsky	St. Michael.
Ballymacoda	Kilmacdonog	St. Peter ad Vincula.
	Kilcreidan	Dedicated to the Holy Cross.
	Garrivow	Dedicated to the B.V.
	Iochtermorow	Dedicated to the B.V.
	Bouchalan	Dedicated to the B.V.
Ballyvourney	Ballyvourney	Ste. Gobineta.
Blarney and Whitechurch	WhiteChurch and Blarney	
	Gara-Cloyne	
Buttevant	Buttevant	Ste. Bridget.
	Temple-Mary	Dedicated to B.V.
Carrigtoohil		
Castlelyons	Castle-Lyons	St. Nicolas.
	Brithway	Ste. Bridget.
	Cool	
Castlemagner	Castlemagner	Dedicated to the B.V.
Coachford	Magourney	St. Colman.
	Ahabollog	St. Eolan.

* This document was kindly given to the author by the present R.C. Bishop of Cloyne, the Right Reverend William Keane, D.D.

Names, Modern.	Ancient.	Patron Saints.
Castletownroche and	Castletown-Town Roche	Dedicated to B.V.
Ballyhooly . .	Ballyhouly .	Dedicated to Nativity of B.V.
	Killaty.	
Charleville . .	Charleville .	Dedicated to Exaltation of the Holy Cross.
Clondrohid.		
Clonmeen . .	Clonmeen . .	St. Furseus.
	Kilcorny . .	St. Nicholas.
Cloyne . . .	Cloyne . .	St. Colman.
	Churchtown .	St. Nicolas.
	Kilteskin . .	Dedicated to B.V.
	Shangarry .	Ste. Machua, sister to Mac Con or Colman.
Conna or Curiglas .	Moguily.	
	Balinoe . .	Ste. Catherine.
	Aghern . .	Ste. Columba.
	Knockmoorny.	
Doneraile . .	Doneraile . .	Dedicated to the Nativity of the B.V.
	Cahirdugan.	
	Temple-Ruane .	St. Ronanus.
Donoughmore .	Donnachmore .	St. Lactine.
Fermoy . .	Fermoy . .	St. Molaisse.
	Clondullane .	Dedicated to the Assumption of B.V.
	Kilcrumper .	Dedicated to the Purification of B.V.
Freemount . .	Kilballane . .	Dedicated to the Assumption of B.V.
	Tullaleas . .	St. Benignus.
	Knock-an-temple	St. Michael.
Glanworth . .	Glanworth .	Dedicated to the Invention of the Holy Cross.
	Dunmahon .	St. Bernard.
	Kilgullane .	Dedicated to the B.V.
	Derryvolane.	
	Ballyclough .	Ste. Catherine.
Glountane . .	Kilsanig . .	St. Sannagh or Sennagh MacCarrðil.
Grenagh . .	Grenach . .	St. Lactine.
Imogeela . .	Mogeely . .	Dedicated to the B.V.
	Clonmult . .	St. Lawrence.
	Dungourney .	St. Peter.
Iniscarra . .	Cloch-Roe . .	Dedicated to the Holy Cross.

Names, Modern.	Ancient.	Patron Saints.
Kanturk.		
Kildorrery . .	Kildarrery .	St. Bartholomew.
	Farrehy . .	St. Colman.
	Moluga . .	St. Molagga.
	Currigdownan .	Dedicated to the Immaculate Conception of B.V.
	St. Nicolas .	St. Nicolas.
Killeagh . .	Killeah . .	St. Farrel.
	Ardagh . .	St. Glassine.
	Dangan . .	St. James.
Kilworth . .	Kilworth . .	St. Martin.
	Macrony . .	Dedicated to the B.V.
	Leitrim . .	As supposed to the B.V.
	Kilmurry . .	Dedicated to the B.V.
Kilnamartara .	Tuathnadroman	St. Lactine.
Liscarroll, and	Liscarroll . .	Dedicated to the Purification of the B.V.
Churchtown . .	Churchtown .	St. Nicolas.
Lisgoold . .	Lisgoold . .	St. Macodom.
	Ballycranan .	Dedicated to the B.V.
	Temple-Beodan .	St. John the Baptist.
	Templenacarrigy	
Macroom . .	Macroom.	
Mallow . .	Mallow . .	Dedicated to the Nativity of the B.V.
Mitchelstown .	Marshalstown .	Dedicated to the B.V.
	Brigown . .	St. Finachin.
Midletown . .	Midleton . .	Dedicated to the B.V.
	Ballynachtrach .	St. Callachan.
	Churchtown, *alias* Inchy na Baccy	B.V.
	Ballyspolan .	St. John the Baptist.
Newmarket . .	Clonfert . .	St. Brandin.
Queenstown . .	Clonmel . .	St. John the Baptist.
	Temple-Robin.	
Rathcormac .	Rathcormick .	Dedicated to the B.V.
(*Shandrum, Patron unknown*)	Gurtroe . .	B.V.
Youghal . .	Youghal . .	Dedicated to the Assumption of the B.V.

The PARISHES of Ross, with the Names of their PATRON SAINTS, as kindly furnished to the author by the Right Rev. Michael O'Hea, D.D., R.C. Bishop of Ross.

	Parishes.	Patron Saints.
1.	Timoleague, and	Nativity of B.V.M.
	Kilmaloody	St. Mulooda.
2.	Abbeymahon, and	St. Bernard.
	Lislee	B.V.M.
3.	Rathbarry, and	St. Michael.
	Ardfield	St. James.
4.	Kilgarave	Nativity of B.V.M.
	Kilnagross	Dedicated to the Holy Cross.
	Temple-O-Malis	St. Malis.
	Temple-Quinlan	St. Quinlan.
5.	Kilmeen, and	St. Marina.
	Castleventry	Dedicated to the Holy Trinity.
6.	Rosscarbery	St. Faughnan, son of Mongach.
	Kilkieran	St. Kieran.
7.	Kilmacobea	B.V.M.
	Fachnabeg	St. Faghna.
8.	Castlehaven, and	St. Barrachane.
	Myross	St. Brigid.
9.	Skibbereen (as believed),	St. Patrick.
	and Creagh	Unknown.
10.	Tullagh	Unknown.
	Cape Clear	St. Kieran.
	Sherkin	St. Connuil.
11.	Affadown	St. Congallus.
	Kilcoe	Unknown.
	Abbeystrewry	Unknown.

ABBREVIATIONS.

Ab. or Abb.	Abbas or Abbathiam.
ad. or adm.	Admittitur, or admissus fuit.
Burke's L. G.	Sir Bernard Burke's "Landed Gentry."
Caulfield MSS.	Manuscripts of Richard Caulfield, esq., F.S.A.
C.B.	Chapter Book.
Chor.	Chorum or choral.
coll. Epi.	Collatione Episcopi.
Cotton	Cotton's "Fasti Ecclesiæ Hibernicæ."
D.R.	Diocesan Registry.
E. Ecca, Eccia, or Ecclia.	Ecclesia.
F.P.	Family Papers.
Imp. improp. impropriata	Impropriator, impropriate.
Lib. Mun.	Liber Munerum Hiberniæ.
M.B. or Mar. Bond	Marriage Bond.
M.L.	" Licence.
M.S.	" Settlement.
MS. T.C.D.	Manuscript in Trinity College Library, Dublin.
P. or Preb.	Prebend. Prebendary.
P.C.	Perpetual Curate or Curacy.
Ptic.	Particula.
R. Rec. Rect.	Rectory or Rector.
R.V. R.I.A.	Royal Visitation in the Royal Irish Academy.
R.V. 1615	Royal Visitation of the year 1615.
R.V. 1634	Royal Visitation of 1634, now in the Consistorial Office, Dublin.
Tax. P. Nic.	Taxation of Pope Nicholas.
U.O.	Ulster's Office.
V. or Vic.	Vicar or Vicarage.
V.B.	Visitation Book.
V.B. D.R.	" in Diocesan Registry.
V.B. 1699. D.D.	Visitation Book of 1699 by Bishop Dive Downes.
Vic. Chor.	Vicar or Vicarage Choral.

RECORDS OF CORK, CLOYNE, AND ROSS.

CORK.

AGLISH.

15—? Dermitius McEglinge.

1581. Feb. 3. Donatus Edmund Moroghen (vice M'Eglinge deprived) was admitted V. de Maall als Aglish. I give the record of his admission entire:—"Idem Epus (Matheus Sheyn) contulit vicariam Ecclisæ Beatæ Marie de Maall als Agalis Donato Edmundi Moroghen Corcagen dioc. clerico per deprivationem dermitii mtt Eglinge tunc vacantem cum dispensatione de non premovendo ad septenium studiorum causa 3 ffebruarii, 1581°. Inductus in pōem dictus donatus per Archidiaconum. Phil. Gold, Registrar." [1st Book of Cork Registry, fol. 51.]

1591. Donatus O'Morough laicus Vicar de Aglis propter defectum sacrorum ordinum et manifestam contumaciam deprivatus. [MS. T.C.D. E. 3. 14.]

1615. July 12. Thomas Davies adm. Vicar de Aglis. [F.F.] He was also P. Inskenny, q. v.

Agglis Rectr. Magister de Mora et Preb. de Kilbrogan. Spectat ad Hospit. de Mora. Ecclesia et cancella in ruinis. Vic. Thomas Davies, Min Legens. Val. 4 li. [R.V. 1615. R.I.A.]

R. de Aglis spectat ad Abb. de Grany et Preb. de Kilbrogan. Cormack Donagh Carty et John Snary Clicus firmarii. Value to Cormack Donogh, 7 li. per an. Vicarius ibm. Thomas Davies. Val. 7 li. per an. [R.V. 1634.]

1634. Decem. 19. Morgan Mundyn. R. Kilnemartery et V. Aglish [F.F.]

Una Rectoria de Aglis spectat ad Mora, altera ad P. de Kilbrogan John Snary. Ecclesia ruinata. Desunt omnia. Vicar. Morgan Mundyn. [V.B., 1639.]

1663. May 21. Bernard Packington, D.D., V. Moviddy, Kilbonane, and Aglis. [F.F.] And also Archdeacon of Cork, q. v.

1674. May 27. Richard Sing, V. Moviddy, Kilbonane, and Aglish, and Kilcully; also V. Whitechurch, in Cloyne. [F.F.] And Archdeacon of Cork, q. v.

B

1688. Sept. 5. ZACHARIAS BRALY, A.B. (per mort. Sing), V. Moviddy, Kilbonane, and Aglis, quibus vicariis rect. imp. unitæ sunt per ltras Dni. Regis. [D.R.]

In 1691. Braly est in Anglia. [V.B., D.R.]

Vide Currograngemore, Ross.

1697. Aug. 27. JOHN WETENHALL (per mort. Braly), V. Moviddy, Kilbonane, et Aglis, et P. Currograngemore, Ross. [F.F.], quibus Vicariis rectoriæ impropātæ de Moviddy et Aglish, per ltras patent. Regis unite sunt cum clausula unionis. [D.R.] He was also Archdeacon of Cork.

Moviddy church in repair. Sermon every Sunday. Sacrament three times a year. [V.B. 1699, D.D.]

"Oct. 16, 1700. Saw Aglish Church. (Aglish means church in Irish.) It stands on the top of a hill.

"Aglish Church built with stone and lime. South wall is down. It lies north-east of Moviddy Church. . . . The church-yard contains at least an English. . . . . has been cut off from the west end about half . . . . by a . . . flax was sowed in it. Memorand.: to speak to the Archdeacon. There seems to be the foundation of a house in the west part of it.

"About five English acres of glebe on the S. of the church near it; belongs . . . . . . About seven or eight Protestant families in this parish; they go to Moviddy Church, which is at least three miles distant from Aglish Church.

"About thirty plowlands in this parish, of indifferent good land. The lands of this parish belonged to the Earl of Clancarty and Colonel Macarthy, of Aglish. —— Croneen was Popish Priest of this parish, and of Ballivourny. Dermot Murphy is now Priest. He lives in Aghabullog parish; he was formerly in the diocese of Cloyne; he has now also the parish of the Ovens.

"The Prebendary of Kilbrogan has in this parish one rectory. Part of this parish lies north of the River Lee. The Incumbent's proportion of the tithes of it was worth £40 per annum. Mr. Harrison received it formerly, in Archdeacon Synge's time." [Dives Downes' Journal.]

Archdeacon Wetenhall died in 1717.

1717 to 1740. GEORGE M'CORMICK appears at visitations as R. V. Moviddy, Kilbonane, and Aglis. [V.B., D.R.] He was also R. V. Kilnemartery, Cloyne, q. v.

On 16 May, 1739, Thomas Blennerhasset, A.M., was admitted to one R. Aglish, vacant by voluntary resignation of William Jackson, P. of Kilbrogan. This R. was, in 1746, restored to Kilbrogan. [D.R.]

1740. November 4. SAMUEL BROME, A.M. (per mort. George M'Cormick), Vic. Kilbonane, R. V. Moviddy, and V. Aglish. [D.R.] He was also Chancellor of Cork, q. v.

1768. July 20. EDWARD KENNY, A.B. [per death of Samuel Brome, D.R.], R. and V. Moviddy, V. Kilbonane and Aglish. [F.F.] He was also P. Inskenny, q. v.

1770. June 16. Edward Kenny memorials to build at Moviddy, and again in 1771, Sept. 27. Both memorials being approved, &c., the Bishop issues a commission to value, Oct. 28, 1791. The return dated 19 Dec., 1791, finds £379 2*s.* 1½*d.* to be the expenditure of Kenny, which sum is certified by the Bishop, and the yearly value of R. and V. Moviddy is certified at £371 5*s.* 6*d.* [D.R.]

1818. June 20. THOMAS ST. LAWRENCE, A.M. (per mort. Kenny), R. V. Moviddy, Kilbonane, and Aglish. [F.F.]

Certified to be under £300 per an. in value.

1831. Protestant population 31.

Vide Currograngemore.

1833. March 28. JOHN HENRY MADRAS, A.B. (per mort. St. Lawrence), V. Aglish. [F.F.] Certified under £400 per an.

In 1833, April 17, a Petty Sessions house in this parish was licensed for Divine Service. [D.R.]

1834, January, the present parish Register commences.

John Henry Madras, son of Rev. John Madras (R. V. Kilcully, q. v.), by Alice Baldwin; was born in the city of Cork, and entered Trin. Coll., Dub., in 1791, where he graduated A.B.

Deacon, 1797, July 25; Priest, 1797, Dec. 21, both at Cork.

1797 to 1798 Curate of Kilmichael; from 1798 to 1801, Curate of Durrus; 1801 to 1813, Curate of Kinneigh; 1813 to 1833, P. C. Nohoval.

He married in 1801, Martha, d. of Richard Evanson, Esq., of Friendly Cove, co. Cork, by whom he had issue: Alice, John, P. Donoghmore Ross, q. v.; Richard, Robert-Conner, Alleyne-Evanson, Elisabeth, and Anne-Connor. He died on 6 July, 1852, and was buried at Desertmore.

1852. July 15. WILLIAM COLBURN, A.M. (per mort. Madras), V. Aglish [F.F.]

In 1852, Aglis was certified by Eccles. Commiss. as of the net annual value of £257 13*s.* 8*d.* [D.R.]

On 24 July, 1856, a new church, with church-yard, built on a new site, was consecrated by name of St. James. [D.R.]

1837. Aglish. A vicarage with cure, 5 miles long by 4½ broad, containing 6,665 acres 1 rood and 39 perches. Gross population 2,782. No Curate employed. Income, composition for vicarial tithes, £310. Seven acres of glebe demised at 10*s.* per acre, £3 10*s.* Subject to visitation fees, 8*s.* 6*d.*; diocesan schoolmaster, 9*s.* No G. H. Incumbent is non-resident, but resides near the parish, and pays £30 a year for house rent. No church. Divine service is celebrated once on Sundays, and on Christmas Day and Good Friday, in a house licensed by the diocesan for the purpose. The Sacrament is administered eight times in the year. The rectorial tithes of five townlands in this parish, compounded for £120, are impropriate, and claimed by Major Philip Cross, as lessee of the impropriator; and the rectorial tithes of three denominations, compounded for £39 2*s.* per annum, are appropriated to the Prebend of Kilbrogan. [Par. Rep.]

1860. £236 annual value. The church, &c., in good order.

There is no Glebe-house, and the glebe of seven acres is set.

The Incumbent resides in adjoining parish, within a short distance of the church.

There is Divine Service every morning on Sundays, and on Good Friday, Ascension, and Christmas Day. Evening service during summer.

Sacrament monthly and on festivals. Ten communicants.

Children are catechised every Sunday in the church by the clergyman. Explanation oral. There is no school, nor are there children to attend one. There are sixty-eight Protestants.

William Colburne, third son of William Colburne, of Cork, esq., by Sarah, d. of William Heard, esq., also of Cork, was born in Cork city, in 1797. He entered T.C.D. as F.C. at the age of seventeen, on 6 Nov., 1815; and graduated B.A. in 1819, and A.M. in 1832.

He was ordained Deacon on 1 June, 1823, and Priest on 21 December same year, both by Bp. of Cloyne.

From 1823 to 1827 he was Curate of Killaspugmullane; and from 1827 to 1852 he served the cure of Blackrock, near Cork.

He married in 1835, Julia, d. of Robt. Coghlan, esq., of Cork, and by her has issue Elizabeth, Charles-Freeman, Sarah-Louise, and Joseph-Capel.

ARDNEGIHY.

1291. Ecclesia de Garthenegeythe is rated at 4 marks. The Vicar receives a half. [Tax. P. Nic.]

1591. E. de Garrinaghihy locus vastatus et desertus vacõe THOMÆ WOOD non admiss. [MS. T.C.D. E. 3. 14.] Wood appears in 1591 as P. St. Michael's, q. v.

1615. Garnehihie, Rector THOMAS DAVIES, Minister legens residens et inserviens curæ. Val. 4 li. per an. Tenet etiam Vic. de Garrycloyne, valor 5 li, et V. de Aglis val. 4 li. per an. [R.V., R.I.A.]

Davies was also P. Inskenny, q. v.

1634. Sept. 5. URBAN VIGORS, R. Ardnegihy, and V. Grennagh, Cloyne. [F.F.]

E. de Ardnegihie Urbanus Vigors Clicus. Predicator est in Anglia. Valet X li. per an. [V.B. 1634.]

In 1637 Vigors became V. Marshalstown, Cloyne, q. v.

1637. Feb. 17. BRYAN ROCHE, R. Ardingihy. [F.F.]

In 1640 he became Vicar of Lisclery, q. v.

1639. BARNARDUS ROCHE appears, "excusatur" [V.B., D.R.] Perhaps Barnardus is the same with Bryan Roche. He does not appear elsewhere.

1663. May 1. PETER MANBIE, R. Ardnegihie. Preb. and Vic. Lisclery, and Vic. Cannaway. [F.F.] *Vide* Lisclery.

1666. This Rectory is vacant, with Peter Manbie's name crossed out. [V.B., D.R.]

1665/6. Feb. 14. PETER HEWIT, R. Ardnegihy, per desertion of Peter Manby. [V.B. of 1669, D.R.]

He appears as R. Ardnegihy from 1667 to 1675. [V.B., D.R.] In 1675 Hewit became Chancellor, and in 1710 Precentor of Cork, q. v.

1675. Feb. 25. HUGO JENKINS, R. Ardnegihie, V. Ballymodan, Rathclarin, and Cannaway. [F.F.]

Jenkins appears until 1679 in V.B. [D.R.] He was again admitted in 1681 V. Ballymodan and Rathclaren, q. v.

1680. Vacant [V.B. of November 3, D.R.]

1681. June 14. JOHN TOM, A.M., R. Ardnegihy. [F.F.]

Tom appears in V.B. 1681 to 1685 [V.B., D.R.] In 1686 he became V. Kinsale, and in 1693 P. Desertmore, q. v.

1686. Mr. ANDREW SYMES appears with the remark "nulls. titula." in V.B. [D.R.] He was instituted to R. Ardnegihy on 7th September, 1687. [F.F.] And he is thus noticed in V.B. of 1689—"Mr. Andrew Symes debet fœda quœdm. ult. visit. et non extraxit ltras ordinum." [D.R.] He appears from 1686 to 1691. [V.B., D.R.]

In 1691 he became V. Fanlobbus, and in 1718 became Precentor of Ross, q. v.

1691. Dec. 7. ALEXANDER OGILBY, A.B., R. Ardnegihy, per resignation of Andrew Symes. [D.R.] Ogleby, or OGilby, or Ogilby, in 1694 became P.C. Ballinaboy, &c., q. v.

1693/4. April 3. CHRISTOPHER SHEARES, A.B., R. Ardnegihy, per cession of Alexander Ogilby. [D.R.] He was also P. Killaspugmullane, q. v.

1694/5. Feb. 7. DANIEL SMITH, A.M., R. Ardnegihy, per cession of Christopher Shears. [D.R.]

In 1696 Smith became also P. Cahirlag, q. v.

1696. Nov. 3. Vacant. [V.B., D.R.]

1696/7. January 7. JOHN DEWEY, A.B., R. Ardnegihy, per mortem Daniel Smith. [D.R.]

Dewey was ordained priest at Cork on 23rd September, 1694. He became a Vicar Choral, Cork, in 1694, and V. Kilcully, and R. Ardnegihy in 1696; all which he retained until his death in 1697.

1698. Sept. 19. SOLOMON FOLEY, R. Ardnegihy, and R.V. Kilcully. [F.F.] per mortem John Dewey. [D.R.] He was also P. Kilnaglory. Appears 1698 to 1704. [V.B., D.R.]

No Protestants, except 2 families. They go to Kilcoan. Ruins of a church. No churchwarden or parish clerk. [V.B. 1699, D.D.]

"Oct. 1, 1700. I saw Ardnegihy Church, which was built with stone and clay; the walls are almost all down, except the west end; this church is about two miles distant from Templeusky Church, to the north of Templeusky Church. There is a ditch about the church-yard of Ardnegihy. The lands of this and the adjoining parishes are for the most part heathy mountain ground. In this parish is a plowland called Bishop's Island, on the left hand of the road from Cork to Rathcormock; it is the estate of Mr. Mitchel. This parish is worth to the Incumbent about £30 per annum. This parish extends from the church towards the north-west, to within three or four miles of Moyallo. The Earl of Barrimore, the Brodericks, and Mr. Mitchel, Prots. and Mr. Roche, Pap. have the greatest part of the estates in this parish. Mr. Richard Wakeham, Prot. David Terry, Pap. who gives the seventh part of his milk to the poor, and Mr. Sarsfield, of Sarsfield Court, on a farm under Mr. Coppinger, of Dublin, live in this parish.

"This parish is an entire rectory. It is worth about £25 or £30 per annum to the Incumbent.

"James Barry is Popish Priest of this parish, and of Kilcoan and Kilshanughan, and Ardnegihy, and Killvulane. Mr. Foley, catechist at St. Barry's, is rector of this parish; he has the profits of it in consideration of his office of catechist. Mr. Sheares had this parish in his titles. The people of this parish go to church either at Rathcormack or Rathcony. No glebe in this parish." [Downes' Tour.]

In 1704 Foley became P. Kilbrogan, q. v.

1704/5. January 5. JOHN POMEROY, R. Ardnegihy, and R.V. Kilcully. [F.F.]

He appears in V.B. of 1723. [D.R.] He was also Chancellor, and afterwards Archdeacon, of Cork, q. v.

1724. Nov. 3. No name appears at this visitation. [V.B., D.R.]

1724/5. Feb. 13. THOMAS RUSSELL, A.M., R. Ardnegihy, and Archdeacon of Cork, per mort. Pomeroy. [D.R.]

He appears 1725 to 1744. [V.B., D.R.] *Vide* the Archdeaconry of Cork.

1745. May 10. JOHN THOMAS ATKIN, A.M., R. Ardnegihy. [F.F.] Per mort. Russell. [D.R.]

John Thomas Atkin, son of Walter Atkin, Treasurer of Cloyne, q. v., was baptized at Middleton, 26th Feb., 1701/2, and entered Trinity College, Dublin, as a pensioner, on 2nd May, 1719, being then eighteen years old. He graduated in that University as A.B., and afterwards A.M. He was ordained priest at Cloyne on 27th February, 1728.

1727, August 9, lic. cur. of Christ Church.

1730 to 1745, P. St. Michael's.

1745 to 1765, R. Ardnegihy.

1747 to 1765, Vic. Chor. Cork.

1752, May 14, lic. cur. of St. Nicholas.

He married in 1728 (M.B., dated 30th October), Margaret, d. of Rev. Mathew Jones, by Bridget, d. of Sir R. Kennedy; and by her, who was also a niece of Edward Jones, Bishop of Cloyne, left issue at his death in 1765 one son, Walter, ancestor of the Atkin family of Leadington, county Cork, for which see Burke's L. G.

1765. Feb. 14. EDWARD BROWNE, A.M., R. Ardnegihy. [F.F.] per mort. Atkin. [D.R.]

Browne, being absent in Great Britain at the time of his preferment to Ardnegihy, obtains a prolongation of the period for reading his assent and consent until 14th May, 1765. [D.R.] He was also P. Killaspugmullane, &c., &c., and Archdeacon of Ross, q. v.

1777. Dec. 15. WILLIAM JEPHSON, A.M., R. Ardnegihy, per mortem Brown. [F.F.] He was Archdeacon of Cork, q. v.

From 1777 to 1796 Ardnegihy was held with the Archdeaconry of Cork, q. v.

1796. June 2. CHARLES HEWITT, A.B. (per mort. Whetham), R. Ardnegihy. [F.F.]

On 1st June, 1797, the Lord Lieutenant and Council order the site of the church to be changed, in compliance with a memorial of incumbent and churchwardens, stating that there is no church, the old one being many years in ruins, and inconveniently situated, and that Edward Hudson had, on 19th April last, granted one acre of the lands of Glenville to the churchwardens for ever, for a new church and churchyard. [D.R.]

In 1803 Hewitt became V. Ballymodan, q. v.

1803. Aug. 1. WILLIAM LEWIS BEAUFORT, A.M., R. Ardnegihy [F.F.]

1804. The present parish registry begins.

1807. Beaufort resides near Cork Cathedral as Preacher Residentiary. [Rep.]

In 1814 he became P. Cahirlag, q. v.

1814. Sept. 2. HONOURABLE GEORGE GORE, A.M., R. Ardnegihy. [F.F.] Certified to be under £500 per annum in value. [D.R.]

Mr. Gore was seventh son of second Earl of Arran. He was born in 1774, and died 27th August, 1844, and was buried at Killala.

He resigned Ardnegihy June 26, 1817, on becoming Dean of Killala.

1817. July 19. THOMAS PHILIP LE FANU, A.M., R. Ardnegihy. [F.F.] Certified under £500 per annum. [D.R.]

Thomas Philip Le Fanu was ordained deacon on 30th April, 1809, by Bp. of Clonfert; and priest on 16th September, 1810 by the same Bishop. He was appointed Assistant Chaplain of the Lying-in Hospital, Dublin, in 1809, and was afterwards one of the Curates of St. Mary's, Dublin, which laborious post he continued to occupy until 1815, when he was selected by Lord Whitworth, the Lord Lieutenant, as Chaplain of the Royal Hibernian School in the Phœnix Park. In 1817 he was promoted to the Rectory of Ardnegihy, and in November, 1823, to that of Abingdon, Emly dioc. He was made Dean of Emly in 1826, but retaining Abingdon. He died on 24th June, 1845, and was buried at Abingdon. His talents as a preacher were of a high order, and he was of refined manners and cultivated mind. His amiability endeared him to his friends, and his benevolence to the poor. He was A.M. and LL.D. of T.C.D.

He was the representative of a noble Huguenot family of Normandy, possessing in that province, and chiefly in the generalité of Caen, many estates, among which were Mondeville, Sequeville, Cresseron, &c. The certificate of Noblesse, officially signed by Guy Chamillart, bearing date 1671, and now in possession of J. S. Le Fanu, esq., of Merrion-square, Dublin, proves their nobility by charter to the year 1595.

On the revocation of the Edict of Nantes, they were deprived of their estates; but having relatives of influence in the Court of Louis XIV., they were permitted to leave France with their personal property, without molestation. Two members of this family, John Le Fanu de Sequeville, and Charles Le Fanu de Cresseron, held cavalry commissions in the army of William III. Charles was upon the King's staff, a brave and excellent officer, and distinguished by being presented from William's hand with his portrait. He afterwards served as major of dragoons under Marlborough. Early in the last century William Le Fanu was the sole representative of this family. He married Henrietta Raboteau de Puggibaut, the only surviving daughter of a Huguenot family, also noble. Her escape from France, when still a child, was accomplished under circumstances of romantic danger, and by the aid and contrivance of a Roman Catholic uncle, who held a considerable post in the Court of France. Of this marriage there were issue several children, sons, who, with the exception of Joseph, all entered the army or the church.

Joseph held the office of Clerk of the Coast in Ireland, and was the eldest of these sons who died leaving issue; by his first marriage to Anne Franklin, he had one son only, William Le Fanu, called to the Irish Bar, who died unmarried in 1817, and is very honourably recorded in Warburton's History of the City of Dublin.

Joseph Le Fanu, married secondly, Alicia, daughter of Thomas Sheridan, and sister of the Right Honourable Richard Brinsley Sheridan. Of this marriage there were three children, who, except the eldest, Thomas Philip Le Fanu, the subject of this notice, died unmarried. His (Joseph's) brother, Captain Henry Le Fanu, of Leamington, co. Warwick, married Elizabeth, the only other sister of R. B. Sheridan.

Dean Thomas Philip Le Fanu, married, in 1812, Emma Lucretia, daughter of the Rev. William Dobbin, F.T.C.D. and D.D., Rector of Finglass and of St. Mary's, Dublin (by his wife Catherine, youngest daughter of Robert Coote, esq., of Ash-hill, co. Limerick, and aunt of Sir Charles Coote, of Ballyfin, bart.) Of this marriage there were three children, Catherine Frances, who died unm.; Joseph Sheridan, barrister, who m. Susan, d. of the late George Bennett, Q.C., of Merrion-square, Dublin, and has issue two sons and two daughters; and William Richard, civil engineer, who m. Henrietta, youngest d. of the late Sir Matthew Barrington, baronet, and has issue three sons and one daughter. [F.P.]

1822. Edward Hudson, M.D., of Dublin (famous for his skill in dental surgery), who had, in 1797, given the site of the church; by his will, dated 9 Sept., 1816, and proved 14 Feb., 1822, in Dublin, bequeathed £500 to assist the public in erecting, in Glenville (Ardnegihy) church-yard, a hollow cone or pyramid for performing his experiments on the pendulum, and for elucidating the phenomena of comets, planets, &c. He desired to be buried in a vault beneath this pyramid. He was father of Edward Gustavus Hudson, Dean of Armagh.

1823. Novem. 18. RICHARD DEANE FREEMAN, A.B., per cess. Lefanu, R. Ardnegihy. [F.F.] This appointment was by the Marquess Wellesley, Lord Lieutenant of Ireland, to whom the nomination was yielded by the Bishop, in courtesy, as the former Incumbent was promoted by the Crown.

1831. Protestant population, 98.

1837. Ardnegihy. A rectory entire, with cure; 12 miles long by 8 broad, containing 15,546 acres and 3 roods. Gross population, 3,715. One Curate employed, at an annual stipend of £69 4*s.* 7½*d.*, British. Composition for tithes, £438 9*s.* 3*d.* 64 acres, 3 roods, and 7 perches of glebe, valued at £20. Subject to visitation fees, 10*s.* 6*d.*; diocesan schoolmaster, 13*s.* 2*d.* No glebe-house. Incumbent is non-resident, from inability of procuring accommodation in the parish: he resides at Charleston, near Middleton. One church, capable of accommodating 200 persons, built about the year 1798, at the cost of £461 10*s.* 9¼*d.* Brit., granted as gift by the late Board of First Fruits. No charge on the parish in 1832 on account of the church. Divine Service is celebrated once on all Sundays, and on the principal festivals. The Sacrament is administered on the three great festivals. [Par. Rep.]

1860. Value £321. The church in good repair. A vestry was built for this church by the Rev. Samuel Dickson Sandes, formerly Curate of the parish. There is no font. The Communion plate consists of a cup and flagon *silvered*, the former gilt inside.

There is no glebe-house nor glebe. There was formerly a glebe of 40 acres, for which a fine of £200 was paid by Board of First Fruits, and a rent agreed on of £30 per an.; but as the agreement was made on an insufficient stamp, the proprietor (Dean Hudson) enclosed these lands in his demesne, and the Incumbent of Ardnegihy was thus deprived of a site on which he had arranged to build a glebe-house, with the help of a loan from Board of First Fruits of £900. Incumbent resides at Fermoy, 10 miles off, and frequently officiates in his church. Curate is constantly resident. Service is celebrated at noon on Sundays, and the four chief festivals. Sacrament monthly. Average of communicants is 7. No school. Protestant population, 40.

Richard Deane Freeman, third son of Edward Deane Freeman, of Castlecor (for a full account of the ancient families of Deane and Freeman, and their alliances to noble houses, *vide* Burke's L. G.), was born at Castlecor, co. Cork, on 11 August, 1789, and was a fellow-commoner of T.C.D., where he graduated with distinction in 1811, and subsequently became A.M.

He was ordained Deacon by Bp. of Cloyne, on 30 Nov., 1811; and Priest in 1812, by Bp. of Limerick, on letters dimissory from Cloyne.

In 1812 he was Curate of Mallow; and in September, 1813, was licensed to Middleton curacy. He was domestic Chaplain for some time to the late Earl of Shannon.

He married, at Kilkenny, in 1812, Ellen, d. of Rev. Rowland Davies, by whom he had issue, six sons (of whom but three, Edward, Rowland, and Richard, now survive), and five daughters, Elizabeth, Mary Jane (died 1861), Ellen, Frances, and Wilhelmina. The youngest son married Miss Rush, d. of Ambrose Rush, J.P., of Taylor's Hill, Galway. One of the daughters, Ellen, is wife to Captain Hamilton Thompson, 59th Regt. Another, Frances, married Major Henry Robert Crew Godley, late of H. M. 28th Regt. [F.P.]

Rev. R. D. Freeman died at Clifton, near Fermoy, on 12th of January, 1863.

1863. Feb. 17. SAMUEL HAYMAN was appointed by the Bishop R. Ardnegihy. His collation will be hereafter mentioned.

S. Hayman (eldest son of Matthew Hayman, esq. of South Abbey, Youghal, by Helen, third dau. of Arundel Hill, esq. of Doneraile), was born at Youghal on 27th July, 1818. He was educated at Youghal by Rev. Thomas Nolan, and afterwards at Clonmel by Rev. Robert Bell, D.D. He entered T.C.D. as a

Fellow Commoner on 18th October, 1835, and graduated A.B. on 2nd July, 1839.

He was ordained Deacon at Cork on 19th September, 1841, and Priest at Killaloe on 14th August, 1842.

From 1841 to 1847 he was Curate of Glanworth; from 1847 to 1849 Curate of Glanmire; and from 1849 to 1863 Curate of Youghal.

He married, at St. Anne's, Belfast, on 26th September, 1854, Emily, dau. (by his first wife, Henrietta, dau. and co-heiress of Samuel Jackson, esq.) of the Rev. Marcus Cassidy, Chancellor of Kilfenora, and Incumbent of Newtownards, co. Down; and by her has issue an only child, Emily-Henrietta-Aline Hayman.

For an account of the very ancient family of Hayman *vide* Rev. Atkin Hayman, V. Ballyclogh, Cloyne, who was the great grandfather of Rev. Samuel Hayman.

The pen of the Rev. Samuel Hayman, during the intervals of parochial duty in the important parishes where he laboured so faithfully as a Curate, has not been idle. He has contributed articles, in prose and verse, too numerous to mention in detail, to various periodicals, including the *Dublin University Magazine*, the *Christian Examiner*, the *Gentleman's Magazine*, and the *Patrician*; of which latter work the fifth volume was inscribed by the editor, Sir Bernard Burke, Ulster, to the Rev. Samuel Hayman, as "one of the ablest contributors to the pages of the *Patrician*, and a constant coadjutor in the author's genealogical works." He has also published the following works:—

1. "The Bible, the Wisdom of a Nation." A Sermon on Deuteronomy, iv. 5–9. (In the *Church of England Magazine*, vol. xx.) London: Edwards and Hughes, 1846.
2. "The Annals of Youghal." First Series. Youghal: J. W. Lindsay, 1848. Medium 12mo, pp. 44.
3. "A Farewell Sermon, preached in Glanmire Church, 18th February, 1849." Cork: The Religious Tract Depository, 1849. Medium 8vo. pp. 32, and Appendix.
4. "An Account of the Present State of Youghal Church (including Memorials of the Boyles), the College, and Sir Walter Raleigh's House." Youghal: J. W. Lindsay, 1850. Medium 12mo, pp. 52.
5. "The Annals of Youghal." Second series. *Ibid.* 1851. Medium 12mo, pp. 20.
6. "The Annals of Youghal." Third series. (The Handbook for Youghal.) *Ibid.* 1852. Crown 8vo. pp. xvi. and 96.
7. "Notes and Records of the Ancient Foundations at Youghal, county Cork, and its Vicinity." Youghal: John Lindsay, 1854. Medium 8vo, pp. 60. [Reprinted in 1855, and again in 1859.]
8. "To-day: its Duties and its Supplies." A Lecture deli-

vered before the Cork Young Men's Association, 27th January, 1857. Dublin: George Herbert, 1857. Small 8vo, pp. 31.

9. "The Annals of Youghal." Fourth series. (The new Hand-book for Youghal.) Youghal: John Lindsay, 1858. Medium 8vo. pp. xxxvi. and 76.

10. "Time and Teaching: A New Year's Address to Sunday-School Teachers." London: Church of England Sunday School Institute, 1860. Small 8vo, pp. 22.

11. "Guide to Youghal, Ardmore, and the Blackwater." With a Map and Sixty Illustrations. Youghal: John Lindsay, 1860. Foolscap quarto, pp. 90.

12. "The Illustrated Guide to the Blackwater and Ardmore." With Twenty-five Illustrations. *Ibid.* 1861. Small quarto, pp. 44.

13. "The Illustrated Guide to Saint Mary's Church, and to the other Ancient Religious Foundations at Youghal." 1862. Small quarto.

14. "Memorials of Youghal." Foolscap quarto. (*In the press.*)

ATHNOWEN.

1581. April 4. WILLIAM FELD, or FIELD. "Vicaria ecclesiæ parochialis beatæ Mariæ de Athenowyn, Corkagen dioc. concessa est per collationem Epī et Inductionem Archidiaconi Willmo feldio clerico dictæ dioc. cui unacum prefata vicaria dispensatio de non premovendo et de non residendo per quinquennium authoritate Epī data est 4 Aprilis, 1581." [D.R.]

1591. R. de Athnowin Abb. Morne et Granie. Vic. ibm. Willmus felde. [MS. T.C.D. E. 3. 14]. William Field was also P. Holy Trinity, q. v.

1611. February 8. WILLIAM HEALY, V. Athnowen. [R.V. 1634.]

1615. Ecclesia de Athnowen, Rectors Magister de Mora et Grany. Vicar William Healy Minister legens. Val. 3 li. Church and chancel in ruins. [R.V., R.I.A.]

"William O Hialyhy (Healy) noe graduate. His wife and children goe to Masse. Hath V. Athnowen in lapse. Val. 14 li." [MS., Probate Court, Dublin.] Healy was also Chancellor of Cork, q. v.

1632. June 5. JAMES CLELAND, Vicar. Athnowen, inducted 14 June. [R.V., 1634.] Cleland became, in 1635, Vicar Kilmaccabee, Ross, q. v.

1634. JAMES HOLLAND appears as V. Athnowen. "R. de Athnowen spectat ad Abb. de Mourne et Graney. Cormack Donogh Carty, et Peregrinus Spencer firmarii. Val. 14 li. per an., Vicar James Holland, sed sub lite. Epūs confert. Val. £14 10*s.* per an." [R.V., 1634.] Holland does not appear elsewhere.

1639. . . . . . JOHN NEWTON, P. Killaspugmullane and V. Athnowen. [F.F.] R. de Athnowen pertinet ad Mora et Grany. Vic. ibm. John Newton. Ecclesia bene et ornata. [V.B. of Nov. 4, 1639, D.R.] *Vide* Killaspugmullane.

1661? . . . . PHELIMY FITZSYMONDS, V. Athnowen and Precentor of Cork, q. v.

1664. June 10. RICHARD CLERKE, Precentor of Cork and V. Athnowen [F.F.], per mortem Phelimy Fitzsymonds [V.B., D.R., 1669], appears to 1685. [V.B., D.R.] *Vide* the Precentorship.

In 1670, Hugolinus Spenser appears as Firmarius of the R. Athnowen, and of R. Brinny and Kilvoynan. [V.B., D.R.]

1686. WALTER NEALE appears as Precentor and R. V. Athnowen. [V.B., D.R.] *Vide* the Precentorship.

He appears in V.B. 1706, Nov. 3. [V.B., D.R.]

1699. No church. Two Protestant families, who go to Carrigrohane. [V.B. 1699, D.D.]

1706. Feb. 11. EVAN DAVIES, R. and V. Athnowen. [F.F.]

He appears in 1715. [V.B., D.R.]

He was also P. Templebryan, Ross, q. v.

1717. RICHARD BALDWIN, Altera R. V. Athnowen, appears 1717 and 1718. [V.B., D.R.]

In 1720 he became P. Kilbrittain, &c., q. v.

1720 to 1724. THOMAS RUSSELL appears in V. B. as Precentor, and R. V. Athnowen. [V.B., D.R.]

In 1724 he became Archdeacon of Cork, q. v.

1724. Feb. 13. JEMMET BROWNE, R. V. Athnowen and Precentor of Cork. [D.R.]

In 1732 he became R. V. Little Island; and in 1733, Dean of Ross, q. v.

1732. March 19. THOMAS RUSSELL, A.M., ad unam R. et V. Athnowen, per resignation of Jemmet Browne. [D.R.] *Vide* Archdeacons of Cork.

1745. June 1. CHRISTOPHER DONNELLAN, D.D., ad unam R. V. Athnowen, vacant per mort. natural. Thomæ Russell. [D.R.] and same day to P. Kilnaglory, on a second collation to the Prebend. [D.R.]

From 1745, the R. V. Athnowen has been held with the Prebend of Kilnaglory, q. v.

BALLINABOY.

The successions to the curacy of Ballinaboy and of all the other impropriate parishes in this diocese, are irregular, and for some periods of time not accounted for: when the curacy was vacant, the duties were performed by the neighbouring clergymen.

1291. Ecclesia de Boye is rated at 12 marks.
Ecclesia de Belachssribrad, rated at 10 marks. [Tax P. Nic.] Between Cullen and Pollyplicke. Could this be Ballinhassig?

1591. EDMUND McBREAN is Curate. "E de Ballinoboy, Willm. Gogan ffir, spectat ad Ab. de Antro. Impr. Edmundus mcbrean cur. nullas exht. lrãs ordm. interdicitur." [MS. T.C.D. E. 3. 14.] McBrean was also Curate of Carrigaline.

1615. RICHARD ALLEN is Curate. "Ecclia de Balliboy, Rector Abb. de Antro. Spectat ad Gilleabby. Richardus Boyle, miles, firmarius. Richardus Allen, minister legens inservit curæ. Ecclesia et cancella in ruinis. Vicaria est indotata per antiquos rotulos sed nullus vicarius." [R.V., R.I.A.] Allen does not appear elsewhere.

1634. WILLIAM ROBINSON is Curate. "Ecclesia de Ballynaboy Spectat ad Abb. de Antro. Comes Cork, integer impropriator. Valet 60 li. per an. Curatus Willmus Robinson habet pro inservicione 50*s.* per an., and the boke-money 50*s.*" [R.V. 1634.]

Wm. Robinson is still Curate in 1639, at which time the church is noted as "bene et ornata." [V.B. 1639.] Robinson appears also as Rector of Templemichael de duagh in 1639.

1666. HUGO SCAMPE appears as Curate of Ballinaboy, Barnahely, Kilpatrick, Tracton, and Inskenny. [V.B., D.R.]
He was also V. Aghadowne, Ross, q. v.

1667. Pertinet ad Comes Shandon. COTTRELL, curatus. [V.B.]

1669. JOHN HARRISON appears as Curate of the nine parishes of which, in Cork diocese, the Earl of Shannon is Impropriator—"nulli vicarii indotati"—namely, the Rectories of Ballinaboy, Kilmoney, Barnahely, Kilpatrick, Tracton, Ballyfiard, Pollypleick, Clontide, and Kinure. [V.B. 1669.]
Harrison appears as Curate up to 1679. [V.B., D.R.] He was, in 1689, V. Cannaway, q. v.

"1676. *Ballineboy* (fo, 7), 13*s.* 3*d.* per plowland raised for walling the church-yard of Ballineboy parish. Benjamin Cotterel and Edward Porter, overseers." [Cork Presentments.]

1680 to 1687. THOMAS DENT appears as Curate of Ballinaboy, Kilmorey, Barnahely, Kilpatrick, and Tracton. [V.B., D.R.] Dent was also from 1682 P. Kilnaglory, q. v.

1688. Mr. BARRY LOVE appears as Curate of Ballinaboy, Kilmorey, Barnahely, Kilpatrick, Tracton, Clonteade, and Kinure. [V.B., D.R.] He was ordained Priest at Cork on 28 September, 1687. He does not appear elsewhere.

1692. July 14. JAMES WADE, A.B., is admitted Curate of Ballinaboy, Barnahely, Kilmoney, Tracton, Kilpatrick juxta Tracton, Ballyfiard, Pollypleick, Clonteade, and Kinure. [D.R.] He was also Vic. Chor. Cloyne, q. v.

1693. May 12. ALEXANDER OGILBY is admitted Curate of Ballinaboy, Barnahely, Kilmoney, Tracton, Kilpatrick juxta Tracton, Ballyfiard, Clonteade, and Kinure. [D.R.]

He appears 1699. [V.B., D.R.]

1699. No church. Many Protestants, who go to Ballimartel. The inhabitants made a proposal for building a church in this parish. [V.B. 1699, D.D.]

"1699. August 18. Ballinebury, upon the river half way betwixt Corke and Kinsale; the church ruinous; the walls were built without lime. Major Rigg's monument there: this church is conveniently situated for several parishes."

"Sept., 1700. I saw Ballinebury church; 'twas rebuilt this last summer with stone and clay, and plaister'd within and slated, but not glaz'd; they were about finishing of it. This church was rebuilt by a voluntary contribution of the parishioners. I gave £5 towards it. It is about 30 foot long, and 18 broad. It stands on the south of the river Bury, at about 200 yards distance from it."

"Sept. 28, 1700. Saw Rinmahon Church, on the south of the river Lee, a mile and a-half below Corke. The church stood about 200 yards distant from the village called Ballintemple, upon the rising ground. The walls of the church are almost quite ruinous, and the bounds of the church-yard are hardly discernible. Ballintemple is one plowland in the parish of Rinmahon. All the tythes of this parish belong to the œconomy of St. Barry's, worth about £30 per an. The lands of this parish belong to Mr. Coppinger, Mr. Roch, Major Clayton. Mr. Coppinger forfeited, in the late rebellion, his interest, being two plowlands. Mr. Synge, as Prebendary of Christ Church, has one plowland, where the black rock is, in this parish, set for about £30 per an. The people of this parish go to Divine Service at St. Barry's, Corke. Captn. Hayes, Hammond (Quaker), at Dundanion, live in this parish—all the rest are Papists. Coleman is Popish priest of this parish, and all St. Barry's parish; his mass-house is near the Red Abby; he has been here three or four years; one Dooly, a priest, assists him."

"Oct. 1700. I saw Barnehely church, which was built with stone, lime, and clay. The walls are above half down. It was about 28 foot long, and 17 broad. The bounds of the church-yard are hardly discernible. There is but one plowland in this parish. This parish is the estate of the Ld. Lanesborough; Mr. Folliot is tenant to it. Henry Gostry, Prot., and John Nevill, Pap., live in this parish. About two English acres of glebe near the sea. The glebe and tythes of the parish belong to Dean Sam Synge, as Impropriator; nothing is allow'd by him to any clergyman for serving the cure; I don't know his pretence for it. The tythes and glebe are set for £6 per an., by lease to Capt. Folliot. The people go to Carrickoline to church. 'Tis thought something ought to be allow'd for serving the cure, tho' it does not appear that they formerly paid tyth. The Coghans, who were the old proprietors, were very powerful, and 'tis likely they withheld the tythes with a high hand."

"Oct. 1700. I saw Ringskiddy and Ballibricken. Ringskiddy and Ballibrickan are one plowland and 15 acres. Ringskiddy makes the point betwixt Carrickoline bay and Raphine brook. There is a heap of rubbish in Mr. Abraham Dickson's orchard at Ballybrickan, which was a church heretofore. Captn. Hayes remembers the walls standing. 'Tis said by the inhabitants that Ringskiddy and Ballibrickan belongs to the parish of Kilgarvan, in the Great Island. Sed Qu."

"The people of both these places pay their tythes to Mr. Folliot, tenant to Dean Synge. Nothing is allowed to any clergyman. Island Creagh, Island Core, and Island Cahill, in the harbour of Corke (being almost unprofitable) belonging to the lands of Ringskiddy. Hallboling Island is the estate of the Crown. There is an old fort on it, built in Queen Eliz. time, now out of repair, formerly the Earl of Corke was governor of it. All these islands, together with Spike Island, belong (as 'tis said) to the Great Island. Ringskiddy and Ballibrickan are the estate of Dean Saml. Synge. Mr. Abraham Dickson lives at Ballybrickan. All these tythes of Ringskiddy and Ballibrickan were formerly enjoyed as mensal tythes belonging to the Bishoprick of Corke or Cloyne, by Bishop Synge, and were by him set to Captain Folliot, about thirty years ago, for about £4 per an. Captn. Hayes, Qu. Dean Davies."

"Ballibricken, 'tis supposed, is the same with Templebracknany in the Visitation Books."

"The people go to Carrickoline to church. Rinmahon parish contains 8 plowlands to the east of Blackrock. The church stood near Captn. Hayes' house, and near the village of Ballintemple, so called from the church near it. Roch and Coppinger had most of these lands which they forfeited in the last rebellion to the king. Captn. Hayes and George Serles live in this parish. No glebe. A plowland in this parish belongs to the Prebendary of Christ Church, worth about £40 per an. All the tythes belong to the œconomy, worth about £30 per an."

"The people come to St. Barry's Church. This parish has been suppos'd to be united to St. Barry's for these forty years last past. They pay tythe of turf and potatoes, &c., in kind, in this and the adjacent parishes." [Downes' Tour.]

Alexander Ogilby, a literate, was ordained Deacon by Bp. of Cork, on 14 June, 1685.

In 1686 he was licensed to teach grammar in the parish of the Holy Trinity, Cork; and same year appears as Vic. Chor., Cork, which post he occupied in 1695. From 1691 to 1693 we find him Rector of Ardnegihy, and in 1693 he was Curate of Ballinaboy and other impropriate parishes near Cork. He was licensed to the curacy of Ballyfeard in 1696. His name disappears before 1704.

1704. MICHAEL BUSTEAD appears as Curate of Ballinaboy, 1704 to 1709. [V.B., D.R.]

In 1715 Bustead became V. Ballyfeard, q. v.

1715 to 1729. EDMOND MOLLOY appears as Curate. [V.B., D.R.] Molloy was Vic. Chor., Cork, q. v., and died in 1735.

1730 to 1744. No mention of Ballinaboy in Visitation Books, but in Cork registry there is an entry, dated 12th June, 1743, to the effect that Eliza Meade "recants" on that day in the Parish Church of Ballinaboy, before James Delacourt, Clk.

1744 to 1755. Mr. JAMES DELACOURT appears as Curate. [V.B., D.R.]

James Delacourt (the eldest son of John de la Court, of Cork, and brother to Robert, ancestor of the Delacour family now in co. Cork), was born at Killowen, co. Cork, in 1709; and when eighteen years old, entered T.C.D. as pensioner, on 29 January, 1727, and graduated subsequently A.B. and A.M.

He was ordained Priest on 24 July, 1737, at Cork.

He held the curacy of Ballinaboy, from 1744 to 1755.

He died unmarried. He is noticed by Smith in his History of Cork, as a poet, and author of the "Progress of Beauty," and the "Prospect of Poetry." [Smith's Cork, vol. ii., p. 427.]

1756 to 1760. JOHN WRIXON appears as Curate. [V.B., D.R.] He was also Vic. Chor., Cork, q. v. He died in 1764.

1766. April 4. JOHN CORKER, A.B., is licensed to be Curate of Ballinaboy, on nomination of Charles, Duke of Dorset, Impropriator of said parish, at stipend of £20.

In 1770 he became V. Killaconenagh, Ross, q. v. [D.R.]

1805. Oct. 7. THOMAS FORSTER SAUNDERS, A.B., is licensed to be Curate of Ballinaboy and Tracton, at £70 per an., on nomination of Henry, E. of Shannon; and he is again licensed, to curacy of Ballinaboy only, on nomination of the same Earl, at £25 per an., on 5 Jany., 1809. [D.R.]

Thomas Forster Saunders was son of Mr. Richard Saunders, of Cork, by Rebecca, d. of George Forster, of Cork, merchant.

He was ordained Priest at Cloyne, on 24 August, 1800.

He married, at Christ Church, Cork, on 12 March, 1807, Barbara Morgan.

1814. August 15. JAMES STEWART, A.B., was licensed as Curate assistant at £25 per an., on nomination of the E. of Shannon. [D.R.] In 1817 Stewart became P. Desertmore, and in 1825 V. Lislee, Ross, q. v.

1817. January 20. HENRY THEOPHILUS HODDER, A.B., is licensed to be Curate at £25 per an., on nomination of E. of Shannon. [D.R.] Hodder became, in 1818, R.V. Leighmoney, and in 1826 Precentor of Cork, q. v.

1819. March 15. THOMAS BEAMISH, A.B., is licensed to be Curate at £25 per an., on nomination of the Earl of Shannon. [D.R.]

1831. Protestant population, 124.

1837. Ballinaboy. A perpetual cure, with spiritual duties annexed, erected within the impropriate parish of the same name; 3½ miles long, by 2¾ broad, containing 7,084 acres. Gross population, 2,887. No Assistant Curate employed. Stipend payable by the Impropriator, £23 1*s.* 6½*d.* Augmentation allowance payable by Ecclesiastical Commissioners out of Boulter's fund, £46 4*s.* No glebe-house. Incumbent is resident, and pays a rent of £25 for a few acres of ground, on which he has, at considerable expense, erected a house for his own convenience. One church capable of accommodating 100 persons, built more than a century ago, but at what cost unascertained. No charge on the parish in 1832 on account of the church. divine service is celebrated twice on Sundays, generally, in summer, and once during the rest of the year, and on the principal festivals. The Sacrament is administered monthly, and on Christmas Day. The tithes of this parish compounded for £500, are wholly impropriate, and belong to the Earl of Shannon; but it is reported that for the last forty years the parish has not paid tithes, the parishioners having, occasionally, during that period, been engaged in giving resistance to his lordship, and alleging that they are at present ready to do so, should he act on the suit still pending, conceiving that there exists, on his lordship's part, no legal claim. [Parl. Rep.]

Thomas Beamish was eldest son of George Beamish, esq., of Clogheen, near Clonakilty, co. Cork.

He was ordained Deacon on 28 February, 1819; and Priest on 7 March, 1824, both at Cork.

1841. AMBROSE HICKEY, P. C. Ballinaboy.

1860. Annual value, £69. Church and everything requisite for divine service in a satisfactory state. No glebe-house or land. Service once each Sunday, and on Christmas and Good Friday.

Sacrament monthly, and at principal festivals. Average of communicants, 12.

Curate catechises every Friday and Sunday in the usual way.

Sixteen children attend a Ch. Ed. School. The Protestant population is 37.

Ambrose Hickey, youngest son of Rev. A. Hickey, R. Murragh, married, in 1843, the only daughter of Captain Archbold, who was first-cousin to the present Lord Bellew.

BALLINADEE,—Treasurers.

1291. Ecclesia de Dowach, rated at five marks. E. de Kylyban at six marks. E. de Rathdruchtin at four marks. [Tax P. Nic.]

1337. J is the initial of the Treasurer. [Plac. Com. Banc. Hib.]

1370. William Gall, Treasurer. [Cod. Clar. 36.]

1591. Dermitius Long, Thesaurar, non exhibuit chartas ordinum. Interdictus et suspensus ab officio et beneficio, fructus sequestrat. defectu sacrorum ordinum. [MS. T.C.D. E. 3. 14.] E. de Dowaughe als Ballynedy vacat sequestrat. pro Regina, the name D. Long being crossed out. [Ib.] Particula de Gortnagrosse sequestrat. [Ib.] E. de Kilgobban vacat per resignationem Dermitii Long et sequestratur ex Scaccario pro primitiis Regineis. Vicar ibm. Mauricius O Contye. [Ib.] E. de Rathdrontin D. Longe sequestr. pro Regina, vacat. [Ib.]

Dermot Long, in 1591, had nine livings, namely, the Treasurership, R. Killanully, Templemichael de duagh, V. Cannaway and Kilmichael, in Cork, and P. Timoleague, R. Tullagh and Creagh, and R. Kilnagross, in Ross.

1607. November 28 . . . Owen, R. Dowaghe, dioc. Cork. [Lib. Mun.] This was probably Richard Owen, who, in 1613, became P. Kilnaglory, q. v.

1615. John Brock, Thesaurarius, in artibus Magister. Valor 4 li. Tenet etiam locum vicarii choralis in Ecclesia Cathedrali, valor duodecem librarum, et prebendam de Inskyne in Ecclia Corcag. valor quinque librarum. Præterea ipse est Ludimagister et docet scholam publicam et recepit stipendium viginti librarum annuatim. homo dignus. [R.V. R.I.A.] Dowagh als Ballinedyn Rectoria spectat ad Tracton. Ecclesia et cancella bene repãntur, cum libris et aliis necessariis. Val. 7 li. per an. Vicarius Robertus Sutton, A.M., Predicator, residens, et inserviens curæ. Val. 7 li. per an. Tenet etiam Vicarias de Kilbrogan et Disertserges per unionem. [Ib.]

Rathdrowen, Rector, John Hussey (R. Templetrine), parcella de Ballineddy. Vicar ibm. Henry Hussey. Kilgobban Particula de Killanedy; but from records it appears to be an entire rectory. Henry Hussey, A.M., is Rector and Vicar. He is also V. Ringrone, and R. Templetrine. [Ib.]

1618. Dnus Epũs univit et annexit Thesauriatui Corcagen. vicarias de Macloneigh et Beatæ Mariæ de Shandon Corcagen. dioc. January 20, 1618. [R.V. 1634.]

Brock was ordained Deacon on 30th October, 1608, and Priest on 31st March, 1610, both by Bp. Cork.

From 1610 to 1634 he appears as Vic. Chor. Cork; from 1615 to 1626 as Treasurer; from 1615 to 1634 as Vic. Chor. Cloyne; from 1615 to 1618 he is P. Inskenny; and from 1615 and 1616 V. Mackloneigh and Shandon.

Brock, in 1616, took the degree of A.M. in T.C.D. He was married, and his fourth son, Richard, born in Cork city, entered T.C.D. as a pensioner, on 26th July, 1641, at the age of 18 years.

1626. June 22. HELSHIAS (or Hilkias) HUSSEY, Treasurer of Cork, per cession of John Brock, with P. Ballindeighie et capellis de Kildarrarie, Cloghane, et Rathdrountine et E. de Kilgobane, et V. Ringroane, united by Bishop to the Treasurership. Installed 24th June. In 1627 he receives also the R. Templetrine, and in 1628, July 5, the Archbishop of Armagh gives him a dispensation to hold all these benefices together. [R.V. 1634.]

[1628. March 20. JOHN JEFFRAY is presented to Parsonage of Ringroane, Ballynidea als Rathdreuton, Kilgobbane, and the . . . . of Car. diocese Cork, with clause of union pro hac vice tantum. [Lib. Mun.] Perhaps this appointment never took effect. He does not appear elsewhere.]

1634 E. de Kilgobban spectat ad Thesaur. E. de Rathdrenton similiter. Particula de Kildarrere et Cloghane similiter. E. de Dowagh als Ballynedy similiter. [R.V. 1634.]

1639. Ecclesia de Ballynadighy spectat ad Thesaurm. idem Hussey curatus. Ecclia bene et ornata. Kilgoban (ruinata) spectat ad Thesaur. Rathdrenton (ruinata) similiter. Particula de Kildarrerie et Cloghane similiter. [V.B. D.R. 1639.]

In 1641 Hussey was plundered by rebels of property to amount of £1,270, besides the loss of Treasurership and Templetrine, worth £300 "communibus annis." [M.S. T.C.D. F. 2. 16.]

Hilkias Hussey, A.B., T.C.D., in 1623. Afterwards A.M. and S.T.D.

Deacon and Priest on 26th January, 1624, by Bp. of Cork.

He was, in 1626, Treasurer of Cork and V. Ringrone, and in 1627 R. Templetrine. He held these livings (except Ringrone, which he resigned in 1634) until 1666, when he was deprived.

He was alive in 1683 and afterwards, for the court books of Cork of that date contain records of proceedings against "Hilkiam Hussey, S.T.D. in casu substr. sallarii sive feod," for which the sentence of excommunication was decreed by the Ecclesiastical Court.

1666. Dec. 21. THOMAS GOODMAN, Treasurer of Cork [F.F.] per deprivation of Hilkiah Hussey. [V.B. 1669, D.R.]

He appears as Treasurer, 1666 to 1680. [V.B. D.R.]

Rectoria de Ballynadee particula et membrum Thesauriatus. [V.B. 1669.]

Goodman was also V. Garrycloyne, Cloyne, R. Rathcony and Shandon, and Templetrine, and in 1675 Precentor of Ross, q. v.

1681. April 29. WALTER NEALE, A.M., Treasurer. [F.F.]

He appears 1681 to 1685. [V.B. D.R.]

In 1686 he became Precentor of Cork. q. v.

1686. March 29. HENRY RYDER, A.M., Treasurer. [F.F.]

Henry Ryder (whom I suppose to have been the son of Thomas Ryder, Secretary to the English Embassy at Paris, who was second son of John Ryder, Bishop of Killaloe, 1613 to 1632), was born at Paris, and was educated at Westminster, Cambridge, and Dublin. He was King's Scholar at Westminster.

1681. September 26, to 1692, P. Mayne, Ossory.
1683. September 17, to 1693, P. Malahidart, Dub.
1685. October 29, to 1686, P. Holy Trinity, Cork.
1686. March 29, to 1687, Treasurer of Cork.
1692. March 30, to 1693, Archdeacon of Ossory.
1692. April 9, to 1693, R. Attanagh and Aharney, Ossory.
1693. June 11, to 1695, Bishop of Killaloe.

He died S.P. on 30th January, 1695/6, and was buried at Clonmethan, county Dublin. His will, dated 12th January, 1695/6, was proved in Dublin on the 12th April following. He was uncle to Rev. Thomas Ryder, P. Brigowne, Cloyne, q. v.

1687. June 30. RICHARD LAPP, A.M., Treasurer. [F.F.]

In 1688 he became Archdeacon of Cork, q. v.

1688. Nov. 2. JONATHAN FALKNER, A.M., of Magd. Oxon, Treasurer. [F.F.]

1699. The church not in good repair. Divine service weekly, every Sunday. [V.B. 1699, D.D.]

"1699. Ballinadehy Church is in pretty good repair, pulpit and seats in half of it." [Downes' Journal.]

1701. July 8. The Bishop certifies that Jonathan Falkner did, since 1690, erect one good dwelling-house, out-houses, garden, orchard, and other necessary improvements, on the glebe lands of Ballynadee, fit and convenient for him and his successors, at the cost of £250. [D.R.]

Jonathan Falkner, A.M. of T.C.D. in 1684, was from 1684 to 1710 P. Cooline, and from 1684 to 1693 V. Bregoge, and from 1684 to 1699 V. Liscarroll.

He married, firstly, in 1693, Jane, d. of ——— White, esq., of Doneraile [Cloyne, M. B.]; and secondly, Grace Masters, of S. Finbar's, spinster. [Cork, Mar. bond, Aug. 7, 1708.] His will, without signature or date, was proved in Cork 9th Feb., 1710. In it he wishes to be buried in the chancel of the church of Ballinadee, "close by his late wife, Jane;" and leaves his present wife, Grace Falkner, universal legatee. [Cork Wills.]

1711. June 30. JOHN MOORE, jun., A.M., Treasurer. [F.F.]

John Moore, jun., A.M., was son of John Moore, Archdeacon of Cloyne, and belonged to the ancient family of More or O'Moore, of Leix, in Queen's county, now extinct in the male line.

He was first, in 1690, Curate of Innishannon, and in 1698 to 1699 was R. Templemichael de Duagh. In 1699 he was made P. Kilbrittain and V. Ballyfeard, which he resigned in

1711, on becoming Treasurer of Cork. He held, in addition to the livings which he obtained in 1699, the Vicarage of Rathclarin, from 1701 to 1714, the V. Innishannon from 1702 to 1738, the R.V. Mackloneigh from 1712 to 1749, the R. Templemichael de Duagh from 1715 to 1746, and the Rectory of Innishannon from 1729 to 1749.

He married Anna Maria Folliott (daughter of Captain John Folliott, by Joane, fifth daughter of Edward Synge, Bp. Cork, sister to Edward Synge, Abp. of Tuam), of St. Finbarry's, in 1700, by whom he had issue Rev. Charles (Rector of Innishannon, q. v.) (born 1717, Pens. T.C.D. 1734), and Pierce; besides daughters, Anna Maria, wife of Boyle Travers, esq.; another daughter, wife to Thomas Corker, of Innishannon, esq., and Catherine, the youngest daughter, wife to Rev. John Meade, of Ballymartle, q. v. He also mentions in his will (dated 1748, and proved at Cork, 1749), Dr. Joseph Leadbetter as a son-in-law. He bequeathed £40 to the poor of Innishannon, Leighmoney, Templemichael, and Ballinadee. He died in 1749.

1749. June 2. JOHN SMITH, A.M., Treasurer. [F.F.] The corps of the Treasurership consists of R. integ. Kilgoban, Rathdowlan, Ballinadee, and one R. Macklonagh. [D.R.]

In 1755, John Smith obtains a commission to view a dwelling-house, barn, and other improvements at the glebe of Ballinadee, which commission is returned on April 8th, and a certificate is granted for £201 10*s.* 4*d.*, on May 19, 1756.

By this return it would appear that quarrymen at Ballinadee worked for 8*d.* a-day; labourers at 6*d.*; a man and horse for 1*s.* per day. Twenty-five dozen of floor tiles cost £1 0*s.* 10*d.* Three tons and one and a-half f. balk timber, £6 7*s.* 6*d.* 3,000 brick, delivered at Ballinadee, came to £1 12*s.* 8*d.* Thirty single deals cost £2 12*s.* 6*d.* Lime for plastering cost 2*s.* per barrel. Slate, 3*s.* per 1,000. "Bought a horse for £3 15*s.*, and sold him again for £2 5*s.* 6*d.*; allowed £1 2*s.* 9*d.*" Hair for plastering, 8*d.* per barrel. The total return is £201 10*s.* 4*d.*; and the certificate states that the house, &c., is very fit and convenient for the residence of John Smith and his successors. [D.R.]

John Smith, A.M., Scholar, T.C.D., in 1736.

Ordained Priest at Cork on 19 December, 1742.

He appears as Curate of Ballymodan, in 1747, and was licensed to that curacy in 1751.

From 1749 to 1770 he was Treasurer of Cork.

He married Elisabeth Lucas, of Desertserges [Cork. Mar. bond of June 5, 1742]. He had issue by her a daughter, Elisabeth (vide the will of Hart Smith, his brother), and died in 1770.

1770. Oct. 9. JAMES WEEKS, A.B., Treasurer (per mort. Smith), and R. Kilgoban, Rathdowlan, Ballinadee, and Macloniegh. [F.F.]

James Weeks, on 24 Feb., 1769, had been licensed to the curacy of Holy Trinity, Cork. He died in Dec., 1775, leaving his widow, Mary Weeks, otherwise Hughes, sole executrix. [Cork Wills.]

I find that a James Weeks, fil. James "generosi," was born in Cork, and obtained Sizarship, T.C.D., on 3 June, 1734, being then sixteen years old, and that the same, or another James Weeks, graduated in the same University, in 1750. In 1668, a Nicholas, fil. William Weeks, born at Loughgur, co. Limerick, entered T.C.D. as a Pensioner.

1775. Dec. 11. JOSEPH WELD, A.M., Treasurer. [F.F.] In 1776 he became R. V. Tullagh and Creagh, and in 1777 became Archdeacon of Ross, q. v.

1776. March 25. JOHN DENIS, A.M., Treasurer. [F.F.]

1777. August 26. John Denis memorials for permission to lay out £40 on the out-offices of Ballinadee, and the Bp. consents, Sept. 3, 1777. In 1778, Nov. 2, a commission to view issues, and the return is made 1778, December 17, finding that Denis had expended £40 10*s.* 7*d.* In this return mason's hire is charged at 1*s.* 7½*d.* per diem, and labourer's at 7*d.* per day. [D.R.]

John Denis, A.M., T.C.D., was from 1750 to 1776, V. Ballymodan, and from 1776 to 1787, Treasurer of Cork. He died 1787.

Among the Cork marriage bonds is one for the marriage of John Denis, Clk., with Mrs. Elisabeth Beven, of Kinsale.

1787. April 25. HON. PERCY JOCELYN, A.B., Treasurer. [F.F.] He was 3rd son of 1st Earl of Roden.

1787, April 25, to 1795, Treasurer of Cork.
1788, Nov. 22, to 1790, R. Tamlaght, Armagh.
1788, Dec. 5, to 1790, Archdeacon of Ross.
1790, March 18, to 1809, Treasurer of Armagh.
1796, January 12, to 1809, P. Disert, Lismore.
1809, August 26, to 1820, Bishop of Ferns and Leighlin.
1820, April 3, to 1822, Bishop of Clogher.

He was deprived of his Bishoprick in 1822, and died in Dec., 1843, and was buried at the New Cemetery, Edinburgh.

Jocelyn resigned the Treasurership of Cork on 4 July, 1795. [F.F.]

On 15 July, 1795, Rev. Wm. Herbert Saunders is appointed Sequestrator of the vacant Treasurership. [D.R.]

1795. Sept. 1. VERNEY LOVETT, A.M., Treasurer. [D.R.] The date of his institution, according to F.F., is July 4, 1795.

1807, Dr. Lovett resides partly at Lismore, where he has a prebend. [Rep.]

On 10 January, 1809, the Bishop certified that Lovett had spent on the glebe, &c., £60 16*s.* 2*d.* [D.R.]

In 1815 he became P. Kilbrogan, and in 1818, R. Kilnagross, Ross, q. v.

1815. Feb. 11. EDWARD ST. LAWRANCE, A.M., Treasurer [F.F], certified under £500 per an. in value. [D.R.] In 1818 he became V. Kilmaccabee, &c., and V. Fanlobbus, and in 1825, Archdeacon of Ross, q. v.

1818. April 25. JAMES STEWART, A.M., Treasurer [F.F.], certified under £500 per an. in value. [D.R.] In 1825, Stewart became V. Lislee, Ross, q. v.

1825. August 24. JOSEPH JERVOIS, A.B., Treasurer. [F.F.]
In 1831 he became R. Ardagh, Cloyne, q. v.

1831. April 20. SOMERS PAYNE, A.B., Treasurer. [F.F.] He was presented by Crown, sede vacante, on letters patent, dated 15 Feb., 1831.

1831. Protestant population, 129.

1837. Ballinadee Union, with cure consisting of:—1. Ballinadee rectory. 2. Kilgoban rectory. 3. Rathdowlan rectory. Extent of union not stated, as the parishes are not contiguous, consisting of 8,466 acres. Gross population, 2,800. One curate employed, at an annual stipend of £75, with the use of the glebe-house and glebe. Tithe composition of Ballinadee par., £581 11*s.* 9*d.*; 8 acres and 15¾ perches of glebe, valued at 30*s.*; per plan. acre, £7 10*s.* Tithe composition of Rathdowlan parish, £35; ditto of two ploughlands in Kilnaglory parish, £35; subject to visitation fees, 9*s.* 6*d.*; diocesan schoolmaster, £1. Ballinadee glebe-house is a condemned building, and unfit for residence; but at the expense of Incumbent, it has been rendered a tolerably comfortable residence for the Curate. Incumbent resides in a neighbouring parish, within three miles of Ballinadee parish, on his own property. One church, situate in Ballinadee parish, capable of accommodating 150 persons, built so many years ago that the date and cost of its erection unknown. No charge on the union in 1832, on account of the church. Divine Service is celebrated twice on all Sundays and on the principal festivals. The Sacrament is administered on the first Sunday in the month and on the festivals. The benefices constituting this union are rectories. [Parl. Rep.]

On 22 August, 1853, a commission condemns the old glebe-house, and recommends a new one to be built on a new site, the value of the old materials being only £30. [D.R.] In 1857, Dec. 23, Bp. certifies that Rev. Somers Payne expended £1,160 on glebe-house and offices; that net yearly value is £481 14*s.* 10*d.*; that £165 3*s.* 6*d.* is necessary to complete the glebe-house and offices; and that £798 6*s.* 2*d.* is the sum of right chargeable on benefice, being two years' income less by the sum of £165 3*s.* 6*d.*, necessary to complete said house, &c. [D.R.]

Somers Payne was ordained Deacon, 1809, Sept. 24, and

Priest, 1810, Sept. 23, both at Cork. He was licensed to the curacy of Kilmichael, in 1809. In 1823 he was R. Ardagh, which he held until he was appointed Treasurer of Cork, in 1831.

He died on 29 May, 1857, leaving issue three sons, Somers Henry (Vicar-General of Killaloe and R. Dunkerrin), James and John Warren, besides a daughter, Mary, wife of Mr. Nash.

1857. July 27. THOMAS TOWNELY MACAN,' A.B., Treasurer, certified to be of the net annual value of £517 6*s.* 7*d.* [D.R.]

1860. No vestry in this church. The glebe-house and offices are in good order. 8 acres of glebe in Incumbent's use. John-Harding Cole is Curate.

Service twice each Sunday in church for eight months of the year; for the other four months it is held once on each Sunday morning in church, and on Sunday evenings in the glebe-house. Service is also held on the principal church holidays.

Sacrament once a month, and at Christmas and Easter. Usual number of communicants, 11.

The children are catechised every Saturday at school, and every Sunday at church, by the Incumbent and Curate.

A Church Ed. School. On rolls, 23; average attendance, 13.

Protestant population, 120.

Thomas Townely Macan, born in co. Armagh, son of Robert Macan; when eighteen years of age entered T.C.D., as Pensioner, on 19 Oct., 1829.

In 1839 he was licensed to the curacy of Knockavilly. In 1850, P. C. Marmullane. In 1855, P. Kilanully, and in 1857, Treasurer of Cork.

He married Belinda, d. of Rev. Thomas Waggett, of Rathclaren, and died in 1860.

1861. January 5. JOHN MURPHY, A.B., Treasurer, certified to be of the net annual value of £451 15*s.* 2*d.* [D.R.]

John, son of John Murphy, esq., of Newtown, co. Cork, by Elisabeth, d. of Samuel Jervoise, esq., of Brade, was born at Newtown, in 1795, and entered T.C.D. in 1813.

He was ordained Deacon at Cloyne, on 10 April, 1825, and Priest at Kildare, on 25 Feb., 1827.

He was curate of Kilbrogan from April to 1 November, 1825, and from that time until 1842 was Curate of Murragh. From 1842 to 1861 he was V. Kilmocamoge, which he resigned for the Treasurership of Cork, in 1861.

He married, in 1826, Alicia, d. of Rev. Charles Smith, Vicar of Kilmocamoge, and has issue by her four daughters.

BALLYDELOUGHY.

1291. Ecclesia de Balyduffloythir, [rated at] 6 marks. The Vicar receives a third part. [Tax. P. Nic.]

1591. E. de Ballidolohir spectat ad Abb. de chore Impr. [MS. T.C.D. E. 3. 14.]

1615. Ballydolohir. Rectoria impropriata Johes. Fitzgerald firmarius. Ecclesia et cancella ruinosa. Nullus curatus. Vicaria vacat et usurpatur per firmarium Rectoriæ. [R.V. R.I.A.] In the V.B. of 1622, in Marsh's Library, it is called Ballidolloghire.

1627. March 20. Richard Jermyn. Rect. integ. de Kilroan et V. de Ballylogher. [F.F.] He was again admitted to R. V. Ballinloghie, dioc. Cork, 28 May, 1633. [Ferguson's MSS. vol. i. p. 97.] Jermyn was also V. Rahan, Cloyne, q. v.

1634. E. de Ballydelohir als Kilroane. Rex est Rector. Johes. Fitzgerald miles tenet. Nullus curatus. [R.V. 1634.]

1639. Ecclia de Ballylogher als Kilroane. Rex est Rector. Curatus Thomas Westmore. Ecclia bene, desunt ornamenta. [V.B., D.R.] Westmore was R. Bretway, Cloyne, q. v.

1666. Eccliam de Ballilogbie als Kilroane Ed. Ffitzgerald tenet. Vicar Samuel Bonner, œgrotat. [V.B. D.R.] Bonner was P. St. Michael's, q. v.

1667. Vacant per mortem Samuelis Bonner. [V.B., D.R.]

1668. John Bayly appears as Vicar, and in 1670 as Rector de Ballydeloghy als Kilroane per litteras pat. dni. Regis. [V.B. D.R.] On 11th July, 1669, he was instituted to the other benefices vacated by the death of Bonner. Bayly appears in 1696. Vide St. Michael's Prebend.

1697. June 17. Valentine French, P. St. Michael's, R. Kilcoane, Templeusky, Ballylogher als Kilroane et Insula parva. [F.F.] French was afterwards Dean of Ross, q. v.

"Oct. 1700. I saw Ballideloughy Church als Killroan. Ballideloghy church, built with stone and clay; half the walls are down; the churchyard is fenct with a ditch. About ten plantation acres of glebe on the south side of the churchyard belonging to the Incumbent. This church is a mile from Racony Church, to the east of Racony. About four and a half plowlands in this parish. The greatest part of this parish was the estate of —— Barry, of Ballideloughy, who forfeited in the late rebellion. Will. Harding, and all the rest of the inhabitants of this parish, are Papists. Cahirlag Church is a mile distant from this church, on the south of Ballideloughy Church.

"Ballideloughy is a village in this parish. The parish is commonly called Ballideloughy, from this village. All the tythes of this parish belong to the Incumbent, worth about £20 or £15 per an. Racony is the next church, in repair, to this parish." [Downes' Tour.]

In 1704, French became Prebendary of Killaspugmullane, since which time the R. V. Ballydeloghy als Kilroane was held with that prebend until 1842.

In 1730, Ecclesia ruinata. [V. B.]

In 1830 the Protestant population of Ballydelohar was 136.

1842. Sept. 2. WILLIAM AUGUSTUS BEAUFORT, A.B., R. Ballydelohar and Templeusky. [F.F.] The Act of Consolidation of these benefices was dated at Council of Dublin 12 Dec., 1846. The total value is given as £390 2*s.* 6*d.*; being thus made up:—Ballydelohar, otherwise Kilroan, rent-charge, £133 2*s.* 6*d.*; ten acres of glebe, £20; Templeusky rent-charge, £237. The Protestant population of Ballydelohar was 73, and of Templeusky, 63. One church at Ballydelohar. On 24 September, 1850, the Bishop certifies an expenditure of £840 on the glebe-house; the annual value of the benefice being £420. [D.R.]

1860. Church, &c., in good order. A glebe-house and ten acres of land in Incumbent's occupation.

Morning and evening service throughout the year on Sundays, and service on principal holydays.

Sacrament monthly; average of communicants, 15; at Christmas, 24; at Easter, 30.

The children are catechised weekly at the school by Incumbent, in Catechism, Scripture, and Liturgy.

A Church Ed. Soc. School, to which the Ladies' Hibernian Society give also £5. About 15 children in course of instruction. Protestant population, 84.

W. A. Beaufort (son of Rev. W. Beaufort, P. Cahirlag, q. v.), entered T.C.D. on 19th October, 1829, being then seventeen years old. He was ordained Deacon on 28th June, 1835, and Priest on 11th September, 1836; both at Cork. From 1836 to 1842 he was V. Brinny.

BALLYFEARD.

1591. R. de Ballefiard spectat ad Ab. de Tracton. Vic. ibm. JOHES. CROMIN; lre ord. sunt cōbuste. [MS. T.C.D. E. 3. 14]. Cromin held also the curacy of Nohoval in 1591.

1615. June 2. MARCUS PAGETT, P. Lisclery, R. Kilmedye als Martelstown, and V. Ballifiard. [F.F.]

1615. Ballefyard spectat ad Abb. de Tracton. Thomas Daunt firmarius. Curatus Marcus Paget, minister et predicator, idem vicarius. Val. £6 13*s.* 4*d.* Ecclesia et cancella repantur. [R.V. R.I.A.]

1634. R. de Ballyfiard spectat ad Abb. de Tracton. Comes Cork Impropriator. Val. £13 13*s*. 4*d*. per an. Nullus curatus. Vicarius ibm. Marcus Paget. Val. £13 13*s*. 4*d*. Epus Confert. [R.V. 1634.]

1639. Pagett appears as Vicar, and John Stukely as curate of Ballyfiard, the Rectory belonging to Tracton. Ecclesia bene, desunt ornamenta. [V.B. D.R., 1639.]

Paget became Dean of Ross, q. v. Stukely became, in 1640, R.V. Glanbarrahan, Ross, q. v.

1666. JOHN BUTLER, V. Ballyfeard; also marked "vacant." [V.B. D.R.]

Butler was also P. Kilbrittain, q. v.

1667. June 29. JOHN MOORE, P. Kilbrittain, R. V. Innishonane, R. Ballymartle, Templemichael de Duagh, Leighmoney, and V. Ballyfiard [F.F.] per desertionem Johannis Butler. [V.B. 1669.] Moore was also Archdeacon of Cloyne, q. v.

1695. Nov. 6. Moore "suspenditur ob negligentiam curæ." And in 1696 the visitation book contains this entry, "Suspensus ult. visit. ob negligent. decrevit sequestrare ad supplendam curam." [V.B. D.R.] On 22nd February, 1696/7, Alexander Ogilby, A.B., is licensed to be curate. [D.R.]

Moore appears as V. Ballyfiard to 1698. [V.B. D.R.]

1699. April 14. JOHN MOORE, junior, P. Kilbrittain, and Vicar of Ballyfiard. [F.F.]

He appears 1709. [V.B. D.R.] In 1711 John Moore, junior, became Treasurer of Cloyne, q. v.

1699. No churchwardens or parish clerk; two or three Protestant families; they go to Tracton, only sometimes Mr. Moore preaches in a house in the parish of Ballyfiard. [V.B. D.D. 1699.]

"1699. August 18. Ballyfiard Church is ruinous, within half a mile of Tracton. Mr. Moore, Vicar." [Downes' Tour.]

"June, 1704. As we go to Tracton from Corke, a long mile on this side Tracton, are the ruins of the Church of Kilpatrick. A long mile to the west of Tracton stood the Church of Ballyfeard; the walls are almost level with the ground. To the south of Tracton, half a mile beyond the great village of Knockmannagh, stood the Church of Bealfoyle; the walls are ruinous. Two long miles to the S.W. of Tracton stands the Church of Noghavale; the church is in good repair, and furnish't with seats; the late Bishop of Corke contributed to the repair of it when he had the Archdeaconry of Corke. Divine service is performed here once a fortnight, and once a fortnight at Tracton by Mr. Ogilby. To the S.W. of Tracton, at four miles distance, stood the Church of Kilmehenoge, on the east side of Oysterhaven, near Mountlong, the church is ruinous." [Downes' Tour.]

1711 ? MICHAEL BUSTEAD, V. Ballyfeard.
He appears in 1715. [V.B. D.R.]
Michael Bustead was also R. Templemichael de Duagh, q. v.

1751. April 1. PETER BRISTOWE, A.M., V. Ballyfeard. [F.F.]
Now vacant by ye nat. death of Rev. Michael Bustead. [D.R.]
Bristowe was also R. St. Paul's, Cork, q. v.

1769. March 16. MATHIAS SPREAD, A.M., per mort. Bristowe. [F.F.]
Spread was also V. Kinsale, q. v.

1771. Feb. 19. JOHN CLIFFE, A.B. [F.F.] per mort. Spread. [D.R.]
John, son of W. Cliffe, of New Ross, county Wexford, esq., was born in 1736, and graduated in T.C.D.

He was licensed to curacy of Carrigrohane on 14th January, 1771, and to that of Killaspugmullane on 17th February, 1772. He became V. Ballyfeard in 1771, and P. Termonbarry, Elphin, in 1775. He held both these livings until his death, on 14th February, 1816, at the age of eighty-three.

1816. March 28. NICHOLAS COLE BOWEN, A.B., V. Ballyfeard, per mort. Cliffe. [F.F.]

1831. Protestant population, 78.

1833. May 7. A school in village licensed for Divine service, [D.R.]

1837. Ballyfeard, a vicarage, with cure, three miles long by two broad, containing 3,000A. Gross population, 1,337. The occasional duties of this benefice are discharged by the Curate of the adjoining parish, at a stipend of £20 per annum. Tithe composition, £130; 9A. 2R. 35P. of glebe, valued at 20*s.* per plantation acre, £6; subject to visitation fees, 15*s.* 5*d.* No glebe-house; Incumbent is non-resident, from his delicacy of health; and as he requires constant medical aid, he resides in the town of Bandon, at a distance of twelve miles from the parish. No church. The rectorial tithes of this parish, compounded for £100, are impropriate, and reputed to belong to the Earl of Shannon. [Parl. Rep.]

Nicholas Cole Bowen was ordained Priest at Cloyne on 6th July, 1806.

In 1816 he became V. Ballyfeard, which he held until his death, in 1837.

1838. Feb. 15. Suspended by Ecclesiastical Commissioners, there having been no Divine service celebrated for the three years ending 1st February, 1833, and a stipend of £75 per annum allowed to a Curate appointed by the Bishop. [Board Minutes of Ecclesiastical Commissioners.]

1860. The Curate is the REV. ROBERT HENRY MEADE. Annual value, £103.

There is no church in this parish, nor any trace of one in the grave-yard, which contains a tombstone of great antiquity, but without any inscription. There was no parish register previous to appointment of present Curate. There is no glebe-house, although there are five acres of glebe in the possession of the Ecclesiastical Commissioners. The Curate resides in his own house, within three miles of the parish.

Divine service is performed once each Sunday, and on chief festivals; and evening service during summer in a school-house duly licensed.

There is a monthly administration of Sacrament. Average of communicants, 6.

On Sundays and week days the children are catechised by Curate and master of the school, which is supported by subscriptions, and in which the books of the National Board are used. The children are 10 in number.

Protestant population, 18.

Robert Henry Meade, fourth son of Rev. Richard Meade, Rector of Ballymartle, was born 25th September, 1809, and graduated in T.C.D. as A.B. in 1832.

He was ordained Deacon at Cloyne on 14th July, 1833, and Priest, at Cork, on 21st July, 1834. He was Curate of Ardfield, Ross, in July, 1833, and in October of same year was Assistant Curate of Ballyfeard. On the death of the Vicar, Mr. Bowen, in 1837, he was appointed Curate of Ballyfeard.

BALLYMARTLE.

1291. Ecclesia de Kylmy, eight marks. [Tax. P. Nic.]

1591. EDWARD M'BRIANY appears as R. de Martelstown als Kilmedye, V. Inchigeelah, and also V. Inchinabacky. [MS. T.C.D. E. 3. 14.]

1591. July 31. DOMINUS JACOBUS MURICE (qu. Maurice) clericus Vicar Ballymartle als Kilmedy. [Ferguson MSS. vol. i. 110.] Murice does not occur in the Cork records.

1611. May 29. NICHOLAS BRIGHT, or BERGHT, is presented to R. Martelstown and Rathclarin. [Lib. Mun.] In 1615 he appears as V. Lisclery, q. v.

1615. June 2. MARCUS PAGETT, R. Martelstown als Kilmedye, P. Lisclery, et V. Ballyfiard. [F.F.]

1615. Kilmiddie als Martelstowne (non residens) R. and V. Mark Paget. [R.V. R.I.A.]

1634. E. de Martelstowne als Kilmiddy, Mark Pagett. Val. £26 6*s*. 8*d*. Vicecomes Kilmallock patronus. [R.V. 1634.]

1637. The advowson of Martelstown was claimed by Pierce, fil. Adam Gold. [Inquis. at King's Old Castle, Cork, No. 415, 13th April, 1637.]

1639. Mark Pagett, Vicar, "Ecclesia bene. Desunt calix et baptisterium." [V.B. D.R.]

Paget became Dean of Ross, q. v.

1662. Feb. 6. JOHN BUTLER, R. Ballymartle als Kilmeedy, and R. Innishannon. [F.F.]

The R. Ballymartle appears in V.B. 1666 as vacant, Mr. Butler's name being struck out by pen.

Butler was also P. Kilbrittain, q. v.

1667. June 29. JOHN MOORE, P. Kilbrittain, R. Ballymartle, and R.V. Innishonane, R. Templemichael de Duagh, and Leighmoney, and V. Ballyfiard. [F.F.]

This admission to Marshalstowne als Kilmedy was per desertion of John Butler. [V.B. D.R. 1669.] Et in presentatione Dni. Regis eo quod Sarsfield patronus est papista. [V.B. 1670.]

Moore was also Archdeacon of Cloyne, q. v.

1679. April 8. THOMAS MEADE, R. Ballymartle, and R. Kilmalooda, in Ross. [F.F.] On letters patent from Crown, dated Feb. 17th. [Lib. Mun.]

In 1692 John Hemlock, parish clerk, did not take out a licence. [V.B. D.R.]

1699. A church served once a fortnight. [V.B. D.D. 1699.]

"1699. Ballimartell Church, betwixt Ballinbuy and Kinsale, about three miles from Kinsale. The church is in good repair." [Downes' Tour.]

Thomas Meade was also P. Inskenny, q. v.

1709. June 9. WILLIAM MEADE is presented to Rs. Ballymartle and Dunderrow. [Lib. Mun.] He was son of his predecessor, who resigned in his favour.

William Meade became, in 1736, Dean of Cork, q. v.

1751. May 14. JOHN MEADE, A.M., is presented to R. Ballymartle [Lib. Mun.] vacant by the vol. resign. of Wm. Meade, Dean of Cork. [D.R.] Admitted 20th May.

In 1746 John Meade had been licensed to the curacy of Ballymartle, Dunderrow, and Cullen.

He was the eldest son of Dean William Meade, and was born in county Cork. He entered T.C.D. as Pensioner on 23rd Nov. 1738, aged eighteen, and took the degrees of A.B. and A.M. in that university.

He m. firstly, in 1748 [M. L. dated 20th April—Cork M.B.] Katherine, d. of Rev. John Moore, R. Innishannon, by whom he had no issue; and secondly, in 1768, Susanna (d. of Rev. Horace Townsend, P. Donoghmore), who died S.P. 1820. [F.P.] In 1787 the Rev. John Meade purchased from his cousin, John, first Earl of Clanwilliam, the family estates of Ballymartle and Ballintubber. He resigned his rectory of Ballymartle in 1794; and died in 1800, leaving his nephew, Richard, the Rector of Ballymartle, his heir.

1794. Feb. 19. RICHARD MEADE, A.B., R. Ballymartle. [F.F.] Pat. dated Feb. 15. [Lib. Mun.] He was nephew to his predecessor.

Richard Meade was eldest son of Rev. William Meade, R. Rincurran, and heir to his uncle's estate of Ballintubber.

He was ordained Priest at Cloyne on letters dimissory from Cork, on 29th September, 1786, having been licensed curate of Ballymartle from 24th March, 1785.

He married Dorothea, d. of Adam Newman, Esq., of Dromore, by whom he had issue two daughters, Mary Townsend and Susan Helena; and six sons—1. William Richard, of Ballymartle, barrister, and representative of the family; 2. John, F.T.C.D., 1832, died 29th June, 1835, S.P.; 3. Richard Newman, Capt. H.E.I.C. fell at the battle of Meanee, in Scinde, 1843; 4. Robert Henry, Curate of Ballyfeard; 5. Horace Townsend Newman, M.D., of Churchill House, Queenstown; 6. Adam Newman, m. 1859, Louisa, d. of Daniel Conner, of Manch, Esq., and has issue. The will of Rev. Richard Meade was dated 24th January, 1807, and proved in Dublin 20th April, 1815. He died on 11th December, 1814.

1815. July 21. ALEXANDER M'CLINTOCK, A.M. [F.F.] Pat. dated June 2. [Lib. Mun.] per death of Rev. Richard Meade, LL.D.

In 1824 M'Clintock became R.V. Glanbarrahan, Ross, q. v.

1824. March 18. HONOURABLE RICHARD BOYLE BERNARD, D.D., R. Ballymartle [F.F.] on letters patent, dated 18th February, 1824.

Mr. Bernard was second son of the first Earl of Bandon. He was born in 1787, and in 1822 was made Dean of Leighlin. He resigned Ballymartle on 29th July, 1826, but retained his deanery until his death, at Leighlin, on 1st March, 1850. He bequeathed £1,000 to the Church Education Society.

1826. August 12. JOHN STOYTE, A.B., R. Ballymartle [F.F.] on letters patent, dated 3rd August, 1826. [D.R.]

1830. Protestant population, 99.

1837. Ballymartle, a rectory, with cure, three miles long by three broad, containing 8,828A. 0R. 15¼P. Gross population, 1,706. No Curate employed. Tithe composition, £424 12*s.* 2*d.*; 8A. 0R. 15¾P. of glebe, valued at £5. Subject to visitation fees, 17*s.* 4*d.* Diocesan Schoolmaster, 17*s.* No glebe-house. Incumbent is resident within the benefice during summer, in a cottage, which he built at his own expense; and during winter in a house in the town of Kinsale, for which he pays a rent of £34 per annum. One church, capable of accommodating 100 persons, but so old and decayed that no record exists of the date and cost of its erection. No charge on the parish in 1832, on account of the church. Divine service is celebrated once on all Sundays, and on the principal festivals. The Sacrament is administered monthly. The benefice is a rectory. [Parl. Rep.]

1860. Church, &c., in good order. Annual value, £323. No glebe-house; three acres of glebe in Incumbent's use. Divine service once on Sundays and festivals. Evening service during summer months. Sacrament monthly; average of communicants, 10; on festivals, 25.

The Rector and his assistants catechise the children on Sundays in Testament, Catechism, and Collects.

There is no school or school-house.

Protestant population, 79.

John Stoyte (son of James Stoyte, esq., of Gloucester-street, Dublin, by Martha, d. of Andrew Moore, esq., of Dublin), was born in 1800, and was educated at Castledawson, Blackrock, Dublin, by Rev. Dr. Leney. He graduated A.B., T.C.D., in 1820.

He was ordained Deacon in 1825, and Priest in 1826, both by the Bishop of Kilmore. From 1825 to 1826 he was Curate of Killeshandra, Kilmore.

He married, in 1844, Elizabeth, d. of William Bleazby, esq., of Ballinacurra, Kinsale, and has by her three sons.

BALLYMODAN.

1291. Ecclesia Ballybudan, rated at seven marks. [Tax. P. Nic.]

1536. Ballymodan was held in commendam with the Bishoprick of Cork. *Vide* Shandon, under the date 1536.

1591. Rector de Ballymodan, Nicholas Thornibt, Vicar John Newman. [MS. T.C.D. E. 3. 14.] Newman was also V. Brinny, same date.

In another MS. of this date there is the following entry—"Rectoria de Ballimodan spect. ad Ab. de Tracton. Vicar ibm. Nicholaus Tompkins." [R.V. R.I.A.] But in another part of same MS. there appears—"Ecclia de Ballymodan Nich. Thomkyns. Vic. ejusdem Richd. Newman."

In 1610 the Earl of Corke and Burlington endowed a classical school at Bandon, with £20 per annum. [D.R.] Newman was also V. Brinny.

1615. Robert Sutton is Vicar. "Rectoria spectat ad Abbathiam de Tracton. Ecclesia et cancella bene repantur cum libris et aliis necessariis; val. 7 li. Vicarius ibm. Robertus Sutton, A.M., minister et predicator residet et inservit curæ; valor 7 li. Tenet etiam vicarias de Kilbrogan et Disertserges per unionem." [R.V. R.I.A.] For Sutton, *vide* Kilbrogan.

1628. August 31. Thomas Wright, Vicar de Ballymodan. [R.V. 1634].

1634. R. Ballymodan spectat ad Abb. de Tracton; valet 40 li. per annum. Comes Cork, Impropriator. Vicarius Thomas Weight predicator; valet 40 li. per annum. Epus confert. [R.V. 1634.]

1639. Weight is still Vicar. "Ecclesia bene." [V.B. 1639.]

Weight was also P. Kilnaglory, Cork, q. v.

1662. Feb. 6. HENRY PARR, V. Ballymodan, R.V. Rathclarin, and V. Templequinlan, in Ross. [F.F.]

He appears in V.B. in 1666. He became R.V. Skull and Kilmoe in 1767, and was also Precentor of Ross, q. v.

1666/7. Feb. 14. PETER HEWET, V. de Ballymodan, per resignation of Henry Parr. [V.B. D.R. 1669.]

He appears 1667 to 1675. Hewett became in 1675, Chancellor, and in 1710 Precentor of Cork, q. v.

1675. Feb. 25. HUGO JENKINS, V. Ballymodan, Rathclaren, Cannaway, and R. Ardnegihy. [F.F.]

He appears to 1679 [V.B. D.R.], and in the margin of that visitation there is this remark opposite his name, "ltræ ord. desunt." In 1681 he was again admitted to Ballymodan and Rathclaren.

1680. July 28. JOHN TOM, A.M., V. Ballymodan, Rathclaren, and R.V. Cannaway. [F.F.]

He appears in V.B. 1680. In 1681 he became R. Ardnegihy, and in 1693 was made P. Desertmore, q. v.

1681. July 30. HUGO JENKINS, A.M., V. Ballymodan and Rathclaren. [F.F.]

He appears 1681 to 1685. [V.B. D.R.]

From 1675 to 1680 Jenkins held R. Ardnegihy, V. Ballymodan, Rathclaren, and Cannaway; he again appears as V. Ballymodan and Rathclaren from 1681 to 1685, when he was deprived for some cause.

1686. March 26. PAUL DUCLOS, A.M., V. Ballymodan, vacant per legitimam privaconem Hugonis Jenkins. [D.R.]

He appears 1686 to 1691. [V.B. D.R.] In 1688 he was made P. Island, Ross, q. v.

1692. April 22. RICHARD GOODMAN, A.B., V. Ballymodan, per cess. Paul Duclos, and same day V. Rathclaren. [D.R.]

In 1736 Goodman is marked "excusatus." [V.B.] He was also, in 1718, P. Desertmore, q. v.

1695. In this year the parish register commences.

"Church in good repair in Bandon. Sermon every Sunday. Very few Papists. Sacrament four times a year. £20 yearly promised by the Earl of Corke to a schoolmaster." [1699. V.B. D.D.]

In 1812 this endowment was increased to £40 per annum by the Duke of Devonshire. [D.R.]

1737. May 5. WILLIAM READER, A.M., V. Ballymodan, per mort. Richard Goodman. [D.R.]

He appears 1737 to 1740. [V.B. D.R.] In 1741 he became V. Kinsale, and in 1745 Archdeacon of Cork, q. v.

1741. March 26. PIERCY MEADE, A.M., V. Ballymodan, per resignation of William Reader. [D.R.] In 1745 Meade became V. Kinsale, q. v.

1745. April 4. WILLIAM MARTIN, A.M., V. Ballymodan [F.F.] per resignation of Piercy Meade. [D.R.]

1747. Dec. 29th. Mr. William Martin, and his Curate, Mr. John Smyth, appear at the Palace, when, after hearing both, the Bishop decreed that £45 be in future paid by quarterly instalments to Mr. S. the Curate, the stipend heretofore being too small for so laborious a cure. [D.R.]

William Martin (son of James Martin, merchant), was born in Bandon, and on 3rd June, 1722, entered T.C.D. as Pensioner, being then eighteen years old. He was a Scholar in 1726, and afterwards A.M.

He was, in 1731, Curate of Templeomalus, Templequinlan, and Kilnagross; and in 1737 was Curate of Abbeymahon, which latter impropriate cure he held, along with V. Ballymodan, until his death in 1750.

In his will he mentions his brothers, Edward and Richard; and administration of his will was granted to his brother-in-law, Rev. William Ellis, P. Island, Ross, in trust for Ann, dau. of Edward Martin, the brother of testator.

1750. March 18. JOHN DENIS, A.M., V. Ballymodan, per death of William Martin. [D.R.]

In 1776 Denis became Treasurer of Cork, q. v.

1776. May 3. JOHN LORD, A.M., V. Ballymodan, per cess. of John Denis. [D.R.]

John Lord was probably of the same family as Daniel Lord, P. of Kilbrogan in 1692. I find a John, son of Edward Lord an apothecary, born in Dublin, was Sizar, T.C.D. in 1734. The V. of Ballymodan died in 1795.

1795. June 17. HENRY HEWITT, A.M., V. Ballymodan, vacant by death of John Lord. [D.R.]

Henry Hewitt was, in 1767, licensed Curate of St. Peter's, Cork; in 1768 Curate of Carrigaline; in December, 1768, Curate of St. Mary Shandon; and in 1770 Thresher's Lecturer in Cork. In 1771 he was made V. Killaconenagh, &c., in Ross; and in 1795 Vicar of Ballymodan. In his will, dated in 1792, he is described as of Clancoole, and mentions his wife, Susannah Judith Browne, otherwise Hewitt (sister of Rev. Thomas Browne, P. Templebryan, Ross, q. v.), and his brother-in-law, Warham Jemmett Browne, of Kinsale. He mentions his late brother, Isaac, and his brother, Rev. Charles, who succeeded him in Ballymodan. He wishes to be buried in Ballymodan, near the wall on the outward part of the church, close adjoining the family tomb, with this inscription over his remains—"Hic jacet corpus Revēndi Henrici Hewitt sed anima cum sanctis." He died in 1803. His widow, Susan Judith, "of Mallow," mentions in her will, dated 1826, and proved in Dublin in 1828, her brother, Warham Jemmett Browne, and her sisters, Sarah Hare and Eliza Latham.

1803. July 11. CHARLES HEWITT, A.B., V. Ballymodan, by death of Henry Hewitt. [D.R.]

Charles Hewitt, the brother of his predecessor, was ordained Deacon at St. Luke's, Dublin, by Bishop of Limerick, on 8th March, 1767, and Priest at Cork by Bishop of Cork, on 25th January, 1768. He was Curate of Desertmore in 1767, and of Murragh in 1775. In 1796 he became R. Ardnegihy, and in 1803 was removed to Ballymodan. His sons, Charles, Isaac, Frederick, and Thomas, and his daughter, Letitia, are mentioned in his brother's will. He died at Clancoole, near Bandon, on 31st March, 1809.

1809. June 15. ROBERT MONTGOMERY, V. Ballymodan, by death of Charles Hewitt. [D.R.] In 1813 Montgomery resigned this preferment, and his name is not entered elsewhere in the Cork records.

1813. August 13. JOSEPH JERVOIS, V. Ballymodan. [F.F.] He was afterwards R. Ardagh, Cloyne, q. v.

Jervois gave £22 15*s.* on August 5th, 1813, towards a fund for erecting in Bandon a Presbyterian meeting-house; and towards the same fund Dr. Kenny, the Vicar-General, gave £34 2*s.* 6*d.*; Rev. E. Kenny, of Moviddy, £11 7*s.* 6*d.*; and Dr. Lovett, £11 7*s.* 6*d.* [Cork Intell.]

Jervois was Provost of Bandon in 1817. [Cork Intell.]

1825. August 26. ARTHUR KNOX, A.B., V. Ballymodan. [F.F.]

He resigned on 16th Nov. 1835, and appears no more in these dioceses.

1831. Protestant population, 2,264.

1835. Nov. 17. HENRY FITZALLEN M'CLINTOCK, A.B., V. Ballymodan. [F.F.]

In 1846 he became R.V. Kilmichael, q. v.

1837. Ballymodan, a vicarage, with cure, 3½ miles long by 2 broad, containing 7,820 acres. Gross population, 9,969. One Curate employed, at a stipend of £75 per annum. Composition for vicarial tithes, £400. Nine acres of glebe, valued at 25*s.* per acre, £11 5*s.*; subject to visitation fees, 17*s.* 4*d.* Diocesan schoolmaster, 17*s.* No glebe-house. Incumbent is resident, and pays an annual sum of £23 for lodging-money. One church, capable of accommodating 800 persons, built about 200 years ago, and enlarged and repaired at different times since by means of parochial assessment, but at what cost not stated. No charge on the parish in 1832 on account of the church. Divine service is celebrated thrice on the first Sunday in every month, and twice on all other Sundays, and on the principal festivals. The Sacrament is administered twenty-six times in the course of the year. The rectorial, consisting of one moiety of the tithes of this parish, compounded for £400, are impropriate, and belong to the Duke of Devonshire. [Parl. Rep.]

1846. May 26. JOHN BLEAKLEY, A.M., V. Ballymodan; certified to be of the net annual value of £207 *5s. 3d.* [D.R.]

1849. August 30. The new church was consecrated to divine uses under the name of St. Peter. [D.R.]

1860. John Bleakley, Rector; G. K. Smyth, Curate. The church in good order. No glebe-house. Ten statute acres of land set to a tenant. The rector resides in the town of Bandon. Divine service twice on all Sundays, and thrice on the third Sunday in each month. There is service also on all Fridays. Sacrament twice each month; average of communicants, 65; and on the three great feasts; average 114. The children are catechised twice a week by the clergymen; 18 boys, and 76 girls and infants, are on the rolls of schools, besides 38 on the rolls of another school in the country part of this parish. The Protestant population is 1,550. The rent-charge is £300, and the value of glebe is £8. Total income, £308, without residence.

J. Bleakley (A.B., T.C.D. in 1826, and A.M. in 1832), was ordained Priest at Cork on 18th December, 1831. He was Curate of Kilgaruffe, Ross, in 1831, and of Holy Trinity, Cork, in 1843.

He married Jane, dau. of the late Colonel Gibbings, of Monkstown, Cork.

BALLYMONEY.

1591. E. de Ballimoney. COR. DONATI, idem V. de Kinneigh. [MS. T.C.D. E. 3. 14.]

1610. Feb. 12. ROBERT SNOWSWELL, R. Crossenhare als Ballymoney et V. Fanlobbus. [R.V. 1634.]

1615. Robert Snowswell, R. et V. Crossenhare als Ballymoney et V. Fanlobbus; ipse inservit curæ. Val. 12 li per an. Ecclesia et cancella bene repantur cum libris. [R.V. R.I.A.]

1634. Robert Snowswell, Rector. Value 15 li. per an. [R.V. 1634.] Snowswell appears in 1639 as Rector, with Thomas Keilly as Curate. "Ecclesia bene, desunt quædam ornamenta præter parvam supellectilem linteam et baptisterium." [V.B. 1639.]

1632. A silver communion cup, weight 9 oz., has this legend, "Ex dono Hellenæ uxoris Antony Stowell gen. mort. August 9th, 1632."

Robert Snowswell, literatus, was ordained Deacon by George,

Bishop of Chester, on 12th June, 1609, and Priest by William, Bishop of Cork, on 23rd September, 1610. In 1610 he was R. Ballymoney and V. Fanlobbus, and in 1614, R. Kilmaloda, Ross. He held all these livings until his death, in or before 1661.

1661? NICHOLAS WINTERBURNE, R. Ballymoney, V. Fanlobbus, and Kinneigh. He was afterwards Treasurer of Ross, q. v.

1664. January 2. ROBERT GOLBORNE, R Ballymoney, and V. Kinneagh and Fanlobbus. [F.F.] In V.B., D.R. 1669, Golborne's admission to these benefices is given as on January 7th, 1664, per deprivation of Nicholas Winterburne, by Convocation at Dublin.

Robert Golborne was seventh son of William Golborne, Bishop of Kildare, by Elizabeth, d. of William Pilsworth, also a Bishop of that See. He died unmarried, in or before 1674. [U.O.]

1674. May 2. ISAAC MANSFIELD, R. Ballymoney, V. Kinneagh and Fanlobbus. [F.F.]

He appears, 1674 to 1688, Nov. 3. [V.B. D.R.] He was also P. Inskenny, q. v.

"An. 1679. (fo. 22.) We do present, that whereas upon a former presentment, anno. 1675, an order was granted to raise £20 upon the parishes of Ballymony and Fanlobbish, which are and were united time out of mind, for the repair of Ballymony, and that the parish of Fanlobish did not contribute anything to the work; and that therefore the parish of Fanlobish ought to pay the summe of ten pounds towards the said work, &c.; and that Brian Wade, &c., &c., are fit persons to oversee the work, and to applot the said summe." [Cork Presentments.]

1688. Feb. 6. ANDREW SYMES, A.B., R. Ballymoney, vacant per mortem Isaac Mansfield; and on 4th Dec., 1691, V. Fanlobish per mort. ejusdem Isaac Mansfield. [D.R.] Symes appears from 1689 to 1718. [V.B.] And in 1718 he became Precentor of Ross, q. v.

"Church in repair; sermon once a fortnight; sacrament thrice a year. About twenty Protestant families. An English school." [V.B. 1699, D.R.]

"1699. —— About seven miles to the west of Bandon, on the south side of the river, is the parish of Ballimony; except one plowland of the parish which is on the north side of the river. The church is large, and the walls and roof are in pretty good repair. Seats in the east end, but not in the west."

"The west end was repaired when Kineigh and Fanlobish were united to it. Contention about a seat gave occasion to the building Kineigh and Fanlobish churches, and dividing the parishes."

"Usually eighty persons at church. Mr. Synge preaches one Sunday at Murragh, the other Sunday at Desert. About twenty-six plantation acres of glebe round the church of Ballymony, divided into five fields."

"A little vicarage house, in good repair, with the glebe well improved. A good garden and orchard. A plowland on the north of the river Bandon is in this parish."

"Drinagh and Kilmine were united pro hac vice to Ballimony. The Vicars Choral have half the tythes of Drinagh. Kilmine lyes to the south-west of Ballimony; Drinagh lyes to the west of Kilmine. Mr Symmes preaches one Sunday at Ballymony, the other at Kilmine."

"1700. Saturday, May 25, I went from Cork to Ballimony. Sunday, May 26, I preach't at Ballimony, and confirm'd about 62 persons in all, viz.: about 36 persons that came out of the neighbouring parishes of Murragh, Dizert, Kilmine, Kineigh, and Fanlobish, and about 26 persons of Ballimony parish. I administered the holy sacrament. About 20 received. There were about 150 persons at church.

"Ballimony Church is in good repair, but a register book is wanting, which Mr. Symmes undertook to get before next Michaelmas.

"In the parish of Ballimony are 19 plowlands, and 9 gneeves. About half the land of this parish is the estate of Mr. Harry Boyle, brother to the Lord Corke. Sir Richard Cox, Counsellor Bernard, Mr. Wade, and Mr. Peter Hewit, are proprietors of all the rest of the lands. Mr. Wade, Mr. Beamish, Mr. Woodroff, Mr. Barrington, Mr. Trench, Mr. Germain, live in the parish. There is a Popish Priest of Fanlobish parish, call'd Charles Carthy, and another at Kineigh, call'd Teigue Murphy. These two divide Ballimony betwixt them. Usually one Priest serves two or three parishes in these parts. About Ballimony there are four Papists for one Protestant. In Fanlobish parish there are ten Papists for one Protestant. The further you go westward, the disproportion betwixt the Papists and Protestants is greater. In the most western parts of the diocese of Corke there is usually twenty Papists for one Protestant. About Bearehaven there are not above five or six Protestant families, most of which are Dissenters. About forty English acres of glebe lye round the church of Ballymony; good land, and well improv'd. There is a small Rector's house. Mr. Symmes designs to enlarge it by building on the old foundations. There are two churchwardens sworn. A chalice, flagon, table-cloth for the Communion table, a Bible, two Common Prayer books. Here, and in the places hereabouts, tyth is paid for potatoes. And for mills, Agistment tythe, viz., a tenth part of the rent of the mill. The clergy don't think it worth the while to demand tythe of turf. Ballimony does not pay first fruits, but it pays 2*s.* per an., twentieth parts. Two Protestant women teach school. Ballymony is worth to the Rector about £50 per an." [Downes' Tour.]

1719 to 1740. SAMUEL BROME appears as R. Ballymony and R. Kilmeen, Ross. [V.B.] In 1731 he became also Chancellor of Cork, q. v.

1737. July 13. The Bishop certifies that Brome expended in improving the glebe-house, £98 11*s.* 2*d.* [D.R.]

1740. March 26. SAMUEL WOODROOFFE, A.M., R. Ballymoney and Killmeen, both vacant per resignation of Brome. [D.R.]

In 1746 Woodrooffe became P. Dromdaleague, and in 1762 was made Precentor of Cork, q. v.

1746. October 25. JOSEPH PRATT, A.M., R. Ballymoney and Kilmeen, in Ross. [F.F.] He was probably of Cabra Castle, co. Cavan. He resigned these livings in 1752.

1752. August 14. CHARLES WYE, A.M., R. Ballymoney and Kilmeen, in Ross, per cessionem Pratt. [D.R.] In 1753, he was also licensed to the curacy of Kinneigh.

1782. The parish Register commences.

Charles, son of Rev. Mossom Wye, born at Dunleer, co. Louth, when sixteen years old, entered T.C.D. as Pensioner, on 28th March, 1710, and was Scholar in 1712. His will is dated 11th April, 1765, and was proved in Cork 16th August, 1784. In it he mentions his son, Francis Wye, and two daughters, Mary, wife of —— Quin, and Elizabeth, his executrix.

1784. August 6. AMBROSE HICKEY, A.B., R. Ballymoney, vacant by death of Wye. [D.R.] In 1796 he became R. Murragh, q. v.

1785. March 21. Hickey memorials to build a new glebe-house; and on 3rd March, 1788, obtains a certificate for having expended £752 3*s.* 1½*d.*, the yearly value of Ballymoney being £315 per an. Hickey reserves his right to a chimney-piece of Italian marble, in the north parlour, and excludes it from his account of expenditure. In 1799, Hickey obtains another certificate for having expended £89 10*s.* 3*d.* in a garden wall, and £1 6*s.* on two farm-yard piers. The tithes of Ballymoney are now valued *over* £400, and the glebe is valued at £60 per an. [D.R.]

1796. May 4. THOMAS HORE, A.B., R. Ballymoney, vacant by resignation of Hickey. [D.R.] In 1798 Hore became Vicar-Choral of Ross, q. v.

1798. March 1. ROBERT MEADE, A.B., R. Ballymoney, vacant by resignation of Hore. [D.R.]

1802. January 13. Meade obtains a certificate of having expended, in additions to the glebe, £295 14*s.* 5*d.*, and that the yearly value of Ballymoney is £643. [D.R.]

1830. Protestant population, 512.

1837. Ballymoney. A rectory, with cure. Seven miles long

by five miles broad, English measure, containing 6,668 acres. Gross population, 3,802. One Curate employed, at a stipend of £75 per annum. Tithe composition, £785. Forty-two acres of glebe, valued at £63; subject to visitation fees, £1 18*s*. Diocesan schoolmaster, £1 5*s*. Ballymoney glebe-house built under the old Acts, in 1788, at the cost of £673 16*s*. 11*d*. Brit., whereof £92 6*s*. 1 *d*. was granted as gift by the late Board of First Fruits, and the residue of £581 10*s*. 9¼*d*. was supplied out of the private funds of the builder. In the year 1798, a further sum, to the amount of £83 16*s*. 6½*d*., was expended on garden wall and piers, under certificate of improvements. The present Incumbent is second in succession to the original builder, and having paid his predecessor £540 12*s*. 2¼*d*., and since expended a certified sum of £272 19*s*. 5½*d*., Brit., he will be entitled to receive from his successor £565 2*s*. 8¾*d*., on account of the building, and in improvement charges. Incumbent is constantly resident in the glebe-house. One church, capable of accommodating 150 persons, but so old a building, that the date and cost of its erection unascertained. No charge on the parish in 1832 on account of the church. Divine service is celebrated twice on all Sundays and once on the principal festivals. The sacrament is administered on the second Sunday in every month, and on the three great festivals. The benefice is a rectory. [Parl. Rep.]

1849. Sept. 3. A new church was consecrated under name of St. Paul. It was built on a site given by the Rector. The ruins of the old church are still in the grave-yard.

Robert Meade, born, 1768; was fourth son of Rev. William Meade, R. Rincurran.

He was ordained Deacon on 1st August, 1790, at Cloyne, on letters dimissory from Cork, and on 26th Sept., 1790 was ordained priest at Cork.

In 1791, he was Curate of Tracton, and in 1796 became Vicar-Choral of Ross, which he held until he was made R. Ballymoney in 1798.

He was, also, from 1796 to 1811, P. Dunsfort, Down; and from 1812 to 1826, R. Templemichael de Duagh.

He married Eliza, daughter of Robert Travers, Esq., and by her had issue, Wm. Robert, (V. Kinsale, q. v.) Robert, died unm., and two other sons and two daughters, who died unm., besides three daughters, of whom the eldest, Barbara, was the wife of Rev. Wm. De Courcy Meade, V. Fanlobbus, q. v. Rev. Robert Meade died 19th March, 1852.

1852. May 27. William Alexander Willock, A.M., R. V. Ballymoney; certified to be worth £604 14*s*. 4*d*. [D.R.]

On 3rd Sept., 1853, Mr. Willock obtains a certificate of dilapidations against his predecessor, to amount of £427 12*s*. 9*d*. [D.R.]

Mr. Willock was a Fellow of T.C.D., and on 29th June, 1854, became R. Cleenish, Clogher diocese.

1854. Dec. 21. SAMUEL BUTCHER, D.D., R. Ballymoney, on presentation of Primate and Archbishop of Dublin. [D.R.]

On 9th May, 1855, Dr. Butcher obtained a certificate of dilapidations against his predecessor, to amount of £504 5*s.* 10*d.*; and on 3rd May, 1859, he obtained a certificate of charge on the benefice for £1,046 18*s.* 6*d.*, the net annual value being £523 9*s.* 3*d.* [D.R.]

1860. Rev. Dr. Butcher, Rector; Rev. W. Mangan, Curate. The church and glebe-house in good order. The Rector is resident whenever his official duties as Regius Professor of Divinity in T.C.D. allow. Divine service twice each Sunday, and afternoon service from March to November in a licensed place of worship at Ballinacarrigy. Sacrament monthly; average of communicants, 31; and at Christmas, 81 communicants. The children are catechised on Fridays and Sundays. 109 children are on roll of schools, maintained by Rector and Church Education Society. The Protestant population is 256. The rentcharge amounts to £588 15*s.*, and the land is worth £63. Total value is £651.

Samuel Butcher (grandson of Thomas Butcher, Esq., of Northampton, and son of Vice-Admiral Samuel Butcher, by Elizabeth-Anne, eldest daughter of Richard Herbert, Esq., of Cahirnane, co. Kerry), was educated at home, and at a public school in Cork. He was Scholar of T.C.D. in 1832, Fellow in 1837, Professor of Ecclesiastical History in 1850, and Regius Professor of Divinity in 1852. He graduated A.B. in 1834, A.M. in 1838, and D.D. in 1849.

He was ordained Deacon in 1839, by Mant, Bishop of Down and Connor, and Priest in 1840, by Plunket, Bishop of Tuam.

He has published several occasional sermons, and introductory lectures as Professor of History and Divinity.

Dr. Butcher is married, and has issue six children.

BRINNY.

1291. Ecclesia de Bryn is rated at 5 marks. [Tax. P. Nic.]

1591. RICHARD or JOHN NEWMAN is Vicar. "R. de Brinny spectat ad Ab. de Grayne. Vicarius ibm. Richūs Nueman. sequestrat. pro Regina." [MS. T.C.D. E. 3. 14.] In another copy John Newman appears as Vicar. Richard Newman was also V. Kilbrogan.

1615. RICHARD WHITE appears as Vicar. "Brinny R. spectat ad Grany. Capt. Tent firmarius. Vicarius Richardus White, minister legens et inserviens curæ. Val. 4 li. per an. [R.V. R.I.A.] White was, in 1634, R. Kilmine, Ross, q. v.

1622. May 4. RANDOL HOLLAND, V. de Brinny. [V.B. 1669.] He appears in 1671 as V. Brinny and Knockevilly, and was also P. Killanully, q. v.

1634. R. de Brinny spectat ad Ab. de Grany. Val. 18 li. per an. Peregrinus Spencer firmarius. Vicarius Randolphus Holland. Val. 18 li. per an. [R.V. 1634.]

1639. "Ecclia bene." [V.B.]

Hugolinus Spencer appears from 1668 to 1694 as Rector of Brinny. In 1689 "procuracones 4 an. debet." In 1695 Mr. Sullevan succeeds Mr. Spencer as Rector impropriator. [V.B.]

1672. April 2. PIERCE BUTLER, P. de Killanully, R. Knockavilly, and V. Brinnie. [F.F.] For Butler, *vide* Killanully.

In March, 1663, Pierce vel Peter Butler, V. Brinny, was accused of adultery sive fornication with Julia Lyde and with Anna Humphreys, and also "de tenendo privatim conventum sive congressum abditum in domo suo in impedimentum Divini cultus publici," &c. [Court Book, D.R.]

1685. May 2. JOSHUA WARREN, A.M., P. Killanully, R. Knockavilly, and Brinny. [F.F.] For Warren, *vide* Killanully.

1685. An attempt of Lord Clancarty to present a Clerk to Knockavilly is thus recorded in the Registry :—"1685, Sept. 28. Presentatio Richi Browne, clici, introducta in officium Registrar. Corcag. die et anno supra dict. sequitur sub tenore verborum sequentum. Revendo in Christo Patri et Dno Dno Edwardo divina providentia Corcag. Epus Donatius Comes Clancarthy verus et indubitatus patronus rectoriæ integræ parochiæ de Knockanilly in Com. Cork. Salutem in Dno sempiternam et cet. Ad ecclíam de Knockanilly prædict. vestræ dioc. modo per resignationem Pierce Butler ult. ibm incumb. jam vacant. et ad nram presentat. pleno jure spect. Dilectum mihi in Xto Richūm Browne, clk. in Art. mag. vestræ paternitati presento, humiliter rogans quatenus prefatum Richūm Browne ad dict. ecclíam admittere, ipsumque Rectorem ejus ecclīæ institut. et induci facere, cum suis juribus et pertinent. universis, cœteraque peragere et adimplere quæ vestro in hac parte incumbent officio pastorali gratiose dignemini cum favore. In cujus rei testim. sigill. meum apponi feci decimo quarto die calendar. October A°. Reg. Dni nri Jacobi 2 di. Anno Domini 1685. Clancarty. (loc. sig.) 28 Sept. 1685. Presentatum fuit hoc instrumentum Rēndo Dno Edwardo Epo per Richūm Browne, clk. intronominatum, cui Dict. Dnus Epus responsum dedit Eccliam esse plenam." [D.R.]

1695. Daniel Comoge is cited "de non fungendo officium Guardiani," &c.; "his child, christened by a Papist Priest, goeth not to church." [V.B. 1695. D.R. Marginal note at Knockavilly parish.]

1696. August 25. RICHARD GOODMAN, P. Killanully, R. Knockavilly, and V. Brinny, vacant per cessionem Warren. [D.R.] In 1718 Goodman resigned Killanully for Desertmore, q. v.

1699. "Every Sunday divine service at Brinny." [V.B. 1699.] "Two Protestant families (at Knockavilly) go to Brinny." [Ib.] "The little church of Brinny, in repair, stands within two miles of Bandon." [Downes' Tour.]

1721. A flagon now (1861) in Brinny Church bears this legend:—"Deo sacrum. In usum Ecclesiæ parochialis de Brinny. Ex Dono Richi Goodman ibidem Vicarii. Anno Redemptionis 1721." A paten, also, has a similar inscription: "impensis Richardi Goodman."

1737. June 28. PERKINS CROFTON, A.M., P. Desertmore, R. Knockavilly, and V. Brinny, per mort. Goodman. [D.R.] For Crofton, *vide* Desertmore.

1768. Dec. 13. JOHN BARRY, A.M., P. Desertmore, R. Knockavilly, and V. Brinny, per mort. Crofton. [F.F. and D.R.] For Barry, *vide* Desertmore.

1778. The silver chalice now (1860), in use in Brinny Church bears this inscription:—"Deo Sacrum. In usum Ecclesiæ parochialis de Brinny. Anno 1778."

1794. June 17. JOHN WHETHAM, R. V. Brinny, and R. Knockavilly, per mortem Barry. [D.R.] He was Dean of Lismore, and Archdeacon of Cork, q. v.

1795. Feb. 21. HON. THOMAS ST. LAWRENCE, A.M., R. and V. Brinny, and R. Knockavilly, per resignation of Whetham. [D.R. and F.F.] St. Lawrence was also Dean of Cork, q. v.

1806. Feb. 24. ROBERT AUSTEN, D.D., R. V. Brinny and Knockavilly, vacant by cession of St. Lawrence; worth £600 per an. [D.R.] Austen was afterwards Treasurer of Cloyne, q. v.

1807. Dr. Austen resides at Brigowne, in Cloyne dioc., which he holds by faculty. [Parl. Rep.]

1809. June 10. Austen takes a second collation to this union on receiving also the union of Castletown and P. Coole, Cloyne. [D.R.]

1810. August 21. WILLIAM LEWIS BEAUFORT, A.M., R. V. Brinny, and R. Knockavilly, certified under £800 per an. in value. [D.R.]

In 1836 he resigned Brinny, but retained Knockavilly. He was also from 1814 P. Cahirlag, als Rathcony, q. v.

1830. Protestant population of Brinny, 249; of Knockavilly, 152.

1832. Brinny Union, with cure, consisting of:—1. Brinny rectory and vicarage. 2. Knockavilly rectory, 5 miles long by 5 broad, containing 11,163 acres. Gross population, 4,133. Two Curates are employed, one for each parish, at stipends to each of £75 per ann.; with the use of a house and 9½ acres of glebe, rent free, and the surplice fees, if any, to the Curate of Brinny parish, in addition. Tithe composition of Brinny parish, £400 ; 9½ acres of glebe, in said parish, valued at £18. Tithe composition of Knockavilly parish, £625 ; 45¼ acres of glebe, in said parish, valued at £43 10*s.* ; subject to visitation fees, £1 6*s.* 5*d.* ; diocesan schoolmaster, £1 8*s.* 3*d.* No glebe-house. Incumbent is non-resident, he resides on his other benefice, in this diocese, which he holds by faculty. One church, situate in Brinny parish, capable of accommodating 300 persons, built about 100 years since, but at what cost unknown, and enlarged in 1813, at an expense of £369 4*s.* 7½*d.*, whereof £276 18*s.* 5½*d.* was granted in way of loan by the late Board of First Fruits, and the residue was raised by subscription, and the sale of some trees in the church-yard. Of the loan aforesaid there remained £76 3*s.* 0½*d.* chargeable on the union in 1832, repayable by annual instalments of £5 2*s.* 6*d.* Divine service is celebrated in the church twice on Sundays in summer, and once in winter, and on the principal festivals ; as also in a private apartment fitted up for the purpose, for want of a church, in Knockavilly parish. The sacrament is administered thirteen times in the year. The benefices constituting this union are rectories ; but a portion of tithes in Brinny parish compounded for £5 is appropriate, and belongs to the Dean of the Cathedral Church of Cork. [Parl. Rep.]

1836. Dec. 29. WILLIAM AUGUSTUS BEAUFORT, A.B., R. and V. Brinny. [F.F.]

In 1842 he became R. Ballydeloher, als Kilroan, q. v.

1842. Sept. 2. JAMES GOLLOCK, A.M., R. and V. Brinny, per cess. of W. A. Beaufort. [D.R.] Gollock became in 1850 V. Desertserges, q. v.

1842. Dec. 16. Mr. Gollock memorials to be permitted to build at Brinny; and on 21 May, 1844, obtains a certificate of charge for a new glebe-house, to amount of £621 10*s.* ; the annual value of Brinny being £310. [D.R.]

1846. April 14. The earliest entry in present register.

1850. Oct. 16. GEORGE BURROWES, A.M., R. V. Brinny, certified value, £309 10*s.* 6*d.* per an. [D.R.] He was also P. Currograngemore, Ross, q. v.

1860. The church and glebe-house in good order ; 9½ acres of glebe in Rector's use. Divine service twice in summer, and once in winter on Sundays, once also on Christmas Day, Good Friday, and Ascension. The children are catechised on Sundays and Fridays. 23 children attend a Church Education School. The Protestant population is 178. The rentcharge is £300. The land is worth £18. Total value of the benefice £318, with residence.

1861. October 17. JAMES STEVENSON, A.M., R. and V. Brinny, vacant by death of Burrowes. [D.R.]

James Stevenson (son of Rev. William Stevenson, Rector

of Kilclonbrock, and Curate of Maryborough, in Leighlin diocese); was born at Mountrath, Queen's county, on 20 Dec. 1827.

He was educated at the Clergy Sons' School, at Lucan, and graduated B.A., T.C.D., in 1849, and M.A. in 1861. He was a Scholar of T.C.D.

He was ordained Deacon on 29 August, 1852, and Priest on 19 Dec. 1852; both at Cork.

He was, in 1852, Curate of Bruhenny and Lackeen, in Cloyne, and in June, 1860, was Curate of Mogeesha.

CAHERAGH.

1317. Dec. 28. GEOFFREY FITZ JOHN DE COGAN is presented by the King (by mandate to the Bishop of Cork), to the church of the Blessed Mary de Catheragh, in the King's gift, by reason of his wardship of the land and heir of John de Cogan. [Tuckey's Cork Remem. p. 18.]

1591. R. de Caheraughe spectat ad Colleg. Youghell. [MS. T.C.D. E. 3. 14.]

1615. TADEUS M'DONNELL O'SULLIVAN is Vicar. "Cathragh: Rectoria spectat ad Coll. de Youghall. Vicarius Tadeus M'Donnell O'Sullivan, minister legens. Val. 8 li. Cancella repata ex parte vicarii, ruinosa ex parte rectoris." [R.V. 1615.] O'Sullivan was also V, Durrus, q. v.

1616. April 12. ANTONIUS RISDON, Vic. de Caragh. [F.F.]

In 1623 he became V. Carrigaline, q. v.

1623. Sept. 8. THOMAS WAY, V. de Caragh, inducted 8th October, 1623. [R.V. 1634.]

1634. R. de Caragh spect. ad Coll. de Youghall. Val. £13 13*s*. 4*d*. per an. Vicarius Thomas Way. Val. £13 13*s*. 4*d*. [R.V. 1634.]

In 1639 Edward Clare appears as Rector, with Thomas Way as Curate of Caheragh. "Ecclia bene, desunt ornamenta." [V.B. 1639.]

Way was also V. Scull, q. v.

1640. May 15. EDWARD CLARE is admitted Rector of Caheragh, on letters patent of the King. [F.F.]

Clare, in 1637, received letters patent for another living. He was probably the same Edward Clare, who was of Killinean, county Carlow, and who married Susan, dau. of Thomas Munday, Porter of Her Majesty's Castle of Dublin, esq. This Edward was second son of Robert Clare, of Dublin, by Joane, dau. of Edward Searle, of Abstain Hall, Herts, England. [U.O.]

1662. April 5. MICHAEL DELAUNE, Clericus, R. de Caheragh, studendi gratia. [V.B. D.R. 1669.]

From 1666 to 1670 Michael de Laune appears as Rector, "*studendi gratia.*" [V.B.]

On 15th Nov. 1672, Michael Delaune receives a patent to R.V. Caheragh, dioc. Cork. [Lib. Mun.]

Michael Delaune (born in London, son of Henry Delaune, "Chiliarchæ," and afterwards of Gurtmore, county Cork, by his wife, a dau. of Richard Boyle, Archbishop of Tuam), was educated at Kinsale, under Dean Boyle, and, when twenty years' old, became a Sociorum commensalis, T.C.D. on 6th May, 1660.

He was ordained Priest on 20th Dec. 1668, and was in that year made Precentor of Ferns and Rector of Enniscorthy. In 1670 he was also Archdeacon of Dublin, having resigned Caheragh. He held his Archdeaconry, and the Precentorship, with Enniscorthy, until his death, on 3rd November, 1675. He was buried in St. Patrick's Cathedral, Dublin. He mentions in his will his elder brother, Richard, of Charleville, county Cork, and another brother, Gideon. [U.O.]

1670. Nov. 25. NICHOLAS BOLTON, R. Caheragh, and R.V. Tullagh, R. Kilsillagh, V. Aghadowne, Cleere, and Donoghmore, in Ross. [F.F.] In 1674 he became also Chancellor of Ross, q. v.

He appears 1671 to 1682. [V.B. D.R.]

1683. Sept. 6. JOHN PATRICKSON, A.M., R. Caheragh, per mort. Bolton. [D.R.]

"In Anglia et sub censura." [V.B. 1691.] "Sub censura." [V.B. 1692.]

1695. Dec. 23. Johes Patrickson, A.M., adm. ad R. Caheragh per nupras calamitates forsan vacant. necnon V. Kinneigh vacant. per cess. Andreæ Symes, et V. Fanlobish per cessionem Johis Fortune. [D.R.] Patrickson was also Precentor of Cloyne, q. v.

No church. Three Protestant families go to Drumdaleige. [V.B. 1699, D.D.]

1718. Nov. 6. Mr. SAMUEL BROME appears as R. Caheragh, Mr. Patrickson's name being crossed out. [V.B.] Brome was, in 1731, Chancellor of Cork, q. v.

1720. MICHAEL PHILPOT appears as R. Caheragh. [V.B. D.R.] And on 17th January, 1727, he is again collated, receiving in addition the P. Dromdaleague. [D.R.]

From 1727 to 1818 Caheragh was held with P. Dromdaleague, q. v.

1818. May 13. RICHARD FRANCIS WEBB, A.B., R. Caheragh, vacant by resignation of Richard Webb. Certified under £300 per an. [D.R.] R. F. Webb became, in 1853, R. Dunderrow, q. v.

1825. The Bishop grants a licence to Webb for three years' non-residence, there being no glebe in the parish. [D.R.]

1830. Protestant population, 131.

1837. Caheragh, a rectory, with cure, 10 miles long by 8

broad, containing 16,521 acres. Gross population, 6,999. One Curate employed, at a stipend of £75 per annum. Tithe composition, £650. Subject to visitation fees, 9*s.*; diocesan schoolmaster, 18*s.* No glebe-house. Incumbent is resident; and considers £45 a-year a reasonable sum to be allowed for house-rent. One church, capable of containing 160 persons, built in 1829, at the cost of £650, British, granted as gift by the late Board of First Fruits. No charge on the parish in 1832 on account of the church. Divine service is celebrated once on all Sundays, and on Christmas Day, Good Friday, and Ash Wednesday. The sacrament is administered monthly. The benefice is a rectory. [Parl. Rep.]

1853. Feb. 17. JAMES SOMERVILLE REEVES, A B, R. Caheragh. Certified to be of the net annual value of £437 8*s.* [D.R.]

1860. The church, &c. in good order. A communion cup and paten of silver. A Flagon and basin plated. No glebe-house or land. Divine service once on all Sundays, and on the usual feasts and fasts. The Sacrament monthly, and at festivals. Average of communicants, 14. The children are catechised on Sundays. Evening service is held during four months of summer; 20 children attend a Church Education school. The Protestant population is 107. The rentcharge amounts to £487 10*s.*

J. S. Reeves is descended from Robert Reve, of Sussex, who came to Ireland *temp.* CHAS. I. *Vide* Burke's L. G.—article, Reeves of Vosterburg. The Rev. Mr. Reeves is son of Thomas Somerville Reeves, esq. by Rebecca, dau. of Isaac Morgan, esq. of Cork. He was ordained in 1849.

CAHIRLAG.

1291. Ecclesia de Cathirlage is rated at 7 marks. [Tax. P. Nic.]

1349. In this year Cahirlag was made a prebendal church by John Roche, Bishop of Cork. One MacCottyr anciently presented to it. [Smith's Cork, B. I. ch. 2.]

1591. E. de Cahirlag als Catherlagg: DAVID TIRRY incūbens, vicarius insulæ parvæ, interdicitur donec prob. se esse ad ordines promot. [MS. T.C.D. E. 3. 14.] Tirry is also P. Lackeen, R. Bretway, V. Carrigtohil, and V. Templebodan, in Cloyne.

1615. June 19. WILLIAM THOMAS is presented to P. Cahirlag, and R. V. Shandon. [Lib. Mun.]

On July 12, 1615, he was admitted P. Cahirlag, R. V. Shandon. [F.F.]

1615. P. de Cahirlag William Thomas, Rector, A.M., et Predicator; val. 8 li. Ecclia in repacōe, cancella ruinosa; Rector obligatur pro reparatione. Tenet etiam R. V. Shandon; val.

12 li.; et P. Cahirultan, Clone; val. 6 li.; et V. Ballimarter; val. 6 li ; et V. Corkbeg, val. 5 li. per an. [R.V. R.I.A.]

1616. Feb. 28. JOHN THOMAS, R. de Cahirlag, and P. Cahirultan, Cloyne, q. v.

1618. Nov. 17. NICHOLAS HALL, Rector de Cahirlag, and Vicar de Christchurch, Cork. [F.F.] In 1619 he became Archdeacon of Ross, q. v.

1634. P. de Cahirlage Nicholas Hall, predicator. Valet 22 li. per an. [R.V. 1634.]

1639. JOHN HALL appears as P. Cahirlag. "Ecclesia non bene, desunt ornamenta." [V.B. 1694, D.R.]

In 1642 he depones to loss of £137 in rebellion of 1641, and his church living, value £76 per an. [MS. T.C.D. F. 2. 17.]

John Hall, from 1638 to 1640, was R. V. Innishannon.

He married, in 1639, Julian Ryan [Cork M. B. of 20th of November, 1639], who was niece to Dermod O'Ryan, of Sallughode, Master of the Rolls. John Hall was an English gentleman, and he left issue by Julian Ryan, a son, John, who married Joanna Stout, of Youghal, and had a son, Richard, who, by Jane Blennerhassett, had issue a son, John, born in 1725, and two daughters, Mary and Joanna Hall. Richard Hall was of Ballycunningham, county Cork. [MS. penes Fisher.]

1661. JAMES COX appears as P. Cahirlag. [V.B. D.R.] He was instituted on June 16th, 1663, as Rector de Cahirlag *per mortem* Nicholai Hall. [V.B. 1669, D.R.] He was on the same day admitted P. Kilmaclenine, Cloyne, q. v.

He appears 1661 to 1683. [V.B. D.R.]

1684. Sept. 5. JASPER COX, A.M., P. Cahirlag, per resignation of James Cox [F.F. and D.R.]

He appears 1684 to 1692. [V.B. D.R.]

Jasper Cox was third son of Rev. James Cox, P. Kilmaclenine, Cloyne, q. v.

He was ordained Deacon on 11th July, 1679, and Priest at Cloyne on 23rd Dec. 1683.

From 1683 to 1693 he was P. Coolstuffe, Ferns; and from 1693 to 1713 he was P. Kilrush, Ferns. He also held, from 1684 to 1694, P. Cahirlag; and from 1688 to 1713 the P. Killrossantie, Lismore.

He died in 1713. He was married; and his third daughter, Bridget, was wife to Rev. Edward Tottenham. No male descendant exists of this line of the Cox family. [Davies.]

1694. Oct. 6. EVAN JONES, A.M., P. Cahirlag, per cession of Cox. [D.R.]

He appears 1694 and 1695. [V.B. D.R.]

Evan Jones, son of John Jones, was born in Wales, and obtained a Sizarship in T.C.D. on 4th Sept. 1677, being then twenty years old.

In 1692 he became V. Templebodane, and in 1693 V. Clonmel and Templerobin, in Cloyne. In 1694 he became P. Cahirlag; and he retained all these livings until his death in 1696.

He left a son, Evan, who, in 1711, entered T.C.D., and died in 1743 P. Kilmainmore, Tuam.

1696. June 15. DANIEL SMITH, A.M., P. Cahirlag, per mort. Jones [D.R.]

Daniel Smith was a Sizar, T.C.D. on 17th November, 1672, and afterwards was A.M., T.C.D.

In 1692 he was Curate of Ballydeloughy. In 1794 he became R. Ardnegihy, and in June of 1696 was P. Cahirlag. He held both livings up to his death, in or before August, 1696.

He married, in 1686, Anne Hewitt, who, as well as her husband, is described in the Cloyne marriage bond as "of Castlelyons."

1696. August 25. RICHARD ROFFEN, A.M., P. Cahirlag. [D.R.]

He appears 1696 to 1724, November 3. [V.B. D.R.]

"October, 1700. I saw the Church of Cahirlag, which is on the top of a hill, on the left hand of the road from Corke to Youghal, built with stone and clay; the walls half down. A ditch about the church-yard. About four acres of glebe, near the church, belong to the Incumbent. Major Clayton, Baron Worth, and Mr. Murragh, have the greatest part of the lands in this parish. About five plowlands in this parish. Alderman Hore and Mr. Gough, Protestants, live in this parish; the rest are Papists. The people of this parish go to church in the Little Island. All the tythes of this parish belong to the Prebendary; they are worth about £45 per ann." [Downes' Tour.]

Richard Roffen entered T.C.D. as a Pensioner on 8th May, 1682.

In 1696 Roffen became P. Cahirlag, and V. Templerobin, Clonmel, and Templebodan, in Cloyne; in 1698 V. Carrigtowill; in 1713 P. Coole, also in Cloyne. He held all these livings up to his death in 1724.

On 11th January, 1696, he signed a bond for marriage with Barbara St. Leger, of Rathcony, spinster; and on 3rd January, 1718, he signed another bond for marriage with Dorothy House, of Ballymodan, widow. [Cork Mar. Bonds.] In his will, dated 18th Sept. 1724, and proved in 1725, he styles himself "Rev. Richd. Roffen, of Rossmore," and mentions only his wife, Dorothy, dau. of Capt. Thomas Gookin. [U.O.] His first wife, Barbara, was dau. of Warham St. Leger, of Heyward's Hill, by Mary Gregory. In 1777 a Richard Roffen (probably a descendant) was Curate of Lisgoold, in Cloyne.

1724/5. Feb. 15. THOMAS SOMERVILLE, A.M., P. Cahirlag. [D.R.]

He appears 1725 to 1732, November 8. [V.B. D.R.]

In 1732 Somerville became R. V. Myros, Ross, q. v.

1732/3. Feb. 16. WILLIAM READER, A.M., P. Cahirlag, per cession of Somerville. [D.R.] In 1745 Reader became Archdeacon of Cork, q. v.

1734. May 14. William Reader gives 5A. 2R. 27P. of glebe to Edward Hoare, of Dunkettle, in exchange for 7A. 1R. 6P. of the lands of Kilcolish for a future glebe, &c. [D.R.]

1745. May 10. JOHN BURGH, P. Cahirlag. [F.F.] In 1749 he became P. Holy Trinty, q. v.

1749. June 22. WILLIAM JACKSON, A.M., P. Cahirlag, R. Little Island, and R. Rathcony. [F.F.]

William Jackson (son, I think, of Rev. William Jackson, D.D.), was born in Dublin in 1713, and became a Pensioner of T.C.D. on 26th April, 1730, when seventeen years old. He was ordained Priest at Cork on 24th July, 1737, for the Curacy of Desertmore, Knockavilly, and Brinny. From 1738 to 1739 he was P. Kilbrogan. From 1739 to 1749 he was P. Templebryan, V. Templequinlan, R. Templeomalus and Kilnagross, in Ross. He was also, from 1745 to 1749, P. Holy Trinity, Cork. In 1749 he resigned his other livings, and became P. Cahirlag and R. Rathcony, which he held until his death in 1767.

He married, in February, 1738, Mary Nash, of Brinny, to whom he bequeathed all his property by his will, dated 19th Feb. 1750, and proved 19th May, 1767.

1767. April 27. CHAMBRE CORKER, A.B., P. Cahirlag als Raherlaghern, and R. Rathcony [F.F.], vacant by death of Jackson. [D.R.] In 1769, May 12, he took a second collation to Cahirlag and Rathconey, on receiving the R. and V. Insulæ parvæ. [F.F.]

1784. July 12. Robert Rogers, esq., of Lota, conveys to the churchwardens half an acre and two perches of land, for ever, for a new church and church-yard at Glanmire. [D.R.]

1784. July 14. The Bishop recommends the Lord Lieutenant to change the site of Rathcony Church to Glanmire. [D.R.]

1784. Nov. 15. The Bishop consents to the union of Rathcony, Cahirlag, and Little Island; their united value being as follows:—Rathcony, £140; Cahirlag, £100; Little Island, £60; in all £300 per an. The union is confirmed by the Privy Council, 3rd March, 1785.

1786. Oct. 24. The new church built in Glanmire is consecrated by the Bishop of Cloyne (the Bishop of Cork being absent in Great Britain for health, &c.), under the name of the Parish Church of Rathcony. [D.R.]

Chambre Corker was son of Thomas Corker, of Cork, by Alice Neville, and was nephew of the Rev. Robert Corker, of St. Burian's, Cornwall. [U.O.]

He was ordained Deacon on 14th April, 1765, and Priest on 19th January, 1766, both at Cork.

He was licensed to be Domestic Chaplain to the Bishop of

Cork (Jemmett Browne), on 26th March, 1766. He became P. Cahirlag and R. Rathcony in 1767, and in 1769 R. V. Insulæ parvæ, and in 1778 Archdeacon of Ardagh. He held all these livings (to which he was collated by his father-in-law), until his death in 1790.

He married Elisabeth, dau. of Jemmett Browne (Bishop of Cork and Archbishop of Tuam), and left issue (besides four daughters, Eliza, who married in 1794 Rev. Philip French; Catherine, wife of Rev. Horatio Townsend; Anna-Maria, and Isabella), two sons, Thomas, who died unmarried; and Chambre, in the army, who was of Dundaniel, and afterwards of Cor Castle, Innishannon. This last Chambre, by his wife, Caroline, dau. of J. Badham Thornhill, of Thornhill Lawn, county Limerick, had issue, *inter alios*, a son, James-Richard Corcor, now the representative of the family, who married, in 1840, Sophia, dau. of John Tonson Rye, esq. late of Rye Court, county Cork. The present family of Cor Castle have resumed the ancient spelling of their name, "Corcor." They have a patent, dated 1696, which enables them to add a ducal coronet to their armorial bearings.

1790. March 18. JOHN CHETWODE, A.M., P. Cahirlag, R. Rathcony, and R. V. of the Little Island, united by Act of Council, 3rd March, 1785. [F.F.]

John Chetwode was a member of a family which can be traced to the LORDS CHETWODE, of CHETWODE, in Doomsday Book. The barony of WAHULL was claimed by a Chetwode, *temp.* JAMES I. *Vide* Burke's Extinct and Dormant Peerages. The Rev. John Chetwode, or Chetwood, was son of Crewe Chetwode, esq. by Anna-Maria, dau. of Allan Holford, county Chester, and relict of Ralph Sneyd, esq. county Stafford.

He was a Scholar of T.C.D. in 1760, and graduated A.M. in 1799. He was ordained Deacon on the 1st, and Priest on 11th of June, 1762, for the stipendiary cure of Desertmore and Brinny. From 1762 to 1799 he was Treasurer of Ross, and from 1799 to 1814 Vicar Choral of Cork. He was also, from 1767 to 1780, R. V. Scull; and from 1780 to 1790 Precentor of Cork; and from 1790 to 1814 P. Cahirlag and R. Rathcony.

John Chetwode was of a highly literary turn of mind, yet never published any work.

He wrote many small pieces in prose and verse, and was an intimate friend of Malone. See Prior's "Life of Malone" for some of his letters. He composed the following lines, not for publication, but as an expression of his feelings upon the death of his young friend, Mrs. Sturgeon (dau. of J. P. Curran). They were intended afterwards to be inscribed as an epitaph on her tomb at Newmarket, but the intention was never carried into effect.

"So late adorned with every grace of mind,
Here gentle Sarah lies, to peace consigned.
Thou soul of harmony! Thy harp unstrung,
Rests the sad emblem of thy tuneless tongue;
Thy pensive grace, thy tasteful genius gone,
Thy wit, thy playfulness for ever flown!
Awhile, to charm the earth, thy powers were given,
But now sublimed they own their native Heaven!"

John Chetwode married Elisabeth, dau. of William Hamilton, esq. and had a son, John, Captain in 33rd Regt. who married Eliza, dau. of G. Patton, Governor of St Helena, and died, leaving an only daughter, Eliza-Constance, wife of Peter Aiken, esq. of Clifton. [B. L. G.] He had also several daughters, of whom the eldest, Elisabeth-Hester, was wife to Robert Wilmot, and bore to him (besides two daughters, Constance-Julia and Anna-Maria), a son, Edward Wilmot, who became heir to the estates of his kinsman, Jonathan Chetwood, of Woodbrook, and took the name and arms of Chetwood by royal licence in 1839. This last-named EDWARD-WILMOT-CHETWODE is now of Woodbrook, Portarlington, and has issue by his wife (the Lady JEAN-JANET ERSKINE, younger dau. of JOHN-THOMAS, EARL of MAR), who died in 1861, a son, KNIGHTLEY-JONATHAN, and three daughters, Alice-Agnes, Fanny-Elisabeth-Isabella, and Janet-Philadelphia.

Among the younger daughters of Rev. John Chetwode were Henrietta-Margaret, Lucy, wife of ——— Hawkshaw; and Mary, wife of William Thompson, Archdeacon of Cork, q. v.

The Rev. John Chetwode died on 13th April, 1814, and was buried, by his desire, in Rathcony church-yard.

1814. July 15. WILLIAM LEWIS BEAUFORT, A.M., P. Rathcony als Cahirlag. [F.F.]

1830. Protestant population of Rathcony, 174; of Cahirlag, 217; and of Little Island, 44. Total, 435.

1837. Rathcony union, 5 miles long by 2¼ broad, with cure, consisting of—1. Rathcony rectory and vicarage, 3½ miles long by 2¼ broad; 2. Cahirlag rectory and vicarage, 3 miles long by 1¼ broad; 3. Little Island rectory and vicarage, 1½ miles long by ¾ broad. The union contains 10,100 acres. Gross population, 5,907. One Curate employed, at an annual stipend of £75, with surplice fees. Tithe composition of Rathcony parish, £500; 14 acres of glebe in said parish let for £18. Tithe composition of Cahirlag parish, £300; 7 acres of glebe in said parish let for £7. Tithe composition of Little Island parish, £180. Subject to visitation fees, £1 7*s.* 6*d.* Diocesan schoolmaster, £1 8*s.* 3*d.* No glebe-house. Incumbent is resident, and pays a rent of £100 a-year for the house he occupies. One church, capable of accommodating 300 persons, built in 1784 by means of private subscription, but at what cost unknown. No charge on the union in 1832, on account of the church. Divine service is celebrated twice on Sundays during the greater part of the year, and once during the rest of it, and on the principal festivals; and a lecture is delivered every Wednesday. The sacrament is administered twelve times in the year, and on the great festivals. The benefices constituting this union are rectories.

William Lewis Beaufort, A.M. and LL.D. of T.C.D. was ordained Deacon on 29th Sept. 1796, and Priest on 25th July, 1797, both at Cork.

In 1797 he was Curate of St. Nicholas; from 1803 to 1814 he was R. Ardnegihy; and from 1814 to 1849 P. Cahirlag. He was also, from 1810 to 1836 V. Brinny; and from 1810 to 1849 R. Knockavilly. He died on 11th December, 1849.

He married, in 1805, Emma-Anne, dau. of Thomas St. Lawrance, Bishop of Cork, and by her had issue, William-Augustus (Rector of Ballydelogher, q. v.); Francis, Thomas St. Lawrance, and William-Daniel, sons; besides five daughters, of whom Frances-Mary-Anne was the eldest.

1850. January 18. JOHN NUN WOODROOFE, A.M., P. R. and V. Rathcony als Cahirlag. [D.R.]

1860. The church, &c., in good order. No glebe-house. The glebe is set. Divine service twice on Sundays, and once on all Thursdays and on chief feasts. Sacrament monthly; average of communicants, 66; and at Christmas and Easter, average, 114. The children are catechised on Sundays and two other days in the week. There are three schools, maintained partly by Church Education Society, at which 8 boys, 14 girls, and 35 infants attend. The Protestant population is 483. The rentcharge of Rathcony is £375; of Cahirlag, £225; and of Little Island, £135. Total rentcharge, £735. The glebe is worth £25 per annum. Total value of benefice, £760, without residence.

J. N. Woodrooffe was ordained Priest at Cloyne on 13th of April, 1834, and on 29th of November, 1834, was licensed to the Curacy of Rathcony.

From 1846 to 1850 he was Chancellor of Cork.

CANNAWAY.

1318. 11. EDWARD II. John Wogan disputes, with William de Wellesley, the right of presentation to Cannaway Church, dioc. Cork. [Pat. Rot.]

1591. DERMITIUS LONG is Vicar. "R. de Keannevy spectat ad Preb. de Killaspugmullan. Vicarius ibm D. Long." [MS. T.C.D. E. 3. 14.] Long was Treasurer of Cork, q. v.

1609. January 22. WILLIAM HEALY, V. Keanway, Cork, and Mocrome, Cloine. [R.V. 1634.] He was Chancellor of Cork, q. v.

1615. Keanvoy Rectoria impropriata. Ecclesia et Cancella bene repantur. Vic. Wm. Healy, minister legens. Val. 30s. [R.V. R.I.A.]

1618. July 7. GEORGE STUKE was instituted to V. Clondroyt et Macrome, Cloine, et V. Canway, Cork, on letters patent of May 27. [Registry of Court of Prerogative, Dublin.] Stuke seems to have held these parishes until 1632 or 1634.

1634. JAMES TREDENNICK appears as V. Cannaway. "R. de Keanvoy spectat ad Abb. de Mora. Cormack Donogh Carty est firmarius. Val. 5 li. per an. Vicarius Jacobus Tredennicke, sed sub lite. Val. 5 li." [R.V. 1634] Tredennick was also R. Shandon, q. v.

1639. THOMAS BANKES was admitted V. Cannaway. [F.F.] He was also V. Holy Trinity, q. v.

1639. "Una R. de Cannaway spectat ad Abb. de Mora, altera ad P. de Killaspugmullane. Vicarius Thomas Bankes. Curatus Nathaniel Gyles. Ecclia ruinata, desunt singula." [V.B.]

1663. May 1. PETER MANBIE, P. Lisclery, R. Ardnigihie, and V. Cannaway. [F.F.]

In V. B. of 1666, the name of Peter Manby is struck out, and the vicarage is marked "vacant." [D.R.]

For Manby, *vide* Lisclery.

1666/7. February 14. PETRUS HEWET, clicus, institutus fuit ad Vicariam ecclise parochialis de Cannaway, per desertionem Petri Manby, in coll. Epi. [V.B. 1669.] Hewet appears again in 1669.

1667 and 1668. DR. BERNARD PACKINGTON appears as V. Cannaway. [V.B. D.R.] Packington was also Archdeacon of Cork, q. v.

1669 to 1675. PETER HEWITT appears as R. V. Cannaway. [V.B.] In the V. B. of 1670, "Rectoria impropriata de Cannaway spectat ad Vicarium ratione confiscationis ejusdem."

Hewett in 1675 became Chancellor, and in 1710 Precentor of Cork, q. v.

1675. Feb. 25. HUGO JENKINS, R. Ardnegihy, V. Ballymodan, Rathclarin, and Cannaway. [F.F.]

He appears to 1679. [V.B. D.R.]

In 1681 Jenkins was again admitted V. Ballymodan, q. v.

1680. July 28. JOHN TOM, A.M., V. Ballymodan, Rathclarin, and R. V. Cannaway. [F.F.]

In 1861 Tom became R. Ardnegihy, and in 1693 was P. Desertmore, q. v.

1681. May 26. JAMES MURPHY, S.T.D., is admitted "ad unam Rectoriam et vicariam de Cannaway." [F.F.] He appears 1681 and 1682. [V.B. D.R.]

James Murphy does not appear elsewhere.

1683. July 19. Daniel M'Owen Sweeny is admitted sequestrator of "unæ R. V. Cannaway." [D.R.]

1683. April 4. JOHN FORTUNE, A.B., "ad unam Rectoriam et ad unam vicariam de Cannaway." [F.F.] In 1695 he became V. Glanbarrahan, Ross, q. v.

On 9 July, 1683, Fortune appoints James Weekes his Proctor in a suit for tithes. [D.R.] He appears as V. Cannaway 1683 to 1688. [V.B.]

1689. JOHN HARRISON appears as V. Cannaway, although in another Visitation Book, of same year, the vicarage is marked "vacant." [V.B.] In 1691 (the rest of the date is torn), "Johēs Harrison, clicus, Divini Verbi predicator, adm. ad V. Cannaway per cessionem Johannis Fortune ultimi incumbentis vacantem." [D.R.]

1699. "No church; no Protestants. Mr. Harrison to converse with the peasants." [V.B. D.D. 1699.]

"1700. October 16. I saw Cannaway Church, which lies to the north-west of Moviddy Church, at about . . . . . distance; the way to the church is stopt, a gap is opened when . . . . . Cannaway Church built with stone and lime, half the walls are standing . . . . . bounds of the church-yard uncertain, whether an inward or out (ward) ditch. Counsellor Long's lands bound upon it. There are the ruins of a house in the church-yard. There is a vault whole; the Priest built an altar in it about a year ago, when some person of note was buried. About three English acres of glebe near the church belong to the Vicar. They lie on the east of the church. There are ten plowlands and a half in this parish; they are pretty good. The Earl of Clancarty had, and Counsellor Long has, an estate in this parish. No other proprietors. No Protestants live in this parish.

"Moviddy is the most convenient church for the inhabitants of this parish to resort to.

"The Prebendary of Killaspugmullane has half the tithes of the four plowlands, and half of Cannaway, and also of the mill. The Earl of Corke has half the tithes of two other plowlands in this parish.

"Mr. Harrison, the Incumbent, has the rest of the tithes, worth about £40 per an.

"Denis Sweny is Popish Priest of this parish and Macromp. No Protestants in this parish. I left with Mr. Harrison four Till. Serm. and six small pr. books. All this parish lies on the south of the river Lee. Mr. Harrison preaches once a fortnight in the parish of Aghabullog, in the diocese of Cloyne." [Downes' Tour.]

John Harrison, in 1669 to 1680, was Curate of Ballinaboy, and of eight other impropriate parishes. From 1669 to 1682 he was Vic. Chor. Cork. In 1671 he was made V. Kilcaskin and Kilkaterne, in Ross, which he resigned that year. From 1671 to 1699 he was Curate of Kilmurry. On 26 Feb. 1684, he was licensed to the curacy of Moviddy and Aglish.

He married Rebecca, neice to the wife of Dr. B. Packington, Archdeacon of Cork.

1715. MR. WALTER HEWETT appears as V. Cannaway. [V.B.] In 1710 he was Curate of Shandon. He was son of another Rev. Walter Hewett, and was born at Ringrone, county Cork, in 1685, and entered T.C.D. on 24 May, 1703.

1717. NICHOLAS SKOLFIELD appears as V. Cannaway. [V.B.] In 1737 he became V. Kilcaskin, Ross, q. v.

1718 to 1744. THOMAS RUSSELL appears as V. Cannaway. [V.B.] He was, in 1724, Archdeacon of Cork, q. v.

1729. May 26. Derby Connellan recants in parish church of Cannaway, before the congregation and Randol Roberts, the Curate. [D.R.]

1745. April 9. GEORGE WILSON, A.M., is admitted "ad unam R. Cannaway et ad V. Cannaway, vacant, per mortem naturalem Thomæ Russell." [D.R.]

George Wilson was, in 1747, Oct. 16, licensed to the curacy of Brinny. In 1743 he was V. Killaconenagh, Ross, whence he was promoted to Cannaway in 1745. He died in 1754.

1754. Sept. 25. THOMAS WATERHOUSE, A.B., R. and V. Cannaway, per mort. Wilson. [D.R.] In 1762 he was Precentor of Cork, q. v.

1757. November 5. THOMAS BROWNE, A.M., R. V. Cannaway, and same day Precentor of Cork, q. v.

1762. May 10. RICHARD BEARE, A.M., R. and V. Cannaway, per mort. Browne. [D.R.] In 1768 Beare was P. Kilbrittain, q. v.

1767. September 8. JOHN SMITH, A.M., R. V. Cannaway. [F.F.] In 1779 he became P. Timoleague, Ross, q. v.

1784. December 7. CHARLES SMITH, A.B., R. V. Cannaway, per cession of John Smith. [D.R.] In 1796 he became V. Kilmocamoge, q. v.

1796. May 4. JAMES BENTLEY GORDON, A.B., R. and V. Cannaway. [F.F.] By resignation of Charles Smith. [D.R.]

1807. Mr. Gordon is also R. Killegny, Ferns, where he resides. He pays £10 for the occasional duties of Cannaway. [Rep.]

He was author of "A History of Ireland," and also of "A History of the late Rebellion."

Rev. J. B. Gordon, held, along with Cannaway, the R. Killegney, Ferns, until his death, on 10 April, 1819. He left an only surviving son, Rev. Richard Gordon : and three daughters, Eliza, wife of Samuel Robinson, of Clonroache, county Wexford ; Catherine, and Harriett, wife of Thomas Jones, of Nutgrove, Rathfarnham, are mentioned in his will, which was dated and proved in 1819.

1819. May 12. JOSEPH CHAPMAN, A.B., R. and V. Cannaway. [F.F.] He does not appear elsewhere in Cork. He resigned in 1825, and became V. Agha and Dunleckney, and R. Templepeter, in the diocese of Leighlin.

1825. June 9. WILLIAM GORE, A.B., R. V. Cannaway. [F.F.]

He was son of Dr. Wm. Gore, Bishop of Limerick, by a daughter of Michael-Prittie Head, esq. of Derrycastle, county Tipperary.

From 1819 to 1825 he was R. Templepeter, Leighlin, and from 1825 to 1830 R. V. Cannaway. In 1825 he was Curate of Kelliestown, Leighlin. He died unmarried, leaving his brother, Nathaniel Gore, esq. of 5, Percy-place, Dublin, his heir. His will was dated from St. Aaresse, near Havre, and was proved in Dublin in 1854.

1830. August 14. RICHARD DAVIES, A.B., R. and V. Cannaway. [F.F.]

1830. Protestant population, 67.

Richard, son of Rev. Simon Davies, R. Macroom, was ordained Deacon on 1 June, 1828, and Priest on 23 August, 1829. He was R. Cannaway, in 1830, and resigned on 2 Nov. 1840. He married Mary, sister of Rev. Maunsell Eyre, R. Innishannon, and by her had a son, Rowland, on officer in the army.

1837. Cannaway, part of rectory and vicarage, with cure, 4 miles long by 2 broad, containing 5,113 acres. Gross population, 1,518. No Curate employed. Tithe composition, £212 6*s.* 2*d.*; 6A. 1R. 36¾P. of glebe, valued at £2 12*s.*; subject to visitation fees, 7*s.* 6*d.*; diocesan schoolmaster, 16*s.* No glebe-house. Incumbent resides in the town of Macroom, about four miles distant. One church, capable of accommodating 150 persons, built in the year 1814, at the cost of £553 16*s.* 11*d.* Brit., granted as gift by the late Board of First Fruits; and new roofed and thoroughly repaired in 1831, at an expense of £96 16*s.* 11*d.* Brit., raised by parochial assessment. No charge on the parish in 1832, on account of the church. Divine service is celebrated once on all Sundays, and on the principal festivals. The sacrament is administered six times in the year. A portion of the rectorial tithes of this parish, consisting of one moiety of the tithe composition of certain plowlands, amounting to £55, is appropriate, and belongs to the Archdeacon of Ross. [Parl. Rep.]

1840. Novem. 11. ROBERT WARREN, A.B., R. and V. Cannaway. [D.R.] Annual value, £161.

1860. Church in good order. No glebe-house. Incumbent lives in adjoining parish. Five acres of glebe, set. Divine service twice on all Sundays, and once on Christmas Day, Good Friday, &c. Sacrament monthly. Average of communicants, 11. No children to attend a school. The Protestant population is 46. Rentcharge, £159 4s. 7½d.; value of land, £2. Total value of benefice, £161 4s. 7½d., *without* residence.

Robert Warren (eldest son of Rev. R. Warren, R. Kilmichael), was born in March, 1794, and entered T.C.D. in July, 1812, and graduated A.B. in 1816.

He was ordained Deacon at Cork, on 3 May, 1819, and Priest at Raphoe, on 16 July, 1820. In 1820 he was Curate of Kilbarron, Raphoe.

He married, in 1825, Mary, second dau. of Dr. Crawford, of Ballyshannon, and has issue four sons and four daughters.

CARRIGALINE.

1291. Ecclesia de Beannier, with its appurtenances, viz.:—Kylneglerath and Anglasse; £33 9s. 8d. [Tax P. Nic.]

12—? RALPH DE KILLANGY was inducted into the vicarage of Beanner, co. Cork, on the presentation of Philip de Prendergast.

12—? MAURICE DE PRENDERGAST was Vicar of Beanner.

12—? STEPHEN DE INSCORTHY, Clk., was admitted in succession to Maurice de Prendergast, on the presentation of Gerald de Prendergast, son and heir of above Philip de Prendergast.

12—? IVER was admitted V. Beanner, on the presentation of Maurice de Rupefort, who married Matilda de Prendergast, daughter and heir of above Gerald de Prendergast; and Maurice de Rupeford (son and heir of said Maurice and Matilda de Prendergast) established his right to the advowson in 1311. [Placita Com. Banci Hib.]

1337. The prebend of Beanner, in St. Finbarry's Cathedral, is in the gift of the heir of Peter de Cogan, a minor. [Placita Com. Banci Hib.]

1386. Oct. 9. THOMAS HARBERG is appointed P. Beavor in ecclesia cathedrali St. Finbarry. [Rot. Canc. Hib.] On 16th Dec., 1386, he was appointed Archdeacon of Ossory; and on 24th June, 1388, the King ratified his estate in that archdeaconry, and in the prebend of Beavor. [Tuckey's Cork Remem. p. 32.] Harberg died in 1405.

1408. EDMUND FITZADAM appears as P. Carrigaline. [Rot. Canc. Hib.]

1414. Feb. 3. JOHN TANNER was presented by Crown to P. Beaver als Carrigaline. [Rot. Canc. Hib.] In 1399 he was Parson of Youghal, and on 17th August, 1408, he was admitted P. Swords, St. Patrick's, Dublin.

1591. EDMUND MCBREAN is Curate. "E. de Bever spectat ad Colleg. de Youghell. Edmundus M'Bre. Cur." [MS. T.C.D. E. 3. 14.] He was also Curate of Ballinaboy.

1615. Bever als Carigaline, Rector, Coll. de Youghall. Val. 24 marcks. Ecclesia et cancella bene repantur. Nullus curatus. Antiqua est vicaria per rotulos sed vacat et usurpatur per firmarium. Dowglasse, particula ejusdem, capella vasta. [R.V. R.I.A.]

1622. Carrigaline. V. usurpatur per firmarium. Douglass pars ejusdem. [R.V. 1622. Marsh's Library.]

1623. June 22. ANTHONY RISDON is presented to V. Carrigaline. [Lib. Mun.] Risdon, in 1615, was V. Aghadowne, Ross, and in 1616, V. Caheragh. He does not appear elsewhere.

1634. ROBERT BECK is Curate of Carrigaline.

"R. Bever als Carrigaline, spectat ad Coll. de Youghall. Val. 40 li per an. Vicariam ibm Coll. de Youghall tenet. Val. 60 li per an. Robertus Beck est Curatus. He hath received, for serving the rectory and vicarage those eighteen years, only 40s." [R.V. 1634.] In 1634 Beck is also Curate of Clonteid.

Beck was, in 1639, Curate of Carrigaline, Tracton, and of Kilcully als Bride als Templebrady, &c.

1638/9. March 26. RICHARD HOWLETT is admitted R. de Carrigaline, on letters patent of 26th November, 1638. [F.F. and Lib. Mun.]

1639. R. Howlett appears as Rector, with Robert Beck as Curate. "Ecclesia bene, deest calix." [V.B.]

Howlett, from 19th Dec., 1635 to 1638, Nov. 28, was Rector of Aghalurcher, Clogher dioc. He does not appear elsewhere in Cork records.

1660. Feb. 19. ROGER BOYLE is presented to R. Carrigoline. [Lib. Mun.]

He appears as R. Carrigaline in V.B. 1666. [D.R.] He was, from 1662, Dean of Cork, q. v.

1667. Ecclesia de Carrigaline als Bever vacat. [V.B.]

1667. November 4. JOHN VEASIE, R. Carrigaline als Bever, vacantem per promotionem Rogeri Boyle ad Episcopatum Dunen. et per litteras patentes Regis. [D.R.] On same day Vesey became Dean of Cork, q. v.

1673. May 5. ARTHUR POMEROY, A.M., is admitted R. Carrigaline, and same day Dean of Cork, q. v.

"Arthur P. being cited, and not appearing or excusing himself in any way, the original citation to be continued against him." [V.B. 1689, Nov. 4.] He is admonished not to neglect the cure of souls in Carrigaline on alternate Sundays. "Sicuti per plures menses," &c.

"1700. Thursday, Sept. 27. I saw Carickoline Church; it is above 70 foot long, built with stone and clay, but the walls are pretty good; well slated, and well furnished with seats. In the church hangs the King's Arms and Table of Marriage. A good vestry built on the north side of the church, at the charge of the Dean of Corke. In the vestry is a chest, where they have a vestry-book and registry for christenings, and book of canons, acts against swearing, and Common Prayer books, and Bible. There is linen for the Communion-table, a pewter flagon, chalice, paten, and basin of silver, and a pewter font. The school is kept in the church, by Rich. Codner, the clerk of the parish. A large church-yard, at least an English acre, well fenc't, and set round with sycamores. There are five small parcels of glebe belonging to the Incumbent of this parish. Not far from the church is the old Castle of Caricko-line, tis almost ruinous; it formerly belong'd to the family of the Coghans, now it is the estate of the Ld. Shannon.

"Near Douglas, in this parish, is a burying-place, in an open field; there is still remaining the foundation of a church, but they were carrying away the stones of the foundation. I charg'd them to carry away no more. The field is part of Sir John Mead's, set to the Potter at Douglass. This was, about 100 years ago, the church of Carickoline parish, before the new church was built, where it now is, in the centre of ye parish. In this parish also there is another burying-place, near a village call'd Balliarban, about four miles distant from Corke, on the left hand of the road from Cork to Carickoline; it is in an open field. There does not appear any foundation of a church, but the ground seems higher about the middle of the burying-place. The Irish bury in this place sometimes. It is thought that there was a church here." [Downes' Tour.]

1709. April. ROWLAND DAVIES, R. Carrigaline, per mortem Pomeroy. Davies was also Dean of Cork, q. v.

He resigned on 10th September, 1717. [Lib. Mun.]

1717. Nov. 6. Carrigaline is vacant. [V.B.] On 4th August and on 14th Oct., 1717, Boyle Davies had letters patent from the Crown to this rectory, but Lord Shannon disputed the presentation. [Lib. Mun. and D.R.]

1717. January 15. SAMUEL WEBBER, A.M., is admitted R. Carrigaline, now vacant by death of Pomeroy, or by resignation of Dr. Rowland Davies, and on the presentation of Earl of Shannon, dated 17th Oct., 1717. He is inducted by the Archdeacon on 16th January. [D.R.] Webber appears 1718 to 1721. [V.B.]

Samuel, son of Edward Webber, "senatoris," entered T.C.D. as a Pensioner on 10th May, 1701, being then twenty-six years of age. In 1716 he was V. Killaconenagh. in Ross; in 1717, R. Carrigaline, and in 1723 he became P. Howth, Dublin. He died in 1742.

1721/2. March 3. BOYLE DAVIES, R. Carrigaline. [F.F.]

He appears in V.B. of 1722. [D.R.] In 1735 he became P. Lisclery, q. v.

1723. The Vestry assigns the seat No. 13 in Carrigaline Church to William Hodder, who paid for it £3 10s. [D.R.]

The Bishop confirms this grant on 30th August, 1762, to the Hodder family, as they had a seat for four generations back in the old church, and subscribed £10 to the new church. [D.R.]

1763. Feb. 6. Rev. John Hickey, Curate of Carrigoline, is appointed Sequestrator, Davies being dead. [D.R.]

1763. May 16. JOHN OLIVER, A.M., is presented to the R. Carrigaline. [Lib. Mun.] He was admitted 6th September, 1763, per mortem Boyle Davies. [F.F.]

John Oliver was third son of Robert Oliver, of Clonodfoy, co. Limerick. He held the Archdeaconry of Ardagh from 1762 along with Carrigaline. He married, in 1761, Elizabeth Ryder, dau. of the Abp. of Tuam. For his issue, *vide* Burke, under *Olivers of Cherrymount*. He died on 23rd November, 1778.

On Nov. 27th, 1778, His Excellency the Lord Lieutenant acquaints the Bishop of his intention to present to Carrigaline, now vacant by death of Archdeacon Oliver. [D.R.] Lord Shannon sends his caveat, Dec. 8, 1778. On Nov. 28th, 1778, Henry Sandiford, Clerk, is appointed Sequestrator; and Hon. Gerald de Courcy is licensed as Curate on Dec. 10, 1778, at £50 per an. [D.R.] William Dickson is presented by Crown, on letters patent of Dec. 11th, 1778, and Lowther Yates, by Lord Shannon, on Dec. 15th, 1778.

1779. April 15. LOWTHER YEATES, B.D., R. and V. Carrigaline. [F.F.] On the presentation of Lord Shannon, after proceedings in Ecclesiastical Courts. [D.R.] Yeates does not appear elsewhere.

1780. April 14. WILLIAM DICKSON, A.B., R. Carrigaline. [F.F.] Vacant by the acceptance of a living in England by Lowther Yates. Wm. Dickson is now presented by the Earl of Shannon on 26th Feb., 1780. [D.R.]

1783. June 2. The Bp. of Cork and the Rector of Carrigaline consent to setting out the boundaries of the cure of the parish church of Douglas. [Chancery Enrolments.]

1784. Feb. 6. THOMAS BREVITOR, A.M., is admitted R. Carrigaline, on letters patent from the Crown, dated 31st December, the last Incumbent, William Dickson, having been promoted to the bishoprick of Down and Connor. [F.F. and Lib. Mun.]

Thomas Brevitor, son of Rev. Thomas Brevitor, P. Templebryan, in Ross, became a Pensioner T.C.D. on 29th June, 1744, and graduated B.A. in 1748, and A.M. in 1765.

He was ordained Deacon on 21st April, 1751, and Priest on 2nd June same year, both at Cork.

In 1751 he was Curate to his father at Templebryan, and in 1765 was Curate of Fanlobbus. He was Vicar-Choral of Cork from 1765 to 1768, and took the curacy of Rincurran in 1766. He became, in 1767, Curate, and in 1784, Rector, of Carrigaline. He died in 1803.

1803. June 11. HORATIO TOWNSEND, A M., R. Carrigaline. [F.F.] On presentation of Richard, Earl of Shannon. The Bishop's letter to institute is dated May 21. [D.R.]

1807. Townsend lives at Courtmacsherry, near the P. Island, which he holds by faculty. [Rep.]

1824. January 31. Carrigaline new Church, built near site of old church, is finished, and on 7th Feb., 1824, is licensed for divine service. [D.R.]

1830. Protestant population, 642.

1837. Carrigaline, alias Beaver, a rectory, with cure; (also Douglas, a chapelry, is attached to this benefice); five miles long by four broad, containing 14,000A. Gross population, 7,375. Three Curates employed at stipends to each of £75 per annum. Tithe composition, £1,080; 6A. of demised glebe, in two parcels, £13 10s. Subject to visitation fees, £1 10s. Diocesan schoolmaster, £2 2s. No glebe-house. Incumbent is non-resident; he is permitted by the Diocesan to reside at his own house at Rosscarberry, being eighty-two years of age, and very infirm. One church and a chapelry in this benefice, distant 3¼ miles from each other, the former capable of accommodating 220, and the latter 280 persons. Carrigaline Church built in 1823, at the cost of £1,846 3s. 1d. Brit., whereof £1,550 15s. 4½d. was granted in way of loan by the late Board of First Fruits, and the residue of £295 7s. 8½d. was raised by subscription. Of the loan aforesaid, there remained £946 9s. 4½d. chargeable on the parish in 1832, repayable by annual instalments of £62 0s. 7½d. Douglas Chapel built in 1785, at an expense of £695 1s. 6½d. Brit., of which sum £369 4s. 7¼d. was a gift granted by the late Board of First Fruits, and £325 16s. 11d. was raised by private subscriptions. No charge on the parish in 1832, on account of the chapelry. Divine service is celebrated twice on all Sundays in the church and chapel, and on the principal festivals, as also on all Wednesdays in the church. The Sacrament is administered monthly, and on the great festivals, in the church and chapel. The benefice is a rectory. [Parl. Rep.]

Horatio Townsend, A.M., was ordained Deacon on 21st, and Priest on 29th September, 1770, by the Bishop of Cork. He was, from 1770 to 1780, Curate of Abbeystrewry, Ross; and from 1780 to 1803, P. St Michael's Cork, and Curate of Carrigaline; from 1785 to 1786, he was R. Dungourney, Cloyne, and from 1786 to 1829, P. Island, V. Kilgaruffe and Desert, in Ross. He was, from 1786 to 1837, V. Kilkerranmore and Castleventry; and from 1803 to 1837, R. Carrigaline.

He was also Sovereign of the Borough of Clonakilty, and agent to the Earl of Shannon.

H. Townsend wrote, besides other fugitive pieces, "A Statistical Survey of the County of Cork," published by Edwards and Savage, Cork, 1813; also, "Observations on Dr. Coppinger's Letter to the Royal Dublin Society," 8vo., Cork, 1811; also, "Observations on Criminal and Civil Judicature in County Cork," published at Cork, in 1817.

The Rev. Horatio Townsend was the third surviving son of Captain Philip Townsend, who was the eighth son of Bryan, who was the second son and heir of Colonel Richard Townsend, of Castle Townsend: (see *Christ Church, or Holy Trinity, Cork, the Rev. Philip Townsend.*) Horatio's mother (Philip Townsend's wife) was Elizabeth, daughter of Thomas Hungerford, of Inchydoney, co. Cork. Horatio Townsend purchased the interest which belonged to his eldest brother, Richard Townsend, M.D., in the paternal estate of Derry, near Rosscarberry, and built a new mansion-house. He married, first, Helena, daughter of the Rev. Robert Meade, of Ballintober, near Kinsale; and, secondly, Catherine, daughter of Archdeacon Corker, Rector of Glanmire, near Cork. By his first wife he had one daughter, by his second wife he had five sons and nine daughters. He died March 26, 1837, aged eighty-seven years. A monument is erected to his memory in the cathedral of Ross. His eldest son, the Rev. Chambre Corker Townsend (see *Kilmacabea, Ross*), succeeded his father in the estate of Derry. His second surviving son, Horace, succeeded him in this rectory.

1837. May 6. HORACE TOWNSEND, A.M., R. Carrigaline [F.F.] On presentation by the Earl of Shannon, dated 2nd May, 1837. [D.R.]

The Rev. Horace Townsend was the second surviving son of the Rev. Horatio Townsend, of Derry, Rosscarberry, as above. In 1829, January 8, he married Anna, daughter of the Rev. Edward Kenny (see *Kilmeen, Ross*); she died, April 2, 1830, without issue. In 1836, February 2, he married Jane Florence, second daughter of Justin M'Cartie, of Carrignavar, co. Cork; by whom he had one son, Horatio, who was born April 1, 1837. He died at Douglas, near Cork, December 19, 1837, aged thirty-four years. His parishioners erected a monument over his remains in the church-yard of Douglas. A monument is also erected to the united memory of himself and two of his brothers, in Ross Cathedral. (See *Kilmacabea, Ross, the Rev. Chambre C. Townsend*).

1838. January 27. JOHN NEWMAN LOMBARD, A.M., R. Carrigaline, on presentation of the Earl of Shannon, dated 22nd January. [D.R.] He was also P. Kilmaclenine, Cloyne, q. v.

1855. Nov. 22. JOHN WATKINS BENN, A.B., R. Carrigaline, on the presentation of Edward William Hartpole Lecky, Esq., dated 12th Nov. 1855, and certified to be of the annual value of £661 10*s.* 6½*d.* [D.R.]

1860. Church in good order. No glebe-house. Five acres of glebe set. Divine service twice on all Sundays, and on the usual feasts and fasts. Evening service during winter in a licensed school-house at Carrigaline. The sacrament monthly, and at chief festivals; average of communicants, 35; 45 children on rolls of school, which is maintained by local subscriptions. The Protestant population is 267.

Douglas Chapel of Ease in good order. Rev. J. Bustead is curate. No glebe-house. Five acres of land set. Divine service twice on all Sundays, and once on usual festivals and fasts. In winter, evening service in a house. 150 children are on rolls of a school kept by local subscribers. The Protestant population of Douglas is 310. Total Protestant population of both parts of this parish is 577. The rentcharge is £810. The land is worth £9. Total value of benefice, £819, without residence.

J. W. Benn (son of James Benn, Esq.) was born in co. Antrim, and when nineteen years old entered T.C.D. as a Pensioner, on 4th November, 1833.

He was Incumbent of St. Paul's, Portarlington, before his admission to Carrigaline.

CARRIGROHANE, PRECENTORS.

1291. Ecclesia de Carrigraffan is rated at 4 marks. There is no Vicar. [Tax. P. Nic.] E. de Corbally, 9 marks. [Ib.]

1337. O is the initial of the Precentor. [Placita Com. Banci Hib.]

1543. June 3. WILLIAM FITZMAURICE FITZGERALD, Chaplain, is appointed Precentor by the Crown, the place being vacant, and at the King's disposal; the late Incumbent being of the Irish nation. [Rot. Pat. 34 Hen. VIII.]

1582. JOHN GOLDE is Precentor. [D.R.] He is called Drumgoulde in a Memoranda Roll of 1585. [Exchequer.]

1591. DIONISIUS CAMBELL appears as Precentor. "Null. cur. alicui cur. ex Relacoe Dni Epi. cont. fructus sequestr. pro amocoe michaelis Dublin."—"E. de Corikippan et E. de Carigrowan spectat ad precentoriam. Nullus curatus."—"Prebenda Scti. ptri. de Carrickruchan—Cambell—nullus curatus."—"Rectoria de Corbally: precent. et Ab. Morne sunt Rectores. Vicaria ibm spectat ad Vic. Chor. DONOGHE O CALE, curatus." [MS. T.C.D. E. 3. 14.]

Cambell was a Scotchman, and was Archdeacon, and afterwards Dean of Limerick. He was also R. Dromcliffe, Killaloe. In 1588 he was appointed coadjutor Bishop of Limerick, and in 1603 was nominated to the sees of Derry, Raphoe, and Clogher. He died, however, before his consecration, in July, 1603, in London. For an account of him and his works, *vide*

"The Miscellany of the Maitland Club," vol. iv. [Lib. Mun. and Cotton.]

1612. Dec. 11. JOHN ALDEN is presented to Precentorship of Cork, the Archdeaconry of Lismore, and the P. St. Munchin's, in Limerick. In 1614 he was admitted V. Cahir cum Clonmell and Grange St. John, in Lismore diocese. [Lib. Mun.]

1613. June 3. ISRAEL TAYLOR, A M., Precentor ex presentatione Elizabethæ nuper Reginæ, on letters patent, dated in the 29th year of her reign. He was installed 3 Nov. 1613. [R.V. 1634.]

1615. Precentor Israel Taylor, A M., Minister et Predicator. Valor 25 li. per an. Tenet etiam R. V. Rathclaren, val 25 li. et V. Clonmel, clonen. val. 12 li., et R. Insulæ Parvæ, val. 7 li. per an. Homo dignus. Carrikippane et Kyrigrohane spectant ad Precentor. Ecclesiæ bene repantur cum libris et omnibus necessariis. [R.V. R.I.A.]

1615. Carrigrohane spectat ad Precentor. Curatus RICHUS ALLEN, Minister legens. Ecclesia et cancella repântur cum libris et aliis necessariis. Corbally (in 1615) spectat ad Precentor. Ecclesia rapâta. cancella in ruinis. The Precentor and Vicars Choral are peremptorily ordered to provide a Curate and repair the chancel. [R.V. R.I.A.]

1634. Carrygrohane spectat ad precentor ; R. de Corbally ad Precentor. et Vicarios Chorales. Val. (of Corbally) 3 li. per an. Vicaria ibm spectat ad Vicarios Chorales. Currikippane, similiter. [R.V. 1634.]

1639. Currikippane spectat ad Precentor. Curatus JASPER TOMPSON. Ecclesia bene et ornata. Clericus Parochialis John Pratt. Carrygrohane similiter—Ecclesia bene, desunt calix et co-opterum. Corbally R. spectat ad Precentor. Ecclesia ruinata, desunt omniaque. Vicaria ibm spectat ad vicarios chorales. Nullus curatus. [V.B. 1639.]

Israel Taylor, A.M., was ordained Deacon and Priest by "Marcum Elien.," on 25 April, 1602.

In 1611, April 20, he was admitted R. Ballymount-Elligott, and V. Kilcummin and Mollahiffe, diocese of Ardfert and Aghadoe.

In 1613 he was Precentor of Cork. In 1614 R. Rathclarin, and Insula Parva, which he held in 1639 and later. In 1615 V. Clonmel, which he resigned in 1618, and in 1615 also V. Clonfert, Cloyne, which he held until 1630.

He received, on 15 March, 1624, a dispensation to hold the Precentorship, Rathclarin and Clonfert, "modo non distent a se invicem ultra spatium 20 milliaria cum clausula permutationis et perinde valere."

In 1641, Taylor, the Precentor, was plundered of property to the amount of £680, besides the loss of his church livings, worth £250 per an. [MS. T.C.D. F. 2. 18]

His will, dated 8 Feb. 1642, and proved 23 June, 1652, is

in Cork Registry. In it he is described as Israel Taylor, Chaunter of St. Finbarrys. He mentions his brother Thomas, and his wife Persis, and says he is "readie to go to sea."

1661. PHILEMON FITZSYMONS appears as Precentor. [V.B. D.R.] He graduated in T.C.D. as A.B. in 1638, and A.M. in 1640.

He resigned Carrigrohanebeg in Cloyne, about 1630. From 1638 to 1640 he was V. Templebodan. He became P. Inniscarra in 1640, and held it and this Precentorship together from 1661 to his death in 1664. He appears as Curate of Youghal in 1639.

1664. June 10. RICHARDUS CLERKE, adm. Precentor et V. de Athnowen, per naturalem mortem Philemii ffitzsymons. Institutus fuit 15 Junii. [V.B. 1669. and F.F.]

Carrigrohane R. spectat ad Precentor. Currikippane similiter. Quatuor vicarii sunt rectores de Corbally. Rectoria ecclesiæ de Kinneigh est particula precentoriatus. [V.B. 1669.]

Richard Clerke graduated A.M. in T.C.D. in 1664. From 1661 to 1663, P. Ballyhay, Cloyne; from 1663 to 1685, P. Tullaghorton, Lismore; from 1664 to 1666, R. V. Rathclaren; from 1664 to 1685, Precentor of Cork, and P. Donoghmore, Cloyne; from 1667 to 1685, V. Carrigrohanebeg, Cloyne; from 1668 to 1671, V. Rathclaren; and from 1668 to 1685, R. Rathclaren. He died in 1685.

1686. WALTER NEALE appears as Precentor, and V. Athnowen. [V.B. D.R.]

He appears 1686 to 1706, Nov. 3. [V.B. D.R.] In the margin of V.B. 1686, he is marked as "non instit." [D.R.] From 1687 to 1699, R. Corbally spectat ad Precentor, Vicaria ad Vicarios Chorales. In 1699 "the Protestants (of Corbally) go to Carrickgrohane." [V.B. of 1699.]

Walter Neale, A.M., was from 1676 to 1686, Archdeacon of Ardfert; from 1681 to 1686, R. Rathcooney; from 1681 to 1707, R. V. Shandon; from 1681 to 1684, P. Templebryan, and V. Templequinlan, Ross; from 1681 to 1686, Treasurer of Cork; from 1681 to 1682, P. Island, Ross; from 1683 to 1707, Chancellor of Ross; and from 1686 to 1707, Precentor of Cork, and V. Athnowen.

Neale was Vicar-General of Cork and Ross. His name disappears from the Cork Records in 1706/7. I find among the Cloyne marriage bonds one dated 1684, between Rev. Walter Neale and Elisabeth Baymond, of Whitechurch; and another between Walter Neale, gent. of Shandon, and Frances Charde, of Coolinie, in the year 1692. I think the Vicar-General was son of Constantine Neale, of county Wexford, and a relative of the Vigors family. A letter of the Rev. Walter Neale on the Gallican Church is printed in the Christian Examiner for 1853.

1706. Feb. 4. ROWLAND DAVIES, LL.D., Precentor. [F.F.] He appears 1709. [V.B.] He became, in 1710, Dean of Cork, q. v.

1710. June 2. PETER HEWET, Precentor. [F.F.]

Peter Hewet was from 1666 to 1675, R. Ardnegihy, V. Ballymodan and Cannaway. From 1671 to 1675, V. Rathclarin; from 1675 to 1676, R. V. Ringrone; from 1675 to 1710, Chancellor of Cork. In 1693 he was Curate of Templetrine. He was from 1710 to 1720, Precentor of Cork; and from 1714 to 1720, R. Templetrine.

He married Alice Wilshire, or Wilson, in 1672. [Cloyne M.B.] And in his will (dated 17 March, 1719/20, and proved 3 Sept. 1720, at Cork) he mentions his wife, Alice, as executrix, and his son, Arthur, and Arthur's son, Peter. He left to the poor of the Alms-house at the Docke 20*s.*; and wishes to be buried "close to my son, at about eight a clock at night," in the chancel of Ringrone Church.

1720. June 29. THOMAS RUSSELL, A.M., Precentor. [F.F.] In 1724 he became Archdeacon of Cork, q. v.

1724. Feb. 13. JEMMET BROWNE, A.B., Precentor of Cork, and R. V. Athnowen, vacant by resignation of Russell. Browne was again admitted on 11 Dec. 1730. [D.R.] In 1733 he became Dean of Ross, q. v.

1732. January 1. PETER WATERHOUSE, M.A., of Christchurch, Oxon, is admitted Precentor. [F.F.]

1739. May 19. Daniel O'Hea recants before the Bishop, and again, on the 20 May, in the parish church of Carrigrohane, *teste* Peter Waterhouse. [D.R.]

Peter Waterhouse entered T.C.D. as Pensioner on 27 Feb. 1720. In 1727 he was made Chancellor of Ross, Vicar Choral of Cork, and R. V. Kilmichael and Inchigeelah. In 1732 he became Precentor of Cork, and retained all these livings (except the Vicarage Choral, which he resigned in 1732), until his death in 1750.

He married, in August, 1730, Mabella Symes, and probably died without issue surviving, as his widow Mabella obtains the renewal of the lease from the Bishop in her own name. The earliest trace of the Cork Waterhouses is the following extract from the parish registry of Christ Church, Cork:—"Mary, the daughter of Thomas Waterhouse and Rachel, his wife, was born the 21 of March, and baptised the 25 of the same, 1659."

Peter Browne, Bishop of Cork, mentions Peter Waterhouse as his cousin, and appoints him a trustee in his will. On 10 Nov. 1729, the Bishop leased to Waterhouse part of the demesne lands of his See, in St. Finbarry's parish, called the half plowland of Farranmacteige, at a rent of £25, and a couple of good fat capons at Shrovetide, or 4*s.* in lieu thereof. This lease was renewed on 28 March, 1751, to Mabella Waterhouse, widow, for twenty-one years, at same rent. [D.R.]

1750. March 28. EDWARD BROWNE, A.B., Precentor. [F.F.] He was also R. V. Mackloneigh, and Archdeacon of Ross, q. v.

1752. May 15. HONOURABLE JOHN CHETWYND, M.A., of Corpus Christi Coll. Oxon., is admitted Precentor, the corps of which consists of R. Currikippane, Corbally, Carrigrohane, and one R. Kinneigh. [D.R.]

He was second son of the 3rd Viscount Chetwynd. He died 1757, and was buried in Cork Cathedral. For his marriage and issue, *vide* Burke's Peerage.

1757. Nov. 5. THOMAS BROWNE, A.M., Precentor. [F.F.]

Thomas Browne, second son of Jemmett, Bishop of Cork, was born in that city in 1729, and entered T.C.D. as Pensioner on 24th Oct. 1746. He was ordained Deacon on 21st April, 1751, and Priest on 2nd June, 1751; both at Cork.

From 1751 to 1757 he was Vic. Chor. Cork; and from 1757 to 1762 Precentor of Cork and R. V. Cannaway. He held also, from 1752 to 1762, the R. V. Little Island. On 23rd Sept. 1754 he was licensed to the Curacy of Killaspugmullane. From 1755 to 1757 he held also the R. V. Kilmichael.

He married (Feb. 1750), Anne, dau. of Rev. David Waterhouse, and by her (who died in Feb. 1756), had two daughters, Alice; and Lydia, wife of Caleb Falkiner, esq.; and one son, Jemmett, who died in 1765.

He died on 9th May, 1762, and was buried in Cork Cathedral.

1762. May 10. THOMAS WATERHOUSE, A.M., Precentor. [F.F.]

He was Curate of St. Nicholas, Cork, in 1753. He became R. V. Cannaway in 1754, R. V. Kilmichael in 1757, and in 1762 Precentor of Cork. He died on 25th Nov. 1762. He was son of Rev. David Waterhouse, and a cousin of the Rev. Peter Waterhouse. His will was proved in Dublin in 1763, and in it several relatives are named, but no wife or children; so, I presume, he died unmarried.

1762. Dec. 2. SAMUEL WOODROOFFE, A.M., Precentor. [F.F.] A Scholar of T.C.D. in 1730.

1765. March 4. A commission issues to value the improvements made by Waterhouse on the glebe-house of Currikippane; on 12th March the return to the commission find £59 7*s.* 8*d.* to be the amount expended. [D.R.]

Samuel Woodrooffe was V. Kinsale from 1736 to 1741, and R. Ballymoney and Kilmeen from 1741 to 1746. He was P. Dromdaleague and R. Caheragh from 1746 to 1762, when he became Precentor of Cork. He also held, from 1746 to 1780, the Precentorship of Ross. He was Vicar-General of Cork and Ross from 1770 to 1772.

He made his will on 29th June, 1760, "being to leave ye kingdom for the recovery of my health." He mentions his wife, Dorothea (who survived him), and his daughter, Mrs. Catherine Mosse; and his nephew, John, son of James Woodrooffe; also his brother, John. The will was proved in Cork, twenty years afterwards, and administration was granted to his widow, Dorothea Woodrooffe.

1780. June 21. JOHN CHETWOOD, A.B., Precentor. [F.F.]

In 1790 he became P. Cahirlag, q. v.

1790. April 12. HENRY SANDIFORD, A.B., Precentor. [F.F.]

1807. Sandiford resides partly on Rathgogan or Charleville. [Rep.]

Henry Sandiford, A.B., was ordained Deacon on 22nd January, 1769, and Priest on 8th October the same year; both at Cork. In 1769 he was Curate of St. Peter's, and from 1770 to 1784 served as Curate of the Holy Trinity. In 1784 he was made P. Donoghmore, in Ross, and also R. V. Kilcully, but resigned both those preferments in 1785, when he became Chancellor of Cork. In 1790 he resigned the Chancellorship, and became Precentor of Cork. He held along with this Precentorship, from 1695 to 1696, the Vicarage of Castlelyons; from 1696 to 1801 the P. Brigowne; and from 1801 to 1826 the Prebend of Ballyhay, in Cloyne. He had been Thresher's Lecturer in Cork from 1773 to 1785. He died in January, 1826, and left issue (besides a daughter, Harriett, wife of Patrick Nugent Savage, esq. then deceased), a daughter, Maria, and a son, Rev. James Sandiford, P. Killenemer, Cloyne, q. v.

1826. March 11. HENRY THEOPHILUS MOORE HODDER, A.B., Precentor; certified under £800 per annum, the corps being the same as in 1752. [D.R.]

1830. Protestant population of Carrigrohane, 163; of Currikippane, 57.

1837. Carrigrohane union, with cure, consisting of—1. Carrigrohane rectory, 3 miles long by 1½ broad. 2. Carrikippane rectory, 2 miles long by 1¾ broad. 3. Corbally vicarage, not stated. Extent of union not stated, but containing 5,310 acres. Gross population of union, 2,961. Two Curates employed, at stipends, to one of £75 per annum and the surplice fees, and to the other of £30 per annum, for occasional duties in part of the union. Tithe composition of Carrigrohane parish, £330; 14 acres of glebe in said parish let for £36. Tithe composition of Carrikippane parish, £280; 3 acres of glebe in said parish let for £7. Composition for the vicarial tithes of Corbally parish, £23 6*s.* 8*d.* Surplice fees, £6 10*s.* Subject to visitation fees, 15*s.* Diocesan schoolmaster, £1. No glebe-house. Incumbent resides in the adjoining benefice, and £60 is considered a reasonable sum to be allowed in way of house-rent. One church, capable of accommodating 70 persons, built about the year 1628. No charge on the parish in 1832 on account of it. A military chapel, capable of accommodating 350 persons, situate in Carrikippane parish, belonging to the Ordnance establishment, at which the parishioners residing in the neighbourhood are allowed to attend. Divine service is celebrated in the church and chapel twice on Sundays in summer, and once in winter, and on the principal festivals. The sacrament is administered monthly, and on the great festivals, in the church and chapel. [Parl. Rep.]

1860. Dr. Hodder, Incumbent; Rev. R. Leslie, Curate. The church in good order. No glebe-house. 21 acres of glebe, of which 7 are set, the rest being in Incumbent's use. Divine service once on all Sundays, and on the chief festivals and fasts, Sacrament monthly, and at festivals; average of communicants, 32. The children are catechised on Tuesdays by the Curate. 45 children attend a school maintained by Incumbent and local subscribers. The Protestant population is 250. The rentcharge of Carrigrohane is £247 10*s.*; of Carrikippane, £210; of Corbally, £17 10*s.*; and of Kinneigh rectory, £168 15*s.* The 17 acres of glebe are worth £43; and a house in St. Finbarry's parish, belonging to the Precentor, is worth £10. Total rentcharge, £632 15*s.* Total value, £685 15*s.* without residence.

In Ballincollig garrison chapel divine service is held on Sunday evenings for the parishioners, and on Sunday mornings and afternoon for the garrison, by the Chaplain, Rev. W. Spedding.

Henry Theophilus Moore Hodder, A.B. (second son of William Henry Moore, esq. who assumed the additional surname of Hodder), was ordained Deacon on 14th August, 1814, and Priest 22nd December, 1816, both at Cork. In 1817 he was Curate of Ballinaboy, in 1818 R. V. Leighmoney, in 1823 Chancellor, and in 1826 Precentor of Cork. He is married.

CULLEN, P.C.

1846. July 27. THOMAS OLDEN was licensed to be Curate of Cullen by the Incumbent, the Dean of Cork. [D.R.]

1847. May 6. Cullen is erected into a perpetual cure, under 11 and 12 G. III., chapter 16. The endowment is the entire glebe of nineteen acres, save one acre set apart for a school-house, and tithes to amount of £55 and three farthings Brit. N.B.—In act of Council, Cullen is said to be endowed with all the tithes, great and small, arising within the parish.

1849. Sept. 8. Cullen new church was consecrated under the name of Christ Church. [D.R.]

Olden is now V. Tullilease, Cloyne, q. v.

1860. August 23. THOMAS DORMAN is admitted P.C. of Cullen. [D.R.]

1860. The Dean is Incumbent; Thomas Dorman, Curate. The church in good order. A new glebe-house and offices, and eighteen acres of land in Curate's occupation. Divine service once on Sundays, and in summer there is also an evening service. Sacrament monthly; average of communicants, 4; and on chief festivals average 14. Eighteen children attend a Church Education School. The Protestant population is 43.

T. Dorman (son of John Dorman, esq.) was born at Kinsale, in 1821, and graduated A.B., T.C.D., in 1847. He was ordained Deacon in July, 1847, by Bp. of Tuam, and Priest in 1848, by Bp. of Killaloe, both on letters dimissory from Cork.

He was Curate of Holy Trinity in July 1847, of Garrycloyne in 1848, and of St. Anne's, Shandon, in September, 1855.

He is married, and has five children.

DESERTMORE.

1591 Preb. de Desertmore. ROBERT STURTON. [MS. T.C.D. E. 3. 14.] He was also Dean of Ross, q. v.

1615. Disertmore Prebend. R. WILSON, A.M., Student in College. Val. £5. Church and chancel in ruins. Curate, Thomas Davies. Minister, legens. Wilson, holds also Drumdalege. [R.V. R.I.A.]

In 1619, Wilson resigned his livings in Cork. He was P. Kilrane, Ferns, from 1626 to 1628, and in 1628, became Dean of Ferns; which preferment, along with P. Donaghmore, Dublin, he held until 1642. He was also Vicar of Finglas, Dublin, where, in 1641, he lost property by the rebellion to amount of "twenty-five hundred pounds." [MS. T.C.D. F. 2. 3.] In 1621 he graduated S.T.B., in T.C.D.

1619. Oct. 26. WILLIAM BOLTON, Preb. de Disertmore. [F.F.] He resigned in 1627, and was subsequently Dean of Ross, q. v.

1627. Oct. 13. THOMAS HOLFORD, adm. P. Desertmore, and installed "per Thomas Wight, decanum Corcagen. ult. Feb. 1627." [R.V. 1634.]

1634. P. Desertmore, Thomas Holford, Predicator. Val. 14 li. per an. [R.V. 1634.]

In 1637, Holford became Treasurer of Cloyne, q. v.

1637. MICHAEL BOYLE (son of Bp. Richd. Boyle) was collated by his father; and this, with other appointments, is complained of by Bp. Wetenhall, in a letter, dated 13th March, 1693, addressed to Bp. T. Tennison, of Lincoln, who was then offered the Archbishopric of Dublin, which, however, he declined to accept. [Lambeth, MSS. 929, p. 14, quoted by Cotton.] Boyle was, in 1640, Dean of Cloyne, q. v.

1639. HOLFORD appears as P. Desertmore, the name Boyle being crossed out. Curate, NATHANIEL WINSMORE, or NINSEMOW. "Navis ecclesiæ ruinata, desunt singula." [V.B., D.R.]

1661. Vacant. [V.B. D.R.]

1663. Bishop MICHAEL BOYLE holds this Preb. by grant from Crown, dated Nov. 17. [Rot. Can. and V.B.] And he retained it after removal to the see of Dublin, until he became Primate.

1678. Feb. 28. JOHN PARKER, Archbishop of Dublin, has a grant of this Prebend in commendam, and retains it until his death in 1681. [Ware.]

He appears, 1681, November 3. [V.B. D.R.]

1681/2. January 4. JOHN TORWAY, A M., P. Desertmore. [F.F.] He does not appear in the visitation books for this prebend. In 1685 he was P. Donoghmore, Cloyne, q. v.

1682. August 21. FRANCIS MARSH, Archbishop of Dublin, P. Desertmore. [F.F.] By grant from Crown in commendam.

1689. PAUL DUCLOS, A.M., appears as P. Desertmore. "Nullus curatus, guardianus, nec clericus parochialis." [V.B.] But in another visitation book of same year the Abp. of Dublin appears, and in 1690 the Archbishop's name is crossed out, and that of Duclos written over it.

Duclos was also P. Island, Ross, q. v.

1691. DOMINUS ARCHIEPUS DUB. appears as P. Desertmore in the years 1691, 1692, and 1693. [V.B.]

1694. Dec. 6. JOHN TOM, A.M., P. Desertmore, per mortem Archiepi Dub. [F.F. and D.R.]

1699. No church; one Protestant family, who go to Moviddy. Mr. Tom preaches six or eight times in a year in Desertmore, at Kilcrea. Six or seven plowlands. Some Papists, married to Protestants, breed their children Papists. [V.B. D.D. 1699.]

John Tom, A.M., of Peter House, Cambridge [Cotton.], was, from 1680 to 1681, V. Ballymodan, Rathclarin, and Cannaway. In 1681 he was licensed to the curacy of Ballydeloghy, and became R. Ardenegihy, which he held until 1686. From 1682 to 1683 he was P. Effin, Limerick, by favour of the Earl of Kildare. From 1684 to 1685 he held the P. Templebryan, &c., in Ross. In 1686 he became V. Kinsale, which he retained until his death, holding along with that vicarage the P. Inskenny from 1688 to 1693, and the P. Desertmore from 1693 to his death. From 1692 to 1698 he held again the P. Templebryan, in Ross, being for that period the holder of three prebends.

He married, firstly, Mary ——? and by her (who was buried 19th June, 1692, in Kinsale), he had issue, Susannah, born 1686; Winifred, born in 1687; William, born in 1688; and Francis, born in 1690. He married, secondly, on 18th Sept., 1692, Deborah Burrows, widow, and by her had issue, St. John, born 1695; Jane, born in 1698; Robert, born 1702, died 1704; and Henry, born in 1703. He died 17th Nov., 1717, and was buried in Kinsale Church; the inscription on his tombstone is still to be seen. His widow, Deborah, married, in 1719, George Coates, esq. [Kinsale Register and Cork M.B.]

1718. April 12. RICHARD GOODMAN, P. Desertmore. [F.F.]

He was a native of county Cork, and son of Rev. Thomas Goodman, Pecentor of Ross, q. v. He entered T.C.D. as Pensioner on 27th March, 1675, being then aged eighteen. He became a Scholar in 1677.

From 1682 to 1691 he was Vicar Choral, Cork; in 1687 he was licensed to the curacy of St. Michael's; from 1689 to 1695 he was R. V. Kilcully; from 1692 to 1696 he was V. Rathclarin, and from 1692 to 1737, V. Ballymodan; from 1696 to 1718 he was P. Killanully, and from 1696 to 1737, R. Knockavilly and V. Brinny. From 1705 to 1737 he was R. Killowen. Besides the Cork livings he held, from 1695 to 1696, the Prebend of Rath, in Killaloe. He died in 1737.

He married Hannah ——? but had no issue; at least, in his will (dated 1736, and proved 1737) he mentions none. He wished to be buried near his mother, in the church of Ballymodan, and bequeathed £20 to the poor of that parish.

1737. June 1. Vacant by death of RICHARD GOODMAN. [V.B. D.R.]

1737. June 28. PERKINS CROFTON, A.M., P. Desertmore, R. Knockavilly, and V. Brinny. [F.F.]

1737. August 1. The Bishop leases to Archdeacon Crofton 6A. 3R. 1P., part of which land was formerly held by Archdeacon Thomas Russell, and three acres formerly held by Rev. John Herbert, and the field called "ye Rock," containing 2A. 2R. 18P., all in St. Finbarry's parish, for twenty-one years, at £8 per an.; and on 10th April, 1741, the Bishop renews Crofton's lease of tenements, &c., in Rosscarbery. [D.R.]

Perkins Crofton, son of Rev. Henry Crofton, was born in the parish of Crossmoline, Killala diocese, and when sixteen years old, entered T.C.D. as a Pensioner, on 9th June, 1720, and graduated afterwards A.B. and A.M.

He was ordained Deacon at Dromore, on May 14, 1727. In 1736 he was made Archdeacon of Aghadoe, and in 1737 became P. Desertmore, retaining his Archdeaconry until his death in 1768. In 1745 he was Vicar-General of Cork and Ross.

He married, in 1740, Elisabeth Uniacke, of Mount Uniacke, co. Cork, [Cloyne, M.B.] dau. of Capt. James Uniacke, by Mary Mathew.

1768. Dec. 13. JOHN BARRY, A.M., P. Desertmore. [F.F.]

He was born in Cork, younger son of Edward Barry, M.D. (who was created a Baronet of Ireland in 1775), by Jane, daughter of Antony Dopping, Bishop of Ossory. When fifteen years of age he entered T.C.D. as Pensioner, on 17th January, 1742.

He was ordained Priest at Cork, on 21st January, 1753, and in same year was V. Killaconenagh, in Ross. He resigned that living in 1756, and held, from 1756 to 1768, the V. Durrus-Kilcrohane. He was P. Kilmaclenine, Cloyne, and P. Desertmore, from 1768 to 1794; and also, from 1778 to 1794, was Dean of Elphin.

He graduated A.M. in 1753, and LL.D. in 1768.

He married, in May 1771, at St Mary's, Shandon, Sarah, dau. of John Bateman, of Oak Park, co. Kerry; and secondly, in 1780, Anne Sican, by whom he had issue a son, Edward, who succeeded to the Baronetcy on the death (without heirs male) of Sir Nathaniel, his uncle. Dean Barry's will was proved on 2nd Sept., 1794.

1794. June 17. JOHN WILLIAM BENNETT, A.B., P. Desertmore, which being under £200 per an. in value, is now episcopally united to R. V. Kilcully, now held by Bennett. [D.R.] He was, in 1799, Treasurer of Cloyne, q. v.

1807. J. W. Bennett lives at Middleton, in Cloyne, which he holds by faculty. [Rep.]

1810. July 28. WILLIAM BUTLER, A.B., P. Desertmore, per mortem Bennett. [D.R.] Butler, in 1817, was P. Ballyhooly, Cloyne, q. v.

1815. A new church was built on the site of the old church of Desertmore, at cost of £553 16*s.* 11*d.*, granted by late Board of First Fruits. [F.F.]

1817. Feb. 3. JAMES STEWART, A.M., P. Desertmore. [F.F.] He was afterwards V. Lislee, Ross, q. v.

1817. May 27. The new church was consecrated under the name of St. John. [D.R.]

1817 Oct. 17. Stewart memorials to build a glebe-house, at estimated cost of £999 18*s.* 7*d.* [D.R.]

1817. Nov 6. The present (1861) parish register begins.

1818. May 5. WILLIAM HARVEY, A.M., P. Desertmore; certified under £300. [D.R.] He became, in 1824, P. Kilnaglory, q. v.

1818. May 18. Harvey memorials for building, and a commission issues 31st March, 1819; and on 3rd June, 1819, the Bishop certifies for an outlay of £999 18*s.* 7*d.*, of which £750 was a loan from Board of First Fruits. [D.R.]

1824. Oct. 19. ROBERT PRATT, A.B., P. Desertmore, certified under £500 per annum in value. [D.R.]

1830. Protestant population, 40.

1837. Desertmore: a rectory, with cure; two miles long by nearly two broad, containing 3,844A. 2R. 23P.; gross population, 1,147; no Curate employed; tithe composition, £350; Fifty acres of glebe, valued at 20*s.* per acre, £50, subject to visitation fees, 18*s.* Diocesan schoolmaster, 11*s.* 3*d.* Desertmore glebe-house built under the new acts, at the cost of £1,015 6*s.* 4½*d.* Brit., whereof £92 6*s.* 1¾*d.* was granted as gift, and £692 6s. 1¾d. as loan by the late Board of First Fruits, and the residue of £230 14s. 1d. was supplied out of the private funds of the builder, to whom the present Incumbent is next in succession; and having paid his predecessor the entire of the sum last named, he will be entitled to receive £173 0s. 6¾d. from his successor on account thereof. Of the loan aforesaid, there remained £408 14s. 8d. chargeable on the benefice in 1832, repayable by annual instalments of £22 14s. 2d. Incumbent is constantly resident in the glebe-house. One church, capable of accommodating eighty persons, built in 1815, at the cost of £553 16s. 11d. Brit., granted as gift by the late Board of First Fruits. No charge on the parish in 1832 on account of the church. Divine service is celebrated once on all Sundays, and on the principal festivals. The Sacrament is administered monthly. The benefice is a rectory. [Parl. Rep.]

Robert Pratt (eldest son of Rev. James Pratt, P. Kilnaglory), left issue, three sons, James, Rev. John (afterwards R. Kilnagross, q. v.), and Robert (afterwards Colonel of 23rd Regt., and C.B., who married, in 1861, May 4, Phœbe-Hester-Jane, eldest daughter of Reverend Robert Bury, of Brooklodge, Carrigrenane, co. Cork), and a daughter, Elizabeth. Rev. Robert Pratt died on 7th February, 1856.

1856. March 18. JOHN QUARRY, A.M., P. Desertmore; certified to be of the net yearly value of £279 13s. 11d. [D.R.] He became in 1859 R. Castrachore, Cloyne, q. v.

On 16th March, 1857, he obtains £205 18s. 1d. dilapidations against his predecessor. [D.R.]

1859. August 23. HENRY CONSTABLE, A.M., P. Desertmore. The yearly value is certified to be £275 14s. 8d. In another certificate of 12th Nov. 1859, the value is given as £323 14s. 3d. [D.R.]

1860. The church, which was built in 1817, in good order. No font. A glebe-house, and 54 acres of glebe, in the occupation of Incumbent. Divine service twice on all Sundays, &c. Sacrament monthly; average of communicants, 9. No school. Protestant population, 22. Rentcharge, £262 10s.; value of land, £51; rent of house in St. Finbarry's parish, belonging to the Prebendary of Desertmore, £2 15s. 4d. Total value of benefice, £316 5s. 4d. with residence.

Henry (son of Robert Constable, of Prior Park, Clonmel, county Tipperary), was born in county Tipperary, and when sixteen years old was entered a Pensioner of T.C.D. He graduated A.B. in 1838, and A.M. in 1842.

He was ordained Deacon by Bishop of Down at T.C.D. Chapel in 1839, and Priest in 1840 by Archbishop of Dublin at Christchurch Cathedral.

From 1839 to 1848 he was Curate of Kilgaruffe, in Ross;

and from 1848 to 1859 was Curate of Athnowen. In 1859 he became P. Desertmore.

He has published one of the essays in "Gold and the Gospel" (London, 1853); also "Parochial Sermons" (London, 1857); also "Essays, Critical and Theological" (London, 1859); and two pamphlets on National Education (Dublin, 1860).

Mr. Constable is married, and has issue.

DESERTSERGES.

1591. R. de Disertsergis Vicar. Chor. Improp. Vicar. ibm. D. LONG. [MS. T.C.D. E. 3. 14.] Long was Treasurer of Cork, q. v.

1615. ROBERT SUTTON, A.M., appears as Vicar of Desertserges, and V. Kilbrogan and Ballinadee. The Rectory of Desertserges belongs to Vics. Choral. Robert Sutton, Minister and Predicator, is Vicar. Val. 6 li. per annum. Church and chancel in repair, with books. [R.V. R.I.A.] For Sutton, *vide* Kilbrogan.

1632/3. March 2. JOHN SNARY is presented to V. Desertserges, and P. and V. Kilbrogan [Lib. Mun.] He was instituted 29th, and installed 31st March. [R.V. 1634.]

1634. R. de Desertserges spectat ad Vic. Chor. Cork. Vic. John Snary. Val. £26 6*s*. 8*d*. per annum. [R.V. 1634.]

1639. John Snary is still Vicar. [V.B. D.R.] *Vide* Kilbrogan.

1661. HUGH DUNSTERVILLE, V. Desertserges, and P. Kilbrogan.

In 1663 he became Archdeacon of Cloyne, q. v.

1666. May 5. BARNABAS HONEYCHURCH, V. Desertserges, per mortem Hugonis Dunsterville. Rectoria de Desertserges spectat ad Vic. Chor. Cork. [V.B. 1669, D.R.]

Honeychurch was also R. V. Murragh, q. v.

1682. August 22. DANIEL LORD, A.M., V. Desertserges, R. Murragh, Garrivoe, and Killowen, all vacant by death of Barnabas Honeychurch. [D.R.]

He appears 1682 to 1704, Nov. 3. [V.B. D.R.] In 1692 he became also P. Kilbrogan, q. v.

1704/5. January 12. JOHN HUNGERFORD, V. Desertserges. [F.F.]

He was also P. Island, Ross, q. v.

1723. Feb. 26. JEMMETT BROWNE, A.B., V. Desertserges, per mortem Hungerford. [D.R.] Browne, in 1733, became Dean of Ross, q. v.

1724. Feb. 13. HARTT SMITH, A.M., V. Desertserges. [D.R.] In 1733 he became Treasurer of Ross, q. v.

1750. August 4. The Bishop certifies that Hartt Smith, in 1747, built from the ground a fit parsonage house and out-offices on Desertserges Glebe, at an expenditure of £181 0*s*. 11*d*.

of which the First Fruits gave £100; and the value of Desertserges Vicarage is certified at £145. [D.R.]

1761. May 6. WILLIAM PRATT, A.B., V. Desertserges, per mortem Hartt Smith. [D.R.] Pratt, in 1769, became Dean of Cloyne, q. v.

1769. June 3. BELLINGHAM SWAN, A.M., V. Desertserges. [F.F.] He was also, from 1768 to 1798, a Vicar Choral of Cork.

B. Swan was son of Edward Swan, of Kilriske, county Dublin, by Jane, dau. of Sir Daniel Bellingham, Lord Mayor of Dublin. He was born in 1703, and matriculated in T.C.D. on 8th Sept. 1719.

He married, firstly, Martha Atkin, of St. Peter's, Dublin [M. L. 2 July, 1739], by whom he seems to have had no issue. He married, secondly, on 24th Feb. 1781, at St. Nicholas', Cork, Mary Berkeley, and by her left issue two daughters, Martha, and Jane, wife of Francis Harris, esq.; and two sons, Bellingham, in the Revenue, who married Mary Harley; and Daniel, who died Sp. [U.O.]

Rev. B. Swan died on 2nd October, 1798, and, according to the dates above given, was ninety-five years old at his death. The statement given in "Easton's Human Longevity," as to his having lived to the age of 102, is therefore incorrect.

1798. Dec. 12. MOUNTIFORD LONGFIELD, A.M., V. Desertserges. [F.F.]

1830. Protestant population, 432.

1837. Desertserges, a vicarage, with cure, 7 miles long by 4 broad, containing 1,400 acres. Gross population, 6,629. One Curate employed, at a stipend of £75 per annum. Composition for vicarial tithes, £730. 72 acres of glebe, valued at 20*s*. per acre, £72. Subject to visitation fees, 19*s*. Diocesan schoolmaster, 19*s*. 6*d*. Desertserges glebe-house is reported to be unfit for the residence of Incumbent, to be small, damp, and incapable of being improved; built about the year 1748, but at what cost unknown, further than that £92 6*s*. 1¾*d*. British, was granted as gift by the late Board of First Fruits for the purpose, and present Incumbent paid his predecessor £18 9*s*. 2¾*d*. on account of it, without having any charge on his successor. The glebe-house is occupied by a yearly tenant, who resides, and keeps the house aired. Incumbent is resident in the benefice. One church, capable of accommodating over 200 persons, built about the year 1805, at the cost of £553 16*s*. 11*d*. British, raised by parochial assessment and private subscriptions. No charge on the parish in 1832 on account of the church. Morning service is celebrated in the church once on Sundays, and on the principal festivals, and Sunday evening service is performed in a school-house in a remote part of the parish. The sacrament is administered eight times in the year. The rectorial, consisting of a moiety of the tithes of this parish, are impropriate, one-half thereof, compounded for £315, belong to the Vicars Choral of Cork, and the remaining half, compounded for £315, is claimed by Lord Kinsale, under different denominations, as Rector of Garrynoe. [Parl. Rep.]

1846. Sept. 17. A faculty is granted for new pews in the Church of Desertserges. [D.R.]

Mountiford Longfield (son of John Longfield, of Longueville, by Elisabeth Foster), was, from 1793 to 1809, P. Timoleague, Ross; and from 1809 to 1850 R. Templenoe and Kilcroghan, in Ardfert diocese. He held also Desertserges from 1798 to his death, on 13th September, 1850.

He married, firstly, Grace, dau. of William Lysaght, esq. and by her had issue Mountiford (now a Judge of the Landed Estates Court, and formerly a Fellow of T.C.D.); and Robert, Q.C., M.P. for Mallow.

He married, secondly, in 1814, Mary Anne Conner; and by her had issue, *inter alios*, George, F.T.C.D.; and Richard, R. Mogeely, Cloyne, q. v.

1850. Oct. 16. JAMES GOLLOCK, A.B., V. Desertserges; certified to be of the annual value of £615 11*s.* 6*d.* [D.R.]

1850. Dec. 2. The old glebe-house and offices are condemned as unfit for residence. On 29th Dec. 1852, the Vicar obtains a certificate of charge for £1,231 for a new glebe-house. The annual value is now stated at £617 10*s.* [D.R.]

1860. The church and glebe-house in good order. The glebe in Vicar's use, excepting 1½ acre in Mr. Longfield's lawn. Divine service once on all Sunday mornings in the church, and on Sunday evenings in a licensed place of worship at Maulnarougy, also on chief festivals, &c. Sacrament monthly, and on festivals; average of communicants, 55. The children are catechised on Mondays and Sundays. 88 children are on rolls of two Church Education schools. The average attendance is 45.

The Protestant population is 437. The rentcharge is £547 10*s.* and the land is worth £55. Total value of benefice, £602 10*s.* per annum, with residence.

James Gollock graduated as A.B., T.C.D. in 1822, and was afterwards A.M.

He was ordained Deacon in 1823, and received Priest's Orders at Cloyne on 1st August, 1824.

In 1825 he was Curate of Ballymodan, and in 1827 of Inniscarra. From 1837 to 1842 he was R. V. Carrigrohanebeg; from 1842 to 1850 R. V. Brinny; and in 1850 became V. Desertserges. He is married, and has issue.

I give an extract from the old registry of Christchurch, Cork, which gives a curious way of spelling Gollock:—

"1660. August 23. Sarah, the daughter of robert gollage, and margret, his wife [was baptised.]"

DOUGLAS.

Douglas is a chapelry in the parish of Carrigaline, and the instrument was dated 2 June, 1783, which assigns to the new district or chapel of Douglas, "by name of the parish or chapelry of Douglas," the following townlands, viz.:—Monriag, Monfieldstown, Roachestown, Knocknamullagh, Oldcourt, Barryarbin, Hilltown, Ballinrea, Balliegurrie, Cusduff, Burnhill, Danebrook, Grange, Montpelier, Scudoalleen, Castletreasure, Maryborogh, Menus, Ballincurrig, Ardclarig, Ardewacleahy, Glebe, Ballinemelagh, Ballinemalagh, Ballygarvers, and Ballyduhig. In this instrument is a clause, "saving to William Dickson and his successors all his and their rights as Rectors of Carrigaline."

1786. Sept. 17. The minister and churchwardens and parishioners of Carrigaline petition the Bishop to consecrate the new Chapel of Ease. And on the 25th October following, it is consecrated under the name of St. Luke, by the Bishop of Cloyne, who acts on behalf of the Bishop of Cork, who was absent in England, and sick.

1788. Sept. 5. Thomas Breviter, writing from Douglas, memorials to build on the glebe of Douglas, which has been hitherto without a house. On 6 July, 1789, he also memorials to build a barn and haggard on one of the glebes of Carrigaline. On 26 April, 1799, a commission finds that Breviter expended £73 13*s.* 9*d.* for enclosing the glebe of Douglas, and £104 8*s.* for erecting a barn and haggard on one of the glebes of Carrigaline. The Bishop, on 19 July, 1799, certifies for £178 1*s.* 9*d.*, being the amount of both these sums. [D.R.]

1791. Nov. 12. Arthur Keily, A.B., was licensed to be Curate of Douglas, at £50 per annum, on the nomination of Breviter. [D.R.]

A. Keily was ordained Deacon in May, 1779, at Cloyne, and Priest at Cork, on 26 Sept. 1790.

He married Dorothea, d. of Edward-Mansel Townsend, esq. by Helena Becher.

1797. Dec. 26. James Sandiford, A.B., is licensed to be Curate, at £50 per an. [D.R.] In 1802 he became P. Killenemer, Cloyne, q. v.

1799. July 13. John Bustead, A.B., is licensed to be Curate, at £50 per annum. [D.R.] In 1834 he became also P. Lisclery, q. v.

For the present state of Douglas, *vide* Carrigaline.

DRINAGH.

1591. DERMICIUS DONATI is Vicar of Drinagh. "R. de Drinaughe Vicar. Chor. Vicarius ibm Dermicius Donati." [MS. T.C.D. E. 3. 14.] He was also V. Kilnemartery, Cloyne.

1615. CON O FARSHAME, an Irishman, is Vicar. "Rectoria spectat ad Vic. Chorales. Vicarius Conno ffarshme hibernus, minister legens. Val. 7 li. per an. Ecclesia et cancella bene repãntur cum libris." [R.V. R.I.A.]

1619. April 10. THADEUS McDONELL O'DONOVAN, Vicar of Drinagh. "Epus univit Precentoriatui Rossen. vicarias de Kilmacabee et Drinagh, 10 April, 1619." [V.B. 1634.]

Vide Precentors of Ross, for O'Donovan.

1634. R. de Drinah spectat ad Vic. Choral, Cork. Vicar Tadeus O'Donovane. Val. X li. per an. [R.V. 1634.]

1635. July 16. JAMES CLELAND, V. Drinah, and V. Kilmaccabee, in Ross. [F.F.] *Vide* Kilmaccabee, for Cleland.

In 1639, James Cleland is marked "excusatur." [V.B. D.R.]

1666 to 1675. JOHN GODFREY appears as V. Drinagh. In the latter year he is marked "absent." [V.B.] He was also P. Currograngemore, Ross, q. v.

1669. Rectoria de Drinagh spectat ad Vic. Chor. Cork. [V.B. 1669.]

1676. Feb. 16. ZACHARIAS BEALY, V. Drinagh, R. Kilmeen, V. Castrumventry, and same day P. Currograngemore, Ross, q. v.

1688. Sept. 24. NICHOLAS BRADY, A.M., V. Drinagh, and R. Kilmeen, in Ross. [F.F.] He was also P. Kilnaglory, q. v. He appears 1688 to 1691, and in the latter year is marked "In Anglia." [V.B.]

1692. Sept. 23. SOLOMON FOLEY, V. Drinagh, R. Kilmeen, and P. Kilnaglory, vacant per cessionem Nicholai Brady. [D.R.] In 1704 Foley was P. Kilbrogan, q. v.

He appears 1692 to 1694, Nov. 3. [V.B.]

1694/5. Feb. 14. ANDREW SYMES, A.B., V. Drinagh, and R. Kilmeen, per cession of Foley. [D.R.] In 1718 Symes became Precentor of Ross, q. v.

He appears 1695 to 1717. [V.B.]

1699. No church; seven or eight Protestant families go to Drumdaleige and Kilmyne, in Ross. [V.B. 1699.]

"1700. Drinagh parish contains 32 plowlands or thereabouts. The church is ruinous. The western part of this parish repairs for divine service to Dromaleague, and the eastern part to Kilmine. 'Tis said there is a Popish schoolmaster in this parish. Ten acres of glebe adjoin to the west side of the church-yard. The Vicar of Drinagh has half of all the tythes; and the Vicars Choral of Cork have the other half. Drinagh lyes more convenient to be joined to Drumaleague or Fanlobbish than to Ballimoney. Drinagh is worth, to the Vicar, about £25 per an. Mr. Tonson and Mr. Scott live in this parish." [Downes' Tour.]

1718. NICHOLAS SKOLFIELD appears as V. Drinagh and Fanlobbish. [V.B.]

He appears 1718 to 1746. [V.B.] He was again collated on 2 January, 1737, on his becoming V. Kilcaskin, Ross, q. v.

1747. January 27. THOMAS BLENNERHASSETT, V. Drinagh and Fanlobbus, vacant by death of Skolfield. [D.R.]

Thomas, son of John Blennerhassett, was born in Kerry, and entered T.C.D. when eighteen years old, on 6 May, 1718. He obtained Scholarship in 1721.

In 1726 he was Curate of Shandon, and from 1739 to 1746 held "unam" R. de Aglish. From 1747 to 1767 he was V. Drinagh and Fanlobbus. In 1742 he was licensed Lecturer of St. Anne, Shandon.

He married Mary Frankland, of Christchurch, Cork, spinster. [Cork M.B. 8 March, 1735.] He mentions in his will (dated 18 Dec. 1760, and proved 18 September, 1767) his daughter, Anne, wife of Thomas Alleyne, and a grandson, Thomas Alleyne. [Cork Wills.]

1767. Sept. 8. RICHARD BEARE, A.M., V. Drinagh and Fanlobbus, per mort. Blennerhassett. [D.R.]

In 1768 Beare became P. Kilbrittain, q. v.

1768. Dec. 21. SIR MICHAEL COX, A.M., V. Drinagh and Fanlobbus, per cess. Beare. [D.R.] Sir Michael was son of Sir Richard Cox, M.P. for Clonakilty, *vide* Baronetage.

He was ordained Deacon at Ardbraccan, by Bp. of Meath on 21 Sept. 1760. He was P. Doon, Emly, and Archdeacon of Cashel, both which livings, with Drinagh and Fanlobbus, he held until his death in August, 1772. In his will (dated 7 Oct. 1769, and proved 2 Feb. 1773), he mentions his wife, Elisabeth Massey, and his son, Richard Eyre Cox, who succeeded to the baronetcy, and was drowned in 1784.

1772. Dec. 21. RICHARD BASSETT, A.B., V. Drinagh and Fanlobbus, per mort. Cox. [D.R.] He does not appear elsewhere in Cork Records. He died in April, 1794. [D.R.]

1794. August 19. Rev. Thomas Waller Evans, of Dunmanway, was appointed Sequestrator on the death of Bassett. [D.R.]

1794. Oct. 9. BRODERICK TUCKEY, A.B., V. Drinagh and Fanlobbus, per mort. Bassett. [D.R.]

Broderick Tuckey, A.B., was ordained Deacon on 3 Oct. 1773, and Priest on 22 January, 1775; both at Cork.

In 1775 he was licensed to the curacy of Killaspugmullane, and in 1777 was Reader at St. Finbarry's. He was Thresher's Lecturer from 1786 to 1795. In 1788 he was P. Killanully, which he resigned on becoming V. Drinagh and Fanlobbus in 1794.

He died in April, 1818. He mentions in his will (dated 22 October, 1806), his sons, Thomas and William and Henry, besides his daughters, Martha, Jane, and Mary. His wife, Martha, was executrix. He was buried at Christ Church, Cork, on 30 April, 1818.

1818. May 13. CHARLETON BROWNE, A.B., V. Drinagh, certified to be under £200, in annual value. [D.R.]

In 1826 he became V. Kilmaccabee and Kilfaughnabeg, Ross, q. v.

1826. July 13. EDMUND STEVELLY, A.B., V. Drinagh. [F.F.]

1830. Protestant population, 321.

1837. Drinagh, a vicarage, with cure, 7 miles long by 3½ broad, containing 12,910A. 2R. Gross population, 4,231. No Curate employed. Tithe composition, £220; 7A. 2R. of demised glebe, valued at 20*s.* per acre, £7 10*s.*; subject to visitation fees, 9*s.* 6*d.*; diocesan schoolmaster, 8*s.* No glebe house. Incumbent is resident, and pays the sum of £20 per annum as rent for a small cottage, exclusive of some land attached to it. One church, capable of accommodating 120 persons, built in 1819, by means of a gift of £830 15*s.* 4½*d.* Brit., granted by the late Board of First Fruits. No charge on the parish in 1832 on account of the church. Divine service is celebrated once on all Sundays, and on Christmas Day and Good Friday. The sacrament is administered monthly, and on the three great festivals. The rectorial, consisting of a moiety of the tithes, compounded for £220, are impropriate, and belong to the Vicars Choral of the Cathedral Church of St. Finbarr's, Cork. [Parl. Rep.]

Stevelly was ordained Deacon on 27 July, 1817, and Priest on 1 Feb. 1818; both at Cork. In 1817 he was Curate of Templemichael de Duagh, and in 1819 was Curate of St. Nicholas. He held Drinagh from 1826, until his death, on 4 June, 1841. He was buried at St. Peter's, Cork, on 8 June, 1841, aged sixty-eight. He married Isabella, dau. of Newbold Russell, esq. and had by her, two sons, George and Newbold.

1841. July 14. JOHN TRIPHOOK, A.B., V. Drinagh. [F.F.] In 1847 he became R. Scull, q. v.

1847. May 3. ROBERT WILLIAM MOLESWORTH, A.M., V. Drinagh. [F.F.] In 1855 he became V. Fanlobbus, q. v.

1855. July 23. WILLIAM MURPHY, A.B., V. Drinagh, certified to be of the annual value of £154 7*s.* 6*d.* [D.R.]

In 1861 he became V. Castroventia, Ross, q. v.

1860. The church in good order. No glebe-house; seven acres of glebe, set. Divine service twice on all Sundays, &c, In winter the evening service is held in the school-house; 75 children are on the rolls of two Church Education Schools. The Protestant population is 290.

1861. August 16. William Meyers Woolsey, A.M., V. Drinagh. [D.R.]

W. M. Woolsey was a Scholar T.C.D. in 1851, and graduated A.B. as Third Senior Moderator and Gold Medallist in Classics, in 1852; and took the degree of A.M. in 1856.

He was ordained Deacon on 11 March, and Priest on 21 Dec. 1855; both at Cork. In 1855 he was Curate of St. Mary, Shandon, and in 1858 was Curate of St. Anne, Shandon.

He married Miss Frances A. Berton, and has issue.

DROMDALEAGUE.

1591. Dromdaleague is vacant. [MS. T.C.D. E. 3. 14.]

1615. Robert Wilson, A.M., is Rector, and Thadeus M'Donnell is Curate. "Drumdalege: Rector non residens; Curatus residens. Rector, Robertus Wilson, A.M., Studens in Collegio Dub. Valor 5 li. per an. Tenet etiam P. Desertmore. Curatus Thadeus M'Donnell, minister legens. Ecclesia et cancella ruinosa. Admonit. ad repandum. [R.V. R.I.A.]

1619. Sept. 11. Edward Goodwin, P. Dromdaleague. [F.F.]

Adm. 23rd Oct. and installed 4th Nov. 1619. [MS. Consist. Dub.] He appears again in 1630.

1620. April 24. Thomas Way is presented to this Prebend. [Lib. Mun.]

Way was also V. Scull, q. v.

1630. Dec. 9. Edward Goodwin is presented by Crown to P. Seskinan, and V. Mothel, Lismore, cum clausula unionis ad P. Dromdaleague, Cork, pro hac vice, &c. [Lib. Mun.]

1634. P. de Drumdaleige, Edward Godwine. Val. 30 li. per an. [R.V. 1634.]

1639. "Edward Godwin excusatus. Curatus Hugo Snary non admissus." [V.B.]

E. Godwin was ordained Priest by "Bernard Limeric. et fenebor," on 10th March, 1610.

In 1615 he appears as V. Aghadowne, Ross. He appears for this Prebend in 1619.

1662. July 28. Henry Rugg, P. Dromdaleague. [F.F.]

He was also Dean of Cloyne, q. v.

1666 to 1671. John Rugg appears as P. Dromdaleague. He has a dispensation in 1666 "studendi gratia." [V.B.]

He was also P. Kilmacdonagh, Cloyne, q. v.

1669. July 15. John Godferry is admitted "V. de Drumalag, per resignaconem Henrici Rugg." [V.B. 1669.]

Godfrey was P. Currograngemore, Ross, q. v.

1672. Aug. 26. Nicholas Winterborne, P. Dromdaleague. [F.F.] He was also Treasurer of Ross, q. v.

1677/8. April 20. SAMUEL SYNGE, A.M. and LL.D., P. Dromdaleague. [F.F.] He is also R. Inchigeelah and Kilmichael.

Samuel Synge, born at Innishannon (son of Edward, Bishop of Cork, by Barbara, dau. and co-heir of William Leatham, of Newplace, county Donegal, esq.), became a Fellow Commoner of T.C.D. when fifteen years old, on 26th January, 1671/2.

From 1674 to 1676 he was P. Lisclery, and P. Inniscarra, Cloyne. From 1677 to 1679 P. Dromdaleague, &c. He held, from 1678 to 1708, the Precentorship of St. Patrick, Dublin; and from 1679 to 1708 the Deanery of Kildare; and from 1696 to 1708 the P. Geashil, Kildare.

He married Margaret, dau. of Michael Boyle, Archbishop of Armagh, and left issue a son, Michael, Lieut.-Col. in the Army; and a daughter, Mary, who married the Rev. Horatio Townsend. [U.O.]

He published "A Sermon on Proverbs, xxiv. 21, preached on 30th January," 4to. Dublin: 1707.

He died on 30th November, and was buried in St. Patrick's on 2nd Dec. 1708.

1679. June 10. CORNELIUS HIGNETT, A.M., P. Dromdaleague and V. Inchigeelagh and Kilmichael. [F.F.] He became, in 1706, Chancellor of Ross, q. v.

"1681. Ten shillings per ploughland to be raised out of the parish of Drummaleigue for the rebuilding the church of the said parish." [County Cork Grand Jury Presentments.]

"1699. Drummalegue lyes about six miles to the south-west of Dunmanway. It belongs to Mr. Hignett. Very coarse country. Mr. Patrickson preaches there once a month, and Mr. Hungerford once a month.

"All the country, from Dunmanway to Bantry, is very coarse mountain, especially on the right hand.

"Caharagh lyes to the south of Drummalegue, and belongs to Mr. Patrickson. No church or divine service but at Drummalegue. We pass through part of Caharagh as we go from Drummalegue."

"Mr. Trix preaches at Skibbareen twice in a month, and at Baltimore and Shirkin.

"1699. Robert Howard, Verger of Ross, says that Caharagh parish is worth about £66 or £70 per annum. It is an intire rectory. That Drummaleague parish is worth £60 per annum. It is an intire prebend."

"Wednesday, May 29th, 1700. I went from Ballimony to Drommaleague. Mr. Patrickson preacht; there were no persons to be confirmed. Drommaleague Church, six miles distant from Dunmanway to the S.W. is in repair; only some of the slates are off. Divine service once a month by Mr. Hungerford for Mr. Hignett, and once a month by Mr. Patrickson for the parish of Caharagh. About 22 or 23 plowlands in this parish.

All this parish, with that part of the rectory in Fanlobish which belongs to the Prebend of Drommaleague, is worth to the Prebendary about £50 per annum. Colonel Sandford, Colonel Freake, Mr. Butler, Mr. Jo. Jarvys, are proprietors of land in this parish. A Bible and one Common Prayer-book. No registry. Mr. Hungerford promised to speak to Mr. Hignett to get one. Felix M'Carthy is Priest of this parish. He was here before the late troubles. Mr. Anthony Butler, and Captain Carthy, a Protestant, live in this parish. It would be very convenient that a minister should reside somewhere in Drommaleage parish, to serve that cure and the cure of Caharagh: divine service to be only at Drommaleage. No glebe in this parish; no houses near the church. In West Carbery the clergy pay the tenth part of the land tax; in East Carbery they pay the sixteenth; and in Barriroe, the fifteenth; and the fifteenth in Ibaun."

"A Protestant schoolmaster complains that Papists teach publick school in this parish. The holy sacrament administered four times in the year. No vessel for the communion. Caharagh Church, about two miles distant from Drommaleage Church to the S.W. lies close to the Island river, on the west side of the river; 35½ plowlands in this parish, of which 29 lie on the west side of the river, and 6½ lie on the east of the said river. There are but 12 Protestant families in this parish. 'Tis thought that there are 40 Papists for 1 Protestant in this parish. No glebe. Will. Guricheen, a very old man, is Priest of this parish. This parish lies convenient to be joined with either Skibbareen, or, perhaps, rather with Drommaleage. Colonel Beecher, Colonel Sandford, Edward Galway, who forfeited in the last rebellion, and the Bishop of Ossory, have the lands of this parish, and Sr. Emmanuel Moore and Colonel Owen, als Beecher. The church is ruinous; the north side is down. Caharagh parish is worth to the Incumbent about £70 or £80 per annum. Mr. Atkins, Mr. George Wood, and Will White, live in this parish. I gave to Mr. Patrickson about 12 Common Prayer and 30 small Prayer-books to be disposed of in Caharagh parish, &c., and Drommaleague, &c." [Downes' Tour.]

1727. January 17. MICHAEL PHILPOTT, A.M., P. Dromdaleague, per mort. Hignett; and same day to Caharagh, per cess. of himself. [D.R.]

He appears 1727 to 1746, May 7. [D.R. V.B.]

Michael Philpott (grandson of Nicholas, who married Anne, sister of Sir Richard Aldworth), was son of Gregory Philpott, by Bridget, dau. of John Evatt, Dean of Elphin.

He was born in county Cork, and when sixteen years old became a Sizar, T.C.D. on 10th May, 1695; and a Scholar in 1699.

From 1715 to 1718 he appears as Vicar of Kilmoe and Scull; and from 1720 to 1746 was R. Caheragh. He held also, from 1727, the P. Dromdaleague; and from 1736 the P. Donoghmore, Ross, until his death in 1746.

He married, firstly, Mary Murray, of Scull, widow [Cork M. B. of 14th Nov. 1700]; and secondly, Katherine Beamish, of Desertserges. [Cork M. B. of 14th May, 1726.] He had a son, Michael, A.M., T.C.D. Curate of Dromdaleague in 1752, who died without issue, and whose relict, Mary Philpott, bequeathed her property to the children of Mr. Andrew Symes, who died in 1775.

1746. July 19. St. John Browne, P. Dromdaleague and R. Caheragh; and same day P. Donoghmore, in Ross, all vacant by death of Michael Philpott. [D.R.] He became, in October, P. Kilbrogan, q. v.

1746. Oct. 9. Samuel Woodroffe, A.M., P. Dromdaleague, and R. Caheragh, and P. Donoghmore, Ross. [F.F.]

In 1762 he became Precentor of Cork, q. v.

1762. Richard Farmer, A.M., P. Dromdaleague and R. Caharagh. [F.F.]

Richard (son of Robert Farmer, esq. by Grace Hovell), was born in Cork, and when sixteen years old entered T.C.D. on 3rd March, 1735. He was afterwards A.M.

He was ordained Priest at Cork on 1st Feb. 1746, and in 1747 was licensed to Kilnaglory curacy. From 1758 to 1762 he was V. Kinsale.

He seems to have been married thrice—first, to Frances Henderson, spinster, of St. Mary's, Cork [M. B. 12th Dec. 1748]; secondly, to Elisabeth, dau. of Robert Freeman, esq. of Ballinguile [Cloyne M. B. 1757]; and thirdly, to Elisabeth Stirling [M.S. 15th July, 1771]. In his will (dated 3rd Oct. 1777, and proved 1st March, 1781), he mentions his wife, Elisabeth Farmer, otherwise Stirling, and three children by a former wife, named Robert, Mildred, and Mary Anne. He also mentions his brother, Captain Edward Farmer, and a kinsman, Jasper Farmer, lately married to his niece, Grace Farmer.

1781. April 25. Joseph Weld, A.M., P. Dromdaleague and R. Caheragh. [F.F.] He was Archdeacon of Ross, q. v.

1781. Nov. 30. Michael Tisdall, A.M., P. Dromdaleague, R. Caheragh, and Archdeacon of Ross, q. v.

1788. Dec. 2. Richard Webb, A.B., P. Dromdaleague, and R. Caheragh. [F.F.]

1807. Webb resides in Kinsale, within a mile of Ringrone, which he holds by faculty. [Rep.]

He resigned on 10th May, 1818, retaining Ringrone, q. v.

1818. May 15. Thomas Tuckey, A.B., P. Dromdaleague; certified under £300 per annum in value. [D.R.]

1830. Protestant population, 567.

1837. Dromdaleague, a rectory, with cure, 6¼ miles long by 4½ broad, containing 17,570 acres. Gross population, 4,870.

One Curate employed, at a stipend of £75 per annum. Tithe composition, £450. Subject to visitation fees, 11*s.* Diocesan schoolmaster, 19*s.* No glebe-house. Incumbent is resident, and pays £40 per annum for house-rent. One church, capable of accommodating 180 persons, built about 50 years, by parochial assessment, but at what cost not stated, further than that the sum of £169 12*s.* 3¾*d.* British, was levied for that purpose, from 1782 to 1790. No charge on the parish in 1832 on account of the church. Divine service is celebrated twice on all Sundays, and on the principal festivals. The sacrament is administered monthy, and at Easter, Christmas, and Whitsuntide. The benefice is a rectory. The Incumbent has, as Prebendary, a revenue (exclusive of the benefice) of £85 7*s.* 8*d.* composition for rectorial tithes of Fanlobbus; and also £2 15*s.* 5*d.* being the rent of a house in city of Cork. [Parl. Rep.]

Thomas Tuckey (son of Rev. Charles Tuckey, Treasurer of Lismore), was a Scholar of T.C.D. in 1798.

He was ordained Deacon on 1st January, 1802, at Cork, and Priest at Cloyne on 6th July, 1806.

He was a Vicar Choral of Lismore from 1812 to 1828, and was P. Dromdaleague from 1818 to his death, on 5th July, 1852.

He left issue, *inter alios*, Rev. Broderick, V. Kilbonane, q. v.; Abraham John, M.D.; and John, youngest son, who married, in 1862, Mary-Elisabeth, youngest daughter of Rev. William R. Townsend, R. Aghada.

1852. August 17. WILLIAM MOORE CROSTHWAITE, A.M., P. Drumdaleague. Net value, £362 11*s.* 9*d.* per annum. [D.R.]

W. M. Crosthwaite (brother of Rev. John Clerke Crosthwaite, Rector of St. Mary at Hill, and St. Andrew's, Hubbard, London, and author of numerous valuable publications, for which *vide* Cotton), was a younger son of Charles Crosthwaite, of Dublin, by Elisabeth, dau. of Benjamin Clarke, esq. also of Dublin.

He was ordained Deacon on 18th Dec. 1831, and Priest on 29th July, 1832, both at Cork. In 1834 he was licensed to the curacy of Innishannon, and from 1838 to 1842 was V. Kilcoe and Cleere. From 1842 to 1852 he was V. Durrus, Kilcroghan, and from 1852 to his death, on 30th December, 1854, was P. Dromdaleague.

1855. Feb. 13. MOUNTIFORD LONGFIELD CONNOR, A.B., P. Dromdaleague. Net value, £363 14*s.* 6*d.* [D.R.]

1856. January 23. Mary Collins and Jane Deasy, widows, and George Robinson (their tenant, at lives renewable for ever), grant half an acre, statute measure, of the lands of Butlersgift, as a site for the new church of Dromdaleague.

1858. Sept. 10. A new church, built by the Ecclesiastical Commissioners, is consecrated under the name of St. Matthew.

1860. The church new. No glebe or glebe-house. Divine

service twice on all Sundays, and once on festivals, &c. Sacrament monthly; average of communicants, 26; and at festivals, average 62. 72 children are on the rolls of a Church Education school. The Protestant population is 414. The rentcharge is £337 10*s.* for Dromdaleague parish, and £64 0*s.* 9*d.* for the rectorial tithes of Fanlobbus in right of the Prebend. There is also a house in Cork, belonging to the P. Dromdaleague, set for £2 15*s.* 5*d.* Total value of the benefice, £404 5*s.* 5*d.*, without residence.

Rev. Mountiford Longfield Connor was, in 1848, Curate of Fanlobbus.

He married a daughter of Rev. Godfrey Smith, of Kinneigh, and has issue.

DUNDERROW.

1291. Ecclesia de Dundirrow is rated at four marks. [Tax. P. Nic.]

1591. Edmond Corbally is Rector ecclesiæ de Dundorvie. [MS. T.C.D. E. 3. 14.]

1615. Hugh Percevall is Rector. "R. de Dundirrowe (nonresidens) Hugo Percevall: ipse inservit curæ. Val. 5 li. per annum. Ecclesia et cancella repantur, cum libris et omnibus necessariis." [R.V. R.I.A.] He was also Dean of Ross, q. v.

1630. Oct. 9. Marcus Pagett, Rector de Dunderrow als Dundervie. [F.F.] per mortem Percivall. [R.V. 1634.] Pagett was Dean of Ross, q. v. E. de Dunderrow. Marcus Pagett, Rector. Alderman Richard Roche, of Cork, patronus. Val. 40 li. per an. [R.V. 1634.] "Ecclia bene, desunt baptisterium et calix." [V.B. 1639.]

1662. Feb. 6. Hugo Dunsterville, R. Dundurrow. [F.F.]

Dunsterville, in 1663, was Archdeacon of Cloyne, q. v.

1666. May 5. William Portman, D.D., R. Dundurrow, per mortem Hugonis Dunsterville, and per presentationem Richardi Roch, Patroni. [V.B. D.R. 1669.]

He appears 1666 to 1675. [V.B. D.R.]

Portman, from 1661 to 1670, was P. Killaraght, Achonry. He was also, from 1661 to 1665 Archdeacon of Elphin. He became R. V. Ringrone in 1665, and R. Dunderrow in 1666, and held both these livings until his death in 1675. He mentions his wife, Grace Portman, as universal legatee, in his will, and wishes to be buried in the church of Ringrone. His will was dated 12th of November, 1675, and was proved in Cork the 4th of January following.

1676. April 3. Thomas Meade, R. Dundurrow. [F.F.] His letters patent to Dundurrogh, dioc. Cork, bear date 1675, Dec. 14. [Lib. Mun.] He appears 1677 to 1709, Nov. 3. [V.B. D.R.]

In 1693 he became also P. Inskenny, q. v.

1709. June 9. WILLIAM MEADE is presented to R. Dundurrow and Ballymartle. [Lib. Mun.] He appears at visitation of May 6, 1752. [V.B.]

In 1736 William Meade became also Dean of Cork, q. v.

1752. May 20. ROBERT MEADE, A.M., R. Dunderrow, (vacant by resignation of William Meade, Dean of Cork) on letters patent of 14th May, 1752. [D.R.]

In 1754 (Feb. 12) a writ of removal is issued from King's Bench against Robert Meade (Francis Kearny, of Garretstown, having established his right to the presentation); whereupon Robert Meade resigns, but is re-appointed on the presentation of Kearny, on April 20, 1754. [D.R.]

Robert Meade was also P. St. Michael's, q. v.

1779. June 7. JOHN KENNY, A.M., R. Dundurrow. [F.F.] By death of Robert Meade. [D.R.]

He was also, from 1796, P. Kilbrogan, q. v.

1815. Feb. 2. MORGAN O'DONOVAN, A.M., R. Dundurrow. [F.F.] By death of John Kenny, LL.D. [D.R.] On letters patent of 14th January, the appointment being in his Majesty's disposal, by the incapacity of Thomas Rochfort, now a Papist. [Lib. Mun.]

1818. The Bishop approves of a memorial to build a glebe-house; and on 4th Feb., 1821, certifies that Donovan had expended £845 6*s.* 10*d.* in the erection of house, &c., the value of benefice being £400 per an. [D.R.]

1830. Protestant population, 112.

1837. Dunderrow: a rectory, with cure; five miles long by two broad, containing 6,371A.; gross population, 2,498; one Curate employed, at an annual stipend of £69 4*s.* 7½*d.* Brit.; tithe composition. £474 0*s.* 8½*d.*; sixteen acres of glebe, valued at 25*s.* per acre, £20, subject to visitation fees, 9*s.* Diocesan Schoolmaster, 7*s.* Dunderrow glebe-house built in 1821, under the new Acts, at the cost of £738 9*s.* 2¾*d.* Brit., granted by the late Board of First Fruits, viz., £230 15*s.* 4½*d.*, in way of gift, and £507 13*s.* 10¼*d.* in that of loan, of which loan there remained £306 5*s.* 2*d.* chargeable on the benefice in 1832, repayable by annual instalments of £19 2*s.* 2*d.* Incumbent is resident in the glebe-house. Exclusive of the moneys aforesaid, Incumbent reports that he has expended £369 4*s.* 7½*d.* Brit., on the house, without having any charge on successor for the repayment of any portion thereof. One church, capable of accommodating 150 persons; built in 1812, at an expense of £461 10*s.* 9¼*d.* Brit., granted in way of loan by the late Board of First Fruits, of which loan there remained £79 0*s.* 3¾*d.* chargeable on the parish in 1832, repayable by annual instalments of £6 5*s.* 6½*d.* Divine service is celebrated once on all Sundays and on the great festivals. The Sacrament is administered monthly, and on the three principal festivals. A portion of the tithes of the parish, compounded for £50 19*s.* 3¾*d.*, is appropriate, and belongs to the Dean and Chapter of the Cathedral Church of St. Finbarr's, Cork. [Parl. Rep.]

Morgan Donovan, or O'Donovan (CHIEFTAIN of the sept of O'Donovan, of Clancahill, *vide* Burke's L. G.) was born in 1769.

He was ordained Deacon at Cork, and Priest at same place, on 23rd September, 1792.

He appears as Curate of Carrigaline in 1795, of St. Peter's in 1797; and in 1815 he became R. Dunderrow, which he held until his death, on 18th October, 1839. He married, in 1795, Alicia, dau. of William Jones, esq., of Cork, and by her had issue, Morgan William, now CHIEFTAIN, and several other children, for whom *vide* Burke's L. G.

1839. Dec. 11. JOHN BEAVOR WEBB, A.B., R. Dunderrow. [F.F.] John Cuthbert Kearney, esq., Patron. The presentation is dated 10th December, 1839. [D.R.]

On 1st Sept., 1841, Webb memorials for liberty to improve; and on 1st August, 1843, obtains the Bishop's certificate for an outlay of £600. [D.R.]

John Beavor Webb (son of Rev. Richard Webb, R. Ringrone) was born in 1803.

He was ordained Deacon on 23rd December, 1827, and Priest on 19th December, 1830, both at Cloyne.

In 1829 he was licensed to the curacy of Ringrone. In 1838 he became R. Templetrine, which he resigned in 1839, when he became R. Dunderrow, which he held until his death, on 5th October, 1852.

He married, on 5th September, 1843, Maria, dau. of Robert Maxwell, esq., of Charleville. [Burke's L. G., WEBB of CAHERAGH.]

1853. Feb. 17. RICHARD FRANCIS WEBB, A.B., R. Dunderrow, on presentation (dated 3rd Feb., 1853) of the Trustees of the late John Cuthbert Kearney, esq.; certified net value, £334 2*s.* 6*d.* [D.R.] Gross value, £375.

1860. The church in good repair; the glebe-house is in good repair; twenty-four acres of glebe are in Incumbent's use; divine service is celebrated once each Sunday and festival at church, and in a school-house on Sunday evenings during summer; the communion is administered monthly; average of communicants is eight; the children are catechised on Sundays by the Minister in New Testament and Church Catechism; a school-house is about to be opened, if funds can be procured; number of children is about 20; the Protestant population is 89; the rentcharge is £355 10*s.* 6½*d.*; the land is worth £20; total value, £375 10*s.* 6½*d.*, with residence.

Richard Francis Webb (eldest son of Rev. Richard Webb, R. Ringrone) was born in 1794.

He was ordained Deacon on 20th April, 1817, and Priest on 3rd May, 1818, both at Cork.

In 1817 he was Curate of Ringrone, and in 1818 became R. Caheragh, which he resigned in 1853, on becoming R. Dunderrow.

He married on 17th September, 1818, Mary, youngest daughter of Rev. Samuel Beamish, and has issue, for whom *vide* Burke's L. G., WEBB of CAHERAGH.

DUNDRINAN.

1591. E. de Drumdrinay als Downedrenan et E. de denarchan als E. de marchan spectant ad Ab. de Antro. nullus curatus. [MS. T.C.D. E. 3. 14.]

1615. Dundrinan Cur. residens. Rector abbas de Antro. Richūs Boyle, miles, firmarius. Curatus WILLIAM HEALY; vicaria vacat et usurpatur per firmarium Rectoriæ. [R.V. R.I.A.]

1634. E. de Dundrinan spectat ad Abb. de Morne. Cormack M'Donogh Carty est firmarius. Valet 8 li. per an. [R.V. 1634.]

1639. E. de Dundrinane als Kilnamartry MORGAN MUNDYN in Cloine dioc. [Cork V.B. 1639.]

Dundrinan disappears from the Cork Visitation Books after this date.

DURRUS.

1591. Rectoria de Durris spectat ad Ab. Scæ Catherine Waterford. Vicarius ibm. CORNELIUS O'SULLIVAN qui propter acceptacionem vicariæ de Kilmo et Skoll deprivatus est. [MS. T.C.D. E. 3. 14.]

"Rectoria de Kilcrohan spectat ad Ab. Scæ Catherine Waterford. Vicaria ibm. vacat et sequestratr." [Ib.]

1615. June 22. THADEUS M'DONNELL O'SULLIVAN is admitted V. Durris, Kilcroghane, Kilcaskin, and Killaconenagh, and R. Kilmanowe and Kilkatherine. [F.F.]

1615. Rectoria de Durrus spectat ad St. Katherine de Waterford. Vicarius est Tadeus M'Donnell O'Sullivan. Val. 6 li. per an. Ecclesia et cancella repāntur. [R.V. R.I.A.]

1615. Rectoria de Kilcroghane spectat ad Ecclesiam Stæ Katherine de Waterford. Vicarius Tadeus M'Donnell O'Sullivane, Minister legens et inserviens Curæ. Valor 3 li. per an. [R.V. R.I.A.] O'Sullivan was also V. Caheragh.

1625/6. Feb. 13. THOMAS BARHAM, V. Durrus and Kilcroghan,

vacant per deprivation of Tade O'Sullevant. Inducted 22nd Feb. [R.V. 1634.] On letters patent of June 9, 1625, vacant by lapse. [Lib. Mun.] On July 10, 1630, Barham was appointed P. Donoughmore, Cloyne, and R. V. Rincurran, Cork, with clause of union to Durrus, Kilcrohan. [Lib. Mun.]

1634. R. de Durrus spectat ad Monasterium Stæ Katherinæ Waterford. Val. 20 li. per. an. Dominus Baro de Esmond est firmarius. ("N.B. This is not in my Lord Esmond's—so if it be not it—speak with John Sharpe.") Vicarius ibm. Thomas Barham. Val. 20 li. per an. [R.V. 1634.]

1634. R. de Kilcroghane spectat ad Monasterium Stæ Katherinæ Waterfordensis, Baro de Esmond est firmarius. Val. 17 li. per an. Vicarius Thomas Barham. Val. 17 li. per an. [R.V. 1634.]

1639. Thomas Barham appears as R. V. Durrus. "Ecclesia bene, desunt ornamenta." [V.B. 1639.] But he is not Vicar of *Kilcroghane* in 1639.

Thomas Barham, A.M., was ordained Deacon by Richard, Bishop of Cork (probably in 1625); and Priest by Malcom, Archbishop Cashel, on 21st December, 1626.

In 1625 he became V. Durrus, Kilcroghane, and Kilmocamoge, which he held until his death, in or before 1663. In 1630, July 10, he was admitted to be one of the Chaplains of Richard, EARL OF CORK, and was also made P. Donoghmore and Kiltegan, Lismore, and also P. Donoghmore, Cloyne, and R. V. Rincurran.

1639. March 29. SOLOMON CLARKE, Vicar de Kilcroghane, taxat. 50s. [F.F.] He appears also in V.B. 1639, with Barham's name crossed out, and the remark, "Ecclesia ruinata, desunt omnia." [V.B. 1639.]

1663. Sept. 22. THOMAS HOLMES, V. Durrus, Kilcroghane, and Kilmocamoge, per mortem Thomas Barham. [V.B. D.R. 1669.]

1704. "Durrus Church stands about a mile distant from the head of Dunmanus bay, N.E. of the bay. The church is uncovered, the walls are standing, built with good, large, square stones, and clay. The land betwixt the head of Dunmanus bay and the church is indifferent good. The church-yard is about an acre of land. There seem to be ruins of a house at the N. end of the church.

The little hill on which the church stands is glebe; 'tis good land. St. Faughnan is the Patron Saint of this parish. In the parish of Durrus, not far from Bantry, by the sea-side, are the ruins of an abbey, which belonged to the Franciscans. I don't hear that there were any other religious houses besides this in ye barony of Beere and Bantry."

"In the parish of Durrus, viz. about 4 mile water, and at about Blackrock, near Bantry, live above 30 Protestant families. Lord Anglesey, Mr. Bernard, Colonel Freake, and the

Earl of Corke have [land in this parish?] Mr. Evanson, Mr. Hutchins. . . . . Hr. Holmes preaches once a month at Mr. Evans's house, in this parish. The Earl of Corke has half the tythes of 12 plowlands in this parish, in the barony of West Carbery. The Vicar has half the tythes of the said plowlands, and all the tythes of the rest of the parish, worth to the Vicar about £26 per an. In this parish are 28 plowlands. Humphrey Sullevane is Popish Priest of this parish and of Kilcroghan; he has been here about 12 years. In that part of Bantry which is in this parish there are 2 English schools kept by women.

"Kilcroghan parish. Major Eyres, of Waterford, Mr. Hull, of Lincon, have the lands of this parish of Kilcroghan. All the inhabitants of this parish are Papists. Earl of Corke has half the tythes of the 3 plowlands of Kilcroghan. Mr. Gideon Delane has half the tythes of all the rest of the parish; he has the same title that he has to the tythes of Kilmacommoge. Mr. Holmes has half of the tythes of the whole parish; the Vicar's tythes of Kilcroghan, with the glebe and book-mony, are worth £16 per an. About 30 plowlands in this parish; all these lands are very coarse, except the Bishop of Corke's lands of Kilcroghan. The ruins of the church are surrounded by the lands of Kilcroghan; the walls are standing. 'Tis about 8 miles in length from the point of Sheepshead to Durrus parish; 'tis about 3 or 4 in breadth. About 12 acres of glebe are round the church." [Downes' Tour.]

Holmes, in 1672, became also V. Killaconenagh and Kilcaskin, in Ross. He disappears from the visitation books in 1714.

1714 to 1734. Richard Davies appears as V. Kilcroghane, Durrus, and Kilmacomoge, and V. Kilcaskin, in Ross. [V.B.]

1729. Dec. 7. John Galway (son of Henry Gallwey, of the the town of Bantry) renounces Popery in the parish church of Kilmocamoge, before Richard Davies, Vicar. [D.R.]

Richard Davies (eldest son of Dean Rowland Davies) was born at Blarney Castle, 24th Nov., 1682, and when fifteen years' old, entered T.C.D. as Pensioner, on 24th April, 1696/7. He was afterwards A.M.

He was P. Ballyhay, Cloyne, from 1709 to 1719; and from 1715 to 1736 held the vicarages of Kilcaskin, in Ross, and of Durrus, Kilcroghane, in Cork diocese.

He married Mary (dau. of Colonel Digby Foulke, by Angel, dau. of Sir Boyle Maynard, Baronet, of Curryglas, co. Waterford), and by her had issue, Rowland (son and heir) of Dawstown, and two daughters, Lettice, wife of Henry White, esq., and Martha, wife of Richard White, esq., the grandfather of the first Earl of Bantry.

Rev. Richard Davies died on 29th April, 1736.

1736. June 28. George Lloyd, S.T.B., V. Kilcroghane, V. Durrus, and V. Kilmacomoge, and same day to V. Kilcaskane, in Ross. [D.R.]

This was, probably, George, son of William Lloyd (Bishop of Killala) who was born at Killala, and entered T.C.D. as Pensioner, on 9th July, 1716, aged fifteen.

He was P. Errew, Killala, from 1731 to 1735, and from 1736 to 1737, held Durrus, &c. He died in 1737.

1737. April 7. JOHN KENNEY, A.M., V. Kilcrohane, Durrus, and Kilmocamoge, per mort. George Lloyd. [D.R.]

In 1745 he took a second collation on 4th Oct. [D.R.]

In 1751 he became P. Kilbrittain, q. v.

1751. April 1. THOMAS MILLERD, A.M., V. Kilcroghan, Durrus, and Kilmocamoge, vacant by resignation of John Kenney. [D.R.]

1753. The flagon, now in use (1861) in Bantry church, bears this legend, "Deo sacrum. The gift of Richard White, esq., to the parish church in Bantry, An. 1753." The chalice and paten have each the following inscription, "Deo sacrum. The gift of the Rev. Thos. Millerd, Vicar of Kilmocamoge, Durrus, and Kilcrohane, to the parish church in Bantry, An. 1754."

Thomas Millerd (son of Hugh Millerd, Mayor of Cork) was, from 1750 to 1751, Vic. Chor. of Cork, and from 1751 to his death, in July 1756, V. Kilcroghan, &c., &c., He was buried at St. Mary, Shandon, on 21st July. He left a son, James, born in 1754, who married Rose Tonson, widow of LORD RIVERSDALE.

1756. July 22. JOHN BARRY, A.M., V. Kilcroghan, Durrus, and Kilmocamoge, vacant by death of Millerd. [D.R.] In 1768 Barry became P. Desertmore, q. v.

1769. March 14. JOHN KENNEY, A.M., V. Kilcroghan, Durrus, and Kilmacomoge, vacant by resignation of John Barry. [D.R.]

John Kenney was afterwards P. Kilbregan, q. v.

1792. 27th November. Order of Lord Lieutenant in Council, on petition of Rev. John Kenney, Vicar of Durrus, Kilcrohan, and Kilmacomoge, stating, that in these three vicarages, contiguous and episcopally united, and in length about 24 miles, there is but one church, at Bantry; in consequence of which the inhabitants of Kilcrohan, and of these denominations of plowlands, (viz., Ardoguina, Ballina, Brahalish, Ballycomane, Carrahavadera, Coolnaharna, Clasadoe, Capanabona, Mr. Hyde's Clonee, Coomkee, Croties, Courcolagth, Dromreagh, Dromderaum, Dromatinnehan, Dromreag, Esknabreeny, Upper and Lower Gurteen, Gerameen, Keiloveemoge, Kealtas, Lisaremig, Murrick, Rooscagh, Rossmore, Ruskinanised, Tedock, and Ueterglina) can't, without *great* inconvenience, resort to it, being from 3 to 8 miles away, but will be within 3 miles at farthest from the new church intended to be built at Carrigbuge, in Durrus parish; therefore the above townlands will be separated from Kilcrohane, and united to Durrus; and per contra, the following townlands of Durrus will be united to Kilmacomoge, viz., Letterlicky, Agagoheen, Arda, Ardevolehane, Beach, Blackrock, Bargurum, Capanalogher Clonee, Dromclogh, Donbittern, Derrigrinagh, Dromacousane, Dromleigh, Gurticlona, Glanlough, Knockikillen, Maulavard, Paurcana, and the Scarts. As the vicarages are now worth—Kilmocamore, £200; Durrus, £220, and Kilcroghan, £80, £500 in all—so, when the separation aforesaid takes place, Kilcrohane will be worth £250, and Kilmocamoge also £250, saving to present Vicar his rights, &c., for his incumbency.

1793. April 16. Edward Herbert Kenney, A.B., V. Durrus and Kilcrohan, per cession, on 15th April, of John Kenney. [D.R.] E. H. Kenney was son of his predecessor. In 1799 he became R. Kilmeen, Ross, q. v.

1799. July 19. Henry Jones, A.B., V. Durrus and Kilcrohan, per cess. of E. H. Kenney, [D.R.]

In 1805 he became V. Lislee and R. V. Kilsillagh, q. v.

1805. Oct. 7. Mason Alcock, A.M., V. Durrus and Kilcrohan, per cession of Henry Jones, [D.R.]

1807. Alcock is non-resident, being infirm. [Rep.]

Mason Alcock, from 1778 to 1805, was V. Lislee and R. V. Kilsillagh, and from 1805 to his death in 1829, was V. Durrus.

It appears by his will (dated 6th May, 1816, and proved 1st Dec. 1829) in which he is stiled Rev. Mason Alcock, of Bandon, that he left issue by his wife, Judith, three sons, Alexander-Man Alcock, m. Martha Jane Morris; Edward Jones, Rector of Kilmeen, Ross, q. v.; and Henry; besides a daughter, Anne.

1829. Oct. 10. Edward Jones Alcock, A.B., V. Durrus and Kilcrohan; certified yearly value under £600. [D.R.] In 1842 Alcock became R. Kilmeen, Ross, q. v.

1830. Protestant population of Durrus-Kilcroghan, 819.

1832. Dec. 10. The Bishop certifies that Alcock expended, since 1st April, 1830, £980 in building a glebe-house, and that £490 is the annual value of the benefice. [D.R.]

1837. Durrus-Kilcrohane, a vicarage, with cure, 19 miles long by 5 broad, containing 23,083A. Gross population, 8,340. No Curate employed. Tithe composition, £490; 51A. of glebe, valued at 20*s.* per acre, £51; subject to visitation fees, £1; diocesan schoolmaster, 12*s.* 6*d.* Durrus-Kilcrohane glebe-house built in 1831, under the old Acts, at the certified cost of £980 Br., supplied out of the private funds of Incumbent, who will be entitled to receive the entire of that sum from his successor. Incumbent is constantly resident in the glebe-house. Exclusive of the moneys aforesaid, Incumbent reports that he has expended a large sum on important improvements, but to what amount not stated, without having any charge on his successor, for the repayment of any portion thereof. One church, capable of accommodating 400 persons, built about 1792, at the cost of £461 10*s.* 9½*d.* Br., granted by the late Board of First Fruits; the greater part whereof falling a few years after, in consequence of its being badly built, the body of the church was rebuilt by the Rev. Henry Jones, Incumbent, at his own expense; the former chancel and tower still standing. In 1832 the church was enlarged, by means of a loan of £188 Br., granted by the Board aforesaid; the whole of which loan remained chargeable on the parish in 1832, repayable by annual instalments of £7 10*s.* 5*d.* Divine service is celebrated twice on all Sundays, and once on the principal festivals, and on several other stated times; during each month, meetings and lectures are held by Incumbent in different and distant parts of the parish, in the dwelling-houses of the Protestants, and in the school-houses. The sacrament is administered monthly, and on the three great festivals. The rectorial tithes of this parish, compounded for £230, are impropriate, and belong, to the amount of £60, to Robert Warren Gumbleton, of Cork, esq. and demised by lease renewable for ever to Nathaniel Evanson, of Friendly Cove, esq.; the residue of the impropriate tithes, amounting to £170, belong to the Earl of Donoughmore, and his lessee, Alexander O'Driscoll, of Shipperton, near Skibbereen, esq. [Parl. Rep.]

1842. June 18. WILLIAM MOORE CROSTHWAITE, A.M., V. Durrus and Kilcrohan. [D.R.]

In 1852 he became P. Dromdaleague, q. v.

1852. August 18. JAMES FREKE, A.B., V. Durrus and Kilcrohan. Net annual value, £308 18*s.* 2*d.* [D.R.]

He obtained a certificate of dilapidation against his predecessor for £56 4*s.* 5*d.*, on 3 Sept. 1853. [D.R.]

1860. James Freke, Incumbent; John Harding Cole, Curate. The church, &c., and glebe-house in good order; 50A. of glebe in Vicar's occupation, and a small glebe in Killeshane, set to a tenant. Divine service twice on all Sundays in the church, and once at two licensed places of worship at Glenlough and Roosha, at the hours of 10 A.M. and 4 P.M. on Sundays. Sacrament monthly and at festivals; average of communicants, 58. 132 children are on the rolls of three Church Education schools. The Protestant population is 536. The rentcharge is £367 10*s.*, and the land is worth £50. Total value, £417 10*s.*, with residence.

James Freke was ordained Deacon on 13 Oct. 1833, and Priest on 5 July, 1834, both at Cork.

In 1840 he was licensed to the curacy of Ardfield. From 1841 to 1842 he was Vicar of Ardfield; and from 1842 to 1852 he was V. Kilcoe and Cleere.

He married Theodosia Elisabeth, dau. of Sir Richard St. George, baronet, and has issue.

FANLOBBUS.

1591. DERMICIUS DANIELIS is Vicar of Fanlobbus. "Rectoria de Fanlobbis spectat ad vicar Chorales. Vic. ibm. Dermicius Danielis, exhibiti sunt tituli." [MS. T.C.D. E. 3. 14.]

1610. Feb. 12. ROBERT SNOWSWELL is instituted to V. Fanlobbus and R. Ballymoney. Inducted 15th Feb. [R.V. 1634.]

In 1615 Snowswell is described as Minister and Preacher. Fanlobbus is valued at 6 li. per an. The church and chancel in good repair, with books. [R.V. R.I.A.]

In 1634 R. de Fanlobbis spectat ad Vic. Choral, Cork. Vicarius R. Snowswell. Val. 16 li. per an. [R.V. 1634.]

In 1639 Snowswell appears as Vicar, with John Godfrey as Curate. "Ecclia bene, desunt quædam ornamenta." [V.B. D.R.]

For Snowswell, *vide* Ballymoney.

16—? NICHOLAS WINTERBURNE V. Fanlobbus, Kinneigh, and R. Ballymoney.

For Winterburne, *vide* Treasurers of Ross.

1664. January 2. ROBERT GOLBORNE, Adm. V. Fanlobbus and Kinneigh, and Rector de Ballymoney, per deprivationem Nicholai Winterburne. [V.B. 1669.]

R. de ffanlobish spectat ad Vic. Chor. Cork. [V.B. 1669.]

Vide Ballymoney for Golborne.

1674. May 2. ISAAC MANSFIELD, V. Fanlobbus, Kinneigh, and Rector de Ballymoney. [F.F.] He was also P. Inskenny, q. v.

He appears from 1674 to 1688 as V. Fanlobish. [V.B.]

1689 to 1690. "Vacant." [V.B. D.R.] N.B. No collation made "propter rebellionem."

1691. Dec. 4. ANDREW SYMES, A.M., adm. V. Fanlobish, per mortem Isaac Mansfield. [D.R.] N.B. Non certificandum eo quod vice hujus vic. collatus fuit idem Symes ad Vicariam de Kinneigh. [D.R.]

For Symes, *vide* Precentors of Ross.

1692 and 1694. Mr. JOHN FORTUNE appears as V. Fanlobbus. [V.B. D.R.]

He was instituted on 1st Dec. 1693, per cess. of Andrew Symes. [D.R.]

In 1695 Fortune became V. Glanbarrahan, Ross, q. v.

1695. Dec. 23. JOHN PATRICKSON, A.M., V. Fanlobish, per cessionem Johis Fortune. [D.R.] He appears as V. Fanlobbus 1695 to 1717. [V.B.]

Patrickson was also Precentor of Cloyne, q. v.

A church designed to be built at Dunmanway. Sermon once a fortnight at present at Fanlobbus. [V.B. 1699, D.D.]

"Thursday, August 10, 1699. I went from Ballimoney to Bantry. I lay at Captain Parker's house. Fanlobish Church is about 3 miles beyond that of Ballimoney, to the west; the country thereabouts is coarse and rocky. The church is covered, but many slates are off; no pulpit nor seats; about half the church is ruinous; the church-yard is well inclos'd. About 14 English acres of glebe round the church. On the south of the church 6 plowlands belonging to the See of Corke; 5 of them on the north of the river Bandon, the sixth on the other side of the river, called Mareagh. The tenants to the Bishop are Sir Richard Cox and Mrs. Moreau. The 5 plowlands contain about 500 English acres; they are set by Sir Richard Cox to an Englishman for 50 li. per an. The sixth plowland is set, worth about £10 per an. These 6 plowlands are the best land thereabouts. Six plowlands belong to the Archbishop of Dublin; they pay a chiefry to the See of Corke; they do suit and service to the manor of Rosse; these are rocky lands.

"The Earl of Corke has two plowlands contiguous to the rest. He pays a chiefry to the See of Corke; but these 2 plowlands are reckoned in the Earl of Corke's manor of Inniskean. The parishioners are generally desirous to have the church at Dunmanway. If this church be not built the church of Fanlobish ought to be repaired forthwith."

"Dunmanway lyes near the centre of the parish; near 30 English families in the town. Divine service three Sundays in the month in a house in Dunmanway. There was subscribed £100 by Sir Richard Cox, and £100 by Mr. Patrickson, towards building a church or chappel of ease at Dunmanway, besides other subscriptions."

"At a mile distant to the west of Dunmanway stands a chappel of ease, ruinous, called Kilbarry Chapel."

"Munday, May 27, 1700. I viewed Fanlobish Church. Fanlobish Church is in the road from Ballimony to Dunmanway. The church stands near the eastern end of the parish; Dunmanway stands nearer the centre. The church is covered, but wants slating; the walls are not good. The church-yard is large, and well fenc't. Sir Richard Cox proposes to build a church at Dunmanway if it could be made the parish church; otherwise to make a chappel of ease there. The 6 plowlands of Nedineagh, belonging to the Bishop of Corke, lye to the south of Fanlobish Church; 5 of them on the N. of the Bandon river, and 1 on the south of the same river; they are good land, and contain in all about 500 acres; the best land thereabouts is set generally for less than 2*s.* an acre. The 5 plowlands of Nedineagh on the N. of the river, are held by Walter Plummer, *terre* tenant, who holds no other land; the sixth plowland is held by Denis Dullea, who holds other contiguous lands. The lands of this parish for the most part belong to the Lord Corke's brother Mr. H. Boyle, Sir R. Cox, the Bishop of Cork, the Archbishop of Dublin, Sir Matthew Dean, Mr. Fenwick,

Mr. Woods, and Ald. Hore, of Corke; Lieutenant Flower, Mr. Fare, and Mr. Plummer, and Mr. Dant, live in this parish, and Mr. Clerk and Mr. White."

"Divine service is performed every other Sunday at Dunmanway for the parish of Fanlobish, and on the same day Mr. Patrickson preaches at Kineigh. The other Sunday he preaches at Drommaleague. The Vicar of Fanlobish has half of the tythes. The Prebendary of Dromaleague has one rectory in this parish, being half the tythes of 14 plowlands; the Vicars Choral of Corke have half the tythes of 40 plowlands. The extent of this and several other parishes, according to the civil account, differs from the extent of them according to the ecclesiastical account. This parish of Fanlobish is worth to the Vicar of it about £50 or £60 per an. There are two churchwardens. There is a registry kept here; 12 acres of glebe adjoin to the east of the church-yard. No parsonage house. Charles M'Carthy is Priest of this parish; and 'tis said he is not a sober man, nor chast; he has been Priest there many years." [Downes' Tour.]

1718 to 1818. Fanlobbus was held with Drinagh, q. v.

1818. June 4. EDWARD ST. LAWRENCE, A.M., V. Fanlobbus, vacant by death of Tuckey; value under £300. [D.R.] He became, in 1825, Archdeacon of Ross, q. v.

1822. July 21. The new church on ancient site was consecrated by name of St. Mary. [D.R.]

1823. June 7. ROBERT KINGSBOROUGH ST. LAWRENCE, A.B., V. Fanlobbus. [D.R.] In 1824 he became Treasurer of Ross, q. v.

1823. Oct. 23. JAMES M'CHEANE, A.M., V. Fanlobbus. [D.R.]

M'Cheyne being Curate of Kilmocamoge, and his Rector being infirm, has his time for reading assent and consent prolonged to 1st March, 1824. [D.R.]

1830. Protestant population, 1,613.

James M'Cheane was ordained Deacon on 18th October, 1812, and Priest on 14th November, 1813, both at Cork. He was Curate of Kilmocamoge for some time; and from 1823 to his death in 1831 was V. Fanlobbus. He married Lucinda, sister to Robert Backas, of Butlerstown, county Waterford, and by her had issue. He left his freehold of Gracy, in the barony of Slieveardagh, county Tipperary, to whichever of his sons should first attain to the age of twenty-one years. [Cork Wills.]

1831. Oct. 26. WILLIAM MEADE, A.B., V. Fanlobbus. [D.R.] William, or *William de Courcy* Meade, was the V. Fanlobbus. [F.P.]

1837. Fanlobbus, a vicarage, with cure, 9 miles long by 5 broad, containing 32,339 acres. Gross population, 11,405. One Curate, employed at a stipend of £80 per annum. Tithe composition, £461 10*s.* 9¼*d.*; 23 acres of glebe, valued at 20*s.* per acre, £23. Subject to visitation fees, £1 3*s.* 3*d.*, diocesan schoolmaster, 16*s.* 8*d.* No glebe-house. Incumbent is resident, and pays the sum of £31 10*s.* per annum in the way of house-rent. One church, capable of accommodating 450 persons, built in 1821, at an expense of £1,384 12*s.* 3¾*d.* British, granted in way of loan by the late Board of First Fruits, of which loan there remaineth £753 4*s.* 10*d.* chargeable on the parish in 1832, repayable by annual instalments of £44 6*s.* 2*d.* Divine service is celebrated twice on all Sundays, and on the principal festivals. The sacrament is administered monthly, and on the three great festivals.

The rectorial, consisting of a moiety of the tithes of this parish, compounded for £461 10*s.* 9½*d.* are appropriate, and belong, as to the amount of £87 7*s.* 8*d.* to the Prebendary of Drumdaleague; and as to the residue, amounting to £374 3*s.* 1½*d.* to the Vicars Choral of the Cathedral Church of St. Finbarr's, Cork. [Parl. Rep.]

1843. March 17. The schoolhouse at Corrigscullihy was licensed for divine service. [D.R.]

William de Courcey Meade (second son of Rev. Richard Meade, of Innishannon, by Mary, dau. of the 25th Baron of Kinsale), was ordained Deacon on 6th July, 1806, and Priest on 12th July, 1807, both at Cloyne. He was, in 1813, licensed Curate of Templemichael de Duagh. From 1818 to 1831 he was P. Inskenny; and from 1831 to his death, on 10th June, 1855, he was V. Fanlobbus. He was also R. Garrivoe from 1832 to 1842. He married Barbara, dau. of Rev. Robert Meade, Rector of Ballymoney, by whom he left issue two daughters.

1855. June 27. WILLIAM ROBERT MOLESWORTH, A.M., V. Fanlobbus; certified value, £330 16*s.* 3*d.* [D.R.]

1860. W. R. Molesworth, Incumbent; J. W. Wakeham, J. M'Cheane, and J. Aldworth, are Curates. The church, &c., in order. No glebe-house; 23 acres of glebe set. Divine service twice each Sunday, and on chief festivals, &c., at the church, and also at a licensed place of worship at Carrigsculley. Sacrament monthly; average of communicants, 48; at Christmas, 108; 165 children are on the rolls of the schools of this parish. There are 7 Protestant teachers, paid by Church Education Society, &c. The Protestant population is 971. The rentcharge is £346 3*s.* 1*d.*, and the land is worth £20. Total value, £366 3*s.* 1*d.* per annum, without residence.

William Robert Molesworth (elder son of Major Bysse-Cole Molesworth, who was fourth son of Robert, the second son of Bysse, seventh son of the first Viscount Molesworth in the peerage of Ireland), graduated A.B., T.C.D. in 1829, and A.M. in 1832. He was ordained Deacon on 18th Dec. 1831, and Priest on 29th July, 1832. From 1842 to 1847 he was V. Ardfield, and from 1847 to 1855 was V. Drinagh.

GARRYVOE.

1610. August 30. THOMAS DAVIES is admitted R. de Garrinow et Killoney. He was inducted 10 August, 1611. [R.V. 1634.]

In 1618 he became also P. Inskenny, q. v.

1634. R. de Garrinowe et Killowen, Thomas Davies. Val. 8 li. per an. Baro de Coursey, Patronus. [R.V. 1634.]

1637. August 12. BERNABAS HONEYCHURCH, R. Garrynowe et Killowen. [F.F.]

He appears in V. B. 1639–1681. Ld. Kinsale, Patron. [D.R.] He was again instituted on 2 April, 1661, "per mortem Thomæ Davyes." [V.B. 1669. D.R.]

Honeychurch, in 1661, became R. V. Murragh, q. v.

1682. August 22. DANIEL LORD, A.M., R. Murragh, V. Desertserges, and on 23 August, R. Garrivoe and Killowen. [F.F.]

On letters patent of 5 July, 1682, to Garrivoe and Killowen rectories. [Lib. Mun.] *Vide* Murragh.

In 1692 Lord became P. Kilbrogan, q. v.

1683. May 24. PETER HEWITT, adm. R. de Garryvoe vacantem per resignationem Danielis Lord et in presentatione Prœhonorabilis Almeric Domini Coursy, Baro. de Kinsale et Rinrone. [F.F. and D.R.] He appears 1683 to 1718. [V.B.]

Garrivoe is said to be part of Desertserges. [V.B. 1699.]

In 1710 Hewitt became also Precentor of Cork, q. v.

1720 to 1763. WILLIAM MEADE appears as R. Garryvoe [V.B. D.R.], *vice* Hewett, deceased.

In 1736 Meade became also Dean of Cork, q. v.

1764. April 5. GEORGE WOOD, A.B., R. Garryvoe [F.F.], *vice* Wm. Meade, deceased.

He was ordained Deacon on 19 Dec. 1742, and Priest on 18 September, 1743. In 1761 he appears as Curate of Kilbrogan. He held from 1764 to his death the R. Garryvoe.

He married, in December, 1748, Jane Beamish, of Kilmalooda, and left his substance to his son, Thomas Wood, of the city of Cork; his other children being provided for. [Cork M.B. and Wills.]

1792. June 13. RICHARD MEADE, A.B., R. Garryvoe, vacant by death of George Wood, and on the presentation of Lord Kinsale. [D.R.]

In 1796 he was also R. Innishannon, q. v.

1799. July 5. HON. THOMAS DE COURCEY, A.B., R. Garrynoe, otherwise Garrivoe, and R. Killowen, otherwise Kilcony. [F.F.] To Garrivoe by cess. of Richard Meade, and to Killowen by cess. of Wm. Noble. [D.R.]

1825. November 9. The Right Hon. and Rev. Lord Kinsale grants the right of presentation to Kilrowan, otherwise Killowen; Garrinue, otherwise Garrinoe, otherwise Garrivoe; Killwoney, otherwise Killowny, Rynroan, or Ringrone, unto John Meade,

Commander of R. Navy, and John S. Newman, in trust, to present Wm. Newman to each and every of said livings; said Wm. Newman, the younger, being only son of Wm. Newman, esq. by Martha, his wife, and first and second cousin to his Lordship, &c. [D.R.]

Thomas (second son of John, 26th Baron Kinsale), was ordained Deacon on 21 Dec. 1797, and Priest on 21 Dec. 1798; both at Cork. From 1799, until his death, in 1832, he was R. Garryvoe and Killowen. In 1822 he became 27th Baron, and died unm. in 1832.

1832. May 15. WILLIAM MEADE, A.B., R. Garrivoe, vacant by death of Lord Kinsale. On presentation of John Meade and John Spiller Newman, esqrs. trustees to late Lord Kinsale. [D.R.] William Meade was also V. Fanlobbus, q. v. He resigned Garrivoe on 22 Feb. 1842.

1842. March 10. WILLIAM NEWMAN, A.B., R. Garrivoe. On presentation of John Meade, esq. dated 24 February. [D.R.]

In 1855 he became also R. Ringrone, q. v.

1860. Garrivoe seems to be a perfect sinecure. In Knox' Index the rentcharge is given as £315 per an. No church; no glebe-house; no return of Protestant population. Accordingly, the present rentcharge reduced from that of 1830 by one-fourth, is £236 *5s.*

GLENGARIFFE.

Glengariffe is a district curacy, formed by deed, dated 31 July, 1861, between the Incumbents of Kilcaskin, in Ross, and Kilmocomoge, in Cork diocese, who pay to the Curate £35 per an., as an endowment for the new church. The Vicar of Kilcaskin, who pays £20 per an. of above sum, has the first, and the V. Kilmocomoge the second turn of the alternate patronage. The Earl of Bantry granted, on 13 April, 1861, 1R. 20P. statute measure of land for a new church at Glengariffe.

1860. Divine service is at present celebrated at half-past twelve o'clock, on Sundays, at the hotel, at Glengariffe. Sacrament six times in the year; average of communicants, *5*. The Curate is Rev. Vincent Lamb, A.B., who was, on 23 January, 1855, licensed to this curacy at £75 per an. on the nomination of the V. Kilmocomoge and the V. Kilcaskin jointly.

A new church, on the site granted in 1861, by Lord Bantry, is now (March, 1863), nearly finished. The designs for it were furnished by the Ecclesiastical Commissioners, and were slightly modified by the Archdeacon of Cork (S. M. KYLE), who originated the idea of placing a church in this romantic locality, and who collected the greater portion of the funds.

HOLY TRINITY.

1291. "Eccia Sce Trinitatis XVmr." [Tax. P. Nic.]

13—? SIMON DE GLANDFORDBRIGG, an Englishman, Chaplain of the Church of the Holy Trinity, dies or resigns in 1381. [Rot. Canc. and Tuckey's Cork Rem.]

1381. Feb. 17. JOHN KINGSTOUN is appointed by the King Chaplain of the Church of the Holy Trinity, *vice* Simon de Glandfordbrigg. [Rot. Canc. and Tuckey's Cork. Rem.]

1386. July 20. THOMAS DE EVERDON is presented by the Earl of Oxford, Lord Lieutenant of Ireland, to the free Chapel of the Holy Trinity. [Rot. Pat. 10 Ric. II.]

Thomas de Everdon was, in 1375, a Canon of St. Patrick's, Dublin. From 1396 to 1399 he was Dean of St. Patrick's, and was P. Clonmethan, St. Patrick's, Dublin, from 1399 to his death.

He held several civil appointments. He was Clerk of the Chancery or Joint Keeper of the Rolls from 1373 to 1377. In 1385 he obtains another patent as Clerk or Keeper of the Rolls, Writs, &c., and in 1401 is again appointed Keeper of the Rolls. He was, in 1399 and 1400, Deputy Treasurer of the Exchequer. From 1406 to 1409 he was Chief Engrosser of the Exchequer.

1386. Oct. 6. THOMAS BARTON is presented by the Lord Lieutenant to the Chapel of the Holy Trinity. [Rot. Pat. 10 Ric. II.]

1414. August 13. RICHARD O'HEDIAN is presented by the Crown to the Chapel of the Holy Trinity. [Rot. Pat. 2 Hen. V.] He took a new patent on 24th June, 1431, and in 1434 had an exemplification made of his old patent of 1444. [Rot. Pat. 10 and 13 Hen. VI.] He was, probably, Archbishop or Archdeacon of Cashel. *Vide* Cotton for his history.

1524. September 1. Master PHILIP GOWLL, Rector of the Church of the Holy Trinity, Cork, is mentioned in a deed of this date, "bonæ memoriæ." [Caulfield MSS.]

1543. DOMINUS DAWYE NAGLE and DOMINUS EDMOND POUCHE, chaplayns and deservitors of Christ's Church, Cork, are parties to a deed of arbitration, dated at Cork, 17th Oct., 1543. [Caulfield MSS.]

Dominus David Nogla, in 1538, witnesses a deed, and in 1552, March 30, "David Nogla, capellanus de markharn in Ecclesia Stœ Trinitatis, Cork," is mentioned in an indenture. [Ib.]

1545. August 3. GEORGE ROCHE, Archdeacon of Cork, and Rector of the free chapel there, is pardoned. [Morrin's Pat. Rolls.] This was, probably, the Chapel of the Holy Trinity.

1572. WILLIAM FELD, or FIELD, was instituted to the P. Holy Trinity. He appears in 1591 "Preb. Gulielmus Feld, idem vicarius de Athnowen; intitulatus ad prebendam anno 1572; ordinatus 1588."—"Rector sive Preb. Scē Trinitatis et vicar.

Athnowen per unionem—deliberand. super unione. Vicarius Scē Trinitatis Roger Skiddy." Field is noted as holding the two benefices, "virtute unionis vitiose." He was also, in 1591, P. Inniscarra, in Cloyne, and R. St. Nicholas. [MS. T.C.D. 3. 14.] Skiddy was P. Lisclery, q. v.

1615. HUGH PERCEVALL, A.M., is Rector, Thomas Bourden is Vicar of the Holy Trinity, and the Dean of Cork is Curate. "Rector S. Trinitatis (non residens) Hugo Percevall, A.M. Val. 4 li. per an. Georgius Lee Decanus Corcagen inservit curæ. Vicarius, Thomas Bourden, minister legens." [R.V. R.I.A.] Perceval was Dean of Ross, q. v. Bourden was V. Kilbonane, q. v.

1628. August 30. JOSEPH FOWLE, P. Holy Trinity, P. Cahirlag et P. St. Michael's. [F.F. as quoted by Cotton.] In 1632 Fowle became Treasurer of Cloyne, q. v.

1634. Rectoria Stæ Trinitatis vacat. Rex est Patronus. [R.V. 1634.]

1637. April 5. JAMES MARGETSON is presented to the P. Holy Trinity. [Rot. Pat. 13 Charles I.] In 1639 he is marked "excusatur." [V.B.] In 1660 he appears again.

1642. March 24. NEPTUNE BLOOD was presented to the P. Holy Trinity. [Pat. Rot. 18 Charles I.]

Neptune Blood, whom Bp. Ryder, of Killaloe, mentions as a "Student in the College of Dublin, a good scholar, and reads the Irish tongue," was ordained Priest on 18th March, 1622, and in that year was presented to the rectory of Yougal-Arra, with a dispensation pro quinquennio, studendi gratia. In 1632 he became Precentor of Killaloe, and in 1641 Archdeacon of Kilfenora. He deponed to the loss of £180 in the rebellion, besides his church living, worth £140 per annum. [MS. T.C.D. F. 2. 22.] In 1642 he became P. Holy Trinity, Cork. In 1663 he became Dean of Kilfenora, R. Killilaye, Kilmora, Carne, R. V. Rathblanagh, R. V. Kilkeedee, and P. Rathderb, in Killaloe. He received, also, in 1663, a dispensation to hold the rectories of Clonferd and Kilbridge; and was, in 1661, a J.P. for Clare, and in 1663 for Westmeath counties. In 1667 he obtained a grant under the Act of Settlement of 208 plantation acres of land, in the barony of Burren, co. Clare.

He married Elisabeth, eldest dau. of Higgat Lone, Dean of Kilfenora, by Mary Baldry, of Suffolk. His son, Neptune, was also Dean of Kilfenora; and the descendants of Dean Blood still possess landed property in the county of Clare.

1660. January 25. JAMES MARGETSON is appointed Archbishop of Dublin, with the Treasurership of St. Patrick's, in commendam, together with the rectory of Galowne, *alias* Dartree, dioc. Clogher, and the prebend of the Holy Trinity, Cork. [Pat. Rot. 12 Charles II.] In 1663 he became Primate of Ireland.

1663? JOHN EASTON or ESTON, Prebendary and Vicar. He was also Chanceller of Ross, q. v.

1664. Nov. 22. BENJAMIN CROSS, R. and V. Holy Trinity, vacant per resignation of John Eston. [F.F. and V.B. 1669.] On letters patent of July 1. [Lib. Mun.] Cross appears 1664 to 1683 as R. V. Holy Trinity. Rex patronus rectoriæ, episcopus vicariæ. [V.B.] Cross was also Precentor of Cloyne, q. v.

1676. A *quare impedit* issues, at suit of the King *v.* Bp. of Cork, *in re* the presentation to the Holy Trinity. [Ferguson MSS. II. p. 132.]

1684. Sept. 3. JOHN PATRICKSON, A.M., is admitted P. and V. Holy Trinity, "per lapsum, prebenda omnino in Rege et vicaria in collatione Epi." [F.F. and D.R.] Patrickson, in 1685, became Precentor of Cloyne, q. v.

1685. Oct. 29. HENRY RYDER, A.M., P. Holy Trinity, on letters patent of 24th September. He was Vicar also on 5th June previous. [F.F. and Lib. Mun.] He became, in 1686, Treasurer of Cork, q. v.

1686. June 25. RICHARD MALLORY, A.M., P. Holy Trinity, and same day R. Ratheoney. [F.F.] On letters patent of June 1. [Lib. Mun.] He became Vicar also on 11th Oct., 1686. Mallory was a Scholar T.C.D. in 1679. In 1686 he became R. Agher and Laracor, Meath.

1686/7. January 22. EDWARD SYNGE, A.M., P. and V. Holy Trinity, per resignation of Mallory, and on letters patent to the prebend, dated 29th Dec. 1686. [F.F. and Lib. Mun.]

1691. Francis Hodder, in consideration of the benefactions of his ancestors, obtains from the Bishop a gallery or seat in the north-west quarter of Christchurch. [D.R.]

Edward Synge (son of Edward, Bishop of Cork, Cloyne, and Ross, by Barbara Latham) was educated at Christ Church, Oxford.

He was, from 1682 to 1686, R. V. Laracor, Meath; from 1686 to 1706, Vicar of Christ Church, Cork, and from 1686 to 1714, Prebendary of Christ Church, Cork. From 1691 to 1714, he was R. Rathclarin, and from 1692 to 1706, was R.V. Kilcolman, Agabulloge, and Aghinagh, in Cloyne. From 1692 to 1714, he was R. Templetrine. He also held, from 1693 to 1702 the P. Lackeen, and from 1702 to 1706, the P. Kilmaclenine. From 1705 to 1714, he was Chancellor of St. Patrick's, and in 1714 was Vicar-General of Dublin.

He was Bishop of Raphoe from 1714 to 1716, and from 1716 to 1741, Archbishop of Tuam.

He married Anne Proud, of the county Cork, and had issue, Edward (Bishop of Ferns), Nicholas (Bishop of Killaloe), Samuel, and George, besides a daughter, who married John Moore, of Raheenduff, in Queen's co.

He published "The Wisdom of being Religious," a sermon, preached at the Castle Chapel, Dublin. 8vo., 1704.

1714. Dec. 7. JOHN SMITH is presented to the rectory of Christchurch, Cork. [Lib. Mun.] He appears, 1714 to 1738, June 9. [V.B.]

This John Smith was the same person, I presume, who was ordained Priest at Cloyne, on 19th Dec., 1714, and who was then A.M. I find among the Cork marriage bonds, one between John Smith, of Clonmel, Cloyne, Clk., and Judith Newman, of Christchurch, Cork.

1738. Sept. 26. JOHN BURGH, or BURKE, is presented to the Prebend of Christchurch, and on 17th October, is instituted "per mortem Johannis Smith." [Lib. Mun. and D.R.] He again received this Prebend in 1749.

1745. Sept. 14. WILLIAM JACKSON, A.M., P. Holy Trinity, per resignation of Burgh. [D.R.] He became, in 1749, P. Cahirlag, q. v.

1749. August 25. JOHN BURGH, P. Holy Trinity, on letters patent of 2nd August, and per resignation of Jackson. [D.R. and Lib. Mun.]

John Burgh, or Burke, was ordained Priest at Cork, on 8th Oct., 1738.

From 1738 to 1745, and from 1749 to 1768, he held this prebend. From 1739 to 1742, he was V. Killaconenagh, Ross, and from 1742 to 1749, R. Rathconey. He was P. Cahirlag from 1745 to 1749. He died in 1768.

1769. June 28. EDWARD DAY, LL.D., P. Holy Trinity, vacant by death of Burgh, and on letters patent of June 14, 1768. [F.F. and Lib. Mun.]

1807. Dr. Edward Day is supposed to be resident in the diocese of Ardfert, of which he is Archdeacon. [Rep.]

Edward Day (eldest son of Rev. John Day, Chancellor of Ardfert, by Lucy, daughter of the Knight of Kerry), was brother to Robert Day, Judge of the King's Bench in Ireland.

He was, from 1768 to 1717, V. Kilsallaghan, Dublin, and R. V. Dunmore, Tuam, &c., &c. From 1769 to 1808, he was P. Holy Trinity, Cork. He was also, from 1770 to 1771, R. V. Rincurran; from 1771 to 1801, R. Killorglin, Kiltallaght, Curranee, Kilcolman, and Knockane, in Kerry; from 1777 to 1782, Chancellor of Ardfert, and from 1782 to 1808 Archdeacon of Ardfert, of which diocese he was also Vicar-General.

He married Barbara Forward, and by her had issue, Rev. Edward Day, whose son is now Rector of Sligo, and Robert, a Barrister.

Another brother of Judge Robert Day was John Day, who, by his wife, Margaret Hewson, had issue, Rev. John Day, Rector of Kiltallagh, who, by his wife, Arabella, dau. of Sir William Godfrey, had issue *inter alios*, Rev. John Day (Dean of Ardfert, who married Eleanor, dau. of Sir John Godfrey), Edward (General in the Army), and Rev. Maurice Fitzgerald Day, Incumbent of St. Mathias, Dublin.

1808. March 5. ROBERT DALY, A.B., P. Holy Trinity, vacant by death of Day, and certified under £100 in yearly value. [D.R.] On letters patent of 29th Feb. [Lib. Mun.] The income arises wholly from lands, the rent of which is £27 13*s.* 10¼*d.*, and the annual renewal fine is, by agreement with the tenant, £369 4*s.* 7½*d.* The total value is £396 18*s.* 5¾*d.* [Parl. Rep.]

The Hon. Robert Daly (brother of the first Lord Dunsandle) was second son of Right Honorable Denis Daly, by the only daughter of the first Earl of Farnham.

He was born in 1783, at Dunsandle, co. Galway, and was educated at Dr. Stock's school, at Delgany, and at Dr. Moore's, Donnybrook.

He entered T.C.D. in 1799, graduated A.B. in 1803, A.M. in 1832, and B.D. and D.D. in 1843.

He was ordained Deacon at Kilmore in 1807, and Priest, at Ferns, in 1808.

From 1807 to 1810, he was Curate of Tomhaggard, Ferns, and from 1810 to 1814, Curate of Newcastle, Dublin. He held, from 1809 to 1843, the P. Holy Trinity, Cork, and from 1814 to 1843, the prebend of Stagonil, and rectory of Powerscourt, Dublin, and from 1840 to 1843, was Dean of St. Patrick's, Dublin. He resigned his three livings in 1843, on becoming Bishop of Cashel, Waterford, &c.

1843. Feb. 18. The appointment of this prebend was now suspended by order in Council, and the revenues were transferred to the Ecclesiastical Commissioners. The Dean and Chapter, on 10th August, 1844, elected, as Honorary Prebendary, the Rev. Charles Leslie, the Vicar of the Holy Trinity. And ever since the Vicars have been also Prebendaries of the Holy Trinity, subject, however, to the severance of the temporalities.

HOLY TRINITY, V.

1525. "DOMINUS DOMINIC TYRRY, Vicarius Ecclesiæ Stæ Trinitatis" is witness to a deed, dated at Cork, 17 July, 1525, anno Regis Henrici 8°, xvii. [Caulfield MSS.]

1571. July 29. Adam Gold bequeaths v marks to Christ Church, Cork, "so that the old faith be set up."

1577. John Teige M'Cartie leaves towards "the reparacion of Christ Church two barrels of barley; and to every poor prieste of said church, xii d." [Cork Wills.]

1581. January 1. DOMINUS DONALDUS DONATI, "sacerdos ecclesiæ parochialis Stæ Trinitatis" is a witness to a deed. [Sarsfield MSS.]

Donaldus Donati appears in 1591 as V. Templeroan, Cloyne, q. v.

1582. "David Lombarde de Corke mercator," in his will proved at Cork, 16 Sept. 1582, leaves "corpus meum sepeliendum in Capella Beatæ Mariæ infra Ecclesiam Sanctæ Trinitatis, Corke, in loco majorum." [Cork Wills.]

1582. "Edmund White, thelder, cittizen of Corcke," in his will (dated the last day of May, and proved 7 June, 1582), desires to be "buried in St. James is chappelle in Christes Churche, in Corcke, wher myne ancestors lie." He gives to "the mayntenance of the waxe of the said church, iijs. iiijd." sterling, and towards the building of the body of the said church, iijs. iiijd. sterling. He was brother to "Sr. Persevall Whyte." [Cork Wills.]

1591. ROGER SKIDDY is Vicar of the Holy Trinity. *Vide* the Prebend.

1615. THOMAS BOURDEN is Vicar. *Vide* the Prebend.

1618. November 17. NICHOLAS HALL, Vicar de Christ Church, and Rector de Cahirlag. [F.F.]

In 1619 he became Archdeacon of Ross, q. v.

1631. September. 7. RICHARD ASHE, A.M., Vicar de Christ Church. [F.F.] Inducted 9 Sept. [R.V. 1634.]

1634. Vicar Christ Church, Richardus Ashe, A.M., divini verbi Predicator. Val. xii. li. per an. Epus confet. [R.V. 1634.]

Ashe was also P. Killaspugmullane. In 1661 he appears as R. Killeagh, Cloyne, q. v.

1639. April 6. THOMAS BANKES, Vicar de Christ Church. [F.F.]

"Ecclesia non bene repatur, ad repandum monit." [V.B. 1639.]

Bankes was also P. Killaspugmullane, q. v.

1643. The old parchment Register of Christ Church was, in this year, given to the churchwardens, Robert Kinge and George White, in consideration of their having given a seat in church to John Bayley, gent. And the earliest entries in this, the oldest and best preserved of the Cork Parish Registers, are those of the burial of the donor and his wife, as follows:—"John Bayly, the elder, late Clerke of the citty and parishe of Christ Church, Cork, deceased the 26 day of July, 1643." "Eleanor Bayly, the wife of the said John Bayly, of Cork, lately deceased the 28 day of January, 1643." The latest entry is dated 1668.

1645. "Phillip, the son of phillip Spenser and of Jaene, his wife, was baptized the 28 of March, 1645."

1644. "Ser Arter hide, knight, was buried the 3 of desember, 1644."

1645. "Collonel henry Braine [O'Brien], desesed, and was buried the seven of Desember, 1645."

1646. "Henery Spenser, Precher of God's word, desesed, and was buried the ix of Aprel, 1646."

1646. "Richard Sterton, who was cruelly mordered by the enemy, disesed, and was buried 24 of Augost, 1646. Sr. Andrew Barott, knight, decesed, and was buried 6 November. 1646. Mr. Cornelius Gray, Precher of God's worde, decesed, and was buried the 28 of January, 1646."

1647. "Mager-generale Evans beeing wounded in the battel att Cnok-nonoss, decesed, and was buried the 2 of Desember, 1647."

"Sr. Williame Bridges, allso beeing wounded in the battel, decesed, and was likwise buried the seconde of Desember, 1647."

1658. "Henery Pepper, Swordberer of the citty of Cork, decesed, and was buried in Christchurch, first of May, 1658. Cateren, wife of Henery Pepper . . . . . was buried 21 Oct. 1658."

1662. "Joshua blood went to the citty of Kilfenora, out of the citty of Cork, with men weeping tears, the seconde daie of Aprill, 1662." [Par. Reg.]

1663? John Eston, or Easton. *Vide* the Prebend.

1664. November 22. Benjamin Cross, Vicar and Prebendary. [F.F.] He appears 1664 to 1683. [V.B. D.R.] *Vide* the Prebend.

"1664. March 30. John Tucker, being 100 and 10, was buried." [Par. Reg.]

1665. "Paid Mr. Joshua Blood, Clarke of the saide church, for 52 weekes allowance from the said parish, determining the 8th May, 1665, £2 12*s*. Mr. John Gartery, Sexton, same period, £1 6*s*." [Christ Church Parish Accounts.]

"1665. May 31. Received from Mrs. Margret pridden, being for soe much left by her late husband, Mr. Richard pridden, by his last will, the use of it, to be distributed to the poore of the said parish on ye 12th of October yearely, wtt one yeares interest, £5 10*s*."

"1665. May 31. From Mr. Neptune Blood, deane of Kilfenora, being in satisfaction of the plate he tocke away (when Minister of the said parish), belonging to the saide parish and church, £14."

"1665. March 25. Paide unto Mr. Benjamin Cross, Minister of said parish, for one yeares allowance from saide parish, determining the 29th September, 1664, £50."

"Paide unto saide Mr. Benjamin Cross, for halfe yeares allowance from the saide parish, determining the 25th of March, 1665, the sum of £25." [Christ Church Accounts.]

"1666. January 10. henrie bill being unfortunately slaine with a great gun" (was buried). [Par. Reg.]

"1676. May 6. Memorandum.—Mr. Timothy Tuckey hath this day paid £26, bequeathed by his father, Timothy, deceased, to the poor of Christchurch parish, the interest thereof to be paid in bread, weekly, for ever. Item—We let out said sum this day to Robt. Gobbe." [Vestry-book.]

"1670. Wee do hereby certifie yt wee saw the disposing of five pounds ster. to the poore of the parish of Christchurch by Richard Perry, being a gift of Left. Samuel Gravener; as witness our hands this 3 day of March, 1670.

"(Signed), "Corne. Covenay.
"Edward Tucker."

1670. "By cash recd. of Wm. Wreen, Shreife of ye citty, esq. to be let out at interest for ye use of ye poore, given by George Savell, £5 to this parish."

1670. "By cash recd. of mr. Haniball Bassett for ye use of £20, left by Alderman Richard Bassett for ye poore. £4 for 2 years' use. [Christchurch Accounts.]

1684. Sept. 3. JOHN PATRICKSON, V. and P. Holy Trinity. *Vide* the Prebend.

1685. June 5. HENRY RIDER, or RYDER, A.M., P. Holy Trinity. He became Prebendary also on 29th October, 1685. [F.F.] *Vide* the Prebend.

1686. May 5. RICHARD HIGGS, V. Holy Trinity, per resignation of Ryder. [D.R.]

Higgs does not appear elsewhere.

1686. Oct. 11. RICHARD MALLORY, A.M., V. Holy Trinity, "per mortem Richardi Higgs." [D.R.] He was also Prebendary, q. v.

1686. January 22. EDWARD SYNGE, A.M., V. and P. Holy Trinity, q. v.

1701. Alderman John Sealy, by his will (dated 6th July, 1701, and proved 14th March following), leaves to his wife, Elisabeth, his property at Coker, in the parish of Wandon, Somersetshire. All his real estate he gives to "Samuel, son of William Sealy, my nephew." He also gives to the parish of Christchurch, Cork, for ever, "one silver flaggon, which at this tyme lies in the hands of Mr. Alexander Doleman, in the city of Bristol." [Cork Wills.]

"1702. In Christchurch parish, at the east end of the church, is a small almshouse (four rooms), wherein are lodg'd six poor women and the old sexton; they have a small weekly allowance of 6*d*. or 8*d*. a-week, paid them by the churchwardens out of the collections for the poor." [Downes' Tour.]

1707. Feb. 11. PHILIP TOWNSEND, V. Holy Trinity, per resignation of Synge. [D.R.]

1712. Jonathan Serrie, of Cork citty, gentleman (will dated 30th May, 1709, and proved 12th Sept. 1712), leaves his "body to be buried in my owne burying place or sepulchre in St. Maries' Isle, in Christchurch, in Cork;" also, "twenty shillings sterling worth of bread to ye English Protestant poore of each of ye two parishes of Christchurch and Shandon, to be distributed ye next day after my burial." [Cork Wills.]

1713. Nov. 16. At a vestry held this day, it was announced that John Perry, late of Youghal, esq. had bequeathed to the poor of Christchurch parish, £100. And the minister, Philip Townsend, being in England, is requested to examine the will and receive the money. [Par. Reg.]

1720. Nov. 27. The first sermon in the new church was preached by Rev. P. Townsend on this day. [Smith's Cork, vol. i. p. 378.]

Philip Townsend, sixth son of Colonel Richard Townsend, of Castletownsend, was born in 1664 at Kilbrittain Castle, near Timoleague, county Cork, and entered T.C.D. as a Pensioner on 20th June, 1684. He at first adopted the military profession, and was a captain in the army, but subsequently entered into Holy Orders, and in 1706 was admitted by Bishop Dive Downes to the Prebend of Lisclery, and by Bishop Crow, of Cloyne, to the R. V. Aghinagh, in Cloyne. These livings, together with the important Vicarage of the Holy Trinity, which he received in 1707, he held until his death. He was buried at the Holy Trinity on the 26th May, 1735.

He married, circa 1705, Helena, dau. of John Galwey, esq. and by her had issue two daughters, Elisabeth (born 1709, died sp.); and Mary, born in 1710 (whom her father calls in his will his only child), who was wife to John Becher, esq. of Aghadowne, near Skibbereen, son of Colonel Thomas Becher, Governor of Sherkin Island, county Cork. Considerable estates were settled on that marriage, which now belong to the present Sir Henry Wrixon Becher, bart. of Ballygiblin, and Creagh, and Castlehyde, county Cork.

Colonel Richard Townsend, the father of Philip Townsend, was descended from the ancient family of that name in the county of Norfolk; and, having settled himself in Ireland, became the founder and common ancestor of the Townsend family in the county of Cork.

In the reign of Charles I. he was a Colonel of Infantry. In the civil wars of that period he would seem to have joined the army which served from 1642 to 1645, under the Earl of Essex, in support of the Long Parliament; but refused to unite himself to that new model of the army which was formed at Cromwell's instance early in 1645. He acted, however, with detached forces, which belonged to Sir Thomas Fairfax's army, in the south-west of England, in the summer of the following year, 1646. He served at that time at the siege of Pendennis Castle, Cornwall, under the immediate command of the Honourable Colonel Richard Fortescue; and was one of the commissioners who were appointed on the part of the besiegers to treat about a capitulation, and who received the surrender of the castle, the 16th August. (See Sprigge, "Anglia Rediviva, History of Army under Sir T. Fairfax," pp. 302–304 (London, 1647; or pp. 306–313, Oxford University Press, 1854); Rushworth, "Historical Collections," part iv. vol. i. p. 295 (London, 1682–1701).

When the House of Commons caused troops to be forwarded to Ireland in the following year, 1647, Cromwell so arranged matters that only those who were opposed to his projects in England were sent thither. Accordingly, upon the 15th June, the Parliament "ordered that Colonel Townsend's regiment be hereby required and commanded forthwith to be shipped and transported into Ireland, for the service of that kingdom. (See Journals of the House of Commons, 1647, p. 211.) On the 13th of the following November, Colonel Townsend commanded the main body of the English infantry at the great battle of Knockninoss, west of Mallow, in the county Cork, which was fought under the Earl of Inchiquin, against the Irish under Lord Taaffe. Subsequently, the English army being in great distress from the want of proper supplies, he united with Lord Inchiquin and others in a "Remonstrance," which was sent to the House of Commons early in the following year, 1648, and which is given by Sir Richard Cox, "History of Ireland," part ii. Appendix, No. 39, p. 140, London, 1689–90; and by Rushworth, "Historical Collections," part iv. vol. ii. p. 1041. And Inchiquin having shortly afterwards renounced his allegiance to the English Parliament, differences upon that subject of a serious character ensued between Colonel Townsend and that nobleman. (See Cox, Ibid. part ii. Charles I. pp. 198–202.)

In the following year, 1649, early in November, Cromwell having invaded Ireland, and taken the towns of Drogheda, Wexford, and Ross, the English garrisons in the county of Cork, in number about 2,500 men, not being able to "endure the thought of joining with the Irish against their own countrymen," united themselves to Cromwell, and proved to be of great service for the general subjugation of Ireland. In this important movement Colonel Townsend, acting with Lord Broghill, Colonel Courtney, Sir Percy Smith, and Colonels Gifford and Warder, took a leading part. (Cox, Ibid. part ii. Charles II. p. 12; "Life of Cromwell," p. 140, London, 1731). Cromwell writes, in particular, at that time, to Speaker Lenthall, that Colonel Townsend had come from Cork, in the "Nonsuch" frigate, to convey to him the submission of the English garrison and Protestant inhabitants of that city; and was with him at Ross (county Wexford), November 14, having, with others, "been very active for the return both of Cork and Youghal to their obedience." (See Despatch of that date in "Letters and Speeches of Cromwell," edited by Carlyle, vol. ii. pp. 94–96; London, 1846.)

After the Irish war, about 1652, Colonel Townsend, it would seem, for a time went back to England. Subsequently he returned to Ireland; and, both during the Protectorate, when so many Irish estates were for sale, and after the restoration of Charles II. in 1660, he made extensive purchases of land. He was seated for a time at Kilbrittain Castle, in the county Cork, and was Member for Baltimore in the Irish Parliament, which met at Chichester House, Dublin, 1661. At the instance of the Earl of Orrery, President of Munster, he was appointed Commander of Militia by the Duke of Ormonde, 1666. (See Orrery's "State Letters," pp. 156, 166, 170, folio, London, 1742); and Smith, "State of the County and City of Cork," vol. i. p. 58, Dublin, 1774). And his purchases were confirmed to him by three several patents, in 1666, 1668, 1679. He finally settled himself at Castle Townsend, in the barony of West Carbery. That site is mentioned in the patent of 1666 by its ancient name, Sleughteige. He became High Sheriff of the county Cork on 12th March, 1671.

His son, Horatio, Captain of the "Lynor," sloop of war, greatly distinguished himself at the siege of Cork by the Duke of Marlborough, which took place in the reign of William III. September, 1690. (See Story, "Impartial History of the Wars in Ireland," p. 141; London, 1693; Smith, Ibid. vol. ii. p. 207). Shortly afterwards, in the same year, November 23rd, an attack was made by a Jacobite party of 500 men, under Colonel O'Driscoll, upon Colonel Townsend's mansion-house at Castle Townsend, which Colonel Townsend, with a garrison of thirty-five men, repelled, with considerable loss to the attacking party. (Story, Ibid. p. 151; Sir Richard Cox, MS. Narrative in Smith, Ibid. p. 211; Miscellany of the Celtic Society, edited by O'Donovan, note, pp. 396–7, Dublin, 1849.)

Colonel Richard Townsend was married, and had issue eight sons and four daughters. Nearly two years after the assault upon his house he died, July, 1692, aged about 84 years, and was buried in Castle Haven churchyard. His will is in the Prerogative Court of the diocese of Ross.

His eldest son, John, had, in 1666, married Lady Catherine Barry, daughter of Richard, second Earl of Barrymore, by the Earl's first wife, Susan, daughter of Sir William Killigrew, knight. John Townsend died before his father, and left a daughter, Susannah. (*See Scull, Cork, the Rev. Richard Townsend*); and a son, Richard Fitz-John (see Colonel Townsend's will), who died after his grandfather's death, a minor, without issue.

Colonel Townsend's second son, Bryan, had, in 1666, been appointed Cornet of Militia Cavalry (see references above to Orrery's State Letters, and Smith's County Cork.) Bryan married, about 1680, Mary, daughter of Edward Synge, Bishop of

Cork, Cloyne, and Ross, and sister of Edward Synge, Archbishop of Tuam.

In the reign of William III. in 1689, Bryan Townsend's name, together with the names of his brothers, Francis and Kingston, appeared in the list of proscribed persons appended to the great Act of Attainder, which was passed by the Irish Parliament under James II. (See the Act, with list, in Archbishop King's "State of the Protestants of Ireland," appendix, p. 348, Cork, 1768; and Macaulay, "History of England," chap. xii. William and Mary, vol. iii. pp. 216–220, London, 1855.) It is not unlikely that Bryan Townsend may have been present at the battle of the Boyne, for we find him at Belfast in 1690, May 21st, only three weeks before the landing of William III. in Ulster, and six weeks before the battle; and in that year he was made Colonel of Militia. (See Diary of Richard Davies, Dean of Cork, edited by Caulfield, Camden Society, p. 115; London, 1857.)

Five years later, in 1695, Colonel Bryan Townsend became Member for Clonakilty in the Irish Parliament. Upon the demise of his nephew, Richard Fitz-John, as above, he inherited the family estates. He had nine sons and five daughters, who have left numerous descendants. And, the male issue of Colonel Bryan Townsend's younger brothers having failed, the Townsends of the county Cork trace their descent from his father, Colonel Richard Townsend, in the *male* line only, through the male issue of Bryan. He died at Castle Townsend in 1726, aged about 78 years, and was buried at Castle Haven.

The Rev. Maurice Fitzgerald Townsend, of Castle Townsend, Vicar of Thornbury, Gloucestershire, is the present head of the family of Townsend in the county of Cork.

See Burke, "Landed Gentry of Great Britain and Ireland," Townsend, of Castle Townsend.

1735. June 13. ISAAC GOLDSMITH, A.M.. V. Holy Trinity, per mortem Philippi Townsend. [D.R.]

Goldsmith was also Dean of Cloyne, q. v.

1740. Sept. 30. "Ordered, that great or loose coats be provided for the bellhours of this parish by the churchwardens thereof. Isaac Goldsmith, Vicar." [Christchurch Vestry Book.]

1769. May 26. WILLIAM PRATT, A.M., V. Holy Trinity, vacant by death of Goldsmith. [D.R.] And also Dean of Cloyne, q. v.

1770. March 28. WILLIAM JEPHSON, A.B., V. Holy Trinity, vacated by death of Pratt. [D.R.] Jephson was also Precentor of Ross, q. v.

1774. August 5. RICHARD PIGOTT, D.D., V. Holy Trinity. [F.F.]

R. Pigott was ordained Deacon in 1752, and Priest on 12th November, 1752, at Cork.

In 1752 he was appointed Reader in Cork Cathedral, and in 1755, April 7, was licensed to the curacy of St. Finbarry.

From 1761 to 1770, he was Vicar Choral of Cork; from 1770 to 1774, P. Lisclery; and from 1774 to 1782, V. Holy Trinity. He died in November, 1782, and was buried in Cork Cathedral.

1782. Nov. 28. ALEXANDER LAMILLIERE, LL.D., V. Holy Trinity. [F.F.] In 1796 he became Archdeacon of Cork, q. v.

In 1782 Dr. Lamilliere resided on White's Quay, Cork. The valuation of his house was £24. [S. Nic. Par. Reg.]

1786. "Paid the bellhours and organ blower, 52 weeks, at 6*s.* 6*d.* per week, £16 18*s.* 0*d.*" "The two bellhours, for attending the churchwardens on their collection, and for distributing the weekly money among the poor, £6 16*s.* 6*d.*" "To advertisements of the time of the patrole, 6*s.* 6*d.*" [Christchurch Vestry Book.]

1796. June 4. WILLIAM NOBLE, V. Christchurch, and R. Killowen. [F.F.]

1804. "Two men attending to ring the bells, &c., at 7*s.* 7*d.* per week, £39 8*s.* 8*d.*"

1805. Nov. 20. "At an adjourned vestry, thanks are voted to Rev. John Quarry, for his "strong and pathetic" charity sermon, whereby the unusually large sum of £184 was collected for the poor of this parish."

1806. April 7. "At a Vestry held in Holy Trinity, &c., thanks are voted to the Rev. Alexander Kennedy, and Rev. Boyle Davies, for their unimpeachable and truly Christian conduct while they have been Curates of this parish; the former, during the period of 21, the latter, 16 years."

"Resolved, also, that a piece of plate, of the value of 50 guineas, be presented to each of these clergymen, with a suitable inscription, as a lasting testimony of the esteem and respect which this Vestry entertain for them."

It was also resolved "that a memorial be presented to the Lord Lieutenant, the Archbishop and Bishop of this diocese, recommending them for promotion." [Vestry Book.]

W. Noble was V. Kinsale from 1780 to 1796, and V. Holy Trinity from 1796 to 1806. He held Killowen from 1796 to 1799.

1806. Sept. 10. JAMES MEARA, A.M., V. Christchurch, vacant by death of Noble. [D.R.]

"1810. 23rd April. £135 17*s.* was paid for taking down part of the steeple of Christchurch."

"Oct. 25, 1810. At an adjourned Vestry it is resolved to 'adjourn the consideration of the erection of a new steeple,' in compliance with the wishes of the majority of the parishioners."

"1816. April 15. £9 2*s.* is voted for washing church linen, and £12 for 4 new surplices; and £34 2*s.* 6*d.* to James Magrath, for singing anthems; £22 15*s.* for sacrament wine; £5 13*s.* 9*d.* for sacrament bread."

"1816. June 3. An annual sum of £50 is voted to each of

the Curates, Alex. Kennedy, and Boyle Davies, as a testimony of respect; but on 17th June, 1816, this is declined by the Curates."

"1822. April 4. Thanks are voted to Miss Sarah French, for her valuable gift of a silver salver for the use of the church." [Vestry Books.]

James Meara was a Scholar of T.C.D. in 1776. He resigned R. Kellistown, in Leighlin, in 1782, and from 1782 to 1823, was P. Aghoure, in Ossory. He also was V. Holy Trinity from 1806 to 1823. And I think he was a Vicar Choral of Tuam, from 1795 to 1812.

He died at Welbrook, co. Kilkenny, in 1823, leaving by his wife, Elisabeth, five sons: Rev. John, James, George, Henry, and Spencer; besides two daughters: Elisabeth, wife of Rev. John Kearney, and Charlotte.

His eldest son, Rev. John Meara, died at Headford, co. Galway, in 1839, leaving issue six daughters.

1824. January 12. JOSHUA BERKELEY, A.M., V. Christchurch. [D.R.]

1824. January 21. The Vestry arrange for a committee, in order to take down and rebuild the church; and on 1st Feb., 1825, they agree to borrow from the Board of First Fruits £13,500 to erect a new church. [Vestry Books.]

Joshua Berkeley (a younger son of Rev. George Berkeley, Vicar Choral of Cork, q. v.) was ordained Deacon at Cloyne, on 24th August, and Priest, at Cork, on September 7, 1800.

He was, on 4th of August, 1801, licensed to the curacy of Carrigaline, and from 1801 to 1825, was R. V. Carrigrohanebeg, in Cloyne. From 1804 to 1825, he was a Vicar Choral, Cork. He died unmarried, on 26th April, 1825.

1825. May 4. CHARLES LESLIE, A.B., Vicar, and in 1844, August 10, Honorary Prebendary of Holy Trinity. [D.R.]

1827. Sept. 10. The Bishop issues a monition to the churchwardens to assess on the parish £3,500 for restoring the church, in consequence of the ruinous state of which the parishioners had been then four years without divine service in the church. [D.R.]

1830. Protestant population, 2,924.

1837. Holy Trinity: a vicarage, with cure, ¼ mile long by ¼ mile broad; gross population, 9,567; two Curates employed, at stipends, to the senior of £75, and to the junior of £50 per annum; from Minister's money, £444; surplice fees, £12 16*s.* 2*d.*; rent of glebe-house, £3 13*s.* 10*d.*, subject to visitation fees, 8*s.*; diocesan schoolmaster, 11*s.* Holy Trinity glebe-house, situate in St. Peter's parish, has been let for the last twenty-nine years, in consequence, as is reported, of its being wholly unfit for the residence of Incumbent from its age and situation; but when, or at what cost, built, unknown. Incumbent is resident in Cork city, though not actually within the benefice, and pays the sum of £52 10*s*. in the way of house-rent. One church, capable of accommodating 2,000 persons, rebuilt in 1828, at a cost of £4,089 18*s*. 5*d*., Brit., raised by parochial assessment. No charge on the parish in 1832 on account of the church. Divine service is celebrated in the church twice on all Sundays, and once on all Tuesdays, Wednesdays, Fridays, and on the principal holidays. Early service is also performed on the third Sunday in each month, and on the three great festivals. The Sacrament is administered thirty-one times in the year. The rectory of the Holy Trinity is appropriated to the prebend of the same name, founded in the Cathedral Church of St. Finbarr's, Cork. [Parl. Rep.]

Charles Leslie (son of John Leslie, of Cork, banker, by Catherine-Mary Hyde) was ordained Deacon on 2nd May, 1819, and Priest on 20th May, 1821, both at Cork.

In 1819, he was appointed Chaplain to the Earl of Donoghmore. He was licensed on 12th Oct., 1819, to the curacy of Blackrock, near Cork, and on 25th September, 1822, to that of the Holy Trinity, which he held until he was appointed Vicar of same place, in 1825.

He died on 8th March, 1846, and bequeathed £50 to the Parochial School, and £10 to the Infant School. His brother, Mathew, of Wilton, co. Cork, was his executor.

1846. April 20. WILLIAM COTTER WILLIAMSON, A.M., Vicar. He was also, in 1846, elected by the Dean and Chapter Honorary Prebendary of the Holy Trinity. [D.R.] Net yearly value, £401 2*s*. [D.R.] In 1861 he became Precentor of Cloyne, q. v.

1853. December 1. JOHN CONNOLLY, A.B., is admitted Vicar, and on 12th April, 1854, is also Honorary Prebendary of the Holy Trinity. The net annual value of the vicarage is £663 1*s*. [D.R.]

1860. The church, &c., in good order; no glebe-house; the Curates are, Gilbert M'Cord and Robert Norcott; divine service twice on all Sundays, and on chief festivals and fasts, and, also on one day in the week, &c., &c. Sacrament twice a month; average of communicants, 118; and at Christmas, 299, and at Easter, 276. There are three schools, (for boys, girls, and infants,) supported by an endowment of £13 16*s*. 11*d*., and by voluntary contributions. Number of children on rolls, 164. Average attendance, 121.

The Protestant population is 1,859.

John Connolly (son of Peter Connolly, esq., by Anne Dowling) was born 3rd Feb., 1806, and was ordained Deacon in 1832. He received Priest's orders at Cloyne, on 14th July, 1833, being then Curate of Curryglass, or Mogeely.

From 1834 to 1848, he was P. C. Tracton, and from 1848 to

1850, Chaplain of Frankfield, near Cork; and from 1850 to 1853, Preacher at Cork Cathedral. He was Chancellor of Cork, from May to December, 1853.

He married, in 1846, Martha, dau. of Rev. John Quarry, LL.D., and has issue one son, John Quarry Connolly, born in 1847.

INCHIGEELAH.

1591. Edmond M'Bryen is Vicar of Inchigeelah. "R. de Inshegewlaughe spectat ad hospit. Morne. Edmundus M'Bryen Vicarius de Inshigulagh deprivatus propter acceptacionem rectoriæ de Mortelstown." [MS. T.C.D. E. 3. 14.] He was also, in 1591, V. Inchinabacky, in Cloyne.

1615. Henry Stone appears as V. Inchigeelah. "Inchigulagh; (residens) Rectoria spectat ad Mourne. Vicarius ibm Henry Stone, minister legens." [R.V. R.I.A.] Stone was also, in 1615, Curate of Kilbrittan and Rathclaren, and Vic. Chor. Cloyne.

1621. Nov. 1. Thomas Holford is admitted V. Inshegulaghe, and on 3rd Nov. is inducted. [R.V. 1634.] In 1637 he became Treasurer of Cloyne, q. v.

1634. R. de Inchogulaghe spectat ad Ab. de Mourne et Antro. Donogh M'Carty ffirmarius. Val. 10 li. per an. Vic. ibm Thomas Holford. Val. 10 li. per an. [R.V. 1634.]

"Thomas Holford, a Reading Minister, noe graduate, and honest by report, hath the vicaridge of Inshegulin in lapse. Val. 10 li." [MS. Probate Court, Dublin.]

1637. Feb. 5. William Dumville, V. Inshegulagh and Clondrohit. [F.F.] Dumville took a degree in T.C.D. in 1637.

1639. "Vacant; William Allen, Curate. Ecclesia bene et ornata." [V.B.]

Perhaps this William Allen was second son of George Allen. If so, he was born at Newcastle, county Limerick, and was educated at Crewkerne, in England. He was a Scholar of T.C.D. on 19 Sept. 1638. [Reg. T.C.D.]

1639 or 1640. Thadeus O'Sheaghan, V. de Inshagulagh. [F.F.]

Thadeus O'Shaughan, or Sheaghan was ordained Priest by the Bishop of Ardfert on 23rd June, 1612. He was admitted V. Dromtariffe, Dryssan, and Cullen, dioc. Ardfert, on 29th August, 1618, ex presentatione Domini Regis Jacobi per litteras patentes 28th August, anno Regni 16°, quas vicarias Rex univit propter tenuitatem fructuum. Inductus est 22nd Sept. 1618. [MS. Consistorial Office, Dublin.]

1663. Sept. 26. George Synge per ltras Dni Regis, studendi gratia, institutus fuit V. de Kilmihill et Inshigula in coll. Epi. [V.B. 1669.] He appears 1663 to 1675. [V.B.] Comes

Cork est Rector. In 1668 Synge was absent *studendi gratia.* [V.B.] In 1674 he was P. Kilbrogan, q. v.

1677. SAMUEL SYNGE, Altera R. V. Inchigulah and Kilmichael, and P. Dromdaleague, q. v.

1679. June 10. CORNELIUS HIGNETT, A.M., V. Inchigulah and Kilmichael, and P. Dromdaleague. [F.F.] In 1706 he became Chancellor of Ross, q. v.

"No Protestants" in this parish in 1699. [V.B. D.D.]

"Oct. 15. 1700. I saw Inchigeelah Church: it is 4 miles to the west of Kilmichael, on the north side of the River Lee, near the river; 'tis about 70 foot long, the walls built with stone and lime are standing uncover'd, the west end hangs over. A good large church-yard, a ditch about it, only three small windows in the church. About 100 plantat. acres of very coarse glebe near the church, belonging to the Incumbent, 'tis set at second-hand for £3 per an. About 23½ plowlands in this parish, the lands westward of ye church are very coarse. These lands are part of the gentry division of the Earl of Clancarty's estate. There were lately 2 or 3 Protestants in this parish, but now there are none. Mr. Brown did preach before the troubles once in three weeks for some time in Mr. Lock's house. Dennis Leary is Popish Priest of this parish, and Kilnemartery, in Cloyne diocese."

"At Gougan Barry, in this parish, lives Dennis Mahony, formerly Priest of this parish, now a hermit, who has built 7 chappels there. He was order'd at Rome to undergo the penance of a hermit, having been guilty of fornication. 'Tis said that St. Finbarry from a cell in this place was remov'd to the bishoprick of Corke. In this parish, 2 miles east of the church, I saw, on the north side of the river Lee, the walls of a church or chappel, call'd Killbarry, the walls built with stone and clay are standing uncover'd. The bounds of the church-yard are discernible; 'tis said to have been a chappel of ease, built by the Learys. This parish was formerly worth £100 per an. now 'tis worth about 40 per an. to the Incumbent. More than half of this parish lies on the north side of the river Lee. There are the ruins of a chappel, call'd Agharus, on the north side of the river, in the north and west corner of this parish, belonging to this parish; but Dean Davies did once pretend it belonged to the diocese of Cloyne, it being mentioned in the Visitation Books of Cloyne. I did not see this chappel. This parish is also called Iveleary, *i.e.* the habitation of the family of the Learys. The Earl of Corke, as Impropriator, has half the tithes of this parish, the Vicar has the other half; the Vicar pays a crown rent of 18s. per an. for this parish. One rectory belonged to the Abbey of Mourne. This parish extends towards the east from the church 3 miles, and towards the west from the church 9 miles." [Downes' Tour.]

1727. Nov. 8. No name appears. [V.B. D.R.]

1727/8. Feb. 1. PETER WATERHOUSE, A.M., R. V. Inchiguilagh and Kilmihill, per mortem naturalem Cornelii Hignett. [D.R.]

He was collated a second time, 31st January, 1732, on becoming Precentor of Cork, q. v.

1750. April 19. PATRICK ELMSLEY, A.M., R. V. Inchigeelah and Kilmichael. [F.F.] Both vacant, per death of Peter Waterhouse. [D.R.]

1750. July 14. The Bishop consents to a memorial for the erection of a glebe-house at Inchigeelah. [D.R.]

Patrick Elmsley was from 1746 to 1749, V. Kilcaskin, Ross; from 1749 to 1750, R. Macloneigh; and from 1750 until his death in 1755 he was R. V. Inchigeelah and Kilmichael.

He does not appear elsewhere in Cork Records. I find among the Cloyne marriage bonds, one for the marriage of Patrick Elmsley, of Crossduff, with Rebecca Sewell, of Kilnemartery, dated in 1757. This might have been a son of Rev. P. Elmsley.

1755. March 18. JOHN BAILY, A.B., R. V. Inshigeelagh. [F.F.] By death of Patrick Elmsley. [D.R.]

1755. August 19. A commission issues (to view the house and offices erected on glebe by late Pat. Elmsley), at request of Francis Elmsley and Thomas Wallis, the executors of Rev. Pat. Elmsley. The return is dated Sept. 22, 1755, and finds £248 18*s*. 1½*d*. to have been the value of the house, &c. when finished; and £218 3*s*. 9*d*. to be the present value; £30 14*s*. 4*d*. being sufficient to put them in as good repair as they were when first completed. According to the detailed account the stone work of the house cost 3*s*. 8*d*. per perch; roofing, 30*s*. per square; slating and rendering, 14*s*. per square; flooring, 30*s*. per square; flagging, 2*s*. 8*d*. per yard. And the stone work of the out-offices, cost 3*s*. 6*d*. per perch; roofing, 20*s*.; and slating, 12*s*. a square. [D.R.]

John (son of Theodore Baily, Medici), was born at Bandon, and when nineteen years old obtained Sizarship, T.C.D. on 28th May, 1718. He afterwards graduated A.B.

He was ordained Deacon at Cloyne on 23rd Sept. 1728. In 1733 he was Curate of Christchurch, Cork, which post he held until 1752, and perhaps longer. From 1743 to 1755 he was R. V. Kilcully.

He married Mary ——? and by her had a son, Theodosius Baily. He left, by his will (dated 24th April, 1773), to his kinsman, John Nash, esq. of Brinny, a silver snuff-box, presented to him with his freedom by the Provost and Corporation of Bandon, on account of a sermon preached before them on 23rd October, 1763.

1773. April 28. EDWARD WEEKS, A.B., R. V. Inshigeelagh [F.F.], per mort. John Baily. [D.R.]

He became in 1791 P. Kilbrittain, q. v.

1791. Feb. 26. GEORGE SEALY, A.M., R. V. Inchigeelah. [F.F.]

In 1794 Sealy became also R. S. Paul's, q. v.

1830. Protestant population, 54.

1837. Inchigeelah, a vicarage, with cure, 6 miles long by 9 broad, containing 40,000A. Gross population, 5,783. One Curate employed, at an annual stipend of £18, with the use of the glebe-house and glebe of 242A. Tithe composition, £400; 242A. of glebe, valued at an entire sum of £80; subject to visitation fees, and diocesan schoolmaster, £2 10*s*. Inchigeelah glebe-house, built under the old Acts, about a century since, but at what cost unknown; the present Incumbent was not chargeable with the payment of any sum to his predecessor, neither has he any demand against his successor, although he expended £36 18*s*. 5½*d*. Brit., in covering the offices with slate, instead of thatch. Incumbent is non-resident, being incapaciated by age and infirmities from discharging duties; he resides in Bath. One church, capable of accommodating 100 persons, built in 1814, by means of a loan of £230 15*s*. 4¾*d*. Brit., granted by the late Board of First Fruits; of which loan there remained £109 16*s*. chargeable on the parish in 1832, repayable by annual instalments of £6 10*s*. Divine service is celebrated twice on Sundays, from March to September, and once during the remainder of the year, and on the festivals. The sacrament is administered monthly and on the three great festivals. The rectorial tithes of this parish, compounded for £125 5*s*. 11*d*. are impropriate, and belong to the Duke of Devonshire. [Parl. Rep.]

1838. June 7. JOHN TORRENS KYLE, A.B., R. V. Inchigeelah, per mortem Sealy. [D.R.]

In 1839 he became R. Clondrohid, Cloyne, q. v.

1839. April 11. HENRY SWANZY, A.M., R. V. Inchigeelah; certified under £400. [D.R.] In 1849 he became R. V. Kilshannig, Cloyne, q. v.

1840. May 14. HENRY EVANS SADLIER, A.M., R. V. Inchigeelah. [D.R.] In 1849 he became P. Ballyhay, Cloyne, q. v.

1847. Nov. 27. The old glebe-house and offices were condemned. [D.R.]

1849. June 14. JAMES WHITE, A.B., R. V. Inchigeelah. Annual value, £379. [D.R.]

1859. Dec. 20. The Bishop certified a charge of £647 1*s*. for a new glebe-house. The old one to be taken down. [D.R.]

1860. The church, &c., and glebe-house, in good order; 240A. of glebe, of which 23 are in the Rector's occupation. Divine service twice on all Sundays, and once on the usual holidays, &c. Sacrament monthly; average of communicants, 8; and on festivals, average 10. 11 children attend a school taught by a Protestant mistress, and maintained by aid of

Church Education Society. The Protestant population is 57. The rentcharge is £300, and the land is worth £80. Total value of benefice, £380 per annum and residence.

James White was ordained Deacon on 21st December, 1823, and Priest on 10th April, 1825, both at Cloyne.

In 1824 he was Reader at St. Finbarry's, Cork, and from 1827 to 1848 he was P. C. Fermoy.

He married, in 1837, Anne Letitia Purcell, of Charleville.

INNISHANNON.

1291. "Eccia de Ymsogenan XVmr." [Tax. P. Nic.]

1542. "Philippus Barry ocke meæ nacōis capitaneus et dnus de Kinelega ac verus patronus Ecclīæ parochialis de Ynyssonan Corcag. dioc. cum consensu omnium fratrum" grants to Patrick Myaghe, and his heirs, besides other things, the advowson of the parish church of Innishannon. This deed is dated 15th Oct. 33 Hen. VIII. [D.R.]

1580. May 14. Alexander Meaghe, or Meade, adm. R. Innishonane. "Rectoria simplex de Inishohnan Corcagen. dioc. concessa est per presentationem patroni et admissionem Epi, facta unione de eadam Rectoriæ simplici de Rinrone quam possidet et tenet Alexander Meaghe ad vitam tantum dicti Alexandri, cui etiam dispensatio de non premovendo et de non residendo per quinquenium de consensu et assensu decani et capituli concessa est Corcagiæ 14 Maij, 1580." [D.R.]

1591. Alexander Meagh, R. de Innishannon, "propter acceptacionem Rectoriæ Insulæ parvæ deprivatus." V. Innishonane, John Nashe, who is also V. Kinsale. [MS. T.C.D. E. 3. 14.] In another part of this MS. Innishannon is said to be "sequestr. pro primitiis Regineis." [R.V. R.I.A.]

1594. June 22. Richard Gibbons is presented to the Rectory and Vicarage, or entire Rectory of Inishonane, dioc. Cork, [Lib. Mun.] in the gift of the Crown by devolved right seu quocunque alio modo de jure, &c. [Pat. Rot. Chanc.] Gibbons does not appear elsewhere.

1615. George Lee (Dean of Cork, q. v.) is R. and V. Inishonan. "Curatus Michael May, minister legens. Ecclesia et cancella repantur." [R.V. R.I.A]

1627. Feb. 28. Joseph Travers, R. V. Innishonane. [F.F.] He was inducted on 24th March, 1632, and instituted on 25th Oct. 1629, according to the Royal Visitation of 1634, but there is some evident confusion as to the dates. In 1635 Travers became Chancellor of Cloyne, q. v.

1634. R. V. Inishonan, Joseph Travers. Val. 60 li. per an. Patronus, Pat. Meagh de Kinsale. [R.V. 1634.] Particula de

Skenavisse spectat partim ad Rect. de Inishonane et partim ad mensam Episcopi. [R.V. 1634.]

1635. August 3. GEORGE HALLYM, R. V. Innishonane. [F.F.] Hallym does not appear elsewhere.

1638. April 28. JOHN HALL, R. V. Innishonane. [F.F.] He became, in 1639, P. Cahirlag, q. v.

He appears in V. B. of 1639, with Antony Hutchins as Curate. "Ecclia bene, desunt ornamenta.'" [V.B.]

1640. August 24. THOMAS FRITH, admissus ad Rectoriam et Vicariam unitam de Inishonane. [F.F.] He was also Archdeacon of Ross, q. v.

1662. Feb. 6. JOHN BUTLER, R. V. Inishonane, [F.F.] on letters patent, dated 29th June. [Lib. Mun.] He was also P. Kilbrittain, q. v.

1666. Vacant, with a stroke through the name of Mr. JOHN BUTLER. [V.B. D.R.]

1667. June 29. JOHN MOORE, P. Kilbrittain, R. V. Innishonan, R. Ballymartle, Templemichael de Duagh, and Leighmoney, and V. Ballyfiard. [F.F.] To Innishannon, &c. "in presentatione regis eo quod Meed patronus est Papista." [D.R.] On letters patent from crown. [Lib. Mun.]

He appears as Rector 1667 to 1691, and as Vicar 1667 to 1702. [V.B. D.R.] John Moore, senior, was Archdeacon of Cloyne, q. v.

1692. Sept. 1. FRANCIS MOORE, A.M., R. Innishannon and Leighmoney, per resignation of John Moore. [D.R.] On letters patent, dated 5th May, 1692. [Lib. Mun.] He was son of his predecessor. [P.P.]

He appears 1692 to 1728 as *Rector*. [V.B. D.R.]

1699. Innishannon. Sermon every Sunday. Sacrament 4 times a-year. Above 20 families of Protestants in this and Lifeny and Templemichael. The church is in good repair. [V.B. D.R. D.D.] At Leighmony is this entry: No churchwardens or parish clerk. 4 plowlands. The Protestants go to Innishonane. [V.B. D.D. 1699.]

Francis Moore (son of John, Archdeacon of Cloyne), was born in the Queen's county, and on 19th January, 1682/3, he became a Pensioner of T.C.D. He was R. Innishannon and Leighmoney from 1692 to 1728. He was also, from 1693 to 1704, R. Templemichael de Duagh.

He had by his wife, Catherine —— ? two daughters, Katherine, wife of William Caulfield, Lieutenant-Governor of Inverness during the late attempt of the Pretender; and Elisabeth, wife of Robert Percy, esq. of Snugborough, county Wicklow.

1702. July 21. JOHN MOORE, jun. A.M., *Vicar* Inishonan, per resignation of John Moore, sen. [D.R.] In 1711 John Moore, jun. became Treasurer of Cork, q. v.

1729. Oct. 30. JOHN MOORE, *Rector* Innishannone and R. Leighmoney, per mort. Francis Moore. On letters patent, dated Sept. 18. [D.R. and Lib. Mun.]

He appears as Vicar 1702 to 1738, and as Rector 1729 to 1749. [V.B. D.R.] He was the Treasurer of Cork, q. v.

1737. John Moore, Vicar of Innoshonane, and the Bishop of Cork, submit their claims to the rectorial part of the tythes of Skemanisk to the award of the Vicar-General, Thomas Russell, and the Registrar, Thomas Weeks, who award the Vicar the possession of the tythes, on payment of an annual head-rent to the Bishop of ten shillings. [D.R.]

1739. July 4. CHARLES MOORE, A.B., V. Inishonan and Leighmony, per resignation of John Moore. [D.R.]

In 1739 the Rectory and Vicarage of Inishonane were consolidated by the Archbishop of Cashel, and in same year the R. and V. of Leighmony were also consolidated. [D.R.]

Charles Moore, A.B., son of Rev. John Moore, Treasurer of Cork, was born 1717, and entered T.C.D in 1734. He was ordained Deacon on 24th July, 1737, and Priest on 8th Oct. 1738, both at Cork.

In 1739 he became V. Innishannon and R. V. Leighmony; the Rectory of Innishannon being afterwards consolidated with the Vicarage. He became also, in 1746, R. Templemichael de Duagh, and retained all the said livings until his death, in 1753.

He married Mary (dau. of Colonel Christopher Rogers, of Lota, by Martha, dau. of Quentin Osborne), and by her left issue three daughters, Martha, Anna-Maria, and Katherine. His will was dated 21st Nov. and proved 21st Dec. 1753. Catherine married, in 1766, on 3rd April, Robert Waller, esq. M.P. for Dundalk; and Martha married Edward Wilmot, esq. ancestor of Wilmot Chetwode, esq. of Woodbrook, Portarlington.

1754. Rectory and Vicarage vacant. [V.B. D.R.]

1755. June 27. ST. JOHN BROWNE, LL.D., is presented to R. V. Innishannon and Leighmoney. [Lib. Mun.] And on July 10 receives a second patent, occasioned by the misnaming Charles Moore (deceased), John Moore in the former patent. [Lib. Mun.] 1760. Sept. 3. By the King's command, Dr. St. John Browne is removed from Innishonane, and re-admitted, on presentation of Francis Kearney, by the Archbishop of Cashel. [D.R.]

Browne was also P. Kilbrogan, q. v.

1760. Feb. 20. Rev. Peter Cortez (who, on the 16th, had taken the necessary oaths, &c.), is licensed by the Bishop to read service in French, preach, and administer the sacraments (according to ye use of the Church of Ireland, and no other) in ye parish church of Inishonane, or wherever else may be appointed for the said French congregation to assemble. [D.R.]

1796. June 18. FORSTER ARCHER, A.B., R. V. Innishannone and Leighmoney, *vice* St. John Browne. [Lib. Mun.]

Forster Archer was ordained Deacon at Cork on 3rd Nov. 1782, and Priest on 5th Dec. 1784, at Cloyne.

In 1782 he was licensed Curate of St. Anne Shandon. He had been partner in a newspaper, and was made Inspector of Prisons by the Government.

1796. July 29. RICHARD MEADE, A.B., R. and V. Innishonane. [F.F.] On presentation of James Kearney, esq. [D.R.]

Richard Meade was, I think, ordained Deacon on 5th Oct. 1777, and Priest on 9th November, 1780, both at Cork. In 1787 he was licensed Curate of St. Paul's.

From 1792 to 1799 he was R. Garryvoe, and from 1796 to 1808 he was R. V. Innishannon.

He married Mary, dau. of JOHN, twenty-fifth BARON KINGSALE, and by her had issue, Rev. Thomas Meade (R. Templetrine, q. v.); Rev. William Meade (V. Fanlobbus, q. v.); and Major-General Frederick Meade, of Belmont. Another son, Michael de Courcy Meade, of the 39th Regiment, was killed at the battle of Vittoria. I think that the following were also children of the above Rev. Richard Meade, namely, "James, third son, and Martha, eldest daughter, of Rev. Richard Meade, of Taxax," who are named in the will (made 1784, and proved 1789), of Catherine Meade, widow of David Meade, of Kinsale, esq.

1808. April 21. THOMAS MEADE, A.B., R. V. Innishannon. [F.F.] On presentation of James Kearney, esq. and on resignation of Richard Meade [D.R.], his father.

Thomas Meade, on 4th July, 1837, became R. Templetrine, q. v.

1830. Protestant population, 438.

1837. Innishannon, a rectory, with cure, 4 miles long by 3 broad, containing 6,678 acres. Gross population, 3,840. No Curate employed. Tithe composition, £632 6*s.* 1¾*d.* Subject to visitation fees, £1 8*s.* 6*d.* Diocesan schoolmaster, £1 5*s.* 10*d.* No glebe-house. Incumbent is resident; and pays an annual rent of £42 for the house in his occupation. One church, capable of accommodating 250 persons, but when, or at what cost, built, unknown. It was partially rebuilt in 1761, at an expense of about £184 12*s.* 3¾*d.* British, raised by subscriptions. No charge on the parish in 1832 on account of the church. Divine service is celebrated twice on all Sundays, and once on the festivals. The sacrament is administered monthly. The benefice is a rectory. [Parl. Rep.]

1837. July 4. JOHN ROGERSON COTTER, A.M., R. V. Innishannon, on presentation of John Cuthbert Kearney, esq. [D.R.]

J. R. Cotter (second son of Sir James Laurance Cotter, by Isabella, widow of George Brereton), was ordained Deacon on

20th June, 1813, at Cork, and Priest on 15th Oct. 1815, at Cloyne.

He was, from 1818 to 1837, R. Templetrine; and from 1837 to 1847 R. V. Innishannon. He died on 18th April, 1847. He married, firstly, Ellen, dau. of Rev. Robert Scott, of Dublin; secondly, Ellen, dau. of Rev. Thomas Hoare, of Castletown, Cloyne; and thirdly, in 1825, Caroline, dau. of Sir Robert Shaw, bart.

1847. Sept. 8. ROBERT HEDGES MAUNSELL EYRE, A.B., R. V. Innishannon, on presentation of John Cuthbert Kearney, esq. Aug. 9th, 1847. [D.R.] Annual value, £474.

1856. July 17. A new church, on new site, was consecrated by name of Christchurch. [D.R.]

1860. R. H. M. Eyre, Incumbent; Alexander Waring, Curate. Church, &c. in order. No glebe-house. No glebe. Divine service twice on all Sundays, and once on chief feasts, &c. Sacrament monthly, and at festivals; average of communicants, 45. 30 boys and 22 girls are on the rolls of male and female schools under the Board of Erasmus Smith. General and Mrs. Meade support an infant school, with 20 children on rolls. The Protestant population is 465. The rentcharge is £474 5*s.* 7*d.*

R. H. M. Eyre, eldest son of Richard Maunsell, esq. by Lady Catherine Hare, took the name of Eyre in compliance with the will of his grand-uncle, ROBERT HEDGES EYRE, esq. *Vide* Burke's L. G.—*article*, EYRE, of Galway.

He was educated at the Luxemburgh School, Dublin, and is a Graduate of T.C.D.

He was ordained Deacon in 1834 by the Bishop of Limerick, for the Curacy of Ballingarry.

He married in 1836 Anna-Maria, eldest dau. of Eyre Evans, esq. of Ash Hill Towers, county Limerick, and has issue five sons and six daughters.

INSKENNY.

1291. "Eccia de Balymolunthil, VImr." [Tax. P. Nic.]

1579. July 2. MAGISTER JOHANNES DONALDUS CORMACUS was appointed Vicar of Inskenny. "Vicaria perpetua de Inskynny, Corkagen dioc. concessa est, per collacionem Epi, M. Joanni Donaldo Cormaco, cum dispensacione de non residendo et de non premovendo per quinquenium, modo dicta ecclesia non defraudetur interim debitis obsequiis, secundo die July, 1579. Inductus est quasi in pōem, 23 die ejusdem. Phil. Goldeus Registrarius." [D.R.]

1581. April 23. RURICUS O'FLYNN is admitted V. Inskenny.

"Vicariam perpetuam Ecclię parochialis et prebendalis St. Jacobi de Inskynny Corcagen. dioc. contulit Matheus Epūs domino Rurico Offlynn presbitero, nulla mentione facta pluralitatis unionis aut alicujus . . . dispensationis, 23 Aprilis, 1581. Inductus est per Archidiaconum, 24° ejusdem mensis." [D.R.] In 1591. Ruricus or Rory Flyn appears as V. Kilbrogan, q. v.

1591. RICHARD SKIDDY (or as in another MS. SKEDDIE) appears as Preb. Inskyny et Vic. St. Barry. [MS. T.C.D. E. 3. 14.]

In another part of this MS. "Rectoria integra de Inskiny que prebenda est, Richd. Skiddy—Vic ibm idem Skiddy exhibuit titulos. Per unionem, deliberand." [R.V. R.I.A.] Skiddy was also a Vicar Choral of Cork.

1615. JOHN BROCK, A.M., Treasurer and Vic. Choral, Cork, is also Preb. de Inskyne, *vide* Treasurership of Cork.

1615. Ballemolemihill; cur. residens Johēs Brock inservit curæ; Ecclesia et cancella in ruinis. [R.V. R.I.A.]

1618. Dec. 1. THOMAS DAVIES is admitted P. de Ballemolemihill als Inskeny, cui prebendæ Epūs univit R. de Dromie als Kilnamarterie, Cloine, et Arnigihie, et V. de Mall als Aglis, Cork. Installed into the Prebend 30th Dec., 1618. [R.V. 1634.]

In 1634, P. Inskeny, Thomas Davies, val. 14 li. per an. [Ib.]

Thomas Davies was ordained Deacon and Priest by "ffranciscum Landanen. Epum," on 30th March, 1602.

From 1610 to 1637, he was R. Garryvoe and Killowen. In 1612, he was Vicar Choral of Cloyne. From 1612 to 1634, he was V. Garrycloyne. From 1615 to 1634, he was V. Aglish and Ardnegihy. From 1618 to 1637, he was P. Inskenny, and from 1618 to 1634, R. Kilnemartery. From 1632 to 1634, he was R. Templensky. From 1623 to 1637, he was V. Cartrachore, in Cloyne, and in 1615 appears also as Curate of Desertmore.

1637. December 21. JAMES BRUCE, P. Inniskenny. [F.F.] He appears in V. B. 1639, with ANTHONY HUTCHINS, as Curate. "Ecclia bene." [V.B. 1639.] Hutchins was also Curate of Innishannon. In 1662, Bruce became R. Dungourney, Cloyne, q. v.

1640. August 16. THOMAS ROBERTS, Preb. Inskenny. [F.F.] He was, in 1661, Chancellor of Cork, q. v.

He was plundered in 1641 of property to the amount of £275, and his living, worth £160 per an. [MS. T.C.D. F. 2. 17.]

1661. THOMAS GOODMAN, A.M., appears as Preb. Inskenny. [V.B.] In 1675 he became Precentor of Ross.

1666. "Vacant," the name THOMAS GOODMAN being crossed out. HUGO SCAMP is Curate. [V.B.]

1667. May 5. JOHN WEBB, P. de Inskinny, per resignation of Thos. Goodman. [V.B. 1669.] Webb, in 1668, became also Chancellor of Cloyne, q. v.

He appears 1667 to 1670. [V.B.]

1671. July 31. ISAAC MANSFIELD, P. de Inskenny. [F.F.]
He appears in 1671 and 1672. [V.B. D.R.] He again appears in 1676.

1674. June 6. ROWLAND DAVIES, P. Inskenny, and R. Mogeesha, V. Carrigtowil cum Kilcurfin, V. Clonmell, and Templerobin. [F.F.] He appears 1674 and 1675. [V.B. D.R.] He was afterwards Dean of Cork, q. v.

1676. Nov. 5. ISAAC MANSFIELD, P. Inskenny. [F.F.]
He appears 1677 to 1688. [V.B. D.R.]

The Bishop, on Nov. 4, 1687, admonished Mansfield, Preb. of Inskenny, Rector of Ballymoney, Vicar of Kinneigh, and Vicar of Fanlobish, to use all diligence "in supplendis respective suis curis." [Addenda to V.B. 1687. D.R.]

Isaac Mansfield, son of William Mansfield, was born in Middlesex, and entered T.C.D. on 10th August, 1666, being then twenty years of age, and in 1667 was elected Scholar. From 1671 to 1682, he was R. Bohillane and Kilmahon, Cloyne. From 1673 to 1674, V. Grenagh, Cloyne. From 1674 to 1688, R. Ballymoney, and V. Fanlobbus and Kinneigh. He held, also, the P. Inskenny from 1671 to 1674, and again from 1676 to 1688. He died in 1688.

1688/9. January 26. JOHN TOM, A.M., P. Inskenny, per mortem Isaac Mansfield. [D.R.] He appears, 1689 to 1692. [V.B. D.R.]

In 1693 Tom became P. Desertmore, q. v.

1693/4. January 9. THOMAS MEADE, A.M., P. Inskenny, per cession of John Tom. [D.R.] He appears, 1694 to 1709. [V.B. D.R.]
In 1704 he was Proctor "Cleri Ross" to Convocation.

"June 1702. Inskeny. The church stood on the left hand of the road as you go from Corke to Bandon, about 3 miles distant from Corke. The walls are standing for the most part, but are very bad; they will be of no use; there is no part of the roof standing. This church was in repair, and divine service in it about 40 years ago. About 9 plowlands in this parish; the prebend is worth about £40 per an. Six acres of glebe near the church belong'd formerly to the Prebendary, 'tis now swallowed up by Mr. Finch, of London, landlord of the adjacent land; 'tis said, 2 acres more, at some distance, belong'd to ye Prebendary, and are now conceal'd. Mr. Piggot's house and Richbilstown are in this parish; Mr. Steadfast lives in it also. Inskeny church is about 2 miles distant from the church of Ballinebuy. There is another place on the east side of this parish, where the Irish bury sometimes their dead." [Downes' Tour.]

Thomas Meade (son of William "generosi") was born in co. Cork; and, when sixteen years of age, entered T.C.D. as Pensioner, on 14th May, 1669. He was Scholar in 1672, and was afterwards A.M. and D.D.

In 1676 he was R. Dunderrow, in 1679, R. Kilmaloda, in Ross, and R. Ballymartle. In 1682 he became R. Rincurran and Taxax, and in 1693, P. Inskenny. All these six livings he held until his death, in 1710. He married, in 1687, Jane Edwards, of Shandon. His will was dated 16th May, and proved 3rd August, 1710. In it he mentions a son, William, and a daughter, Elizabeth, both younger children, besides another daughter, Margaret, wife of a "reverend good clergyman." He left the Rev. George Synge his executor. Synge was R. Taxax, and was his son-in-law.

1710. July 11. BOYLE DAVIES, A.M., P. Inskenny. [F.F.] In 1717/8 he took a second collation. [D.R.]

In 1735 he became P. Lisclery, q. v.

1735. August 23. HART SMITH, A.M., P. Inskenny. [D.R.] He was also Treasurer of Ross, q. v.

1761. May 6. EDWARD KENNY, A.B., P. Inskenny, vacant by the death of Hart Smith. [D.R.]

1808. The union, formed by the Bishop in 1768, consists of P. Inskenny, R. V. Moviddy, V. Kilbonane (R. imp.), and V. Aglish; one rectory of Aglish being impropriate, and the other belonging to Kilbrogan. Kenny holds, also, Templetrine by faculty. [Rep.]

Edward Kenny (son of John Kenny "generosi") was born in co. Cork, and entered T.C.D. as Pensioner, when sixteen years old, on 4th June, 1745, and became a Scholar in 1748.

He was ordained Deacon on 21st April, and Priest on 2nd June, 1751.

In 1751 he was Curate of Kilbrittain, and in 1752, of Knockavilly. From 1757 to 1761 he was Vicar Choral, Cork; and in 1761 became P. Inskenny; in 1768, R. V. Moviddy, Kilbonane, and Aglish; and in 1769, R. Templetrine; all which he held until his death, in 1818. He also held R. V. Kilmichael from 1762 to 1777.

He died 23rd April, 1818, *unmarried*, and bequeathed £10 to the poor of Moviddy parish.

1818. May 30. WILLIAM MEADE, A.B., P. Inskenny. Certified under £300. [D.R.] In 1831 he became V. Fanlobbus, q. v.

1830. Protestant population, 75.

1831. Dec. 9. RICHARD LEE, A.M., P. Inskenny, certified to be under £500. [D.R.]

1837. Inskenny: a rectory, with cure; 3½ miles long by 3 broad, containing 3,810A.; gross population, 1,290; one Curate employed, at a stipend of £75 per annum; tithe composition, £369 4s. 7½d., subject to visitation fees, 6s.; Diocesan schoolmaster, 15s.; no glebe-house; Incumbent is non-resident, from inability of procuring suitable accommodation; he resides in the city of Cork, within two miles of his benefice; one church, capable of accommodating 100 persons, built in 1805, by means of a loan of £553 16*s.* 11*d.* Brit., granted by the late Board of First Fruits; no charge on the parish in 1832 on account of the church; divine service is celebrated once on all Sundays and on the principal festivals; the sacrament is administered monthly and on the great festivals; the benefice is a rectory; there is no revenue attached to this prebend exclusive of the benefice; the Prebendary, as such, has no duties except preaching three or four times a year in the cathedral. [Parl. Rep.]

Richard Lee was ordained Deacon on 10th Feb., 1811, and Priest on 29th September same year, both at Cork. He was licensed Curate of St. Ann, Shandon, in 1811; and from 1831 to his death, on 26th Nov., 1853, was P. Inskenny. He married Ann Lawless, of Cloyne, and had issue four sons, Paul-Giles, John, Richard-Thomas, and James.

1854. January 3. WILLIAM SHERRARD, A.B., P. Inchonny. Net value per an., £248 3*s.* 7*d.* [D.R.]

1860. The church is considered unfit to be repaired, and requires to be rebuilt; no glebe-house; no glebe; divine service twice on Sundays during summer, once in winter, and on usual holidays; sacrament monthly, and at the great feasts; average of communicants, 13; seventeen children are on the rolls of a Church Education school; the Protestant population is 97; the value of this benefice is £276 18*s.* 5*d.* per annum (rentcharge) *without* residence.

William Sherrard was ordained Deacon on 13th October, 1833, at Cork, and Priest, at Cloyne, on 13th April, 1834. He was, in 1834, licensed Curate of Ballymoney.

KILBONANE.

1582. July 30. DOMINUS JOHANNES BRETHNAGH is admitted V. Kilbonane.

"Epus contulit vicariam ecclesiæ parochialis Stæ Marie de Kilbonneayn Corck. dioc. domino Johanni Brethnagh, presbitero, 30° Julii, 1582. Inductus est quasi in pōem 26° Augusti. Phil Goldeus Registrarius." [D.R.] Brethnagh was Vicar of Scull, in 1581.

1591. RURICUS O'FLYNN appears as V. Kilbonane. "R. de Kilvoynan spectat ad Abb. de Grayne. Vicarius Roricus o'flin." [MS. T.C.D. E. 3. 14.] In 1591 he was deprived of Knockavilly Rectory for accepting this benefice. He was also V. Kilbrogan.

1615. THOMAS BOURDEN appears as Vicar of Kilbonane. "Kilvoynan residens. Rectoria spectat ad Grany. Capt. Tent firmarius. Vicarius ibm Thomas Bourden, minister legens et inserviens curæ. Val. 50s. per an. Ecclesia et cancella in ruinis." [R.V. R.I.A.]

1634. R. de Kilvoynane spectat ad Abb. de Grany. Cormack Donogh Carty est firmarius. Val. £6 6s. 8d. per an. Vicarius ibm Thomas Burden, predicator. Val. £6 6s. 8d. per an. [R.V. 1634.]

In 1639 Burden is still Vicar. "Ecclesia bene. Hewne O'Harrylan et Eman. O'Gare detinent ornamenta." [V.B. 1639.]

Thomas Burden, "studiosus," was ordained Deacon and Priest by Miler, Archbishop of Cashel, on 12th May, 1606.

From 1615 to 1618 he appears as Vicar of Holy Trinity, and from 1618 to 1621 as P. Kilmaclenine, Cloyne. He also was from 1615 to 1634, R. Insulæ parvæ. He took a degree in T.C.D. in 1618.

1663 to 1833. Kilbonane was held with Aglish, q. v.

1830. Protestant population, 53.

1833. March 25. EDWARD WEBBER WARREN, A.B., V. Kilbonane, certified under £300 per an. [D.R.]

1833. April 19. The parlour of the Vicar's house, at Agharloe, was licensed for divine service. [D.R.]

E. W. Warren was 5th son of SIR ROBERT WARREN. *Vide* Burke's Baronetage.

He was ordained Deacon at Cork, on 29th Sept. 1796, and Priest at Cloyne, on 13th November of same year. He was Curate of Templemartin in 1796. He died on 20th September, 1833, leaving an only son, Robert, and a daughter, Mary-Augusta.

1833. Oct. 25. WILLIAM RUXTON NASH, A.M., V. Kilbonane. [D.R.] Nash seems to have been always non-resident. He got three years' licence for non-residence on May 1, 1834, and this was renewed from time to time, until 1856. [D.R.]

1837. Kilbonane, a rectory and vicarage, with cure, 2½ miles long by 2 broad, containing 4,910A. Gross population, 1,740. One Curate employed, at a stipend of £75 per annum. Tithe composition, £352 3s. 9d.; 9A. of glebe, let at an annual rent of £9; subject to visitation fees, 7s. 6d.; diocesan schoolmaster, 10s. No glebe-house. Incumbent is non-resident, by licence of the diocesan, in consequence of ill-health; he resides at present at Cove, but generally at Blackrock, in the county of Cork. One church, capable of accommodating eighty persons, built in 1834, at a cost of £150 Brit.; whereof £75 was contributed by Incumbent, and £75 raised by subscriptions. Divine service is celebrated once on all Sundays, and on Christmas Day, Ash Wednesday, and Good Friday. The sacrament is administered nine times in the year. The church in this parish, in which there never had been one until 1834, is reported to be in want of many necessaries to complete it. The benefice is a rectory. [Parl. Rep.]

1844. April 30. The new church, on new site, was consecrated under the name of St. Mark. [D.R.]

W. R. Nash (grandson of Rev. W. Nash, P. Brigowne, Cloyne, q. v.), was son of William Nash, esq. by Amelia Spread. He was ordained Deacon on 15th October, 1815, and Priest on 14th September, 1817, both at Cloyne.

In 1817 he was Curate of St. Peter's, Cork, and in 1830 was Thresher's Lecturer. In August, 1833, he became V. Kilcaskin, Ross, which he resigned in a few months for Kilbonane. He married —— ? dau. of Henry Milward, of Cork, and relict of —— Nash, esq. He died in 1856.

1857. Dec. 23. BRODRICK TUCKEY, A.B., V. Kilbonane, certified to be of the net value of £299 *5s.* *3d.* per an. [D.R.]

1860. The church in good order. No glebe-house; 9A. of glebe in Vicar's use. Divine service twice on all Sundays and once on the usual holidays. Sacrament monthly; average of communicants, 9. 15 children attend a Church Education school. The Protestant population is 59. The rentcharge is £274 *2s.* *9d.*, and the land is worth £7. Total value, £281 *2s.* *9d.* without residence.

Brodrick Tuckey (eldest son of Rev. Thomas Tuckey, P. Dromdaleague), was ordained Deacon on 19th September, 1841, at Cork. He was Curate of this parish in 1854.

KILBRITTAIN.

1579. Mr. PHILIP GOULD appears as P. Kilbrittain in a document wherein Mathew, "Busshopp" of Cork and Cloyne, gives sentence in a dispute between Mr. Philipp Goulde, Prebendary of Kilbrittain, and a person, name illegible, "of Ballincoursay, in the county of Cork, gent." concerning the tithes of the "westerne half of Kylshenygyn." Date "consecrationis meæ Septimo." (A.D. 1579.) [Roch MSS. Brit. Mus. 19, 868.]

1591. E. de Kilbrittain et Kilshiniham, prebenda nata, Phil. Golde. [MS. T.C.D. E. 3. 14.] Gold was also Archdeacon of Cork, q. v.

1615. EDWARD BECHER appears as Prebendary, and Henry Stone as Curate of Kilbrittain. "Kilbrittan prebenda, Edward Becher, studendi gratia. Val. 4 li. Curatus Henricus Stone minister legens. Ecclesia et cancella repantur. Becher tenet etiam R. de Knocknevilly. Val. 10 li. Henry Stone inservit curæ. [R.V. R.I.A.] Stone was V. Inchigeelagh, q. v.

1617. March 16. JOHN BRADISHE, P. Kilbrittain, and R. V. Knockavilly. [F.F.] On letters patent, dated Feb. 27. [Lib. Mun.]

Bradishe, in 1610, was appointed V. Moyeleggy als Modeligo, and V. Kilmolash, Lismore; and in 1617 he was made P. Modeligo, and also P. Kilbrittain, &c. He vacated the P. Modeligo in 1620. In 1617 he took a degree in T.C.D.

1627. Oct. 12. JOHN POWELL, P. de Kilbrittain. [F.F.]

He appears in 1634 as P. Kilbrittain, "Predicator." [R.V. 1634.]

John Powell was ordained Deacon on 4th June, and Priest on 24th December, 1626, by "Theophilum Epūm Landanen." From 1627 to 1638 he seems to have been P. Kilbrittain. In 1628 he was made Vicar Choral, Cork; in 1630 V. Clonfert, Cloyne; in 1632 V. Kilmeen, Ardfert; and in 1634, Vicar Choral, Ross.

In 1642 Powell depones to the loss of £250 by the rebellion, besides the loss of his living, worth, *communibus annis*, £70 per an. [MS. T.C.D. F. 2. 18.] N.B.—The living was his Vicar Choralship.

1638. Sept. 25. JOHN CHAPELL, D.D., is presented to P. Kilbrittain by the Crown. [Pat. Rot.] In 1639 he became Dean of Ross, q. v.

1639. This Prebend is marked vacant. BARNABAS HONNYCHURCH is Curate. [V.B. 1639.] Honnychurch was, in 1661, R. Murragh, q. v.

1661 to 1666. JOHN BUTLER appears as P. Kilbrittain. [V.B.] He vacated in 1666 the P. Kilbrittain, R. V. Innishannon, R. Ballymartle, V. Ballyfeard, R. Templemichael de Duagh, and the R. Leighmoney.

1666. Vacant, a stroke being drawn through the name of JOHN BUTLER. [V.B.]

1667. June 29. JOHN MOORE, P. Kilbrittain, R. V. Innishonane, R. Ballymartle, Templemichael de Duagh, and Leighmoney, and Vicar of Ballyfiard, vacant per desertion of John Butler. [V.B. D.R. 1669.]

He appears 1667 to 1698, in which latter year he is marked "Mr. John Moore, sen. excusat." [V.B. D.R.]

John Moore was also Archdeacon of Cloyne, q. v.

1699. April 14. JOHN MOORE, Jun., A.B., P. Kilbrittain, and V. Ballyfiard, per resignation of John Moore, sen. [D.R.] In 1701 John Moore, jun. was also Vicar of Rathclaren.

No church. Three Protestant families near Templetrine. [V.B. 1699.]

In 1711 John Moore, jun. became Treasurer of Cork, q. v.

1711. July 31. PIERCE GOOLD, A.M., P. Kilbrittain. [F.F.] On 9th December, 1714, Goold is presented to the Rectory of Rathclarin on letters patent. [Lib. Mun.]

Pierce Gould (son of Pierce Goold "generosi") was born in Cork, and when nineteen years old entered T.C.D. as a Pensioner, on 18th March, 1696. He was Scholar in 1698, and A.M. in 1706.

He was ordained Deacon on 21st September, 1701, and Priest on 20th September, 1702, both at Cork. From 1706 to 1711 he was Vicar Choral, Cork; and from 1711, to his death in 1715, was P. Kilbrittain, with which he held in addition, from 1714, the Rectory of Rathclaren.

1715. Sept. 10. ANDREW SYMMES, A.M., P. Kilbrittain, with R. V. Rathclaren. [F.F.] In 1718 he became also Precentor of Ross, q. v.

1719. June 30. THOMAS RUSSELL, A.M., P. Kilbrittain, and R. V. Rathclaren. [F.F.] He was also Precentor of Ross in succession to Symes. In 1724 Russell became Archdeacon of Cork, q. v.

1720. June 29. RICHARD BALDWIN, A.M., P. Kilbrittain, and R. V. Rathclaren. [F.F.]

Richard Baldwin was son of Richard, "causidici," and was born in Cork. When sixteen years old he entered T.C.D. as Pensioner, on 16th May, 1697, and in 1701 was a Scholar.

From 1712 to 1720 he was Vicar Choral, Cork, and from 1714 to 1720 was Curate of St. Mary, Shandon. He also held the V. Athnowen from 1717 to 1720. From 1720 to his death in 1742 he was P. Kilbrittain, R. V. Rathclaren, and R. V. Kilcully.

He married Mary, sister to Stephen, and daughter of Benjamin Winthrop, of London, and by her left issue Charles, Winthrop (who was born 1735, and entered T.C.D. in 1741); and Stephen; besides two daughters, Bridget, wife of Henry Wrixon, of Glenfield; and Anne, wife of George Sealy, of Bandon. His will was dated 1742, and proved 1743.

1742. March 24. THOMAS WHITE, A.M., P. Kilbrittain, and R. V. Rathclaren. [D.R.] He became in 1751 P. Kilnaglory, q. v.

1751. March 29. JOHN KENNY, A.M., P. Kilbrittain, and R. V. Rathclaren, per resignation of Thomas White. [D.R.]

John Kenny, A.M., the elder, was licensed in 1727 to the Curacy of St. Peter's, Cork. From 1728 to 1737 he was V. Ringrone, and from 1730 to 1737 was also P. Kilnaglory. He appears in 1734 as Curate of St. Finbarry's. From 1737 to 1751 he was V. Durrus-Kilcroghane, and from 1751 to his death in 1768 was P. Kilbrittain and R. Rathclaren. He also held, from 1744 to 1768, the Rectory of Templetrine.

He married Judith Brown, of St. Mary Shandon, sister of Jemmett, Archbishop of Tuam, [Cork M. B. of April 3, 1728], by whom he had a son, William (baptized at St. Mary Shandon, Cork, in 1734); also an elder son, Edward, P. Inskenny, q. v.; and another, John, P. Kilbrogan, q. v.

1768. Dec. 21. RICHARD BEARE, A.M., P. Kilbrittain, and R. V. Rathclaren, vacant by death of John Kenny the elder. [D.R.] Beare was Vicar-General of Cork and Ross.

Richard Beare (member of a family settled near Cloyne in

1633, and afterwards at Beare Forest, near Mallow), was born at Mallow, being the son of Richard Beare *generosi;* and when sixteen years old he entered T.C.D. as Pensioner, on 18th June, 1728. He graduated A.M. in 1759.

He was licensed to the Curacy of St. Mary Shandon in 1736, and to that of Kinsale in 1740, and to that of St. Paul's, Cork, in 1747. From 1751 to 1760 he was Curate of St. Peter's. He was, from 1759 to 1762, P. St. Michael's; from 1762 to 1767 R. V. Cannaway; from 1767 to 1768 V. Fanlobbus and Drinagh; and from 1768 to his death in 1770 P. Kilbrittain and R. V. Rathclaren. He married on 14th August, 1739, Mary, eldest dau. of Richard Sympson, of Cork, esq. but had no issue surviving at his death.

His will was dated 16th June, 1770, and proved 26th April, 1771; and in it are mentioned an elder brother, William, and a younger, named John. [Davies.]

The family of Beare derived their name from the barony of Beare, and were a branch of the sept of O'SULLIVAN BEAR. A sister of the Rev. Richard Beare was grandmother of RICHARD BEARE TOOKER, esq. of Cork, who possesses the family papers.

1770. Dec. 28. SAMUEL HALES, A.M., P. Kilbrittain, and R. V. Rathclaren. [F.F.] Hales was afterwards D.D.

Samuel Hales, from 1733 to 1762, was Curate of Templemartin, holding also from 1751 the Curacies of Moviddy, Kilmurry, Dunisky, and Cannaway, &c. From 1755 to 1762 he was also R. V. Kilcully. In 1762 he was Reader at St. Finbarry's. From 1762 to 1769 he was R. V. Little Island; from 1769 to 1770 P. Lisclery; and from 1770 to his death in 1782 he was P. Kilbrittain and R. V. Rathclaren.

In 1745 he was a member of the Loyal Protestant Society at Moyallow.

He married, in May, 1746, Helen Hingston, of Aglish, by whom he had issue a son, William (F.T.C.D. and author of the Chronology); and three daughters, Sarah, Helen, and Elisabeth. Samuel Hales died 12th Nov. 1781, aged 72; and his wife, Helen, died 3rd March, 1787, aged 61. Both lie in St. Anne's churchyard, Dublin, between the church and schoolhouse, where a flat stone marks their grave. Sarah, the daughter, married, in 1774, Mr. John Hill, junior, of Drogheda.

1782. March 11. WILLIAM JEPHSON, D.D., P. Kilbrittain, and R. V. Rathclaren. [F.F.] He was also Precentor of Ross, q. v.

1791. Feb. 16. EDWARD WEEKES, A.M., P. Kilbrittain, R. V. Rathclaren, per mortem Jephson. [F.F.]

1792. July 17. Ed. Weekes, there being no glebe-house at Rathclaren, memorials to build one; and Bishop approves, 31st July, 1792. Commission to value issues 1794, May 10, and makes its return on 21st May, 1794, finding that Weekes had expended £797 8*s.* 8½*d.* and that the parish of Rathclaren exceeds per annum £350, in addition to £50, value of house and twenty acres of land. The Bishop certifies for above amount, May 24, 1794. [D.R.]

Edward Weekes, son of Thomas Weekes, was born in Cork; and when fifteen years old entered T.C.D. as Pensioner, on 13th May, 1746, and graduated A.B. in 1750, and afterwards A.M.

He was ordained Priest by the Bishop of Clogher on 8th September, 1754.

In 1759 he was licensed Curate of Dromaleague, in 1763 of Kilnaglory, in 1768 of St. Peter's. From 1771 to 1773 he was R. V. Kilcully; from 1773 to 1791 R. Inchigeelagh; and from 1791 to 1794 P. Kilbrittain. He was also, in 1786, licensed Curate of Ballinadee and Ballinaboy. He was twice married, and had a daughter, Elisabeth, by his first wife. By his second wife, Elisabeth (dau. of Edward Richardson, by Catherine Baillie), he had several daughters. He bequeathed to poor of St. Peter's, £5; of St. Paul's, £3; and to poor debtors in county Cork gaol, £2 5*s.* 6*d.* He desired to be buried in the church-yard of Upper Shandon, Cork. He died 10th April, 1794.

1794. June 26. THOMAS BARRY, A.B., P. Kilbrittain, R. V. Rathclaren. On 13th August, 1795, he was a second time collated. [F.F.]

1830. The Protestant population of the union is 140.

1831. May 3. On death of Thomas Barry the Rev. Henry Somerville and Robert Barry, esq. were appointed sequestrators. [D.R.]

Thomas Barry, A.B. (second son of Charles Barry, who was eldest son of Charles, eldest son of Humphrey, the youngest brother of James Barry, L.C.J. and first Lord Santry), was descended from the Barrys of Dungourney, county Cork.

He was born in 1744, and was ordained Priest at Cloyne on 8th February, 1773.

From 1794 to his death, in 1831, he was P. Kilbrittain. He married a daughter of St. George Ryder, esq. of the county Cork, and by her had issue three sons, John (Captain, 36th Regiment); Robert, and St. George (who married a daughter of Eustace Stawell, esq. of Coolmain); and one daughter, Dorothea, the wife of William Hamilton, esq. who had issue by her two sons, Thomas and Robert Hamilton. The Rev. T. Barry desired in his will to be buried in the church of Kilbrittain.

1831. Sept. 15. BENJAMIN SWETE, A.B., P. Kilbrittain, under £300. [D.R.]

1832. April 18. The inhabitants of Kilbrittain are ordered to attend Rathclaren Church. The Bishop wished to unite those two parishes, but was prevented. [D.R.]

1834. Dec. 19. The newly erected schoolhouse at Kilbrittain was licensed for divine service. [D.R.]

1837. Kilbrittain, a rectory, with cure, 3½ miles long by 1 broad, containing 4,651A. 1R. 38P. Gross population, 1,607. No Curate employed. Tithe composition, £410. 5 acres of glebe in Incumbent's occupation, valued at 20*s.* per acre, £5. Subject to diocesan schoolmaster, 6*s.* 8*d.* No glebe-house. Incumbent, not being able to procure a residence in the parish, resides, with the Diocesan's permission, within a quarter of a mile of it, and pays the sum of £40 per annum for house-rent. No church. Divine service is celebrated once on Sundays, Good Friday, and Christmas Day, in a school-house licensed by the Bishop, and during the summer months once every fortnight on a week-day. The sacrament is administered 14 times in the year. The benefice is a rectory. The P. Kilbrittain has also a revenue of £7 7*s.* 8*d.* arising from the rent of a house and concerns in Cork, but no duties, except preaching in the cathedral three or four times a-year. [Parl. Rep.]

Benjamin Swete (eldest son of John Swete, esq. of Floraville), was ordained Deacon at Cloyne on 24th August, 1806; and in 1810 was licensed to the Curacy of St. Mary Shandon.

He married (in 1811, on July 8, at St. Nicholas, Cork), Eliza Jane Lennox, eldest dau. of H. Bigger, esq. of Richmond Lodge, by whom he had issue Hewson-Bigger, Benjamin, M.D., Rev. Charles John, Richard-Warren, Arthur-Warren, Sally-Anne (wife of Marshal N. Cummins), Elisabeth, and Lucia. He died on 18th November, 1849.

1850. January 18. JOHN EGAN, A.B., P. Kilbrittain. Net value, £288 10*s.* 5*d.* [D.R.]

John Egan, in 1821, was licensed Curate of St. Finbarry's; and in 1824 was librarian and catechist at that cathedral. From 1850 to his death on 17th June, 1855, he was P. Kilbrittain.

In his will he desired to be buried in the vaults of Ballymodan Church, at a cost of not more than £40. Having no relative living, he gives all his effects to the two schools near Lucan for educating the children of the clergy.

1855. July 23. ROBERT HALBURD, A.B., P. Kilbrittain. Net value, £280 13*s.* 9*d.* [D.R.]

1860. No church. No glebe-house. The glebe is set to a tenant. The Incumbent resides in Ballymodan parish. Divine service once on all Sundays, and on Christmas Day and Good Friday, in a licensed place of worship. Sacrament monthly, and at festivals; average of communicants, 10. Twelve children attend a Church Education school. The Protestant population is 60. The rentcharge is £307 10*s.* The land and premises in Cork are worth £12. Total value, £319 10*s.* per annum, without residence.

R. Halburd was ordained Deacon on 1st June, 1823, and Priest on 10th June, 1827, both at Cloyne.

In 1832 he was licensed Curate of Dunderrow, and from 1840 to 1855 was P. Killanully.

He married, firstly, a Miss Travers; and secondly, a Miss Johnson.

KILBROGAN.

1481. "M." was Rector and Vicar of Kilbrogan. [Pipe Roll, p. 15.]

1591. Richard Newman appears as Vicar of Kilbrogan. "Preb. de Kilbrogan: Ab. graine et hosp. mor. sunt Rectores. Vicarius ibm Richs. Newman." [MS. T.C.D. E. 3. 14.]

In another V. B. of same date, Rory flynn appears as Vicar. Flynn was Vicar of Inskenny in 1581, and in 1591 was also V. Kilbonane and R. Knockavilly.

1615. Robert Sutton appears as Vicar. "Kilbrogan vic. residens. Magister de Mora et Grany sunt rectores. Geraldus Aylmer et Wilhelmus Sarsfield, milites, sunt firmarii. Val. 3 li. Ecclesia et cancella repantur. V. Robertus Sutton, inserviens curæ. Val. 4 li." [R.V. R.I.A.]

Sutton was also V. Desertserges and V. Ballinadee.

1628. Sept. 28. Baptist Hassell, P. Kilbrogan. [F.F.]

1632. March 29. John Snary, A.M., is admitted P. and V. Kilbrogan, and V. Desertserges, installed 31st March, on letters patent, dated 2nd March. [R.V. 1634.] He was ordained Deacon on 23rd May, and Priest on 29th of September, 1624, by John, Bishop of Sodor and Man. 1634. R. de Kilbrogan spectat ad Ab. de Mora. Cormack Donogh Carty firmarius. Valet. 20 li. per an. Preb. and V. de Kilbrogan John Snary. Val. 37 li. per an. [R.V. 1634.]

He appears in 1639 as Preb. Rec. and Vic. Kilbrogan. [V.B. 1639.]

On 11th May, 1635, Snary received a second patent, uniting the rectory of Kilbrogan to the P. and V. Kilbrogan and Desertserges, already held by him. [Lib. Mun.] And he was a second time admitted, on 29th May, 1635. [F.F.]

In 1642 he deposes before the Royal Commissioners, that in 1636 he was molested in a rebellious manner by one Cormac Carthy (probably Cormack Donogh Carty, the firmarius, mentioned above), but was re-established by the Lords of the Privy Council; yet that the said Cormac held him in suit to the loss of £400, entered on his glebe-lands, and plundered him of cattle, &c. till restored by order of the Judges of Assize. The said Cormac and his party came again (in the rebellion), and plundered him of tithes, &c., value £110 per annum. [MS. T.C.D. F. 2. 17.]

1661. HUGH DUNSTERVILLE, A.M., appears as P. Kilbrogan. [V.B.] Dunsterville, in 1663, was also Archdeacon of Cloyne, q. v.

1666. May 6. JOHN EASTON, A.M., P. Kilbrogan. [F.F.] He was also Chancellor of Ross, q. v.

1669. Oct. 14. RICHARD SYNG, P. Kilbrogan, per mortem Johis Eston. [V.B. D.R. 1669.] He was again instituted on 15th May, 1671, on receiving the Chancellorship of Ross and other benefices. [F.F.] In 1674 he became Archdeacon of Cork, q. v.

1674. June 5. GEORGE SYNGE, P. V. Kilbrogan, R. V. Aghinagh, V. Aghabollig, and Kilcolman. [F.F.]

1688. Mrs. Maria Bull, of Bandon, widow, bequeaths £40 to the poor English Protestants of Bandon, and to Kilbrogan parish church twelve pounds for a silver flagon, for the communion, if celebrated in both kinds. [Cork Wills.]

George Synge (son of George, Bishop of Cloyne) was born at Cork; and when sixteen years old, entered T.C.D. as Pensioner, on 27th February, 1665.

From 1663 to 1675, V. Inchigeelah and Kilmichael; from 1671 to 1674, P. Lisclery and P. Inniscarra; from 1674 to 1692, P. Kilbrogan, R. V. Kilcoleman, Agabulloge, and Aghinagh. He was also, from 1681 to 1692, R. Templetrine. In 1682 he held also R. Agiapallin, in Meath.

He married, in 1681, Mary (dau. of Thomas Hewytt, of Bandon bridge, gentleman); and he married, secondly, in 1687, Margaret Freke, of Templebryan, in Ross.

In his will (dated 12th September, 1692, and proved 22nd of March following) he wishes to be buried near his first wife, in the chancel of Kilbrogan, and mentions his son George (afterwards R. Taxax, q. v.), and his daughter, Elisabeth, both minors, in 1692. He mentions also his *brother*, Woodley, and his *brother*, Lap. His widow, Margaret, married in 1695, Thomas Salmon, of Cork, gentleman.

1692. December 7. DANIEL LORD, A.M., P. R. V. Kilbrogan, per mortem Georgii Synge. [D.R.]

1699. A good church in Bandon. Sacrament four times a year. [V.B. D.R.]

1700/1. "Friday, the 14th March, I went to Bandon. On Saturday morning, after prayer, I examined Mr. Mills and Mr. Christie, in Mr. Lord's church. On Sunday, the 16th of March, I preach't in the same church, and after sermon I ordained the aforesaid persons Deacons, and administered the holy sacrament. There were about 800 persons at church, of which number about 40 received the holy sacrament. On Monday, the 17th ditto, I examined the children of both the parishes in Bandon in the church catechism. I distributed amongst them 4 Bibles, and 28 Common Prayer Books, and 100 of Acheson's Devotions."

"I returned to Corke on the said 17th of March, 1700/1. No Papists are suffered to live within the walls of Bandon. The Earl of Corke, in his leases, has obliged all the tenants not to admit Papists." [Downes' Journal.]

Daniel Lord, son of Richard Lord, was born in Dublin, and when fourteen years old entered T.C.D. on 3rd January, 1671, as a Pensioner, and graduated afterwards D.D. He was Curate of Liscarroll, Cloyne, in 1662. From 1681 to 1693, he was P. Killaspugmullane. He was R. Garryvoe from 1682 to 1683. From 1682 to 1704, R. V. Murragh and Desertserges. From 1683 to 1704, R. Killowen, and from 1692 to 1704, P. Kilbrogan. He was Proctor Cleri Corcagen. to Convocation in 1703. In his will, dated 25th Nov., 1704, and proved 26th Dec., 1705, he is styled "Rev. Daniel Lord, D.D., Minister in Bandon bridge," and he desires burial "in ye chancel of my own parish of Bandon bridge, as near the body of my daughter Frances as may be." He mentions his wife Dorcas, his daughters Bridget and Dorcas, his eldest son, Daniel (to whom he leaves his lease of "ye 12th lot, on St. Stephen's-green, Dublin, which he holds in fee from ye city of Dublin"), and his younger sons, Richard, Benjamin, William, Joseph, Edward, and John, who are all minors at the date of the will. [Cork Wills.] I think the Rev. John Lord, V. Ballymodan, was either his son or his grandson.

1704. January 5. SOLOMON FOLEY, P. R. and V. Kilbrogan, and R. and V. Murragh. [F.F.]

1726. Sept. 25. Cornelius Murphy recants in the parish church of Moragh, *teste* John Frier, Curate. [D.R.]

Solomon Foley (son of Samuel Foley, armiger,) was born in Clonmell, co. Tip., and was a younger brother of Samuel Foley, Bishop of Down. He entered T.C.D. as Pensioner on 2nd April, 1679, being then sixteen years old. He was a Scholar in 1681.

From 1692 to 1694 he was R. Kilmeen and V. Drinagh; from 1692 to 1704, P. Kilnaglory; from 1698 to 1704 he was R. Ardnegihy and Kilcully; from 1704 to 1738 he was P. Kilbrogan. He seems to have held the P. Dunsford, Down, from 1694. He was Proctor Cleri, Cork, to Convocation in 1703.

He wishes (in his will, dated 12th Feb., and proved 2nd of March, 1738) to be buried in the chancel of Kilbrogan, near his deceased wife. He mentions his daughter, Mrs. James Jackson, and their child, Susannah Jackson, and another daughter, Susannah, the wife of Rev. Robert Clellan, or M'Clellan.

1738/9. Feb. 26. WILLIAM JACKSON, A.B., P. R. and V. Kilbrogan, one R. Aglish, and R. V. Murragh, vacant by the death of Sol. Foley. [D.R.] In 1749 Jackson became P. Cahirlag, q. v.

1739. May 4. WILLIAM ROBINSON, A.M., P. R. and V. Kilbrogan, and R. V. Murragh. [F.F.] Without the one R. of Aglish, which was not restored to Kilbrogan until 1746, *vide* Aglish.

William Robinson (son of Rev. Thomas Robinson) was born at St. Michael's, Lancashire; and when fifteen years old, entered T.C.D. as Pensioner, on 14th June, 1693.

From 1716 to 1739 he was R. Tullagh, and from 1736 to 1739, R. Creagh, in Ross. From 1739 to his death, in 1746, he was P. Kilbrogan.

He married Anne Moorcroft, and by her had issue a son, Thomas Robinson, who married Dorothy, dau. of Samuel Townsend, of Whitehall.

1746. October 9. ST. JOHN BROWNE, LL.D., P. Kilbrogan and R. V. Murragh. [F.F.] He was again collated on 3rd June, 1749, and a third time, on 21st April, 1750, on receiving other additional preferments. [D.R.]

1746. January 27. Thomas Blenerhassett voluntarily renounces the one rectory of Aglish (to which he had, by mistake, been collated by the late Bp.) in favor of the Preb. of Kilbrogan, to whom it rightfully belongs. [D.R.]

St. John Browne, a native of Cork (son of Edward Browne, "Senatoris Corcagiensis"), was educated at Middleton, under Mr. Chinnery, and when eighteen years old entered T.C.D. (Tutor, Dr. Gilbert) on 7th May, 1729. [Reg. T.C.D.] He graduated afterwards A.M. and LL.D. He was a younger brother of Jemmett Browne, Bishop of Cork, for whom see Deans of Ross.

He was ordained Priest at Cork on 3rd Oct., 1736.

He was licensed on 3rd August, 1737, to the curacy of Killowen, near Kinsale, and on 3rd of April, 1738, to that of Ringrone, and on 28th Oct., 1742, to the curacy of Rincurran and Taxax.

In 1746 he was made P. Donoghmore, Ross, and P. Dromdaleague, both which he resigned in October, 1746, for the P. Kilbrogan, which he held until his death in 1796. He also held, from 1749 to 1796, the R. Killowen, and from 1750 to 1774, was Chancellor of Ross. He was also, from 1755 to 1796, R. Innishannon and Leighmoney.

He married in 1738 [M. B. dated July 20] Amelia St. George, of the parish of St. Multose, Kinsale, and by her had issue Rev. Thomas Adderly Browne (Chancellor of Ross, q. v.), Rev. St. John Browne, (B.A., and Scholar of Trinity College, Cambridge, who was ordained Deacon and Priest in Cork in 1770, and who was Curate of Rincurran in 1772, of Murragh in 1774, and in 1774 removed to Canterbury diocese, and died Sp.), and Sir St. George Sackville Browne, K.C.B., Lieut.-General in the Army. The Rev. Dr. Browne, of Kilbrogan, married, secondly, on 16th Nov., 1776, Mrs. Elisabeth Hodder, at St. Nicholas', Cork. His will was dated 3rd October, 1791, and proved 28th January, 1796

1796. January 20. JOHN KENNY, LL.D., P. R. and V. Kilbrogan. [F.F.]

1807. Dr. Kenny is Vicar-General. He resides at Kilbrogan, and holds also, by faculty, Kinneigh and Dunderrow. [Rep.]

1811. The Bishop approves of a memorial to build, and on 8th Dec., 1813, confirms a return of commission, which finds that Kenny had expended £3,104 8*s.* 6*d.*, and that the yearly value of Kilbrogan was £1,588 15*s.* [D.R.]

John Kenny, LL.D., (son of John Kenny, P. Kilbrittain,) was brother to Rev. Edward Kenny, P. Inskenny.

He was ordained Deacon on 24th May, and Priest on 4th of October, 1761, both by Bp. of Cork.

He was, on 25th May, 1761, licensed to the curacy of Rathclarin; and on 2nd June, 1762, to that of Aglish, Moviddy, and Dunisky; and on 4th June, 1762, to that of Kilmurry, Templemartin, and Cannaway.

From 1762 to 1771 he was P. St. Michael's, Cork; from 1771 to 1796, Vic. Choral, Cork; and from 1796 to his death, in 1814, P. Kilbrogan. He was also, from 1763 to 1771, R. V. Kilcully; from 1764 to 1769, R. Ringrone; from 1768 to 1769, R. Templemichael de Duagh, and V. Kinneigh; from 1769 to 1793, R. Durrus; from 1779 to 1814, R. Dunderrow; from 1796 to 1801, P. Donoghmore, Cloyne; and from 1801 to 1814, V. Kinneigh. He was also Vicar-General of Cork and Ross from 1772. He published "A Thanksgiving Sermon, preached at Bandon, on 16th Feb., 1797," 8vo. Cork, 1797.

He married Mary Herbert, of Muckrus, who died in 1803, and by her had issue, an eldest son, Rev. Edward Herbert Kenny, (R. Kilmeen, Ross, q. v.); Robert, second son, (who was Capt. R. N., and married a daughter of Colonel Kearney, and died Sp. in 1826); Rev. Thomas Kenny, (P. Donoghmore, Cloyne, q. v.); and Rev. Arthur Kenny, F.T.C.D., who died in Brussels about 1856. He also left a daughter, Mary, who wrote "Letters on Prejudice," and died unmarried.

The Rev. Dr. Kenny died on or about 25th, and was buried on 27th December, 1814, in the church-yard of Ballymartle.

1815. January 14. VERNEY LOVETT, P. R. and V. Kilbrogan, and Rect. of Aglish. [F.F.]

He resigned 4th June, 1818, and became R. Kilnagross, Ross, q. v.

1818. June 13. HORATIO TOWNSEND NEWMAN, A.M., P. Kilbrogan, certified to be under £700. [D.R.] In 1842 he became Dean of Cork, q. v.

1830. Protestant population, 1,477.

1833. Oct. 14. The school-house at Carhue was licensed for divine service. [D.R.]

1837. Kilbrogan: a rectory and vicarage, with cure; 5 miles long by 3 broad, containing 7,255A. 1R. 0P.; gross population, 5,710; two curates employed, at annual stipends of £75 to each; tithe composition, £650; 32 acres of glebe in Incumbent's use, valued at 40*s.* per acre, £64, subject to visitation fees and diocesan schoolmaster, £2 10*s.* Kilbrogan glebe-house built in 1813, under the new acts, at the cost of £2,861 10*s.* 9¼*d.* Brit., whereof £1,384 12*s.* 3¾*d.* was granted in way of loan, and £92 6*s.* 1¾*d.* in that of gift, by the late Board of First Fruits, and the residue of £1,384 12*s.* 3¾*d.* was supplied out of the private funds of the builder, to whom the present Incumbent is third in succession; and having paid his predecessor £1,107 13*s.* 10¼*d.*, he will be entitled to receive £738 9*s.* 2¾*d.* from his successor on account of the sum last named. Of the loan aforesaid there remained £659 1*s.* 4*d.* chargeable on the benefice in 1832, repayable by annual instalments of £38 15*s.* 5*d.*

Incumbent is constantly resident in the glebe-house. One church, situate in the town of Bandon, capable of accommodating 800 persons, built in 1625, but at what cost unknown; and enlarged in 1829 by means of a loan of £200, granted by the late Board of First Fruits; of which loan there remained £176 chargeable on the parish in 1832, repayable by annual instalments of £8.

Divine service is celebrated thrice on the first Sunday in each month, and twice on all other Sundays, and once on every Wednesday evening; and service is celebrated in a school-house twice on Sundays in summer, and once in winter, and on the principal festivals. The sacrament is administered in the church twice in each month, and in the school-house monthly. The benefice is a rectory. The P. Kilbrogan has also a revenue of £39 2*s.* arising from the composition rent of the rectorial tithes of Aglish parish, enjoyed as Prebendary, but no duties, save preaching in the cathedral about three or four times in the year. [Parl. Rep.]

1842. April 9. HONORABLE CHARLES BRODRICK BERNARD, A.M., P. Kilbrogan. [D.R.]

1860. C. B. Bernard, Incumbent. R. H. Loane and James O'Sullivan, Curates. The church and glebe-house in good order. 32 stat. acres of glebe in Incumbent's use. Divine service thrice on the first Sunday in each month, and twice on all other Sundays. Service is held also on one day in the week, and on the usual holidays. Sacrament twice each month, and twice on the great festivals. The average of communicants at the monthly celebrations is 83. Over 200 generally receive on Christmas Day. 223 children are on the rolls of the schools, which are under the Church Education Society. The Protestant population is 1,038. The rentcharge of Kilbrogan is £487 10*s.*; of the R. Aglish, £29 6*s.* 6*d.* The land is worth £64. Total value of benefice, £580 16*s.* 6*d.*, with residence.

Charles Brodrick Bernard, of Balliol College, Oxford, A.M., (son of James, second EARL of BANDON), was born 4th January, 1811. He was ordained Deacon on 28th of June, 1835, and Priest on 11th September, 1836, both at Cork. In 1835 he was licensed Curate of Desertserges. From 1840 to 1842, he was V. Kilmocamoge, and in 1842 became P. Kilbrogan.

He married, in 1843, Jane-Grace Freke, sister to the present LORD CARBURY, and has issue.

KILCOAN.

1291. "Eccia de Kylcoan. Vmr." [Tax. P. Nic.]

1591. "E. de Kilcoan JACOBUS VERNAM, presentat: nondum admissus; respicitur in crast." [MS. T.C.D. E. 3. 14.]

1615. "Kilcoane. Rector THOMAS WESTMORE, Minister legens et inserviens curæ. Val. 4 li. per an. Ecclesia et cancella ruinantur." He holds also a Vic. Chor. Cloyne, and the Vicarage of Kilmahon, Cloyne. [R.V. R.I.A.] Westmore was also, in 1615, R. Bretway, Cloyne, q. v.

1627. March 20. RICHARD JERMYN is admitted R. V. Kilcoane, vacant per cessionem Thomæ Westmore. Inducted 26th May, 1628. [R.V. 1634.] In 1666 Jermyn was V. Rahan, Cloyne, q. v.

1634. E. de Kilcoan Richard Jerman, R. and V. Predicator. Valet XII li. per an. Alderman Thomas Coppinger, of Cork, is Patron. [R.V. 1634.]

1639. FRANCIS FREDERINGHAM appears as R. Kilcoan. "Ecclia de Kilcoan: ffranciscus ffredringham, idem curatus, excusatur. Ecclia ruinata, desunt omnia. Richard Caldwell clericus parochialis." [V.B. D.R.] Frederingham was also V. Clonmel, Cloyne, q. v.

1666. SAMUEL BONNER appears as R. Kilcoan; "ægrotat." [V.B.] He was also P. St. Michael's, q. v.

1667. "Vacat per mortem BONNER." [V.B.]

1668. JOHN BAILY appears as P. St. Michael's, R. Kilcoan, Templeusque, and R. V. Insulæ parvæ. [V.B. D.R.] He was instituted to these benefices on 11th July, 1669, per mortem Samuelis Bonner. [V.B. 1669.] *Vide* St. Michael's.

1697. June 17. VALENTINE FRENCH, P. St. Michael's, R. Kilcoan, Templeusque, Insulæ parvæ, and Kilroan, per mortem John Bayly. [D.R.] *Vide* St. Michael's.

1699. Sermon once a fortnight at Mr. Mitchell's house. Sacrament four times a year. A church ought to be built either here or in some other of Mr. French's parishes. [V.B. D.R.]

In 1704 French took the P. Killaspugmullane, and resigned St. Michael's. Since that time Kilcoan was held with Killaspugmullane, q. v.

KILCULLY.

1291. "Eccia de Kilcully IIImr. Vicar. cap. dimid." [Tax. P. Nic.]

1591. "E. de Kilcully spectat ad Abb. de Chore. Regina." [MS. T.C.D. E. 3. 14.]

1615. "R. de Kilcully impropr. Heres Johis Fitzgerald militis est rector. Vicaria usurpatur per Rectorem. Ecclesia et cancella bene repãntur. Nullus Curatus." [R.V. R.I.A.]

1634. "E. de Kilcully. Rex est Rector. Johēs Fitzgerald miles tenet hanc vicariam. Nullus Curatus." [R.V. R.I.A.]

1639. "Rex est Rector. Wm. Gilsland, Curatus. Ecclia ruinata, desunt omnia." [V.B. D.R.]

1666. Ecclesia de Kilcully. Rector impropriator Edward Fitzgerald. Vicaria vacat. [V.B.]

1667. July 31. Bernardus Packington, D.D., iustitutus fuit V. Kilcully, in coll. Epi. [V.B. 1669.] In 1670 he is Rector also "ratione confiscationis ejusdem." [V.B.] He was Archdeacon of Cork, q. v.

1674. May 27. Richard Sing is admitted to V. Kilcully, and also to the Archdeaconry of Cork, q. v.

1688. The R. V. Kilcully are vacant by the death of Sing. [V.B.]

1689 to 1695. Richard Goodman appears as R. V. Kilcully. [V.B.] In 1718 he was P. Desertmore, q. v.

1696. Nov. 3. Vacant. [V.B.]

1696/7. Feb. 1. John Dewey, A.B., V. de Kilcully cui R. de Kilcully unita est per ltras patentes Dni Regis. [D.R.] Dewey was R. Ardnegihy, q. v.

1698. Sept. 19. Solomon Foley, R. V. Kilcully, and R. Ardnegihy, per mortem Dewey. [D.R.] In 1704 Foley became P. Kilbrogan, q. v.

1699. No churchwardens nor parish clerk. The people go to Shandon. It belongs to the catechist in St. Finbarry's. [V.B. D.R.]

1704/5. January 5. John Pomeroy, R. V. Kilcully, and R. Ardnegihy. [F.F.] In 1717 he became Archdeacon of Cork, q. v.

1717. Nov. 6. Vacant. [V.B.]

1718. Nov. 6. Bartholomew Salter appears as R. V. Kilcully. [V.B.] In 1720 he became V. Ringrone, q. v.

1720 to 1742. Richard Baldwyn appears as R. V. Kilcully. [V.B.] He was also P. Kilbrittain, q. v.

1743. March 30. John Bayley, A.B., R. V. Kilcully, vacant by the death of Rev. Richard Baldwyn. [D.R.] In 1755 Bayley became R. Inchigeelah, q. v.

1755. March 18. Samuel Hales, A.M., R. V. Kilcully. [F.F.] In 1770 he became P. Kilbrittain, q. v.

1762. June 11. Thomas Browne, A.B. (vice Hales resigned), R. V.

Kilcully. [D.R.] In 1763 he became P. Templebryan, Ross, q. v.

1763. January 28. JOHN KENNY, R. V. Kilcully, per resignation of Rev. Thos. Browne. [F.F.] In 1796 Kenny was P. Kilbrogan, q. v.

1771. January 1. EDWARD WEEKS, A.B., R. V. Kilcully, per resignation of John Kenny. [D.R.] In 1791 Weeks was P. Kilbrittain, q. v.

1773. May 1. JOHN MADRAS, A.M., R. V. Kilcully, per resignation of Edward Weeks. [D.R.]

John Madras (son of —— Madras, of Amsterdam), was ordained in 1739 as Minister of the French Church in Cork city, and he held that post until his death in 1773. He was also Precentor of Ross from 1745 to May, 1773.

He married, firstly, Anne ——, by whom (whose will was dated 1752, and proved 1754) he seems to have had no issue; and secondly, he married, in 1768, Alice (dau. of Henry Baldwin, of Curravody, county Cork, by Alice Warren), by whom he had issue, Rev. John Henry Madras (V. Aglish, q. v.), and a daughter, Anne-Eliza, who married, in 1789, Robert Longfield Conner, esq. of Fort-Robert, and bore to him three daughters, of whom Mary was wife of her cousin, Arthur, son of Roger Conner, esq. and Elizabeth was wife to George Roger O'Conner, brother to Arthur. The Rev. John Madras was buried at the French Church, in Cork. His will was dated 22nd April, 1769, and proved 25th May, 1774.

1774. January 26. CHARLES COOTE, A.B., R. V. Kilcully, per death of John Madras. [D.R.] In 1775 Coote became Vic. Chor. Cork, q. v.

1775. January 20. ACHILLES DAUNT, A.M., R. V. Kilcully [F.F.], per cession of Chas. Coote. [D.R.]

Achilles Daunt, born in county Cork (son of Henry Daunt, *generosi*), was educated at Middleton, under Rev. George Chinnery, and entered T.C.D. when fifteen years old, on 20th Oct. 1729.

He was ordained Deacon on 8th October, 1738, and Priest on 19th December, 1742.

In 1743 he was Curate of Tracton, and in 1751 of Ballyfeard, Nohaval, and Kilmonoge, all which curacies, Tracton inclusive, he held until his death, in 1784.

He married, in 1747, Frances French, of Moviddy.

1784. Dec. 31. HENRY SANDIFORD, A.B., R. V. Kilcully, by death of Achilles Daunt. [D.R.] In 1790 Sandiford became Precentor of Cork, q. v.

1785. June 6. FRANCIS ORPEN, A.B., R. V. Kilcully, by resignation of Sandiford. [D.R.] In 1786 Orpen became R. Dungourney, Cloyne, q. v.

1786. March 8. EDWARD SANDIFORD, A.B., R. V. Kilcully, by resignation of Francis Orpen. [D.R.] On March, 19, 1787, Sandiford takes a second collation on receiving, in addition, the V. Kilmaccabee, Ross, q. v.

1793. August 2. Thomas Gregg, esq. is appointed Sequestrator, on the death of Sandiford. [D.R.]

1793. Dec. 3. JOHN WILLIAM BENNETT, A.B., R. V. Kilcully. [F.F.] In 1799 he became also Treasurer of Cloyne, q. v.

1810. May 19. ROBERT HOARE, A.B., R. V. Kilcully, vacant by the death of Bennett, and certified under £200 in value. [D.R.]

1830. Protestant population, 25.

1832. Kilcully, a rectory and vicarage, with cure, 2 miles long by 1½ broad, containing 1,750A. Gross population, 447. No Curate employed. Tithe composition, £127 19s. 8*d.*; subject to visitation fees, 8s.; diocesan schoolmaster, 8s. 6*d.* No glebe-house. Incumbent, although non-resident within the benefice from inability to procure suitable accommodation, resides in the county of the city of Cork, within a mile and a-half of the parish, and considers £35 a year to be a reasonable sum for house rent. No church. The benefice is a rectory. [Parl. Rep.]

Robert Hoare was ordained Deacon at Cork on 1st Nov. 1778, and Priest at Cloyne on 21st Sept. 1781. He was Curate of Desertmore in 1781. He resigned Kilcully in 1833, and died in 1839 or 1840, leaving his wife, Dorcas, sole executrix. He mentions in his will his nephews, William Barry Hoare, William Newenham Hoare, and Henry Hoare.

1833. April 20. NICHOLAS DUNSCOMBE, A.B., R. V. Kilcully, under £200 in value. [D.R.]

1833. May 2. An apartment in Mrs. Ireton's is licensed for divine service. [D.R.]

Nicholas Dunscombe, born circa 1775, was fifth son of Nicholas Dunscombe, of Mount Desert, by Mary, only child of Thomas Parker, of Inchigaggin. He was ordained Deacon on 28th October, and Priest on 21st December, 1797, at Cork.

He was, in 1798, Curate of Carrigrohane, and was from 1833 to his death in 1838, R. Kilcully. He died 1st August, 1838, unmarried.

1838. August 5. Samuel Swayne Beamish, A.B., is appointed Sequestrator. On 12th Nov. 1838, the appointment of a Clerk to this benefice is suspended, because there was no divine service for three years ending 1st Feb. 1833; and £50 of the income is allocated to a Curate, the remainder being set apart to form a fund to build a church. [Board Minutes of Ecclesiastical Commissioners.]

1838. Nov. 20. S. S. Beamish is licensed to be Curate of Kilcully.

1846. Dec. 19. H. J. O'Brien, LL.D., is appointed Curate.

1849. September 10. A new church (built partly in consequence of the exertions of Rev. Dr. O'Brien), is consecrated under the name of St. Mary.

1852. August 11. The suspension of any appointment of a Clerk to Kilcully is removed.

1852. August 14. HENRY JAMES O'BRIEN, LL.D., is admitted R. V. Kilcully, net annual value, £85 11*s.* 5*d.* [D.R.]

1860. The church of St. Mary's, Kilcully, is Gothic in style, with vestry, porch, font of cut stone, open benches, &c., and accommodates eighty persons; cost of erection, £700. The communion plate is of "pewter, silvered," supplied by Ecclesiastical Commissioners. There is no glebe-house or land.

The Incumbent of this small parish is also diocesan schoolmaster, and resides in Cork. Divine service is performed in Kilcully once every Sunday and on chief festivals. The sacrament is administered monthly; average of communicants, 12. There is no school. The Protestant population of Kilcully is 28. The rentcharge is £95 19*s.* 9*d.*

H. J. O'Brien was born in Cork on 22nd May, 1812. He was educated by William Maginn, LL.D., and entered T.C.D. in 1826. He graduated A.B. in 1830, LL.B. in 1837, and LL.D. in 1839.

He was ordained Deacon on 13th August, 1837, at Cork, and Priest in November of same year (on letters dimissory from Cork), by Bishop Knox, of Limerick.

In 1837 he was Curate of St. Mary Shandon; in 1840, Assistant Curate of St. Luke's; in 1844 he was Curate of Kilcully; and in 1852, R. V. Kilcully. In 1840 he was appointed by the Lord Lieutenant diocesan schoolmaster at Cork.

He married, on 2nd July, 1834, Maria Elisabeth, only surviving daughter of George Shaw, esq.

KILLANULLY.

1291. "Eccia de Kyllynnelith VIIImr." [Tax. P. Nic.]

1591. Killanullie: Rector, D. LONG. [MS. T.C.D. E. 3. 14.] He was also Treasurer of Cork, q. v.

1615. EDWARD CLERKE, A.M., appears as Prebendary. "Killanully Preb. residens. Edrus Clerk, A.M., minister et predicator. Val. £6 13*s.* 4*d.* Ecclesia et cancella in ruinis. Tenet etiam vicarias de Kynneagh et Murragh, val. 12 li. per annum." [R.V. R.I.A.] Clerke was Dean of Cloyne, q. v.

1623. Sept. 9. RANDOLL HOLLAND, P. Killanullie cui Epūs univit et annexit R. Knockavilly et V. de Brynie. Installed 11th Sept. 1623. [R.V. 1634.]

1634. Randolphus Holland P. de Killanully, val. 15 li. per annum. [Ib.]

1639. "Ecclia bene, desunt ornamenta." [V.B.]

From 1623 to 1671 Holland appears as P. Killanully. [V.B.]

In 1642 Holland depones to loss of goods to amount of £109, and his living, worth, communibus annis, £135. [MS. T.C.D. F. 2. 16.]

Randulphus Holland, A.M., was ordained Deacon and Priest by the Bishop of Cork on 2nd January, 1614. From 1615 to 1620 he appears as R. Kilmeen, Ross; from 1615 to 1629 V. Kilmichael; from 1621 R. Knockavilly; from 1622 V. Brinny; and from 1623 P. Killanully.

Zachariah, fourth son of Rev. Randolph Holland, was born at Dundaniel, county Cork, and became a Pensioner of T.C.D. in 1641, when seventeen years old. Randolph, the father, was appointed Chaplain to the Archbishop of Armagh on 15th July, 1628. A family of Hollands, among whom the name Randol occurs, was settled in the county Limerick.

1672. April 2. PIERCE BUTLER adm. Preb. Killconnollie als Killanullie et ad R. de Knocknyvillie et V. de Brinnie. [F.F.]

On 6th April, 1686, Pierce Butler became R. Clanbehy, Kilmore, Dromodecaher, and Kilmane-prior, in the diocese of Ardfert and Aghadoe.

1685. May 2. JOSHUA WARREN, A.M., P. Killanully, R. Knockavilly, and V. Brinny, per resignation of P. Butler. [D.R.]

From 1687 to 1696 neither churchwarden nor parish clerk appears. [V.B. D.R.]

In 1694 Warren was cited to show cause why he should not be deprived "propter pluralitatem beneficiorum." [Addenda to V.B. 1694.]

Joshua Warren became P. of Rath, Killaloe, on 27th Sept. 1697. He died in 1701.

Two sons of Rev. Joshua Warren, named Stafford and Thomas, entered T.C.D. in 1700. They were born in the county Meath.

1696. August 25. RICHARD GOODMAN, A.B., P. Killanully, R. Knockavilly, and V. Brinny, per resignation of Warren. [D.R.]

Goodman, in 1718, became P. Desertmore, q. v.

1699. "The walls of the church standing; the Protestants go to Carrickgoline. Four plowlands in this parish." [V.B. 1699. D.D.]

"Saturday, Sept. 28, 1700. I saw the church of Killanully; 'tis not far from the river Awne-buy. The walls are standing, built with stone and clay, uncovered. It is about 2 miles from Carrickoline Church. The bounds of the church-yard are hardly discernible. There is about an acre of glebe, belonging to the Incumbent, near the church. Mr. Burstian and Mr. Bayly live near the church."

"An. 1702. Killanully Church is ruinous, only the walls

standing. There is a large stone altar at the east end, and a stone font is lying upon the ground.

"The church-yard is not inclos'd. The church stands on the north side of the river Bury. Ballinebury Church stands at two miles distance to the east of it. The Prebend is worth to Mr. Goodman about £18 per an. communibusannis." [Downes' Tour.]

1718. June 23. THOMAS RUSSELL, A.M., P. Killanully. [F.F.] In 1724 he became Archdeacon of Cork, q. v.

1720. Nov. 17. Russell leases the tithes, &c., of Killanully for £40 a-year. [D.R.]

1719. July 21. THOMAS SOMERVILLE, A.M., P. Killanully. [F.F.] He became, in 1732, R. Myros, Ross, q. v.

1724/5. Feb. 16. LEWIS LACROIX, P. Killanully. [D.R.] In 1726 and 1728 Lacroix is admonished to reside on his prebend on pain of suspension. [D.R.]

He appears 1725 to 1737. [V.B. D.R.]

Lacroix was ordained Deacon at Cork on 22nd December, 1700, and from 1700 to 1724 was a Vicar Choral, Cork.

1738 to 1741. JOHN HERBERT, A.M., appears as P. Killanully. [V.B. D.R.]

This was probably John (son of Arthur Herbert), born in county Kerry, at Castleisland, who entered T.C.D. aged seventeen, on 3rd of June, 1716. He was ordained Deacon on 11th August, 1723, and Priest on June 5, 1726. He was Treasurer of Ardfert from 1728 to 1741. He married in 1733 Mary Gibbings, of St. Peter's. He died in 1741.

1741. Dec. 8. ISAAC GOLDSMITH, A.M., P. Killanully, per mort. John Herbert. [D.R.] Goldsmith was also Dean of Cloyne, q. v.

1763. January 22. EDWARD COTTRELL, A.M., P. Killanully. [F.F.]

Edward (son of Alderman Francis) Cottrell, was born in Cork, and when sixteen years old entered T.C.D. as Pensioner, on 2nd June, 1724. He graduated afterwards A.M. He was ordained Priest at Cork on 24th July, 1737. In 1737 he was Curate of Passage, and in 1742 Curate of St. Finbarry's. He was P. Killanully from 1763 to 1788. He died in 1788, leaving a son, Francis-Edward, and a daughter, Mary.

1788. Feb. 23. RICHARD WEBB, A.B., P. Killanully. [F.F.] In 1788 he became P. Dromdaleague and R. Ringrone, q. v.

1788. Dec. 2. BRODRICK TUCKEY, A.B., P. Killanully. [F.F.] He resigned on 9th October, 1794, for V. Drinagh, q. v.

1795. April 2. JAMES STOPFORD, A.M., P. Killanully. [F.F.] In 1797 he became P. Killaspugmullane, q. v.

1797. Sept. 4. HENRY ST. ELOY, P. Killanully. [F.F.] He held also along with this living the P. Edermine, in Ferns, from 1806 to his death in 1827. In his will he wishes to be buried at Prospect, near his late wife, and mentions his second wife, Susannah, dau. of John Nun, esq. of Gorey. He left to the poor of Gorey £5.

1827. Nov. 1. RICHARD ROTHE, A.B., P. Killanully. Certified under £200. [D.R.] In 1829 he became R. V. Kilmichael, q. v.

1829. Dec. 22. JOHN JOHNSON, A.B., P. Killanully. Certified under £200. [D.R.]

1830. Protestant population *not returned.*

1833. April 17. The schoolhouse at Killanully was licensed for divine service. [D.R.]

1837. Killanully, a rectory, with cure, 3 miles long by 2½ broad, containing 3,500 acres. Gross population, 631. No Curate employed. Tithe composition, £170. 5 acres of glebe, valued at 30*s.* per acre, £7 10*s.* Subject to visitation fees, 11*s.* Diocesan schoolmaster, 14*s.* 6*d.* No glebe-house. Incumbent is non-resident, from want of accommodation; he resides in Carrigaline village, within a quarter of an hour's ride of the benefice, and pays the sum of £31 10*s.* a-year for house-rent. No church. Divine service is performed once on Sundays, and on the principal festivals, in a school-house, built by W. H. Newenham, of Coolmore, esq. The benefice is a rectory. The Prebendary has no separate revenue as such, nor any duties, except preaching in the cathedral in rotation with the other members of the chapter. [Parl. Rep.]

John Johnson was ordained Deacon at Cork on 13th April, 1823, and Priest at Cloyne on 21st December following. From 1823 to 1829 he was P. C. of Templebredy, and from 1829 to his death on 11th June, 1837, was P. Killanully.

He married Catherine, sister of Rev. Henry Theophilus Moore Hodder.

1837. Aug. 24. RICHARD LLOYD, A.B., P. Killanully. [F.F.]

Richard (son of Richard Lloyd, esq. by Jane, dau. of Thomas Austen, esq. of Waterfall, county Cork), was a grandson of Rev. Richard Lloyd, R. Rathcormack, and was born at Rathcormack on 27th May, 1767.

He was ordained Deacon on 1st August, 1790, at Cloyne, and Priest, at Cork, on 26th Sept. 1790. From 1791 to 1837 he was P. C. Marmullane, and from 1837 to his death on 6th Feb. 1840, was P. Killanully.

He married on 20th March, 1802, Mary, dau. of James-Franklin Morrison, of Cork, by Elisabeth (eldest dau. of Archdeacon Michael Davies, of Cloyne), by whom he had issue, besides a daughter, Richard Lloyd, esq. of Passage West, who married, in 1836, Margaret, dau. of Edward Knapp Piersy, esq.

1840. March 16. ROBERT HALBURD, A.B., P. Killanully. [D.R.] In 1855 he became P. Kilbrittain, q. v.

1855. August 25. THOMAS TOWNLY MACAN, A.B., P. Killanully. Certified annual value, £120 4*s.* 8*d.* [D.R.] In 1857 he became Treasurer of Cork, q. v.

1857. Sept. 28. RICHARD LONGFIELD, A.B., P. Killanully. Net

value, £129 8s. 4d. [D.R.] In 1858 he became R. Mogeely, Cloyne, q. v.

1858. Nov. 16. MELIANUS SPREAD CAMPION, A.B., P. Killanully. Net value, £117 11s. 10d. [D.R.]

1860. No church. No glebe-house. About an acre of glebe let. Divine service twice on all Sundays, and once on the usual holidays, in a licensed schoolhouse. Sacrament monthly, and at chief festivals; average of communicants, 8. A few children attend a Church Education school. The Protestant population is 10. The rentcharge is £127 10s. The land is worth £2. Total value, £129 10s. per annum, without residence.

M. S. Campion (son of T. S. Campion, D.D., V. Ballynoe, Cloyne, q. v.), was born in the county Waterford, and when seventeen years old entered T.C.D. as Pensioner, on 6th Nov. 1826. He was ordained Deacon on 11th January, 1835, at Cloyne, and was for some years Curate of Mogeely, in that diocese.

He married Arabella Peard, by whom he had issue an only child, Thomas-Spread, who died at the age of six years, in 1863.

KILLASPUGMULLANE.

1291. "Eccia de Kylasputmullan IIIImr. Vicar cãpit dimid." [Tax P. Nic.]

1591. THOMAS GIBBONS is Prebendary, and MAURICE M'DERMOT is Curate. "Preb. Killaspugmullane Thomas Gibbons. Suspend. fructus sequestr. D. Mauritius m'dermot curatus." [MS. T.C.D. E. 3. 14.] M'Dermot was also R. Marmullane, q. v.

1615. Killaspugmullane, Prebenda residens MANASSES MARSHALL, A.B., Minister and Preacher. Value £8. He holds also the Preb. of Kilmacdonagh, in Cloyne, worth £24. Two churches, in good repair, with books. [R.V. R.I.A.] He was Archdeacon of Cork, q. v.

1619. October 23. THOMAS WAY is instituted P. Killaspugmullane cui prebendæ Epũs univit V. de Scoll. Installed 4th Nov. 1619. [R.V. 1634.] *Vide* Scull.

1626. April 7. RICHARD ASHE, A.B., is admitted P. Killaspugmullane, and installed 15th July, 1626. [R.V. 1634.] In 1661 he was R. Killeagh, Cloyne, q. v.

1634. P. Killaspugmullane Richs. Ashe, Predicator. Valet XIX li. per an. [R.V. 1634.]

1639. April 8. THOMAS BANKES, P. Killaspugmullane. [F.F.] He was also V. Holy Trinity, q. v.

1639. JOHN NEWTON, P. Killaspugmullane and V. Athnowen. [F.F.]

1639. Nov. 4. John Newton appears. "Ecclesia bene. Desunt ornamenta et liber." [V.B. D.R.]

In 1641 Newton was plundered by the rebels of his goods and chattels, and of his church livings, worth together £50 per an. [MS. T.C.D. F. 2. 17.]

1663. Sept. 7. WILLIAM SMITH, D.D., P. Killaspugmullane. [F.F.] *Per mortem Richi. Ash* (sic). [V.B. D.R. 1669.]

Dr. Smith appears in the Visitation Books up to 1681.

William Smith, from 1661 to 1662, was P. Subulter, Cloyne; and from 1661 to 1681 R. V. Rathcormack, Cloyne, and P. Lulliaghmore, Kildare. From 1663 to 1681 he was P. Killaspugmullane, and also P. Modeligo, Lismore. From 1664 to 1666 he was V. Ballyspillane, and from 1666 to 1681 P. Ballyhooly, Cloyne. He was also, from 1673 to 1681, Treasurer of Limerick. He died in 1681 the Incumbent of six livings, in five different dioceses.

In his will (dated 11th September, 1681, *from Limerick*), Dr. Smith mentions his children, William, Edward, and Mary; also his brother-in-law, Rev. John Norcot, of Ballygarret.

1681. May 3. DANIEL LORD, A.M., P. Killaspugmullane. [F.F.]

He appears 1682 to 1692. [V.B. D.R.]

In 1692 he became P. Kilbrogan, q. v.

1693/4. April 3. CHRISTOPHER SHEARES, A.B., P. Killaspugmullane, per cession of Daniel Lord ultimi incumbentis, and same day R. Ardnegihy. [D.R.]

He appears 1694 to 1704, Nov. 3. [V.B. D.R.] In the latter V. B. Mr. Valentine French is Curate, but there are no churchwardens. [D.R.]

"Oct. 1, 1700. I saw Killshanaghan Church. It was built with stone and clay, and is altogether ruinous; only the west end is standing, cover'd with ivy; it was a very small church. Elder trees grow within the church. It is on the left hand of the road from Cork to Rathcormock, about eight miles distant from Corke. The bounds of the church-yard are discernible. This parish, together with Killvillane, and a particle in Canaway, belongs to the Prebendary of Killaspugmullane, worth altogether £30 per an. at least. The Earl of Barrimore has the most considerable estate in this parish. Will. Bible is the only Protestant in this parish, except one that came lately from Imokilly. James Barry is Popish Priest of Killaspugmullane, viz. of Killshanaghan and Killvillane, and also of the parish of Kilcoan; he has been here eight years at least; he is also Priest of the parish of Ardnegihy. The Prebendary of Killaspugmullane has all the tythes of this parish; they are worth to him about £20 per an. The people of this parish go to church either to Rathcormack or Racony. No glebe in this parish."

"Oct. 1700. I saw Killvolane Church; forsan the proper

name is Killmullane or Killaspugmullane. Killvolane Church was built with stones and clay; the stones are good square stone; 'tis about 46 foot long and 17 foot broad; half the walls are down. There is no glebe belonging to this parish. A ditch round a small church-yard. This church lies to the S.E. of Templeusky Church; 'tis about two miles distant from Templeusky, and about two miles from Rathcony Church, to the north-east of Rathcony Church; 'tis about a mile from Kilcoan Church to the north-west of Kilcoan Church. Part of this parish was formerly the Duke of York's estate; now 'tis Mr. Thomas Brodrick's. Lord Barrimore has also an estate here. Mr. Will. Harding, Papist, John Dixon, and Thomas Harding, live in this parish. The Prebendary of Killaspugmullane has all the tythes of this parish; they are worth at least £10 per annum; the people of this parish go to Rathcony Church. [Downes' Tour.]

Christopher (son of Humphrey Sheares, of Cork), was born at Cork, and when twenty years old entered T.C.D. as a Pensioner, on 2nd May, 1680.

He held, for a short time, the R. Ardnegihy, which he vacated in 1694. From 1694 to 1704 he was P. Killaspugmullane; and from 1696 to 1704 he was also P. Ballymore, Armagh. He died in 1704. It appears by his father's will, dated and proved in 1703, that Christopher had a son, Henry, and two daughters, Elisabeth and Dorothy. The father, Humphrey, made a bequest to the parish of Castlelyons, Cloyne, q. v.

1704/5. Feb. 3. VALENTINE FRENCH, P. Killaspugmullane. [F.F.] In 1717 he became Dean of Ross, q. v.

1731. July 4. On this Sunday Terence O'Brien renounces Popery in the parish church of Killaspugmullane.

1732. Nov. 8. No name appears. [V.B.]

1732/3. Jan. 1. JEMMET BROWNE, A.M., vice French deceased, P. Killaspugmullane, et unam R. V. Cannaway, R. Kilcoane, Templeusky, Ballydeloghie als Kilroan, and R. V. Insulæ parvæ. He is again admitted to same on 28th June, 1733. [D.R.]

He appears 1733 to 1743, June 1. [V.B. D.R.]

Browne was also Dean of Ross, q. v.

1743. Nov. 11. PHILIP SYDNEY SMYTH, fourth VISCOUNT STRANGFORD, is presented to Preb. Killaspugmullane, R. Templeusque, Kilkoan, and Kilroan als Ballydeloghy, and one R. Cannaway. [Lib. Mun. and D.R.]

In 1752 LORD STRANGFORD became Dean of Derry, which he resigned in 1769 for the Archdeaconry of Derry, which he held until his death, on 29th April, 1789.

LORD STRANGFORD was born on 14th March, 1715, and entered T.C.D. as Nobilis on 13th Oct. 1733. He graduated afterwards as LL.D.

He was elected in 1745 a member, and in 1760 President of the Moyallow Loyal Protestant Society.

He married in 1741 Mary, dau. of Antony Jephson, of Mallow Castle, M.P., and by her had issue an only son, Lionel, fifth VISCOUNT STRANGFORD, who took holy orders.

1752. May 11. EDWARD BROWNE, A.M., P. Killaspugmullane, &c. as held by Lord Strangford. [D.R.] He was also R. V. Mackloneigh, and Archdeacon of Ross, q. v.

1777. Dec. 15. JEMMET BROWNE, A.B., P. Killaspugmullane, &c. [F.F.]

Jemmet Browne (son of Edward, Archdeacon of Ross), married, in 1784, Frances (dau. of John Blennerhasset, by Frances, dau. of Edward Herbert, of Muckruss), and by her had issue two sons, Jemmet and Rev. John; besides three daughters, one of whom, Frances, was wife to Rev. Frances Fox, a nephew of LORD FARNHAM. The Rev. Jemmet Browne lived at Riverstown, county Cork, and his will was dated 27th Oct. 1786, and proved 21st June, 1797. He died on 3rd March, 1797.

1797. August 29. JAMES STOPFORD, A.M., P. Killaspugmullane, &c. [F.F.]

James Stopford (son of Joseph Stopford, who was brother to Thomas, Bishop of Cork and Ross), was nephew to the first Earl of Courtown.

He was ordained Deacon on 1st May, 1768, at St. Kevin's, Dublin, by the Bishop of Cork; and Priest on 11th September of same year, by the Bishop of Cork, at Cork.

He was licensed to the Curacy of Innishannon on 26th May, 1768, and remained there for several years. From 1786 to 1797 he was P. Killavery, in Meath; and from 1795 to 1797 held Killanully Prebend, in Cork. From 1797 to his death on 27th September, 1823, he was P. Killaspugmullane. He desires in his will to be buried in the tomb built by himself, in the church-yard of Kilroan als Ballydelogher. He bequeathed twenty guineas to the poor of Killaspugmullane.

1823. Oct. 22. EDWARD ST. LAWRANCE, LL.D., P. Killaspugmullane, &c. [F.F.]

In 1825 he became Archdeacon of Ross, q. v.

1830. Protestant population of Templeusque, 63; of Kilcoan, 26; of Ballydelohar, 73; of Ballinalty, 24; of Ballyvinny, 0. Total of union, 186.

1838. Sept. 22. A new church, built at expense of Ecclesiastical Commissioners, in the parish of Kilcoan, is licensed for divine service. [D.R.]

1837. Killaspugmullane union, 7 miles long by 4 broad, with cure, consisting of—1. Templeusque rectory, 5 miles long by 1¼ broad; 2. Kilcoane rectory, 3 miles long by 1¼ broad; 3. Ballydelohar rectory, 1½ miles long by 1 broad; 4. Ballinalty rectory, 3 miles long by 2½ broad; 5. Ballyvinny rectory, 1¼ long by 1 mile broad. The union contains 21,755 acres. Gross population, 6,639. One Curate employed, at a stipend of £75 per annum. Tithe composition of Templeusque parish, £316; Kilcoane, £244 12*s.* 3¾*d.*; Ballydelohar, £177 10*s.* 16A. 0R. 31⅝P. (statute measure) of glebe in said parish, valued at £2 per plantation acre, £20. Tithe composition of Ballynalty parish, £276 18*s.* 5½*d.*; Ballyvinny, £92 6*s.* 1¾*d.* Subject to visitation fees, about £1 10*s.* Diocesan schoolmaster, £1 5*s.* No glebe-house. Incumbent is resident, and pays a sum of £40 per annum for house-rent. One church, situate in Ballydelohar parish, capable of accommodating 200 persons; built in 1829, by means of a gift of £650, granted by the late Board of First Fruits. No charge on the parish in 1832, on account of the church. Divine service is celebrated twice on Sundays in summer, and once in winter, and on the principal festivals. The sacrament is administered twelve times in the year. The benefice is a rectory. The P. Killaspugmullane has a separate revenue of £46 3*s.* 1*d.* from the rectorial tithes of Cannaway, but no duties, save preaching occasionally in the the cathedral. [Parl. Rep.]

1842. August 26. JOHN ABRAHAM BOLSTER, A.M. (vice St. Laurence, deceased), P. Killaspugmullane, the corps of which consists of R. Kilcoan and Ballynalty Rectory als Kilshanahan, with Ballyvinny Rectory, and the one R. of Cannaway. [D.R.]

1851. August 5. The new church is consecrated, but no name of dedication is mentioned in the registry. [D.R.]

1860. One church. No glebe-house. Incumbent resides in the adjoining parish. Divine service on all Sundays, &c. Sacrament monthly: average of communicants, 12. A Church Education school. The Protestant population is 57. The rentcharge of Kilcoan is £183 9*s.* 2*d.*; of Ballynalty, £207 13*s.* 9*d.*; of Ballyvinny, £69 4*s.* 6*d.*; of one R. Cannaway, £46 3*s.* 1*d.* Total rentcharge, £506 10*s.* 6*d.*, without residence.

J. A. Bolster graduated A.B. in 1826, and A.M. in 1837. He was ordained Deacon on 23rd December, 1827, and Priest on 30th November, 1828, both at Cloyne.

In 1829 he was licensed to the Curacy of Killaspugmullane. From 1836 to 1842 was R. V. Inchinabacky.

He is married, and has issue.

KILLOWEN.

1610 to 1682. Killowen was held with Garrivoe, q. v.

1682. August 23. DANIEL LORD, A.M., is admitted R. Garrivoe et Killowen, and on 24th August, R. V. Murragh, and V. Desertserges. [F.F.] He resigned Garrivoe in 1683, but retained Killowen until 1704. In 1683, Sept. 6, he was again admitted to Killowen. [F.F.] "Killowen is said to be part of Murragh." [V.B. 1699. D.D.] *Vide* Murragh.

1705. July 16. RICHARD GOODMAN, R. Killowen. [F.F.] He appears 1705 to 1736, July 14. [V.B. D.R.] In 1718 he became P. Desertmore, q. v.

1737. June 1. Vacant per mortem RICHI GOODMAN. [V.B. D.R.]

1737/8. January 19. THOMAS BARRY, A.M., is instituted to R. Kilcony, als Killowen. [D.R.]

He appears 1738 to 1749. [V.B. D.R.]

Thomas Barry (brother to Sir Edward, the father of John, P. Desertmore), was son to Edward Barry, M.D., and was born in Cork, and educated by Rev. Edmond Molloy. When eighteen years old, he entered T.C.D. as a Pensioner, on 9th July, 1729, and in 1733 obtained a Scholarship.

He was ordained Deacon on 1st of June, and Priest on 27th of July, 1735, by the Bishop of Cork.

In 1735 he was made a Vicar Choral, and in 1737, R. Killowen, both which appointments he held at his death. He was killed by a fall from his horse on 19th May, 1749, and was buried on 20th of May, in the church-yard of St. Mary, Shandon. He held also, in 1742, the curacy of Killaspugmullane.

1749. June 2. ST. JOHN BROWNE, LL.D., R. Kilcony, als Killowen. [F.F.] On presentation (of May 20, 1749) of Gerald, Lord Baron of Kinsale. [D.R.] Browne was also P. Kilbrogan, q. v. He died in 1796.

1796. June 4. WILLIAM NOBLE, R. Killowen, and V. Holy Trinity. [F.F.] He was presented to Killowen by John, Lord Kinsale. [D.R.] *Vide* the V. Holy Trinity for Noble.

1799. July 5. HON. THOMAS DE COURCY, A.B., R. Killowen and Garrivoe [F.F.]; to Killowen by resignation of Noble; and to Garrivoe by resignation of Richard Meade; to both on presentation of John, Lord Kinsale. [D.R.] *Vide* Garrivoe.

1830. Protestant population, 18.

1832. May 22. JOHN STEWART, R. Killowen, on presentation of John Meade and John Newman Spiller, esqrs. trustees to late Lord Kinsale. [D.R.] Stewart resigned on 27th April, 1840, for Templetrine, q. v.

1837. Killowen, a rectory, with cure, ¾ of an Irish mile long by ¾ broad, containing 1,260A. Gross population, 432. No

Curate employed. Tithe composition, £140 12*s.* 9*d.* No glebe-house. Incumbent is non-resident from inability of obtaining accommodation; he resides at Bandon, and pays the sum of £21 a year for house rent. No church. Divine service is celebrated once on all Sundays and on the great festivals in a private dwelling-house. The sacrament is administered twelve times in the year. The benefice is a rectory. [Parl. Rep.]

1840. October 17. RICHARD THOMAS MEADE, A.B., R. Killowen, (on presentation of the same patrons as those in 1832), dated 5th October, 1840. [D.R.] Meade, in 1856, became R. Templetrine, q. v.

1849. August 31. A new church and church-yard were consecrated, the church under the name of St. John. [D.R.]

1856. July 9. JOHN PRATT, R. Killowen, on presentation of Lord Kinsale, dated 14th June, 1856. [D.R.] His Lordship gave his turn of nomination to the Bishop.

In 1858 Pratt became R. Kilnagross, Ross, q. v.

1858. Sept. 6. ROBERT WILLIAM DELACOUR, R. Killowen, on presentation of Lord Kinsale, dated 3rd August, 1858. The net value is £94 19*s.* 6*d.* [D.R.]

1860. The church in order. A glebe-house and five acres of glebe in Rector's use. Rev. James Smith is Curate. Divine service twice on all Sundays, and on the usual holidays. Sacrament monthly and at festivals; average of communicants, 29. About 27 children attend a Church Education Society school. The Protestant population is 60. The rentcharge is £105 9*s.* 6*d.* The land is worth £5. Total value, £110 9*s.* 6*d.* per an., with residence.

R. W. Delacour (son of James Delacour, esq. of Mallow), was ordained in 1846.

He married Eliza, dau. of Frederick Hyde, esq. of Hollywood, county Kerry, and has issue.

KILMICHAEL.

1591. Rectoria Sci Michaelis spectat ad prebend de Kilbrogan. Vic. ibm DERMICIUS LONGE, Thesaurarius. [MS. T.C.D. E. 3. 14.]

1615. RANDOLPH HOLLAND appears as V. Kilmichael. "Kilmighell. Abbas de Antro rector. Richūs Boyle, miles, firmarius. Vicarius Randol Holland, Studens in Collegio. Val. £6 13*s.* 4*d.* Ecclia repāta. Cancella ruinata." [R.V. R.I.A.] Holland, in 1623, became P. Killanully, q. v.

1629. Sept. 9. EDWARD CLERKE, A.M., is admitted V. Kinneigh and Kilmichael, united by Bishop to Deanery of Cloyne. [R.V. 1634.] For Clerke, *vide* Deans of Cloyne.

1634. R. de Kilmichael spectat ad Abb. de Antro et Mourne. Cormack Donogh Carty, firmarius. Val. IV li. per an. Vic. ibm Edward Clerke. Val. IV li. per an. [R.V. 1634.]

1639. V. Edward Clerke. It is also marked vacant. Curate, Richard Burden. "Ecclia non bene, habent ornamenta." [V.B. D.R.]

1640. Oct. 2. EDWARD WORTH, V. de Kilmichael. [F.F.] In 1644 he was Dean of Cork, q. v.

1640 (circa). THOMAS HENSEY, V. Kilmichael and Kinneigh. [F.F.]

1663. Sept. 26. GEORGE SYNGE, V. Kilmichael and Inchigula, per litteras patentes Regis, studendi gratia, in collatione Epi. [V.B. D.R. 1669.]

In 1674 he became also P. Kilbrogan, q. v.

1677. SAMUEL SYNGE appears as V. Kilmichael and Inchigeelah. [V.B. D.R.] He is also P. Dromdaleague, q. v.

1679. June 10. CORNELIUS HIGNETT, A.M., V. Kilmichael and Inchigeelah, and P. Dromdaleague. [F.F.] In 1706 he was also Chancellor of Ross, q. v.

1699. Some few English there. No church. Ought there not to be care taken that divine service be performed there sometimes? No churchwardens nor parish clerk. [V.B. 1699. D.D.] "On the north of Fanlobbus lye Kilmichael and Inchigeelah in a coarse country. The people are all Irish, except one or two families. No church nor divine service." [Downes' Tour.]

1727/8. Feb. 1. PETER WATERHOUSE, R. and V. Kilmichael and Inchigeelah, per mort. Hignett. He is again admitted 1st January, 1732. [D.R.] In 1730 he was also Precentor of Cork, q. v.

1728. April 23. Edmund Barrett renounces Popery in the parish church of Kilmichael. [D.R.]

1750. April 19. PATRICK ELMSLEY, A.M., R. and V. Kilmichael and Inchigeelah, per mort. Waterhouse. [D.R.] *Vide* Inchigeelah.

1755. April 25. THOMAS BROWNE, A.M., R. V. Kilmichael, per mortem Elmsley. [D.R.]

In 1757 Browne became Precentor of Cork, q. v.

1757. November 5. THOMAS WATERHOUSE, A.M., R. V. Kilmichael, per cession of Browne. [D.R.]

In 1762 Waterhouse became Precentor of Cork, q. v.

1762. May 13. EDWARD KENNY, A.B., R. V. Kilmichael, per cession of Waterhouse. [D.R.] Kenny was P. Inskenny, q. v.

1777. December 17. THOMAS BREVITOR, A.M., R. V. Kilmichael and Macloneigh. [F.F.] In 1784 he became R. Carrigaline, q. v.

1778. August 15. Kilmichael and Macloneigh parishes are united for ever by the Lord Lieutenant and Privy Council, with consent of the Archbishop of Cashel and of the Bishop of Cork, and on the petition of Brevitor, who states that there is but one church in the episcopal union of Kilmichael and Macloneigh, in the parish of Kilmichael; and no glebe-house in either. He states the value of Kilmichael to be £250, and of Macloneigh to be £150, and says he intends to build on Macloneigh glebe. [D.R.]

1784. Dec. 4. The Bishop certifies for improvements on the glebe, £120 3*s.* 3*d.* The yearly value of the benefice is £388. Brevitor's memorial to build was dated 17th July, 1778. He did not expend much on the house, as his successor had to build a new residence.

1784. Feb. 18. GEORGE SACKVILLE COTTER, A.M., R. V. Kilmichael and Macloneigh. [D.R.] In 1797 he became R. Igtermurragh, Cloyne, q. v.

In Feb. 1791, Cotter memorials for permission to build a new house on a different part of the glebe of Macloneigh. The Bishop certifies, on 3rd Feb. 1797, that Cotter expended on such house £509 17*s.* 4*d.*, that the glebe at Macloneigh is worth £80, and that the tithes of Kilmichael and Macloneigh are worth £350. [D.R.]

1797. June 20. ROBERT WARREN, R. V. Kilmichael and Macloneigh. [F.F.]

1799. January 11. Robert Warren memorials for liberty to erect a barn and offices, and the Bishop approves same day. In 1803, 25th April, a commission to value issues, and the Bishop, on Sept. 23, 1805, certifies that Warren expended £697 3*s.* 6*d.*; the yearly value of the benefice being £700 per an. [D.R.]

Robert Warren (fourth son of the first baronet SIR ROBERT WARREN, of Warren's Court, county Cork), was ordained Deacon at Cloyne, by letters dimissory from Cork on 29th September, 1786, and Priest at Cloyne, also on letters from Cork, on 1st August, 1790.

On 28th October, 1791, he was licensed to the curacy of Aglish, &c., and from 1797 to his death in 1829 was R. V. Kilmichael. In 1799 he seems to have held also the curacy of Magourney.

He married Margaret, dau. of Kingsmill Pennefather, M.P. for Cashel, and by her had issue, Rev. Robert (R. Cannaway, q. v.), and Richard, M.D., who married Margaret, dau. of William Pennefather.

1829. December 2. RICHARD JEPHSON ROTHE, A.B., R. V. Kilmichael and Macloneigh. [D.R.]

1830. Protestant population, 107.

1837. Oct. 2. Rothe memorials for liberty to renew the roof of the glebe-house at Macloneigh, at cost of £232, which sum a commission returns as duly expended on 11th June, 1839. [D.R.]

1837. Kilmichael union, 10 miles long by 6 broad, with cure, consisting of:—1. Kilmichael, part of rectory and vicarage, 6 miles long by 6 broad. 2. Macloneigh rectory, 4 miles long by 3 broad. The union contains 23,713A. Gross population, 7,686. No Curate employed. Tithe composition of Kilmichael parish belonging to Incumbent, £692 6*s.* 2*d.*; 7A. of glebe in said parish, valued at 25*s.* per acre, £8 15*s.* Tithe composition of Macloneigh parish, £250; 48A. of glebe in said parish, valued at 25*s.* per acre, £60; subject to visitation fees, 18*s.* 4*d.*; diocesan schoolmaster, £1 2*s.* 9*d.* Kilmichael glebe-house built under the old Acts in 1784, at the cost of £111 7*s.* 7¼*d.* Brit., the dwelling-house being then thatched. A new glebe-house erected on a new site in 1797, at a certified charge of £470 12*s.* 11¼*d.* Brit.; and a further expenditure of £643 10*s.* 11*d.*, made under certificate of improvements in 1805. The present Incumbent is third in succession from the original builder; and having paid his predecessor's executors £889 16*s.* 11*d.*, on account of the building and improvement charges, he will be entitled to receive about £553 16*s.* 11*d.* from his successor. Incumbent is resident in the glebe-house. The rectorial, or one-half of the tithes of 13,500 plan. acres in Kilmichael parish, compounded for £273 5*s.* 8*d.* are impropriate, and belong to the Duke of Devonshire; the remaining half of these tithes, and the whole tithes of the rest of the parish belong to Incumbent. One church, in which there is divine service once on all Sundays, and on Christmas Day and Good Friday. The sacrament is administered monthly. [Parl. Rep.]

Richard Jephson Rothe (son of George Abraham Rothe, by Salisbury, dau. of Lorenzo H. Jephson, esq. of county Tipperary; which George-Abraham was eldest son of Richard Rothe, of Mountrath, county Kilkenny, by Catherine D'Alton; which Richard, last named, was eldest son of Michael Rothe, esq. of Butler's Grove, who died circa 1746), was from 1827 to 1829, P. Killanully, and from 1829 to his death on 26th April, 1846, R. Kilmichael.

He married on 18th October, 1830, Letitia (dau. of Thomas St. Lawrence, Bishop of Cork), who died in 1833, bequeathing to her husband her lands in East Carbury, county Cork.

1846. May 23. HENRY FITZALLEN M'CLINTOCK, R. V. Kilmichael and Macloneigh; certified value, £713 14*s.* 5*d.* [D.R.]

1846. July 25. A commission finds £155 19*s.* 10*d.* to be the amount of dilapidations against Rothe's representatives. [D.R.]

1860. One church and a glebe-house; 48A. of glebe in Rector's use. Divine service once on Sundays and the usual holidays; evening service in the glebe-house. Sacrament monthly; average of communicants, 17. 11 children attend the parish school. The Protestant population is 46. The rentcharge of Kilmichael is £519 4*s.* 7*d.*, of Macloneigh, £187 10*s.* The glebe of Kilmichael is worth £8 15*s.*, and that of Macloneigh is worth £60. Total value of benefice, £775 9s. 7d. with residence.

H. F. M'Clintock (eldest son of the late Alexander M'Clintock, R. Glanbarrahan, Ross, q. v.), was from 1835 to 1846, V. Ballymodan.

KILMOCAMOGE.

1550. May 14. McDermot O'Mulriane, of Kylmocowoge, Clerk, is pardoned. [Morrin. Pat. Rot. 4th Edw. VI.]

1591. E. de Kilmochomog als Killmachumocke spectat ad Ab. Scē Catherine Waterford. Vicaria vacat. [MS. T.C.D. E. 3. 14.]

1612. 10th James I. Gibson is presented to V. Kilmaconnock, dioc. Cork. [Lib. Mun.]

1615. R. Kilmacomoge spectat ad Eccliam Katherinæ Waterfordensis. Vicarius ibm Gawinus Gibson, minister legens et inserviens curæ. Valor 5 li. Ecclia in repatione, cancella ruinata. [R.V. R.I.A.]

1627. May 20. Marcus Pagett, V. de Kilmacomoge. [F.F.] He was afterwards Dean of Ross, q. v.

1634. R. Kilmacomoge spectat ad monasterium Stæ Katherinæ Waterford. Comes Corke firmarius. Val. 20 li. per an. Vicarius ibm Marcus Pagett. Val. 20 li. per an. [R.V. 1634.]

1639. R. Kilmocamoge Baro de Esmond. Vicarius Marcus Pagett. Curatus Wm. Bird. Ecclesia bene. [V.B. D.R.]

16—? Thomas Barham, V. Kilmocamoge and Kilcroghane, and Durrus, q. v.

1663. Sept. 22. Thomas Holmes, V. Kilmocamoge, V. Durrus, and Kilcrohane, vacant by death of Thomas Barham. [V.B. D.R. 1669.]

"1699. Kilmacomogue joins to Caharagh, about two miles before we come to Bantry, and lyes westward of Caharagh; the church stood three miles to the north-east of Bantry; 'tis ruinous; there is a cabin built on purpose for a chapel in Bantry; 75 plowlands and 8 gneeves in the parish of Kilmacomoge; about 150 persons usually at church in Bantry; three Sundays in four Mr. Holmes preaches in Bantry; the fourth Sunday he preaches in Captain Evanson's house, at Four-mile-water, in the parish of Durrows. Kilmacomoge being 3 plowlands, belongs to the See of Corke, set for £12; well set; and Innishbegclary, an island, set for £14, is worth about £35 per an. The 3 plowlands of Kilmacomoge are better land than the land about it, but 'tis small measure. The rectory of Kilmacomoge belongs to St. Catherine's Abby, of Waterford."

"Kilchroghan lyes to the south-west of Bantry, about five

miles, at the nearest, and about twelve miles at the furthest part distant from Bantry; no church, nor Protestants. Kilcroghan, 3 plowlands, belonging to the see of Corke, worth at least £20 per an., is set to Sir Richard Hull for £5 per an.; the land is better than the other land in that parish; indifferent measure. The rectory of Kilcroghan belongs to St. Catherine's, Waterford, except the rectory of the 3 plowlands of Kilcroghan, which belongs to the Earl of Cork."

"Anno. 1699. Most part of the parish of Kilcroghan is the joynture of Mrs. Peyton; the estate belongs to the Hulls for the most part. The greatest part of the barony of Bere and Bantry is the estate of the Earl of Anglesey; Mr. Davys has an estate about Bantry and Whidy Island worth about £500 per an., out of which he pays a chiefry to the Earl of Anglesey of £100 per an., and quit rent £150 per an. The parish of Durrows lyes close to the town of Bantry, to the south, and Kilcroghan to the south of Durrows, they both lye betwixt Bantry bay and Dunmanus bay. There was a chappel of ease in the parish of Durrows, near Bantry, before the year 1641. Bantry bay runs about twenty miles up into the land. Bantry town stands within three miles of the highest part of the Bay. Mointer-Vary, in the parish of Kilcroghan, is the lowest point on the east side of the mouth of the Bay, and Great Island opposite to it on the west. The Bay runs from the sea to the north-east. Barracks for one company of foot are building at Bantry. Durrows and Kilcroghan are united pro hac vice to Kilmacomoge. Some Protestants in Durrows; three Sundays in four Mr. Holmes preaches at Bantry, the fourth Sunday he preaches at Four-mile-water for the parish of Kilcroghan and the adjacent parts of Durrows. No divine service in any place westward of Bantry within less than twelve miles, in Kerry, at Glanerought. The ruins of an abbey lie within quarter of a mile of Bantry. Two little schools kept in Bantry; 31 plowlands in the parish of Durrows. The Earl of Corke has the moiety of the tythes of 12 plowlands; the Vicar has the remainder of all the tythes; the Vicar's share is worth about £30 per annum; 30 small plowlands in Kilcroghan parish; the rectory belongs to the Abbey of St. Catherine's, Waterford, the estate of Sir Ellis Layton; the lease of this, from the King, expired in the Earl of Essex's time, and was then renewed by Sir Ellis Layton; only the rectory of the three plowlands of Kilcroghan belongs to the Earl of Corke."

"The vicarage is worth about £16 per annum; Bantry bay runs from the sea to the north-east above 20 miles into the land; it branches itself into little creeks: on one of them stands Bantry or Oldtown; on another, Newtown; on another, Ballilicky; on another, the Snave. The bay is generally about a league broad. About a mile below Bantry are four or five little islands, as Horse Island, Hog Island, Cony Island, &c. Whidy Island is about 2 miles from Bantry, very good land; about 1,000 English acres are set for about £80 per an. by Mr. Davys to Mr. Bemish; frost seldom continues, nor snow on this island; the biggest ships may come on the west of Whidy with safety. Berehaven side of the bay is coarse rocky mountain, hardly passable; there the cane apples, or Arbutus, grow on the sides of the most steep and rocky mountains. A river runs down a steep side of the hill; springs generally on the tops of the hills, and bogs on the tops of the rocky mountains; Pilchers were taken generally in this bay heretofore; few of late. Beds of escalops about the Horse Island, they are large.

	Plowlands.	Gneeves.
Kilmacomoge, . . .	75	8
Durrus, ...	11	2
Kilcaskane, . . .	10	6
Killaghaninagh, . . .	74	3
Killmannah, . . .	9	9
Killkatiern, . . .	14	3

"The whole charge on the barony of Bere and Bantry for the half year's land tax, £88 19*s.* 11*d.*

"Charge on the tythe, £8 19*s.* 11*d.*

"Charge on the barony, deducting the tythe, £80.

"Each plowland pays, half-yearly, 8*s.* 2½*d.*

"In the parish of Kilmacomoge the Irish observe Macomoge's day as a festivall, and generally each parish observes a patron day; and in the whole diocess of Corke generally the Irish observe St. Finbarry's day as a festivall. In the whole diocess of Rosse the Irish observe St. Faughnan's day as a festivall. The parish of Kilmacomoge is worth about £30 per an. to Mr. Holmes.

"The Bay of Bantry is a good harbour; ships of great burden, of a thousand tuns, may come within Whidy Island; no shallows nor hidden rocks in the bay. The French men-of-war, being above 20, came into the bay in 1689. The ships laden with ammunition, &c., came up to the bay. The English and French men-of-war engag'd betwixt Great Island and Mointervary." [Downes' Tour.]

From 1663 to 1769 Kilmocamoge was held with Durrus, q. v.

1769. March 14. JOHN KENNEY, A.M., V. Kilmocamoge, Durrus, and Kilcroghan. [F.F.] In 1796 he was P. Kilbrogan, q. v.

In 1793, April 16, Kenney resigned Durrus, Kilcroghan, and in 1796 he resigned Kilmocamoge.

1792. November 27. An order was made by the Lord Lieutenant and Privy Council to change the site of the church of Kilmocamoge and Durrus. [Lib. Mun.]

1796. May 4. CHARLES SMITH, A.B., V. Kilmocamoge. [F.F.]

1814. July 9. Lord Bantry leases for ever to the Vicar about 20 plantation acres of the lands of Cappanology for a glebe, at the annual rent of £147 7*s.* 9*d.*; and on 3rd August, 1814, the Bishop receives a memorial and estimate for a house on said glebe, at cost of £1,390 10*s.* 9*d.* for house, and £639 10*s.* 6*d.* for offices. On 27th Sept., 1816, the Bishop certifies the yearly value to be £1,200 12*s.* 6*d.*, and Smith's expenditure to be £2,902; from which latter sum the loan of £1,500 from First Fruits being deducted, the charge on benefice is fixed at £901 5*s.* [D.R.]

1815. Oct. 23. Richard, Earl of Bantry, grants for ever two roods and thirteen perches of land in Bantry for a church-yard and site of new church. On 13th July, 1816, an order is obtained from Privy Council to change the site.

Charles Smith was ordained Deacon on 24th August, 1784, at Cork, and Priest on 5th December, same year, at Cloyne.

He was licensed to the curacy of Castlemartyr, on 22nd Nov., 1784, and held that curacy in 1786.

From 1784 to 1796 he was R. V. Cannaway, and from 1796 to his death in 1825, was V. Kilmocamoge.

He married, firstly, Elisabeth Forsayeth; and, secondly, in 1790, Jane Kenah, of Igtermurragh. He left issue John, his eldest son, and Rev. Godfrey C. C. W. Smith, his youngest son (R. Kinneigh, q. v.), besides 3 daughters, Margaret, Ellen, and Alicia, wife of Rev. John Murphy, Treasurer of Cork, q. v.

1825. March 10. HENRY EVANS SADLIER, A.B., V. Kilmocamoge. [D.R.] In 1849 he became P. Ballyhay, Cloyne, q. v.

1830. Protestant population, 948.

1837. Kilmocomogue: a vicarage, with cure; 14 miles long by 12 broad, containing 56,910A.; gross population, 14,483; one Curate employed, at a stipend of £75 per annum; tithe composition, £625; 10 acres of glebe let for £10; 32¼ acres of glebe in Incumbent's occupation, rented at four guineas per acre, £135 9*s.*, subject to visitation fees, 7*s.* 8*d.*; diocesan schoolmaster, 18*s.* Kilmocomogue glebe-house built under the new Acts, in 1816, at a cost of £2,307 13*s.* 10¼*d.* Brit., whereof £1,384 12*s.* 3¾*d.* was granted in way of loan, and £92 6*s.* 1½*d.* in that of gift by the late Board of First Fruits, and the residue of £830 15*s.* 4¾*d.* was supplied out of the private funds of the builder, to whom the present Incumbent is next in succession; and having paid his predecessor's representatives the entire of the sum last named, he will be entitled to receive £623 1*s.* 6½*d.* from his successor on account thereof. Of the loan aforesaid there remained £817 9*s.* 4*d.* chargeable on the benefice in 1832, repayable by annual instalments of £45 9*s.* 2*d.* Incumbent is constantly resident in the glebe-house. Exclusive of the monies aforesaid, the builder is reported to have expended £369 4*s.* 7½*d.* on the glebe-house, without having any charge on his successor for the repayment of any portion thereof. One church, capable of accommodating 500 persons, built in 1818, at the cost of £1,938 9*s.* 2¾*d.* Brit., whereof £1,384 12*s.* 3¾*d.* was granted in way of loan by the late Board of First Fruits, and the residue of £553 16*s.* 11*d.* was raised by private subscriptions. Of the loan aforesaid there remained £1,023 10*s.* 2*d.* chargeable on the parish in 1832, repayable by annual instalments of £48 14*s.* 8*d.* Divine service is celebrated in the church twice on all Sundays, and on the principal festivals, as also in a private house, four miles from the church, on Sunday mornings, and at the glebe-house on Sunday evenings. Service is also performed in the church on all Thursdays, and a lecture is delivered in a part of the parish remote from the church on every Wednesday evening. The sacrament is administered monthly, and on Christmas Day. The rectorial tithes of this parish, compounded for £561 15*s.*, are impropriate, and belong to the Earl of Donoughmore. [Parl. Rep.]

1840. May 12. HON. CHARLES BRODRICK BERNARD, A.M., V. Kilmocamoge. [D.R.] In 1842 he became P. Kilbrogan, q. v.

1842. July 2. JOHN MURPHY, A.B., V. Kilmocamoge. [D.R.] In 1861 he became Treasurer of Cork, q. v.

1860. The outside wall of the church requires repairs, and is very unsightly. The church was built about 1818. It is oblong, with tower, in which is a porch, and with vestry, but without transepts or spire. The interior was completely altered in 1859, and was fitted with benches. There is a gallery at the west end. A font of Bath stone (octangular, 3 feet 2 inches high, and 2 feet 2 inches at its greatest breadth) was given by the EARL of BANTRY, who erected also at the east end a stained-glass memorial window, in memory of the late COUNTESS of BANTRY, his deceased wife, to whom is inscribed a mural monument on the north wall of the church. The west end window was also fitted with stained glass by the present LORD BANTRY. There is a glebe-house and 32½ acres of glebe in Vicar's use. There are two other glebes, one of 8 the other of 4 acres, in remote parts of the parish, which are let to tenants. Divine service twice on all Sundays, &c. Sacrament monthly, and at festivals; average of communicants, 45; 66 children are on the rolls of the schools, which are aided by the Church Education Society.

The Curate is Rev. A. B. Wilson. The Protestant population is 396. The rentcharge is £468 15*s.* There are 43 acres of land, worth £75 per an., but as the enormous rent of £135 9*s.* has to be paid to Lord Bantry for 32½ acres of the glebe, th Vicar suffers an annual loss of £60 9*s.* by their occupation.

The Vicar also pays £15 yearly to the Curate of Glengariffe, q. v. His income, after these outgoings, may be set down as £393, with residence.

1861. January 17. RICHARD CHARLES FAULKNER, A.B., V. Kilmocamoge. [D.R.]

Mr. Faulkner was ordained in 1847. From 1851 to 1861 he was licensed Curate of Middleton. He was educated at Portora Royal School, Enniskillen.

He married Mary (dau. of Abraham Chatterton, esq., of Cork, by Jane, dau. of Rev. Fitzgerald Tisdall, R. Kilmoe, q. v.), and has issue.

KILMOE.

1581. Sept. 4. DERMITIUS M'CORMUCK MACARTY, R. Kilmoe. "Idem (Epus) contulit unam Rectoriarum Ecclise St. Brandain de Kilmo, viz., Rectoriam in feodo Ecclesiastico dno dermitio M'Cormuck Macarty, presbitero, 4° Septembris, 1581. Inductus est quasi in poẽm eodem die per Phil. Gold." [D.R.]

1591. CORNELIUS O'SULLIVAN appears as V. de Kilmoe. "Rectoria de Kilmo spectat ad Colleg. de Youghell. Cornelius O'Sullivan, vicarius de Kilmo et vicarius de Skull et vicarius de Durrus, interdicitur donec probavit se promot. ad sacros ordines." [MS. T.C.D. E. 3. 14.]

1615. THOMAS WAY appears as Vicar. "Kilmoe: Rector Collegium de Youghell. Vicarius ibm Thomas Way, Minister et predicator, inserviens curæ. Valor 8 li." [R.V. R.I.A.] 1634. Rectoria de Kilmoe in fundo spectat ad Coll. de Youghall. Val. XX li. per an. Rector in feodo Ecclesiastico est Thomas Way, predicator. Val. 20 li. per an. Comes. Corke est patronus. [R.V. 1634.] Way is also V. Scull, q. v.

1619. August 18. DERMITIUS O'COGHLAN, V. de Kilmoe. [F.F.] But the date given in R. V. of 1634, is 3rd July, 1619, and inducted 29th November, 1619.

1634. Vicarius de Kilmoe Dermot O'Coughlan, predicator. Epus confert. Val. 20 li. per an. [R.V. 1634.] O'Coughlan is still Vicar in 1639. "Ecclesia bene, desunt singula." [V.B. 1639.]

Dermitius O'Coghlan, diaconus, was ordained Priest by John, Bishop of Cork, on 6th December, 1618.

Dermitius O'Coghlan, or Coughlan, is said to have been Incumbent in 1641, when he was driven to England by the wars, and died in that kingdom. His son, Thadeus, was father of Dermitius Coughlan, whose relict, Sarah, aged about 80, is mentioned in some law case of Rev. Paul Limerick, R.

Kilmoe, temp. 1723. [Nichols' Topographer, vol. II. pp. 344 to 356.]

1637. March 3. GEORGE HORSEY is presented to V. Kilmowe. [Lib. Mun.] In 1638 he became Dean of Ross, q. v.

1639. April 29. JOHN STANHOP is presented to R. Kilmowe, dioc. Cork. [Lib. Mun.]

1663/4. January 29. JOHN EVELAYE, Dean of St. Faghanan, Ross, is presented to the Rectory and Vicarage of Kilmo, dioc. Cork. [Lib. Mun.] He was instituted on 15th June, 1664. [F.F.] *Vide* Deans of Ross.

1666. Kilmoe and Scull are vacant. [V.B. D.R.]

1667. May 15. HENRY PARR, R. V. Kilmoe and Scull, per resignacõn Johīs Eveleigh. Rectoriæ sunt in presentatione Regis, vicariæ in collatione Episcopi. [V.B. 1669, D.R.] On letters patent. [Lib. Mun.] He became on same day R. V. Creagh, in Ross. [F.F] Parr appears as R. and V. from 1667 to 1674. [V.B. D.R.]

Parr was also Precentor of Ross, q. v.

1674/5. April 23. JOHN EVELEIGH, Vicar Kilmoe and Scull. [F.F.] He appears in 1675. [V.B. D.R.]

1675. June 30. WILLIAM HULL, Rector de Kilmoe and Scull. [F.F.] On letters patent of June 3. [Lib. Mun.] He appears as Rector from 1675 to 1722. [V.B. D.R.]

Hull was Treasurer of Ross, q. v.

1676. May 26. JOHN GIBSON, Vicar de Kilmoe and Scull. [F.F.] He appears 1677 to 1691 as Vicar. [V.B. D.R.]

1692. Sept. 6. WALTER BRUCE, A.M., Vicar Kilmoe and Scull, per cess. of John Gibson. [D.R.] He appears 1692 to 1699 as Vicar. [V.B. D.R.] Bruce was a Vicar Choral of Ross from 1686 to 1688.

1699. Feb. 13. JOHN VYSE, Vicar Kilmoe and Scull, per mortem Walter Bruce. [D.R.] He appears as Vicar in 1704. [V.B. D.R.]

John Vyse, literatus e Jesu Coll. Cambridge, was ordained Deacon at Cork on 20th September, 1696, and Priest at Cork on 20th March, 1697. From August, 1699, to the end of that year, he was a Vicar Choral of Cork. From 1699 to 1704 he was V. Kilmoe and Scull.

"1699. Skull parish, about 50 plowlands, the rectory being half the tythes; the Vicar has the other half, and the glebe and bookmony. The vicaridge is worth about £40 per an.; the rectory is worth about £32 per an. In this parish, and in other parishes that lie on the sea, the Rector and Vicar agree as well as they can with the fishermen for the tythe of fish, sometimes 40*s.* for a sain, and sometimes 5*s.*; sometimes 10*s.* per boat for hook fishing. Half the tyth is paid by those that come out of other parishes; the other half is paid in the parish where the fishermen dwell."

"1699. Kilmoe parish, 25 plowlands. The rectory being half the tythes, is worth about £16 per an.; the vicaridge being the other half of the tythes, and the glebe and bookmony, is worth about £20 per an."

"On Munday, the 3rd of June, 1700, I left Skibbareen, and went to Skull that night. I lodg't at Mr. Bruce's house, at Derrineha, near Skull. Skull parish extends six miles eastward from the church, and to the west about three miles. The church walls are standing, and good, made of stone and lime, 84 foot long and 24 broad. It stands near the center of the parish. June 4th, 1700. An act of vestry was made for raising 12*s.* off each plowland for the repairs of the parish church. In this parish are the ruins of a chappel, near Dunmanus Castle, called Kilkanget. 84 plowlands are in this parish. 3 Sundays in 4 divine service at Skull in a house; the 4th Sunday at a house in Kilmoe parish. The 12 plowlands of Skull belong to the Bishop of Corke; they lie round the church. These lands extend a mile and a-half from the church, towards the north, and take in part of Mount Gabriel. These 12 plowlands include Castle Island, the Middle and West Calves, and Carthy's Island, all which are in the parish of Skull. These 12 plowlands are as good as any thereabouts, but they are small measure.

"The bay that goes up to Ballidehob is called Loughtrasnah. John Prouce, a good old man, is the parish clerk of this parish and Kilmoe. There are about 4 Protestant families in this parish, and about 400 Papist families. Daniel Carthy is Popish Priest of the eastern part of this parish; he has been here ever since before the late troubles. No glebe in this parish. No registry-book, nor Bible, nor Common Prayer-book. A silver chalice and plate, the gift of Mr. Hull, the Rector, are in the hands of Mr. Randolph Warner. The Bishop of Corke, Colonel Beecher, Earl of Castlehaven, Mr. Hull and the Earl of Corke have the lands of this parish; and Mr. Sullivan, a Protestant. Mr. Hull, Mr. Bennett, Dan O'Hea, Armiger How, and Anthony Allen, live in this parish. Mount Gabriel, in the parish of Skull, is a haunt of wolves; there are no trees nor shelter, except rocks and bogs. It is the highest hill in those parts, only Hungry Hill and other hills in Beerhaven are higher. From the top of Mount Gabriel we saw Dunmanus bay, the lands of the town of Kilcroghan, beyond Dunmanus bay, and also Bantry bay, with the hills of Beerhaven. We saw also from thence Ballineskellix Islands, in Kerry. Mr. Bennet saies he has heard that the Bishop of Corke has some estate thereabouts. On the Skellix, the gannet, as big as a goose, breeds. There is a small lough on the top of Mount Gabriel. From the rocks of Derrinetragh we saw Castle Island, belonging to the Bishop of Corke. It lies to the S. a mile from shore; the tenant pays to Mr. Hull for it £8 per an. There is an old Irish castle on it. Beyond Castle Island lies Carthy's Island, and the Three Calves, good land, belonging to the Bishop of Corke. From the same rocks we saw Horse Island, belonging to the Countess of Castlehaven; the West Inniskeanes, good land, belonging to the Bishop of Corke; the East Inniskeanes and Hare Island, forfeited lately by Coppinger, and granted to Dr. Lesley; Cape Clear and Shirkin, belonging to Colonel Beecher; Long Island, belonging to the Earl of Corke; and Goat Island, belonging to Mr. Hull. There is a high steep rock in the sea, called the Fastnet, which, with Cape Clear's western point and Crookhaven, make an equilateral triangle, each side three leagues. The shore on these parts is all rocky. The O'Mahons had above 100 plowlands formerly in this country."

"Tuesday, June 3, 1700. After prayers in the church of Skull, I confirmed about 40 persons that came out of the parishes of Skull and Kilmoe. I dispos'd of about 14 Common Prayer-books, and 35 small Prayer-books, for Skull and Kilmoe. The Middle and West Calves are in the parish of Skull, and the East Calf and the two Skames are in the parish of Aghadown. Some people live upon the East and Middle Calf, but none on the West Calf. The church of Skull is uncovered; the walls are standing, well built, with lime and stone. It is about 84 foot long and 24 foot broad."

"At a vestry held in Skull Church on June 4, 1700, Thomas Bennett and John Sullivan were chosen churchwardens of Skull, they were then and there presented to the Bishop of Corke, and sworn before him. At the same vestry, 12*s.* on each plowland in the parish of Skull was assest for the repairs of the Church of Skull. It was agreed that only 30 foot in length should be repaired. I promised £5 towards the repairs of Skull, and paid it. There are 84 plowlands in this parish. This parish is about 9 miles in length and 6 miles in breadth. 3 Sundays in 4 there is divine service at Mr. Bennett's house in Skull, and the fourth Sunday Mr. Vyse preaches at Mr. Coghlan's house, in the parish of Kilmoe. John Prouce, a good old man, is Clerk of this parish and Kilmoe. The parish of Skull extends 6 miles eastward from the church, it reaches to the west about 3 miles and a half from the church. In this parish are the ruins of a chappel near Dunmanus Castle, called Kilkanget. The bay that goes up to Ballidehab is called Loughtrasnagh; several islands, viz., Castle Island, &c., lie in this bay. Daniel Leahy, a convert, teaches school in this parish at Gortineroagh. This parish is worth to the Vicar about £50 per an. No glebe-house in this parish; no collections, but at the sacrament. They pay tythes of fish; the tenth fish. As to those that are remote, the Minister generally agrees with them for so much a boat. There is a Bible, but no Common Prayer-books. Sacrament three times in the year."

"On Thursday, the 6th of June, I went to Kilmoe and Crookhaven, and returned to Skull the same night.

"Kilmoe: the church is ruinous, the walls that are standing are bad, built with stone and clay. The church stands about a mile from Crookhaven, to the westward near the head of Barlycove bay. 8A. of glebe on the north of the church; good land, set for £20 per an. There are the ruins of a vicaridge house joining to ye church-yard. Crookhaven town lies on the south side of the haven; there were formerly (viz. before 1641) 200 houses there. It yielded £300 per an., rent. There are the ruins of a small fort on the east end of the town, built by the King. There are also the walls of an old castle about the middle of the town, which they say was formerly a prison. There are the ruins of a chapple at the west end of the town. One end of the chapple is dedicated to St. Mullagh, 'tis said some glebe belonged to this chapple. Missen Head lies to the south-west of Crookhaven town; the Three Castle's Head lies to the north-west of Missen Head; off of Crookhaven Head lies the rock, call'd the Aldern. Barlycove is an open bay to the south-west of Crookhaven. The church of Kilmoe is dedicated to St. Briana, als Brandon, whose festival is observed in this parish. About 9 Protestant families in this parish. There are about 200 papist families in this parish. The Earl of Corke, Bishop of Corke, Colonel Beecher, Mr. Hull, Mr. Arthur Hide, and Thadeus Coghlan, have the lands of this parish. Mr. Pierce Arnot, Thadeus Coghlan, and Mr. Mahon, a late convert, and Thomas Dyer, the tide-waiter, live in this parish. Tiege Coghlan is Popish Priest of the parish of Kilmoe, and of the western part of the parish of Skull, he has been here for about eight years. On the hill near Castlemehaga, which lies on the north side of Crookhaven bay, grows the Arbutus; I saw some of them, they grow out of the clefts of the rocks on the side of the rock looking to the south; the mould was black, wash'd down from the hill into the clefts; I suppose 'tis good rich earth. A young Irishman, a Papist, teaches school in this parish of Kilmoe, about the middle of it. This parish is very hilly and rocky. This parish is worth about £25 per an. to the Vicar. This parish has 42 plowlands in it, 'tis about 6 miles in length from east to west, and about 3 miles in breadth.

"The Rectories of Skull and Kilmoe are in the gift of the Crown, worth £60 per an.; the vicaridges in the Bishop of Corke's gift, are worth £70 per an. These two rectories, as 'tis said, belong'd formerly to the College of Youghal, the Lord Strafford wrested them out of the hands of the Earl of Corke.

"Kilmoe parish. No books, nor any Registry of Kilmoe.

About 7 or 8A. of glebe on the north of the church, near it, 'tis good land. There are about 9 Protestant families in this parish, and about 200 Papist families; the Bishop of Corke's land about the church is very good, 'tis set to the terre-tenant for about 2*s.* per acre. Carrenmore, also Carrenoglaven, belonging to the Bishop of Corke, lies to the east of Missen Head. The ruins of a chapple are at Crookhaven, 'tis said there is some glebe belonging to it, but 'tis concealed."

"Teige Coghlan is Papist Priest of Kilmoe, and the western part of the parish of Skull, he has been so for eight years. The Earl of Corke, Colonel Beecher, the Bishop of Cork, Mr. Hull, Mr. Hide, and Thadeus Coghlan, a Protestant, have the lands of this parish. Mr. Pierce Arnot, Thadeus Coghlan, and Mr. Mahon, a late convert, and Thomas Dyer, the waiter, live in this parish. Before the 1641 wars there were 200 houses in Crookhaven. Crookhaven harbour is a very good one. The parish church of Kilmoe stands at the head of Barlycove; the walls standing are bad, built of stone and clay; set for 20*s.* per an."

"The ruins of a vicaridge house within the north of the church joining to the church-yard; part of the chappel of Crookhaven is said to be older than the rest, and that it was dedicated to St. Mullagah. The Church of Kilmoe was dedicated to St. Brianah, als Brandon, whose festival is kept in the parish of Kilmoe on the 16th of May. Barlycove is an open bay to the south-west of Crookhaven; Missen Head is the western point of this bay; Three Castles Head lies to the north-west of Missen Head, in Kilmoe parish; in all the O'Sullivan's country they observe as a holiday St. Rooane's Day." [Downes' Tour.]

1705. Aug. 20. USHER SMITH, Vicar of Kilmoe and Scull. [F.F.]

In 1711 Smith became Vicar Choral, Cork, q. v.

1715 to 1718. MICHAEL PHILPOT appears as Vicar of Kilmoe et Scull. [V.B. D.R.]

In 1720 Philpot was R. Caheragh, and in 1727, P. Dromdaleague, q. v.

1720 to 1754. PAUL LIMERICK appears as Vicar of Kilmoe et Scull. [V.B. D.R.] And from 1723 to 1754, as *Rector and Vicar* of Kilmoe and Scull. [V.B. D.R.]

1724. January 23. The Bishop certifies that Limerick has expended £600 in building a glebe-house at Scull. [D.R.] An account of a suit concerning the Glebe of Kilmoe will be found in Nichols' Topographer and Genealogist, vol. ii., pp. 344–356.

Paul Limerick (son of Paul Limerick), was born in Derry, and entered T.C.D. as Pensioner, on 16th June, 1708. He obtained Scholarship in 1711. He appears as V. Killaconenagh, &c., in Ross, in 1718, and as Vicar of Scull and Kilmoe from

1720 to 1755, being also Rector from 1723 to 1755. He died in March of 1755, and was buried at St. Mary Shandon, Cork, on 30th March, 1755.

In his will, dated 25th March, 1755, he mentions two sons, William (who had a son Paul), and Robert, besides four daughters, Bridget (wife of Benjamin Sullivan, ancestor of the O'SULLIVAN MORE, and of SULLIVANS, BARONETS, of Thames Ditton, Surrey), Mary, Anne, and Mrs. White.

1755. Kilmoe and Scull are both vacant. [V.B. D.R.]

1755. Sept. 4. BENJAMIN PROSSER, R. V. Kilmoe, per mortem Paul Limerick. [D.R.] On letters patent of 22nd July, to the Consolidated R. and V. of Crookhaven, als Kilmoe. [Lib. Mun.] From this time Scull was held separately.

1762. Oct. 29. RICHARD ORPEN, A.M., R. V. Kilmoe, vacant by death of Prosser. [D.R.] Orpen resigned in October, 1764.

Richard Orpen (eldest son of Rev. Thomas Orpen, of Killowen, *vide* ORPEN, of GLANEROUGH, in Burke's L. G.), was born in county Kerry, and when seventeen years old, entered T.C.D. as a Pensioner, on 14th of April, 1743. He obtained Scholarship in 1746, and graduated B.A. in 1747.

In 1758, September 11, he was licensed to the curacy of Kilnaglory. From 1762 to 1764 he was R. V. Kilmoe, and from 1764 to 1770 he was R. Valentia, Dromod, Cahir, Killinane, Prior, and Glanbeagh, in the diocese of Ardfert. He died in 1770.

He married, Mary (dau. of Mathew Hutchinson, and relict of James French), and by her had issue Richard-Thomas Orpen (of Lirias, High Sheriff of county Cork, who died unmarried), and several daughters.

1765. June 11. SAMUEL STONE, A.M., R. V. Kilmoe. [F.F.] On letters patent of April 11. [Lib. Mun.]

Samuel Stone (son of Samuel Stone "Ducis"), was born in co. Derry, and when fourteen years old entered T.C.D. as Pensioner, on 17th September, 1737. He graduated A.M., in 1755.

From 1765 to 1769 he was R. V. Kilmoe, and from 1769 to 1799 was R. Culdaff, co. Donegal. He died in 1799, and mentions in his will his brother, Guy Stone, P. Kilroot, Connor dioc., who married, in 1760, Margaret Bryanton, and had issue four sons, Samuel, Richard, Guy, and William, besides a daughter, Anne. [U.O.]

1769. August 4. ARTHUR HYDE, A.M., R. V. Kilmoe, vacant by resignation of Stone. [D.R.] The Bishop collates for this turn.

In 1772 Hyde became R. St. Anne, Shandon, q. v.

He resigned Kilmoe in October, 1786. [Lib. Mun.]

1787. March 30. ARTHUR HYDE, junior, A.B., R. V. Kilmoe. [F.F.] On letters patent of 17th March. [Lib. Mun.] In 1791 he was Precentor of Ross, q. v.

1791. November 23. FITZGERALD TISDALL, A.M., R. V. Kilmoe. [F.F.] The Bishop collated this turn. Tisdall resigned on 23rd March, and took a second collation on 15th of April, 1808. He resigned finally on 25th April, same year, for the Union of Kenmare, Kilmackeloge, Templenoe, Kilcroghan, &c., in Ardfert dioc.

Fitzgerald Tisdall (son of Michael, Archdeacon of Ross, q. v.), was Scholar T.C.D. in 1780. He was ordained Deacon, at Cork, on 1st Nov., 1785, and Priest, at Cloyne, on 29th Sept., 1786.

From 1786 to 1791 he was Curate of Holy Trinity, Cork. From June to Nov. of 1791 he was Vicar Choral of Cork, and from 1791 to 1808 R. V. Kilmoe. He exchanged Kilmoe for Kenmare, &c., in Ardfert dioc.; and in 1809, on the morning of Easter Day, was murdered at a place called Priest's Leap, near Kenmare, as he was returning homewards. He was a J.P. for Cork county, and at the time of the expected French invasion got up a yeomanry corps, at Crookhaven, of which he was commandant.

He married in August, 1788, Mary (dau. of William Jameson, esq., by Hannah, dau. of Thomas Farren, esq.), and by her had issue Michael (in the Customs, now of Rockhouse, Clifton), Fitzgerald, and George-Canning (who both died Sp.), and two daughters, Mary, the younger, relict of Mr. Devereux, and Jane, wife of Abraham Chatterton, of Cork, who had issue by her two sons, Hedges-Eyre, Barrister-at-law and Q.C., and Abraham-Thomas, of Cork; besides a daughter, Mary, wife of Rev. Richard C. Faulkner, R. Kilmocamoge, q. v.

1808. September 15. STEPHEN DUNLEAVY, A.M., R. V. Kilmoe. [F.F.] He resigned on 3rd Nov., 1818. In 1820 he was V. Urigare, Limerick. From 1799 to 1808 he had been R. Kenmare, Ardfert. In 1794 he was Chaplain of the Kerry Militia.

He married Catherine, dau. of William Townsend Gun, esq., of Rattoo, co. Kerry, and by her had issue George, and Diana, and Mary-Frederica, wife of T. C. Ponsonby, esq.

1818. Dec. 17. FRANCIS LANGFORD, A.M., R. V. Kilmoe. [D.R.] On letters patent, dated 20th November. In his Majesty's gift for this turn. [Lib. Mun.] From 1795 to his death, on 9th February, 1842, he held, along with Kilmoe, the R. Kilcornan, Limerick diocese.

1830. Protestant population, 630.

1837. Kilmoe: a rectory, with cure; 7 miles long by 3 broad; gross population, 6,889; one Curate employed, at a stipend of £100 per annum; tithe composition, £500; 12A. 0R. 24P. of glebe, set for £8 8s., subject to visitation fees, and diocesan schoolmaster, £1 12s.; no glebe-house; Incumbent is occasionally resident within the benefice, but resides, for the most part, on his other benefice, in the county of Limerick. One church, capable of accommodating 300 persons, built upwards of a century ago, by Bishop Browne, at his own expense; no charge on the parish in 1832 on account of the church; divine service is celebrated on Sunday mornings, and on the principal festivals, in the church; and on Sunday evenings, in the school-house; the sacrament is administered monthly and at the festivals. The benefice is a rectory. [Parl. Rep.]

Francis Langford died on 9th February, 1842, leaving issue by his wife Margaret Lucinda (dau. of Rev. Walter Stewart, by Agnes, dau. of Rev. Thomas Orpen), three sons, George-Walter (of Adare), Francis, and John Thomas, besides two daughters, Charlotte, wife of John Limerick, esq., of Ardnance, co. Cork, and Anna-Maria, wife of James O'Callaghan, esq., of Rock Cottage, co. Cork.

1842. Feb. 18. WILLIAM ALLEN FISHER, A.B., R. V. Kilmoe. [D.R.]

1843. July 26. St. Brendan's Chapel of Ease was formed into a district church. [D.R.]

1860. W. A. Fisher, Incumbent; J. P. Myles, Curate. The church and chapel in good order; no glebe-house; the glebe is let for £9 per an.; divine service twice on all Sundays, both in church and chapel, besides frequent services on ship-board in Crookhaven harbour; sacrament monthly, and at festivals, in both churches; the average number of communicants is 14 at the parish church, 10 in the other; there are four Church Education schools, at which about 94 children attend; the Protestant population is 513; the rentcharge is £375, and the land is worth £9; total value, £384, without residence. There is also in Kilmoe parish a church, called Templenaboit, or the church of the poor, which was built in 1847 by the inhabitants of the district during the famine. The money sent to Mr. Fisher for relief of the destitute, instead of being distributed in alms gratuitously, was employed in giving labour, and procuring materials to erect this church. No horses were employed at it, and all the work was done by hand. Besides the erection of a place of worship in a poor locality, occupied by Protestants, and distant about four Irish miles from Scull or Kilmoe churches, Mr. Fisher found also this benefit from his proceedings, namely, that while in the neighbouring districts the rates for relief of the poor were enormously high, in this district they were comparatively little. Mr. E. H. Hopley is the Curate of Templenaboit Church, in which there is divine service twice on all Sundays, besides an early service at 8 A.M. on Sundays in a licensed place of worship at Lissacha, a place in the same district. The sacrament is administered monthly, at Templenaboit, and at festivals; the average of communicants is 37. 57 children are on the rolls of a Church Education school.

The protestant population of this portion of Kilmoe parish is 509.

William Allen Fisher (son of Joseph Devonshire Fisher, esq., by Margaret Allen, of Greenfield, near Kanturk), married, on 14th Feb., 1844, Anna, youngest daughter of Rev. Thomas Carson, R. Kilmahon, Cloyne, and has issue three sons, Joseph Devonshire, Thomas-Carson, and William-Allen-Waggett; and two daughters, Eliza, and Margaret Allen.

KILMURRY.

1591. E. de Kilmurry, MORRICIUS MCDERMOTT. [MS. T.C.D. E. 3. 14.] He was also R. Templeusky, q. v.

1615. Clonherkin als Kilmurry. Ecclesia et cancella penitus ruinantur. Vicarius nullus nec Curatus. [R.V. R.I.A.]

1634. E. de Clonherkin als Kilmurry, spectat ad Ab. de Antro. Comes Cork firmarius. Gully Ceugh, ye farmour, hath ye book-money. BENJAMIN HEARICE, Curatus, habet £4 pro inservicione curæ. [R.V. 1634.] Hearice was R. V. Lislee, Ross, q. v.

1639. E. de Kilmurry, spectat ad Ab. de Antro. Curatus est NATHANIEL GYLES. Ecclesia ruinata, desunt ornamenta. [V.B. D.R. 1639.] In 1666 Giles was V. Clonmel, Cloyne, q. v.

1667. Rector, Comes Cork; Vicar, THOMAS MURRAY. [V.B. D.R.]

1669 and 1670. JOHN GODFREY is Curate. [V.B.] He was P. Currograngemore, Ross, q. v.

1671 to 1699. JOHN HARRISON is Curate. [V.B.] In 1689 he was V. Cannaway, q. v.

1700. March 17. THOMAS MILLS is appointed Curate. [D.R.]

Mills was born in Cork (son of John Mills "conario"?). When nineteen years old he obtained Sizarship in T.C.D. on 6th July, 1694.

He was ordained Deacon on 16th March, 1700, at Kilbrogan, and Priest, on 21st September, 1701, at Cork, by the Bp. of Cork. On 2nd January, 1700, he was licensed to teach school in Bandon; and on 17th March following was licensed to this cure. He died between 17th February and the 3rd of March, 1720, leaving a few trifles to the Minister of Ballymodan, Mr. Richard Goodman.

1752. May 21. SAMUEL HALES is licensed to be Curate, at a stipend of £10. [D.R.] In 1770 he was P. Kilbrittain, q. v.

1762. June 4. JOHN KENNEY, the younger, A.B., is licensed as Curate, at £10. [D.R.] In 1796 he was P. Kilbrogan, q. v.

No Curate seems to have been licensed for many years after Kenney vacated this curacy. The duties were performed by the clergymen of the neighbouring parishes, for a small—almost nominal—remuneration. The Duke of Devonshire was Rector impropriator.

1840. October 27. The lodge of Sir Augustus Warren is licensed for divine service. [D.R.]

1847. March 5. A new church, in Kilmurry parish, is licensed for service, and is consecrated under the name of St. Andrew, by the Bishop of Killaloe, on the 7th of Dec. following. [D.R.]

1848. January 8. EDWARD GEORGE JONES is licensed to the curacy of Kilmurry, at £100 per an. [D.R.] He seems to have been Curate for some years previously.

1860. One church; no glebe-house; there are 14½ acres of glebe, of which 5 are in Curate's use. Divine service twice each Sunday, and also on the usual holidays; sacrament monthly, and at festivals; average of communicants, 18. No school. Protestant population, 85. The rectory is impropriate in the Duke of Devonshire.

KILNAGLORY.

1291. "Eccia de Kylneglory IIImr." [Tax. P. Nic.]

1591. "Preb. sive Rector de Kilneglorie, EDMUNDUS BRENNAUGHE. Idem Vicarius ibm—non exhibuit chartas ordinum,—exhibuit titulos ad prebendam; allegat titulos vicariæ combustos.—privand. vicaria." [MS. T.C.D. E. 3. 14.] He does not appear elsewhere.

1613. Nov. 15. RICHARD OWEN, P. Kilnaglory, R. Taxas, V. Kinsale, and P. Donoghmore, Cloine. [R.V. 1634.]

1615. Kilnaglorie: Richūs Owen, A.M., minister et predicator, ipse inservit curæ. Val. 4 li. Tenet etiam V. Kinsale, val. 10 li. et R. Taxax, val. 5 li. Ecclesia repāta, cancella in ruinis. [R.V. R.I.A.]

1626. March 17. Rev. Richard Owen, P. Kilnaglory, gave £20 towards a library, for use of the cathedral. [Tuckey, Cork Rem.] 1634. P. Kilnaglory, Richard Owen. Value, 80 li. per an. [R.V. 1634.]

Richard Owen, from 1613 to 1629 was V. Kinsale, and from 1613 to 1634 was R. Taxax, P. Kilnaglory, and P. Donoghmore, in Cloyne. From 1625 to 1634 he was also R. Rincurran; and from 1625 to 1631 was P. Donoghmore and Kiltegan, in Lismore diocese.

In 1631, July 28, the Archbishop of Armagh gave him a dispensation to retain Kilnaglory, Donaghmore, Rincurran, and Taxax, "cum clausula perinde valere et permutationis." [R.V. 1634.]

1634/5. Feb. 11. THOMAS WEIGHT, P. Kilnaglory. [F.F.] He appears in V.B. 1639. "Ecclesia bene, desunt calix," &c. [V.B. D.R.]

Thomas Weight, A.M., was ordained Deacon and Priest, by

John, Bishop of Oxford, on 23rd October, 1619. He was probably brought over to Ireland by the Boyle family.

In 1620 he became P. Kilmacdonogh, Cloyne (per cession of Roger Boyle), and in 1628 was also V. Ballymodan. In 1634 he became, in addition, P. Kilnaglory. He was also, from 1628 to 1640, Rector of Aglishdrinagh, in Cloyne; and from 1628 to 1630 Vicar of Aglishdrinagh. He appears for nearly all these livings in 1639. He was, in 1628, elected Dean of Cork, by the Chapter, but his appointment was set aside by the Crown. He was, in 1628, S.T.B.

1661. Vacant. [V.B. D.R.]

1662. July 28. EDWARD BULLEN, Preb. Kilnaglory. [F.F.] He appears in 1670. [V.B. D.R.] In 1662 he was V. Castlemagner, Cloyne, and in 1667, R. Templeroan, Cloyne. He vacated these three livings in 1670. For a notice of the Bullen family, *vide* Donoughmore, Cloyne, under Rev. Richard Bullen.

1671. May 11. ROWLAND DAVIES, Preb. Kilnaglory. [F.F.] He appears 1671 and 1672. [V.B. D.R.] He was afterwards Dean of Cork, q. v.

1674. August 25. "Sub sequestracone," with Theo. Veasy's name in the margin. [V.B.]

1675. No name appears. [V.B.]

1676. April 5. THEODORE VESEY, P. Kilnaglory. [F.F.] He appears 1677 to 1681. [V.B. D.R.]

"1681. The church and church-yard of Kilnaglory to be repaired, and thirty-eight pounds to be raised for that purpose, by distress, if need be." [Cork Presentments.]

Theodore Vesey (son of Rev. Thomas Vesey) was born at Coleraine, where he received his education; and, at seventeen years of age he entered T.C.D. as a Pensioner, on 30th April, 1658. He was a Scholar in 1660.

From 1666 to 1669 he was V. Clonmeen, Roskeen, and Kilshannig; and from 1666 to 1676 P. Cooline, in Cloyne. From 1669 to 1682 he was V. Kinsale, and R. V. Rincurran. From 1670 to 1682 he was R. Taxax; from 1675 to 1682, P. Lackeen, in Cloyne, and from 1676 to 1682 P. Kilnaglory. He died, in 1682, the incumbent of four livings.

Theodore Vesey was brother to John Vesey (Dean of Cork, q. v.), Archbishop of Tuam, and ancestor of the Lords DE VESCI.

Theodore was married, and had a son, Theodore, born at Kinsale in 1672, who entered T.C.D. in 1692.

1682. Oct. 10. THOMAS DENT, A.M., P. Kilnaglory. [F.F.] He appears 1682 to 1687. [V.B. D.R.]

Thomas Dent (son of Thomas "armiger") was born in London, and entered T.C.D. as Pensioner, on 2nd of April, 1670, at the early age of thirteen. He graduated A.M., in 1682.

In 1675 he appears as P. Droghta, Clonfert. From 1680 to 1686 he was Curate of Ballinaboy. In 1679 he was a Vicar

Choral of Cork. From 1681 to 1688 he was P. Island, V. Desert and Ardfield, in Ross; and from 1682 to 1688 he was P. Kilnaglory. In 1688 he resigned, or was deprived of all his livings in Cork and Ross.

1688. July 9. NICHOLAS BRADY, A.M., P. Kilnaglory [F.F.], vacant per cessionem Thomæ Dent, et per deprivationem Thomæ Dent. [D.R.] Brady appears 1688 to 1691. In the latter year he is marked "In Anglia." [V.B. D.R.]

Of Dr. Nicholas Brady, whose name will be remembered as long as the present version of the Psalms remains in our Books of Common Prayer, some fuller account than usual will be acceptable. He was descended from the noble and once powerful family of O'GRADY, which boasts an equal antiquity and a common lineage with that of O'BRIEN from the ancient kings of Ireland. [*Vide* Keating, vol. ii. p. 401, ed. 1809, and O'Brien's Irish and English Dictionary, p. 514. *Vide* also the families of O'GRADY and the Lords INCHIQUIN and GUILLAMORE, in Burke's L. G. and Peerage.] The first of the O'Grady family who took the name of Brady seems to have been SIR DENIS O'GRADY, als BRADY, knight and chief of his name, or "nacion," to whom King HENRY VIII. granted by letters patent, dated 5th January, 1543, the following lands (which had previously belonged to the ancestors of Sir Denis), namely, the manors, lordships, towns, &c., of Thoymcreny (Tomgrany), Finnagh, Kyllachulybeg, Killachulymore, Seamboycronayn, Killokenedy, Clony, Killchonmrian, Enockeim, Parchayne, and the moiety of Kiltulla. Sir Denis O'Grady, als Brady, died (circa 1569), in Limerick, in a house, called the "Archdeakan's Courte," belonging to himself, having had issue four sons, Edmond (d. Sp. 27th December, 1576), Donald (d. Sp.), John, and Hugh.

The third son, John O'Grady, als Brady, was heir to his brothers Edmond and Donald, and surrendered to Queen Elizabeth all his estates on 26th of July, 1582. Her Majesty regranted to John O'Grady and to his brother, Hugh, with limitation to the heirs, not of John, but of Hugh Brady, the same estates which are described as the manors, lordships, &c., of Tomgraney, Ballyduff, Ballynock, Aghrim, Ithnatty, Ballymollowin, Ballymarrane, Ashrymdowgin, Fassabeg, Fassaghmore, Tyronethy, Toare, Rathyny, Tullaghary, Ballycoin, Twilaghgory, Chrony, Finaghe, Killuckwillibeg, Killuckwillimore, Knockeyprighane, Killockenedy, Seambocthcronane, O'Grady's Island, alias Illan-I'Gradye, Kilsulla, Skarriff, in the county of Clare, aliter Thomond; also "unum domum lapideum infra civitatem Limerici vulgariter vocatum le Archdeaken's Courte," in the parish of St. Michael's, Limerick. John O'Grady, by his wife, Katherine Bourke, had issue a son, Donogh O'Grady, of Fassaghmore, ancestor, according to Sir

William Betham, of several of the present families of O'Grady, in the county Limerick, and elsewhere.

Hugh O'Grady, alias Brady, fourth son of Sir Denis, was born at Dunboyne, county Meath, and obtained by conveyance from his brother, John, the lands of Tomgrany and Scariff, &c., mentioned in above patents. He was educated in England, and was Rector of St. Mary, Aldermary, London (*vide* Shirley's Letters in Illustration of the Church in Ireland, page 188; London, Rivington, 1851); and from 1563 to 1584 was Bishop of Meath. He married, firstly, a widow (whose dau. married Geoffrey Pinchbeck (or Pichebek, Chief Registrar of the High Commission for Ecclesiastical Causes in Ireland, and a kinsman of SIR WILLIAM CECIL, the first LORD BURGHLEY), by whom he had no issue; and secondly, Alice (dau. of Right Hon. SIR ROBERT WESTON, Lord Chancellor of Ireland), by whom he left issue at his death, on 13th Feb. 1584/5, three sons, Lucas, Nicholas, and Gerald, besides a dau. Elisabeth. His relict, Alice, in 1585, married Sir Jeffery Fenton, Secretary of State in Ireland, and bore to him SIR WILLIAM FENTON and Alice, wife of the first EARL of CORK, who erected to her memory the huge monument in St. Patrick's Cathedral. Of the Bishop's children, Elisabeth died unmarried, and was buried in St. Patrick's; Gerald, the youngest son, was a "student of Trinitie Colledge," and died Sp. having previously married Joane (dau. of William Conway, of Dublin, who was buried at St. Patrick's, in 1633), who married, after Gerald's death, Mathew Trott, esq., of London. Lucas or Luke, the Bishop's eldest son, as one of the Chieftains of the County of Clare, signed the treaty between Queen Elizabeth and the Lords of that county on 17th August, 1585; and was, I think, in 1591, though a layman, R. Bruhenny, Cloyne, q. v. He married Agnes Evans, by whom he had a son, Luke, born at Rosscarbery, in 1623, and a dau. Alice, wife of Laurance Clayton, of Mallow, brother to SIR RANDOLL CLAYTON. The last-named Luke was heir to the property of Tomgrany and Raheens, county Clare, which remained in that branch of the Brady family until sold in the Incumbered Estates Court to the present proprietor, Mr. Moreland.

The Bishop's second son, Nicholas, was appointed Escheator of Connaught, in 1606, no doubt through the interest of the first EARL of CORK, who had married, in 1603, his half-sister, Alice Fenton. That Earl appears, from papers now in the possession of Lord Inchiquin, to have been joint proprietor with the Bradys of their Clare estates, and in the Down Survey of 1641, was owner of ten denominations of land in that county, including Scariff and Fassaghmore, while Mr. Brady was owner of eleven, among which were Tomgraney and Raheens. Nicholas Brady was probably brought by the same nobleman to Bandon (which was re-built or re-edified by the Earl, in 1641), where he acquired a property in the town and neighbourhood, which remained in the family until recent times. He afterwards removed to England, and died, leaving a son, Major Nicholas Brady, of Richmond, in Surrey, and of Bandon, county Cork, who married Martha, the dau. and heiress of Luke Gernon, esq. of Cork ("a Judge of singular meekness and probity," who was Second Justice of the Presidency Court of Munster, 1618 to 1660), by whom he had issue, besides an elder son, whose descendants have been long settled in England, Nicholas Brady, the P. Kilnaglory.

The foregoing statement of the descent of Dr. Brady from Sir Denis O'Grady, chief of his name, has been taken from the family pedigree, certified by Sir Wm. Betham, and verified by reference to the will of Bishop Hugh Brady, and by documents in the Ulster Office, &c. The following account is taken from the second edition of Vol. II. of the "Biographia Britannica," enlarged by Dr. Andrew Kippis, fol., London, 1780, with some slight alterations and additions from the family papers, now in the possession of Antonio Brady, esq., of Stratford, near London:—

Nicholas Brady, born at Bandon, co. Cork, on 28th of October, 1659, was educated for a time by Dr. Tindall, of Cork; and when twelve years old, was removed to Westminster School, then under the care of the celebrated Dr. Busby. Brady was much thought of by his master, and was elected King's Scholar at Westminster; and from thence was sent to Oxford as a Student of Christchurch. After continuing there four years he went to Dublin, where his father then resided, and commenced B.A., and in the following year, 1688, graduated A.M. His degree of D.D. was afterwards presented to him on account of his uncommon merit, and brought over to him to England by Dr. Pratt, then Travelling Fellow, and subsequently Provost of that University.

He was ordained Priest, at Cork, on 28th September, 1687, by Bishop Whetenhall, to whom he was Chaplain. In 1688 he was appointed P. Kilnaglory, R. Kilmeen, V. Drinagh, and V. Castroventia, in the diocese of Ross, all which he resigned in 1692. He was, in 1690, Minister of St. Catherine-Cree, and Lecturer of St. Michael's, Wood-street, London. He was afterwards Minister of Richmond, in Surrey, to which post he was invited by the gentlemen of that place in consequence of the high esteem they had conceived for him during a retreat which he had made thither while he was translating the Psalms. The vicarage of the Holy Trinity of Stratford-upon-Avon was given to him by the great Earl of Dorset, and the rectory of Clapham, by Dame Rebecca (relict of Sir Richard) Atkins, Baronet, on 21st February, 1705/6. He died Rector of Clapham, and Minister of Richmond, on 22nd of May, 1726, and was buried at Richmond on the 26th of May. Dr. Thomas Stackhouse, author of the "History of the Bible," preached his funeral sermon.

Dr. Brady was a zealous promoter of the late happy Revolution, and an eminent sufferer for it. In 1690, when the troubles broke out in Ireland, by his interest with King James' general, MacCarty, he thrice prevented the burning of Bandon town, after three several orders given by that Prince to destroy it. The same year, having been deputed by the people of Bandon, he went over to England to petition the Parliament for a redress of some grievances they had suffered while King James was in Ireland.

Dr. Brady was Chaplain to the Princess of Wales, to King William and Queen Mary, and to Queen Anne; also, to the Duke of Ormond's troop of Horse Guards.

Dr. Brady had the character of being a person of most obliging, sweet, affable temper, a polite gentleman, an excellent preacher, and a good poet. His qualifications would undoubtedly have raised him, it was said, to some of the greatest dignities in the church, if the singular humanity and benevolence of his disposition would have suffered him to have run in with the violence of either prevailing party.

He published, in conjunction with Mr. Tate, Poet Laureate, the well-known version of the Psalms, which first appeared in 1698. Of the numerous and various editions of this work a collection has been made, at great expense, by Mr. James Lenox, of New York. The opinions of learned men as to the merits of the versification, and also as to the share Dr. Brady had in the composition of the several pieces, are nearly as various as the different editions.

He published also:—

1. The Rape, or the Innocent Impostors; a tragedy. [Anonymous.] 4to. London, 1692.

2. A Sermon, preached at Whitehall, London, before the King and Queen, on October 23, 1692. 4to. London, 1693.

3. A Sermon on Matthew xvi. 26. 4to. London, 1693.

4. A Sermon, preached at the Funeral of Thomas Shadwell, esq., on Revelation xiv., part of verse 13. 4to. London, 1693. Shadwell was successor to Dryden in the office of Poet Laureate, and was succeeded in that office by Tate, the colleague of Brady in the versification of the Psalms.

5. A Funeral Sermon, on Eccles. vii. 2. 4to. London, 1694.

6. A Sermon before the Incorporated Society of Apothecaries of London. 4to. London, 1695.

7. A Sermon on occasion of the late horrid Plot. 4to. London, 1696.

8. Church Music Vindicated, a Sermon on St. Cecilia's Day,

preached in St. Bride's Church, London. 4to. London, 1697.

9. A Sermon on the Death of King William. 4to. London, 1702.

10. Sermons: 3 volumes. 8vo. London, vol. i., 1704; vol. ii., 1706; vol. iii., 1713.

11. A Thanksgiving Sermon for the Victory of Blenheim. 4to. London, 1705.

12. A Thanksgiving Sermon on the Union of England and Scotland. 8vo. London, 1707.

13. A Sermon on Acts viii. 14–17, on the Antiquity and Usefulness of Episcopal Confirmation. 4to. London, 1708.

14. A Thanksgiving Sermon, on Nahum i. 15. 8vo. London, 1713.

15. The Æneid of Virgil, in Verse, 4 vols. 8vo. 1726.

16. Sermons; three additional volumes, published after his death by his eldest Son. 8vo. London, 1730.

17. A Sermon, on Psalm cxviii. 23, 24. 4to. London, 1738.

The Rev. Nicholas Brady married, on the 29th June, 1690, Letitia (daughter of Edward Synge, Bishop of Cork, as Sir Wm. Betham has stated, or if the account of William Brady, of Sydenham, be preferred, she was Letitia, grand-daughter of that Bishop, and daughter of Richard Synge, who died Archdeacon of Cork in 1688, bequeathing to his daughter Letitia £500). Dr. Brady had issue by this lady four sons and four daughters.

Nicholas, the eldest, R. Tooting, Surrey, and LL.B., was baptized at St. Catherine-Cree Church, on 23rd March, 1692/3, and died on 11th December, 1768, and was buried at Clapham. He was married to Martha, dau. of William Lethulier, esq., of Clapham; and had issue an only son, William Brady, esq., of Sydenham, who married Susannah Le Keux, and died Sp. on 12th Sept., 1773. George, the second son of Dr. Brady, was born on 26th July, 1705; the third son has not been found in any registry; the fourth, Thomas, was baptized on 23rd September, 1707, at Richmond. Of the four daughters, Elisabeth, Letitia, Mary, and Martha, the last died unmarried, and the others married respectively Mr. Morgan, Mr. Woodhouse (a Quaker), and a Mr. Paton.

Dr. Brady's fourth son, THOMAS, with whose issue we are now concerned, married Eleanor, dau. of Rev. Dr. Cheyne, of Clapham, believed to have been of the family of the Cheynes, LORDS NEWHAVEN; and by her had issue (besides a daughter Letitia, wife of John Collins, esq., of Woolmers, Herts), a son, Nicholas William, born at Richmond in 1734, who was precluded from a learned profession by an impediment in his speech, and was therefore brought up to business. He came to Ireland in 1761, and established himself in Dublin, having previously married, on 4th Nov., 1758, at St. Clement Danes Church, in London, Dorothea Creighton, of Penrith, Cumberland. He died on 18th May, 1808, leaving issue *inter alios* Francis Tempest Brady, his eldest son, who died on 11th April, 1821, leaving issue Sir Nicholas William Brady, eldest son (Alderman, and Lord Mayor of Dublin, who was knighted by King George IV.); Maziere Brady, second son (now Lord Chancellor of Ireland), and Rev. Francis Tempest Brady, Chancellor of Lismore, for whom *vide* Kilworth, in Cloyne. He had also six daughters, Mary, Eliza, Letitia-Synge, Mary Anne (who all died unmarried), Charlotte (wife of John Mollan, esq., M.D., of Fitzwilliam-square, Dublin), and Dorothea (wife of Rev. David-Carlisle Courtenay, Rector of Glenarm, in the diocese of Connor).

The second son, MAZIERE BRADY, LORD CHANCELLOR of IRELAND, married, firstly, Eliza-Anne, dau. of Beaver Buchanan, esq., of Dublin; and, secondly, on 15th Dec., 1860, Mary, dau. of Rt. Hon. John Hatchell. Chancellor Brady has issue by his first wife, who died 15th June, 1858, 1. Francis-William Brady, Q.C. (who married on 7th Nov., 1847, Emily-Elisabeth, youngest dau. of Dr. Kyle, Bishop of Cork, and has issue a son Maziere-Kyle, born 25th March, 1849, and a daughter Marion-Eleanor); 2. Maziere-John Brady, esq., (who, by his wife Elisabeth, youngest dau. of Rev. Robert Longfield, V. Clonfert, Cloyne, q. v. has issue Robert-Maziere, Emily-Augusta-Mary, and Maude-Cherry-Elisabeth); 3. Eleanor (wife of Rev. Benjamin Hale Puckle, Rector of Graffham, Ely); 4. Charlotte; and 5. Eliza.

1692. Sept. 23. SOLOMON FOLEY, A.M., P. Kilnaglory, and V. Drinagh, and R. Kilmeen, per cession of Nicholas Brady. [D.R.]

1699. The church not yet repaired, but an assessment was made for the repairs. At present the Protestants go to Inniskarrow. The repairs ought to be hastened. [V.B. 1699. D.D.]

In 1704/5 Foley became P. Kilbrogan, q. v.

1704/5. January 5. THOMAS DERHAM, P. Kilnaglory. [F.F.]

1704. Feb. 8. David Thyrry, junior, renounces Popery in the parish church of Kilnaglory. [D.R.]

Thomas Derham, in 1699, on 2nd March, was licensed to the Curacy of the Holy Trinity, Cork. In 1699 he was Vicar Choral, Cork, and Rector of Creagh, in Ross. In 1701 he was R. Killeagh, Cloyne, and in 1704 became P. Kilnaglory. He held all those preferments to his death in 1705. He was Proctor "Cleri Rossen," to Convocation in 1704. He took degrees in T.C.D. in 1701 and 1704.

He married Mary Vaughan, of Golden Grove, county Tipperary. [M. B. Dec. 22, 1704.] She afterwards married the Reverend Mr. Prince, Vicar of Uffington, Berks, and by him had a daughter, wife to the Archbishop (Laurence) of Cashel.

1705/6. March 6. CHIDLEY COOTE, A.M., P. Kilnaglory. [F.F.]
He appears 1706 to 1730, July 28; but in another V.B. of 1730, this prebend is marked vacant. [V.B. D.R.]

Chidley Coote (grandson of the first Baronet, *vide* Burke) was born in the county Roscommon, being son of Chidley Coote "Ducis," by Catherine Sandys.

He entered T.C.D. as Pensioner on 1st March, 1693, being then sixteen years old, and graduated afterwards A.M. and D.D.

He was ordained Deacon on 16th September, 1699, and Priest on 5th April, 1701/2, both at Cork.

From 1705 to 1730 he was P. Kilnaglory; and from 1709 held also the P. Effin, Limerick. He was Proctor "Cleri Aghadoe" to Convocation in 1704. He died in 1730, leaving by his wife, Jane Evans, sister of the first LORD CARBERY, a numerous family; Charles, his third son, was Dean of Kilfenora, and had issue (by his wife, Catherine Bathurst) Charles Henry (the father of EYRE, LORD CASTLECOOTE), and a daughter, Grace, wife of Henry Bathurst, Bishop of Norwich.

1730/1. January 21. JOHN KENNEY, A.M., P. Kilnaglory, per mortem Coote. [D.R.] In 1751 he was P. Kilbrittain, q. v.
He appears 1731 to 1736. [V.B. D.R.]

1737. July 9. CHRISTOPHER DONNELLAN, B.D., P. Kilnaglory. [F.F.]
In 1745, June 1, he took a second collation to P. Kilnaglory and R. V. Athnowen. [D.R.] He was also P. Inniscarra, Cloyne, q. v.

1751. March 28. THOMAS WHITE, A.M., P. Kilnaglory and R. V. Athnowen, consolidated this year. [D.R.]

Thomas White (grandson to William White, who married Anne, dau. of Thomas Bowles), was the second son of Swithin White, by Anne, dau. of Alderman William Ballard, of Cork. [Dunscombe.]

He was born at Mallow in 1700, and when eighteen years old entered T.C.D. as a Pensioner, on 27th April, 1718, and subsequently took the degree of A.M.

He was ordained Deacon on 25th September, 1726, and Priest on 28th May, 1727, both at Cork.

From June, 1727, to the end of that year, he was a Vicar Choral of Cork. From the beginning of 1728 to 1742 he was R. Rathcooney; from 1742 to 1751 he was P. Kilbrittain; and from 1751 to 1777, when he died, he was P. Kilnaglory.

He married, in August, 1728, Mary Farthing, then of the parish of St. Dominick, and by her had issue a son, Richard, who died in 1730.

The Rev. Thomas White was buried on 17th August, 1777, in the church-yard of St. Nicholas, Cork.

1777. August 23. ROBERT AUSTEN, D.D., P. Kilnaglory, and R. V. Athnowen. [F.F.]
In 1785 he became Archdeacon of Cork, q. v.

1785. April 25. JAMES PRATT, A.M., P. Kilnaglory, and R. V. Athnowen. [F.F.]

1807. March 12. The Bishop approves of Pratt's memorial to build at Athnowen; and on 21st Nov. 1809, he certifies that Pratt has expended in erecting a glebe-house £961 18*s.* 7*d.*, the value of Athnowen being £490 7*s.* per an. [D.R.]

James Pratt (son of Robert Pratt, esq., Portrieve of Castlemartyr, by Sarah, dau. of Richard Williams, esq.), was a Scholar of T.C.D. in 1766, and afterwards took the degree of A.B. and A.M.

He was ordained Deacon on 18th of December, 1768, and Priest on 17th February, 1771, both at Cloyne. From 1768 to 1782 he was Curate of Igtermurragh, Dungourney, &c. From 1782 to 1785 he was Chancellor of Cork, and from 1785 to 1824 he was P. Kilnaglory, which preferment he resigned on 18th October, 1824.

He married, in 1775, Anne Rugge, of Kilcredan; and mentions in his will (dated 7th Nov. 1825, and proved 1st Dec. 1827), Robert (P. Desertmore, q. v.); Henry, married to Sarah Fitton; Richard; John, who married Mrs. Frances Hawkes; James; and Sarah.

1824. Oct. 19. WILLIAM HARVEY, A.M., P. Kilnaglory. [D.R.]

1830. Protestant population, 55.

1837. Athnowen union, 7 miles long by 5 broad, with cure, consisting of Athnowen rectory and vicarage, and Kilnaglory rectory, containing 8,554A. 1R. 10¾P. Gross population, 3,075. One Curate, employed at a stipend of £75 per annum. Composition for the tithes of Athnowen parish, £425; of Kilnaglory parish, £325. 14 acres of glebe in Incumbent's use, valued at 30*s.* per acre, £21. Subject to diocesan schoolmaster, £1 2*s.* 6*d.* Athnowen glebe-house, built under the old Acts in 1810, at a certified cost of £980 4*s.* 10*d.* British, whereof £92 6*s.* 1¾*d.* was granted as gift by the late Board of First Fruits, and the residue of £887 18*s.* 8¼*d.* was supplied out of the private funds of the builder, to whom the present Incumbent is next in succession; and having paid his predecessor the whole of the sum last named, he will be entitled to receive £665 19*s.* from his successor on account thereof. Incumbent is usually resident in the glebe-house. One church, capable of accommodating 100 persons; but when built, or at what cost unknown. No charge on the union in 1832 on account of the church. Divine service is celebrated once on all Sundays, and on the principal festivals. The sacrament is administered monthly, and on the principal festivals. The benefices constituting this union are rectories, but a portion of tithes in Kilnaglory parish is received by an Ecclesiastical Incumbent. The Prebendary of Kilnaglory has also a separate revenue, arising from rent of houses, to the amount of

£5 10*s.* 9*d.*, but no duties, save preaching occasionally in Cork Cathedral. [Parl. Rep.]

William Harvey was ordained Deacon at Cloyne on 8th of October, 1809, and Priest at Cork on 23rd Sept. 1810. From 1810 to 1824 he was R. V. Wallstown, Cloyne; and from 1824 to his death, on 27th August, 1839, he was P. Kilnaglory. He also held, from 1815 to 1818, the V. Killaconenagh, in Ross; and from 1818 to 1824 the P. Desertmore, Cork.

He left issue two daughters, Elisabeth and Constance-Alice.

1839. Nov. 26. THOMAS DUKE MOORE, A.M., P. Kilnaglory, and R. V. St. Mary's, als Athnowen; certified under £600 in annual value. [D.R.]

1846. Dec. 28. A commission reports that Moore expended £140 in improvements on the glebe-house; and that the net annual value of the benefice is £340 17*s.* 6*d.* [D.R.]

Thomas Duke Moore was son of William John Moore, and grandson of William Duke Moore, of Summer-hill and Buckingham-street, Dublin.

From 1833 to 1839 he was V. Aghadowne; and from 1839 to his death, on 17th September, 1847, he was P. Kilnaglory.

He married Alicia-Dorothea, dau. of SAMUEL KYLE, Bishop of Cork, and left issue five daughters, Alicia-Dorothea, Annette, Elisabeth, Frances-Mary, and Emily-Elisabeth.

1847. Nov. 27. EDMUND LOMBARD, A.M., P. Kilnaglory, and R. V. St. Mary's, als Athnowen. [D.R.]

1860. E. Lombard, Rector; H. Wilmot, Curate. The church and glebe-house in good order. 20 acres of glebe in Rector's use. Divine service once on all Sundays and usual holidays, and evening service during the summer months. The sacrament monthly; average of communicants, 42. About 12 children attend a Church Education school. The Protestant population is 107. The rentcharge of Athnowen is £318 15*s.*; of Kilnaglory, £243 15*s.* The land is worth £21, and the houses belonging to the Prebendary of Kilnaglory are worth £5 10*s.* 9*d.* Total value, £589 0*s.* 9*d.* with residence.

Edmond Lombard (eldest son of Rev. John Lombard, R. V. Kilshannig, Cloyne, q. v.), was ordained Deacon at Cloyne on 18th October, 1821, and Priest, also at Cloyne, on 14th April, 1822. From 1836 to 1847 he was R. V. Monamimy, Cloyne.

He married, in 1836, Elisabeth, dau. of John Longfield, esq. of Longueville, county Cork.

KINNEIGH.

1591. CORNELIUS DONATI appears as Vicar of Kinneigh. "Rectoria de Kineighe. Precent. et vicarii Chorales sunt rectores. Vic. ibm Cornelius donati. Exhibiti sunt tituli, Dominus deliberavit super iisdem." [MS. T.C.D. E. 3. 14.]

1615. EDWARD CLERKE, A.M., appears as V. Kinneigh. "Vicarii Chorales et Precentor sunt rectores. Vicarius Edrūs Clerke, A.M., minister et predicator. Val. 9 li. per an. Ecclesia et cancella bene repantur cum libris." [R.V. R.I.A.] Clerke was also Dean of Cloyne, q. v.

1634. R. de Keneagh spectat ad Vic. Chorales et Precentor. Cork. Vicar, Edward Clerke. Val. 20 li. per an. [R.V. 1634.] Clerke is still Vicar in 1639. "Ecclesia bene et ornata, Curatus, Richard ——." [V.B. 1639. D.R.]

1640. THOMAS HENSEY, V. Kilmichael, and Kinneigh. [F.F.]

16—? NICHOLAS WINTERBURNE, V. Kinneigh.

He was afterwards Treasurer of Ross, q. v.

1664. January 7. ROBERT GOLBORNE, V. Kinneagh, per deprivationem Nicholai Winterburne, clerici, per Convocationem apud Dublin, ob non confirmitatem. [V.B. D.R. 1669.] On the same day he became V. Fanlobbish, and R. Ballymoney, q. v.

He appears 1666 to 1672. [V.B. D.R.]

1674. May 2. ISAAC MANSFIELD, V. Kinneigh, Fanlobbus, and R. Ballymoney. [F.F.] He was also P. Inskenny, q. v.

He appears 1674 to 1688. [V.B. D.R.]

1682. "The church of Kineigh to be repaired." [County Cork Grand Jury Presentments.]

1689. The vicarage is vacant. [V.B.]

1690 and 1691. Mr. JOHN FORTUNE appears as V. Kinneigh. [V.B.] He became, in 1695, V. Glanbarrahan, Ross, q. v.

1692. April 11. ANDREW SYMES, A.B., V. Kinneigh, per mortem Mansfield. [D.R.] In 1695 he resigned, but in 1718 appears again as V. Kinneigh.

1695. Dec. 23. JOHN PATRICKSON, A.M., V. Kinneigh per cessionem Andrew Symes. [D.R.] He appears 1695 to 1717. [V.B. D.R.] He was also Precentor of Cloyne, q. v.

1699. A sermon once a fortnight at Kinneigh, by Mr. Patrickson. The church not in good repair. [V.B. 1699. D.D.]

"1699. About five miles to the west of Bandon, on the north side of the river, adjoining to the parish of Murragh, begins the parish of Kineigh. Near the river is Inniskean, a little market town, in the parish of Kineigh. The parish church of Kineigh stands three miles from Inniskean, to the north-west. Inniskean is the Earl of Corke's Estate.

"Kineigh: 30 plowlands in this parish. Half the tythes of 14 plowlands belong to the Chantor, half the other 16 to the

Vicars Choral. Kineigh Church is out of repair. Divine service once a fortnight at Inniskean, by Mr. Patrickson.

"Munday, May 27, 1700. I went to Kineigh; the parish church stands three miles distant from Ballimony to the N.N.W. The west end of the church is cover'd, but the wall-plates give way; the partition betwixt that part of the church which is cover'd and the east end, which is uncovered, is not plaister'd. A high round tower stands in the S.W. corner of the church-yard. A door was in the north side of the church, and, it is thought, opened into a vestry. 'Tis supposed this church was formerly a cathedral. The church-yard, being an acre, is well inclos'd with a stone wall. About 30 acres of glebe lie round the church of Kineigh. The country about Kineigh is indifferent coarse. Mr. Woods, and Mr. Ware, and Mr. Woodly live in this parish. Towards the north, at about a mile distance from the church of Kineigh, begins the parish of Inchigeulah. There is no church northward of Kineigh Church nearer than Macromp, which is seven miles distant. Kineigh Church ought to be kept in repair, and divine service, at least, continued once a fortnight. Kineigh parish is worth to the Incumbent about fifty pounds per an. The lands of this parish belong chiefly to the Lord of Corke's brother. The country about Kineigh is indifferent coarse. But few Protestants live to the north of Kineigh. A stone is in the S.W. corner of the Church of Kineigh, counted very sacred, which the Irish solemnly swear upon. This church is accounted amongst the Irish very sacred. The Vicar's house, built with stone and thatch't, is standing, and there are the ruins of a barn and stable. There is a tradition amongst the Irish that formerly in the church-yard there was a well that had great medicinal vertues, and that the concourse of people being very chargeable to the inhabitants, they stop't it up. Half a plowland of Kineigh, lying near the church to the west, belongs to the Bishop of Corke, and contains about 60 English acres, indifferent coarse land. The Vicar of Kineigh has half the tithes of Kineigh. The Chantor of Corke has one rectory, and the Vicars Choral another. These two rectories are nearly equal in value." [Downes' Tour.]

1718. Nov. 6. Mr. ANDREW SYMES appears as V. Kinneigh. [V.B.] He was also Precentor of Ross, q. v.

1720. SAMUEL BROOME appears as V. Kinneigh. [V.B. D.R.] And he took a second collation on 15th Feb., 1731, on becoming Chancellor of Cork, q. v.

1768. Sept. 19. JOHN KENNEY, A.M., V. Kinneigh, per mortem Broome. [D.R.] In 1796 he became P. Kilbrogan, q. v.

1769. March 4. MICHAEL TISDALL, A.M., V. Kinneigh. [F.F.] In 1781 he became Archdeacon of Ross, q. v.

1781. June 8. STEPHEN BAGGS, A.M., V. Kinneigh. [F.F.] In 1782 he became R. V. Myros, Ross, q. v.

1782. April 1. MEADE SWIFT, A.M., V. Kinneigh. [F.F.] He took afterwards the name of Dennis, and in 1796 became a Vicar Choral of Cork, q. v.

1794. September 3. Armiger Sealy, Curate, and Edward Wood and Alexander Nicholls, Churchwardens, petition the Bishop to consecrate the new church, built near the foundation of the old church by the Commissioners of First Fruits; and it is accordingly consecrated same day, under the name of Christ Church. [D.R.]

1796. January 7. THOMAS KENNEY, A.B., V. Kinneigh. [F.F.] In 1801 he became P. Donoghmore, Cloyne, q. v.

1799. Sept 1. Kenney memorials for permission to build a glebe-house; and the Bishop approves on 15th Nov., 1800. [D.R.] The house was built, but no charge for it was ever made on his successors.

1801. Nov. 4. JOHN KENNEY, LL.D., V. Kinneigh. [F.F.] He was also P. Kilbrogan, q. v.

1815. March 10. ABRAHAM HAMILTON, A.M., V. Kinneigh, vacant by death of Kenney, and certified under £500 per annum in value. [D.R.]

1830. The Protestant population is 392.

1837. Kinneigh: a vicarage, with cure, 10 miles long by 6 broad, containing 13,539A. 2R. Gross population, 5,708. Two Curates employed, at stipends to the senior of £69 4*s.* 7½*d.* Brit., and to the junior of £75 Brit. per annum. Composition for vicarial tithes, £450; 45½A. of glebe, valued at 20*s.* per acre, £45 10*s.*; subject to visitation fees, 11*s.*; diocesan schoolmaster, £1 11*s.* Kinneigh glebe-house, built in 1798, under the old Acts, but at what cost unknown, as it was defrayed out of the private funds of the builder, without subjecting his successor to any charge on account of the house, which is reported to be unfit for residence, having been originally intended for offices. Incumbent is non-resident; he resides occasionally on his other benefice, but more generally at Florence Court, being domestic chaplain to the Earl of Enniskillen. One church, capable of accommodating 120 persons, built in 1790, at an expense of £461 10*s.* 9¼*d.* Brit., granted as gift by the late Board of First Fruits. No charge on the parish in 1832 on account of the church. Divine service is celebrated once on all Sundays and on the principal festivals. The sacrament is administered monthly and on the three great festivals. The rectorial, consisting of one moiety of the tithes, compounded for £450, are appropriate, and divisible in equal moieties between the Chantor and the Vicars Choral of the Cathedral Church of St. Finbarr's, Cork. [Parl. Rep.]

Abraham Hamilton, from 1801 to 1815, was R. Clonmany, Derry; from 1815 to 9th February, 1847, R. Kinneigh; and from 1822 to 1856, Rector of the Union of Manorhamilton, in Kilmore diocese.

He died on 16th December, 1861, at 8, Rutland-square, Dublin, and desired to be buried in the vault of his family at Drumholm, county Donegal.

1847. Feb. 18. GODFREY CLARKE CHARLES WILLIAM SMITH, A.B., V. Kinneigh; certified net value, £305 18s. [D.R.]

1847. May 24. The old glebe-house and offices are condemned; and on 31st July, 1849, the Bishop certifies that Smith has expended £1,100 in erecting a new glebe-house, &c., and that the certified yearly value, exclusive of poor rates, is £400 per an. [D.R.]

1856. August 27. A new church, on new site, is consecrated under name of St. Bartholomew. [D.R.]

1860. G. Smith, Vicar; James Clarke, Curate. The church in order. The glebe-house is in good order, and the glebe is in Incumbent's use. Divine service twice on all Sundays during summer in the church, and once in winter, and on the usual holidays. Evening service during the winter months is held in the school-house. Sacrament monthly; average of communicants, 30; and on festivals, average 68. 72 children are on the rolls of two Church Education schools. The Protestant population is 341. The rentcharge is £337 10s. The land is worth £45 10s. Total value, £383 per annum, with residence.

G. C. C. W. Smith (youngest son of Rev. Charles Smith, V. Kilmocamoge, q. v.), was ordained Priest at Cloyne on 10th June, 1827.

On 19th May, 1830, he was licensed to the curacy of Kilmeen. He is married, and has issue.

KINSALE.

1291. "Eccia de Kesaly IIImr." [Tax. P. Nic.]

1377. PHILIP BARRY, Vicar of the Church of Kinsale, is mentioned. [Tuckey, C. R., p. 27.]

1383. January 28. The King committed to John Horsington, Proctor of the house of Saints Peter and Paul, Bath, the custody of the profits of the Rectories of Kinsale, S. John Evan, in the *fairgh*, near Cork, and of Legan (Castlelyons), in county of Cork. [Tuckey, p. 30.]

1406. JOHN NUGENT is presented to V. Kinsale. [Pat. Rot. Hen. VII.]

1412. RICHARD PELLYN is presented to V. Kinsale. [C.R.O. 13 Hen. IV.]

1446. January 3. "DOMINUS HENRY GLASSANE, Vicar de Kynsale," is witness to a deed. [Sarsfield and Tyrry MSS.] He is also a witness to a deed in 1447. [MSS. penes R. Caulfield.]

1488 to 1498. DOMINUS PHILIP COPENER, son and heir of Richard Copener, is Vicar of Kynsale. [Sarsfield and Tyrry MSS.]

1528. October 28. "DOMINUS JACOBUS CURSY vicarius, et DOMINUS WALTER YONG, Rector de Kinsale," are witnesses to a deed of above date. [MSS. penes R. Caulfield.]

1545. Dec. 7. THOMAS BARNARDE is presented to V. Kinsale, "upon the backe of Yoghull," in the diocese of *Limerick*, in the presentation of the Crown, "pleno jure." [Morrin's Pat. and Close Rolls, p. 110.]

He was Rector of Old Rosse, Ferns dioc. from 1541, January 2, to 10th Nov. 1545. [Pat. Rot. Morrin, vol. i. pp. 83 and 110.] On 1st August, 1558, he was presented by Crown to V. Ballynestellock, in the diocese of Kildare. [Morrin, vol. i. p. 402.]

1552. May 12. RICHARD BARRETT, Chaplain, is presented to V. Kynsale, in the diocese of Cork. [Pat. Rot. Morrin, vol. i. p. 282.]

1557/8. January 20. Geoffry Galway, Burgess of Kinsale, makes his will, in which he directs his body to be buried in the chapel of the B. V. Mary, in the parish church of Kinsale, which he had erected. He bequeaths, among other legacies, 40*d.* to Thomas Gerode. [Pat. Rot. Morrin, vol. i. p. 445.]

1558. Oct. 31. THOMAS GERROD is presented to the Rectory of St. Milock of Kynsale, in the diocese of Cork. [Morrin, vol. i. p. 402.]

He was also R. Ringrone. He died in 1571.

15—? STEPHEN SERRET, Vicar of Kinsale, died in 1571.

1571. Sept. 27. DAVID ROCHE, "Scolar," is instituted "ad vicariam Ecclise Sancti Ayultose de Kynshall nunc vacantem de jure et de facto per mortem dni Stephani Serret ultimi incumbentis ibidem." The mandate to induct is signed by Magister Patricius Roche, Archdeacon of Cork and Cloyne, and Magister Andrew Skiddie, Armiger, the Commissaries of Dominus Richard Dixon, the Bishop, who is absent. The induction is made by Eugenius dali, the deputy of the Archdeacon. The record of this institution is written on a mere rag of paper, and is nearly destroyed. There is mention of a dispensation "in defectu ætatis" and for non-residence, in this document. [First Book of Cork Reg.]

1579. July 20. DOMINUS JOHANNES EGERTON, a Presbyter of the diocese of Dublin, is collated to the Vicarage perpetual of the parish church of St. Multose, Kinsale. [D.R.]

1591. "Rectoria de Kinsale spectat ad Prior Bath. JOHANNES NASH, V. de Kinsale et V. de Inishonan citatus." [MS. T.C.D. E. 3. 14.]

In another part of same MS. ROBERT STURTON, the Dean of Ross, is Vicar.

1613. Nov. 15. RICHARD OWEN is admitted P. Kilnaglory, R.

Taxax, and V. Kinsale, and P. Donoughmore, Cloyne. [R.V. 1634.]

1615. Kinsale, residens. Rex est Rector. Dominick Roch, firmarius, tenet. Spectat ad Abb. de Bath in Anglia. Val. 5 li. per annum. Ecclesia repata, cancella in repatione. Vicarius Richardus Owen ipse inservit curæ, parvi valoris. [R.V. R.I.A.] Owen was also P. Kilnaglory, q. v.

1629. Sept. 6. JOHN JOHNSON, V. Kinsale. [F.F.] He was collated on 16th Oct. and inducted 21st Oct. 1629. [R.V. 1634.]

1634. R. de Kinsale Rex est Rector. Val X li. per an. Vicarius John Johnson, Predicator. Val. X li. per an. Epus confert. [R.V. 1634.]

John Johnson, A.M., was ordained Deacon and Priest by Lancelot, Abp. of Dublin, on 24th June, 1622. From 1627 to 1634 et seq. he was R. V. Aghinagh, Cloyne; from 1629 to 1637 he was V. Kinsale. From 1634 to 1637 he held R. Taxax. He was presented to V. Killery and Killenumery, Ardagh, in 1629, and also in 1639 to V. Athenry, Tuam. [Lib. Mun.] From 1632 to 1637 he also held V. Moviddy.

1637. October 13. JONAS STEWELL, Vicar de Kinsale. [F.F.] He appears in 1639. "Ecclesia bene et ornata." [V.B. 1639. D.R.] He appears up to 1668 in the Visitation Books. [D.R.] Stewell, or Stawell, was also Archdeacon of Ross, q. v.

1669. July 23. THEODORE VESEY, R. V. Kinsale, and R. V. Rincurran, vacant per mortem Jonæ Stowell. [V.B. 1669. D.R.] In 1676 Vesey was P. Kilnaglory, q. v.

The King is patron of the rectory, and the Bishop of the vicarage. [V.B. 1670.] In 1674 "Vesey est in Anglia." [V.B. D.R.]

1682. Sept. 11. RICHARD LAPP, A.M., V. Kinsale. [F.F.] He appears 1682 to 1685. [V.B. D.R.] In 1688 he became Archdeacon of Cork, q. v.

1686. June 11. JOHN TOM, A.M., V. Kinsale, per cession of Lapp. [D.R.] He appears 1686 to 1717. [V.B. D.R.] In 1693 he was also P. Desertmore, q. v.

When James II. landed in Kinsale, "the Vicar of Kinsale was among those who went to pay their duty; he was presented by the Bishop of Chester, and was not ungraciously received." [Macaulay, Hist. Eng. iii. p. 170.]

"1699. At Kinsale the water is about 200 yards broad. On the west side of the river is the old fort, on the top of the hill; it is now neglected. There is a small block-house at the point of the same hill, with about seven embrasures, near high-water mark, and a little store-house in it, but no guns. The new fort is about a quarter of a mile below the block-house, on the east side of the river. It has five bastions of stone—those two that look towards the mouth of the harbour, with the curtine betwixt them have many embrasures, with guns planted in them. There are two tires of guns below the south curtine that faces the mouth of the harbour; the west curtine that looks across the water has one tire of guns below it. There are about 140 guns in all; 200 are designed. Several of the guns are off the carriages, and the carriages are laid up. There is a hill on the east of the fort, within 200 yards; it overlooks the fort. One of the bastions which looks towards the land is call'd the cittadell, and is enclosed on the inward side towards the fort. The channel runs within 100 yards of the new fort. There is a sort of a barr a little below the new fort, so that first and second rate ships can't well pass, unless it be at high water. The old head of Kinsale is the extreme point of land on the west side of the water. Pallisados, at the foot of the walls of the new fort, towards the land, were made in King James's time; pallisados on the counterscarp were made about the year 1694. The walls of the fort that face towards the land were not well made, the inside being nothing but rubbish, viz., the walls towards the land. The English, in 1691, attack'd the fort on the east side; they beat down the N.E. bastion from a battery plant'd on the side of the hill, at about 200 yards distance. Lord Marleburrough, after thirteen days' siege, had it surrendered to him by Sr. Ch. Cotter." [Downes' Tour.]

1718 to 1729. Nov. 6. EMMANUEL HUNGERFORD appears as Vicar of Kinsale. [V.B. D.R.] He was also P. St. Michael's, q. v.

1720. Thurston Haddock, esq. of Kinsale, leaves £5 to the Protestant poor of Kinsale. [D.R.]

1730. Sept. 14. JOHN JEPHSON, A.B., V. St. Multose, Kinsale, per mortem naturalem Emanuelis Hungerford. [D.R.] In 1735 Jephson became Archdeacon of Cloyne, q. v.

1736. July 5. SAMUEL WOODROOFFE, A.M., V. Kinsale, per cession of Jephson. [D.R.]

Woodrooffe became, in 1762, Precentor of Cork, q. v.

1741. March 26. WILLIAM READER, A.M., V. Kinsale. [D.R.] In 1745 he became Archdeacon of Cork, q. v.

1745. April 4. PERCY MEADE, A.M., V. Kinsale. [F.F.]

Percy Meade (son of Dominick, Archdeacon of Cloyne, q. v.), was born in county Tipperary, and educated in Dublin by Dr. Sheridan. When seventeen years old he entered T.C.D. as Pensioner, on 3rd January, 1727. He subsequently graduated A.B. and A.M. In 1734 he was Curate of Kinsale, and in 1736 of Ballymartle and Dunderrow. From 1741 to 1745 he was V. Ballymodan.

He married Elisabeth (dau. of Henry Tonson, of Spanish Island, county Cork, by Elisabeth, dau. of Sir Richard Hall), relict of Major John Reading, who died in 1727. He had issue one daughter, Elisabeth, wife of John Rye, esq., of Rye Court, county Cork.

1747. August 26. BARTON PARKINSON, D.D., V. Kinsale, per mortem Percy Meade. [D.R.]

B. Parkinson (son of Richard Parkinson *generosi*), was born in Lancashire, and when nineteen years old entered T.C.D. as Pensioner on 26th May, 1724. He became a Scholar in 1728, and afterwards took the degrees of A.B. A.M. and D.D. He was licensed to the Curacy of St. Peter's, Cork, on 5th October, 1734, and in same year was appointed Surrogate.

Dr. Parkinson was twice married; by his first wife he had (I think) no issue. He married, secondly, Ellen, dau. of Michael Goold, esq., of Jamesbrook, and had issue by her a son, Thomas, who died in 1746; and two daughters, Jane and Sarah. Dr. Parkinson died in 1758, and in his will desired to be buried with his children, six foot deep in the north-east corner of St. Peter's church-yard, in Cork. His daughter, Sarah, was the administrator to his will; and Jane was wife to William Hill, esq., of Cloyne, father of Henry Hill, esq., of Cork, architect.

1758. Sept. 14. RICHARD FARMER, A.M., V. Kinsale, per mortem Parkinson. [D.R.] In 1762 he became P. Dromdaleague, q. v.

1762. Dec. 11. MATTHIAS SPREAD, A.M., V. Kinsale. [F.F.]

1767. In this year Lord de Clifford endows a classical school at Kinsale with £50 per annum, and also a large house, which was formerly the residence of Mr. Southwell, his ancestor. [D.R.] The school premises thus granted were estimated in 1858 as worth £41 2*s.* per annum, and the income from land was £27 13*s.* 10*d.* The state of the school generally was unsatisfactory. [Parl. Rep.]

Matthias Spread was son of William Spread, esq. who, in 1702, obtained a conveyance from the Trustees of Forfeited Estates of half a plowland, 131A. 2R. 16P. of the town and lands of Ballycaneen, in the North Liberties of Cork, at a rent of 8*s.* 10*d.* Matthias was born at Ballycaneen; and when eighteen years old entered T.C.D. on 20th May, 1727, and became a Scholar in 1729.

He was nominated in 1734 to Rathcormack Curacy. In 1749, Sept. 18, he was licensed to be Lecturer at St. Anne Shandon; and in 1752 was licensed to the Curacy of St. Paul's. He held from 1762 Kinsale, and from 1769 the V. Ballyfeard in addition, until his death in 1771.

He married, firstly, in 1738, Elisabeth Fitzgerald, of St. Peter's, who died in 1749, in the end of May. He married, secondly, in January, 1750, Elisabeth Boiteau, widow, of the parish of St. Paul.

He left issue surviving by his second wife, Edward (V. Ahern, Cloyne, q. v.); and John, his youngest son, besides a daughter, Lucy-Ann, wife of a Mr. Wood.

1771. Feb. 19. THOMAS ADDERLY BROWNE, LL.B., V. Kinsale, per mortem Spread. [D.R.] He became, in 1774, Chancellor of Ross, q. v.
1780. Dec. 4. WILLIAM NOBLE, A.B., V. Kinsale, per cession of Browne. [D.R.] In 1796 he became V. Holy Trinity, Cork, q. v.
1796. June 6. HENRY JONES, A.B., V. Kinsale. [F.F.] He became, in 1805, V. Lislee, Ross, q. v.
1799. July 27. SAMUEL BEAMISH, A.B., V. Kinsale. [F.F.]

1807. Beamish is non-resident. [Rep.]

1811. The Bishop approves of a memorial to build a glebe-house at Kinsale; and in September, 1812, he certifies for an outlay of £866 1s. 10½d. (portion of which was advanced by First Fruits); and that the yearly value of Kinsale is £175. [D.R.]

Samuel Beamish, of Mount Beamish, county Cork, was ordained Deacon on 16th October, 1774, and Priest on 24th August, 1777. He was licensed to the Curacy of Templebryan, in Ross, on 30th August, 1775. He held Kinsale from 1799 to 1826, when he resigned in favour of his son.

He married Mary (dau. of Joshua Hamilton, by Mary, dau. of Sir Richard Cox, of Dunmanway), by whom he had issue, *inter alios*, Mary, wife of Rev. R. F. Webb, of Caheragh; and Henry Hamilton Beamish, R. Taxax, q. v.

1826. April 4. HENRY HAMILTON BEAMISH, A.B., V. Kinsale; certified under £200 per annum in value. [D.R.] In 1829 he became R. Taxax, q. v.

1830. The Protestant population was 1,070.

1832. July 6. JAMES THOMAS BROWNE, A.B., V. Kinsale, vacant by resignation of Beamish. [D.R.]

1837. Kinsale, a vicarage, with cure, 1½ miles long by ½ broad, containing 550 acres. Gross population, 6,897. No Curate employed. Minister's money, £80. Composition for vicarial tithes, £16 11s. 3d. Three acres of glebe, worth £7. Pew rents, £12; surplice fees, £7. Subject to 17s. 4d. visitation fees; and £2 5s. for diocesan schoolmaster. The glebe-house was built under the old Acts, in 1811, at cost of £784 12s. 3¾d. British, whereof £461 10s. 9¼d. was a gift, and £323 1s. 6½d. a loan from First Fruits. Of the loan, £101 was chargeable on the benefice in 1832, repayable by annual instalments of £5 19s. Exclusive of the monies aforesaid, it is reported that the builder expended £184 12s. 3d. British, and the present Vicar £50, British, on the premises, without having any charge on their successors. Incumbent is resident in the glebe-house.

One church, capable of accommodating 1,200 persons, but so ancient that the date and cost of erection are unknown. No charge on the parish in 1832 on account of the church. Divine service twice on all Sundays, besides a third service on the first Sunday in every month; service also twice a week, and on principal festivals. The sacrament is administered twice each month from Easter to October, and on Christmas Day, Easter Day, Whit Sunday, and once a month during remainder of year. The rectorial tithes, consisting of one moiety, are compounded for £16 11*s.* 3*d.* They are impropriate, and belong to Thomas Cuthbert Kearney, esq.

James Thomas Browne (son of Henry Browne, esq. of Ballinvoher, near Farrahy, by Isabella, dau. of William Galwey, esq., of Mallow), was born at Mallow on 15th July, 1803, and graduated A.B. T.C.D in 1826, M.A. in 1832, and in 1841 became A.M. of Cambridge. He was ordained Deacon on 10th June, and Priest 23rd Dec. 1827, both at Cloyne. He was Curate of Rahan, Cloyne, in 1827, and of Kinsale in 1828. From 1832 to 1838 he was V. Kinsale, which he resigned on 10th Dec. 1838. He was Incumbent of St. Edmund's, Northampton, in 1846.

He married, in November, 1834, Martha, dau. of John Abbott, esq. of Cork, by whom he had issue two sons. He married, secondly, Sarah Elisabeth, dau. of General Greenstreet, H.E.I.C., and has issue five sons and four daughters.

1838. Dec. 20. WILLIAM ROBERT MEADE, A.B., V. Kinsale. [D.R.]

W. R. Meade (eldest son of Robert Meade, Rector of Ballymoney), was ordained Deacon at Cloyne on 29th Sept. 1819, and Priest at Cork on 20th May, 1821, on letters dimissory from Cloyne. From 1826 to 1839 he was R. Templemichael de Duagh; and from 1839 to his death, on 21st of May, 1852, he was V. Kinsale.

He married Margaret, dau. of Richard Lewis, esq., by whom he had no issue.

1852. June 2. RICHARD GRAVES MEREDYTH, A.B., V. Kinsale; certified yearly value, £128 4*s.* 8*d.* [D.R.] He obtained, on 10th Oct. 1853, £132 9*s.* 10*d.* dilapidations, against his predecessor. [D.R.] In 1861 he became R. Knockavilly, q. v.

1856. Dec. 31. JOHN WRIGHT HOPKINS, A.B., V. Kinsale; certified yearly net value, £89 12*s.* 1*d.* [D.R.]

1860. St. Multose, Kinsale. The church, &c., in good order. The glebe-house is in good repair. Two acres of glebe let. Divine service twice on all Sundays, and once on Wednesdays and festivals. Sacrament monthly. The average of communicants is from 90 to 150. 21 boys, 19 girls, and 25 infants attend the schools, which are supported by subscriptions, and managed by trustees. The Protestant population is 700. The net annual income of Kinsale is returned as £82, with residence. The rentcharge is £12. The land is worth £4. £55 4*s.* 10*d.* is paid as Minister's money, and the remainder is from other sources. Since the vacancy of Taxax parish (1863) a union of that small parish to Kinsale has been under the consideration of the Privy Council.

J. W. Hopkins was ordained Priest at Cork on 3rd June 1849. He is married, and has issue.

KNOCKAVILLY.

1291. "Eccia de Cnocbile Xmr." [Tax. P. Nic.]

1591. RURICUS FLIN appears as Rector of Knockavilly. "E. de Cnocknovilly, Ruricus flin, incumbens respicitur in prox. pro titulis." [MS. T.C.D. E. 3. 14.] In another part of same visitation book, Roger Flynn, "rector de Knocknoville" is deprived "propter acceptacionem rectoriæ de Kilboynan." Flynn was also V. Kilbrogan.

1615. EDWARD BEECHER appears as R. Knockavilly, and P. Kilbrittain, q. v. "Knockevilly Rectoria integ. Edwardus Becher, studii gratia, inservit curæ. Val. 10 li." [R.V. 1615.]

1617. March 16. JOHN BRADISHE, P. Kilbrittain, and R. V. Knockavilly, on letters patent of Feb. 27. [F.F. and Lib. Mun.] *Vide* Kilbrittain.

1621. April 5. RANDAL HOLLAND, R. de Knockenyvilly als Knockaveely. in Coll. Epi. [V.B. 1669.] In 1623 he became P. Killanully, q. v.

1634. Knockavilly is valued at 35 li. per an. "Comes de Muskerry, patronus." [R.V. 1634.] In 1639 "Ecclia bene, desunt ornamenta." [V.B. D.R.]

1622 to 1810. Knockavilly was held in union with Brinny, q. v.

1810. August 21. WILLIAM LEWIS BEAUFORT, A.M., was admitted R. Knockavilly, and R. V. Brinny. He resigned Brinny in 1836, but retained Knockavilly till his death in 1849. He was also, from 1814, P. Cahirlag, q. v.

For the population in 1830, and for the statistics of the parish in 1832, *vide* Brinny.

1832. Nov. 8. W. L. Beaufort gives to Joseph Garde 13A. 2R. 30P. English statute measure, of the glebe lands of Knockavilly, in exchange for 19 acres English statute measure, of the lands of Raheen, which, lying near the site of the old ruined church of Knockavilly, are more suitable for any new church or glebe-house which may hereafter be built. [D.R.]

1834. April 14. An apartment in the house of Abraham Haynes, farmer, at Lissgrovin, is licensed for divine service. [D.R.]

1844. May 14. A new church on new site (built by Ecclesiastical Commissioners) is consecrated under the name of St. James. [D.R.]

1850. January 3. WILLIAM JOHNSON, A.B., R. Knockavilly, per mortem Beaufort; certified value, £458 8*s*. 6*d*. [D.R.] In 1861 Johnson became Chancellor of Cloyne, q. v.

1860. The church in order; no glebe-house; 45½ acres of glebe set to a farmer; Rector resides at Innishannon; divine service once on all Sundays and usual holidays in the church, and evening service during summer in a licensed schoolhouse. Sacrament monthly; average of communicants, 19; and at chief festivals, average 28. 9 children are on the rolls of a Church Education school. The Protestant population is 68. The rent-charge is £468 10s.; the land is worth £43 10s.; the total value is £512 per annum, without residence.

1861. January 28. RICHARD GRAVES MEREDYTH, A.B., R. Knockavilly. [D.R.]

R. G. Meredyth (son of Thomas Meredyth, D.D., F.T.C.D., by Eliza, dau. of Dean Richard Graves), is a descendant of John Meredyth, who died in 1594, and who, with his brother Richard, Bp. of Leighlin, was buried in St. Patrick's Cathedral, Dublin.

He was a Scholar, T.C.D. in 1829, and was ordained Deacon on 13th August, 1837, and Priest on 24th Feb., 1838, both at Cork. He was some time Chaplain of the Foundling Hospital, Cork. In 1845 he was Curate of Rincurran. From 1852 to 1856 he was V. Kinsale, and from 1856 to 1851 P. Timoleague, Ross.

He married, in 1841, Maria, dau. of Thomas Johnston, esq., of Fort Johnston, county Monaghan, by Martha, dau. of Rev. Dr. Hingston, Vicar-General of Cloyne. His only son, Thomas Richard E. Meredyth, was accidentally killed by a gun-shot wound, at Fort Johnston, on 24th August, 1862, at the early age of eighteen.

LEIGHMONEY.

1291. "Eccia de Lachmoin Vmr." [Tax. P. Nic.]

1591. "THOMAS WOODE, Rector de Shanbally, and Vicarius Ecclesiarum respective de Rosbery Tisbery et Leighmony Corkagen. dioces., deprivatus beneficiis respective propter defectum sacrorum ordinum et pluralitatem beneficiorum." [MS. T.C.D. E. 3. 14.] In another MS. of same year THOMAS LEIGH is Rector and Vicar de Leighmoney—"presentat—non admiss—Dno respex." Leigh appears as R. Rincurran. Woode was also P. St. Michael's, q. v.

1615. "Leighmoney residens. Rector et Vicarius, JOHANNES HONICHURCH, minister et predicator. Val. 3 li. per an. Ecclesia et cancella in ruinis. Tenet etiam R. Templemichael de Dowagh." [R.V. R.I.A.]

1617. June 10. STEPHEN VEIGHNING, R. and V. Leighmony [F.F.] He was also P. Currograngemore, Ross, q. v.

1634. Leighmony, R. and V. Stephen Veighning, predicator. Richard Roch fils. John patronus. Valet 20 li. per an. [R.V. 1634.]

1639. THOMAS BOYLE appears as R. Leighmoney. "Ecclia ruinata." [V.B 1639.] He was, in 1629, V. Ardfield, and in 1630, V.

Timoleague, in Ross. He resigned in 1633 the R. V. Kilsillagh, in Ross. In 1632 he was V. Clondrohid, Cloyne. The most of above livings he vacated before 1639.
166—? JOHN BUTLER, R. Leighmoney, *vide* Kilbrittain.
1666. Vacant. [V.B.]

1667 to 1796. Leighmoney was held with Innishannon, q. v.

1796. March 3. On the death of Rev. Dr. St. John Browne, the Rev. Peter Foley is appointed Sequestrator of Leighmoney. [D.R.]

1796. May 11. James Kearney, esq., of Garretstown, withdraws his presentation of a Clerk to Leighmoney, having seen a paper which induces him to think himself mistaken with respect to his right of presentation to this benefice. [D.R.]

1796. Oct. 12. JOHN KINGSTON, A.B., R. V. Leighmoney. [F.F.]

1799. April 17. JOSEPH WRIGHT, A.M., R. V. Leighmoney, vacant by death of Kingston. [D.R.] He was also V. Aghadowne, Ross, q. v.

1806. Wright resides at Aghadowne. [Parl. Rep.]

1812. March 27. ALEXANDER KENNEDY, A.B., R. V. Leighmoney, *vice* Wright, who resigned on 21st March. [D.R.]

Alexander Kennedy was ordained Deacon on 29th of September, 1786, and Priest on 9th December, 1787, both at Cloyne, on letters dimissory from Cork.

From 1789 to 1826 he seems to have been Curate of the Holy Trinity, Cork.

From 1806 to 1812 he was P. Donoghmore, Ross, and from 1812 to 21st September, 1818, he was R. V. Leighmoney. He then resigned.

He married, on 20th June, 1789, Sarah O'Callaghan, who died on 24th January, 1817.

1818. Oct. 9. HENRY THEOPHILUS HODDER, A.B., R. V. Leighmoney, certified under £200. [D.R.] In 1826 he became Precentor of Cork, q. v.

1826. March 30. JOHN FORSAYETH, A.B., R. V. Leighmoney, certified under £200. [D.R.]

John Forsayeth was ordained Priest at Cloyne on 29th September, 1786.

He seems to have been Curate of St. Peter's, Cork, from 1783 to 1826. He held Leighmoney from 1826 to his death in 1828. He taught a school in Henry-street, Cork, for many years.

He was, in 1805, October 7, appointed Thresher's Lecturer, in Cork.

He was buried at St Nicholas, Cork, on 16th of September, 1828.

1828. Sept. 20. JOHN NASH WRIGHT, A.B., R. V. Leighmoney, certified under £200. [D.R.]

1829. Sept. 29. Wright memorials for liberty to reside at

Creaghe, paying £10 per an. for the occasional duties of this parish to Rev. Robert Halburd. The total value of Leighmoney is £110. He is licensed accordingly for three years non-residence, on 2nd March, 1830. [D.R.]

1830. Protestant population, 97.

1830. July 18. The present parish register begins.

1833. In May, an apartment, in the house of the steward of Captain Herrick, at Shippool, is licensed for divine service. [D.R.]

1837. Leighmoney: a rectory and vicarage, with cure, two miles long by one broad, containing 2,736A.; gross population, *855*; one Curate employed for the occasional duties, at a stipend of £10 per annum; tithe composition, £110 0*s.* 5½*d.*, subject to diocesan schoolmaster, 3*s.* 9*d.*; no glebe-house; Incumbent is non-resident; by permission of the Diocesan, he resides in the parish of Creagh; no church; divine service is performed once on all Sundays, in a school-house, with the Bishop's permission, and on Christmas Day and Good Friday; the sacrament is administered monthly, and on the festivals; the benefice is a rectory. [Parl. Rep.]

John Nash Wright (eldest son of Rev. Joseph Wright, V. Aghadowne, Ross, q. v.,) was ordained Deacon, at Cork, on 1st January, 1802, and Priest, at Cloyne, on 12th December, 1802, on letters dimissory from Cork, for the curacy of Tullagh and Creagh, in Ross. In 1806 he was Curate of Tullagh only, and afterwards he again became Curate of Creagh. Leighmoney being distant from his residence, and his health becoming impaired, he resigned it on 8th January, 1841. He received an address and testimonial of regard from the parishioners of Creagh on retiring from that curacy.

He married, on 22nd June, 1819, Horatio-Nelson (dau. of Thomas Stocken Triphook, esq., of Ballinadee, by his wife, Charlotte Vokes). He had issue by her nine sons (Joseph, Thomas, John, Thomas-Triphook, William, Robert, Richard, William, and Henry); and four daughters, Horatio-Jane, Maria-Sophia, Elisabeth-Margaret, and Charlotte-Helena.

1841. January 19. JOHN MEADE, A.B., R. V. Leighmoney. [D.R.]

1860. The church has been in ruins from time immemorial. No glebe-house; no glebe. Divine service once on Sundays, and on festivals, in a licensed school-house. Sacrament monthly; average of communicants, 9. Incumbent resides in his own house, within a short distance of the parish. 6 children attend a Church Education school. Protestant population, 34. The value of the benefice is £82, arising from rentcharge.

John Meade, eldest son of John Meade, Collector of Customs at Kinsale (who was son of Rev. William Meade, Rector of Rincurran), by Alice, dau. of Rev. Chamber Corker, P. Cahirlag, was born 26th July, 1792, and was educated at Rev. Dr.

Coghlan's school, at Glanmire. He obtained two classical premiums in T.C.D., where he graduated A.B. in 1813.

He was ordained Deacon on 24th Dec., 1815, at Cork, and Priest, in January, 1819, also at Cork.

He was, in 1815, Curate of Templemichael; in 1818, of Ballymartle; and in 1833, of Leighmoney.

He married, on 26th July, 1816, Sarah, dau. of George Wood, esq., and has issue three sons, John, Richard-William, and Edward-Southwell; and two daughters, Eliza and Alice-Corker. The Rev. John Meade is the possessor of the family estate of Ballintobber.

LISCLERY.

1291. Ecclesia de Lystlerith is rated at 8 marks. [Tax. P. Nic.]

1332. This Prebend was founded by John de Ballyconingham, Bishop of Cork. It was anciently named Sanctæ Brigidæ de Lisly Clerigy. One Meagh, or O'Mide, anciently presented to it. Taxed in K. B. at £3. Proxy, 6*s.* 9*d.* [Smith's Cork, vol. i. p. 64.]

1502. The advowson of St. Nicholas de Lysinclery is given to the church of the Holy Trinity, Cork, for the augmentation of divine service, by James Myagh, the Patron. I give the deed entire. "Sciant presentes et futuri quod Ego Jacobus Myagh, civis civitatis Cork, verus patronus Ecclesiæ prebendalis Sti. Nicholai de Lysinclery Cork. dioc., dedi, &c. in puram et perpetuam elemosinam Ecclesiæ prebendali Stæ Trinitatis infra muros Cork, duas acras terræ cum pertinentiis in tenemento de Lysinclery unacum advocatione juris patronatus dictæ Ecclesiæ Lysinclery —Habendum, &c. dictæ ecclesiæ in augmentationem divini cultus in eadem ecclesia in perpetuum de capitalibus dominis feodi per servicia inde debeta, &c. ita quod tocies quocies contingет rectoriam Sancti Nicholai vacasse, quod quatuor legales homines de probioribus dictæ ecclesiæ, parochianis nomine ipsius ecclesiæ unum dignum presbyterum aut clericum ad rectoriam prefatam presentabunt, in eadem ecclesia deservire, &c. In cujus rei testimonium sigillum meum cum sigillo maioratus Cork civitatis officii presentibus duxi apponendum. Datum apud Cork X die Octobris Anno Dni. milessimo quingentessimo secundo. Testibus Edmundo Goull, maiore Cork—Georgio Roche, burgense—Dno Mauricio Whitt, Ricardo Sydda et aliis." [Caulfield MSS.]

1591. Roger Skyddy appears as Prebendary, and Thomas Woods as Vicar of Lisclery. Skiddy is also "R. particulæ de Liscornan." [MS. T.C.D. E. 3. 14.] In another part of this visitation book,

Skiddy is called "Rector de lesclerie et Rector Scti nichli de lisclery." Of Thomas Wood, it is noted, "nihil exhib—privat. ——comit. custod. mar." This means, I suppose, that Mr. Wood had neither orders nor titles to produce, and that he was deprived and given into custody for some misconduct.

1615. June 2. MARCUS PAGETT, P. Lisclery, R. Ballymartle, and V. Ballyfeard. [F.F.] He was afterwards Dean of Ross, q. v.

1615. "Liscleary Prebenda; non-residens. Rector Mark Paget, minister et predicator. Val. 20 marcarum. Ecclesia et cancella in ruinis. Vicarius Nicholas Bright, minister et predicator." [R.V. R.I.A.]

Nicholas Bright was ordained Deacon and Priest by John, Bishop of Gloucester, in 1600. From 1611 to 1614, Bright was R. Rathclarin, and from 1611 to 1615, R. Ballymartle. From 1615 to 1617 he was V. Lisclery. In 1615 he is found also as Treasurer of Killaloe, and Vic. Choral of Limerick; and on 17th October, 1629, he is admitted V. Drumcliffe, als Grormath, in Killaloe.

Bishop Ryder gives Bright the character of "a minister and preacher, a man of good conversation."

1617. July 19. RICHARD SUTTON was admitted Vicar of Lisclery, and P. St. Michael's, q. v.

16—? NICHOLAS HALL, Preb. and Vicar of Lisclery. In 1619 he became Treasurer of Ross, q. v.

1626. Oct. 20. CHARLES COLDWELL, Preb. Lisclery, per cessionem Nicholai Hall. [R.V. 1634.]

1634. P. Lisclery, Charles Coldwell, Predicator. Val. 15 li. per an. Vicarius Nicholas Hall. Val. XII. li. per an. [R.V. 1634.]

Charles Coldwell, literatus, was ordained Deacon on 31st of March, 1625, and Priest on 28th of June, 1626, both by Michael, Bishop of Waterford and Lismore.

In 1626 he was P. Lisclery, and R. Bohillane and Kilmahon, in Cloyne; in 1628 he was Vicar Choral, Cloyne; and in 1631 he was also V. Ballygourney, Cloyne. He held most of these livings in 1634.

1634. Feb. 1. JOHANNES BINNS, V. Lisclery. [F.F.] He was, in 1641, Treasurer of Cloyne, q. v.

In 1639, Charles Coldwell appears as P. and John Binns, as V. Lisclery—"Ecclesia bene, desunt ornamenta." [V.B. D.R.]

1640, *circa*. BRIAN ROCH was admitted V. Lisclery. [F.F.]

From 1637 to 1640, or 1639, Roch was R. Ardnegihy, and V. Ballyvourney, Cloyne.

1661. Lisclery is vacant. [V.B.]

1662. July 24. ROGERUS BOYLE admissus ad Prœbendam de Lisneclearie et ad vicariam ejusdem. [F.F.]

In a few months Boyle became Dean of Cork, q. v.

1663. May 1. PETER MANBIE, P. and V. Lisclery, als Lesley-Clerrigge, and R. Ardnegihy, and V. Cannaway. [F.F.]

Peter Manby, besides his preferment in Cork, held from 1660 to 1661, a minor canonry in St. Patrick's, Dublin, and from 1666 to 1670 was Chancellor of St. Patrick's. In 1670 he became First Canon of Kildare, and in 1672, Dean of Derry.

1681. Dec. 19. John Graham informs the Archbishop of Canterbury that the Archbishop of Dublin "dyed this day;" and recommends the translation to Dublin of the Bishop of Kilmore and Ardagh, and that either Dean Manbie of Derry, or Dean Bladen of Dublin, be made Bishop of Kilmore, &c. [Rawlinson MSS. Oxon.]

In 1688 Manbie was made an Alderman of Derry, and on 21st July, 1688, James II. granted him a dispensation to hold his deanery, notwithstanding his professing the Roman Catholic religion. After the battle of the Boyne he went to France; and died in London, 1697. *Vide* Cotton for a list of his works.

1666. Vacant. [V.B. D.R.]

1667. JOHN VEASIE appears as P. and V. Lisclery. [V.B. D.R.] On 3rd September, 1667, he was made Dean of Cork, q. v.

1668. Vacant. [V.B. D.R.]

1669. Oct. 26. THOMAS WILCOX, P. and V. Lisclery, per resignation of John Veasy. [V.B. 1669.] Wilcox appears at the visitation of 1670, and in 1671 became P. Brigowne, Cloyne, q. v.

1671. May. 15. GEORGE SING is admitted to P. V. Lisclery, als Lisleyclerigge, V. Inchigeelah, V. Kilmichael, and P. Inniscarra, and V. Mathea, in Cloyne. [F.F.] In 1674 he became P. Kilbrogan, q. v. He appears in 1671 and 1672, as P. and V. Lisclery. [V.B. D.R.]

1674. June 5. SAMUEL SING, P. and V. Lisclery, and P. Iniscarra, Cloyne. [F.F.] In 1677 he became P. Dromdaleague, q. v. He appears in 1674 and 1675. In the former year he is marked as "in Anglia, studendi gratia." [V.B. D.R.]

1676. Oct. 26. ROWLAND DAVIES, P. V. Lisclery, P. Inniscarra, and V. Grenagh. [F.F.] In 1710 he was Dean of Cork, q. v.

He appears 1677 to 1706. [V.B. D.R.]

"The Protestants go to Carrickgoline." [V.B. 1699. D.D.]

1706. Feb. 11. PHILIP TOWNSEND, A.M., P. and V. Lisclery. [F.F.] He was also V. Holy Trinity, q. v. He appears 1709 to 1734. [V.B. D.R.]

1735. August 23. BOYLE DAVIES, A.M., P. and V. Lisclery, per mortem Phil. Townsend. [D.R.]

Boyle Davies, the second son of the Dean of Cork, was born "at Blarney Castle, 29th daie of December, 1683, at four minutes past eleven of the clock, afternoon." His godfathers were Capt. John Folliott and Alderman Thomas Kitchingham; his godmothers were Mrs. Margaret Singe and Mrs. Elisabeth Colthurst.

He entered T.C.D. as Pensioner on 14th Feb. 1698, being then sixteen years old. He became a Scholar in 1701, and subsequently graduated A.M.

He was P. Inskenny from 1710 to 1735, and from 1735 to 1763 was P. Lisclery. He also held from 1721 to 1763 the Rectory of Carrigaline. In 1713 he appears as Curate of Christchurch, Cork. He died on Wednesday, January 19, 1763. The freedom of the city of Cork was given to him by special grace on 23rd September, 1710.

Boyle Davies was author of "A Sermon preached at St. Peter's Church, in the city of Corke, on the 29th day of September, being the anniversary of the surrender of that city to the victorious arms of the great and glorious King William, of blessed memory, in the late happy revolution of these kingdoms in the year of our Lord 1690, and published at the special request of the loyal Corporation of that city, by the Reverend Boyle Davies, M.A., Corke. Printed by George Bennett, and are to be sold at his shop, 1720."

He married, firstly, in May, 1709, Mary Bond, of Christchurch, Cork, widow (she was dau. of Richard Travers, by Elisabeth, or Eleanor, dau. of Jonas Stawell, Archdeacon of Ross), and by her had issue four sons and six daughters, all of whom died young, or unmarried, save Mary, who was wife to W. Thomas Spiers, esq.

His second wife was Mary, dau. of Thomas Tuckey, esq. of Cork, and this marriage took place in April, 1724. By this lady he had issue, besides Boyle and Thomas, both clergymen, who died Sp. (*vide* Index), a third son, Richard (born 1731, died Sp. in 1755), and a fourth, Robert, M.D., who was born on 17th November, 1735, and died 5th September, 1789. This Robert married at Dublin, on 14th March, 1763, Jane, only dau. of Ven. Christopher Isaac, Archdeacon of Emly, and by her had issue (besides two sons, who died unmarried), Rev Boyle Davies (*vide* Index), and an only dau. Mary Jane, who married in 1795, her cousin, Rowland Morrison, of Tivoli House, county Cork.

1763. January 22. ISAAC GOLDSMITH, A.M., P. and V. Lisclery. [F.F.] He was also Dean of Cork, q. v.

1769. May 12. SAMUEL HALES, A.M., P. and V. Lisclery, *vice* Goldsmith, deceased. [F.F.] In 1770 Hales became P. Kilbrittain, q. v.

1770. Dec. 28. RICHARD PIGOTT, B.D., P. and V. Lisclery. [F.F.] In 1774 he became V. Holy Trinity, q. v.

1774. August 5. ROBERT AUSTEN, D.D., P. and V. Lisclery. [F.F.] He resigned for P. Kilnaglory in 1777, August 23, and on 26th August, was appointed Sequestrator of Lisclery during its vacancy. [D.R.] He was afterwards Archdeacon of Cork, q. v.

1777. Oct. 7. WILLIAM WALLER, A.B., P. and V. Lisclery. [F.F.] He was second son of Samuel Waller, esq. of Newport, county Tipperary, the brother of Sir Robert Waller. [U.O.] He died in 1823, being also Rector of Maryboro', Leighlin.

1823. April 19. JOHN FORTESCUE, A.M., P. R. and V. Lisclery. [D.R.]

1824. The inhabitants of Barnahely and the eastern part of Lisclery are ordered to resort to the new church of Carrigoline. [D.R.]

1830. Protestant population is 89.

1833. May. 16. A slated house on the lands of Dromgorrihy in this parish was licensed for divine service. [D.R.]

John Fortescue was Chancellor of Cork from 1790 to 1823, and from 1823 to his death in August, 1833, he was P. Lisclery.

1834. Feb. 22. JOHN BUSTEED, A.B., P. and V. Lisclery, net value, £116 13*s.* 4*d.*, arising from the rectorial tithes of Lisclery, which form the corps of the Prebend. The revenues of the vicarage amounting to £93 6*s.* 8*d.* for the vicarial tithes, are now appropriated by the Ecclesiastical Commissioners, the vicarage being suspended. [D.R.]

1837. Lisclery: a vicarage, with cure, 4½ miles long by 3 broad, containing 6,738A. 2R. 1¾P. Gross population, 2,804. One Curate employed for the occasional duties of this parish, at a stipend of £10 per annum. Composition for vicarial tithes, £93 6*s.* 8*d.* No glebe-house. Incumbent is non-resident; he resides in the city of Cork. No church. The rectorial tithes of this benefice, compounded for £116 13*s.* 4*d.*, are appropriated to Lisclery prebend. N.B.—The *vicarage* is suspended. [Parl. Rep.]

1860. There is neither church nor licensed place of worship, nor divine service, nor glebe-house, nor school, nor parish clerk, nor register in this parish. The Incumbent is non-resident. The Protestant population is 32. The rentcharge is £87 10*s.* arising from the *rectorial* tithes.

John Busteed was ordained Deacon on 10th of May, 1799, at Douglas, by the Bishop of Cork, and Priest on 1st Sept. 1799, at Cloyne, on letters dimissory from Cork. On 13th July, 1799, he was licensed to be Curate of Douglas, which cure he still holds along with this prebend.

LITTLE ISLAND.

1291. "Eccia de Insula XLs. vicar. capit dimid." [Tax. P. Nic.]

15—? PHILIP SARSFIELD, Rector of Sti. Lappani de insula. He died circa 1582.

1582. July 5. DOMINICK SARSFIELD is admitted "ad rectoriam simplicem ecclię parochialis Scti Lappani de insula parva als Inishvieneyl Corcagen. dioc. vacantem per mortem PHILIPPI SARSFIELD ultimi incumbentis." [D.R.]

He was inducted on July 9, 1582. This admission was on the presentation of the parishioners of the Holy Trinity, Cork, of which I give the copy entire.

"Reverendo in Christo patri ac domino Matheo, Corcagen. et Clonen. Epō, aut vicariis generalibus Corcagen: parochiani Ecclię Sctę Trinitatis, Cork, veri patroni rectorię simplicis ecclesię Scti Lappani de insula parva Corcagen. dioces. Saltem. Ad rectoriam prefatam jam de jure et de facto per mortem Philippi Sarsfield ultimi ibidem incumbentis vacantem, et ad nostram presentationem spectantem: Dilectum nobis in Christo Dominicum Sarsfield clericum indole et natalibus probum presentamus et presentatum fore volumus per presentes. Vestram paternitatem in Domino obsecrantes quatenus pfatum Dominicum, sic per nos presentatum et divino cultui in pfata nostra ęde Sctę Trinitatis frugi et utilem futurum, ad pdictam Rectoriam simplicem vestra auctoritate admittatis et admissum faciatis. In hujus presentationis testimonium sigilla nostra opposuimus et nomina subscripsimus. Dat Corcagię quinto Junii, 1582. Patrick Galwey, Maior; James Creagh, bailiff; Adam Goole, bailiff; Andrew Skiddy, recordor; William Tirry, James Hore, churchwarden; Philip Martell, Edmond Tirry, Christopher Galwey, Thomas Sarsfield, Morris Roch, David Tirry fitz Oliver, Robert Tirry Scoolemaster, Thomas fitz John, Charles Field, Patrick Gold, John Miaghe, ffrauncis Martell, Gerald Gold, James Roch, John ffaygan, John Skiddy, Patrick Tyrry, John Skiddy, Dominick Meaghe, Ricd. Pounch, William Goole fitz Walter, John pounch fitz Patrick, Piers Gold, Robert Coppinger, James Close, Dominick Gold, George Roch, Rd. Downy, John Verdon, David Nash, John Morroghe, Rd. Roch, James Morrogh." [Cork Registry.]

1591. ALEXANDER MEAGH or MEAD is Rector, and DAVID TIRRY is Vicar. "Rector insule pve. als Rector Sci lupani de insula, Alexander Meagh, respicitur in crast. idem Rector de Inishonan et contumax [deliberand] pro ejus amocōe nisi venit. Vicarius ibm David Tirry, interdicitur ut supra." (*Vide* Cahirlag). [M.S. T.C.D. E. 3. 14.]

1614. May 6. ISRAEL TAYLOR is presented "ad *Rectoriam* Insulę parvę" and R. V. Rathclarin. [Lib. Mun.] He was admitted on 6th of April, 1615, and inducted on 27th April, 1615, as R. Insulæ parvæ et R. V. Rathclarin, ex presentatione Regis Jacobi, dat. 6th March. [R. V. 1634.] He was Precentor of Cork, q. v.

1615. THOMAS BOURDEN (V. Kilbonane, q. v.) appears as *Vicar*, and TAYLOR as *Rector* of Little Island. "Rector, Israel Taylor, minister et predicator. Val. 7 li. Vicarius, Thomas Bourden, minister legens. Val. 3 li. Ecclia et cancella bene repantur cum libris." [R.V. R.I.A.]

1634. R. de Insula parva; Israel Taylor, Rector. Rex est patronus. Val. X li. per an. Vicarius, Thomas Bourden. Epus patronus. Val. 5 li. per an. [R.V. 1634.]

1639. RICHARD BENNETT (Vicar Choral, Cork, q. v.) appears as *Vicar*, with TAYLOR still as Rector Insulæ parvæ. Ecclesia bene, desunt ornamenta." [V.B.]

16—? SAMUEL BONNER, R. V. Insulæ parvæ. He was also P. St. Michael's, q. v.

1667. P. R. and V. Insulæ parvæ, vacant per mortem SAMUELIS BONNER. [V.B. D.R.]

1668. JOHN BAYLEY appears as R. V. Insulæ parvæ, and as R. Kilcoan and Templeusky. [V.B. D.R.] On 11th July, 1669, he is instituted to R. V. Insulæ parvæ, per mortem Samuelis Bonner. [V.B. 1669.] He was also P. St. Michael's q. v.

1697. June 17. VALENTINE FRENCH, P. St. Michael's, R. Kilcoan, Templeusky, Kilroane, and R. V. Insulæ parvæ. [F.F.] In 1704 French became P. Killaspugmullane, and in 1717 Dean of Ross, q. v.

1699. Insula parva. "No churchwardens; 2 plowlands; one Protestant family—Alderman Rogers'; divine service and sermon once a fortnight; sacrament four times a year." [V.B. 1699. D.D.]

"Oct. 1700. I saw the church in Little Island, built with stones and lime, in good repair; there is a pulpit and desks, but no seats; a tomb in the church, belonging to the Courthy's family; the church is about 40 feet long and 20 broad; the church-yard inclos'd by a good stone wall; no glebe in this parish. 2 plowlands and a half in this parish; the lands belong to Major Clayton and the Solicitor-General, Brodrick. No inhabitants in this parish but Captain Wakeham and a dozen of Irish families. All the tythes of this parish belong to the Incumbent; they are worth about £12 per an. Mr. French preaches here once a fortnight, the other Sunday he does no duty in all his parishes. William Dooly is Popish Priest of this parish and Cahirlag, &c.; he lives in Carricktoghill; he has been many years in these parts." [Downes' Tour.]

1732. January 1. JEMMET BROWNE, A.M., P. Killaspugmullane et unam R. V. Cannaway, R. Kilcoan, Templeusky, Kilroan et R. V. Insulæ parvæ, per mortem Val. French. [D.R.] He was, in 1733, Dean of Ross, q. v.

1743. Nov. 5. ARTHUR ECHLIN is presented by Crown to R. V. Little Island, vacant by promotion of Jemmet Browne to the Bishoprick of Killaloe. [Lib. Mun. and D.R.]

Arthur, son of Rev. John Echlin, was born in Antrim; and on 18th March, 1724, entered T.C.D., being then nineteen years old.

From 1743 to 1752, when he died, he was R. V. Little Island. Either this, or another Arthur Echlin, was licensed to the curacy of St. Peter's, Cork, on 5th September, 1751.

1752. Feb. 19. THOMAS BROWNE, A.B., R. V. Little Island, vacant by death of Arthur Echlin. [D.R.] Browne became Treasurer of Ross, and Precentor of Cork, q. v.

1762. May 13. SAMUEL HALES, A.M., R. V. Little Island, vacant by death of Thomas Browne. [D.R.] In 1770 he was P. Kilbrittain, q. v.

1769. May 12. CHAMBRE CORKER is instituted to R. V. Little Island. He was also P. Cahirlag and R. Rathcoony. [D.R.]

From 1769 to present time the R. V. of the Little Island were held in union with Cahirlag Prebend, q. v.

MACLONEIGH.

1591. DERMITIUS LONG (Treasurer of Cork, q. v.), is V. Macloneigh. "R. de Cloineighe; Thesaur. et hospit. Morne sunt Rectores. Vic. ibm Dermicius Long." [MS. T.C.D. E. 3. 14.]

1615. JOHN BROCK (Treasurer of Cork, q. v.), appears as Vicar. "Clonegh. Mourne et Thesaurarius Rector. Vicarius Johēs Brock. Curatus Willmus Healy, minister legens." [R.V. R.I.A.] Healy was also Chancellor of Cork, q. v.

1618. Jan. 20. John Brock, the Treasurer, receives the V. Macloneigh, et V. beatæ Mariæ de Shandon united to the Treasurership. [R.V. 1634.]

1634. Una R. de Cloneigh spectat ad Abb. de Morne. Cormack Donogh Carty firmarius. Brock Curatus. Val. 7 li. per an. Altera R. spectat ad Thesaurarium. Vic. ibm Johēs Brock. Val. 7 li. per annum. [R.V. 1634.]

1637. Jan. 3. ROBERT KEMPE, V. Macloneigh and Moviddy. [F.F.] He appears in V.B. 1639 as "excusetur." [D.R.]

1640. Feb. 12. WILLIAM BEARDE, R. MacCloneagh and Moviddy. [F.F.]

1666. Vacant. [V.B. D.R.]

1667 and 1668. JOHN WEBB appears as V. Macloneigh. [V.B.] He was also Chancellor of Cloyne, q. v.

1669. October 29. RICHARD BROWNE, V. Macloneigh, Macromp, and Ballyvourney, vacant per desertionem Johis Webb. [V.B. 1669.] For Browne, *vide* Macroom, Cloyne. "Rectoria una de Macloneigh est particula Thesaur." [Ib.]

1694. In a list of churchwardens at the end of a V.B. of this date, is mentioned the churchwarden of Macloneigh "Robert Powell vulneratus a latronibus."

1699. "Two Protestant families; they go to Macromp, in Cloyne diocese." [V.B. 1699.]

"Oct. 15. 1700. I saw Mackloneigh Church, near the river Lee, on the south side of it; the walls built with stone and lime, are standing uncover'd, about 60 foot long; the bounds of the church-yard are discernible, 'tis uncertain whether the inward or outward ditch. About 40 English acres of glebe lying round the church, belong to the Vicar; 'tis good land. No house near the church. Barry Swiney is Priest of this parish, and of Kilmichael. This church lies near the Lee, on the south side of the river; the town of Maclony is a mile distant towards the north-west. There are eight and a-half plowlands in this parish; all the lands were the estate of the Earl of Clancarty; for the most part good land; the Powels and about six families more of Protestants are in this parish. A proportion of the tythes of two plowlands in this parish, viz., of Killbarry and Killnaghrounagh, belongs to the Treasurer of St. Finbarry's; and 'tis said the proportion is half the said tythes. The monastery of Mourne Abby or Preceptory had the rest of the rectory; 'tis now enjoy'd by the Vicar, according to King Charles the Second's grant by the Act of Settlement. Farrenavaragan being half a plowland, containing at least eighty English acres, belongs to the Bishop of Corke. It lies contiguous to the glebe of Macloneigh; 'tis very good land, set by Mr. Warren, the Bishop's tenant, to Mr. Browne, for £9 per an.; it lies near the river Lee; half ye tithes of the lands of Coolcour and Slevins, lying on the north of the river Lee, belongs to the vicarage of Macloneigh. No churchwardens in this parish; there are generally no churchwardens in the parishes where the churches are out of repair; I left with Mr. Browne 7 "Tillotson's Sermons" and 12 small Prayer-books. No schoolmaster here, nor in Kilmichael, nor Inchigeelah, &c. Some people fancy that this was formerly a Bishop's see, but I could find no reason for any such belief."

"Oct. 15. 1700. I saw Kilmichael Church, built with stone and lime, about 50 foot long, besides the west end which is divided by a wall; it looks like a house; the walls of the church are standing uncovered; the bounds of the church-yard are discernible; it lies south-west of Macloneigh, at two miles distance. About 6 English acres of glebe lie round the church, belonging to the Incumbent. About 24 plowlands in this parish; a great part of it indifferent good land. The Earls of Cork and Clancarty have the lands of this parish. Mr. Edward Jermin and about 7 families of Protestants more live in this parish; this parish is worth at least £40 per an. to the Incumbent. The Earl of Corke, as Impropriator, has half the tithes of this parish. The Vicar has the other half. This church seems fittest to be rebuilt, on account of its situation being nearest the centre of those parishes, whose churches are ruinous." [Downes' Tour.]

1712 to 1749. JOHN MOORE appears for "Altera R. V. Macloneigh." [V.B.] He was Treasurer of Cork, q. v.

1749. June 2. PATRICK ELMSLEY, A.M., R. V. Macloneigh. [F.F.] Vacant by death of John Moore. [D.R.] In 1750 Elmsley became R. V. Inchigeelah, q. v.

1750. May 14. EDWARD BROWNE, A.B., R. V. Macloneigh. [F.F.] He was also Archdeacon of Ross, q. v.

1777. Dec. 17. THOMAS BREVITOR, R. V. Macloneigh and Kilmichael. [F.F.] In 1784 he became R. Carrigaline, q. v.

1778. August 15. Order of Council for uniting the parishes of Macloneigh and Kilmichael. [Lib. Mun. Vol. II. p. 176.] From this date Macloneigh has been held with Kilmichael, q. v.

MARMULLANE.

1591. "E. de murmullan. MAURICIUS M'DERMOTT, incumbens. idem R. de Kilmorey." [MS. T.C.D. E. 3. 14.] He is also Curate of Killaspugmullane and Rathcoony, and R. Templeusky, q. v.

1615. July 20. JOHN TWYNBROOKS, R. de Marmullane and R. V. Titeskin, Cloyne. [F.F.]

1615. Johannes Twinebroke, A.B., Rector. Val. 4 li. Ecclesia et cancella ruinata. [R.V. R.I.A.] *Vide* Kilteskin, in Cloyne.

1618. Dec. 15. SIRACH GILSLAND, R. Marmullane. [F.F.] Gilsland was, in 1639, R. Murragh, q. v.

1634. Rector de Marmullane, Siracke Gilsland, Predicator. Val. 7*s.* per annum. [R.V. 1634.]

1636. Feb. 3. THOMAS BENNET, Rect. integ. de Marmullane. [F.F.] He was, in 1639, a Vicar Choral, Cork, q. v.

1637. June 3. ROBERT CREWE, R. de Marmullan. [F.F.] He appears in 1639. "Ecclia ruinata, desunt omnia." [V.B. 1639.] Crewe, or Crues, was, in 1635, appointed Vicar Choral, Cork. He is mentioned as the terror of the rebels, in the letter of Urban Vigors, *vide* Marshallstown, Cloyne.

1669. Quatuor vicarii chorales sunt Rectores de Marmullane. ptic. ad chor. [V.B. 1669.]

1687 to 1696. No churchwardens nor parish clerk. In latter year "plurima illicita in ibi perpetrantur." In 1698 Phil. Bernard is churchwarden. In 1699. spect. ad Chor. [V.B. D.R.]

"Oct. 1700. I saw Killmurry church, als Murmullane. The

The walls are almost quite down; they were built with stone and clay; the bounds of the church-yard are discernible; the church is about four miles from Corke, not far from the river, within less than a mile of the Passage, on the same side. About three English acres of glebe lying round the church belong to the church of St. Finbarry's, set to the *Terre* tenant for about 40*s*. per an.; the whole parish is but one plowland; there is but one constable for this parish and Monkstown; all the tithes of this parish were set this year for about £8, by Capt. Hayes; they belong to the œconomy of St. Barry's, but the Vicars Choral pay 20th parts to the King for it. Mr. Burstead lives in this parish, and three or four Protestants more; the lands of this parish belong, forty acres, to John Parsons, and forty acres to Roch, of Dunderrow, and forty acres to Konan; the people go to Carrickoline to church, or St. Barry's; this parish, time out of mind, is supposed to be united to the parish of St. Barry's." [Downes' Tour.]

1733. April 29. Mrs. Mary Ronayne recants in parish church of Marmullane teste Thomas Somerville, and on 23rd Dec. Edwd. Ronayne *similiter*, teste Edmond Molloy, Minister. [D.R.]

1737. Edward Cottrell is nominated Curate of Marmullane by the Dean and Chapter. [D.R.] He was afterwards P. Killanully, q. v.

In 1775, May 19. Thomas Maginn is licensed as parish clerk and schoolmaster of Marmullane, on the nomination of Edward Cottrell, Curate. [D.R.]

1785. Sept. 15. The Dean and Chapter lease the tithes and Ecclesiastical dues of Marmullane to Rev. Jonathan Bruce, to hold them as long as he shall continue Curate of the same. [D.R.] Bruce was afterwards Curate of Kilbolane, Cloyne, q. v.

1788. Oct. 22. The Dean and Chapter lease to Rev. John Townsend the tithes and due of Marmullane, to hold as long as he shall continue Curate of the same. [D.R.]

John Townsend (eldest son of John Townsend, of Courtmasherry, who was married to Elisabeth, dau. of Colonel Reddish, and who was the second son of John Townsend and Catherine Barry, *vide* Scull, 1780–1793, *the Rev. R. Townsend*) was ordained Deacon on 23rd April, 1775, and Priest on 5th May, 1776, both at Cork.

In 1776 he was Curate of Island, Ross, and from 1788 to 1791 was Curate of Marmullane.

He married Martha, dau. of Carrē Williams, esq., of Ashgrove, county Cork, and had issue a daughter, Martha, who was wife to Carrē-Columbine Williams, esq., of Cork.

1791. Oct. 28. Richard Lloyd, A.B., is admitted Perpetual Curate of Marmullane, under Dean and Chapter. [F.F.] He is to have the great and small tithes, and all dues, &c. [D.R.] He became, in 1837, P. Killanully, q. v.

1812. August 21. The Dean and Chapter endow the Curate of Marmullane with the glebe, 6A. 3R. 23P., and with all great and small tithes, and erect it into a perpetual curacy. The Bishop confirms the same in September, 1812. [D.R.]

1814. May 10. Richard Lloyd obtains a certificate of having, since 14th June, 1813, spent £539 7*s.* (part of which was advanced by the Board of First Fruits) in building a new glebe-house at Marmullane. [D.R.]

1830. Protestant population, 221.

1837. Marmullane: a perpetual cure, with spiritual duties annexed, erected within the parish of the same name, appropriated to the Dean and Chapter; 1 mile long by ¾ broad, containing 465A.; gross population, 1,459. No assistant Curate employed. Tithe composition, £69; 7 statute acres of glebe, valued at 35*s.* per acre, £12 5*s.* Marmullane glebe-house built in 1814, under the new Acts, at the cost of £461 10*s.* 9¼*d.* Brit., whereof £415 7*s.* 8¼*d.* was granted in way of gift, and £46 3*s.* 1*d.* in that of loan, by the late Board of First Fruits, of which loan there remained £12 18*s.* 5½*d.* chargeable on the benefice in 1832, repayable by annual instalments of 18*s.* 5½*d.* Incumbent is resident in the glebe-house for seven months in the year; but owing to the exposed situation of it, he resides in another house in the parish during the rest of the year, and pays the sum of £36 18*s.* 5*d.* for the rent of said house. One church, capable of accommodating 250 persons, but so old that the date and cost of its erection are unknown; in 1808 the eastern end of it was taken down, enlarged, and rebuilt, at an expense of £185 15*s.* 4½*d.* Brit., whereof £93 9*s.* 2¾*d.* was subscribed by the parishioners, and £92 6*s.* 1¾*d.* contributed by the Dean and Chapter of Cork; no charge on the parish in 1832 on account of the church. Divine service is celebrated twice on Sundays in summer, and once in winter, and on the principal festivals; a service and lecture have also been delivered once a week during the summer months within the last year or two; the sacrament is administered monthly, and on the great festivals. The Curate is endowed with the tithes of this parish, which is appropriated to the Dean and Chapter of Cork. [Par. Rep.]

1837. WILLIAM COTTER WILLIAMSON is P. C. Marmullane. He became, in 1860, Precentor of Cloyne, q. v.

1837. Nov. 7. A commission finds £57 19*s.* 7*d.* dilapidations against Richard Lloyd, late Incumbent. [D.R.]

1842. WILLIAM TOTTENHAM DAY, P. C. Marmullane. He became, in 1861, R. Rathclaren, q. v.

1850. THOMAS TOWNELY MACAN, P. C. Marmullane. He became, in 1857, Treasurer of Cork, q. v.

1854. RONALD MACDONNELL, P. C. Marmullane.

1854. Feb. 10. He obtains £37 9s. 8d. dilapidations against his predecessor, Macan. [D.R.]

Ronald MacDonnell, younger brother of the Dean of Cashel, is the sixth son of the Provost of T.C.D., by Jane, dau. of Dean Richard Graves, of Ardagh. The Provost (Richard MacDonnell) is son of Robert MacDonnell, by Susannah Nugent, of county Waterford, and grandson of Richard MacDonnell, by Miss Sandes.

Ronald MacDonnell was educated at Portora Royal School, and was a Scholar of T.C.D. in 1844, and First Senior Moderator in Ethics and Logics in 1845. He was ordained Priest, at Cork, on 3rd June, 1849, for the curacy of Agabulloge, in Cloyne, and from 1854 to 1857 was P. C. Marmullane. In 1857 he was promoted by the Crown to the incumbency of Monkstown, Dublin.

He married Jane, dau. of Edward Rotheram, esq., of Crossdrum, and has issue.

1857. THOMAS T. HALLARAN, P. C. Marmullane.

He was ordained in 1854.

1860. The church and glebe-house in good order; 6¼ acres of glebe in Incumbent's use. Divine service twice on all Sundays, and once on the usual holidays, and on all Wednesdays throughout the year. Sacrament monthly, and at chief festivals; average of communicants, 62. 46 children are on the rolls of a Church Education school; the *permanent* Protestant population is 311. The rentcharge is £51 15s.; the land is worth £22, and there is an augmentation of £35; total value, £108 15s., with residence.

MONKSTOWN.

This ancient parish seems never to have had any Incumbent from the dissolution of the abbey to which it belonged until 1835. There is little notice of it in the diocesan records, except what here follows:—

"Oct. 1700. I saw Monkstown Church; the walls, built with lime and sand, are standing; the timber of the roof is up, and some slates on it; the timber is beginning to decay. There is no sign of the bounds of the church-yard. There are two tombs on the south side of the church belonging to the family of Archdeacons, who were the antient proprietors of Monkstown. There are three plowlands in this parish, the lands of which belong to the Lord Primate Boyle. Mr. Callaghan, Protestant, lives at Monkstown, in a good square castle, with *flankers*. This church was repaired when Mr. Hodder lived at Monkstown, above twenty years ago. Monkstown is near the harbour of Cork, over against the Cove. From Monkstown we see the Island of Halleboling, Spike Island, &c. There is no tythe paid, nor allowance made to any clergyman out of this parish; 'tis pretended by the inhabitants 'tis tythe-free; the tythes are set together with the lands to the tenants. The people of this and the adjacent parishes go to Carickoline Church—viz., those of Barnehely and Kilmurry. No glebe in this parish. The lands of this parish belonged to the Abby of St. Catherine's, of Waterford. Colonel Hunks had these lands in Cromwell's time. Hunks was supposed to be concerned in the murther of King Charles I.; he sold them to Primate Boyle before the Court of Claims, who made good Hunks his title in the Court of Claims. He gave about £400 for it to Hunks. The same person is Popish Priest of this parish and Carickoline, Kilmurry, and Templebredy, and Barnahely, and Ringskiddy. 'Tis alledg'd in these parts that Abby lands pay no tythe. The tythes of this parish have been set formerly for above £20 per an.; they are now worth £20 per an. John Archdeacon, before 1641, was paid no tythe out of these lands." [Downes' Tour.]

1830. Protestant population, 241.

1831. June 20. Daniel and Gerard Callaghan, esquires, of Cork (being tenants to Lords Longford and De Vesci), grant, at nominal rent of one peppercorn, one rood of land at Monkstown for a church; and on 28th July, the Earl of Longford and Viscount De Vesci lease the same land for ever, at same rent of one peppercorn. [D.R.]

1831. July 28. Thomas, Earl of Longford, and John, Viscount De Vesci (being appointed patrons to nominate a Vicar, either jointly or alternately), grant £50 per annum for ever out of the lands of Monkstown (of which they are tenants in common) as an endowment for Monkstown. [D.R.]

1833. January 10. A building, intended for a parish church, is licensed for divine service. [D.R.]

1833. Sept. 6. ARTHUR GEORGE HARPER HOLLINGSWORTH, A.M., is licensed to officiate in the building in Monkstown not yet consecrated; and on 13th August, 1835, he is instituted to the Vicarage of Monkstown, on presentation of Lord De Vesci. [D.R.]

A. G. H. Hollingsworth was ordained Priest at Cloyne on 15th of Feb. 1829. He married, in 1825, Miss Margaret Mountford, of Cove.

He resigned Monkstown on 11th January, 1836, and is now Vicar of Stowmarket, in Suffolk, England.

1836. Feb. 26. ALEXANDER STUART, A.M., Vicar, on presentation of

Lord De Vesci. [D.R.] In 1842 Stuart became Archdeacon of Ross, q. v.

1837. Monkstown, a vicarage, with cure, 3½ miles long by 2 broad, containing 2,504A. 1R. 1¾P. Gross population, 2,199. No Curate employed. From stipend payable by Impropriator, £50; pew rents, £4 7*s.* 6*d.*; surplice fees, £1 1*s.* 3 acres of glebe, valued at £5 per acre, £15. Augmentation allowance, payable by Ecclesiastical Commissioners out of Boulter's Fund, £25. Monkstown glebe-house is reported to be almost unfit for residence, being very old, and in very bad repair. Incumbent does not state when it was built, at what cost, or from what funds supplied, but adds, "that no money has been expended on it as such, having been only lately made a glebe-house." Incumbent is usually resident in the glebe-house. One church, capable of accommodating 270 persons, built in 1832, at the cost of about £1,500, British, raised by subscriptions. No charge on the parish in 1832 on account of the church. Divine service is celebrated twice on Sundays from May to November, and once during the remainder of the year, and on Christmas Day, New Year's Day, Ash Wednesday, and Good Friday. The sacrament is administered monthly, and on the festivals. The tithes of this parish, compounded for £90, are wholly impropriate, and belong to Lord De Vesci; but it is reported that they have never been demanded or paid as such. The glebe is subject to a rent of £25. [Parl. Rep.]

1839. August 3. THOMAS GIBBINGS, A.M., V. Monkstown, on presentation of Lord De Vesci, dated 19th June, 1839. [D.R.] In 1851 Gibbings became Treasurer of Cloyne, q. v.

1851. March 21. GEORGE HAZLEWOOD, V. Monkstown, on presentation of Lord De Vesci, dated 14th March, 1851. £63 18*s.* 4*d.* certified value. [D.R.]

1860. G. Hazlewood, Incumbent; J. J. Sargent, Curate. The church in good order. No glebe-house or land. Divine service twice on all Sundays, and once on the usual holidays. Sacrament monthly, and at festivals; average of communicants, 46. There is also divine service at Glenbrook, in a licensed place of worship, twice on all Sundays, and once on holidays, the same as at the church. Sacrament at Glenbrook monthly, and at festivals; average of communicants, 10. 19 children are on the rolls of a Church Education school. The Protestant population is 600.

MOVIDDY.

1591. NICHOLAS O'FLYNN is Vicar of Moviddy, but in another copy of the visitation book of same year WILLIAM O'FOY appears. "Willmus o'foy, als o'ffeehy, interdicitur donec prob. se esse ad ordines sac. prom." [MS. T.C.D. E. 3. 14.]

1615. WILLIAM HEALY (Chancellor of Cork, q. v.), appears as Vicar of Moviddy. "Rect. imp. spectat ad Mourne. Vicarius William Healy, minister legens. Valor 4 li. Ecclia repāta, cancella ruinosa. [R.V. R.I.A.]

1632. June 5. JOHN JOHNSON, A.M., V. Moviddy, per deprivation of William Healy. Inducted 6th August. [R.V. 1634.]

1634. R. de Moviddy spectat ad Ab. de Morne. Cormack Donogh Carty firmarius. Val. 16 li. per an. V. John Johnson sed sub lite. Epus confert. Val. 8 li. per an. [R.V. 1634.] Johnson was V. Kinsale, q. v.

1637. January 3. ROBERT KEMPE, V. Moviddy and Mackcloneigh. [F.F.]

1639. Rectoria spectat ad Ab. de Morne. Vic. Robert Kempe excusatur. [V.B. D.R.]

1640. Feb. 12. WILLIAM BEARDE, R. Moviddy and Mackcloneigh. [F.F.]

1663 to 1833. Moviddy was held with Aglish, q. v.

1830. The Protestant population of Moviddy was 85.

1833. April 19. HUME BABINGTON, R. V. Moviddy; certified under £600 in value. [D.R.]

In April, 1833, a commission finds £150 2*s*. 4*d*. dilapidations against St. Lawrence. 1835. Feb. 19. Bishop certifies that Babington (since 13th July, 1833) hath expended £242 7*s*. 10*d*. in repairs and improvements, according to memorials, &c. 1854. March 21. He obtains a certificate for £167 19*s*. 10*d*. improvements, the net yearly valuation being £459 15*s*. 4*d*., not calculating poor rates. [D.R.]

1837. Moviddy, a rectory and vicarage, with cure, 3 miles long by 4½ broad, containing 9,562A. 1R. 5¼P. Gross population, 2,718. No Curate employed. Tithe composition, £570 13*s*. 10*d*. 82 acres of glebe, valued at 15*s*. per acre, £61 10*s*. Subject to visitation fees, 9*s*. Diocesan schoolmaster, 17*s*. 6*d*. Moviddy glebe-house built under the old Acts, at the cost of £349 19*s*. British, supplied out of the private funds of the builder, to whom the present Incumbent is second in succession; and having paid his predecessor £262 9*s*. 3*d*., and since expended £242 7*s*. 10*d*. on improvements, he will be entitled to receive from his successor £356 15*s*. 4½*d*. on account of the building and improvement charges. Incumbent is resident in the glebe-house. One church, capable of accommodating 120 persons; but when built, at what cost, or from what funds supplied, not stated. No charge on the parish in 1832 on account of the church. Divine service is celebrated once on Sundays, and on the principal festivals. The sacrament is administered monthly. The benefice is a rectory. [Parl. Rep.]

1860. The church and glebe-house in order. 74 acres of glebe in Vicar's use. Divine service once on all Sundays, and on usual holidays, and on Sunday evenings during summer. Sacrament monthly; average of communicants, 9. No school. The Protestant population is 47. The annual value is £428 from rentcharge, and £55 from land. Total, £483, with residence.

H. Babington was ordained in 1827; and in 1836 married Esther, dau. of Richard Neville Nettles, esq., of Nettleville, county Cork. He has issue. [Burke's L. G.]

MURRAGH.

1591. DANIEL O'HENNEHAN appears as Vicar of Murragh. "Rectoria de Maraughe als moraghe spectat ad ab. grayne per usurpationem. Vic. ibm per ijos. annos Daniel O'Hennehan, idem Rector de Kilmine; obtinuit utrasque per licent." [MS. T.C.D. E. 3. 14.]

1615. EDWARD CLERKE (Dean of Cloyne, q. v.), is Vicar of Murragh. "Mayrath (residens) Rector Edrus Clerk, minister et predicator. Valor 4 li. Ecclesia et cancella repãntur cum libris." [R.V. R.I.A.]

1624. Nov. 24. SIRACH GILSLAND, R. Murraghe, quam rect. et rect. de Marmullane Epus unvit. Inductus fuit, 30th Nov. 1624. [R.V. 1634.]

1634. R. de Morraghe, Siracke Gilsland, predicator. Val. 12 li. per an. [R.V. 1634.]

1639. Gilsland appears. "Ecclesia bene, deest coopērterum." [V.B. 1639.]

In 1642, Oct. 22. Gilsland depones to loss of £48, besides his Rectory of Morrath. [MS. T.C.D. F. 2. 15.]

Syracus Gilsland, *literatus*, was ordained Deacon on 26th of June, 1616, and Priest on 9th Feb. 1618, both by the Bishop of Waterford and Lismore.

From 1618 to 1636 he was R. Marmullane. In 1624 he became a Vicar Choral of Cloyne, and also R. Murragh. In 1618 he took a degree in T.C.D.

1661. April 2. BARNABAS HONEYCHURCH, R. V. Murragh, per mortem Sirach Gilsland. [V.B. D.R. 1669.] He appears 1661 to 1681. [V.B. D.R.]

Barnabas Honeychurch was ordained Deacon and Priest on 18th Dec. 1633, by Richard, Bishop of Cork.

From 1633 to 1667 he was R. V. Kilsillagh, in Ross, and from 1666 to his death in 1682 was Vicar of Desertserges. He also held from 1637 to 1682 the R. Garrivoe and Killowen, and from 1661 to 1682 was R. V. Murragh. He appears also in 1639 as Curate of Kilbrittain and Ringrone. In his will (dated 30th May, 1682, and proved on 1st of March following) he mentions his son, Roger. He desired to be buried in Murragh parish.

1682. August 22. DANIEL LORD, A.M., R. V. Murragh and V. Desertserges. [F.F.] He appears 1682 to 1704. [V.B. D.R.]

1699. Church in repair. Sermon once a fortnight. [V.B. 1699. D.D.]

"1699. Murragh lyes higher up the river Bandon; a church near the river, at the south-west corner of the parish; about 80 persons at church on Sunday. The walls and roof of the church in pretty good repair; a pulpit and communion table; no seats but one; not flag'd; the church-yard inclos'd; about 30 acres of glebe near the church; good land. Over against Murragh, on the south side of the river Bandon, lyes the parish of Desert; the church is about half an English mile from the church of Murragh; the church walls and roof in pretty good repair; a pulpit and several seats; a communion table. A good church-yard, but not inclosed; about 60 acres of glebe joining to the church-yard; half the glebe is claimed by the Vicars Choral; Mr. Lord pays them 30*s.* per an. for it; about 80 persons at church on Sundays. 'Tis supposed the Earl of Corke has, in his possession, several acres belonging to the glebe. Mr. Synge, the Curate, lives at a pretty good house, within a quarter of a mile of the Church of Desert. Garrivoe, a rectory in Desert parish, being half the tythes of 14 plowlands, is a *sinecure*, in the gift, it is said of the Lord of Kinsale. Killowen is a rectory, *sinecure*, in Murragh parish."

"Tuesday, May 28, 1700. I view'd Murragh and Desert, and returned to Ballimony. Murragh parish lyes on the north side of the river Bandon; the church is in good repair, it stands near the river; the church-yard is fenc't. Divine service here once a fortnight, and once a fortnight at Desert, performed by Mr. Synge, Curate to Mr. Lord. John Lamb is Parish Clerk to both parishes. There are two churchwardens in this parish. The Clerk teaches school. 17 plowlands in this parish. The sacrament administered four times a year in this church; catechizing in part of the summer. Daniel Hurley, a quiet man, Popish Priest, serves this and three or four contiguous parishes: he has been here since before the late troubles. There are more Protestants than Papists in this parish. There are about 100 Protestant families here; about twenty of these families are Dissenters; they go to Bandon. There was a registry bought lately; a Bible and two Common Prayer-books, Linnen, a silver chalice and paten, and pewter flagon and plate. About 40 acres of glebe round the church; very good land, set for about £5 or £6 per annum. The rectory is worth to Mr. Lord about £70 per annum. They pay tythes of potatoes in this parish, and in all this country. Few poor here belonging to this parish. The Earl of Corke has almost all this parish; Captain Bernard, Thomas Ware, live in this parish. Desertsurgis parish lyes on the south side of the river Bandon; it reaches to within two miles of Bandon. The church is in good repair. Divine service once a fortnight by Mr. Synge, Curate to Mr. Lord. The sacrament four times in ye year. Mr. Synge has £30 per an. for serving this cure, and the cure of Murrogh, besides the English Bookmoney. Two churchwardens in this parish. The Protestants are equal to the Papists in number; there are about 150 families of Protestants in this parish. The Clerk teaches school for this parish and Murragh. No Popish schoolmasters in this parish; 30 plowlands in this parish. There is a registry lately bought; a Bible and Common Prayer-books lately bought. A rate made for linnen, &c., for the communion. About 60 acres of glebe, good land, round the church, worth about £10 per an. Half the tythes of this parish belong to Mr. Lord, the Vicar, the other half belongs to the Vicars Choral of Corke, and to Mr. Hewit, as Rector of one part of this parish; the Vicars Choral have also half the glebe. Dennis Mahony is Popish Priest of this parish. Mr. Henry Boyle, brother to the Earl of Corke, Mr. Gookin, Counsellor Bernard, Sir Richard Cox, Purser Atkins, Mr. Richard Beamish, Mr. Wade, Mr. John Beamish, Alderman Love, of Corke, have most of the lands in this parish. Major Herbert Love, Mr. Charles Gookin, Mr. Richard Beamish, live in this parish.

"Tuesday, the 28th May, 1700. I went to see the churches of Murragh and Desert. Murragh Church is on the north of the Bandon river, near the river; it is in repair, only the east end and some part of the south side hangs over; 'tis built, as the other churches generally are, with stone and clay, slated; there is a pulpit, desk, and one pew. A good church-yard, fenc't; 'tis undermined by the river; part of it is worn away. This parish is worth about £70 or £80 per an. to the Incumbent. The glebe lies round the church, containing about 30 acres. There was formerly a vicarage-house within the church-yard. There are Common Prayer-books, but they borrowed the Bible from Desert. Two churchwardens. The lands of this parish belong almost intirely to the Earl of Cork. Captain Bernard lives in this parish; some Dissenters live in this parish. Mr. Lord, the Incumbent, allows £30 per annum, and the obventions of the Protestants to Mr. Synge, for serving the cures of this parish and Desert. Divine service here once a fortnight, and Mr. Synge preaches at Desert once a fortnight. Desert Church in good repair, well furnish't with seats, a very good roof. A table-cloth, pewter flagon and silver cup that serves both Murragh and Desert. There is a Bible, but Common Prayer-books are wanting. The church-yard fenc't; about 100 acres of glebe round the church, part of it is boggy; heretofore the glebe was set for £8 per annum. Two churchwardens. This parish is worth about £60 per an. to the Incumbent. The Incumbent has half the tythes of this parish; the other half is enjoyed partly by the Vicars Choral of Corke, and partly by Mr. Hewit, who had his rectory by the presentation of the Lord of Kinsale. Divine service here once a fortnight." [Downes' Tour.]

1692 to 1796. Murragh was held with Kilbrogan, q. v.

1796. May 7. Ambrose Hickey, A.B., R. V. Murragh. [F.F.]

1808. Order of Council for changing site of Murragh Church. [Lib. Mun.]

In January, 1808, a commission finds that Hickey had expended (after memorial, &c.) £1,905 13*s.* 5½*d.* in building a glebe-house and offices, and that the yearly value of Murragh was, for three years last past, over £900 per an. And in 1809, January 12, the Bishop certifies for £1,055, expended by Hickey, *over and above* £850 advanced to him by First Fruits. [D.R.]

1811. April 18. Murragh new church was consecrated by name of St. Patrick. It was built on about three roods Eng. Stat. meas., of the lands of Farrenthomas, granted by Thomas Ware, esq.

1812. June 15. Hickey makes another application to build offices, &c. (the value of Murragh having increased), which is granted by the Bishop, who, in 1813, Oct. 15, issues a commission to value, which reports on June 2, 1814, that Hickey spent £69 2*s.* 7*d.* "in erecting a range of offices fit to contain cars, carts, straw, and sheep," and that the yearly value of Murragh is £1,150. The Bishop certifies for these amounts on 12th Oct. 1814. [D.R.]

Ambrose Hickey was a Scholar of T.C.D. in 1770, and afterwards took the degree of D.D.

He was ordained Deacon on 16th May, 1773, at Kildare, and Priest on 5th April, 1774, at Cork.

From 1775 to 1780 he was Curate of Innishannon. From 1780 to 1784 he was P. Donoghmore, in Ross. From 1784 to 1796 he was R. Ballymoney, and from 1796 to his death in 1826 he was R. Murragh.

He married Jane, dau. of Falkiner Herrick, esq., of Shippool, by Sarah, dau. of Thomas Bousfield, esq., of Cork, and had issue two sons, William, Rector of Mulrankin, Ferns, but better known as "Martin Doyle," and Ambrose, Incumbent of Ballinaboy, q. v. He left, also, three daughters, Eliza, wife of Rev. Anthony Edwards, Jane, and Anne.

1826. July 7. ROBERT KINGSBOROUGH ST. LAWRENCE, A.M., R. V. Murragh, certified under £600 per an. [D.R.] In 1824 he was made Treasurer of Ross, q. v.

1830. The Protestant population is 374.

1837. Murragh: a rectory and vicarage, with cure; 3 miles long by ¾ broad, containing 8,000A. 2R. 2P.; gross population, 3,270; one Curate employed at an annual stipend of £75 Brit.; tithe composition, £851; 37A. 0R. 16P. of glebe, valued at 18*s.* per acre, £33 7*s.* 9½*d.*, subject to diocesan schoolmaster, £1 6*s.* 8*d.* Murragh glebe-house built in 1808, under the new Acts, at the cost of £1,850 15*s.* 4½*d.* Brit., whereof £784 12*s.* 3¾*d.* was granted in way of loan, and £92 6*s.* 1¾*d.* in that of gift, by the late Board of First Fruits, and the residue, of £973 16*s.* 11*d.* was supplied out of the private funds of the builder, as well as a further sum of £63 16*s.* 2¾*d.* under certificate of improvements; the present Incumbent is next in succession to the builder, and having paid his predecessor £1,037 13*s.* 1¾*d.*, he will be entitled to receive £657 13*s.* 10¼*d.* from his successor on account of the building and improvement charges; of the loan aforesaid there remained £84 17*s.* 11*d.* chargeable on the benefice in 1832, repayable by annual instalments of £5 1*s.* 3*d.* Incumbent is usually resident. One church, capable of accommodating 300 persons, built in 1810, at the cost of £507 13*s.* 10¼*d.* Brit., granted in way of loan by the late Board of First Fruits, of which loan there remained £107 16*s.* 1*d.* chargeable on the benefice in 1832, repayable by annual instalments of £5 14*s.* 6*d.*; divine service is celebrated once on Sundays, and on the principal festivals; the sacrament is administered monthly, and on Christmas Day; the benefice is a rectory. [Parl. Rep.]

1860. R. St. Lawrence, Rector; Thomas Bennett, Curate. The church and glebe-house in order; part of the glebe is let, and some is in the Curate's occupation. The Rector is non-resident. Divine service twice in summer on Sundays, and once in winter, and on the usual holidays; evening service in winter at the glebe-house. Sacrament monthly, and at festivals; average of communicants, 25. 52 children are on the rolls of a Church Education school. The Protestant population is 223. The present rentcharge is given as £514, and the land is worth £33; total value, £547, with residence.

NOHOVAL AND KILMONOGE.

1291. "Ecclesia de Neoffal" is rated at 5 marks,—"Ecclesia de Kylmonog," at 4 marks. [Tax. P. Nic.]

1591. E. de Noffall et E. de Kilmonoge spectant ad Archidiaconatum. Particula de Belagh est p'cella. Curatus JOHES CROMIN. [MS. T.C.D. E. 3. 14.] Cromin was also V. Ballyfeard.

1615. Noffal; Archidiaconus Rector et Vicar. Curatus, HUGO PERCEVALL (Dean of Ross, q. v.) minister et predicator. Ecclesia et cancella ruinantur. Kilmahavock consimiliter est ut Noffal per omnia nisi quod ecclesia hic repata est et cancella est in ruina. [R.V. R.I.A.]

1634. E. de Neoffal ad Archid. Kilmonoge similiter. [R.V. 1634.]

1639. E. de Neoffoll ad Archid. Ecclia reparat., habent ornamenta. Curatus, JOHN FULHAM. Particula de Belagh est p'cella. E. de Kilmonoge ad Archid. Ecclesia bene. Curatus, John Fulham. [V.B. 1639.]

1669. Spectant ad Archidiaconatum. [V.B. D.R.]

1687 to 1699. Nohoval ad Archid. Kilmonoge similiter ut Nohoval. [V.B.]

1699. Nohoval: divine service and sermon once a fortnight in the church, which was lately repaired. The Protestants of Kilmonoge go to Nohoval. [V.B. 1699. D.D.]

"1704. June. Nohoval church in good repair, and furnisht with seats. The late Bishop of Cork (Edward Wetenhall) contributed to the repair of it when he had the Archdeaconry of Cork. Divine service here (at Nohoval) once a fortnight, and once a fortnight at Tracton, by Mr. Ogilby." [Dive Downes' Tour.]

1720. February 2. RANDOL ROBERTS was licensed to be Curate of Nohoval and Kilmonoge. [D.R.] He became, in 1724, a Vicar Choral, Cork, q. v.

1726. A cup and paten were "Presented to Nohoval Church, by Elisabeth Pomeroy, 1726."

1745 is the earliest date of an ancient parish register, now the private property of a gentleman, whose ancestor was formerly Curate. It ends Sept. 15, 1784.

1751. September 5. ACHILLES DAUNT, A.M., is licensed to be Curate of Nohoval and Kilmonoge, at £20. [D.R.] He became, in 1775, R. V. Kilcully, q. v.

1784. Nov. 18. ROBERT FORSAYETH, A.B., is licensed to be Curate of Nohoval and Kilmonoge, at £25. [D.R.]

1785. The present parish register begins.

Robert Forsayeth (son of Samuel, and nephew of John, Archdeacon of Cork, q. v.), was a Scholar of T.C.D. in 1780, and was ordained Deacon on 25th January, 1783, at Cork, and Priest, at Cloyne, on 5th December, 1784.

He was licensed, in January, 1783, to be Curate of St.

Peter's, at £40; and in 1784 was Curate of Ballyfeard, at £10, and also of Tracton. He was also a Vicar Choral of Cashel from 1782 to 1791. He became, in 1798, R. Kilfithmore, Cashel.

He married Miss Jane Evans, of Cashel, by whom he had issue, besides eight children (all now deceased), Richard-Martin Forsayeth, M.D., Templemore.

1802. September. WILLIAM DWYER, A.B., was licensed Curate of Nohoval and Kilmonoge, at £60. [D.R.] He was also R. Templeroan, Cloyne, q. v.

1808. June 22. BLANEY MITCHELL was licensed to be Curate of Nohoval and Kilmonoge, at £75. [D.R.]

1810. September 23. ANTHONY SIMKINS, A.B., was licensed as Curate of Nohoval &c. [D.R.]

1812. ANTHONY EDWARDS, A.B., was licensed Curate of Nohoval, &c., at £75. [D.R.]

1813. October 2. JOHN HENRY MADRAS was admitted Curate of Nohoval, &c. [D.R.] In 1833 he became V. Aglish, q. v.

1815. March 1. The deed of endowment was signed, by which (under the Act 11th and 12th Geo. III., chap. 16) Nohoval was erected into a perpetual cure, with spiritual duties annexed, comprising the parishes of Nohoval and Kilmonoge. This perpetual cure was endowed with all the glebe of Nohoval, and the entire tithes, great and small, of the plowland of Nohoval, and the sub-denominations of Curravah, containing 2 gneeves; Ballyhorkin, 1 gneeve; and Ballinreenarrig, 2 gneeves. [D.R.]

1816. Feb. 21. Madras memorials to build; and on 8th August, 1817, he obtains a certificate of having laid out £624 4s. on a house. [D.R.]

1830. Protestant population, 151.

1832. Nohoval, P. C., comprises the parishes of Nohoval, 3 miles long by 1¼ broad, and Kilmanogue, 4 miles long by 1½ broad, appropriated to the archdeaconry, containing 5,462A. 2R. 15P.; gross population, 2,477; tithe composition, £75; augmentation allowance, out of Boulter's fund, £23 2s.; 2A. 2R. 7P. of glebe, valued at 36s. per acre, £4 11s. 7d. Nohoval glebe-house built in 1816, under the new Acts, at the cost of £461 10s. 9¼d. Brit., granted by the late Board of First Fruits, viz., £415 7s. 8¼d. in way of gift, and £46 3s. 1d. in that of loan; there remained £24 chargeable on the benefice in 1832. repayable by annual instalments of £1 10s. Exclusive of moneys aforesaid, Incumbent reports that he has expended £114 12s. 11d. on the house, without having any charge on his successor. One church, situate in Nohoval village, built more than a century, but at what cost unknown. No charge on the parish in 1832 on account of the church. Divine service is celebrated once on Sundays, and on Christmas Day and Good Friday; the sacrament is administered twelve times in the year; the benefices comprised within this perpetual cure are rectories. [Parl. Rep.]

1833. April 6. WILLIAM ROBINSON TOWNSEND, A.B., P. C. Nohoval, Kilmonoge, and Dunisky. [D.R.] In 1837 he became R. V. Aghadda, Cloyne, q. v.

1833. April, 25. Townsend obtains £64 17*s.* 4*d.* dilapidations against Madras. [D.R.]

1837. August 10. CHARLES ROBERT ADAMS, A.M., P. C. Nohoval. [D.R.] In 1826 he was R. V. Carrigdownan, Cloyne, q. v.

1844. Feb. 13. JOHN CECIL ROGERS, P. C. Nohoval and Kilmonoge, vacant by death of Rev. C. Adams. [D.R.]

1848. A font and bell were given to the church by the Archdeacon; cost of both, £10.

1860. Incumbent, S. M. Kyle; Curate, Rev. J. C. Rogers; the glebe-house is in good repair; a quarter of an acre of land is in the occupation of the Curate. Divine service on Sundays and festivals; the sacrament is administered monthly; the average of communicants is 14. 32 children are on the rolls of a Church Education Society school; average attendance, 18. The Protestant population is 105. The annual value is £90 7*s.*; arising, from tithe £56 5*s.*; from Boulter's fund, £23 2*s.*; and £11 from land.

J. C. Rogers (son of Rev. George William Rogers, Rector of The Rowers, Ossory, who was son of George Rogers, the Chancellor of Dromore, who was son of Thomas Rogers, esq., of Lisburn) was educated at home and at Delgany, county Wicklow. He became an A.B., T.C.D., in 1839.

He was ordained Deacon at Limerick in 1840, and Priest, at Cork, on 19th Sept., 1841.

In 1840 he was Curate of Carrignavar; in 1842, of Kilbolane; and in 1844, of Nohoval.

He married, in 1859, Louisa Russel, granddaughter of the late General Arnold, and has issue one son, Cecil-George-William.

RATHCLARIN.

1291. "Eccia de Rathlaryn IIIImr." "Eccia de Boryon (Burrin?) VIIImr." [Tax. P. Nic.]

1591. "R. vacat. sequestrat. Vicar, MAURICIUS O'CONTYE." [MS. T.C.D. E. 3. 14.]

1611. May 29. NICHOLAS BERGHT, or BRIGHT, is presented to the Rectory of Mortelstown and Rathclarin. [Lib. Mun.] He appears in 1615 as V. Lisclery, q. v.

1614. May 6. ISRAEL TAYLOR is presented ad R. V. Ratholarin et R. de Insula parva. [Lib. Mun.] He was instituted on 6th April, 1615, ex presentatione Regis Jacobi dat. 6th March,

1615, and inducted into Rathclarin on 18th April, and into R. Insulæ parvæ on 27th April, 1615. [R.V. 1634.]

1615. Rathclarin (Curatus residens) Israel Taylor, Rector. Henry Stone, minister et predicator, curatus. Burrin (residens) R. ignotus. Vicarius ibm idem Taylor. [R.V. R.I.A.] Stone was also V. Inchigeelah, q. v.

1626. June 30. JOHN NEWMAN is presented to R. Rathclarin, dioc. Cork, and R. V. Lislee, dioc. Rosse, by the Crown, with clause of union, pro hac vice tantum. [Lib. Mun.] In 1634 he was presented to the Vicarages of Kildrum and Garfinagh, dioc. Ardfert. [Lib. Mun.]

1634. ISRAEL TAYLOR appears again as R. de Rathclarin et particula de Burrin. Idem est Vicarius. Val. 50 li. per an. [R.V. 1634.] Taylor was also Precentor of Cork, q. v.

1639. Israel Taylor appears as R. Rathclaren cum particula Burren. "Ecclesia bene, desunt ornamenta. Curatus ARTHUR VAMUR monitus ad extrahend. litteras licentiæ." [V.B. 1639.]

1662. Feb. 6. HENRY PARR, V. Ballymodan, R. V. Rathclarin, and V. Temple O'Quinlan, in Ross. [F.F.] In 1666 he appears again.

1664. June 10. RICHARDUS CLERKE institutus R. V. Rathclaren, per desertionem Henrici Parr in coll. Epi. [V.B. 1669.] He appears again in 1668.

1666. HENRY PARR appears as R. V. Rathclarin "excusat." [V.B. D.R.] Parr was Precentor of Ross, q. v.

1667. Vacant by resignation. [V.B. D.R.]

1668. May 23. RICHARD CLERKE, R. V. Rathclarin. [F.F.]

He appears as *Rector* 1668 to 1685, and as *Vicar* from 1668 to 1671. [V.B. D.R.] Clerke was Precentor of Cork, q. v.

1671. June 1. PETER HEWITT, *Vicar* of Rathclarin. [F.F.]

He appears as Vicar 1672 to 1675. [V.B. D.R.] In 1710 he was Precentor of Ross, q. v.

1675/6. Feb. 25. HUGO JENKINS, V. Ballymodan, Rathclarin, Cannaway, and R. Ardnegihy. [F.F.]

In 1680 he resigned, but in 1681 appears again.

1680. July 28. JOHN TOM, A.M., is admitted Vicar of Ballymodan, Rathclarin, and Cannaway. [F.F.] He appears in 1680 as Vicar. [V.B. D.R.] In 1694 Tom was P. Desertmore, q. v.

1681. July 30. HUGO JENKINS, A.M., is admitted Vicar of Rathclarin and of Ballymodan, q. v. He appears 1681 to 1685. [V.B. D.R.]

1685. March 24. RICHARD LAPP, A.M., R. et V. Rathclarin, vacant per mortem Richi Clarke et privaconem Hugo Jenkins. [D.R.] Lapp appears 1686 to 1691 as R. and V. [V.B. D.R.] In 1688 he was also Archdeacon of Cork, q. v.

1691. Nov. 3. At this visitation there is this remark, but crossed out—"D. Epus tenet in commendam." [V.B.]

1691. Dec. 29. EDWARD SYNGE, A.M., is admitted *Rector* of Rathclarin, per mortem Richi Lapp. [D.R.]

Synge was *Rector* of Rathclarin to 1714. He was also P. Holy Trinity, q. v.

1692. April 22. RICHARD GOODMAN, A.B., is admitted *Vicar* of Ballymodan, and V. Rathclarin, per mort. Lapp. [D.R.]

He appears 1692 to 1695 as Vicar. [V.B. D.R.] In 1718 Goodman was P. Desertmore, q. v.

1696. Vicarage vacant. [V.B.]

1696. Feb. 22. THEOPHILUS WRAGGE, A.M., is admitted Vicar of Rathclarin, per cession of Goodman. [D.R.]

1699. Rathclarin church in repair. Divine service once a fortnight. [V.B. 1699. D.D.]

Theophilus Wragge was ordained Priest on 16th of April, 1685, in Capella apud Bishopscourt, Cork. From 1687 to 1696 he was Curate of Brinny and Killanully, &c.; and from 1696 to his death in 1701, he was Vicar of Rathclarin. His name was sometimes spelt "Ragg."

1701. March 31. JOHN MOORE, jun., is admitted Vicar of Rathclarin, per mortem Theophili Wragge. [D.R.] Moore was also P. Kilbrittain. He became, in 1711, Treasurer of Cork, q. v.

1714 to 1831. Rathclaren was held with Kilbrittain, q. v.

1830. The Protestant population of Rathclarin is 140.

1831. Sept. 2. SAMUEL MOORE KYLE, A.M., R. V. Rathclarin; certified under £600. [D.R.]

In 1833 Kyle became Archdeacon of Cork, q. v.

1833. July 12. THOMAS WAGGETT, A.M., R. V. Rathclarin. [D.R.]

1837. Rathclarin, a rectory, with cure, 3½ miles long by 2½ broad, containing 5,728 acres. Gross population, 2,775. The yearly income is, from composition, £650; 24 acres of glebe, valued at 30*s.* per acre, £36. Subject to visitation fees, 18*s.*; and diocesan schoolmaster, 10*s.* 6*d.* Rathclarin glebe-house, built under the old Acts in 1794, at the cost of £828 8*s.* 0¼*d.* British, whereof £92 6*s.* 1¾*d.* was granted as gift by the late Board of First Fruits, and the residue of £736 1*s.* 10½*d.* was supplied out of the private funds of the builder, to whom the present Incumbent is third in succession; and having paid his predecessor £368 0*s.* 11*d.* he will be entitled to receive £184 0*s.* 5½*d.* from his successor, on account thereof. Incumbent is resident in the glebe-house. One church, capable of accommodating nearly 200 persons, built about the year 1650, but at what cost unknown. No charge on the parish in 1832 on account of the church. Divine service is celebrated twice on Sundays in summer, and once in winter, and on the principal festivals. The sacrament is administered monthly, and on the festivals. The benefice is a rectory. [Parliamentary Report.]

1844. Nov. 15. The annual value is certified to be £517 10s. [D.R.]

1860. The church and glebe-house are both in want of repair. 24 acres of glebe are in Rector's use. Divine service in the church twice on all Sundays in summer months, and once in winter and on the usual holidays. Evening service during winter months is held in the glebe-house. Sacrament monthly; average of communicants, 16. 26 children are on the rolls of the Church Education school; the average in attendance is 17. The Protestant population is 139. The rent-charge is £413 7*s*. 3*d*. The land is worth £18. Total value, £431 7*s*. 3*d*., with residence.

Thomas Waggett (second son of Alderman Thomas Waggett, of Cork, by Eliza Sealy), was born in 1790.

He was ordained Deacon on 14th November, 1813, and Priest on 31st July, 1814, both at Cork. He was Curate of St. Peter's in 1815, and of St. Paul's in 1822. In January of 1833 he became P. Timoleague, in Ross; and in July of same year was removed to Rathclarin, where he continued until his death on 8th May, 1861.

He married Belinda Saunders, and by her had issue, *inter alios*, a son Thomas, now settled near Bandon.

The family of Waggett was formerly settled at Spittle, near Buttevant, where Robert Waggett lived, who married Anne, dau. of Christopher Crofts, of Buttevant. Robert Waggett died 1681. The late Recorder Waggett was son of Christopher, elder brother to Alderman Thomas Waggett. The male line of this branch is now extinct. The representatives in the female line are the Very Rev. Thomas Carson, Dean of Kilmore; and Nicholas Dunscombe, esq., of King Williamstown House, county Cork.

1861. May 31. WILLIAM TOTTENHAM DAY, A.M., R. V. Rathclarin. [D.R.]

W. T. Day (fourth son of Richard Day, of Youghal), was ordained Deacon at Cork on 13th August, 1837, and Priest, the same year, at Limerick, on letters dimissory from Cork. From 1837 to 1842 he was P. C. Templebrady; from 1842 to 1850 P. C. Marmullane; and from 1850 to 1861 V. Kilkerranmore, Ross.

He married Alicia, third dau. of Rev. J. Quarry, R. St. Mary, Shandon, and has issue five children.

RATHCONY.

1291. "Eccia de Rathcona VIIImr." [Tax. P. Nic.]

1591. "Rectoria integra de Rathcony. HUGH LANGLEY, laicus, tenuit sex menses." [MS. T.C.D. E. 3. 14.] "MAURICIUS M'DERMOT, Cur. per dimid. anni, monite ad recipiend. ordines infra annum et ad certificand. postea." [R.V. 1591. M.R.I.A.] M'Dermot was R. Templeusky, q. v.

1615. Rathconie (residens) Rector integer JOHANNES GOLD (P. St. Michael's, q. v.), minister legens; ipse inservit curæ. Val. 9 li. Ecclesia et cancella ruinate; but the Rector is bound to repair within a fixed time. [R.V. R.I.A.]

1618. March 5. GEORGE STUKELY, R. de Rathcooney. [F.F.]

1628. Sept. 3. JOSEPH FOWLES, P. St. Michael's, als. Shanbally, et R. Rathconye united by Bishop. [R.V. 1634.]

1634. E. de Rathcony Josephus ffowles. Valet 26 li. per an. [R.V. 1634.] Fowles was also Treasurer of Cloyne, q. v.

1637. July 27. GEORGIUS KELLY, adm. ad Rectoriam integram de Rathconye et ad P. St. Michael's, q. v.

He appears in 1639, with WILLIAM GILSLAND as Curate, "bene omnia." [V.B. 1639. D.R.] Gilsland was also Curate of St. Michael's.

16—? HEZECHIAH HOLLAND, R. Rathconey, and R. V. Shandon. He does not appear, save in the following extract from the Visitation Book of 1669.

1661. April 26. THOMAS GOODMAN, R. de Rathcony, and R. V. Shandon, per mortem Hezechiæ Holland. [V.B. 1669. D.R.] He appears 1661 to 1680. [V.B. D.R.] In 1675 he became also Precentor of Ross, q. v.

"1676. July 27. We find and present that the parish church of Rathcony was, at the assizes held in Corke, the 29th day of May, 1675, presented to be out of repair, and that the same ought and should be repaired, and made up by the parishioners of said parish; and forasmuch as Templemichael parish, being four plowlands and a-half, in the barony of Barrymore, was always reputed to be joyn'd with the said parish of Rathcony, viz., the parish of Rathcony and Templemichael; the inhabitants of the said four plowlands and a-half of Templemichael shall and ought to contribute towards the building and repairing and erecting the said church of Rathcony; and that, with the approbation of the Reverend Father in God, Edward, Lord Bishop of Corke, Cloyne, and Ross, the same be built as appertaineth; and that the overseers named in the said presentment, with Edward Gallway, gent., joined with them, shall equally and indifferently applot, levy, and collect, with the Bishop's approbation and consent, within the said two parishes, what money, not exceeding £36 sterling, shall or will build or finish the said church." [Cork Grand Jury Presentments.]

1681. May 3. WALTER NEALE is admitted "ad Rectoriam de Rathcony." [F.F.] He appears 1681 to 1685. [V.B. D.R.] In 1686 he became Precentor of Cork, q. v.

1686. June 3. RICHARD MALLORY, A.M., R. Rathcony, per resignation of Walter Neale. [D.R.] He appears 1686. [V.B.]
Mallory was also P. Holy Trinity, q. v.

1686. Dec. 4. DOMINIC MEADE, A.B., R. Rathcony, per cession of Mallory. [D.R.] He appears 1687 to 1692. [V.B.] He was also Archdeacon of Cloyne, q. v.

1692. Feb. 7. VALENTINE FRENCH, A.M., R. Rathcony, per resignation of Dominic Meade. [D.R.] In 1718 French became Dean of Ross, q. v.

1697. June 28. CORNELIUS HIGNETT, A.M., R. Rathcony, per resignation of Valentine French. [D.R.] He appears 1698 to 1726, November 3. [V.B. D.R.] Hignett was also Chancellor of Ross, q. v.

1699. Sermon once a fortnight. [V.B. 1699. D.D.]

"1700. Oct. 1. I saw Rathcony Church, built with stone and clay; 'tis in good repair, and has a good roof, and is well furnished with seats and pulpit. The communion table is rayl'd in, and the walls are plaistered on the inside. There are Common Prayer-books and a Bible, and a silver chalice and pewter flagon. The old seats were destroy'd in the time of the late troubles. There have been new ones built since. Captain St. Leger's father got this church repaired about twenty years ago by a presentment at the assizes. About 9 plowlands are in this parish; the lands are the estates of Mr. Evans, Captain St. Leger, and Counsellor Galway, who has a tomb in the church. Captain St. Leger, Colonel Rogers, Herbert Love, live in this parish, and Coppinger, a Papist, and Captain Finch, Protestant. The church-yard is fenct, but a gate is wanting. Colonel Rogers and Will. Kemp are churchwardens. No English school; there would be above twenty scholars there. The church is about two miles from Corke. Cornelius Curtin is Popish Priest of this parish and Templeusky, and Ballideloughar and Rathcony. He has been here at least eight years. This parish is an intire rectory; 'tis worth about £40 per an. to the Incumbent. Mr. Hignet preaches here once a fortnight. About 7 English acres of glebe near the church, westward of the church, belong to the Incumbent, and are set for 30*s.* or 40*s.* per an." [Downes' Tour.]

1727. Nov. 8. No name appears. [V.B. D.R.]

1727/8. January 22. THOMAS WHITE, A.M., was collated to Rathcony, vacant per mortem Cornelii Hignett. He was inducted on 25th January. [D.R.] In 1751 White became P. Kilnaglory, q. v.

1734. April 7. A certificate is issued of the recantation of Anstace Cahill, in the parish church of Rathcony. [D.R.]

1742. March 24. JOHN BURGH, A.M., is admitted to the entire Rectory of Rathcony, vacant by resignation of White. [D.R.]

In 1745 Burgh became P. Cahirlag. And from that time to the present the R. V. Rathcony has been united with the P. Cahirlag, q. v.

RINCURRAN.

1291. "Ecoia de Rincorran, IXmr." [Tax. P. Nic.]

1531. EDMUND DE BARRY, Rector de Rynchorran, is witness to a deed, dated, "in monasterio Beatæ Marie de Kynsale feria vi. post festum Sti. Brandani Ao. Di. 1531." [Browne's MSS.]

1591. R. de Rincurran, vacat per resignat. THOMÆ LEIGH. Vic. ibm D. LONG. [MS. T.C.D. E. 3. 14.] Long was Treasurer of Cork, q. v. Leigh appears also as R. V. Leighmoney.

1615. Rector, HUGO PERCEVAL, A.M., minister et predicator, ipse inservit curæ. Ecclia ruinosa spatiosa nunc in repacoe. Nulla cancella ibm per vigenti annos elapsos sed Rector contribuit cum parochianis in repacoe Ecclesiæ. [R.V. R.I.A.] Perceval was Dean of Ross, q. v.

1625. Feb. 23. RICHARD OWEN is presented by Crown to R. V. Rincurran and R. Taxax. [Lib. Mun.] He was inducted 10th April, 1626; and on 29th May, 1627, was admitted and instituted by James, Archbishop of Armagh, "ad R. and V. Rincurran quas Carolus Rex per literas patentes dat. apud. Dublin, 23rd Feb. anno regni primo univit. [R.V. 1634.] He appears again in 1630.

1630. July 10. THOMAS BARHAM is presented to P. Donoghmore, Cloyne, and R. V. Rincurran, in Cork, with clause of union pro hac vice to V. Durrus-Kilchrohan, in said Barham's possession. [Lib. Mun.] He was admitted and instituted on 9th August, 1633, by James, Abp. of Armagh, and was again admitted to Rincurran, on 24th Aug. 1633. [R.V. 1634.] Barham was V. Durrus, q. v.

1630. Sept. 17. RICHARD OWEN, R. and V. Ringcurran. [F.F.]

1734. R de Rincurran, Richard Owen. Rex est patronus durante minoritate Gould minoris. Vic. ibm Richard Owen. Val. 10 li. per an. Nullus, Curatus. [R.V. 1634.]

Owen was also P. Kilnaglory, q. v.

1634. July 19. ROBERT MILNER is presented to R. V. Rincurran. [Lib. Mun.]

Milner is R. V. Rincurran in 1639. "Ecclesia bene, deest pulpitus." [R.V. D.R.]

1666 to 1668. JONAS STAWELL appears as R. Rincurran. [V.B. D.R.] He was also V. Kinsale, and Archdeacon of Ross, q. v.

1669. July 23. THEODORE VEASIE, V. Kinsale, and R. V. Rincurran als Ryconran, both vacant per mortem Jonæ Stawell. [V.B. 1669.] He appears 1669 to 1681. [V.B. D.R.]

In 1676 Vesey became P. Kilnaglory, q. v.

1682. Sept. 26. THOMAS MEADE, A.M., R. V. Rincurran, and R. Taxax. [F.F] On letters patent of August 30. [Lib. Mun.] In 1693 he was also P. Inskenny, q. v. He appears 1682 to 1709. [V.B. D.R.]

1699. The Protestants go to Kinsale, and the Fort. [V.B. 1699. D.D.]

1709. June 9. JONATHAN SMEDLEY is presented to R. V. Rincurran. [Lib. Mun.] He appears to 1720. [V.B.] In 1720 he became R. Ringrone, q. v.

1717. Galfrid anglice Jefrey Wild bequeaths to the poor £5. [Cork Wills.]

1720. November 3. WILLIAM CROSSE is presented to R. V. Rincurran. [Lib. Mun.] He was also Dean of Lismore.

Crosse does not appear in any visitation book; and in that of Nov. 3, 1721, the name of Smedley appears with "vacant" added. [D.R.] From this it would seem that Crosse was never instituted.

William Crosse was, from 1719 to 1720, Dean of Ferns, and from 1720 to 1722, Dean of Lismore and R. Rincurran. In 1722 he became Rector of St. Mary's, Dublin; and in 1723, Dean of Leighlin; which two latter appointments he held until his death in 1749.

He had issue by his wife Anne —— ? *inter alios* Margaret, born 1726, died 1727; William, born 1728, and buried in 1729; and Phineas, baptized 6th of June, 1736.

Dean Crosse was buried at St. Mary's, Dublin, on 12th of November, 1749. [Par. Reg. of St. Mary's.]

1722. August 2. JOHN FRANCIS, Dean of Lismore, is presented to R. V. Rincurran. [Lib. Mun.]

He appears 1722 to 1724, Nov. 3. [V.B. D.R.]

John Francis was, from 1665 to 1705, P. St. Michael's, Dublin; and from 1705 to 1722, Rector of St. Mary's, Dublin; and from 1722 to 1724 Dean of Lismore, and R. V. Rincurran. He was also, in 1693, appointed to V. Talpestown, R. Ballymartin and Ballywalter, in Down and Connor, and to V. Attannagh, Agharney, &c., Ossory; and in 1694 to R. Catherlogh and Killesheen, Leighlin; he was, from 1695 to 1723, Dean of Leighlin.

He left issue by his wife Anne, three sons, Richard, Philip, and Tench; and a daughter, Mary, wife of Joshua Baggs, esq. His will was dated 25th of September, 1724, and proved 25th of January following. His son Philip was the Translator of

Horace, and his grandson, Sir Philip, was the reputed Author of Junius.

1724. July 2. THOMAS SHERIDAN, A.M., is presented to R. V. Rincurran. [Lib. Mun.] He was instituted 19th July, 1724, per mort. John Francis. [D.R.]

He appears 1725 to 1729. [V.B. D.R.]

Thomas Sheridan, the son of Patrick Sheridan, a gentleman who possessed a small estate near Kilmore, in Cavan, was a near relative of Patrick Sheridan, Bishop of Cloyne, and of William Sheridan, his brother, Bishop of Kilmore. By the help of the last-named prelate, Thomas Sheridan, when twenty years of age, was enabled to enter T.C.D. as a Pensioner, on 18th Oct., 1707. He subsequently attained the degree of D.D. in that University.

Having entered into holy orders, he became a schoolmaster; and was so much esteemed in that capacity as to have sometimes made £1,000 in a year by his school. He was soon distinguished by the friendship of the celebrated Swift; and his correspondence with the great Dean of St. Patrick's forms almost the entire of one of the volumes of Swift's Miscellanies. By the Dean's interest Sheridan was appointed Chaplain to the Lord Lieutenant, and in 1724 R. V. Rincurran, which he exchanged in 1730 for the V. Dunboyne and Kilbride, in Meath diocese. The latter preferment he exchanged also in 1734 for the Mastership of the Royal School at Cavan. He lost in money, however, by his successive changes; and after disposing of the Cavan school for about £400, he fell into bad health, and died on 10th Sept., 1738, aged about 51 years.

His character is given at some length by another friend of Swift, the fifth EARL of CORK, who describes Sheridan as a man well versed in books and in the Greek and Latin languages, but ignorant of the value of money, careless, and improvident. His fortunes at the Castle of Dublin were marred by his negligence in preaching at Cork, on the 1st of August, the anniversary of King George's accession, on the text, "Sufficient unto the day is the evil thereof." He lost, by this unlucky sermon, his post of Chaplain to the Lord Lieutenant, LORD CARTERET, who, although accustomed to the petulance of Swift, never pardoned Sheridan's ill-timed, if not unintentional, joke upon his Sovereign.

Dr. Sheridan remained, says Lord Cork, despite his disgrace at the Viceregal Court, "a punster, a quibbler, a fiddler, and a wit. Not a day passed without a rebus, an anagram, or a madrigal. His pen and his fiddlestick were in continual motion."

Yet, though thus unfortunate in life, and deemed worthy of no higher promotion than a Cork living or a Cavan school, Sheridan was fortunate in transmitting the genius he undoubtedly possessed in a high degree to his descendants. He left issue by his wife, Elisabeth McFadden, a lady of worth and talent, two sons, Richard and Thomas, and four daughters, Anne, Elisabeth, Meliora, and Esther. His son Thomas became a famous actor, philologist, and lexicographer, and was father (by his wife, Frances, a granddaughter of SIR OLIVER CHAMBERLAINE), of the celebrated statesman, dramatist, and orator, RICHARD BRINSLEY SHERIDAN, as also of an elder son, Charles Francis Sheridan, Secretary-at-War in Ireland, and author of "The History of the Revolution in Sweden in 1772."

R. B. Sheridan, the statesman, was twice married—first, to Elisabeth-Anne, dau. of Thomas Linley, and afterwards to Esther-Jane Ogle, dau. of the Dean of Winchester. His son by the first marriage, Thomas Sheridan, married Caroline Henrietta, dau. of Colonel Callender, and left issue, *inter alios*, Richard Brinsley Sheridan, of Frampton court, county Dorset, Charles-Kinnaird Sheridan, Attaché to the Embassy at Paris; Helen-Selina, wife of the fourth, and mother of the fifth LORD DUFFERIN and CLANEBOY; Caroline-Elisabeth-Sarah, wife of HON. G. C. NORTON; and Jane Georgina, wife of EDWARD ADOLPHUS, DUKE OF SOMERSET.

1730. Oct. 16. JOHN JEPHSON, A.B., R. V. Rincurran, per cession of Sheridan, on letters patent of 14th September. [D.R. and Lib. Mun.] In 1735 he was also Archdeacon of Cloyne, q. v.

He appears 1730 to 1742, June 9, but in latter year with his name crossed out. [V.B. D.R.] In 1742, June, Rev. William Reader, V. Kinsale, is appointed Sequestrator of Rincurran and Taxax, on the death of John Jephson. [D.R.]

1742. Aug. 13. DR. JEMMETT BROWNE (Dean of Ross, q. v.) is admitted R. V. Rincurran and Taxax. [D.R.]

1743. November 5. RICHARD TAYLOR is presented to R. V. Rincurran and R. Taxax. [Lib. Mun.]

1743. March 30. An act of Council was passed for removing the site of the parish church of Rincurran. [Lib. Mun.]

Richard, son of Berkeley Taylor, was born in Cork, and when seventeen years old entered T.C.D as Pensioner, on 29th July, 1723.

The Reverend Richard Taylor, of Kinsale, made his will on 24th of October, 1764, leaving his gold watch and seals, and gold-headed cane to "John Gill, doctor in physick, and now Sovereign of Kinsale." He gives the residue of his estate to his niece, Sarah Westropp. This will was proved on 29th Nov., 1765. On the 25th of November, 1764, was "buried at Cove, the Rev. Mr. Taylor, of Kinsale, passenger to Bristol, who died on board." [Cork Wills and Par. Register of Cove.]

1766. March 18. RICHARD GODLEY, A.M., R. V. Rincurran and Taxax. [F.F.] On letters patent of February the 7th. [Lib. Mun.] Vacant by death of Richard Taylor. [D.R.] He resigned in 1767.

1767. July 3. WILLIAM MEADE, LL.B., R. V. Rincurran and Taxax, on letters patent of May 14, vacant by resignation of Richard Godley. [D.R.]

William Meade, fourth son of Dean William Meade, was born in county Cork in 1728, and entered T.C.D. on 5th June, 1745, being then seventeen years old. He graduated B.A. in 1749, and was afterwards LL.B.

He was ordained Deacon on 6th October, and Priest on 8th of December, 1754.

He was licensed to the curacy of Kilmoe and Scull on 7th Oct., 1754, and on 9th of August, 1756, to that of St. Nicholas, in Cork. He got letters dimissory to Clogher Diocese, on 3rd of January, 1763, and became Rector of Derryvullan, Clogher. He was Rector of Rincurran and Taxax from 1767 to 1769.

He married, in 1759, Martha, dau. of Colonel Richard Bourne, of Burren, by whom he had issue (besides two daughters, Martha and Helena, who both died unmarried), four sons, of whom the youngest, Robert, was Rector of Ballymoney, q. v., and Richard, the eldest, was R. Ballymartle, q. v. William, the second son, was M.D., and married Catherine, dau. of Hewitt Poole, of Mayfield, and died Sp. John, the third son, was born in 1767. He was Collector of Customs at Kinsale, and succeeded to the estates of Ballintubber. He married Alice, dau. of Chambre Corker, P. Cahirlag, q. v., and by her had issue four sons, John, R. Leighmoney, q. v.; William, R. Inchinabacky, Cloyne, q. v.; Richard (of Kildare-street, Dublin, who married Catherine, dau. of W. Stephens, esq., and had issue at his death, in 1861, three sons and two daughters); and Edward, died unmarried.

1770. Feb. 14. EDWARD DAY, LL.D., R. V. Rincurran and Taxax, on letters patent of 28th October, 1769, vacant by death of Wm. Meade. [D.R.] He was also Prebendary of the Holy Trinity, q. v.

1772. January 14. DAVID COPE, A.M., R. V. Rincurran and Taxax, per resignation of Edward Day. [D.R.] On letters patent of October 3, 1771. [Lib. Mun.] Cope does not appear elsewhere in Cork or Cloyne.

1788. Oct. 16. THOMAS ADDERLEY BROWNE, LL.B., R. V. Rincurran and Taxax, per resignation of Cope. [D.R.] On letters patent of December 30. [Lib. Mun.] Browne was also Chancellor of Ross, q. v.

1793. Earliest date in present vestry books.

1795 is the date on the plates at present used in Rincurran parish for collecting alms.

1798 July 6. ARTHUR JOHN PRESTON, A.B., R. V. Rincurran and Taxax, per death of T. A. Browne. [D.R.] On letters patent of June 18. [Lib. Mun.]

1807. Preston resides partly on his other benefice in Kildare. [Rep.]

Arthur John Preston was second son of Rev. Nathaniel Preston, by Alice Dillon, and was grandson of Nathaniel Preston, of Swainstown, county Meath.

He was from 1793 to 1809, Second Canon of Kildare, and from 1809 to 1844, Dean of Limerick. He held also from 1798 to 1809 the R. Rincurran; and from 1808 to 1809 the Deanery of Kildare; and from 1809 to 1833 the P. Lulliaghmore, Kildare.

He married, in 1794, Araminta-Anne, dau. of William Beresford, third son of MARCUS, EARL OF TYRONE, and by her had issue, *inter alios*, Arthur John, who succeeded his father in the P. Lulliaghmore, Kildare; and William-Richard, Lieut.-Col. 45th Regt. Dean Preston married secondly, Isabella Shepherd, and had issue a daughter, Elisabeth.

1809. August 15. THEOPHILUS BLAKELY, A.M., R. V. Rincurran and Taxax. [F.F.] On letters patent of August 3. [Lib. Mun.]

Theophilus Blakely was from 1807 to 1809, R. Lyons, and V. Kill, Kildare; from 1809 to 1811, R. Rincurran; and from 1811 to 1824, Dean of Connor, and R. Islandmagee. From 1824 to 1839 he was Dean of Achonry; and from 1839 to 1855, Dean of Down. He married Emily-Catherine, dau. of Edward Ball, esq., by Catherine Cuthbert, and by her had issue six children, all now dead. The Dean married secondly, Mary-William, dau. of John Stewart, esq., and by her had issue a son, Alexander Theophilus, Captain Royal Artillery, and two daughters, Mary, wife of Robert Spankie, esq., and Isabella-Chalmers. The Dean died on 1st December, 1855.

1811. Sept. 21. THOMAS GRAVES, A.M., R. V. Rincurran and Taxax, on letters patent of May 24. [D.R.]

Thomas Graves was eldest brother of the celebrated Richard Graves, Dean of Ardagh, and was the eldest son of Rev. James Graves, Vicar of Kilfinane and Darragh, Rector of Ballingarry, Dunmoylan, and Castlerobert, and finally R. Croom and Adare, in Limerick diocese, who married Jane, dau. of Rev. Thomas Ryder, P. Brigowne, Cloyne.

Thomas was born in 1745; was educated at Kilkenny, and became a Scholar of T.C.D. in 1763.

He was from 1771 to 1828, R. Ballymacelligott and Nohoval-Kerry, in Ardfert. He held therewith, from 1784 to 1802, the Deanery of Ardfert; from 1802 to 1811, the Deanery of Connor, and Rectory of Islandmagee; and from 1811 to 1828, the Rectory of Rincurran.

Rev. Thomas Graves was author of a "Sermon before the Association for Discountenancing Vice," preached on 12th June, 1800. 8vo. Dub. 1801.

He was a man of great literary acquirements, and to his mode of instructing his younger brother was due, in a great measure, that brother's success in college. Several portions of his correspondence are preserved in a very interesting memoir of Dean Richard Graves, prefixed to the edition of the Dean's works published by his son, the P. Brigowne, Cloyne.

Thomas Graves married Anne, dau. of John Dunleavie, esq., and by her had issue, James William (Lieut.-Col. 18th Royal Irish), his eldest son; and John-Crosbie Greaves, his second son; and two other sons, who were in the army.

His second son, John-Crosbie, was a barrister, Commissioner of Bankrupts, and for many years Magistrate of the Head Office of Police in Dublin. He married a dau. of Rev. C. Perceval, R. Bruhenny, and had issue four sons, besides a dau., married to Von Ranke, the Prussian Historian.

John, the eldest, is Inspector of Poor Laws, and resides at Cheltenham; James Perceval, the second son, is dead; Robert Perceval, the third, is in holy orders; and the fourth son, Charles, is F.T.C.D., President of the Royal Irish Academy, and Dean of the Chapel Royal, Dublin Castle.

Thomas Graves, Rector of Rincurran, lived to the age of eighty-three, and was able to officiate in his church a few days previous to his death. He died in November, 1828, and was buried, according to his wish, in the grave-yard of St. Catherine's, in the parish of Rincurran, near his wife. He left bequests to the poor of Rincurran and of Ballymacelligott parishes.

1829. January 15. JOHN BAGWELL CREAGH, A.M., R. V. Rincurran. [D.R.]

1834. Protestant population, 291.

1837. Rincurran: a rectory and vicarage, with cure, 7 miles long by 1½ broad in its greatest breadth; but in many parts not half a quarter in breadth, containing 5,186A. 3R. 28P. Gross population, 3,758. No Curate employed. Tithe composition, £461 10*s.* 9*d.*; 3A. of glebe, valued at £5; subject to visitation fees, £1 3*s.* 6*d.*; diocesan schoolmaster, £2 5*s.* No glebe-house. Incumbent is resident, and pays the sum of £44 a-year for house rent. One church, capable of accommodating 150 persons, built many years since, but at what cost, unknown. No charge on the parish in 1832 on account of the church. Divine service is celebrated once on Sundays and on the principal festivals. The sacrament is administered monthly. The benefice is a rectory. [Parl. Rep.]

J. B. Creagh (son of Arthur Gethin Creagh, of Laurentinum, by Isabella Bagwell, and grandson of Michael Creagh, esq., of Liscarroll, county Cork), was born on 26th Dec., 1772, and was ordained Deacon on 24th of August, 1800, at Cloyne.

From 1802 to 1813 he was licensed Curate of Doneraile and Templeroan. He was, in 1814, V. Carrigamleary, and in 1829, R. V. Ringcurran, both of which parishes he held until his death, at Kinsale, on 13th of February, 1846.

He married, in 1797, Gertrude, dau. of John Miller, esq.,

and by her had issue seven sons and five daughters, for whom *vide* Burke's L. G.—article CREAGH, of BALLYANDREW.

1846. August 8. BENJAMIN MORRIS, R. V. Rincurran; certified annual value, £312 12*s*. 3¾*d*. [D.R.]

Benjamin Morris was son of William Morris, by Mary, dau. of Shapland Carew, of Castleboro', and was grandson of William Morris, of Waterford, esq. [U.O.]

He was ordained Deacon at Cloyne on 14th September, 1817, and for many years was Curate in the diocese of Ossory. He died, shortly after his admission to Rincurran, at Attanagh Glebe, in Ossory, leaving issue by his wife, Elisabeth (dau. and co-heiress of Maurice Nugent O'Conor, esq., of Mountpleasant, in Queen's county), three children, William, of Mountpleasant, Maurice O'Conor, and Marie-Catherine.

1846. Dec. 17. RALPH SADLEIR, R. V. Rincurran, on letters patent of 3rd of December. [D.R.]

Ralph Sadleir (son of Thomas Sadleir, eldest brother of the late Provost of T.C.D., *vide* Burke's L. G.), entered T.C.D. on 22nd Oct. 1832, and graduated B.A. in 1837, and D.D. in 1852.

He was ordained Deacon on 25th April, 1838, by the Bishop of Elphin, and Priest on 23rd Dec. 1838, by the Archbishop of Dublin. He was licensed to St. Mark's Curacy, Dublin, on 18th Jan. 1838, and to that of St. Anne's, Dublin, on 26th Dec. 1840. From 1846 to 1848 he was R. Rincurran, and on 4th November, 1848, he became P. Castleknock, Dublin.

He married Letitia-Sarah-Georgina, dau. of the late Provost Sadleir, and has issue one child, Franc.

1848. Dec. 28. ANDREW NOBLE BREDIN, A.M., R. V. Rincurran. [D.R.] He resigned on 12th of August, 1851, exchanging for the Rectory of Taney, diocese of Dublin, which he held until 1857, when he became P. Dunlavin, Dublin. In 1858 he became R. Clonbulloge, Kildare, where he shortly afterwards died.

1851. Sept. 5. WILLIAM HENRY STANFORD, R. V. Rincurran, on letters patent of 12th of August; certified value, £312 16*s*. 7*d*. [D.R.]

W. H. Stanford (son of William Stanford, of Cavan, a descendant of Bishop Bedel, of Kilmore; and brother to C. S. Stanford, R. St. Thomas, Dublin), was Curate of Slane, dioc. Meath, of some parish in England, and of Taney, dioc. Dublin, before he came to Rincurran. He died on 22nd Feb. 1856, leaving three sons and two daughters.

1856. Sept. 18. ACHILLES DAUNT, A.B., R. V. Rincurran, on letters patent of 26th of March, 1856. Annual value, £316 18*s*. 3*d*. [D.R.]

1860. A. Daunt, Rector; John Cooke, Curate. The church in order. No glebe-house. 4 acres of glebe let. Divine service thrice on all Sundays, and on chief festivals, and on every alternate Tuesday. Sacrament monthly, and at festivals;

average of communicants, 70. 59 children attend a Church Education school. The Protestant population is 260. The rentcharge is £346 3s. The land is worth £4. Total annual value, £350 3s. per an. without residence.

Achilles Daunt (grandson of Isaac Heard, late M.P. for Kinsale), was a Scholar, T.C.D. in 1852, and graduated A.B. in 1856. He was ordained in 1855.

He married on 24th February, 1863, Catherine Mary, eldest dau. of the late Rev. John Leslie, R. Kilcredan, Cloyne.

RINGRONE.

1291. "Eccia de Ruion Xmr." [Tax P. Nic.]

1542. DOMINUS WALTER YONG, Rector de Rinron, is mentioned in a deed concerning the advowson of Inishannon, dated Oct. 15, 1542. [Browne MSS.]

15—? THOMAS GEROD. R. Ringrone. He died in 1571. He was, from 1558 to 1571, Vicar of Kinsale also.

"In dei noie amen. Visis cognitis et intellectis meritis circumstanciis causæ controverciæ seu contentionis motæ inter Reverendum patrem Ricardum Cork et Clonem Episcopum ex una parte, allegantem Ecclesiam de Corrowraine Cork dioc. simpliciter et mere suæ esse collacois, et superiorem consilium et comitatem villæ de Kinsale, quibus non competit jus patronatus Ecclæ parochialis de Rinrone, parte ex altera, allegantes dictam Eccliam de Corrowraine capellam et parcellam esse ejusdem Ecclæ de Rinrone et ita esse et fuisse et longissimi temporis prescriptionem de quo aliter non existet memoria hominum. Verum quia, &c., allegationem superioris, &c., de Kinsale fundatam esse de jure et fuisse veram idcirco nos Magister Pat. Roche, Archd. Cork et Clon. ac Leonardus Palmer generos. general Commissarii seu officiales curiarum et causarum ecclesiasticarum, &c., declaramus dictam Eccliam de Corrowraine esse et fuisse capellam ad Eccliam de Rinrone spectantem, &c. 12 die October, 1570.—(Signed), PATRICIUS, Archidiaconus, LEO PALMER." [Browne MSS. fol. 16.]

1571. January 20. THOMAS BROCKLEY is presented to the Rectory of Ringrone by the Sovereign, Council, and Burgesses of Kinsale. "Reverendis magistris decano et capitulo Ecclæ Corck, seu vicariis generalibus pro dispositione Juris vel per capitulum sede vacante deputatis,—nos ROBERTUS MIAGHE, Superior villæ de Kinsall, Consilium, Burgenses et coitas ejusdem saltim. Cum ad nos jus presentandi idoneam personam ad rectoriam ecclæ parochialis de Rynerone nunc ad p'sens de jure et de facto per mortem Dni Thomæ Gerod ultimi inibi incumbentis vacantem spectare dignoscitur, vris discretionibus dilectum nobis in christo dnum Thomam Brockley vicarium ejusdem putamus. Rogantes quatenus ipsum ad eandem Rectoriam admittent ac cetera quæ in hac p'te vro incumbent officio facere dignemini, cum omni favore, vel a vobis fieri expectamus. Datum apud Kinsale vicessimo die Januarii, Ao. 1571. Sub testimonio nri communis sigilli. Registered the xxvij of Februarie." [First Book of Cork Registry, fol. 15.]

1580. May 14. ALEXANDER MEAGHE, the Rector of Rinrone, is also admitted Rector of Innishannon, q. v.

1591. ROBERT STURTON (Dean of Ross, q. v.), appears as R. V. Ringrone "cum capella Killorem—Ecclia de Borrowrane capella de Rinerone Anexa." [MS. T.C.D. E. 3. 14.]

1615. Rinrone Rector (non residens) JOHANNES IRISH (R. V. Rathcormack, Cloyne, q. v.), minister et predicator. HENRY HUSSEY, A.M., minister et predicator est Vicarius. Tenet etiam R. de Templetrine et Killanody (Ballinadee). Val. 16 li. Ecclesia et cancella de Ringrone bene repantur cum libris et aliis necessariis. Val. 30 li. per an. [R.V. R.I.A.]

1626. June 22. HELICIAS HUSSEY, A.M., is admitted *Vicar* de Ringrone, and Treasurer of Cork, q. v.

[1628. JOHN JEFFRAY was presented, but not, I think, admitted, to the Parsonage of Ringrone and Ballinadee, q. v.]

1634. R. de Rinrone, John Irish. The Earl of Cork had the presentation from the Lord Courcey, and did present the said Irish unto the said benefice, and did agree with hym uppon the said presentation that the said Irish should have IV li. per an. for serving the cure, and the Earl of Cork 55 li. per. an. It is leased by the Earl of Cork to Hesiah Hussey, of Bandonbridge, for 60 li. per an. Vicar ibm. Hilshias Hussey. Val. 25 li. per an. Epus confert. [R.V. 1634.]

1634. August 31. THOMAS FULLER, or FULWAR, is admitted Rector de Ringrone. [F.F.] In 1639 he was also Chancellor of Cork, q. v.

1634. December 22. Fuller is presented to Vicarage of Ringrone, with clause of union pro hac vice tantum to the Rectory of Ringrone now held by him. [Lib. Mun.]

Fuller appears in V. B. of 1639, with Barnabas Honnychurch as Curate. "Ecclia bene et ornata." [V.B. D.R.]

In 1641 Fuller became Bishop of Ardfert, retaining Ringrone in commendam; and in 1661 he was made Archbishop of Cashel.

1661. August 31. THOMAS HACKET is appointed R. V. Ringrone and Dean of Cork, q. v.

166–? SAMUEL HINDE, or FINDE, R. V. Ringrone.

1665. August 20. WILLIAM PORTMAN, D.D., is instituted R. V. Rinroan, per desertionem Samuelis Hinde (ffinde?), on presentation of the Sovereign and Burgesses of Kinsale, to the Rectory, Vicaria in coll. Epi. [V.B. 1669.] Portman was also R. Dunderrow, q. v. He appears at the visitation of 1675.

1675/6. January 22. PETER HEWITT, R. V. Ringrone, and Chancellor of Cork. [F.F.] In 1710 he became Precentor of Cork, q. v.

Feb. 8, 1676. THOMAS WARD is presented to Rectory of Ringrone. [Lib. Mun.] But he does not appear in the visitation books. He was afterwards Dean of Connor.

1720. May 26. JONATHAN SMEDLEY, A.M., is admitted Rector de Ringrone, per mortem Petri Hewitt, on presentation of Gerald, Lord Kinsale, dated 30th April, 1720. [D.R.] Jonathan, son of John Smedley, was born in Dublin, and entered T.C.D. as Pensioner on 18th September, 1689, when eighteen years old.

From 1709 to 1720 he was R. Rincurran; and in 1720 was appointed R. Ringrone, which he held for a very short time. From 1718 to 1724 he was Dean of Killala; and from 1724 to 1727 Dean of Clogher. In 1723 he was also appointed V. Knockmark, Meath.

The following account of his works, &c., is extracted from Cotton.

He published the following pieces :—

1. A Sermon on the Queen's Accession. 8vo. London, 1714.

2. A Sermon on the Anniversary of the Irish Massacre. 4to. London, 1715.

3. A Sermon on January 30. 8vo. London, 1716.

4. A Sermon on the Birthday of the Prince of Wales. 4to. London, 1716.

5. Eight Sermons on several subjects. 8vo. 1719.

6. Poems. 8vo. 1721.

7. A Specimen of an Universal View of all the eminent Writers on Holy Scripture. Folio. 1728.

Of his "Specimen," &c., "being a Collection of the Dissertations, Explications, and Opinions of Learned Men in all ages concerning the difficult passages and obscure texts of the Bible," Mr. T. H. Horne observes, that it contains only the first chapter of Genesis. The work which it announced was never published. There is an engraved portrait of Dean Smedley. Early in 1728 he proceeded to Fort St. George, in the East Indies, on a clerical mission. See a notice of him in "Swift's Works," by Sir W. Scott, vol. xiv.

The full title of Dean Smedley's Sermon, No. 2, is—"A Sermon to the Protestants of Ireland residing in London, preached at the Church of St. James, on October 23, the day of the Rebellion in 1641. By Jonathan Smedley, A.M., Rector of Rincurrane, in Ireland." It is dedicated to Mrs. Elizabeth Hales, of Putney, and the author subscribes himself "your dutiful son."

1720 to 1729. EMANUEL HUNGERFORD appears as *Rector*. [V.B. D.R.] Hungerford was also P. St. Michael's, q. v.

1720 to 1727. BARTHOLOMEW SALTER appears as *Vicar*. [V.B. D.R.]

B. Salter was born at Youghal, and was son of John Salter, gentleman. He entered T.C.D. when twenty-one years old, on 9th June, 1702.

He was ordained Priest at Cloyne on 19th Dec. 1714. In 1717 he was Curate and Lecturer at Holy Trinity, Cork. From 1718 to 1720 he was R. V. Kilcully; and from 1720 to his death, in 1727, was Vicar of Ringrone. He was also, on 1st Dec. 1720, licensed to be Curate of Templetrine.

1728. Oct. 7. JOHN KENNY, A.M., *Vicar*, per mortem B. Salter. [D.R.] In 1751 he was P. Kilbrittain, q. v.

1730. May 30. WILLIAM MEADE was admitted Rector, per mortem Emanuelis Hungerford, on presentation of Sovereign and Burgesses of Kinsale. [D.R.] In 1730 the rectory and vicarage were consolidated by the Archbishop of Cashel. [D.R.]

1737. April 7. St. John Browne, A.M., is licensed to be Curate of Ringrone, on nomination of William Meade, who promises him the vicarial part of the parish as fully as it was enjoyed by John Kenny, the late Vicar thereof. [D.R.] Meade was also Dean of Cork, q. v.

1764. April 10. JOHN KENNY, the younger, R. Ringrone, vacant by death of William Meade, in coll. Epi for this turn. [D.R.] He was, in 1796, P. Kilbrogan, q. v.

1769. March 3. THOMAS KEEFFE, A.B., to consolidated R. and V. Ringrone, vacant by death of William Meade, last Incumbent, on presentation of Sovereign, Burgesses, and Commonalty of the town of Kinsale, by their instrument, dated 21st March, 1764, which the Bishop hath hitherto deferred to accept, on account of a suit to this time subsisting relative to the right of presentation, which presentation belongs of right for this turn to said Sovereign, &c. [D.R.] In 1768 titles were made out for Mr. Keeffe to Ringrone; but Mr. Kenny and he not agreeing, they were never granted. [D.R.]

Thomas Keeffe (son of John Keeffe, who married Jane, dau. of Jonas Stawell, grandson of the Archdeacon of Ross), entered T.C.D. as Pensioner on 8th Feb. 1732. He was ordained Priest at Cork on 19th Dec. 1742. He was licensed on 23rd Sept. 1742, to the Curacy of Ballymartle, Dunderrow, and Cullen; and on Feb. 11, 1746, to the Curacy of Ringrone. On 17th May, 1755, he was licensed to the Curacy of Killowen. From 1769 to his death in 1788, he was R. V. Ringrone.

He married, in Dec. 1741, Miss Mary Travers, of Kinsale.

1788. Oct. 18. RICHARD WEBB, A.B., R. V. Ringrone, per mortem Keeffe. [D.R.]

1830. Protestant population, 136.

1832. Ringrone, a rectory and vicarage, with cure, 7 miles long by 5 broad, containing 10,000 acres. Gross population, 4,813. One Curate employed, at a stipend of £75 per annum.

Tithe composition, £750. Three roods of glebe, valued at £1. Subject to visitation fees, £3; diocesan schoolmaster, 18s. No glebe-house. Incumbent, although non-resident in the benefice, resides within a quarter of a mile of it, in the town of Kinsale, and pays £60 a-year for house-rent. One church, capable of accommodating 150 persons, built about the year 1780, by subscription and assessment, but at what cost unknown. No charge on the parish in 1832 on account of the church. Divine service is celebrated once on Sundays, and on the principal festivals. The sacrament is administered monthly, and on the festivals. The benefice is a rectory. An alternate turn of presentation to this benefice belongs to the Diocesan, and to either Lord De Clifford or Lord Kinsale. [Parl. Rep.]

Richard Webb (eldest son of George Webb, of Trumpington, county Cambridge, *vide* B. L. G.), was born 11th May, 1755. He was ordained Deacon on 1st Nov. 1778, and Priest on 19th Nov. 1780, both at Cork. On 5th Nov. 1784, he was licensed to the Curacy of St. Nicholas, Cork. From 1788, Feb., to Dec. 1788, he was P. Killanully. From 1788 to 1818 he was P. Dromdaleague and R. Caheragh; and from 1788 to his death on 6th Feb. 1836 he was R. V. Ringrone.

He married, in 1793, Eliza, dau. of Francis Browne, of Kinsale; and left issue two sons, Richard-Francis (R. Caheragh, q. v.), and John (R. Dunderrow, q. v.)

1836. May 26. THE HONOURABLE ANNESLEY GORE, A.B., R. V. Ringrone, on presentation (dated 6th May) of John Meade, John Newman, William Russell, and Sophia, Baroness De Clifford. [D.R.]

A. Gore was nephew of the third, and brother to the fourth Earl of Arran. He was fourth Canon of Kildare, from 1834 to 1840, and R. Ringrone from 1836 to 1840. He resigned on 3rd November in that year.

1840. Nov. 18. JOSHUA BROWNE RYDER, A.B., R. V. Ringrone, in coll. Epi pro hac vice. [D.R.]

1844. May 9. A new church, built by Ecclesiastical Commissioners, on new site, is consecrated under the name of St. James; also a church-yard is consecrated. [D.R.]

J. B. Ryder was the eldest son of Rev. John Ryder, Chancellor of Cloyne, q. v. He was ordained Deacon on 8th Oct. 1809, and Priest on 30th Oct. 1811. From 1840 to his death, on 20th June, 1855, he was R. V. Ringrone.

He married, on 21st Nov. 1812, at the Foundling Hospital, Cork, Lucinda, dau. of Michael Wood, esq., of Cork. By her (who died on 24th January, 1861) he had issue, *inter alios*, Margaret-Wood, born 1813; and Michael-Wood, born in 1818.

1855. August 6. WILLIAM NEWMAN, A.B., R. V. Ringrone, on presentation, dated 2nd August, of Elisabeth H. Meade, widow, and executrix of the will of John Meade, Captain, R.N. the last surviving trustee, &c. Certified annual value, £504 15s. 3d. [D.R.]

1860. William Newman, Rector, and George C. Nash, Curate. The church in order. No glebe-house. The glebe (¾ of an acre) is let. Rector lives in Kinsale. Service once on Sundays and holidays at the church, and on Sunday evenings at Coolmain school-house. Sacrament monthly and at festivals; average of communicants, 11. There are two Church Education schools, one at Oldcourt, at which an average of 6 children attend; another at Coolmain, where the average attendance is 18. The Protestant population is 130. The rent-charge is £562 10s. per an. The land is worth £1. Total value, £563 10s. per an. *without* residence.

William (son of James Newman, esq.), was born in London, and when twenty-one years old entered T.C.D. as Pensioner, on 4th Nov. 1833.

He was ordained Deacon at Cork on 19th Sept. 1841. In 1842 he became R. Garryvoe, and in 1855 R. Ringrone. He holds both benefices.

He is married, and has issue.

SCULL.

1581. July 4. "Vicariam Ecclisæ parochialis Stæ Marie de Scoll, Corcagen. dioc., contulit Epus dno JOANNI BRETHNAGHE presbitero, cui quidem vicarie Rectoriarum ejusdem Ecclisæ unacum ob tenuitatem univit, 4 Julii, 1581. Archidiaconus sigillum suum apposuit quinto die ejusdem mensis, Julii. Phil. Goldeus Registrarius." [Dioc. Reg.] *Vide* Kilbonane.

1591. "Rectoria de Scholl Coll de Youghell. Vic. ibm CORNELIUS SWILLIVAN" (or O'SULLIVAN). [MS. T.C.D. E. 3. 14.]

Cornelius O'Sullivan, Vicar de Durrus, propter acceptacionem vicariæ de Kilmoe et Skoll deprivatus circiter 1591. [Ib.]

1615. Scooll. Rector Coll de Youghell. Vicarius, THOMAS WAY, idem V. de Kilmoe. [R.V. R.I.A.]

1634. R. de Scoole spectat ad Coll de Youghall. Val. 30 li. per an. Comes Cork, patronus. It is alledged by the Dean and Chapter of Cork that it belongeth to them. Vic. ibm Thomas Way, val. 30 li. per an. Epus Confert. [R.V. 1634.] On 3rd July, 1634, Thomas Way is presented to V. Skull and Caheragh. [Lib. Mun.]

In 1642 Thomas Way, of Scull, depones to loss of £1,252, besides the benefit of his R. and V. of Scull, and V. Caheragh, worth, communibus annis, £250. [MS. T.C.D. F. 2. 15.]

Thomas Way, "de Kinsale," was ordained Deacon and Priest by William, Bishop of Cork, on 27th Oct. 1605.

He appears as V. Scull from 1615 to 1640. From 1619 to 1626 he was P. Killaspugmullane, and from 1620 to 1630 P. Dromdaleague, and from 1623 to 1640 was V. Caheragh.

1637. July 25. WILLIAM BURLEY, Rector de Scull. [F.F.] In 1639 Burley appears as Rector, and Way as Vicar of Scull. "Ecclesia bene, desunt omnia." [V.B. 1639. D.R.]

William Burley was, from 1625 to 1630, V. Bruhenny and Inchinabacky, Cloyne; and from 1630 to 1666? P. Tipper, Dublin, and V. Cahir. He was also, from 1634 to 1640, Dean of Clonmacnoise; and from 1640 to 1666, Dean of Emly. From 1630 to 1640 he was R. Scull.

1640/1. January 28. FRANCIS COCKMAN, Rector de Scull. [F.F.] On letters patent of November 27, 1640. [Lib. Mun.] Cockman was A.M. in 1645. In that year, on Sept. 1, he was instituted to the P. Tassagart, St. Patrick's, Dublin, of which cathedral he had been a Minor Canon. He died in 1646. [MS. in Consistorial Office, Dublin.]

16—? JOHN EVELEIGH, R. V. Scull and Kilmoe, q. v. He was, in 1661, Dean of Ross.

1666. The rectory and vicarage are both vacant. [V.B.]

1667 to 1755. Skull was held with Kilmoe, q. v.

1755. July 16. GEORGE RUSSELL, R. V. Scull, vacant by death of Paul Limerick. [D.R.] On letters patent of July 8, from the Crown. [Lib. Mun.]

On 29th March, 1757, Russell (having paid Wm. Limerick, the executor of his predecessor, £400,) obtains a certificate of dilapidations against Limerick for £54 10*s.* 10*d.* [D.R.]

George Russell, A.B., of Oxford, was ordained Priest on 6th Oct. 1754. He was licensed to the curacy of St. Nicholas, Cork, on 7th Oct. 1754, and from 1755 to 1767 was R. V. Scull. He died in 1766 or 1767.

1767. Feb. 21. JOHN CHETWOOD, A.B., R. and V. Scull, vacant by death of Russell, and in the Bishop's collation for this turn. [D.R.] In 1790 he became P. Cahirlag, q. v.

1780. June 26. ANDREW DOWNES is presented to R. V. Scull, vacant by resignation of Chetwode. [Lib. Mun.]

In 1782 Downes is R. V. Tullagh and Creagh, Ross, q. v.

1780. Nov. 1. RICHARD TOWNSEND, A.M., R. V. Scull, now vacant by the resignation of Andrew Downes, late Incumbent. [D.R.]

Richard Townsend was the eldest son of John Townsend, who was the fourth son of Bryan, the second son and heir of Colonel Richard Townsend, of Castle Townsend. The mother of the Rev. Richard Townsend was Catherine, dau. of Colonel James Barry, of Lisnegar, Rathcormack, by his wife Susannah, who was the only daughter of John (the eldest son of Colonel

Richard Townsend) by his wife, LADY CATHERINE BARRY. [*Vide* V. Holy Trinity, *Rev. Philip Townsend.*]

Richard Townsend was ordained Priest, at Cork, on 29th April, 1753.

In 1752 he was Curate of Donoghmore, Cloyne; and in 1753, of Dromdaleague.

From 1759 to 1780 he was R. V. Myros, Ross; and from 1780 to 1793, R. V. Scull. He was also, from 1764 to 1793, V. Rathbarry, Ross. He held, also, from 1764 to 1780, the Vs. Kilmaccabee and Kilfaughnabeg; and from 1768 to 1780, was P. Currograngemore, Ross.

He married Susannah, daughter of Colonel Alexander Gay; and died, May 17, 1793, without issue.

Through the above Lady Catherine Barry, daughter of Richard, second EARL of BARRYMORE, the descendants of John Townsend, fourth son of Bryan Townsend, trace descent from Lord Barrymore's maternal grandfather, Richard Boyle, the great EARL of CORK, and lay claim to the extinct de Barri peerage. See Caulfield's note on Diary of Rowland Davies, Dean of Cork, p. 95; Camden Society, London, 1857.

1793. August 2. The Rev. Philip French, of Scull, was appointed Sequestrator. [D.R.]

1794. Feb. 24. JOHN WHETHAM, R. V. Scull. [F.F.] On letters patent of Dec. 19, 1793. [Lib. Mun.]

Whetham was Dean of Lismore and Archdeacon of Cork, q. v. In June, 1794, he resigned Scull.

1794. July 12. ANTONY TRAIL, A.M., R. and V. Scull. [F.F.]

In 1795 the Bishop approves of Trail's memorial for leave to expend £101 16*s.* 2*d.* on the glebe-house, and £314 12*s.* 6*d.* on the offices of Scull. In 1799 the Bishop certifies for an outlay of £416 8*s.* 8*d.* as duly expended, and returns the yearly value of Scull as £500. In 1801 a further expenditure of £26 11*s.* 5*d.* is certified, the value of the benefice being stated as £600 per an. [D.R.]

1807. Trail resides in Connor diocese. [Rep.]

Anthony Trail (nephew to James Trail, Bishop of Down and Connor) was son of Rev. Robert Trail by Jean Dow, and grandson of Mr. Trail, who married Miss Haldane.

From 1777 to 1781 he was P. St. Andrew's, Down; and from 1782 to 1831, was Archdeacon of Connor. He held, also, from 1794 to 1830, the R. V. Scull, which he then resigned in favour of his son.

He married Agnes, dau. of William-Watts Gayer, LL.D., Clerk of the Irish House of Lords; and by her had two sons, William (now of 3, Ely-place, Dublin), and Robert (who succeeded his father in his Cork living). Antony Trail died in 1831.

1830. November 29. ROBERT TRAIL, A.M., R. V. Scull, on letters patent, from the Crown, of 22nd Nov. 1830. [D.R.]

1830. Protestant population, 1,898.

1836. Sept. 2. A school-house in townland of Lissacabee is licensed for divine service.

1837. Skull: a rectory and vicarage, with cure, 16 miles long by 6 broad, containing 49,873A. 0R. 12P.; gross population, 15,252. Two Curates employed, one for the eastern, and the other for the western divisions of the parish, at annual stipends to each of £80 Brit. Tithe composition, £850. 63 acres of glebe, valued at £100. Subject to visitation fees, 17*s*; diocesan schoolmaster £1 10*s*. Skull glebe-house in excellent order, built in 1721, and repaired during the late incumbency at an expense of £408 18*s*. 6¾*d*. Brit. Incumbent is next in succession to the improver; and having paid his predecessor £306 13*s*. 9¼*d*., and since expended about £35 Brit., he will be entitled to receive £230 14*s*. 3¼*d*. from his successor on account of the improvement charges. Incumbent is resident in the glebe-house. Exclusive of the moneys aforesaid, the improver, who was the father of the present incumbent, is reported to have expended £1,437 4*s*. 7½*d*. Brit. on the premises, without having any charge on his successor for the repayment of any portion thereof. One church, and a chapel of ease in this parish, distant 4½ miles from each other, the former capable of accommodating 250, and the latter 180 persons. The church, situate at Skull, built in 1721, but at what cost, or from what funds, unknown. The chapel of ease, situate near Ballydehob village, in the eastern division of the parish, built in 1829, by means of a gift of £650 Brit., granted by the late Board of First Fruits. No charge on the parish in 1832 on account of either the church or chapel of ease. Divine service is celebrated once on Sundays in the church and chapel of ease respectively, and on Sunday evenings in school-houses, one at a distance of four miles from the parish church. Four private weekly services are also celebrated for the benefit of the scattered population of this parish, and a week-day service has also been latterly performed in the church and chapel. The sacrament is administered twelve times in the year in each. The benefice is a rectory. [Parl. Rep.]

In 1847, £152 2*s*. was certified to have been expended by Robert Trail on the glebe-house. [D.R.]

Robert Trail (son of his predecessor) married Anne, sister to Sir Edmund Hayes, of Drumboe Castle, county Donegal, and by her had three sons and five daughters. His exertions in his parish, during the famine years, for the spiritual and temporal welfare of his flock were injurious to his health, and he died on 21st April, 1847. He wrote a Translation of Josephus' Holy War, which was published after his death.

1847. May 3. JOHN TRIPHOOK, A.B., R. V. Scull. [D.R.]

1847. July 9. A commission finds £218 dilapidations against

Trail's executors. In 1849, Feb. 17, the annual value of Skull is certified to be £637 10*s*. [D.R.]

1854. Sept. 3. A new church, on new site, is consecrated under the name of the Holy Trinity. [D.R.]

1857. June 16. £342 6*s*. 9*d*. is certified for improvements at Scull, the net yearly value being £574 6*s*. 7*d*. [D.R.]

1860. J. Triphook, Rector; Richard Hayes, Curate. The parish church is in good order. There is also a chapel of ease at Ballydehob. The glebe-house in order. 63 acres of glebe, of which one-half is in the Rector's use, the other is let. Divine service twice on all Sundays in both church and chapel, and once during summer, at 10 A.M., on Sundays, at Lesheeneen. Sacrament 12 times yearly at the church, average of communicants, 35; and also at the chapel, average 33. There are two Church Education schools, at one of which 69, and at the other 98, children are on the rolls. The Protestant population of one division of the parish is 515, of the other 735. The total Protestant population is 1,240. The rentcharge is £637 15*s*. per an., with residence.

John Triphook (whose father was born in London, and settled in Ireland circa 1788, and whose mother was Miss Trophina Vokes, of Limerick) was born on 10th Sept., 1796, and after graduating in Dublin University, was ordained Deacon on 19th May, 1822, for Castlehaven curacy, and Priest, on 13th April, 1823, both at Cork.

In 1825 he was Curate of Tullagh.

From 1829 to 1841 he was V. Ardfield; and from 1841 to 1847, he was V. Drinagh.

He married, firstly, in December 1824, Maria, dau. of Rev. Joseph Wright, V. Aghadowne, &c., and by her had issue two sons, Thomas-Dawson and Joseph-Robert; and one daughter, Jane-Anne. Mr. Triphook married, secondly, on 1st Dec., 1848, Jane-Ellesmere, dau. of John Noble, esq., of Lisnaskea, county Fermanagh.

Joseph-Robert Triphook, the second son of Rev. John Triphook, entered T.C.D. in 1848, and graduated A.B. in 1853. He was ordained Deacon, at Cork, on 18th Dec., 1853, for the curacy of Aughrim, in county Galway. He was transferred to the curacy of Nenagh in Oct. 1854; and in 1859 became Precentor of Killaloe, and Rector of Latteragh. He married, on 3rd August, 1854, his cousin, Elisabeth-Margaret-Sophia Triphook, and by her had issue, surviving, three sons, John-Crampton (born 18th May, 1856), Robert Dawson (born 24th April, 1859), and Victor-Albert (born 28th August, 1861); and three daughters, Annie-Elisabeth, Josephine-Jane, and Charlotte-Maria.

ST. ANNE, SHANDON.

"The church of St. Anne was begun to be built, upon the old foundation where St. Mary, Shandon, stood, anno 1722, and is to be made a distinct parish on the demise or removal of the present Incumbent. It was erected by a subscription, and is a very neat plain church. The steeple is of hewn stone, 120 feet high, with a handsome spire, fifty feet more, erected the last summer; also a musical ring of bells, chimes, and clock; which building being on an eminence, is a great ornament to the city. It was designed after the model of St. Mary's, in Limerick." [Smith's Cork, vol. i. p. 376.]

1772. ARTHUR HYDE, A.M., is admitted to the Rectory of St. Anne's, vacant by the death of Dr. George Tisdall, and on the presentation of Arthur Hyde, esq., of Castlehyde, the patron for this turn. [D.R.]

1772. The present parish register begins.

1785. May 26. Lord Muskerry sells his perpetual advowson or right of alternately presenting to St. Mary's, St. Anne's, and St. Paul's, for £600, to Richard Longfield, of Castlemary. [D.R.]

Arthur Hyde (son of George Hyde, who was son of Arthur Hyde, of Castlehyde, by his second wife, Mary, dau. of Colonel George Evans), was born in county Cork, and when sixteen years old entered T.C.D. as a Pensioner, on 28th September, 1744, and graduated A.B. in 1748.

He was ordained Deacon on 23rd June, and Priest on 9th July, 1751. On 24th June, 1751, he was licensed to the Curacy of Clonfert; and on 29th June, 1753, to that of Castlemartyr. From 1754 to 1793 he was R. Litter; from 1761 to 1769 R. Culdaff, Derry; from 1769 to 1787 R. V. Kilmoe; and from 1772 to 1805, when he died, R. V. Shandon.

He married, on 14th October, 1756, Anne, only dau. of Benjamin Green, esq., by Alicia, dau. of Arthur Bernard, esq., of Palace-Anne, county Cork. By her he had issue Rev. Arthur Hyde (Precentor of Ross from 1791 to 1815, q. v.); and five daughters, Alice, Ann (died 1760), Sophia, Mary-Elisabeth, and Ann (born 1766).

1805. April 22. WARHAM LEADER, A.B., R. St. Anne's, Shandon, on the presentation of William Leader, of Cork, esq., patron for this turn. [D.R.]

1813. John Symson, of Cork, leaves by his will, dated on 2nd March, £1,000 for the poor of St. Anne's. He died in 1816.

1817. June 3. Alderman John Forster died, leaving £50 to the poor of this parish. Mr. Rogerson also left £100.

Warham Leader (third son of William Leader, esq., of Cork, Barrister-at-Law, and of Mount Leader, county Cork, by his wife, Margaret, dau. of Warham St. Leger, esq., of Heyward's

Hill, county Cork), was ordained Deacon on 1st Sept., 1799, and Priest on 24th August, 1800, both at Cloyne. He was, from 1805 to his death on 26th October, 1818, Rector of St. Anne, Shandon.

He married, on 10th October, 1817, at Cove, Henrietta, youngest dau. of Robert Atkins, esq., of Firgrove, near Mallow, but had no issue. His relict, Henrietta, married Rev. Mathew Moore, Rector of Cahirconlish, Limerick.

Rev. Warham Leader was brother to the late NICHOLAS PHILPOT LEADER, esq., M.P. for Kilkenny; and was uncle to NICHOLAS PHILPOT LEADER, now M.P. for Cork county.

1818. Nov. 5. RICHARD LONGFIELD CONNER, A.B., R. St. Anne's, Shandon, on presentation of Colonel Richard Longfield, of Castlemary, patron for this turn. [D.R.]

1824. Oct. 26. The tithe composition of St. Anne, Shandon, as fixed for twenty-one years, is to be £260 3*s.* 9*d.* The average price of oats for seven years, ending 1st Nov., 1821, was 15*s.* per barrel. [D.R.]

1834. The Protestant population was 3,551.

In April, 1834, R. L. Conner, A.M., gets three years' licence for non-residence, which licence was renewed from time to time on the ground of ill-health. [D.R.]

1834. August 25. Thomas Johnson, shipbroker, sells, for £40, the site of a new chapel of ease, which was licensed for divine service on 30th June, 1837, and consecrated by the name of St. Luke on 21st October, 1837. [D.R.]

1837. St. Anne's, Shandon, a rectory, with cure, 3 miles long by 1½ broad, containing 2,777 acres. Gross population, 23,350. Two Curates employed, at an annual stipend to each of £75, British. Tithe composition, £240 3*s.* 3*d.* Minister's money, £325. Surplice fees, £73. Rents of houses, £52 12*s.* 4*d.* Subject to visitation fees, 6*s.* 8*d.*; diocesan schoolmaster, 16*s.* 7*d.* No glebe-house. Incumbent is non-resident, by permission, in consequence of ill-health; he resides near Innishannon, in the county of Cork. One church, capable of accommodating 700 persons, built more than a century, but at what cost unknown. No charge on the parish in 1832 on account of the church. Divine service is celebrated in the church twice on Sundays, and on every Wednesday and Friday. The sacrament is administered monthly, and on the great festivals. The benefice is a rectory. [Parl. Rep.]

1860. R. L. Conner, Rector; John Lee and W. M. Woolsey are the Curates. The church in order. No glebe or glebe-house. The Rector resides at Innishannon. Divine service twice on all Sundays, and once on the chief holidays, and on all Wednesdays and Fridays throughout the year. Sacrament twice a month; average of communicants, 52; also on the chief festivals; average 124. 30 boys are on the rolls of the *Green Coat* school; average attendance, 20. Another school, for girls, has 26 on roll, and an average attendance of 19. A third school, for infants, has 28 on roll, and an average attendance of 20. The Protestant population is about 1,100. There is also a chapel of ease in this parish called St. Luke's. Protestant population of this district is 1,846. The Rev. R. F. Clarke is Chaplain; and Rev. Justin M'Carthy is Assistant Chaplain. Divine service is celebrated in this chapel twice on all Sundays, and once on holidays, and on Thursday evenings. Sacrament twice a month; average of communicants, 75; and at Christmas and Easter, average, 140. There are 3 schools in St. Luke's district, at which there is an average attendance of 27 boys, 18 girls, and 60 infants. The rentcharge of St. Anne's is £180 2*s.* 6*d.* The minister's money, paid by the Ecclesiastical Commissioners, is £610 14*s.* 7*d.* The total income is £790 17*s.* 1*d.*, exclusive of surplice fees, &c.

R. L. Conner, grandson of Roger Conner, esq., of Connerville, by Ann, only sister of Viscount Longueville, was second son of William Conner, Lieut.-Col. Cork Militia, by Mary, dau. of Thomas Grant, esq., of Kilmurry; and was born in Youghal in 1785.

He was ordained Deacon at Cork on 6th Dec., 1807, and Priest, at Cloyne, on 8th October, 1809. He was for some time Curate of Clondulane, in Cloyne; and from 1818 to present time has held the R. St. Anne, Shandon.

He married, on 30th Sept., 1817, at St. Paul's, Cork, Frances-Gertrude, second dau. of William Honner, esq., of Round Hill, county Cork, and has issue, now surviving, seven children. His second son, Rev. Richard Mountiford Conner, born 7th July, 1823, after a distinguished undergraduate career, obtained a Fellowship in T.C.D. in 1851.

ST. FINBAR (VICARS CHORAL).

"In a MS., wrote by Robert Travers, register, anno 1628 (transcribed from an ancient roll), p. 10, are those words:—Concessio Richardi episcop. Corcagiensis, prebendariis ecclesiæ Cathedralis, Corke, ut propter exilitatem nullum habeant vicarium, sed presbiterum anualem qui parochianiis suis deserviat. Dat. Crast, annuntiat. B. M. 1278.—Note, according to Sir J. Ware, Robert MacDonogh was Bishop of Cork at this time; but his name was Richard, as appears from this MS. And in the same page is as follows:—Concessio Magistri hospitalis de morn ejusdem tenoris prebend de Moyallo. Dat. die ascentionis Beat. Virginis, anno 1298.—In the same MS. p. 10 :—De proprietatibus Vicariorum ecclesiæ Cathedralis. Concessio iisdem Vicariis facta per Walterum episcopum, Philip decanum, et capitulum Corcagiæ, 204 pedum terræ in longitudine jacent. inter ecclesiam predictam ex parte orientali, et curiam episcopi ex parte occidentali, in latitud. 200 pedum, inter viam regiam ex parte Australi, et viam quæ ducit ad curiam predict, ex parte Aquilon. Dat. Crastino purificationis anno 1328. Appropriatio Vicariæ de Corbally per Johanem episcop., Geraldinum decanum, et Capitulum Corcagi. iisdem Vicariis facta. Dat. 5 Novembris, 1348. Quæ appropriatio predict. confirmata fuit per Edwardum regem anno regni sui 22° per suas litteras patentes. Teste Walter de Bermingham justic. Hiberniæ. Collatio iisdem fact. per Milonem episcop. Corcagiens. eccles. parochialis de Desertserges, 3° Junii, 1431. Concessio ecclesiæ Beat. Mariæ de Narde iisdem Vicariis facta per Jordanum episcop. Corcagiensis. Dat. 3° Septemb., 1441. Concessio ecclesiæ Kilroan iisdem, per eundem episcop. anno 1447. Donatio ecclesiæ parochialis de Drynagh et particulæ de Drumlag. in parochia de Desertserges, facta iisdem Vicariis, per Robertum Coggan, anno 1437, et confirmat. per eundem episcop. anno 1456. Donatio iisdem Vicariis facta per Edmund Riddefort, rectoriæ Fanlobbis et Kineagh, confirmata per Jordanum episcopum Corcag. et Cloniensis an. 1477. Legatio iisdem Vicar. per Will. Nogle terrarum nuncupatar. Clasdow, *alias* Clasduff, Boirnecarty, Ynerynybrenig, &c. There were anciently only two Vicars Choral in this cathedral, as appears from an inquisition taken anno 1370, and the same is observed in the instrument relating to Cahirlag, p. 25 of the same MS." [Smith's Cork, vol. 1, p. 64, &c.]

1591. The four Vicars Choral are PHILIP GOLD (Archdeacon of Cork, q. v.; he died 1612); EDMUND CORBALLY, JOHN MARTELL (died 1610); and RICHARD SKIDDY. [MS. T.C.D. E. 3. 14.] For Martell, *vide* Chancellors of Cork. Corbally was R. Dunderrow, q. v. Skiddy was P. Inskenny, q. v.

1610. Feb. 20. JOHN BROCK (per mortem John Martell) is admitted Fourth Vicar Choral. Installed 23rd February, 1610. [R.V. 1634.] In 1615 he was Treasurer of Cork, q. v.

1615. Ecclesia Cathedralis in bene statu, bene reparata, ornata libris et omnibus necessariis. In this year three of the Vicars are Dignitaries, viz., Dean GEORGE LEE; the Archdeacon MICHAEL BOYLE; and the Treasurer, JOHN BROCK. "Quartus vicarius choralis ecclesiæ est THOMAS LLOYD, A.M., minister et predicator, (val. 12 li.) Capellanus Domini Presidentis. Tenet etiam vicariam de ffiddowne in Diocesi Ossoriensi Valor. viginti octo Librarum." The value of each Vicar Choralship is 12 li. [R.V. R.I.A.]

Boyle was Archdeacon of Cork and Cloyne, Dean of Lismore,

&c. He became Bishop of Waterford in 1619, but held this Vicarage Choral until his death, in 1635.

1615. "Killonay spect. ad Vicarios Chorales Ecclie Corcagiensis. Nulla Ecclia. Cancella ruinata; sed Decanus et vic. chorales admoniti providere curatum et cancellam repāre; et Episcopus admonetur convenire parochianos ad repāndum Ecclíam." [R.V. R.I.A.]

1617. "The seconde daie of Aprill, 1617, William, by God's providence, Bishop of Cork, Cloine, and Rosse. To the inhabitants of Gill abbey, and of and upon the abbeys of St. Augustine and St. Dominicke, the waste churches and chappells of St. John the Baptist, St. Nicholas, St. Stephen, St. Bridgit, and of and upon the lands and within the p'cints of the saide abbeys, churches, chappells, and of, upon, and within everie of the same without the south gate of the cittie of Corke, and to everie of the said inhabitants greeting in our Lord God everlasting. Knowe ye that I have (by my ordinary power soe far ffoorth as the lawes and statutes of the land will suffer and p'mitt) ordained and appointed, and by these p'sents doe ordaine and appointe the vicars choralls of the cathedrall church of St. ffinbarry bye Cork aforesaide, vicars of the p'rishe churches of the same nowe being, and their successors, of the said inhabitants and of evrie of them, to have the charge and cure of soules, being places adjacent and p'sons, and the nexte dwellers neare to the said p'rishe church of St. ffinbarries aforesaid, and no other p'per and peculiar p'rishe church or churches, other than of the abbeys and dissolved religious houses belonginge to the same. Willing and requiring by these p'ntes the said inhabitants to resorte from tyme to tyme, and at all tymes hereafter upon Sundaies and holidaies appointed in the church of England and Irelande to the said p'rishe church of St. ffinbarries; and to pay to the viccars, p'rish clerke and sexton of the same, and to noe other, such ryghts and duties, as for weddings xxtnings and burialls, and other such spirituall and ecclesiasticall services, are or shalbe due and payable. In witness whereof I have to these p'ntes set my hand and episcopall seale. Given at Bishop's courte the daie and yeare above written. "William Corke, Cloine, Ross."

1626. Rev. Richard Owen, P. Kilnaglory, gave £20 to the Cathedral Library.

1628. Oct. 28. EDWARD JOHNS was admitted a Vicar Choral, and installed 12th Nov., 1628. [R.V. 1634.] He was still a Vicar Choral in 1641. [MS. T.C.D. F. 2. 16.]

Johns was, in 1640, R. Aglishdrinagh, Cloyne, q. v.

1631. Feb. 25. JOHN BYNNS, A.M., is admitted Vicar Choral, and installed 27th Feb. 1631. [R.V. 1634.] He was, in 1640, Treasurer of Cloyne, q. v.

1634. Edward Johns, John Brock, Michael Boyle, and John Binns, appear as Vic. Chor. [R.V. 1634.]

1634/5. Feb. 10. NICHOLAS HALL is admitted a Vicar Choral. [F.F.] He was also Archdeacon of Ross, q. v.

1635. April 9. ROBERT CRUBS was admitted a Vicar Choral. [F.F.] He became, in 1637, Rector of Marmullane, q. v.

1639. NICHOLAS HALL (*vide* supra), EDWARD JOHNS (*vide* supra), THOMAS BENNETT (Rector of Marmullane, 1636 to 1637), and ROBERT BAYLEY (who is also Curate of St. Peter's), are the Vicars Choral. [V.B. 1639.]

1641. April 27. RICHARD BENNETT was admitted a Vicar Choral. [F.F.] He was also Vicar of the Little Island in 1639. He took a degree in T.C.D. in 1641.

In 1641 the Vicars depose to loss of church-rents, to amount, per annum, of £90 10*s*., during the rebellion. MS. T.C.D. F. 2. 10.]

1651. Mr. Richard French left £1 per an. to poor of St. Finbarry.

1661. SAMUEL BONNER has the four places. [V.B. D.R.] In 1662 he became P. St. Michael's, q. v. He died in 1666 or 1667.

1666 to 1668. The four places are vacant. [D.R. V.B.]

1669. JOHN HARRISON (V. Kilcaskin, Ross); JOHN BAYLY (P. St. Michael's); WILLIAM LOVE (organist in 1685); and JOHN WEBB (P. Inskenny, and Chancellor of Cloyne), are the Vicars Choral. [V.B. 1669.]

Harrison appears 1669 to 1682, and Bayly 1669 to 1672. [V.B. D.R.]

In 1670 only Harrison and Bayly appear: "alii vacant." [V.B. D.R.]

1672. On a salver, weighing 26 oz. 19 dwts., is this inscription, "Deo sacratum Eccles. et Cathedral. St. Finbarry's, Corcag. 1672. Hic est Panis qui de cœlo descendit Qui manducat hunc panem vivet in æternum."

1674. JOHN TINDALL (he appears 1674 to 1686), WILLIAM SCROGGS (R. Kilnemartery, Cloyne, q. v.), who appears as Vic. Chor. Cork, 1674 to 1680, MATHEW ROMIER, and JOHN HARRISON are the Vicars Choral. [V.B. 1674. D.R.] In 1677 Romier's place is marked vacant. [V.B. D.R.]

1675. August 31. A visitation book of this date has the following notice of the tower of St. Finbarry's:—"Epus admonuit Decanum et Cap. ad tegend, et vitecis (sic) claudend. turrim." &c. [V.B.]

1679. THOMAS DENT appears as a Vicar Choral. [V.B. D.R.] In 1680 he was licensed to the cure of Ballinaboy. In 1682 he became P. Kilnaglory, q. v.

1680. JOHN GRIFFITH appears as a Vicar Choral. [V.B. D.R.] In 1684 he appears as R. V. Kilsillagh, in Ross. In 1685 he became a Minor Canon and Vicar Choral of St. Patrick's, Dublin. He appears as Vic. Chor. Cork, 1680 to 1685. [V.B.] On 4th Dec. 1685, he was suspended at the visitation. [Addenda to V.B. 1685.]

1681. EDWARD HINDE (*vice* Scroggs ?), appears as Vicar Choral. [V.B.]

1682. RICHARD GOODMAN (*vice* Hinde), appears as a Vicar Choral from 1682 to 1691. [V.B.] In 1718 he became P. Desertmore, q. v.

An assault committed on the person of this clergyman gave occupation to the Ecclesiastical Court of Cork about this time. The following is a specimen of the entries relative to the case :

"Negotium injectiōis manuum violentarum in Richum Goodman, Vic. Chor. : per Robtum Rogers, Alderman. Corcag. Civit." [Court Book of 1683. D.R.]

1683 to 1691. THOMAS GOODMAN (*vice* Harrison), appears as Vicar Choral. [V.B.] In 1719 he was R. Templetrine, q. v.

1683. Mr. William Smart left £8 per an., and his widow £4 per an. to the poor of St. Finbarry.

In 1684, the Goodmans are admonished to discharge their duties as Vicars Choral, and to attend on every Sunday and holiday in the cathedral. Richard is called to answer articles for having celebrated a marriage without banns or licence, and both Richard and Thomas are desired not to preach without licence. [Addenda to V.B. 1684.]

The following documents, extracted from the Visitation Books of 1684 and 1685, attest the zeal of Bishop Edward Synge to maintain the daily choral service in the cathedral, which seems to have been grossly neglected by the officials in ancient and modern times :—

"November 20, 1684. Acta habita, &c.——Quo die : Quoad obsequia et quotidiana ministeria vicariorum Choralium organistæ et ceterorum membrorum Chori ecclīæ Cathed. St. finbarry Corcagiensis, Dnus Epūs ordināciones et decreta sua subscripta sermone Anglicano perspicue intelligenda, servanda, observanda, apparenda et ab ipsis respective perimplenda et obtemperanda registrari et insinuari mandavit, quorum tenor sequitur et est talis. Whereas, both by the general complaint of people, and by our owne observacion it appeareth to us, that the publiq service of God is grossly neglected by the Vicars Chorall of the Cathedral Church of St. ffinbaries, Corke, and through their example (or as wee have reason to beelieve through the advice and approvement of some of them) by the organist, and others of the quire, contrary to orders made and provided in our primary visitacion, in the year 1679, as allsoe to other orders of the same import in ye visitacion of the yeare 1680, both given under our hand and seale. Wee, therefore, for the effectual reformacion thereof, doe order, decree, and injoyne as followeth :—ffirst, that all the fower Vicars Chorall, the organist, and all members of the quire, doe from this day forward attend every Lord's Day att the canonicall hours, morning and evening, all (saving the organist) in their surplices, and from and after the first Sunday in Advent next ensuing, dayly, and every day in the weeke, att the same canonicall hours, morning and evening, and in the same habitt then and there to perform the service of the church, in the best melodies that they can, according to cathedrall use. Secondly, that they all take care to behave themselves with such seriousnesse, gravity, and devotion in all parts of their office, as becomes the worship of God, especially that they avoyde laughing, talking, and even needelesse whispering to one another in service time, as allsoe all indecent postures and gestures of body. Thirdly, that if any of the Vicars Chorall and other members of the quire being present att service shall willfully forbear to sing, chant, or answer in their course, such their willfull silence shall bee interpreted and punished as totall absence for that weeke. Provided neverthelese that if the Deane of the said cathedrall shall perceive or knowe any of the Vicars Chorall to bee diligent in their studyes, and improveing themselves in theologicall learning, it shall and may be free for him att his pleasure to dispense with the absence of such two of them upon ordinary days of the weeke, or upon any p'ticular incident occasion, as he sees fitt, yet soe that there bee always two of the said Vicarrs morning and evening ever in constant attendance. And in case one of the said two, whose course of attendance it is, should bee through sickness or business enforced to bee absent, he shall provide some other of his brethren to attend in his roome. All these orders and injunctions wee decree and require to bee observed by the said Vicars Chorall, organist, and other quire men, as they will answeare the neglect of God's service, and bringing it into contempt with the people, before God's Tribunall att the last day; and in the meane while before us att our next visitation sub pœna juris et contemptus, and before the Deane ordinarily under such mulcts, fines or punishments as have beene usuall or are canonicall in this case.

"Given under our hand and seale mannuall this 20th day of November, pendente visitacione Chori, Anno Dni. 1684.—E. Corke (seal) Rosse."

A dispute having arisen among the Vicars Choral concerning the payment of the organist, the following decree is pronounced by the Bishop on 25th November, 1684:—

"Whereas upon full hearing what the Vicars Choral have to say in defence of their owne claims, and after several admonitions that if they had any further evidences to justify their claims they should produce them, as likewise upon due examination of all such records, old visitation books, and all other papers relating hereto, which have come to my hands, there appears no evidence or color of evidence that the small tithes of St. ffinbarries did of old belong to the Vicars Chorall of said church, but rather that they were (as is alleadged by the Reverend Dr. Arthur Pomeroy, Deane of the said church), cast in amongst other things by the said Deane and Chapter for the encouragement of the said Vicars, and towards the mainteining of an organist. And whereas we have seene an order or determination made by the most Rev. Father in God, Thomas, Lord Archbishop of Cashell, in his triennial visitation, Ano. Dni. 1676, that the Vicars Chorall injoying such means as therein specified, and p'ticularly the small tithes of St. finbarie's not reserved to the œconomy, the organist of the said church should enjoy the full benefitt, that is, as wee conceive, his share or full dividend of the said means, wee do therefore order and require that the Vicars Chorall observe the said determinacion of ye most Rev. the Archbishop of Cashell, and that they forthwith pay unto ye p'sent organist such arrears of salary as are to him due, and for the future, at ye usuall times of paiment, do from time to time pay him his share or part as it becomes due, and that they certifie their obedience to this our order, under the hand of the said organist, by Christmas Day next ensuing, under the pain of sequestracion of all their benefices till such time as the said organist shall be satisfied and paid such arrears as are, by the adjustment of the said Deane, now due to him." [Addenda to V.B. 1684.]

"The addresse of the Bishop and Clergy of Cork and Rosse to King James ye Second.

"To the King's Most Excellent Majestie.

"The most humble address of the Bishop and Clergy of the Diocesses of Corke and Ross, in Ireland."

"Though wee have already, most of us, in the addresse made by the body of our countye, and by severall corporacions therein, given such demonstracions of our zeale towarde your sacred Majestie, as wee have had opportunity for, as well by word as by example, according to our bounden Duty exciting and animating our neighbours to the vowes and practice of all faith and Allegiance, yett considering the clergy of these three nations can never pay sufficient Thankes and duty to your Majestie for your most graciouse promise to protect and maintain our Religion as by law established,—Wee most humbly crave leave, afresh and apart by ourselves, to present our vowes to God and your Majestie, that as our lives are not deare to us in comparison of our Religion and Loyaltye, soe wee will not fayle, though with the perill of our lives (God being our helper), according to our uttmost power by the strictist tyes of our Religion (which abhorrs all Resistance or unfaithfulness to Princes), to secure to your Majestie both our owne and our people's Loyaltie and obedience, and wee will incessantly importune the Throne of Grace to preserve your Majestie's sacred person from all violence, treachery, or any evill accidents, till it please Him by whom Kings reign, that in a good old age you exchange your crowne. Dated at Corke, Mar. 16, 1684/5.

Deane of Corke. E. Corke, Rosse.
Chanter, &c. D. of Rosse."

[Second Book of Cork Registry, fol. 55.]

"1685. Dec. 4. William Love, the organist, is ordered to attend dayly. Love is satisfied to resign if he be paid what is due to him."

"1685. Dec. 15. In Chapter-house—at visitation of Dean, and Chapter, and Quire—present only Walter Neale, Thesaur., Row. Davies, P. Lisclery, and Henry Ryder, P. Holy Trinity. The Bishop decreed as follows:—

"'Whereas the service of God is not a little slighted and neglected by the common sort of people, as may be conseived by reason of the very seldom attendance of them, whom in duty it concerns to attend itt, to the very great scandall of our Church and itts Constitution amongsts its adversaries. ffor the more effectuall Redress hereof as farr as in us lies, wee order, decree, and enjoyne as followeth:—

"'1. That all Dignitaries and Prebendaries, when they come to preach their Turns in Course, doe, from and after the ffeast of ye Nativity of our Lord next ensueing, reside and attend att and during divine service in their Surplices and habitts belonging to their degrees, att the least three days of the weeke into which their course falls, att morning and evening prayer in the Quire of Saint ffinbarrie's. And that for this purpose those of them who have manse houses, provide and reserve to themselves Lodgeings in their manshouses.

"'2. That the orders and Rules of the attendance of the Vicars and members of the Quire affixt up in the vestry being now by reason of Interlinacons very *untertaynd* be writt over again fairly, and made in all things to agree with the orders deliver'd to the Quire in my Visitacion of the year 1684, and Reinforced this p'sent Visitacion.

"'3. That the Organist attend ordinarily att morning and evening prayers every day from and after the ffeast of St. Thomas the Apostle next ensueing, then and there to discharge his duty for the more regular p'forming the chorall service and improveing of the Quire.

"'4. That the Virger alsoe attend, as the Organist is before required, ordinarily every day for the keeping better order in the Church.

"'All these orders Wee decree and Enjoyne to be observed respectively by those whom they concern, under paine of admonicion for the ffirst, and suspension for the second offence.

Given under my hand and Episcopall Seale this fifteenth day of December, Ao. Di. 1685.'" [Addenda to V.B. of 1685.]

1686 to 1695. ALEXANDER OGLEBY (*vice* Griffith) appears as Vicar Choral. [V.B.] He was not admitted until 23rd January, 1694. His appointment was by the Dean, and the Bishop disputed it. In 1693 he became P. C. Ballinaboy, q. v. He was suspended from his Vicar Choralship on 11th January, 1694. [Addenda to V.B. 1694.]

1686. Thomas Goodman seems to have resisted the efforts of the Bishop to improve the choral service, as all the Vicars Choral, *but especially Thomas Goodman*, and the choristers, are again admonished to attend the daily choral service,—" constanter et quotidie attendere choro Cathedralis et in ibi cantare." Goodman's absence from the holy communion is also censured. [Addenda V.B. 1686.]

1687. WILLIAM DENNY (*vice* Tyndall) appears as a Vicar Choral. [V.B.] In 1688 he became V. Whitechurch, Cloyne, q. v.

1688. " The Bishop admonisht the Vicars Choral to attend the dayly service of the church at the usual times," &c. "Item, Mr. William Denny, a Prebendal Vicar Choral of ye Cathedral Church of St. Finbarry's, Cork, being duely cited to appear and undergoe this visitation, Mr. Denny's Vicar's place (is decreed) vacant." [Addenda V.B. 1688.]

1688 to 1693. ANDREW SYMMES (*vice* Denny) appears as a Vicar Choral. [V.B.] In 1718 he became Precentor of Ross, q. v.

" Declaratio recognito et Protestatio Dni Edwi. Corcagen. et Rossen. Epi circa acta and gesta Arthuri Pomeroy, Decani Cork:—

"' Whereas, I, Edward, Lord Bp. of Cork and Rosse, was yesterevening, in ye face of ye congregation in ye church of St. ffinbarry, near Cork, besides other abuses and oppositions given me, contrary to all canons, law, and good order, charged with injustice and wrong, with having p'varicated in my opinions and practices, with disobedience of divers of his Majesty's proclamations and commands, and haply with several like enormities which I could not take notice of or doe not remember, for ye clearing thereof of my selfe from all these injust imputations, although my innocency is sufficiently known to all my brethren of ye chapter who are in or about ye citty, all who, except my accuser, are ready to attest it, yet to ye end noe scruple may sticke with ye people in whose hearing I was accused, or anywise blast my ministry towards them or others, I have thought fitt publickly to declare:—In generall, yt blessed be God, in whose feare I speake it, I have, through his grace, lived in ye faithful discharge of my duty with all good conscience, and setting aside my infirmityes, am free from these or any other like vile offences. I never, yt I doe remember, willingly and deliberately invaded ye right of any p'son in my life; and where, through passion or ignorance, I have done any verbal wrong or otherwise injured any, I still made as suddaine and as ample a satisfacion as I could; nor doth (I thanke God) my conscience at p'sent accuse me of allowing my selfe either in doing wrong, or in ye practice of any knowne sin, or neglect of any knowne Christian duty. And in particular as to yt act of mine wherein I was charged with wrong and injustice, I do avow it was just and good my right and duty to doe, namely, to finish my visitacion, which because ye principall day for it fell on ye Lord's Day, a time unfitt for any businesse (if it may be deferred) but devotion, I adjourned till munday, and ye one of ye principall p'sons whose assistance wee needed to redress some things amiss willfully absenting himself, I was forced to adjourne it ye seconde time, hoping I might obtaine ye said p'sons p'sence, which by law and his canonicall oath he was bound unto, which I say I was in going about, was both my right and duty, as all clergymen, who will not be willfully blinde, doe plainly see and acknowledge; nor did I intend any violence or rigour, but all candor and brotherly love in my proceedings, as my brethren, to whom I communicated my intentions beforehand, knew and know. As to ye charge of prevaricating in my opinions and practices, I confess I know not well what that means; but not to indulge ye temptation of reflecting upon any other, I answer as to ye matters I suspect designed by ye accuser, namely, ye strict pressing all parts of ye churche liturgie as at p'sent it stands. I have conferred with ye most learned men I could meet with, I have read, studied, and prayed, I have determined nothing rashly, I have been candid in declaring my judgement before my subscription and since, both in private and publick. My opinion, as to such points as I suspect meant, was in print, and dedicated to your two primates, yt now are of England and Ireland, before I was made a Bishop; it hath been publisht again on another occasion since; what is enjoined by our church I have proved to be lawful, what I conceived more excellent I frankly declared; in ye mean time I never practiced contrary, either to what by ye law, Ecclicall, antient, and moderne, I might doe, or to what in conscience I approved, though for peace sake and obedience, which I wish all may affect as much as I doe, I have denied myselfe some satisfaction; and as to ye expedience of some things, I have sacrificed my private sentiments to such constitucions as I have been informed by some of ye principall Authors ye necessity of times would p'mitt, though I have now lived to see those very reasons, which were other mens as well as mine, generally p'vail amongst ye most learned in ye English church, and this I need not be ashamed nowe to owne; but in all this, I say, noe man reasonably can affirme there is any thing of p'varicacion.'

"As to ye last point I can recollect charged upon me, of disobeying his Majesties proclamation, though they may be taxed thereof who make illegall assemblies of persons incapacited for such purposes as they called them to, yet I, in visiting legally ye clergy, can be noe more supposed to act agt those proclamacions yn ye civill magistrates by calling people to courts of justice or civill governt, or ye parochiall ministers for assembling ye people togeather to ye worship of God, to both which Episcopall visitacions have a singular conducency. Having now shewne how unjuste this charge was, I might expose it alsoe as most irregular, and proceed immediately to censure; but instead thereof I onely add, yt as to all p'sonall affronts and injuries done me in ye whole action, I, from my heart, intirely forgive, and humbly beg God, through Jesus Christ, through whom alone I hope for mercy, to forgive ye author of them all; and as to ye wrong done to ye order in which God hath been pleased to place me, and to ye Episcopall power and jurisdiction, I deferre ye righting of that to more favourable, I mean more peaceable times, which God hasten, when I believe a nationall Synod, if any such sitt in our age will noe more approve . . . . [The rest of this line is *torn.*] a diocesan Synod can be now had doth; and in ye meantime I further declare myselfe to be in p'fect charity with all and every of my breathren, my accuser not excepted, and in a word, with all ye world; and I give notice yt as being soe I intend ye next Lord's Day, in ye next p'rish church where ye Lord's Supper, according to our use, is celebrated, if I can gett thither, if not, in my own chappell, to receive ye wholy cōmunion, where I envite any peaceable, well-disposed Christians to meet me, and soe conclude with pt of ye Angell's hyme, not in ye words of a certaine bad translation, peace be to men of good will, but peace on earth, peace be to all men, peace be to men yt have good will, and as to those who doe not, God give ym a good will yt they may have peace, goodwill to mankinde.

"Lecta, recognita et probata fuit haec declarāo recognitio et protestatio a nobis in Ecclīa Cathedrali St. ffinbarry corcag. die Jovis octavo scilicet die mensis Nov. Ano Dni. 1689.—Edrds. Corcagiensis et Rossensis." [D.R.]

1692 to 1696. Valentine French (*vice* one of the Goodmans) appears as Vicar Choral. [V.B.] He was not admitted until 29th Dec. 1694. [D.R.] His appointment was probably in dispute between the Dean and Bishop. In 1692 there were but three Vicars, Ogleby, French, and Symes.

French became, in 1717, Dean of Ross, q. v.

1694 to 1697. John Dewey (*vice* Symes), appears as Vicar Choral. [V.B. D.R.] At the visitation of 1694 Dewey was ordered to take out a proper licence within a month, on pain of suspension. [Addenda to V.B. 1694.] And, accordingly, he was formally admitted on 11th January, 1694/5. [D.R.] Dewey became, in 1696, R. Ardnegihy, q. v.

In 1694 and 1695 there are but three Vicars, Ogleby, French, and Dewey. In 1696 only two (French and Dewey), appear. [V.B. D.R.]

1695. April 25. The Bishop causes the following memorandum to be inserted in the registry:—"His Grace of Cashel claymes *the right* of visiting the first year of his accession, but waives it (out of favour to the clergy, and by reason of the late calamities, and because they were so lately visited by his predecessor), until the three years should be compleate." [D.R.]

1698. BENJAMIN WALL, JOHN VYSE, and EDMUND MOLLOY, are the Vicars Choral, the fourth vicarage being vacant. [V.B.] Of Wall there is no further mention, except that in 1697 his name is to a marriage bond, as Benjamin Wall, of St. Finbarry's, Clerk. Vyse was admitted on 2nd August, 1699, [F.F.] and in February of 1699/700 became V. Kilmoe and Scull, vacating his Vicarage Choral. Molloy was admitted on 6th Sept. 1698 [F.F.] per mortem John Dewey, and continued a Vicar Choral until his death in 1735. [V.B.] Molloy was for many years P. C. Ballinaboy.

"Abstract of the decision of William, Archbishop of Cashel, touching the right of presenting to the Vicarages Choral, now disputed by Dean Pomeroy against the Bishop of Cork. The Bishop of Cork's claim is, that some of his predecessors founded and endowed the College of Vicars Choral out of episcopal lands.

"This foundation is proved by the Vicar's hall and houses (the ruins still to be seen) and lands called Vicar's lands or acres, all, both houses and lands, being encompassed by the Bishop's land.

"Also, by a grant of certain proffitts to Vicars Choral, made by Dominick, Bishop of Cork, 1554. This original grant now to be seen and read by me (*i.e.*, by the Archbishop.)

"The Archbishop of Cashel refers to Sir James Ware De Præsulibus Hiberniæ, p. 168, who says of Walter le Rede (translated from Cork to Cashel, 1330) 'Cum adhuc Epūs esset Corcag. Vicariis ibm habitaconem comodam assiguavit.' He refers also to the same author, *de Archiepis Casil et Tuam*, published 1626. Ware, noted in margin, says he had this Ex Archivis Corcag. ecclisæ. The Bishop also quoted R. V. 1634, out of Prerogative Office, by which it appeared that Brock, Johns, and Binns, were admitted and instituted by the Bishop, with mandate to ye Dean to install. The Bishop also urged that Michael Boyle, the first Bishop after the Restoration, exercised his right without contest; and that Dean Roger Boyle, afterwards Bishop of Clogher, acted merely as his commissary in appointing to the Vicarages Choral.

"Dean Pomeroy alleges per contra that, since his being Dean, he has collated to the Vicarages Choral, and by his own right appointed William Scroggs, Mathias Kenion, John Tindal, Edward Hine, Thomas Dent, Thomas Goodman, Alexander Ogilby, William Denny, and John Dewey; but the Bishop contested these appointments, and several of these persons took out fresh titles from the Bishop.

"Dean P. also alleges that the Dean is Ordinary of the Cathedral, and therefore collates; but the Archbishop of Cashel says he might also on those grounds claim to appoint the Prebendaries.

"Dean Pomeroy also alleges that Dean Fitzgerald (father to the present Bishop of Clonfert), before ye warrs, upon a contest, carried the disposal of the Vicarages Choral from the Bishop of Cork; but the Archbishop says that he spoke to the Bishop of Clonfert, who recollects nothing about it; and that even if it were true that the then Bishop, by reason of infirmities, or that Bishop Synge (when the gout had rendered him incapable of government) permitted the Dean to do as he pleased, yet that this could weigh little against prescription and long possession.

"On the whole, the Archbishop of Cashel decides that the Bishops of Cork, as *founders*, &c., have the right of collation. March 26, 1698." [D.R.]

1699. HENRY GOUGH and THOMAS DERHAM, besides VYSE and MOLLOY, are the Vicars. [V.B.] Gough appears 1699 to 1711. He became afterwards P. Templebryan, Ross, q. v. Derham was admitted 1699, July 22, and continued a Vicar Choral until his death in 1705. [D.R.] He held Creagh, in Ross, and Killeagh, in Cloyne, along with this Vicarage Choral, for many years, and died P. Kilnaglory, q. v.

"1700. The parish of St. Barry's contains sixteen plowlands. All the tythes of corn of the sixteen plowlands in this parish belong to the œconomy of St. Barry's. All the rest of the tithes of these sixteen plowlands belongs to the Vicars Choral of St. Barry's. The Dean and Chapter receive the œconomy part, and are supposed to be the Incumbents. No church belongs to this parish, except the Cathedral of St. Barry's. No glebe belongs to this parish, only the manses, belonging to the Dean, Dignitarys, and Prebendarys, which are reckon'd part of this parish. The Prebendarys' and Dignitarys' gardens pay the small tythes to the Vicars, but the Dean's garden does not pay tithe. Bishopscourt, and the marshes belonging to the Bishop, are reckon'd as part of this parish. No tythe is paid out of Bishopscourt, nor out of the nearest marsh; but the other marshes, even while they were in the Bishop's occupation, in Bishop Michael Boyle's time, paid tythe. This parish extends to the western stone bridge, and so runs by the west end of the stone fort, up to the sign of the mitre; from thence to

Gallow's Green and the spittle lands, and to Killindrindownagh lands, belonging to St. Dominick's Abby. Here some small fields, and a small street, which are in this parish, are not in the mannor of St. Barry's, but in the city. All the rest of this parish, together with severall other lands in several other parishes, belongs to the mannor of St. Barry's. The tyth belonging to the œconomy in this parish is worth about £40 per an. The tyth belonging to the Vicars Choral in this parish is worth about £30 per an. There was one mass-house in this parish—'tis now ruinous. No meeting-house in this parish. In St. Barry's parish 'tis thought there are two Papists for one Protestant. There are not above four or five families of Dissenting Protestants in this and the united parishes. The parishes of St. John, Rinmahon, St. Stephen's, St. Nicholas, and St. Mary de Narde (where the King's stone fort stands) have been united time out of mind to this parish. Six shillings and eight pence was paid heretofore to the Bishop of Corke out of the spittle lands of St. Stephen's. Bishop Synge received it from John Fournacres, paiable on Easter Munday. When Bishop Michael Boyle was here he liv'd in the city; the Bishop and Mayor used to go to St. Barry's Church together, but when they came to the middle of the eastern stone bridge, the Bishop took the right hand of the Mayor, and the sword and other ensigns were left in Alderman Field's house, at the foot of the bridge, till they returned from church. Captain Hayes saies he has seen this twenty times done. St. Dominick's Abby, Red Abby, or St. Augustine's Abby, and Gill Abby, are in the south suburbs of Corke's, and within the union of St. Barry's. The inhabitants come to St. Barry's Church, but they pay no tithes, neither out of the sites of the Abby, nor out of the lands belonging to them. The lands of the parish of St. Barry belong chiefly to the Bishop of Cork, the Earl of Cork, Dean Davys, Ignatius Gold (lately forfeited to the King), Captain Travers, Mr. Pigott, Alderman Charters, and Mr. Webber. Mr. Piggot, Alderman Chartres, Lieutenant Parker, and Collector Trench, live in this parish. Mr. Synge, &c., in the verge of the cathedral. There is a particular constable for the verge, chosen at the Court Leet of the Manor; there are two other constables in the mannor, chosen at the Quarter Sessions in the city. There is an alms-house in this union in St. Nicholas parish, near Southgate: a house, but no maintenance. Colman Sarsfield is Popish Priest of this and the united parishes. He has been here about four or five years. He has a mass-house near Red Abby. He was bred at Bordeaux, in France, in the Irish seminary, which is a small college, governed by a superior and prefect, subject to the visitation of the Archbishop of Bordeaux. The French King allows £200 per an. for the support of the college, wherein are maintained about twenty-four young Irish scholars, clergymen, or designed for clergymen. They are generally poor, and the college receives generally £200 per an. (besides the King's allowance) from private benefactors. These scholars usually go to the Jesuit's College to be instructed in philosophy and divinity. Sarsfield, the Priest of this parish, saies mass twice every Sunday morning, and the rest of the Priests in Ireland, by order from the Pope, have the privilege of saying two masses in one day, by reason of the great extent of most parishes or unions. There are no churchwardens in any of the united parishes of St. Nicholas, &c. The churchwardens of St. Barry's serve for all the united parishes, and have done so time out of mind." [Downes' Tour.]

1700. Nov. 16. LEWIS LACROIX (per cess. of John Vyse) is admitted Vicar Choral. [D.R.] In 1724 he resigned, and became P. Killanully, q. v.

"1702. One Smart, by his will, left £8 per an., and his wife left by her will £4 per an. to the English poor of the parish of St. Barry's, to be disposed of by the Dean and churchwardens; this £12 for ever yearly is to be paid out of lands in the barony of Fermoy. One Gylbert left 20*s*. yearly to the poor of St. Barry's; 'tis payable by old Captain Hayes." [Downes' Tour.]

1704. July 9. William Supple recants in the cathedral. [D.R.]

"1704. St. Dominick's Abby, in the south suburbs of Corke, belong'd to the Dominicans. Half a plowland, call'd Killinrindowny, and the lands and houses, and mills near the Abby, belong'd to this Abby. One Gold had the propriety of this Abby formerly; now it is the estate of Captain Cross. This Abby is supposed to be in St. Barry's parish." [Downes' Tour.]

"Patribus Dominicanis in Suburbio Corkagiensi circa an. 1229 cœnobium construxit Philip Barry, a quo originem trahit comes de Barrimore." [Bruodini propugnaculum Cathol. veritatis.]

"1704. Gill Abby, in the south suburbs of Corke, belonged to the Canons regular of the Order of St. Augustin. It was formerly called Monasterium de antro St. Finbarri. Gilla Æda O'Mugin, Abbot of this Abby, was Bishop of Corke about 1172. The half plowland of Gill Abby, and the half plowland of Ballygaggen, belong to this Abby. The Earl of Corke's marshes are part of the half plowland of Gill Abby. This Abby, with the lands belonging to it, are the estate of the Earl of Corke. This Abby is said to be in St. Barry's parish. The 25th of September, yearly, is observed as a festival in the diocese of Corke, as dedicated to St. Finbarry."

"1706. April 3. William Walsh, als Bury, *not much to be credited*, living in Bandon-street, in St. Barry's, saies that he is 81 years old; that he heretofore received the Bishop's rent for Bishop Boyle and Bishop Synge. He received £7 per annum cheifry out of Tuogh Canaway, in the barony of Muskerry, from the Longs, who were proprietors of the estates both all Boyle's time and all Synge's time. He received £7 per annum cheifry out of the twelve plowlands of Ballivorny, in the barony of Muskerry, from the Hierlighy's, all Boyle's time and all Synge's time. Out of Knockilishine, near Timoleague, he received 40*s.* from James Barry, the proprietor. From one Thomas Bateman, a Mugletonian, he received £3 per annum cheifry for Balliduan, near Cloghnikilty, all Boyle's and Synge's time. He saies his grandfather paid 13*s.* per annum cheifry for the Bishop's defence, to secure his estate from Esq. Barret, for Curribaghagh, in the barony of Barretts, in the parish of Inniskarra. This was paid to Bishop Lion. This estate came to Friar Ulick [or Alick] Barret, who died twelve years ago. Upon his death, Pourdon, Coulthrust, and others, got possession of it. Leenagh, nine acres beyond the Lough near Corke, was a common belonging to St. Barry's. It was inclos'd about twelve years ago. He receiv'd from Bishop Synge 10 li. per annum from Sir Peter Courthop for the stone fort. Courthop was governor of the fort. Captain Folliot was captain-lieutenant in the fort. Formerly where the fort stands there stood the church of Templecroghenigh, or Holy Cross. The church-yard of this church was where the Bandon road goes betwixt the fort and the barracks. The Bandon road at that time went through the place where the barracks are built. John Gerald's houses are built on the old church-yard." [Downes' Tour.]

1706. April 22. PIERCE GOOLD, A.M. (*vice* Derham), is admitted a Vicar Choral. [F.F.] In 1711 he resigned, and became P. Kilbrittain, q. v.

1711. June 1. USSHER SMYTH, A.B. (*vice* Gough), is admitted a Vicar Choral. [F.F. Cotton.]

Ussher Smyth was born in county Cork, and was son of Francis Smyth, of Rathcoursey, county Cork, esq., by Maria, dau. of Beverly Ussher, by Jane, dau. of Sir Percy Smyth, of Ballinatray. [U.O.]

He entered T.C.D. as Pensioner, ætat 18, on 2nd Feb. 1698, and become a Scholar in 1702.

From 1705 to 1711 he was V. Kilmoe, and from 1711 to 1712 was a Vicar Choral of Cork.

1711. July 31. JOHN KENNEY, A.M. (*vice* Goold), is admitted a Vicar Choral. [F.F. Cotton.] In Feb. 1711/2, he became P. St. Michael's, q. v.

1711/12. April 2. RICHARD DAVIES, A.M. (*vice* Kenney), is admitted a Vicar Choral. [F.F.]

Richard Davies (a near relative of Dean Rowland Davies), was from 1671 to 1684, V. Clonfert, R. Knocktemple, and V.

Tullilease, in Cloyne. He was also in 1671 a Vic. Choral of Cloyne. From 1697 to 1711 he appears as Curate of Youghal, and from 1711 to 1712 he was Vicar Choral of Cork. He was buried in St. Finbarry's church-yard, on 5th August, 1712, aged eighty-two.

1712. October 1. WILLIAM CRONE, A.M. (*vice* Davies), is admitted a Vicar Choral. [F.F.]

1712. October 7. RICHARD BALDWIN, A.M. (*vice* Smyth), is admitted a Vicar Choral. [F.F.] He appears to 1719, and in 1720 became P. Kilbrittain, q. v.

1716/17. March 21. NICHOLAS SKOLFIELD (*vice* Crone, deceased), is admitted a Vicar Choral. [F.F.] In 1717 he became V. Cannaway, and in 1737, V. Kilcaskin, Ross, q. v.

1717. August 13. SAMUEL BROME, A.M. (*vice* Skolfield), is admitted a Vicar Choral. [F.F.] In 1718 he became P. Currograngemore, Ross, and in 1731, Chancellor of Cork, q. v.

1719. September 29. WILLIAM ELLIS, A.M., is admitted a Vicar Choral, per resignation of S. Brome. [D.R.] And on same day he was licensed to the Curacy of Carrigrohane. He resigned the Vicarage Choral in 1723, and became P. Island, Ross, q. v.

1720 to 1747. WILLIAM FULTON (*vice* Baldwin), appears as a Vicar Choral. [V.B.] In 1735 he was also V. Garrycloyne, Cloyne, q. v.

On the 4th June, 1720, Lacroix was admonished by the Bishop for neglecting to attend ye service some days this week, and was threatened with further proceedings at next visitation. [V.B. D.R.]

1720. Dean Davies left £10 to the Protestant poor of St. Finbarry's.

1723. Edward Wetenhall left £100, and Mr. Samuel Lugg left £25 to the poor of St. Finbarry's.

1724. July 14. JEMMETT BROWNE, A.B. (*vice* Ellis), is admitted Vicar Choral. [F.F.] He was at this time Treasurer of Ross, and in Feb. 1724/5, he resigned this Vicarage Choral, and became Precentor of Cork. He was afterwards Dean of Ross, q. v.

1724/5. Feb. 15. RALPH DAVENPORT, A.M. (*vice* Jemmett Browne), is admitted a Vicar Choral. [D.R.]

In 1724 Archdeacon Pomeroy bequeathed to the Bishop of Cork, £100 for building and supporting a charity school at St. Finbarry's.

Ralph Davenport was son of Charles Davenport, and was born at Innishannon, county Cork. When eighteen years old he entered T.C.D. as Pensioner on 7th June, 1707, and obtained a Scholarship in 1711.

In 1725 he was Curate of Holy Trinity, Cork, and from 1724 to his death in 1727 was a Vicar Choral of Cork.

1724/5. March 8. RANDOLPH ROBERTS, A.M. (*vice* Lacroix, resigned), is admitted a Vicar Choral. [D.R.]

Roberts was Vicar Choral from 1724 to his death in 1753. He held in 1720 the Curacy of Nohoval and Kilmonoge, and in 1729 that of Cannaway.

He was ordained Deacon on 20th Sept. 1719, and Priest on 12th June, 1720, both at Cork. He was a grandson of Rev. Thomas Roberts, Chancellor of Cork.

1727. June 15. THOMAS WHITE, A.M. (per mort. Davenport), is admitted Vicar Choral. [D.R.] He became in 1751, P. Kilnaglory, q. v.

1727/8. Feb. 1. PETER WATERHOUSE, A.M. (per resignation of White), is admitted a Vicar Choral. [D.R.] In 1732 he became Precentor of Cork, q. v.

In 1730 Mrs. Shearman bequeathed £10 per an. to the school at St. Finbarr's; (Latin to be taught); the master to be appointed by the Bishop.

1732/3. Feb. 16. PETER BRISTOW, A.M. (*vice* Waterhouse), is admitte a Vicar Choral. [D.R.] In 1741 he became also R. St. Paul's, q. v.

In 1733 Emanuel O'Hea, and in 1734 Alexander M'Carthy and John Barrett, recant in St. Finbarry's Cathedral. [D.R.]

Dean Carlton left, in 1735, £100 to the Poor of St. Finbarry's.

1735. August 1. THOMAS BARRY, A.B. (per mortem Molloy), is admitted Vicar Choral. [D.R.] In 1747 he became also R. Killowen, q. v.

1747/8. January 4. JOHN THOMAS ATKINS, A.M. (per mortem Fulton), is admitted Vicar Choral. [D.R.] He was also R. Ardnegihy, q. v.

1749. May 29. EDWARD BROWNE, A.B. (per mortem Barry), is admitted Vicar Choral. [D.R.] In the same year he was made Archdeacon of Ross, q. v.

1750. March 28. THOMAS MILLERD, A.M. (*vice* Browne), is admitted a Vicar Choral. [D.R.] He resigned on 1st April, 1751, and became V. Durrus, q. v.

1751. June 3. THOMAS BROWNE, A.B. (*vice* Millerd), is admitted Vicar Choral. [D.R.] He resigned in 1757, on becoming Precentor of Cork, q. v.

1751. Mrs. Eliza Farthing leaves £100 to the poor of this parish.

1752. Oct. 31. The four Vicars Choral (as some of them have cure of souls in different parishes, or through their infirmities cannot without great difficulty attend to their duty in the cathedral, and in order that the service on them incumbent may regularly be performed in case of their necessary absence), petition the Bishop to allow one Reader to attend such service in their behalf, for which each is willing to allow £10 each by the year; and they present Richard Pigott, A.B., for his Lordship's licence, as such Reader. Pigott is accordingly licensed "to do the whole duty belonging to said Vicars Choral," at a stipend of £40 per annum, on 14th Nov. 1752. [D.R.] Pigott, who had been ordained Deacon on 24th May, 1752, by the Archbishop of Dublin, at St. Patrick's, was, in 1774, V. Holy Trinity, q. v.

1753. October 12. JOHN WRIXON, A.B. (per mortem Roberts), is admitted Vicar Choral. [D.R.]

John Wrixon, born at Glenfield, county Cork, was the son of Henry Wrixon, esq., and entered T.C.D. as a Pensioner, on 3rd Feb., 1730, aged seventeen.

He was licensed on 17th June, 1747, to the curacy of Clonmeen and Roskeen, and in 1751, May 7, to that of Killaspugmullane. From 1756 to 1760 he appears as Curate of Ballinaboy. He continued Vic. Chor. Cork, until his death in 1764.

He married Catherine, sister of Rev. Thomas White, P. Kilnaglory. [Duns.]

1757. Nov. 7. EDWARD KENNEY, A.B. (*vice* Thomas Browne) is admitted Vicar Choral. [D.R.] He resigned in 1761, and became P. Inskenny, q. v.

1761. May 8. RICHARD PIGOTT, B.D., (*vice* Edward Kenney). [D.R.] He resigned on becoming P. Lisclery in Dec., 1770. He was afterwards V. Holy Trinity, q. v.

Emanuel Pigott, esq., leaves £100 to the poor in 1762.

1764. April 30. CARLETON BARRY, A.M., (*vice* Wrixon) is admitted Vicar Choral. [F.F.]

He was a son of Edward Barry, M.D., (and was either son or brother of Edward Barry, M.D., who was created a Baronet in 1775). He was born in Cork, and entered T.C.D. as Pensioner, on 10th July, 1737, at the age of fifteen. [Reg. T.C.D.]

He held this vicarage choral until his death in February, 1768. He was buried at St. Andrew's, Dublin.

1765. January 6. THOMAS BREVITOR, A.M., (*vice* John Thomas Atkin) is admitted a Vicar Choral. [D.R.] He resigned in 1768. He was R. Carrigaline, q. v.

1765. Mr. James French leaves £5 a year to the poor of this parish.

1768. Feb. 12. WILLIAM JEPHSON, A.B., (per mortem Carleton Barry) is admitted Vicar Choral. [D.R.] He resigned in 1774, on becoming Archdeacon of Cork. He was, in 1773, Precentor of Ross, q. v.

1768. August 2. BELLINGHAM SWAN, A.M., (*vice* Brevitor) is admitted a Vicar Choral. [D.R.] In 1769 he received the V. Desertserges, q. v.

1769. March 17. GEORGE BERKELEY, A.M., (per mortem Bristowe) is admitted a Vicar Choral. [D.R.]

George Berkeley (son of Rev. Robert Berkeley, Treasurer of Cloyne, and nephew to George, Bishop of Cloyne) was ordained

Deacon, on 9th July, 1758, at Cloyne, and Priest, on 26th August, 1759, at Cork.

He was licensed on 23rd May, 1759, to be Curate of Middleton.

From 1766 to 1789 he was R. V. Whitechurch, Cloyne; and from 1769 to 1804, a Vicar Choral of Cork. From 1777 to 1801 he was R. V. Carrigrohanebeg, in Cloyne; and from 1784 to 1804, Precentor of Killala. He was also R. V. Nathlash and Kildorrery from 1789 to his death in 1804.

He married at Midleton, on 12th of Feb., 1772, Mrs. Ursula Browne, of Coolcower, and by her had issue five sons, Richard, and Robert (twins), George, Joshua, and Sackville-Hamilton. He also had a daughter, Anne.

Of his five sons, Richard (by his wife Sarah Atkins), had two sons, George, in holy orders, and Robert, Q.C., who married Clara De Moleyns, and has issue. The three next all died unmarried; and the fourth, Sackville-Hamilton, became a General in the Army; and by his wife, Elisabeth Murray, had ten children, viz., Combermere-George-William, Joshua, Sackville-Hamilton, Robert, and James; Anne, Mary, and Louisa (daughters), and two other children, who died young.

1771. January 1. JOHN KENNEY, A.M., (*vice* Pigott) is admitted a Vicar Choral. [D.R.] In 1796 he became P. Kilbrogan, q. v.

1775. January 14. CHARLES COOTE, A.B., (*vice* Jephson) is admitted Vicar Choral. [D.R.] In 1778 he resigned.

This Charles Coote was probably third son of Robert Coote, esq., of Ashhill, county Limerick, by Anne, dau. of Bartholomew Purdon, esq.

In 1774 he was Curate of Castlemagner and of Ballyclogh, in Cloyne. From 1774 to 1775 he was R. V. Kilcully, and from 1775 to 1778 he was Vicar Choral, Cork.

"Isaac, by Divine Providence, Lord Bishop of Cork and Ross, To our beloved John Maginn, greeting. We hereby give and grant to you the office of Schoolmaster of the parish of St. Finbarry, Cork, in our diocese of Cork, with full power and authority to teach and instruct children in the English tongue, writing and arithmetick, and other lawful and honest documents, allowed and approved of by the laws and statutes of this Kingdom, within the said parish; and we appoint you Schoolmaster in said parish during our will and pleasure, with all wages, stipends, salaries, and all other profits and emoluments of the office of a Schoolmaster in the said parish, payable under the will of Mary Shearman, late of the city of Cork, widow, deceased, or otherwise however. You having first taken all the oaths required by law in this behalf to be taken, and subscribed the declaration, oath of abjuration, and two first canons. In testimony whereof we have caused our Episcopal Seale to be thereunto affixed. Dated 29th September, 1777. Thos. Gregg, Dep. Reg." [D.R.]

1778. Feb. 7. MICHAEL TISDALL, A.M., (*vice* Coote) is admitted a Vicar Choral. [D.R.] In 1781 he resigned, and became Archdeacon of Ross, q. v.

1778. Mr. W. Smith, organist, leaves £200 to the poor.

1781. Nov. 24. JOHN DRURY, A.M., (*vice* Tisdall) is admitted a Vicar Choral. [D.R.]

John Drury was, from 1758 to 1771, P. Stagonil; and from 1771 to 1791, P. Kilmactalway, Dublin. He was, also, from 1775 to 1791, Chancellor of Kildare. From 1780 to 1781, he was also P. Currograngemore, Ross; and from 1781 to 1791, a Vicar Choral of Cork. He also held, from 1787 to 1789, the P. St. Michael's, Dublin; and from 1789 to 1791, was P. St. John's, Dublin. He died in 1791.

1791. June 3. FITZGERALD TISDALL, A.B., (*vice* Drury, deceased) is admitted a Vicar Choral. [D.R.] He resigned in 1791. He became R. V. Kilmoe, q. v.

1791. Dec. 22. ARTHUR HYDE, junior, A.B., (*vice* F. Tisdall) is admitted Vicar Choral. [F.F.] And same day Precentor of Ross, q. v.

1796. April 16. MEADE DENNIS, A.B., (*vice* John Kenney) is admitted a Vicar Choral. [D.R.] He resigned in 1809.

Meade Swift, als Dennis, was, from 1782 to 1796, V. Kinneigh; from 1796 to 1809, Vicar Choral, Cork; and from 1809 to his death in 1841, Rector of the Union of Lynn, Moyliscar, and Carrig, in Meath.

He was the son of Thomas Swift, esq., of Lynn, county Westmeath, by the only sister of LORD CHIEF BARON DENNIS, who was created BARON TRACTON in 1780. His uncle dying without issue in 1782, Meade Swift took the name and arms of Dennis. He married Delia Sophia, daughter of Morley Saunders, esq., of Saunders Grove, county Wicklow, by whom he had Thomas Stratford Dennis, esq., of Fort-Granite; Rev. Meade Paul Dennis; John Dennis, M.D.; James-Aldborough Dennis; and Rev. Morley Dennis; besides five daughters.

1799. Feb. 27. JOHN CHETWOOD, A.M., (*vice* Swan) is admitted Vicar Choral. [D.R.] Along with this vicarage choral he held, until his death in 1814, the P. Cahirlag, q. v.

1804. January 28. JOSHUA BERKELEY, A.B., (*vice* George Berkeley) is admitted Vicar Choral. [D.R.] In 1824 he became also V. Holy Trinity, q. v.

1805. Bishop Stopford bequeathed £100 to the Dean of Cork, the interest only to be applied to the benefit of the poor of St. Finbarry's. Also, he gives, by his will, 100 spinning wheels, at 7*s.* each, to 100 of the poorest women, as the Dean or the Curate may appoint. He also left *all* his books to the library of St. Finbarry's.

1809. December 7. ROBERT EVANS, A.B., (*vice* Meade Dennis) is admitted a Vicar Choral. [D.R.]

In 1781 Robert Evans became R. Lynn, Moyliscar, and Carrig, in Meath diocese, *vice* George Evans, resigned. He held that Union until 1809, when he became, by exchange, a Vicar Choral of Cork. He died in 1831.

1814. May 17. JOHN HENRY GOULDSBURY, A.B. (*vice* Chetwood), is admitted to a vicarage choral, certified value under £300 per an. [D.R.] He always resided in the town of Boyle, in the diocese of Elphin, where he held another benefice.

J. H. Gouldsbury was a Scholar, T.C.D., in 1765.

He was, from 1785 to 1819, P. Tighbohine, Elphin; and from 1819 (?) to 1825 (?) R. Ardcarne, Elphin; and from 1825 to 1831, P. Oran, Elphin. He was, also, from 1814 to 1831, a Vicar Choral of Cork.

He died on 30th August, 1831, aged eighty-five, in the town of Boyle, where he had resided for 61 years. A tablet to his memory is in Boyle Church.

1816. March 9. HONORABLE GEORGE DE LA POER BERESFORD (*vice* Arthur Hyde) is admitted to a Vicarage Choral, certified under £300 per an. in value. [D.R.] Beresford was also P. Inniscarra, Cloyne, q. v. He resigned in 1826.

1825. May 4. THOMAS ST. LAWRENCE (*vice* Joshua Berkeley), is admitted Vicar Choral. [D.R.] He was also P. Currograngemore, Ross, q. v. He died in 1833.

1826. July 13. JOHN WARBURTON, A.M. (*vice* G. Beresford), is admitted Vicar Choral. [D.R.]

John Warburton (son of Charles Warburton, or Mongan, Bishop of Cloyne) was, from 1811 to 1816, Precentor of Ardfert.

He holds to the present time (1862), from 1825 a Vicarage Choral in Cloyne; from 1826 a Vicarage Choral in Cork; from 1818 the Precentorship of Limerick; from 1814 the R. Kill and Lyons, Kildare; and from 1829 the R. Drumcliffe, Killaloe.

He is married, and has issue.

1831. April 16. SAMUEL GEORGE ROGERS, A.B. (*vice* Evans), is admitted a Vicar Choral on letters patent of March 9, *sede vacante.* [D.R.] In 1839 Rogers became also R. V. Nathlash, Cloyne, q. v.

1831. Sept. 9. SAMUEL MOORE KYLE, A.B. (*vice* Gouldsbury), is admitted a Vicar Choral. [D.R.] In 1833 Kyle became also Archdeacon of Cork, q. v.

1832. The four Vicars Chorals have amongst them an average gross income of £1,558 11*s.* 6*d.* calculated on an average of three years, ending 1st November, 1831, exclusive of two-thirds of the tithes of Corbally parish, valued at the annual sum of £67 9*s.* 8*d.*; no part of which was received during those three years. Their income arises from one-third of composition rent of St. Finbarry's, £300; from part of Desertserges parish, £315; of Fanlobbus, £373 13*s.* 1*d.*; from portions of tithes of

Kinneigh, £225; of Drinagh, £220; and of Kilroan, £70. And from rents of houses and lands reserved by lease, £54 18*s.* 5*d.* They pay as outgoings £75 to the Reader or Curate of St. Finbarry; and £168 to the Choir, and to their Syndic, £77 18*s.* 6*d.*; and to their Runner, £6 6*s.*; they also pay £10 for the occasional duties of Kilroan parish. Their net annual income is £305 6*s.* 9*d.* for each Vicar Choral. [Parl. Rep.]

1833. March 15. THOMAS HENRY TORRENS, A.B. (*vice* Thomas St. Lawrence), is admitted a Vicar Choral. [D.R.]

T. H. Torrens (eldest son of the Venerable John Torrens, Archdeacon of Dublin), was ordained in 1827.

He was, from 1832 to 1858, R. Carnalway, Kildare; and from 1833 to 1858, Vicar Choral of Cork. He died on 29th Nov., 1858, having had issue by his wife, Miss Richardson, of Somerset, near Coleraine, one son, who has since died.

1834. The Protestant population of St. Finbarry's is 1,826.

1842. Feb. 2. The appointment of Vicars Choral was suspended by an Order in Council.

1860. The Dean and Chapter are the Incumbents of the parish of St. Finbarry. Frederick Dobbin is Curate; and Isaac Morgan Reeves is Reader and Catechist. The cathedral church is an unsightly edifice, and there is nothing within its walls to compensate for the deformity of its exterior. The choral service is neglected, and there is no daily service. Divine service is performed twice on Sundays, and once on the usual holidays, and also on all Wednesdays and Fridays; but the choir do not attend except on Sundays and Christmas Day. The sacrament is administered monthly; average of communicants, 51; and at Christmas and Easter; average 119. The children of the parish are instructed by the clergyman on one day of the week, as are also the school children. 32 boys (with an average attendance of 27); 27 girls (average attendance, 23); and 68 infants are on the rolls of the schools, which are supported by a small endowment, the collections at the cathedral on Sunday evenings, and by voluntary contributions. The Protestant population, inclusive of Frankfield district, is about 1,000.

At Frankfield (a chapel within this parish, served by the Curate and the Catechist of the cathedral alternately), there is divine service on all Sunday mornings. Sacrament monthly; average of communicants, 11; and at Christmas and Easter; average, 29. 17 children attend a Church Education school. The Protestant population of the district (including the Dean's household) is 124.

At St. Michael's (Blackrock), a Chapel of Ease to St. Finbarry's, there is also divine service twice on all Sundays, and once on the usual holidays, and on Wednesdays in Lent. Sacrament monthly and on festivals; average of communicants,

45. About 40 children attend a Church Education school. The Protestant population of this district is 640.

1863. A sum of money has been subscribed for the erection of a new cathedral on the old site. The plans have been chosen, and there is a fair prospect that Cork will soon possess a decent cathedral church, in which, it is to be hoped, the choral service will be used daily throughout the year.

ST. JOHN.

"Juxta Corkagiam monachis Benedictinis sub titulo Sti Johannis Evangelistæ monasterium fundavit Johannes Rex Angliæ et Dominus Hiberniæ." [Bruodini propugnac. Cathol. Veritatis.]

1591. E. Sci Johis Evangeliste spectat ad Prior Bothon. imp. [MS. T.C.D. E. 3. 14.]

1615. Scti Johannis Evangelistæ Rectoria spectat ad Priorem de Bath; nulla Ecclia, nulla cancella, nullus curatus. [R.V. R.I.A.]

1634. E. Sti Johis Evangelistæ. Rex est Rector. John Gratrix de Cork generosus tenet hanc rectoriam. Nullus curatus. Valet 14 li. per an. [R.V. 1634.]

1639. St. John's. THOMAS ROBERTS, Curatus. Ecclesia ruinata, desunt omnia. [V.B. 1639. D.R.] Mr. Thomas Roberts also appears as lay Proxy for St. John's, and pays IIIs. fees. [V.B.]

Roberts was presented to the rectory of St. John of Jerusalem circa 1636, by King Charles I., who gave him a lease for 61 years, by patent dated 2nd July, 1638, of lands called Wasterfield and Terenure, als Ballinure, part of the late dissolved priory of St. John of Jerusalem. [Betham MSS.]

Roberts was afterwards Chancellor of Cork, q. v., He died in 1664.

1664. July 12. JOHN PARRY, D.D., is presented to the rectory of St. John of Jerusalem. [Lib. Mun.] He was son of Edward Parry, Bishop of Killaloe. John Parry was, in 1660, Treasurer of Christ Church, Dublin; in 1666, Dean of Christ Church; and in 1672 Bishop of Ossory.

1666. May 21. EDWARD SING is presented to the rectory of St. John of Jerusalem. [Lib. Mun.]

In 1667, St. John's is said to belong to Grany, and Edward Sing appears for it at visitation. If this Edward Synge was the same person who was afterwards Abp. of Tuam, he must have been a mere child when he obtained his patent.

1675. May 20. ROWLAND DAVIES is presented to the rectory of St. John of Jerusalem. [Lib. Mun.] In 1709 Davies was Dean of Cork, q. v.

1679. Dec. 15. By letters patent of this date the rectory of St. John of Jerusalem is granted to the Bishop of Cork, to maintain a Priest Vicar Choral in the Cathedral of St. Finbarry, Cork. [Lib. Mun.]

The patent states the reason of this grant as follows:—

"CAROLUS s'c'dus dei grā Angl', Scot', Franc', et Hibn' rex fidei defensor et cet.—omnibus ad quos p'sentes lrē nrē p'venînt saltm. CUM intelligim' quod incole paroch' Sanct' Johīs p'p' civit' n'ram Corcag' et jacent' in com' d'ce Civit' in regno n'ro Hib'niæ ex homin' memoria dependebant et adhuc depend' sup' Eccliam Cathedral' Sanct' Fynbarry, Corkagen' p' oībus pastoral' officiis et inde fruuntur eis:—Et informat' quod a felice restauracōe n'ra dca Ecclia Cathedral' destitut' fuit omni Choral' servic' ex inopia opportunar' dotation':—Ac etiam intelligent' dict' rector' Scī Johīs jam vacant' esse et ad n'ram donacōn et libām disposicōem n'ram (p'plenum jus et patronatu' n'rum) spectan' et p'tin':—SCIATIS igitur quod nos, de grā n'ra spīali ac ex certa scīa et mero motu n'ris, de et cum assensu et consensu p'dilect' et p'q'mfidel' consanguinei et conciliar n'ri Jacobi Duc' Ormon' loc' ten' n'ri genāl' et genāl Gubnator' n'ri regni n'ri Hibnīæ, necnon s'c'd'm tenor' et effect' quar'd'm l'rar' n'rar' manu n'ra p'pria signat' dat' sub signeto n'ro apud cur' n'ram de Whitehall vicessimo septimo die Octobr' anno r'ni n'ri tricessimo primo annoq' d'ni millimo sexcentessimo septuagessimo nono, et nunc in rotul' Cur' n're Cancellar' in d'c'o r'no n'ro Hibniæ irrot'lat', DEDIMS concessim's et contulim's, ac p' p'sentes dam's Dil'c'o nobis in Xrō reverend' in Xrō p'ri Edrō Corkagen' et Rossen' Epō, et succ' suis Epīs Corkagen', d'c'am integram rector' Sanct' Johīs p'pe Corkag' unacum ōibus et olod' terr' tenement' debit' p'fic' decim' commodit' jurisdicion' et emolum't quibuscunque tam sp'ual q'm temporal' dcē integr' rector' Sanct' Johīs p'pe Corkag' quoquomodo spectan' et p'tinen,'—HABEND' et tenend' d'cam integr' rector' Scī Johīs p'pe Corkag' cum o'ibus suis jur' membr' et p'tin' universis p'fat Edrō Corkagen' et Rossen' Epō et success' suis Corkagen' Epīs inp'petuum p' et ad usum et sustentacōem unius sacerdot' Vicar' Choral' qui lib'os parochie Scī Johīs p'd' in medio Ecclie Cathedral' Sanct' Fynbarry Corkagen' secund' leges Ecclie Angl' catechisabit; ac etiam p' sustentacōe unius laici Vicar' Choral' et tot Cantor' aut chorist' quousque reddit' dict' rector' extend'; et q'mlibet eor' quotidie in d'co Cathedral' aut Chor' Sanct' Fynbarry secund' choral' usum Ecclisæ Hibnie officiar'. REDDEND inde nobis hered' et succ' n'ris solt ad manus Vicethesaurar' sive gen'al receptor' n'ri hered' et succ' n'ror' d'c'i r'ni n'ri Hib'nie p' tempore existente ad recept' Scrii n'ri hered' et succ' n'ror' d'ci rni nri Hib'nie tot' et tal' redit' reservacon' et offic' quot jam p' ead' solut' sunt solvend' ad festa Pasche et Sancti Michlis Arch'i p' equal porcon' annuatim ab et immediate post dict' integr' rector' Scī Johīs eveniet in possess' d'c'i Edri Corkag' et Rossen' Ep aut successor' suor' Corkagen' Epor' PVISO semp' et firmiter injungend' mandam's quod p'fat Edrūs Corkag' et Rossen' Epūs irrolulabit vel irrotulari causabit has l'ras n'ras patent' in alta cur' n'ra Cancellar' in d'co r'no Hibniæ infra sex menses p'xim' post dat' har' l'rar' n'rar' patent'. Eo quod, &c., aliquo statuto et cet. In cujus rei testimoniu' has l'ras n'ras fieri fecim's patent.' Teste p'fat loc' ten' n'ro Gen'ali et Gen'ali Gub'natore dci r'ni n'ri Hibnie apud Dublin, decimo quinto die Decembr' anno r'ni n'ri tricessimo primo.

"Irrot' vicessimo die Decembr' anno R' R' Caroli S'c'di tricessimo primo."

I also give a translation of the foregoing:—

Charles the Second, by the grace of God, of England, Scotland, France, and Ireland, King, defender of the faith, and soforth. To all to whom these, our present letters, shall come, greeting.

Whereas, We understand that the inhabitants of the parish of St. John, near our city of Cork, and lying in the county of the said city, in our Kingdom of Ireland, were since the memory of man dependent, and still are dependent, upon the Cathedral Church of St. Finbarry, of Cork, for all pastoral offices, and thence enjoy them; and being informed that from our happy restoration the said Cathedral Church has been destitute of all choral service, from want of a fitting endowment; and, moreover, understanding that the said rectory of St. John is now vacant, and appertaining and belonging to our gift and free disposition (by our full right and patronage).

Know ye, therefore, that We, of our especial grace, certain knowledge, and mere motion, by and with the assent and consent of our well-beloved and faithful cousin and counsellor, James, Duke of Ormond, our Lieutenant-General and General Governor of our Kingdom of Ireland, and also according to the term and effect of certain letters signed with our own hand, and sealed with our seal, at our Court of Whitehall, the twenty-seventh day of October, in the thirty-first year of our reign, and in the year of our Lord one thousand six hundred and seventy-nine, and now enrolled in the Rolls of our Chancery of our said Kingdom of Ireland, We have given, granted, and conferred, and by these presents We do give, grant, and confer on our well-beloved in Christ, our rev. father in Christ, Edward, Bishop of Cork and Ross, and his successors, Bishops of Cork, the said entire rectory of St. John, near Cork, together with all and all kind of land, tenements, debts, profits, tithes, commodities, jurisdictions, and emoluments whatsoever, as well spiritual as temporal, to the said entire rectory of St. John, near Cork, in any manner appertaining and belonging.

To have and to hold the said entire rectory of St. John, near

Cork, with all its rights, members, and appurtenances whatsoever, to the said Edward, Bishop of Cork and Ross, and his successors, Bishops of Cork, for ever, for and to the use and support of one Priest Vicar Choral, who shall catechise the children of the Parish of St. John aforesaid in the midst of the Cathedral Church of St. Finbarry, of Cork, according to the laws of the Church of England. And, moreover, for the support of one lay Vicar Choral, and so many singers or choristers as the rents of the said rectory extend to, and that every of them shall daily officiate in the said cathedral or choir of Saint Finbarry, according to the choral usage of the Church of Ireland.

Returning thereout to us, our heirs and successors, to wit, at the hands of our Vice-Treasurer or General Receiver of us, our heirs and successors of our said Kingdom of Ireland for the time being, at the receipt of the Exchequer of us, our heirs and successors of our said Kingdom of Ireland, so much and such rents, reservations, and offices as now are paid for the same. To be paid at the feasts of Easter and Saint Michael the Archangel, by equal portions, yearly, from and immediately after the said entire rectory shall come into the possession of Edward, Bishop of Cork and Ross, or his successors, Bishops of Cork.

Provided always, and firmly enjoining, We command that the said Edward, Bishop of Cork and Ross, shall enrol, or cause to be enrolled, these our letters patent in our High Court of Chancery in our said Kingdom of Ireland, within six months next after the date of these our letters patent, although, and soforth. Any statute, and soforth.

In witness whereof We have caused these our letters to be made patent. Witness our said Lieutenant-General and General Governor of our said Kingdom of Ireland, at Dublin, the fifteenth day of December, in the thirty-first year of our reign.

Enrolled on the twenty-first day of December, in the thirty-first year of the reign of King Charles the Second.

"1700. St. John's Church stood to the east of Red Abby; it is ruinous, and has been so for eighty years. Several parcels of glebe, some in the north suburbs of Corke, belong to this parish, and all the tithes of this parish, which was formerly the possession of the priory of St. John of Jerusalem. They were lately given by the King for the maintenance of the quire of St. Barry's. There was formerly a house near the church, where they entertained the Knights of St. John of Jerusalem, in their travels. Mr. Thomas Roberts heretofore held this priory by lease from the Crown during his life, after him Mr. Parry, and then Mr. Edward Synge, enjoy'd it during Mr. Parry's life. Upon Parry's death Dr. Wetenhall, Bishop of Corke, got the King's patent appropriating it to the quire, paying the former rent reserved. The glebe and tythes are worth about ——. The people of this parish go to St. Barry's Church. The parish has been supposed to be united to St. Barry's, ever since the dissolution of the priory. The church-wardens of St. Barry's serve for this and the adjacent parishes, and also for the three Abbys in the south suburbs."

"An. 1702. A little beyond Red Abby, to the east, stood St. John's Church, the side walls are standing, but the gable ends are down. They bury sometimes in the church; but there are no signs of the bounds of the church-yard, as there are gardens all round the church. Betwixt Red Abby and St. John's Church is the mass-house, a long cabin, that will contain about 400 persons. St. John's Church and parish belong'd to the knights of St. John of Jerusalem. Upon the dissolution of that order it came to the Crown, and was leased from the Crown in Charles the First's time. The lease being expired, Mr. Roberts (Clerk) got a presentation of it from the Crown, and it has been ever since in the possession of the church. About the year 1664, Mr. Edward Synge had the intire rectory of St. John of Jerusalem. About the year 1694, Mr. Rowland Davys got a presentation of it from the Crown, as being vacant; but Bishop Synge compounded with Mr. Davys, and gave him some other livings, and kept St. John's for his son. Upon Bishop Synge's death, Bishop Wetenhal coming to the see got a patent from the Crown, appropriating the parish of St. John's to the use of the quire of St. Finbarry's.

"1704. Red Abby, in the south suburbs of Corke, belong'd to the monks of St. Augustine. Some gardens and houses near the Abby belong'd to it, and a small piece of ground and mill, call'd Ballivracks, near Douglas, belonged to the Abby. This Abby, with the lands, &c., belonging to it, is the estate of my Lord Primate Boyle. The lands of this and the other Abbys pay no tithes. This Abby is said to be in St. John's parish." [Downes' Tour.]

"Non procul a Corcagia ordini eremitorum Sti Augustini, regnante Edwardo primo, cœnobium fundavit DERMITIUS CARTHÆUS vulgo Macarthæus fuscus." [Bruodini propugnaculum Catholicæ veritatis.]

1860. Without reference to the chapter books of the cathedral, which have not latterly been accessible to inquirers, it is impossible to trace the uses to which the revenues of St. John have been applied. It may, however, be fairly presumed that they have been appropriated always to the maintenance of the Choir, or of the Curate, or Reader, at the cathedral. The present Reader, Rev. I. M. Reeves, was appointed by the Bishop of Cork, in 1850, to the Vicarage of St. John of Jerusalem; but it does not appear that he is either the *Priest* Vicar Choral, whose duty was to catechise *in medio ecclesiæ*, or the *lay* Vicar Choral, who was to attend daily to the choral service in the cathedral, under the patent of CHARLES II.

Isaac Morgan Reeves (eldest son of T. S. Reeves, esq., *vide* CAHERAGH, *Rev. James S. Reeves*) was educated at T.C.D., where he obtained a Senior Moderatorship in Ethics and Logics in 1841. He graduated B.A. in 1842, and M.A. in 1853.

He was ordained Deacon at Kilkenny, by the Bishop of Ossory, on 21st Dec. 1844, and Priest at Cavan, by the Bishop of Kilmore, on letters dimissory from Cork.

In 1844 he was Curate of Douglas, in the parish of Carrigaline, to which he was licensed on 29th May, 1847. His licence was transferred from Carrigaline to the Holy Trinity on 3rd July, 1850. He was, in the latter year, appointed by the Dean of Cork to the curacy of St. Finbar's, and at the same time to the Vicarage of St. John of Jerusalem by the Bishop. In February, 1858, having resigned the curacy of St. Finbar's, he was appointed by the Bishop to be also Reader in the Cathedral.

He married Anna-Maria-Toke (dau. of Rev. Henry Bouchier Wrey, R. Tawstock, Devon, and granddaughter of SIR BOUCHIER WREY), by whom he has issue a daughter, Helen-Wrey, born 26th October, 1860.

ST. MARY, SHANDON.

1291. "Eccia de Sandona VIImr. Vicar capit dimid." [Tax. P. Nic.]

1462. In a charter of this date, of King Edward IV., the churches of St. Mary Shandon, and St. Catherine, are named. [Mason's Parochial Survey.]

St. Mary, Shandon, R. and V. "Heredes Domini de Rupefort" present to the Rectory; the Bishop collates to the Vicarage. [Clarendon MSS. No. 36, Brit. Mus.]

1523. Sept. 4. "Dominus Willūs Oflioyn, presbyter parochialis S. Katerinæ" is a witness to a deed. [Sarsfield MSS.]

1536. In this year DOMINICK TIRREY, Rector of Shandon, became Bishop of Cork and of Cloyne. [Tuckey, p. 47.] In a letter from the King to the Mayor and citizens, &c., of Cork, and to the officers and subjects at Bandon, it is stated that by reason of the tenuity of the bishoprick, Tirrey had the vicarage of Cork (St. Mary, Shandon), and the parsonage and vicarage of Bandon (Ballymodan), granted to him in commendam. June 11, 18th Hen. VIII. [Pat. Rot.]

1582. March 14. DOMINUS DONALDUS DONATI Y CONOGHER is presented to V. Mariæ de Shandon—"decimo quarto die ejusdem mensis (Martis 1582), dnus donaldus donati y Conogher, presbiter per honorabilem virum Geraldum comitem Kildarie cōmendatus et presentatus ad vicariam p'petuam Ecclesiæ beatæ Marie de Shandon; admissus est per supradictum Epum ad dictam vicariam et inductus est quasi in poem per magistrum Philippum Goldeum archidiaconum Corcagen. P. Goldeus Registrarius." [D.R.]

1583. April 30. MAURICIUS DERMICII Y DALY is admitted Rector of St. Mary, Shandon. "Rectoria simplex Ecclie parochialis beatæ Mariæ de Shandon juxta civitatem Corkagen. dioc. Corkagen. concessa est dno Mauricio dermicii y daly p'bitero, qui quidem dūs Mauricius institutus est per presentationem honorabilis viri dni Barrymore decān. noie vicecomitis de Buttivant, admissione decani et capituli, et inductus per Archidiaconum ultimo die Aprilis, Ao. Di. 1583. Phil Gold. R." [D.R.]

1591. Rector Ecclesiæ Mariæ de Shandon PHILIP MARTELL. Vicarius ejusdem EDMUND NELSON, laicus. [MS. T.C.D. E. 3. 14.] In another part Johēs Martell is Rector, and Edmond Nelson is marked "dispens—ejus amocōe per ijos annos—laicus obtint per 2os annos." And in the list of persons cited before the royal commission is DANIEL M'DONOGH, Vicar de Shandon, and Vicar de Walestown.

1591. "E Scē Catherine spectat ad ab. de Chore. Vas. RICHARD SKIDDYE, Cur." [R.V. 1591.]

1615. June 19. WILLIAM THOMAS is presented to R. V. Shandon, and P. Cahirlag, q. v. [Lib. Mun.] He was instituted on 12th July, 1615. [F.F.]

1615. Shandon (residens) R. et V. William Thomas, minister et predicator. Ecclesia bene repāta, cancella in repātione. Ipse inservit curæ. [R.V. R.I.A.]

1615. October 29. JOHNSONNES FENTON, adm. Rector de Shandon. [F.F.]

1616. April 17. JOHN BROCK, *Vicar* de Shandon. [F.F.] He is still Vicar in 1634. He was also Treasurer of Cork, q. v.

1617. July 17. The Sequestration of R. Shandon, dioc. Cork, was granted to John Gratrix, of Cork, *generosus*. [MS. Prerogative Court, Dublin.]

1617. Nov. 29. The Sequestration of the Prebend or Rectory of Shandon, dioc. Cork, was granted to Edmund Murfy, of Cork. [Ib.]

1617/8. January 23. JOHN HULL, *Rector* de Shandon. [F.F.] He was also Precentor of Cloyne, q. v.

1617. William, Bishop of Cork, Cloine, and Rosse, orders the inhabitants of St. Francis, commonly called Shandon Abby, St. Cattalin, als St. Catherine, and of all places without the north gate of the cittie of Cork to "resorte, from tyme to tyme, and at all times hereafter," upon Sundays and holidaies appointed in the church of England and Ireland, to the parishe church of St. Mary, Shandon, and to pay to the Vicar, Parish

Clerk, and Sexton of the same, and to noe other, such ryghts and duties as for weddings, christnings, and burialls, and other such spirituall and ecclesiastical services are or shalbe payable. The Vicar of St. Mary, Shandon, is by this Act ordained to have the charge and cure of souls and persons within the precincts of St. Francis, St. Catherine, Gill Abby, &c. His successors to have the like charge, &c. [D.R.]

1627. A cup of silver now in use bears the following legend: "THIS CVP WAS GIVEN TO THE CHURCH OF ST. MARY, SHANDON, WITHOUT CORKE, THE YEAR, 1627, BY MARGERIE, THE WIFE OF THOMAS HVET." A small paten accompanies this cup, without inscription.

1628. April 12. JAMES TREDENNICK, *Rector* de Shandon [F.F.], to which the Bishop united the R. V. Kilgulane, and V. Mogeely, Cloine. [R.V. 1634.]

1634. R. de Shandon, James Tredennick, predicator. Val. XII li. per an. Comes Barrimore, patronus. Vicarius de Shandon, John Brocke, predicator. Val. XII li. per an. Comes Kildare, patronus. [R.V. 1634.] E. de Sta Katherina, Rex est Rector. Johēs Fitzgerald, miles, tenet hanc ecclìam. [Ib.]

In 1666 "St. Catherine prope Shandon, Edward Fitzgerald est impropriator," and in 1667 "spectat ad Shandon ratione confiscationis ejusdem et per litteras patentes regis." [V.B. D.R.]

James Tredennick, "Clīcus, divini verbi predicator," was ordained Deacon and Priest by William (Lyon), Bishop of Cork.

In 1615 he appears as V. Grenagh, R. V. Marshalstown and Kilgulane, in Cloyne. In 1628 he is R. Shandon; in 1629 V. Mogeely, in Cloyne; and in 1634 V. Cannaway.

1637. March 10. RICHARD GEADINCH, *Vicar* de Shandon, and on 21st July, 1638, *Rector* de Shandon. [F.F.]

1639. R. and V. de Shandon, Richūs Geadinch compt per procuratorem Thomam Banks, Ecclesia bene et ornata. George Kelly, the Curate, is to take out a faculty. St. Catherine, particula de Shandon. [V.B. D.R.]

Geadinch, on 20th April, 1639, was admitted V. Stradbally, in county Waterford. [F.F.]

16—? HEZECHIAH HOLLAND, R. V. Shandon, and R. Rathcoony. He does not appear save in the following entry from the visitation book of 1669.

1661. April 26. THOMAS GOODMAN, R. and V. de Shandon, prope Cork, and R. Rathcoony, per mortem Hezechiæ Holland. Comites Kildare and Barrimore, patroni. [V.B. 1669. D.R.] Goodman appears in 1680, as R. V. Shandon, and in 1670 he is also R. St. Catherine, per letters patent of the King. [V.B. D.R.] In 1675 he was also Precentor of Ross, q. v.

1666. Sept. 28. A grant is made, under the Act of Settlement to Goodman and his successors, Ministers of Shandon, of "a front house and housteade, a backside, and garden," at a rent of £1 2s. 6d.

1681. May 20. WALTER NEALE, R. and V. Shandon. [F.F.] He appears 1681 to 1706. [V.B. D.R.] He was also Treasurer, and subsequently Precentor of Cork, q. v.

1688. A cup and paten of silver both bear this legend:—"The Guift of Ellin Taylor to the Church of St. Mary, Shandon, 1688."

1690, *circa*. The old parish church, near Shandon Castle, was demolished by the Irish.

1693. The site of the present church, part of the forfeited estate of Ignatius Goold, Merchant, was granted by Viscount Sidney, Lord Lieutenant of Ireland; and in 1696 the church was built, and ready for erection of pews, &c. [Vestry Book.]

1693. Over the west door of this church, on a stone, is this inscription, in gold letters:—"Ad Edificandum Templum Hoc Quantulum est Agri Donum Parochiæ Sanctæ Mariæ de Shandon Dedit Nobilissimus Dominus Henricus Vicecomes Sydney Hyberniæ Prorex. An. Domini MDCXCIII. Cujus Memoriæ in Æternum floreat." [Smith's, Cork, vol. i. p. 375.]

"1700. St. Francis' Abby, in the north suburbs of Cork, belong'd to the Franciscans. Half a plowland near the Abby, and several other parcels of land in the country, belong to this Abby. This Abby, with the lands belonging to it, is the estate of the Earl of Orrery. This Abby is said to be in Shandon parish."

"May, 1700. St. Francis's Abby is on the north side of the Lee, in the north suburbs of Cork. The site of it contains a few gardens on the side of the hill near the Abby. It is the estate of the Lord Orrery, and before the late troubles was held and inhabited by Mr. Rogers, Thomas Cooke, and others. In King James's time, a new chappel was built by the Friars on part of the Abby, but not where the former chappel stood. Some Friars lived there. In the time of the siege, the Abby, with the rest of the suburbs, was burnt. A good strong steeple remains standing. The chappel that was lately built, having been burnt with the Abby, was repaired by Mr. Morrison, a merchant, and is now used by him as a warehouse."

"1702. The hospital in Shandon parish.—One Stephen Skiddy long since settled twenty-four pounds per annum (payable by the Company of Vintners in London, out of certain houses in that city) upon the Mayor and Corporation of Corke, to be bestowed by them upon ten poor people, which they accordingly did. The said annuity of 24 li. per an. was duly paid to the year 1644; and what was farther due to the year 1660, Sir Robert Coppinger, the last Papist Mayor, got into his hands, and never accounted for it.

"From the year 1660, or soon after, the said annuity was paid into the hands of Christopher Rye, Alderman of the city of Corke, a third part being for some years defalkt on account of the fire of London. The said Alderman Rye, upon his account with the city a little before his death, appeared to have disburs'd about eighty pounds of this said mony (so received by him) for the use of the Corporation, and to have besides remaining in his hands 114 li., for which he offer'd his bond, which, by neglect, was never taken. And the said Rye's executors having no assets remaining, and his heir deriving under a settlement, the said 114 li. is irrecoverably lost. From the death of Alderman Rye the said annuity was received by Robert Rogers, Alderman of the said city of Corke, who, out of it, has rebuilt the said house for the said ten poor people (which was fallen down), and fairly accounted with the city. From the time that the said house has been rebuilt, the said money, as it comes in, is applied to the use intended by the donor."

"An. 1702. This hospital is sufficient for the reception of twenty poor people. There are in it at present, of old men and women, sixteen. Eight of these have tenpence weekly, besides their lodgings, the other eight have nothing besides lodging."

"In Shandon parish is Bretridges Hospital, joyning to the fore-mentioned hospital. Captain Bretridge, about the year 1678, by will, settled some lands in the barony of Duhallo, for the maintenance of seven poor Protestants of the Church of England. Each of them to have eighteen pence a week and twenty shillings apiece on St. Simon's and St. Jude's day, yearly, for clothing. And if there be any overplus, it is to be laid out in putting out as apprentices poor boys of the city of Corke. The lands were heretofore set for 36 li. per annum.

"An. 1702. There are now but five poor men in the hospital, the rent of the lands not being sufficient for the whole number. The Mayor, Recorder, and Sheriffs of Corke, are governors of the hospital. Mr. Hartstonge, the grandson of Capt. Bretridge, is to nominate the poor men during his life, afterwards the Mayor and Sheriff of Corke, and the Minister of Shandon, are to nominate them." [Downes' Tour.]

1706/7. April 5. HENRY MAULE, R. V. St. Mary, Shandon. [F.F.]

1707. He repaired the parsonage of St. Mary, Shandon, and obtained a certificate for an outlay thereon of £150. [D.R.]

1711. Maule copies the old register. In 1716 he gives up certain buildings for use of the charity schools. [Par. Reg.]

1713. A large alms-basin, weighing 22 oz. 9 dwts., is inscribed "Deo DD Prenobilis Viri Robertus Comes de Kildare et Jacobus Comes de Barrimore alternatim Patroni Ecclesiæ Stæ Mariæ de Shandon in Civitat. Corcag. et in usum Eccles. Prædict. 7 Decembris, 1713."

1713. Two large flagons, weighing respectively 72 oz. 12 dwts., and 71 oz. 11 dwts., are inscribed "Deo DD Rector et Parochiani Ecclesiæ Stæ Mariæ de Shandon in Civitat. Corcag. et in usum Eccles. prædict. 24 Decembris, 1713."

1715. A large silver cup, weighing 23 oz., bears the monogram I.H.S., surrounded by a nimbus or glory, and is inscribed "Deo DD Et in usum Eccles. Paroch. Stæ Mariæ de Shandon in Civitat. Corcagiens. et Diocæsi prædict. April 26, An. Dom. 1715. Quid retribuam Domino." A paten, weighing 12 oz. 5 dwts., has the same inscription and date; and a larger paten or alms-basin, weighing about 26 oz., has the same inscription and date.

1720. Dr. Maule, in a petition to the Primate, states that he is Rector of St. Mary, Shandon, worth £300; of Mourne Abbey, worth £90; and also was lately presented to ye deanery of Cloyne, worth £60 per an., which he can't hold without a faculty. He states also that there is constant service in St. Mary Shandon, and in Mourne Abbey, by his Curates; and that he has built both a church and a parsonage at Mourne Abbey, at his own expense; and that the Churches of St. Mary, Shandon, and Mourne Abbey, are "but about ten miles" distant from ye corps of ye deanery of Cloyne. On 21st June, 1720, the Primate consults the Bishop of Cork, who affirms the above statement of Maule to be true, and recommends the issuing of a faculty for Maule to hold the three livings, which is thereupon granted. [D.R.]

1720. George Simpson, of Cork, gentleman, gives by will (dated 30th July, 1719, and proved 4th Feb., 1720) £3 unto ye poore children of ye charity schoole of St. Mary, Shandon. [D.R.]

1723. Sept. 7. An order in Council was passed for dividing the parish of St. Mary, Shandon, and erecting a new parish of St. Paul. [D.R.]

1724. An almshouse was built and endowed by Abraham Morris, esq., for four poor men and four poor women, Protestants.

Maule was also Dean of Cloyne, q. v.

1726. Sept. 24. JAMES WARD is appointed by the Crown R. V. St. Mary, Shandon, and Dean of Cloyne, q. v. He was instituted on 3rd of January, 1726/7. [D.R.]

1736. Nov. 20. GEORGE TISDALL, A.M., is admitted on the presentation of the Earl of Kildare, dated 11th Nov., to the R. V. St. Mary, Shandon, and R. St. Catherine, prope Shandon, vacant by death of James Ward. [D.R.]

1737. Daniel Thresher, merchant, of Cork, by will bearing date 9th January, 1737, bequeathed to ye Mayor, Sheriffs, and Common Council of Cork for the time being, £250, to be laid out in lands in fee-simple, the rent and profits to be paid to such clergyman as the Bishop of Cork for the time being may appoint, who shall, every first Sunday in the month, read morning service, and preach a sermon (in the parish church of St. Mary's, Shandon, or in any other church in Cork city the Bishop may select) at an early hour, so as not to interfere with other services, but to be convenient for servants and others who can't attend the usual service; and who also shall catechise, after evening service, the children, and instruct the adults who attend in the principles of religion. [D.R.]

In 1738, Oct. 27, an order in Council divides the parish of St. Mary, Shandon, and erects a new parish of St. Anne. [Lib. Mun.]

In 1750, Dr. Tisdall is suspended for one month, for having shut out from his church the Rev. Mathias Spread, a lecturer, appointed by the Bishop. [V.B. D.R.]

1758. September 11. Michael Tisdall is appointed Thresher's lecturer. [D.R.]

1770. Nov. 30. Richard, Earl of Barrymore, sells for £1,500, the next presentation to St. Mary, Shandon, and St. Anne, Shandon, unto Arthur Hyde, of Castlehyde, esq. [D.R.]

George Tisdall, the first of his family who came to Cork from Louth, was born in Dublin in 1706, and was son of William Tisdall, esq., of Mount Tisdall, county Meath, by Frances, dau. of Hon. Robert Fitzgerald, and sister of the 19th EARL of KILDARE. He entered T.C.D. on 12th June, 1722, when seventeen years old, and was afterwards D.D. He held the R. St. Mary, Shandon, from 1736 to 1772.

He married, on 17th March, 1727, Frances, dau. of George Canning, esq., of Garvagh, county Derry, and had issue Rev. Michael Tisdall, Archdeacon of Ross, q. v.; a daughter, Lettice (born 1741), and other children.

1772. May 25. RICHARD GIBBINGS, A.B., R. V. St. Mary, Shandon, and R. St. Catherine, near Shandon. [F.F.]

1785. August 24. Robert, Duke of Leinster, sells the next presentation to St. Mary, Shandon, to George M'Carty Portis, of Belfast, who, on 5th Dec., 1787, assigns the same to Waddell Cunningham, John Alexander, Valentine Jones, and Christopher Salmon, of Belfast. They sell it to John and Robert Leslie, who act in behalf of Rev. John Leslie, of Dublin. The Leslies, in 1790 (Dec. 8), sell it to Thomas Lloyd, of Prospect, county Limerick, for £750; who, in 1805, December 21, sells it to Sampson Stawell, of Kilbrittain, for £1,200.

Richard Gibbings, born 15th Feb., 1746, was eldest surviving son of Bartholomew Gibbings, by Elisabeth, eldest dau. of Venerable Richard Wight, Archdeacon of Limerick. Bartholomew was son of Thomas Gibbings, by Anne, dau. of Robert Conran; and Thomas was son of Captain John Gibbings, of Gibbings Grove, who died 23rd Dec., 1678, aged fifty-five.

Richard Gibbings was licensed to the curacy of Clonfert, Cloyne, on 11th July, 1771, and to the curacy of St. Mary,

Shandon, on 26th Feb., 1772. He was R. V. St. Mary, Shandon, from 1772 to 1807, when he resigned.

He married, firstly, on 23rd Sept., 1773, Alice, dau. of Arthur Hyde, of Castlehyde, M.P. for Cork county, and by her had no issue. He married, secondly, Catherine, dau. of John Odell, High Sheriff for county Limerick, and sister to Colonel William Odell, M.P. for Limerick county, and for some years a Lord of the Treasury. By this lady he had (besides Thomas, Treasurer of Cloyne, q. v.) an eldest son, Bartholomew, of Gibbings' Grove, county Cork.

Rev. Richard Gibbings died on March 5, 1812, at his seat, Gibbings' Grove.

1807. January 7. JOHN QUARRY, A.B., R. V. St. Mary, Shandon, and R. St. Catherine, near Shandon, on presentation of Sampson Stawell, *vice* Gibbings, resigned. [D.R.]

1819. The Protestant population was 1,190; the Roman Catholic, 11,718. [Mason.]

1824. Feb. 17. It is ordered that the inhabitants of St. Catherine resort to St. Mary, Shandon, until a church be built in St. Catherine, or this order be revoked. It is stated that the parish or district of St. Catherine has been for a great length of years held with the parish of St. Mary, but no record has been found in the registry of the parish of St. Catherine having been united by Bishop or charter to St. Mary's, or any other parish. [D.R.]

1830. The Protestant population is 1,666.

1832. St Mary's, Shandon, union: 2 Irish miles long, by 1½ broad, with cure, consisting of:—1. St. Mary's, Shandon, rectory and vicarage. 2. St. Catherine, near Shandon, rectory. The union contains 2,246A. 2R. 33P. Gross population of both parishes, 16,018. One Curate employed, at a stipend of £75 per annum. Tithe composition of St. Mary, Shandon, £25; Minister's money, £86 11*s.* 2½*d.*; rents of houses, £95 10*s.* 9½*d.*; surplice fees, £22 17*s.* 2*d.*; subject to visitation fees, £1; diocesan schoolmaster, 9*s.* No glebe-house for the residence of Incumbent. Incumbent is resident, and pays the sum of £42 a-year for house rent. One church, capable of accommodating 1,000 persons, built by means of parochial assessment, in 1693, but at what cost unknown. No charge on the parish in 1832 on account of the church. Divine service is celebrated thrice on the first and fourth Sundays in each month, and twice on all other Sundays; and service and a lecture are delivered on every Tuesday and Thursday. The sacrament is administered twice in each month, and on the great festivals. The benefices constituting this union are rectories; but the denomination of the union called St. Catherine's is reported to be the estate of the Earl of Cork, who claims entire exemption from tithes, or any payment to the Rector on account thereof, as Impropriator. The Incumbent is also Chaplain of the gaol of the city of Cork. [Parl. Rep.]

John Quarry was ordained Deacon on 10th May, 1799, at Douglas, Cork, and Priest on 1st September, 1799, at Cloyne, on letters dimissory from Cork.

He was licensed on 7th Oct. 1805, to the curacy of St. Mary, Shandon, and from 1807 to his death on 1st June, 1837, was R. V. St. Mary, Shandon.

He married, on 20th August, 1807, at St. Nicholas' church, Miss Mary Busteed, and by her left issue, Rev. John, eldest son (V. Castrachore, Cloyne, q. v.), Michael, Jephson-Busteed, and three daughters, Mary, Martha, and Alicia.

The Rev. John Quarry, LL.D., was buried at St. Mary, Shandon, on 5th June, 1837, aged sixty. He was author of a statistical account of this parish in Mason's Parochial Survey of Ireland.

1837. July 18. WILLIAM CHADWICKE NELIGAN, LL.D., R. V. St. Mary, Shandon, and R. St. Catherine, on the presentation of Rev. Robert Longfield, dated 8th July, 1837. [D.R.]

1838. Feb. 24. Dr. Neligan was appointed Thresher's Lecturer. [D.R.]

1860. W. C. Neligan, Rector; R. P. Foley and T. H. Gollock, Curates. The church in order. No glebe-house. No glebe. Divine service twice each Sunday and once on all church holidays, and on all Wednesdays and Fridays. Sacrament twice a month; average of communicants, 43; and at Christmas and Easter, average 108. The schools are maintained by Moses Deane's endowment (£60 per annum), and by voluntary contributions; 52 boys, 31 girls, and 49 infants are on the rolls. The average attendance is 34 boys, 20 girls, and 31 infants. The Protestant population is about £1,500. The sum paid by the Commissioners as Minister's money is now (1863), £270 15*s.* 5*d.*; the tithe is £18 15*s.*; the rents of houses amount to £95 10*s.* 9*d.* The total value is £385 1*s.* 2*d.*, without residence. The next presentation to this benefice will rest with his Grace the Duke of Leinster.

W. C. Neligan (son of Rev. Frederick Neligan, Rector of Kilmastulla, Cashel dioc. and grandson of Rev. Lawrence Neligan, Rector of Golden, Cashel diocese), entered T.C.D. in 1821, and graduated A.B. in 1828, A.M. in 1832, and LL.D. in 1836.

He was ordained Deacon at Cloyne on 1st June, 1828, and Priest at Killaloe in September of same year. He was licensed on 31st July, 1830, as Chaplain of the Cork Episcopal Mariners' Church. He was licensed to the Curacy of St. Peter's on 9th July, 1833.

He married, on 3rd Dec. 1839, Rachel, second dau. of Henry Longfield, esq., of Waterloo and Seacourt, county Cork. He has issue two daughters, Elisabeth, and Mary-Longfield.

ST. MICHAEL.

1291. "Eccia de Sanbally IIImr. vicar capit dimid." [Tax. P. Nic.]

1326. According to an ancient roll, this church was made prebendal in 1326, by Philip, Bishop of Cork. [Smith's Cork, vol. i. p. 64.]

1591. "E. de Shanbally als. Shenavallie THOMAS WOOD incumbens interdicitur defectu ordinum et titulorum; vacat per ijos annos." [MS. T.C.D. E. 3. 14.] In same MS. D. LONG, the Treasurer, and Prebendary of Killanully, appears as *Rector* of St. Michael's.

Thomas Wood, in 1591, appears as R. Shanbally, V. Rosbery, Tisbery, and Leighmoney, and as R. Ardnegiby.

1615. JOHN GOLD appears as P. Shanbally;—"Preb' de Shanbally, John Gold. Valor 3 li." [R.V. R.I.A.] He was also R. Rathcony, and V. Kilcoe, Ross.

1617. July 19. RICHARD SUTTON is admitted Rector of St. Michael's and Vicar de Lisclery. [F.F.]

1628. Sept. 3. JOSEPH FOWLES is admitted P. St. Michael's als. Shanballie, and R. Rathconye, united by Bishop. [R.V. 1634.]

1634. E. de Shanbally als. St. Michael's Josephus Fowles, predicator. Val. 4 li. per annum. [R.V. 1634.]

Fowles was also Treasurer of Cloyne, q. v. He died in 1637.

1637. July 27. GEORGE KELLY is admitted Preb. St. Michael's, and R. Rathcony. [F.F.] He appears in 1639 with Mr. Gilsland as Curate. "Ecclesia ruinata, desunt omnia." [V.B. 1639. D.R.] Kelly was also, in 1639, Curate of Shandon.

He married, in August, 1640, Elisabeth Lanyon, "widdowe." [Cork M.B.]

On May 16, 1642, "George Kellie" depones to losses in respect of his church livings, the Rectory of Rathcony and Prebend of St. Michael's, both worth communibus annis three score and five pounds. [M.S. T.C.D. F. 2. 15.]

1662. July 28. SAMUEL BONNER, A.M., P. St. Michael's. [F.F.] He was also R. V. Insulæ parvæ, V. Ballydeloghy and Kilcoan. In 1662 there was a bond for marriage, signed on 13th October, 1662, between Samuel Bonner, of St. Finbarrie's, Clearke, and Catherine Needum, of the south suburbs of Cork, widow. [Cork M.B.] In the Visitation Book of March 15, 1666, Samuel Bonner is marked "ægrotat."

1667. Vacant by death of SAMUEL BONNER. [V.B. D.R.]

1668. JOHN BAYLIE appears as P. St. Michael's. [V.B.] On 11th July, 1669, he is instituted to P. Shanbally als. St. Michael, R. Templeusky, R. Kilcoan, and R. V. Insulæ parvæ, all vacant by death of Samuel Bonner. [V.B. 1669.] He was also Vicar Choral, Cork, in 1669.

In 1685 Bayley was suspended, &c., "for not appearing at ye 4 last visitations." [V.B. D.R.]

John (son of John Bayley), was born in Cork, and was educated at Hardford West, county Pembroke. He entered T.C.D. on 21st October, 1664, was elected Scholar in 1665, and graduated A.B. in 1669. This John Bayley was probably of the same family as John Bayly, who, in 1643, gave a parchment register to the parish of the Holy Trinity, q. v.

1697. June 17. VALENTINE FRENCH is admitted P. St. Michael's, R. Kilcoan, Templeusky, Ballydeloughie als. Kilroan, and R. V. Little Island, per mortem John Bailey. [D.R.] French appears from 1698 to 1704. [V.B. D.R.] In 1705 French became P. Killaspugmullane, and in 1718 Dean of Ross, q. v.

Oct. 1700. "I saw St. Michael's Church, built with stone, and clay, and lime; the walls are half of them down; it is about 50 foot long; a partition, with an arch, runs through the middle of it; a ditch about the church-yard. 'Tis said by the country people this church was never made use of for divine service, and that it was a place for the clergy to meet in. There is no sign of any graves either in the church or church-yard. In the church, on the sides of the altar, are niches for holy water, &c. There are four plowlands in this parish. Mr. Thomas Brodrick and Mr. Evans have the lands of this parish. Mr. Atkins and Mr. Murphy are all the Protestants that live in this parish. The people of this parish go to Rathcony church. The Prebendary of St. Michael has all the tythes of this parish, worth about £12 per annum. No glebe in this parish."

"Kilcoan Church als. Knockra was built with stone and clay. The walls are half down; 'tis about 2 miles distant from Mr. Mitchell's house, to the south-east of the house. The church-yard is unfenc't, and the way to the church is stopt up. I ordered it to be immediately open'd. The church is about a mile from Kilvolane church, to the east of Kilvolane. The bounds of this diocese is within a mile of this church, towards the east. Gold, Murragh (Papist), have estates in this parish, and also Sir St. John Brodrick. Mr. Mitchell, Protestant, at Barnetstown, als. 5 mile house, and Mr. Gold, Papist, live in this parish; and several other Protestants live here also. They go to Racony church. No glebe found. Eight plowlands in this parish. This parish is commonly called Knockra, from a village of that name in this parish, where Gold, the principal person of this parish, lives. All the tythes of this parish belong to the Incumbent; they are worth about £40 per an. Mr. French did, since the late troubles, preach once a month in Mr. Mitchel's house, in this parish; but he has not for this last year and a half preacht there." [Downes' Tour.]

1705. July 23. HENRY HARRISON, Preb. St. Michael's. [F.F.] He was son of Rev. Henry Harrison, V. Castlelyons, Cloyne, q. v.

He entered T.C.D. on 3rd May, 1698, when seventeen years old, and was a Scholar in 1702. He died in 1711.

1711/12. Feb. 15. JOHN KENNEY, A.M., P. St. Michael's. [F.F. Cotton.]

John Kenney, son of Edward Kenney, was born at Kinsale, and when nineteen years old entered T.C.D. as Pensioner, on 15th June, 1690, and became Scholar in 1695.

In 1699, Feb. 24, he was licensed to the Curacy of St. Peter's. In 1711 he was P. St. Michael's, and Vicar Choral of Cork. He died in 1712.

1712. Dec. 19. ANDREW SYMMES, P. St. Michael. [F.F] In 1718 he became Precentor of Ross, q. v.

1715. Nov. 3. MR. ANDREW SYMES' name is crossed out. [V.B. D.R.]

1715. Nov. 4. EMMANUEL HUNGERFORD, A.M., P. St. Michael's. [F.F.]

E. Hungerford (son of Colonel Richard Hungerford, of the Island, Inchidonie, county Cork, by Mary, dau. of Sir Emanuel Moore, bart.), was born in county Cork, and when eighteen years old entered T.C.D. as Pensioner, on 18th January, 1699.

He was a Surrogate. In 1715 he was P. St. Michael's; in 1717 V. Kinsale; and in 1720 R. Ringrone. He held all these livings till his death, in 1729 or 1730.

He left issue three sons, Thomas, Richard, and John; and a dau. Mary. His will was dated 18th March, 1729, and proved 7th April, 1730.

1730. May 6. JOHN THOMAS ATKIN, A.M., P. St. Michael's, per mortem Emanuelis Hungerford. [D.R.] In 1745 he became R. Ardnegihy, q. v.

1745. May 10. ARTHUR SAYERS, A.B., P. St. Michael's. [F.F.] He appears at visitations from 1745 to 1759, May 23. [V.B. D.R.]

A. Sayers (son of Edward, Chancellor of Cloyne, q. v.), was born at Doneraile, county Cork, and when nineteen years old entered T.C.D. as Pensioner, on 19th June, 1718.

He was ordained Priest at Cloyne on 23rd Sept. 1728. In 1727 he was nominated to the Curacy of Doneraile. In 1730 he became Rector of Templeroan, Cloyne; and in 1745 was P. St. Michael's, Cork, both of which livings he held until his death, in 1759.

He married Miss Martha Lindsay, of St. Andrew's, Dublin. [M.L. 15th Oct. 1728.] He left issue, a son, Edward, M.D., who married Elisabeth, eldest dau. of William Lysaght, esq., of Mount North, county Cork, and by her had issue several children.

1759. August 6. RICHARD BEARE, A.M., P. St. Michael's, per mortem Sayers. [D.R.] In 1768 he was P. Kilbrittain, q. v.

1762. May 13. JOHN KENNEY, jun., A.B., P. St. Michael's, per resignation of Beare. [D.R.] In 1796 he was P. Kilbrogan, q. v.

1771. January 1. ROBERT MEADE, A.M., P. St. Michael's, per resignation of Kenney. [D.R.]

R. Meade (second son of William, Dean of Cork), was born in Cork, and when seventeen years old entered T.C.D. on 12th Nov. 1739, and graduated A.M. in 1747.

He was ordained Deacon on 21st December, 1748, and Priest on 2nd April, 1749, both at Cloyne.

He was licensed to the Curacy of Inniscarra, Cloyne, on 22nd Dec. 1748. From 1752 to 1779 he was R. Dunderrow; and from 1771 to 1779 he held also the P. St. Michael's.

He married, in 1753, Charlotte, dau. of J. Nesbitt, esq., M.D., and by her left issue two daughters, Helena (wife of Rev. Horace Townsend, R. Carrigaline, q. v.), and Joanna.

His will was dated 9th Feb. and proved 16th Feb. 1779.

1779. Feb. 15. ISAAC MANN, P. St. Michael's, per mortem Robert Meade. [D.R.] Mann being in ill-health, is permitted to defer reading his assent and consent until his health be restored, or until 12th May, 1779. [D.R.] He died in a short time.

1779. June 7. JOSEPH WRIGHT, A.B., P. St. Michael's, per mortem Mann. [D.R.] In 1780 Wright became V. Aghadowne, Ross, q. v.

1780. Nov. 2. HORATIO TOWNSEND, A.B., P. St. Michael's. [F.F.] In 1803 he became R. Carrigaline, q. v.

1803. Nov. 2. EDWARD MITCHELL CARLETON, P. St. Michael's. [F.F.] The Bishop's mandate to institute is dated 17th October, 1803. [D.R.] In 1825 Carleton became R. V. Carrigrohanebeg, Cloyne, q. v.

1807. Carleton resides in adjoining parish. [Rep.]

1825. June 16. FRANCIS JONES, A.M., P. St. Michael's; certified under £100 per annum in value. He is again collated on 15th Dec. 1826, when it is certified under £200 per annum in value. [D.R.] In 1833 Jones became V. Castrachore, Cloyne, q. v.

1830. Protestant population, 8.

1832. St. Michael, a rectory, with cure, 3 miles long by ¾ broad, containing 1,995A. 2R. Gross population, 529. One Curate employed for the occasional duties, at a stipend of £10 per annum. Tithe composition, £129 9*s*. 0¾*d*. Subject to diocesan schoolmaster, 5*s*. No glebe-house. Incumbent is non-resident; he resides at Macroom, on his other benefice. No church. The benefice is a rectory. There is no separate revenue belonging to this Prebendary. [Parl. Rep.]

1833. July 23. WILLIAM RYDER, A.B., P. St. Michael's. [D.R.] In 1834 he became Archdeacon of Cloyne, q. v.

1834. May 9. WILLIAM COLLINS, A.B., P. St. Michael's; certified under £200 in value. [D.R.]

1860. No church. No glebe. No divine service. The Incumbent is non-resident. He serves the Curacy of Mogeesha,

Cloyne. Mr. George Keyburn, Curate of an adjoining parish, performs the occasional duties. There are no registries. The Protestant population is 7. The rentcharge is £97 2*s.* 8*d.*

William Collins was ordained Deacon at Cork on 31st July, 1814, and Priest at Cloyne on 15th Oct. 1815.

On 28th September, 1816, he was licensed to the Curacy of Kilmahon; in 1820, January 18, to that of Killeagh; and in 1826 to that of Carrigtowil, Cloyne.

In 1834 he became P. St. Michael's; and in 1840 R. V. Kilcummer, Cloyne, both which he held until his death in 1860. He was buried at Carrigtowill on 11th June, 1860.

1860. August 28. HORACE TOWNSEND FLEMING, A.M., P. St. Michael's, vacant by death of Collins. Net value, £96 17*s.* 11*d.* [D.R.]

H. T. Fleming was a Scholar, T.C.D. in 1846. He was licensed to the Curacy of Rathcony on 28th Dec. 1852.

He married, on 12th Feb. 1863, Emma Catherine, dau. of the late Richard Rothwell, esq., D.L., of Rockfield, county Meath.

ST. NICHOLAS, CHANCELLORS.

Notices of St. Bridget (the ancient corps of the Chancellorship), of St. John, St. Stephen, St. Mary de Narde, St. Dominick, and St. Magdalene, are given under this parish of St. Nicholas.

"The Church of Narde was anciently possessed by Gill-Abbey. Anno 1270, the parish of Narde was granted to Reginald, Bishop of Cork, by Prince Edward, then Lord of Ireland, by donation from his father, King Henry III., *for the relief and amendment of the state of the Church of Cork*, as the record saith; as also the Chapel of St. Peter, at Cork, to hold in frank almoigne. Dated 20th of May, that year. But A.D. 1299, King Edward I. recovered against Robert, Bishop of Cork, by writ of right of advowson, the patronages of the same churches, viz., St. Mary, of Narde, in the suburbs of Cork; the Church of Kilmanock, Nochynvall, and that of St. Peter's, of Dungarvan, in the suburbs of that city. The Bishop's defence as to the advowson of St. Mary, of Narde, Kilmanock, and St. Peter's, was through the above-named grant. But judgment was given against him, because King Edward, when he made the grant, had no right to the said advowson, his father, King Henry, being then alive, and the Prince having at that time nothing in Ireland but by his father's gift, which shows that the Prince was no other than a Viceroy or Lord Lieutenant. As to the Church of Nochynvall, judgment was given against the Bishop by default." [Smith's Cork, vol. i. p. 65, &c.]

1337. D. —— appears as Chancellor. [Placita Com. Banci Hib.]

1370. PHILIP GALL is Chancellor. [Cod. Clar. 46.]

1402. MICHAEL KENEFEG is Chancellor. [Rot. Pat. 3. Hen. IV.]

1552. THOMAS WALSHE is named as Chancellor in this year. [Coppinger. MSS. Cork.]

1571. JOHES MARTELL. "Institutus ad Cancellar. 1571 ordinatus anno 1581." He appears as Chancellor in 1591, with this remark, "delib. sup. dispensis. ltris."; (which is, I suppose, a contraction for "deliberandum super dispensationis litteris ordinum." St. Bridget, in this year, is thus noticed: "E. Scē Brigide spectat ad Cancellarium." In another part of same MSS. it is styled, "Prebend Scē brigide." [MS. T.C.D. E. 3. 14.]

John Martell appears in 1591 as V. Clonmell and Templerobin, in Cloyne, and as Vicar Choral of Cork. He died 1610.

1581. Alderman William Galwey, of Cork, died in this year, seized of the advowsons of Kilgoban and St. Nicholas, Cork. He left Edmund, his son and heir. [Ferguson MSS. Vol. ii. p. 226.]

1588. August 13. John fitz James Barrett, Prior of St. Stephen's, by Corcke, signs an indenture. The Prior is a marksman. [Roche MSS. Brit. Museum.]

1591. "Rector Ecclię Scti Nicholai Pat Corbally ps" i.e. presens. In another part it is marked "Vacat." [MS. T.C.D. 3. 14.] "E. bte marie de Nard spectat ad vicar chorales." In another part it is marked, "Capella libera." [Ib.]

1610. Feb. 10. WILLIAM HEALIHY was instituted Chancellor. Installed 16th Feb., 1610. [R.V. 1634.]

1615. Cancellarius Ecclesiæ Willmus Healy, minister legens, residens. Valor 4 li. Tenet etiam vicariam de Clondrought in dioc. Clonensi, vicariam de Mocrone in eadem dioc. et vicariam de Moviddie in dioc. Corkag. que tres vicariæ non extendunt valorem 10 li. Scē Brigitte, Prebenda est cancellarii, curæ inserviens cancellarius. Cancella bene cum libris, &c. Ecclesia ruinata. [R.V. R.I.A.]

1615. St. Nicholas. Nulli inhabitantes. [Ib.] St. Mary de Narde spectat ad vicarios chorales, parochiani confluunt ad Ecclesiam Cathedralem. [Ib.]

William Healy, or Healihy, from 1609 was V. Macroom, in Cloyne, and V. Cannaway, Cork; from 1610 he was Chancellor of Cork; and from 1611 V. Athnowen; from 1618 he was V. Clondrohid, in Cloyne. From 1615 to 1632 he was V. Moviddy. In 1615 he was also Curate of Macloneigh. In 1632 Healy was deprived or resigned.

1632. June 5. MARCUS PAGETT, A.M., is admitted Chancellor, and on 18th June he was installed. The chancellorship is nevertheless marked "Sub lite." "E. Stæ Bridgit spectat ad Cancellar." [R.V. 1634.]

Pagett was afterwards Dean of Ross, q. v.

1634. E. Sti. Nicholai vacat. Vicecomes Kilmallock patronus. Valet 18 li. per an. 14*s.* XXies paid to the Bpp. [R.V. 1634.]

1634. Ecclesia Beatæ Mariæ de Narde demolitur ad edificaconem novi munimenti de Corke. [Ib.]

1639. THOMAS FULWAR appears as Chancellor—St. Bridgitt ad Cancellar. bene. [V.B. 1639. D.R.] Proxies for St. Bridget, 1*s.* [Addenda to V.B. 1639.] B. M. de Narde demolitur. [Ib.]

1639. In this year THOMAS ROBERTS is Rector of St. Nicholas. "Ecclesia ruinata." [V.B. 1639. D.R.] In 1661 he is also Chancellor of Cork.

Thomas Fuller, or Fulwar, in 1633, resigned R. Ardcanny, in Limerick. From 1634 to 1641 he was P. Killinemer, Cloyne, and from 1634 to 1665, R. Ringrone. He was Curate of Killowney under the Vicars Choral in 1639. From 1639 to 1660 he was Chancellor of Cork. From 1641 to 1660 he was Bishop of Ardfert, with this chancellorship and R. V. Ringrone in commendam; and from 1660 to 1667 was Archbishop of Cashel. He died, aged seventy-four, on 31st March, 1667, and was buried at St. John's, Cashel.

1661. THOMAS ROBERTS appears as Chancellor. [V.B. D.R.]

Thomas Roberts (born 1599, died 1664) was the first of the family of Roberts, of Glastonbury, who settled in Ireland. [Betham MSS.]

In 1636 he was granted by Charles I. the rectory of St. John of Jerusalem.

From 1637 to 1640 he was P. Coole, Cloyne; from 1639 to 1664 he was Rector of St. Nicholas. From 1640 to 1661 he was P. Inskenny, and from 1641 to 1664 P. Donoghmore, Cloyne. From 1661 he was also Chancellor of Cork, and from 1663 Vicar of Whitechurch, Cloyne, until his death in 1664.

Roberts was twice married. By his first wife, Elisabeth, he had one son, Francis, born in 1642, who entered T.C.D. as a Fellow Commoner when nineteen years old, on 6th July, 1661, and who was a J.P. for Cork county in 1666. To Francis Roberts the lands of Britfieldstown, in that county, were granted under the Act of Settlement. The Chancellor married, secondly, Dorothy, daughter of Richard Boyle, Archbishop of Tuam, by whom he had three sons. She had been previously married to Capt. Greenfield Halse, and also to Henry Turner. A member of this family was, in 1809, created a Baronet. The Chancellor died in 1664. [Fisher.] Michael and William Roberts, both Fellows of Trinity College, Dublin, are descendants of Chancellor Roberts.

1664. July 15. HENRY PARR was admitted Cancellarius, per mortem Thomæ Roberts, in coll. Epi. [V.B. 1669. D.R.] Rectoria Stæ Brigittæ prope Cork, est particula et membrum Cancellariatus, Cork. [V.B. 1669. D.R.] Parr appears 1664 to 1674. [V.B. D.R.] He was also Precentor of Ross, q. v.

1666 to 1670. St. Nicholas is marked vacant. In 1670, "Rector St. Nicholai vacat pauper, in collatione Epi." [V.B. D.R.] In 1669, "Rector St. Nicholai prope Cork, spectat ad Vic. Choral." [V.B. 1669.]

1669. The four Vicar Choral, "sunt rectores Stæ Mariæ de Narde." [V.B. 1669.]

1675. Vacant. [V.B. D.R.]

1675. January 22. PETER HEWET was admitted Chancellor of Cork, and Rector of Ringrone. [F.F.] He appears from 1675 to 1709. [V.B. D.R.] In 1710 he became Precentor of Cork, q. v.

1699. St. Bridget ad Cancell. St. Nicholas ad chorum. St. Mary de Nard ad Vicarios Chorales spectat. [V.B.]

"1699. The Blew Boy's Hospitall at Corke, was founded by William Worth, esq.—Abstact of the deed. Indenture between Will. Worth, esq., and the Mayor and Constables of the Staple of the City of Corke. The said Mayor and Constables to have possession of the lands, &c., all the Spittle lands, St. Stephen's Chaget, East and West Ballinaght. They paying 20 li. yearly for four scholars in Dublin College. The rest in trust for a schoolmaster, and poor boys to be taught to read, write, and arithmetic. The Mayor and Common Council of the city of Corke are to be Governors of the said hospital, and to choose the master and poor boys, all of ye Protestant religion, as by law established. The poor boys to have blew coats and caps, with other clothing, meat and drink and lodging. The Mayor and Common Council to make rules for the government of the hospital. The schoolmaster and poor boys to continue during the pleasure of the Mayor and Common Council. Leases in the south liberties to be made for twenty-one yeares of expiration, on paying half a years rent for fine. The rest only for twenty-one years in possession for the full rent. The Mayor and Constables of the staple are to set the leases, with the consent of the Mayor and Common Council of the city of Corke. The aforesaid 20 li. per an. to be paid to four scholars in Dublin College, equally divided amongst them, the natives of the city and county of the city of Corke, and for want of them the natives of the county of Corke, for want of them the natives of any other county in Ireland alwaies to be preferr'd, all which natives and none other shall be named and chosen by the Bishop of Cork and his successors, the Mayor of Corke and his successors for the time being, William Worth, esq., and his heirs, and the Provost of the said college and successors, or any two or three of them, whereof the said Will. Worth and his heirs shall be alwaies one. The schoolmaster to have 25 li. per an. salary for teaching the poor boys [and to have 10 li. per an. for each poor boy's diet, clothing, &c.]—[and 5 li. per an. to the Receiver or Steward]—[The boys not to be admitted before eight years old, not to stay after fourteen]. And that then or sooner such boys shall be put apprentices to such trades, and for so long time as the Mayor and Common Council shall think fit, which boys shall, at such time, have one suit of decent apparel, with other necessaries provided out of the rents of the premises. And if the expences of the boys, &c., exceed the income, the Mayor and Council may lessen the number of boys."

"1700. St. Bridget's Church stood where the fort called the Cat is now built, on the south side of the Cat. There is no appearance of the ruins of the church. The ruins did appear before the last war. This parish contains the place where the barracks are built, and the houses on the south and east of the barracks to the Spittle lands and St. Nicholas parish. The plowlands Maglin and part of Curriheen, near Kerrigrohan, pay all their tythes to the Chancellor of St. Barry, as belonging to this parish, of which the Chancellor has the intire rectory. No glebe in this parish. The whole tythe of this parish is worth about £8 per an., and belongs to the Chancellor of St. Barry's. The people of this parish go to St. Barry's. The Lord Romney has an old estate in this parish, and Counsellor Welsh. More than half of the people in this parish are conforming Protestants."

"St. Nicholas Church stood to the west of Red Abby; it has been ruinous time out of mind. It is supposed to be united to St. Barry's. The church-yard is inclosed, but there is a way through it. Some houses, viz., Piper's holding, &c., near the church-yard, belong to this parish. The houses, glebe, and all the tythes of this parish belong'd formerly to the priory of St. John of Jerusalem, now to the quire of St. Barry's."

"St. Mary's de Narde Church stood in the place where the King's stone fort now stands, the ruins of it do not remain. The stone fort was built in Queen Elizabeth's time, and was raised higher by Cromwell. The west side of the street coming from the south bridge and up to the mitre, and also the north side of the fort belong to this parish. There is no distinct Constable in this parish, nor in St. Nicholas. There are two Constables for St. Nicholas, St. John's, &c., in the south suburbs, within the city jursdictions. No glebe belongs to this parish, nor tythes, except the tythes of some gardens, which are worth little or nothing. The tythe belongs to the Vicars Choral of St. Barry's. There is no valuation of the houses in this parish, nor in St. Nicholas, nor the adjacent parishes, for the support of the Ministers. No churchwardens here."

"St. Stephen's Church stood where the new hospital is now building. No ruins of the church appear. This parish contained half a plowland. This half plowland belonged to the Lepers' Old Hospital of St. Stephen's. This plowland was set lately for £150 per an. The tythe of these lands belong'd also to the hospital, it was set for £10 per an. Three plowlands on the north side of the river Lee, called Ballineboght, belong'd to this hospital. These lands are in Shandon parish, and are worth about £120 per an. Several houses are built in this parish of St. Stephen's; the people go to St. Barry's. This parish is said to be united to St. Barry as the other parishes are. The Bishop of Corke formerly received six shillings and eight pence yearly out of these lands, or tythes, either as a chiefry or as proxeys. John Foreacres paid it to Bishop Synge. There was formerly a prior of St. Stephen's."

"1702. St. Nicholas Church stood above Mr. Morrison's house, in the street going to Red Abby. The walls are standing, and there is a good church-yard belonging to it, on the south side of the church. In the street going to the Red Abby is an almshouse, built by the father of Mr. Ronan, of Ronanscourt, and by him settled on such poor as his heir shall place in it. The heir is to repair it. It is a good stone house, four rooms on a floor; twelve in all; there are about twenty persons in it at present, of which three are men, the rest women. Before Mr. Ronan was restored to his estate, and since the late troubles, a Protestant had the disposal of the house, under, as I suppose, the Lord Romney, who fill'd it with Protestant poor; but Mr. Ronan being restored to his estate about two years ago, he has ever since, as the Protestants died, fill'd their places with Popish poor. There are now about six Protestants, widows; and fourteen Papists, in the house. The poor have no allowance, except their house-room, except those Protestants in it that are on the church-book in St. Barry's, who have seldom above twelve pence apiece per week, and about 1*s.* 6*d.* per quarter out of Smart's legacy."

"1702. St. Stephen's Church stood where North's Blew-coat Hospital now stands. The south side of the Hospital-court wall stands upon the foundation of the north side of the church. There is no sign of a church-yard." [Downes' Tour.]

1710. Sept. 20. JOHN POMEROY, A.M., Chancellor of Cork. [F.F.] In 1717 he became Archdeacon of Cork, q. v.

1717. August 30. GILES EYRE was admitted Chancellor of Cork. [F.F.] He was also Archdeacon of Ross, q. v.

"1720. The church of St. Nicholas, pursuant to the Act of Parliament for the union and division of parishes, was begun to be erected on the 19th of January, 1720, a church being wanted in the south part of the city by the increase of the Protestant inhabitants. This work was chiefly promoted by Bishop Brown, and by the joint and cheerful contribution of other well-disposed persons, by whose assistance it was completed in 1723, and the first sermon preached therein on the 1st of September, by Archdeacon Eyre. It is a small, neat church; has a pretty gallery on the W. end, and is well pewed. The altarpiece and pulpit are well carved, and adorned with fluted columns of the Corinthian order. The Incumbent is supported by a voluntary subscription of the inhabitants. Here is early service and sacrament every fourth Sunday of the month." [Smith's Cork, vol. i. p. 380.]

1721. The earliest register of St. Nicholas begins.

1730. Nov. 1. SAMUEL BROME, A.M., Chancellor of Cork. [D.R.] He was collated, secondly, on 15th February, 1731/2, to the Chancellorship, with Kinneigh Vicarage. [D.R.]

1752. August 3. The union of St. Nicholas was formed (in pursuance of an Act of Parliament, 25th George II.), by the Bishop of Cork, and approved by Archbishop of Cashel, on 21st October, and by Dean and Chapter, 25th August, 1752. [D.R.]

The Act (25th Geo. II. chapter 23, sections 10 and 11), recites, "that St. Nicholas parish, in Cork, is so small, and so intermixed with other small parishes, that there is no provision for a minister, that the church is in danger of ruin, and that there is no church whatever for those other parishes; it is enacted, that the Bishop of Cork, with approbation of the Archbishop, and with the consent of the Dean and Chapter, and majority of the adjacent parishioners of the south suburbs of Cork, may, at vestry in St. Nicholas Church, unite such parishes to St. Nicholas parish for ever; the inhabitants to be liable to such taxes, &c., as those of the old parish of St. Nicholas have been liable to. The said united parish shall be the corps of the Chancellorship of St. Finbarry's, as the parish of St. Bridget's was before; and the Chancellor of St. Finbarry's shall be Rector of said union. [Statutes of Ireland.]

1757. Feb. 15. Rev. S. Brome received £100, legacy of Serjeant John Stokes, which was funded for use of the poor. [Vestry Book.]

Samuel Brome (son of Thomas Brome), was born in Derry, and when seventeen years old entered T.C.D. as a Pensioner, on 9th July, 1706.

Brome, from 1717 to 1718, was a Vicar Choral of Cork; and from 1718 to 1768 held the P. Currograngemore, in Ross. He also held, from 1718 to 1720, R. Caheragh; and from 1718 to 1740 R. Ballymoney; and from 1719 to 1740 the R. Kilmeen, in Ross. From 1730 to 1768 he was Chancellor of Cork; and from 1731 to 1768 V. Kinneigh. From 1740 to 1768 he held also the union of Aglish, Kilbonane, and Moviddy.

He died on 17th July, 1768, and was buried at the Cathedral of Cork.

1768. July 20. ROBERT AUSTEN, A.M., Chancellor of the Cathedral of St. Finbarry, and R. St. Nicholas, St. Bridget, St. John of Jerusalem, St. Stephen, St. Mary de Narde, and St. Dominick. [F.F.] In 1785 Austen was Archdeacon of Cork, q. v.

1774. August 13. Alexander Lamilliere, A.M., Chancellor of Cork. [F.F.] In 1796 he was Archdeacon of Cork, q. v.
1782. Nov. 28. James Pratt, A.B., Chancellor of Cork. [F.F.] In 1785 he became P. Kilnaglory, q. v.
1785. June 6. Henry Sandiford, A.B., Chancellor of Cork. [F.F.] In 1790 he became Precentor of Cork, q. v.
1790. April 12. John Fortescue, A.B., Chancellor of Cork. [F.F.] In 1823 he became P. Lisclery, q. v.
1823. October 10. Henry Theophilus Moore Hodder, A.M., Chancellor; certified under £200 in value. [D.R.] In 1826 Hodder became Precentor of Cork, q. v.
1826. April 6. John Newman Lombard, A.M., Chancellor. [D.R.] He was also P. Kilmaclenine, Cloyne, q. v.

1830. The Protestant population of the union is 2,321.

1832. St. Nicholas union, 1 mile long by 1½ broad, with cure, consisting of—1. St. Nicholas rectory, in part; 2. St. Bridget rectory; 3. St. John rectory; 4. St. Stephen rectory; 5. St. Mary rectory; 6. St. Dominick rectory; 7. St. Maglene rectory. Gross population of union, 17,374. One Curate employed, at an annual stipend of £75, with a share of contingent fees, and an addition of £30 per annum, supplied by voluntary contribution. Within the last year a second Curate has been appointed, with the special charge of the House of Industry, which is within this parish, at a salary of £75, British, per annum, supplied by voluntary contributions. Tithe composition of part of St. Nicholas parish, £57 14*s.*; of St. Maglene rectory, £21. Minister's money, £210. Surplice fees, £24. Subject to diocesan schoolmaster, 10*s.* 8*d.* No glebe-house. Incumbent is resident; and pays a sum of £60 per annum for house-rent. One church, capable of accommodating 800 persons, built in 1723, but at what cost, or what funds supplied, unknown. No charge on the union in 1832 on account of the church. Divine service is celebrated thrice on the first Sunday in each month, and twice on all other Sundays, and on the principal festivals; and one service on every Friday, and on all Thursday evenings. The sacrament is administered twice in each month, and on the principal festivals. A portion of the rectorial tithes of St. Nicholas parish, forming part of this union, and compounded for £108 0*s.* 10*d.*, is impropriate; and belongs, to the amount of £62 4*s.* 9*d.*, to the Messrs. Meade; to the amount of £4 19*s.* 9*d.* to Mr. Benjamin Deeble; and the residue of £40 16*s.* 4*d.* to the lessees of Spital lands Corporation. The Chancellor has also a separate revenue of £6 14*s.* 9½*d.*, rent of tenements reserved by lease, and also fines for renewal to the average annual value of £2 4*s.* [Parl. Rep.]

1836. Nov. 30. The House of Industry was licensed for divine service on application of the Minister and parishioners of St. Nicholas. [D.R.]

1838. March 3. WILLIAM HALL, A.M., Chancellor, certified under £300 in value. [D.R.] In 1849 Hall was R. V. Kilshannig, Cloyne, q. v.

1840. July 8. The Free Church in St. Nicholas parish was licensed for divine service. [D.R.]

1841. Dec. 3. WILLIAM COTTER WILLIAMSON, A.M., Chancellor. [D.R.] In 1860 he became Precentor of Cloyne, q. v.

1846. May 2. JOHN NUN WOODROOFFE, A.M., Chancellor. Certified annual value, £206 3*s*. 3*d*. [D.R.] In 1850 he became P. Cahirlag, q. v.

1847. Feb. 24. A faculty is granted for taking down, and rebuilding, on old site, the old Church of St. Nicholas, the parishioners having lodged £500. [D.R.]

1850. January 25. RICHARD WALTON MARMION, A.M., Chancellor. [D.R.] In 1862 he became R. Kilmeen, Ross, q. v.

In 1850. March 21. The new Church of St. Nicholas was consecrated. [D.R.]

1853. May 21. JOHN CONOLLY, A.B., Chancellor. Certified annual value, £491 14*s*. [D.R.] In Dec. 1853, Conolly became V. Holy Trinity, Cork, q. v.

1854. January 19. NICHOLAS COLTHURST DUNSCOMBE, A.B., Chancellor. Certified annual value, £361 8*s*. 0½*d*. [D.R.] In 1862 Dunscombe became R. Macroom, Cloyne, q. v.

1856. April 18. The licence for divine service was transferred from the Mission School-house, Cove-street, to the large upper room in Buckingham-house, No. 1, White-street, in St. Nicholas parish. [D.R.]

1858. January 5. GEORGE WEBSTER, A.M., Chancellor. Certified annual value, £283 19*s*. 1*d*. [D.R.]

1859. July. The organ formerly in use in Christchurch Cathedral, Dublin, is now purchased for £450, and erected at the western end of St. Nicholas Church.

1860. G. Webster, Incumbent; Caleb Clifford, and John Nicholson, Curates. The church is in good order. No glebe or glebe-house. A house in St. Finbarry's parish is reported to belong to the Chancellor, but it is claimed by the Ecclesiastical Commissioners. Divine service thrice on all Sundays, twice on all Wednesdays, and once on all Fridays, &c., throughout the year. [In 1863 there was a choral service on Sundays and on Wednesday evenings, and service every day throughout the year. All these services are well attended.] The holy communion is administered twice each month; average of communicants, 109; and twice at Christmas and Easter, average 193. [In 1863, the holy communion is celebrated on every Sunday.] The schools are supported by Moses Deane's bequest, the National Board of Education, and by voluntary contributions. 69 boys, 94 girls, and 96 infants, are on the rolls. The average attendance is 44, 60, and 58 respectively. The children are instructed on every day, from 10 to 11 A.M., by the Incumbent and one of the Curates. The Protestant population, exclusive of the inmates of the poorhouse and the Refuge, is about 1,900. The amount of minister's money now (1863) paid by the Ecclesiastical Commissioners to the Rector of St. Nicholas is £358 18*s.* 10*d.* The tithes of St. Nicholas (£43 5*s.* 6*d.*), of St. Magdalene (£15 15*s.*), and rents of houses, &c., &c., make the gross value amount to about £475 per annum.

There is also in this parish a licensed place of worship, called the Free Church, of which the Rev. H. C. Finny, and Rev. Robert William Forrest are Chaplains. Divine service twice on all Sundays, and on the usual holidays, and on a weekday. Sacrament monthly; average of communicants, 146; and at Christmas and Easter, average 168. No school. No district is assigned to this chapel.

George Webster (son of Michael Webster, esq.) was born in Dublin, and when sixteen years old matriculated as a Pensioner in T.C.D., on 3rd May, 1847. He graduated A.B. in 1852, and A.M. in 1856.

He was ordained Deacon, at Dublin, on 25th Sept., 1853, and Priest, at Killaloe, in September, 1854. He was, in 1853, Curate of Castlemacadam, county Wicklow; in 1854 junior, and in 1856 senior Curate of Donnybrook, Dublin. In 1857 he was appointed domestic Chaplain to the Bishop of Cork, and Preacher and Librarian at Cork Cathedral.

He married, on 7th May, 1859, Gertrude-Adeline, the only daughter of the late William St. John Smyth, Chancellor of Down, R. Ballymoney, and private Chaplain to Bishop Mant. He has issue by her, two sons, Reginald-Godfrey-Michael, and George-Arthur, and a daughter, Blanch-Eveline.

Mrs. Webster died on 21st Nov., 1862, and was buried in the vaults of St. Nicholas' Church, where a stained glass window (for which already £100 has been subscribed) will be placed to perpetuate her memory.

Mr. Webster is domestic Chaplain to Dr. Fitzgerald, Bishop of Killaloe.

He has published—1. Notes of Lectures on the New Testament. 8vo. Parker and Bourne, London. 2. Witness of the Spirit. 3. Amusements—A Lecture, &c. 4. The Importance of Studying the Evidences of Christianity. 5. Why are Sponsors appointed? 6. Spiritual Organizations. 7. The Scripture Doctrine of Election. 8. The Scripture Doctrine of Imputed Righteousness. 9. The Scripture Doctrine of the Sovereignty of God. 10. The Scripture Doctrine of Perseverance. 11. The Scripture Doctrine of Sober-mindedness. 12. The Scripture Doctrine of Regeneration. Almost all the above works were published by Messrs. Hodges and Smith,

Dublin. The last six are tracts, which have had an extensive circulation, and to which about twenty *answers* were published by various writers.

1862. The variance between the gross and net value of this benefice, as set down in the Irish Church Directory, requires explanation. The apparent value of St. Nicholas in 1862 was £432 4*s.* 4*d.*, arising from £358 18*s.* 8*d.* minister's money, £63 5*s.* 8*d.* rents and rentcharges, and £10 surplice fees. His actual payments to two Curates and for house-rent were £204 8*s.* His apparent income would, therefore, be the difference between £432 4*s.* 4*d.* and £204 8*s.*, namely, £227 16*s.* 4*d.* Instead of this the actual income of the Chancellor was much more, in consequence of a clause in the recent Act of Parliament, by which the Ecclesiastical Commissioners are obliged to pay, in addition, to the Incumbents of all parishes receiving minister's money, an allowance of 25 per cent. on all the items of necessary expenditure, such as house-rents, stipends to Curates, &c., &c.

For instance, in 1862, the Chancellor received as follows:—

	£	s.	d.
Minister's money, . . .	£358	18	8
Rents and rentcharges, . .	63	5	8
Surplice fees, ...	10	0	0
Allowance of 25 per cent. on £211 15*s.* 1*d.*, necessary expenditure,	52	18	8
Total income, . . .	£485	3	0

His expenditure in same year was—

	£	s.	d.
For stipend of two Curates, at £75 per an. (income tax deducted),	£144	8	0
House rent, ...	60	0	0
Income tax on minister's money,	13	9	4
Income tax on allowance of 25 per cent., ...	1	19	8
Poor-rate and income tax on rents and rentcharges, . . .	8	12	1
Expenses of collection of rents, &c.,	5	9	6
Total expenditure, .	£233	18	7

	£	s.	d.
Total income, ...	£485	3	0
Total expenditure, . . .	233	18	7
Net value in 1862, .	251	4	5

The Chancellor is also Chaplain of the poorhouse, for which he receives £60 per annum.

His real income in 1862 from all sources, after the above expenditure, was £311 *4s. 5d.*

It is to be remarked, that in all parishes receiving minister's money a Curate whose stipend is £100 per annum costs the Rector but £75 per an.; or a Curate at £75 costs the Rector but £56 *5s.* It is also to be noted that the true value of any benefice which is entitled to minister's money varies with the poor-rate, or income tax, or as often as any change takes place in the items of necessary expenditure, or in the number of Curates employed.

The income of the chancellorship may in future years be increased by an addition of nearly £300 per annum, if there be no renewals granted to the present tenants of their holdings. The previous Chancellors took fines, and renewed leases at a merely nominal rent.

ST. PAUL.

1726. Sept. 19. EDWARD SAMPSON, A.M., is presented to the Rectory of St. Paul, in the city of Cork, vacant by promotion of Dr. Henry Maule, the last Incumbent. He was instituted 3rd Oct. 1726. [Lib. Mun. and D.R.]

"The church of St. Paul was built by a subscription of the parishioners; the ground on which it stands was granted by the Corporation to the late Bishop Brown, May 14, 1723; and divine service was, for the first time, celebrated therein by the Rev. Edward Sampson, October the 9th, 1726. By an Act for the union and division of parishes, &c., the East Marsh, belonging to St. Mary, Shandon, and Dunscomb's Marsh, in the parish of Christ Church, were, by the consent of the respective Incumbents, made one entire parish, called the parish of St. Paul, which, by a valuation on houses, affords a suitable maintenance for an Incumbent." [Smith's Cork, vol. i. p. 380.]

Edward Sampson, son of Richard Sampson, was born in Cork, and when seventeen years old entered T.C.D. as Pensioner, on 21st June, 1702.

He was, from 1726 to 1727, Rector of St. Paul's, Cork, and also Vicar Dunboyne and Kilbride, in Meath. He resigned both these livings, and in 1728 became Archdeacon of Aghadoe.

He married Clotilda-Barbara, dau. of —— Lisle, esq., and by her left issue, at his death in 1734, a son, Edward; and three daughters, Barbara (who married Henry Pilkington, esq., of Tore), Alice, and Anne. [U.O.]

1727. July 27. GEORGE SANDFORD, A.M., R. St. Paul's, vacant by resignation of Sampson, and on presentation of the Earl of Kildare, dated 3rd July, 1727. [D.R.]

George, son of Henry Sandford, was born in Dublin; and when sixteen years old entered T.C.D. as Pensioner, on 9th July, 1716. Perhaps this is the same George Sandford who was, in 1749, made Dean of Ardfert.

1733. June 9. JOHN HERBERT, A.M., R. St. Paul's, vacant by resignation of Sandford, and on presentation of the Earl of Barrymore, dated 22nd May, 1733. [D.R.] Herbert was also P. Killanully, q. v.

1741. August 15. PETER BRISTOW, A.M., is presented to R. St. Paul's, vacant by death of Herbert, by the Earl of Kildare, the patron. [D.R.]

Peter Bristow (son of Roger Bristow), was born in county Antrim, and when eighteen years old entered T.C.D. as Pensioner, on 12th May, 1719. He graduated A.M. in 1761.

In 1732 he was a Vicar Choral of Cork; in 1741 R. St. Paul's; in 1751 V. Ballyfeard; and in 1761 R. V. Agabulloge, Cloyne, all which he retained until his death, which took place in January, 1769, at Bath.

He was author of a comedy, "The Harlequins." London. 8vo. 1753.

1769. May 6. SAMUEL MEADE, A.B., R. St. Paul's, vacant by death of Bristow. Richard, Earl of Barrymore, patron. [D.R.]

Samuel, son of Samuel Meade, "generosi," was born in Cork, and when eighteen years old became a Pensioner of T.C.D., on 7th Dec. 1739. He was a Scholar in 1743.

From 1761 to 1768 he was Curate of St. Peter's, Cork. In 1769 he became R. St. Paul's; in 1777 Sacrist of Clonfert and Archdeacon of Kilmacduagh; and in 1784 R. Kilnemartery, Cloyne. He held all these livings until his death in 1788.

He married Abigail Cope, sister of Walter Cope, Bishop of Ferns. In the marriage licence, dated 29th April, 1758, he is described as "Rev. Samuel Meade, of Tuam." By her he left a daughter, Arabella Sarah Abigail, wife of Nicholas Archdall, of Springfield, near Leaslip, who afterwards inherited the fortune of his wife's uncle, the Bishop, and took the arms of Cope. [*Vide* COPE of DRUMMILLY, in Burke's L. G.] The Rev. Samuel Meade married, secondly, in 1769, Grace Townsend, of Clondrohid [Cloyne Mar. Bonds], but by her had no issue. In his will (dated 1st Oct. 1784, and proved at Cork, 1788), he desires to be buried near his first wife, in the family vault, near the chancel of Christchurch, Cork. He bequeaths to the poor of St. Barry's £3; to the poor of Christchurch and St. Paul's, £3 each; and to Walter Cope, Bishop of Ferns, he leaves his "plate corkscrew," given to him in 1755 by his kinsman, Robert Maynard, esq., who died at his table (in the town of Hammersmith, near London) in the presence of several gentlemen, "he at the same time desiring me to get my crest put on it close to his own."

Archdeacon Meade was buried on 17th May, 1788, at Christchurch, Cork.

1789. March 18. THOMAS BUCHANAN, the younger, A.B., R. St. Paul's. [F.F.] Vacant by death of Meade, and on presentation of Thomas Buchanan, the elder, of Tipperary, in the county Tipperary. He was admitted by the Dean and Chapter of St. Finbarry, as Guardians of Spiritualities, *sede vacante*. [D.R.]

Thomas Buchanan, junior, was a Scholar of T.C.D. in 1784.

On 16th of October, 1788, being presented to the Rectory of St. Paul's, he received letters dimissory for Priest's orders to any other Bishop. [D.R. Cork.]

He married, on 15th April, 1790, Anne Allen, at Christchurch, Cork, and by her had issue. He died on 1st May, 1794.

1794. October 9. GEORGE SEALY, LL.D., R. St. Paul's, on presentation of Right Honourable Richard Longfield. [D.R.]

1807. Dr. Sealy resides in Cork, and holds Inchigeelah by faculty. [Rep.]

1817. April 22. The thanks of the parish are voted by vestry to Winthrop Baldwin, esq., of Bath (the maternal uncle of Rev. Dr. Sealy), for his gift of £200 towards a new roof for the church. On 21st Dec. 1817, the church was reopened for divine service. [Par. Vestry Book.]

1830. Protestant population, 936.

1837. St. Paul, a rectory, with cure, not one-sixth of a mile long, not one-fourteenth broad. Gross population, 4,845. Two Curates employed, at annual stipends—to the senior, of £69 4*s.* 7½*d.*; and to the junior, of £50, British. Income from Minister's money, £250. Small dues, £16. Subject to visitation fees, 14*s.* 5*d.* Diocesan schoolmaster, 11*s.* No glebe-house. Incumbent is non-resident, being incapacitated from officiating in consequence of advanced age; he resides at Bath. One church, capable of accommodating 600 persons, built in 1726, but at what cost unknown. No charge on the parish in 1832 on account of the church. Divine service is celebrated twice on Sundays, and on the principal festivals; and a short service on all Wednesdays and Fridays. The sacrament is administered monthly. The benefice is a rectory. [Parl. Rep.]

George Sealy (son of George Sealy, esq., of Bandon, by Anne, dau. of Rev. Richard Baldwin, P. Kilbrittain), was ordained Deacon by the Bishop of Waterford and Lismore, and afterwards was ordained Priest by the Bishop of Cork, on 4th March, 1781.

He was licensed to the Curacy of Kilbrittain and Rathclaren on 24th March, 1780.

He was V. Inchigeelah from 1791 to 1838; and R. St. Paul's from 1794 to 1838. He died 29th of May, 1838, and was buried near his wife, in the Abbey Church, Bath.

He married, in 1791, Alicia, dau. of Antony Lane, esq., but

by her had no issue. He took the name of BALDWIN on succeeding to the property of his maternal uncle, Winthrop Baldwin, esq., of Bath.

1838. July 26. FRANCIS DE MONTMORENCI ST. GEORGE, A.B., R. St. Paul's, on presentation of his Grace the Duke of Leinster. [D.R.]

1860. The church in order. No glebe. No glebe-house. Incumbent resides at Blackrock, by reason of ill-health. Divine service twice on all Sundays, &c. Sacrament monthly; average of communicants, 54; also at Christmas and Easter; average, 74. 30 boys, 20 girls, and 50 infants (the average attendance being respectively 25, 16, and 40), are on the rolls of the schools, which are maintained by voluntary contributions. The Protestant population is under 500. The yearly income is £251 7*s.* 2*d.* from minister's money, and *one-fourth of any necessary expenditure.*

Francis, son of Thomas Bligh St. George (who was son of Sir Richard St. George, bart., of Woodsgift), by Hannah, dau. of Sir Hercules Langrishe, was born in Dublin, and when sixteen years old entered T.C.D. on 22nd October, 1827. He is married, and has issue.

ST. PETER, ARCHDEACONS.

1157. January 1. On this day died PATRICK M'CARTHY, Archdeacon of Cork. [Cod. Clar. and MS. T.C.D. F. 1. 18.]

1180. REGINALD appears as Archdeacon. [Cod. Clar. and MS. T.C.D. F. 1. 18.] He confirmed under his seal the donation of the church of St. Nessan, made by the Bishop and Chapter to the Monks of St. Thomas Abbey, Dub. [King's Collections.]

1225. In this year GILBERT, Archdeacon of Cork, became Bishop of Cork. He died 1238. [Ware.]

1236. REGINALDUS OFIN appears as Archdeacon. [MS. T.C.D. F. 1. 18.]

In 1270, Prince Edward granted to Reginald, Bishop of Cork and his successors, the right of patronage and advowson of Nard and Kilmehannock and of the chapel of St. Peter's, at Cork. May 20, date of grant which was resumed after the Prince came to the throne. [Rot. Pat. 54. Hen. III.]

1291. "Jūrdicō Archid. Corcag. Cs.—Eccia de Dunbolg VIImr. —Eccia bī Petri XIImr. [Tax. P. Nic.]

1323. (16th Edward II.) JOHN appears as Archdeacon of Cork. [Rot. Com. Banc. Turre Berm.]

1337. D. is the initial of the name of the Archdeacon. [Placita Com. Banci. Hib.]

1346. WILLIAM EPWORTH, Archdeacon of Cork, was a royal Commissioner for collecting a subsidy, granted this year by the Parliament held at Kilkenny. The Archbishop of Cashel (Kelly) excommunicated him, and all others concerned in collecting this subsidy. [Ware.]

1365 to 1370. NICHOLAS DE BARRY is Archdeacon. [MS. T.C.D. F. 1. 18.]

1375 to 1385. ROB. ROCH is Archdeacon. [MS. T.C.D. F. 1. 18.]

1407. October 15. WALTER GALLE was appointed by the Crown Archdeacon. [Rot. Canc.]

1408. JOHN REDE, appointed Archdeacon by the Pope, is confirmed by the King on March 18. [Rot. Pat. 10. Hen. IV.]

1430. RICHARD SCURLAG is Archdeacon. "On the death of Bishop Milo Fitzjohn, in 1430, the custody of the See of Cork was committed to Nicholas, Bishop of Ardfert, and Richard Scurlag, Archdeacon of Cork." [Tuckey, p. 298.] Scurlag is Archdeacon in 1431. [MS. T.C.D. F. 1. 18.]

1437. JOHN BRASYLL, Archdeacon of Cork, appears in a mandate, signed 6th August, 1437, concerning the admission of a Clerk to Templeusky. [Caulfield MSS.]

1471. Feb. 6. On this day DIONYSIUS HERLEY, Archdeacon of Cork, is pardoned by the King for all offences committed against the Crown. [Rot. Pat. 11 Henry VII.] He appears as Archdeacon in 1495. [MS. T.C.D. F. 1. 18.] In 1496 *Donatus Hyerlachy*, LL.B., Archdeacon of Cork, witnesses a deed. [Sarsfield MSS.]

1500. "BARRY MORE was slain by his own kinsman [or brother], DAVID BARRY, Archdeacon of Cork and Cloyne. David was slain by Thomas Barry and Muinter O'Callaghan. The Earl of Desmond disinterred the body of David in twenty days, and afterwards burned it. [Annals of Ireland.]

1544. GEORGE ROCHE, Archdeacon, appears. [Rot. Pat.]

August 3. 36°. Hen. VIII. Pardon is granted by the King to George Roche, Archdeacon of Cork, Rector of the Free Chapel there. [Morrin.]

George Roche was third son of Morris Roche, who mortgaged Mitchelstown to Philip Barry. [Roche MSS. Brit. Mus.]

1555 to 1582. PATRICK ROCHE, Archdeacon, appears. [Dioc. Reg.] In 1554 he was Vicar-General of Cork and Ross. [Sarsfield MSS.]

Before the appointment of Bishop Skiddy, in 1557, to the See of Cork, the clergy and inhabitants of Kinsale petition Queen Mary for the appointment of Patrick Roche, Archdeacon of Cork, to the Bishoprick of Cork. [MS. Cotton, Titus B. XI. 252.]

1565. July 3. Dominus Patricius Roche, Archdeacon of Cork, is a witness to a deed. [Browne MSS.] Patrick Roche appears also in 1571 as Archdeacon of Cork and Cloyne. [D.R.]

Archdeacon Patrick Roche was third son of Edmund, who

was third son of Richard Roche, by his second wife, Ellys Yonge, of Kinsale. The last-named Richard Roche was eldest son of John, the eldest son of Morris Roche, who mortgaged Mitchelstown to Philip Barry. [Roche MSS. Brit. Mus.]

1582. PHILIP GOULDE is Archdeacon of Cork. [Dioc. Reg.] He was Vicar-General of Cork and Cloyne. He appears again in 1591.

1585. Sept. 9. THOMAS WETHERHEAD is appointed by letters patent Archdeacon of Cork and Cloyne. [Cotton.] He was Warden of Youghal from 1587 to 1591, and on 20th July, 1589, was appointed Bishop of Waterford and Lismore. He died in 1592. [Ware.]

1591. PHILIP GOLD appears as Archdeacon of Cork and Cloyne. [MS. T.C.D. E. 3. 14.] In this visitation the Archdeacon takes rank next to the Dean. The remark "del. sup' dispens," follows his name, in allusion to his holding other benefices. "E. Scī Petri spectat ad Archīnum." In another part of same Visitation Book Gold is mentioned as Archdeacon, and WILLMUS FIELD as "Rector ecclesiæ parochialis S. Petri, Cork, citatus." [MSS. T.C.D. E. 3. 14.] In 1591, E. de Danesky spectat ad Archinum. [Ib.] E. de Dunbolloig spectat ad Ab. de Chore. Regina. [Ib.]

1594. April 16. "Richard Skydde, now Chapelaine of our lady chapell in the church of St. Peter's," is mentioned in a deed made by the churchwardens of St. Peter's. [Roche MSS. Brit. Mus.]

1606. Feb. 6. Philipp Gould, esquier, Archdeacon of Cork, John Goule, Minister and P'rish Priest of the church of St. Peter's, in Corck, and others, made an indenture. [Roche MSS. Brit. Mus.]

1609. Philip Gould, Archdeacon, grants a tombe in St. Peter's. [Roche MSS. Brit. Mus.]

Philip Gold or Gould was P. Kilbrittain from 1579 to 1591, and appears as Archdeacon of Cork from 1582 to 1585, and also from 1591 to 1612; and from 1583 to 1612 as Archdeacon of Cloyne. In 1587 he was also a Vicar Choral of Cork, and he held likewise the P. Glanworth, Cloyne, from 1591 to 1612.

Archdeacon Philip Gold was married to Helena, sister to Patrick Sarsfield, as appears by a curious document now among the Roche MSS. in the Brit. Museum, which purports to be a certificate from John Copinger, Priest, S.T.B., formerly of Acquitain, who acts by virtue of a faculty from "Reverendissimo patre Christophero Hollenodio, Soc. Jes. in Hib." Copinger grants a dispensation to Dr. Philip Goulde and Helena Sarsfield, who after many years intermarriage find that they were consanguineous in third and fourth degree. This dispensation or certificate was granted by Copinger, "non plus in favorem Helenæ quæ semper in Catholica fide perseverabit sed et in favorem Philippi qui licet beneficia ecclesiastica ab hereticis obtenta possideat et teneat, tum pro viribus catholicam fidem fovebat et catholicis ubique fovebat et favit, qui juxta sacram scripturam boni et honesti viri omen et nomen obtinet, qui potuit facere malum et non fecit," &c.

Archdeacon Gold was also custodian of the church plate of St. Finbarry's, as Vicar Choral; and on 8th September, 1587, signs an acknowledgment of having received "of my brethorne, thother three Vicars of the said St. Barry's, one old senser of silver, not gilt, two challices, with their pattenes, duble gilt, and one pix, duble gilt, all belonging to the said church, and comytted to my kepinge to thuse of the same, and taken for that p'pose oute of the hands of Sir Roger Skiddy, Preste, now Warden of Youghal, who had the kepinge of the same afore me the said Philip." On the 9th January, 1612, Mrs. Ellen Gold, the Archdeacon's widow, gives up the above plate to some person whose name is illegible, who also signs a paper stating that he has received them to the use of the cathedral church. [Roche MSS. Brit. Mus.]

Mrs. Ellen Gold, the widow, also gives up in due form to John Travers, the Registrar, "the booke of laste wills and testaments, containing in it thirty-four leaves and seaven lines, wrytten" on the 9th January, 1612, in presence of her brother Patrick Sarsfield, and others. [Cork Reg.]

1613. January 7. MICHAEL BOYLE, D.D., is admitted Archdeacon of Cork and Cloyne. [Cotton.]

1615. Archidiaconus Ecclesiæ (non-residens) Michael Boyle antea Decanus Lismorensis, Theol. Doc., minister et predicator, valoris 16 li. Tenet etiam locum vicarii choralis ad val. duodecem librarum et prebendam in dioc. Clonensi val. 40 li., vocatam Glanor. [R.V. R.I.A.] Sti Petri prebenda est Archidiaconi. Curatus Johannes Gold, minister legens. [Ib.] Dunisky spectat ad Archid. Nulla Ecclesia, nulla cancella, nullum servitium. [Ib.] Prebenda de Donbolloge vacat et usurpatur per heredem Johis Fitzgerald. Vicaria vacat et usurpatur. Ecclesia et cancella bene teguntur stramine, sed nullus curatus. [Ib.]

1615/6. January 17. MANASSES MARSHALL, Archdeacon of Cork [F.F.] and of Ross. In 1615 he appears as P. Killaspugmullane and P. Kilmacdonogh, Cloyne.

1625. March 7. EDWARD FINCH is appointed Archdeacon of Cork and Cloyne. [Lib. Mun.]

1627. A small silver cup, originally gilt, is inscribed with this legend, "This cup was made for the Church of St. Peter, in Cork, in the year 1627. Richard Cooke, and William Potter, churchwardens."

1634. MICHAEL BOYLE, D.D., appears as Archdeacon. [R.V. 1634.]
Rectoria Scti Petri spectat ad Archidiacōn. [R.V. 1634.]

E. de Dunisky similiter. [Ib.] E. de Dunbullog Rex est Rector. Johēs Fitzgerald miles tenet vicariam. Nullus Curatus. [Ib.]

Michael Boyle, D.D., of Oxford (son of Michael Boyle, of London, merchant, and cousin of the great EARL of CORK) was educated at Merchant Tailors' school, and became a Fellow of St. John's College, Oxford.

He appears to have held from 1613 to 1635 the two Archdeaconries of Cork and Cloyne, and from 1613 to 1627 the P. Glanworth. He was Dean of Lismore from 1614 to 1621, and Bishop of Waterford and Lismore from 1619 to 1635; he held also from 1622 to 1635 the Treasurership of Waterford, and from 1615 to 1635 was a Vic. Chor., Cork.

He married Dorothy, dau. of George Fish, of South-hill, Bedfordshire, and relict of Dr. Condall, Bishop of Lincoln. He married, 2ndly, Christian, dau. of Thomas Bellott, of Chester, and left no issue by either of his wives.

He died at Waterford, on 29th December, 1635, and was buried at that cathedral. [U.O.]

1636/7. April 23. WILLIAM STEERE, Bishop of Ardfert, was admitted to the Archdeaconry of Cork and Cloyne. [F.F.]

William Steere, D.D., was, from 1612 to 1615, Treasurer of Ardfert, and from 1618 to 1627 Dean of Ardfert. From 1628 to 1637 he was Bishop of Ardfert, and from 1636 to 1637 Archdeacon of Cork and Cloyne.

"The Right Reverend Father in God, William Stears, late Lord Bishop of Ardfert and Aghadoe, in the county of Kerry, was second sonne of William Stears, Parson, of Barnesby, by London, in Kent, in the Kingdom of England. He tooke to wife Ellinor, daughter of Randall Maynwarring, sonne of John Maynwarring, second sonne of Sir Randall Maynwarring, of Peever, in Cheshire, in the said Kingdome of England, Knight, and relict of William Gunn, of Limerick, Parson, by whome the said Lord Bishop had no issue. The said Lord Bishop departed this mortal life at Ardfert, the 21st of January, 1637, and was interred in the Cathedral Church of Ardfert aforesaid. The truth of the premises is testified by the subscription of the said Ellinor, relict and executrix of the said Lord Bishop, whoe hath returned this certificat into my office, to be there recorded. Taken by me, Thomas Preston, esquire, Uluester King of Arms, the 23rd of May, 1638." [Funeral Entries, Ulster Office, vol. 7, p. 284.]

1639. The Archdeaconry is vacant.—"Ecclesia Sti Petri spectat ad Archidiac. vacat—ruinata—desunt ornamenta—Curatus, Robertus Baly, compt." [V.B. 1639. D.R.] E. de Dunesky spectat ad Archinum. [Ib.] Ecclesia de Donbollig Doms. Johēs Fitzgerald. Curatus, Thomas Swift. Ecclesia ruinata desunt omnia. [Ib.]

1641. August 17. MARTIN TINLY is presented to the archdeaconry of Cork. [Lib. Mun.]

In 1640 the name of the Archdeacon of Stafford, diocese of Lichfield, was Martin Tinley. [Le Neve's Fasti.]

Martin Tynly was, in 1638, Treasurer of Dromore; in 1640 Archdeacon of Stafford, dioc. Lichfield, and in 1641 Archdeacon of Cork. In 1642 he was Vicar of Paulswalden, Herts.

He married, Frances, daughter of Bazill Smith, who was Clerk of the parish of St. Andrew, Holborn, in London. He had issue by her, Martin, born in 1638, died same year; Frances, born at Lisneygarvey, county Antrim, where her father was Parson; Elizabeth, also born at Lisneygarvy, in 1641, and buried at Marresbie Church, in Cumberland, near Whitehaven, on 4th January, 1641; and Anne, born 9th December, 1642, at Paulswalden, Herts, where her father was Vicar. To Archdeacon Tinly, in 1645, on 21st March, was born another son, Martin, "born at Bazill Smith's house, in St. Andrew's Court, against the church."

The Archdeacon's death and burial is thus recorded:— "Martin Tynly, Clarke, sometime Archdeacon of Stafford, and late Archdeacon of Corke, died in Bazill Smith's house, his father-in-law, Clk of this parish, 31st Jan., buried 2nd Feb., 1646." [Extracts from the parish Register of St. Andrew, Holborn, furnished by Archdeacon Cotton.]

1662. July 5. BERNARD PACKINGTON, D.D., Archdeacon of Cork [F.F.] per mortem Martini Tinley. [D.R.]

R. Sti Petri Corke pticula et membrum Archidiaconatus Corkag. [V.B. 1669.] Rectoria de Dunbullog similiter. [Ib.] R. de Dunusque similiter. [Ib.]

1666. Sept. 28. A grant is made under the Act of Settlement to Packington and his successors, ministers of St. Peter's, of "a back house, and another back house and garden to the wall in Dominick Terry's lane, in Cork, at 19*s.* 6*d.* rent. [Records of Ireland.]

Bernard Packington, A.M., resigned on 9th Nov., 1660, his vicarage of Cheswicke, in county of Middlesex, and diocese of London. [MS. Consistorial Office, Dublin.] In 1661 he was a D.D. and R. Bruhenny, in Cloyne; in 1662 Archdeacon of Cork; in 1663 V. Aglish, Kilbonane, and Moviddy; in 1664 V. Whitechurch, Cloyne, and in 1667 V. Kilcully. He held all these livings (except Bruhenny) until his death in 1674.

He married Rebecca Exham, and by her left issue two sons, William (Lieut. in the Army), and Bernard, besides a daughter, who married Lieut. Theophilus Carey, and bore to him Richard, Susannah, and Elisabeth Carey.

Dr. Packington, in his will, "professes to dye a true sonne of the Church of England, according to the primitive constitution, suitable to the precepts of Christ and his holy Apostles." He wishes to be buried in St. Peter's Church, "within the rayle, in a tombe there, on the south side of the communion table." He gives £5 towards the enlarging of the quire and chappell of St. Finbarries, and £5 towards hanging up the bells in the steeple now begun at St. ffinbarries. He gives also ten shillings worth of bread to the prisoners in the north-east of Cork, and ten shillings to those in the south-east of Cork.

The Archdeacon died in May, 1674, and was buried at St. Peter's. His relict, Rebecca, makes her will, and dies in 1683. She mentions her nephews, John Exham, in Leighlinbridge, in the county of Catherlogh, gentleman, and Nathaniel Exham, his brother; also other nephews, John, of Charleville, and Joseph, of Cork, sons to her brother Henry, deceased. She was buried near her husband, in St. Peter's.

The arms of Packington are, "part per chevron, in base three garbs, in chief three mullets (spur rowels), the crest a garb." Dr. Packington was probably a near relative of Sir John Packington, Baronet, who fought at the battle of Worcester, on the side of King Charles II.

1674. May 27. Richard Synge is admitted Archdeacon of Cork, and Vicar of Moviddy, Kilbonane, Aglish, Kilcullie, and V. Whitechurch, in Cloyne diocese. [F.F.]

Richard Synge, son of George, Bishop of Cloyne, was born in Dublin, in 1646, and was educated at Cloyne, by Mr. Goffe. He entered T.C.D. as Pensioner, on 9th June, 1662, being then sixteen years old. He was nephew to Edward Synge, who was Bishop of Cork, Cloyne, and Ross 1663 to 1679.

From 1669 to 1674 he was P. Kilbrogan, Cork, and R. V. Aghinagh, Kilcoleman, and Agabulloge, in Cloyne. From 1671 to 1674 he was also Chancellor of Ross. From 1674 to his death in 1688 he was Archdeacon of Cork, and Vicar of the five parishes mentioned above in his titles to the archdeaconry.

He was, on 4th March, 1680, appointed to the commission of the peace for Cork county.

He married Elisabeth, whom I suppose to have been Miss Elisabeth Clarke (relict of William O'Connor, esq.), who is mentioned in Burke's L. G., edition of 1840, vol. ii., p. 1346, as having been married in 1671 to Rev. Richard Synge—there said, *erroneously* (I think) to be a son of Bishop Edward Synge. Richard Synge, however, in his will (dated 1686) calls his wife *Elisabeth, the dear companion of his youth*, and leaves to her for her life his house and lands near Bridgnorth, county Salop, and his house, in Bandon, then leased to his brother George, P. Kilbrogan, q. v. After his wife's death he leaves the said property to his son Richard, to whom he leaves £30 per an. for his maintenance at College.

He mentions also his son-in-law, Rev. William Denny, V. Whitechurch, Cloyne, q. v., and his daughter Letitia, to whom he leaves £500, and who was afterwards wife to Dr. Nicholas Brady, P. Kilnaglory, q. v. Archdeacon Synge's son, Richard, is, I think, the same person who, on 23rd Sept., 1694, was ordained Deacon at Cork, although a literate, and who was, on 20th March, 1696, ordained Priest at Cork.

1688. October 31. RICHARD LAPP, A.M., Archdeacon. [F.F.] The corps of the Archdeaconry in 1688 was "E. Kilmonoge, Dunisky, Naoffoild, et Vic. Donbullog seu decimæ quatuor carrucat. de Carrinavarr in parochia de Dunbullog ex antiquo unitæ una cum Rect. de Dunbullog per ltras patentes Dni Regis eidem vicariæ seu decimis de Carranavarr." N.B. This vicarage of Dunbullog was not in V.B., but was inserted in the title, by order of the Bishop, who found it elsewhere. [D.R.]

Lapp appears as Archdeacon from 1688 to 1690. [V.B. D.R.]

Richard Lapp, son of Thomas Lapp, "Mercatoris," was born at Bandon, and entered T.C.D. as a Pensioner, on 13th May, 1674, being then sixteen years old. [T.C.R.]

He was, from 1682 to 1686, V. Kinsale; from 1685 to 1690 P. Templebryan, and V. Templequinlan, in Ross, and R. V. Rathclarin. He was, from 1687 to 1688, Treasurer of Cork; and from 1688 to 1690 Archdeacon of Cork.

1691 to 1696. The Archdeaconry was held in commendam by Bishop EDWARD WETENHALL. [V.B. D.R.]

Before 1691 there is no mention of churchwardens or parish clerk for St. Peter's. In 1694 two churchwardens appear; and in 1695 Mr. Daniel Smith is Curate, succeeded by Cornelius Hignet, in 1696, who "non extraxit litteras curatiæ." [V.B. D.R. 1691–1696.]

1697. April 23. JOHN WETENHALL is admitted Archdeacon, per cessionem et desertionem Rēndi in Christo Patris Edwardi Epī Corkag. &c. ultimi incumbentis vacant. [D.R.] On 14th August he received also the Vicarages of Moviddy, Kilbonane, and Aglish.

1699. Dunbullog spectat ad Archid. No churchwardens nor parish clerk. [V.B. D.R.] In 1704 Jac Kean est clericus parochialis de Dunbullog. [V.B.] Dunbullog, in 1699, has no churchwarden, no parish clerk, and but one Protestant, who goes to Moviddy. [V.B. D.R.]

"Oct. 1700. I saw Dunbullog church, which was built with stone and lime. The walls are standing for the most part; the church is about 60 foot long; a partition wall runs through the middle of it, without any arch. There is a church-yard, about an acre, with a ditch about it. About 3 English acres of glebe, on the east side of the church, belongs to the Archdeacon. The ditch which bounds the glebe on the north side is broken down. The greatest part of this parish lies north of the church. About five plowlands are in this parish; the tythes are worth about £23 per an. To the east of Dunbullog church is the church of St. Michael, at about half a mile's distance. About a mile to the east of St. Michael's church is the church of Templeusky. Sir St. John Brodrick and Mr. Piggot have the greatest part of this parish. Redmund Barry (Papist), Thomas May, and —— Smith, Protestants, live in this parish, in which there are no more Protestants. The people of this parish go to Corke to church. Peter Murrogh is Popish Priest of this parish, and Kilcully, &c. He was tried at the assizes at Corke, about 1698, as being Vicar-General of the diocess of Corke. He pleaded that the Popish Bishop had some time ago displac'd him, and so he was acquitted. All the tythes of this parish belong to the Archdeaconry of Corke." [Downes' Tour.]

"1702. In St. Peter's parish there is an alms-house (in St. Peter's-lane, near the steeple), which was rebuilt not long since, when Mr. Browne, the town clerke, was churchwarden of St. Peter's, at the expence of 40 or 50 pounds, which he laid out for the parish, and afterwards forgave it, with the interest. There are 4 rooms in it, sufficient for 8 people. There are now in it but 6, viz., 2 men and 4 women, who receive 12*d.* per week from the churchwardens of St. Peter's. Besides the weekly collections in the church, there is £4 per annum paid out of 2 new houses, not far from the church, being the gift of Captain Bretridge, and also the interest of £40, at the rate of 8 per cent., charged by Mr. Browne, town clerk, on some houses on the East Marsh (he having received the said £40 from the parish), for the relief of the poor of the parish of St. Peter's. Captain Bretridge gave also 20*s.* yearly for a sermon on St. Simon's and St. Jude's Day in St. Peter's church, out of the above said houses. The £40 above mentioned was given by Alderman Newenham to the parish for the poor. The Minister of St. Peter's has a house in a lane, on the east side of the street, in Christchurch parish, but not far from St. Peter's church. This house was assigned to the Minister according to the Act of Settlement. 'Tis divided into 2 tenements, one of which is held by Dr. Barry at nine pounds per annum rent. The south side of the house hangs over. The timber in the upper part, I fear, is decaying. A weaver lives in the other tenement; 'tis less than Dr. Barry's. The weaver paies £12 per annum. The Archdeacon is obliged by his lease to repair the houses for the tenants."

"In St. Peter's parish, in a lane, near the wall, is a meeting-house of the Presbyterians. It is a large room; the seats and galleries will hold about 400 people. In the same parish, in another lane, near the water, is the Quaker's meeting-house, a neat room; the benches and galleries will hold about 200 people. Adjoining to it is a large room, where a Quaker teaches school at present. In the meeting-house is a long seat, next the wall, raised a step or two above the floor, where the speakers preach."

"The house of the Minister of Christchurch is in Watergate-lane, in St. Peter's parish, over against Christchurch. It was exchanged for another house in Christchurch parish, assign'd to him according to the Act of Settlement. There is a little garden plot behind the house. The walls and main timber are pretty sound and good, but the window frames, and some of the timber in the back front, are decaying. This house is set by Mr. Synge to one person for £12 per annum. The tenant sets it for about £16 per annum. Mr. Synge keeps it in repair. There are at present 7 families in the house. The old proprietor, in King James' time, upon the breaking the Act of Settlement, took possession of the house, but could get no tenant for it, so that after the troubles it was much out of repair. The Minister of St. Peter's parish has, by way of exchange, a house in the parish of Christchurch, which house was appointed to be the house of the Minister of Christchurch, according to the Act of Settlement." [Downes' Tour.]

1704. Alderman William Allwin, by his will (dated 19th Feb. 1703, and proved 26th January, 1704, bequeathed "unto the English poor of St. Peter's, £20, to be disposed of by the Minister and churchwardens for an annual revenue for the said poor, and the interest to be paid them yearly at Easter for ever." [Cork Wills.]

1709. April 6. "Hugh Hovell, of citty of Cork, gent." makes his will, of which the following is an extract—"Item, I leave £10 ster. to buy a tomestone, to be laid over my father's grave in St. Peter's church; my father and mother's names, and the time of their decease, and given by me, all to be cutt in plain characters. Item, I leave £40 sterling, which I desire may be laid out on the erecting of a pirimide or an obliqq of freestone or limestone, to stand a convenient distance in the street of Cork, over right the front of the new Exchange: my name and arms to be hewn on said pirimide, the time of my decease, and what else my 2 trustees think fitt." [Cork Wills.]

1714. The following is inscribed on a large silver salver, weighing 20 oz.—"In usum Ecclie St. Petri Corcagiensis anno Domini 1714."

1716. Thomas Browne, of Cork city, gentleman, in his will (dated 28th Dec. 1713, and proved 14th Feb. 1716), wishes to be buried in his own tomb in St. Peter's, and mentions a former deed, by which he gave to the Minister and churchwardens of St. Peter's and their successors for ever, to the use of the poor of said parish, one annuity of £5 12*s.* sterling, issuing out of two houses in Brown-street, one in his own tenancy, the other in that of Rev. Evan Davies. [D.R.]

John Whetenhall (son of Edward, Bishop of Cork, by Philippa, dau. of Sir William Doyly, bart.), was born in Essex, and educated at Ross, county Cork, by Mr. Hickson. When seventeen years of age he was entered a Fellow Commoner, T.C.D. on 24th April, 1685.

From 1697 to 1717 he was Archdeacon of Cork, V. Moviddy, Kilbonane, and Aglish; and P. Currograngemore, in Ross. In 1703 he was summoned to the Convocation in Dublin.

Archdeacon Wetenhall left no issue by his wife, Ann ——? and desired in his will (dated 1715, Feb. 17, and proved 8th May, 1717), to be buried near his mother, in the cathedral of St. Finbarry. He left £10 to the poor of St. Peter's, and £5 to the poor of St. Finbarry.

1717. August 30. John Pomeroy, A.M., Archdeacon. [F.F.]

1718. On two silver flagons is inscribed, "Deo sacrum in usum Ecclisæ St. Petri corcag. Qui ex te bibit non sitiat in æternum. Dec. 25, 1718, ex dono Johannis Pomeroy Archidiaconi Corcagiensis."

1719. On two small patens of silver, weighing 9 oz. 18 dwts. and on one silver basin, weighing 19 oz. is inscribed, "In usum Ecclisæ St. Petri, 1719."

On one large cup of silver is inscribed, "In usum Ecclisæ St. Petri, Cork, A.D. ex dono Danielis Crow armigeri civitatis Corcagiensis Aldermanni."

John Pomeroy (son of Dean Arthur Pomeroy), was ordained Deacon on 22nd Dec. 1700, and Priest on 31st May, 1702, both at Cork.

From 1704 to 1724 he was R. Ardnegihy and Kilcully; and from 1710 to 1717 was Chancellor; and from 1717 to 1724 Archdeacon of Cork.

He married, in 1716, Elisabeth, dau. of Edmund Donellan, esq., of Cloghran, county Roscommon, and by her had issue, *inter alios*, two sons, born in Cork, Arthur and John, who entered T.C.D. the same day, 19th Sept. 1739, aged respectively sixteen and fifteen years. Arthur, the eldest, was created Viscount Harberton; and John was a Lieutenant-General in the army, and a Privy Councillor in Ireland.

The Archdeacon died in the spring of 1725, having shown himself a most generous benefactor to the poor; for by his will, dated September 24, 1724, he bequeathed £100 towards building or supporting a charity school in St. Finbar's parish, and £60 worth of his own books to found a parish library there: also, £180 to the Bishop and the Archdeacon of Cork, in trust, for clothing and keeping to school poor children of St. Peter's parish; £50 to the Minister and churchwardens of St. Peter's parish, to be put out to interest for the use of the poor of said parish; and £5 to the poor of each of the country parishes of which he was Incumbent. [Board of Char. Bequests.] In the library a marble tablet has been deservedly erected to his memory, bearing the following inscription:—

"Scholæ hujus et Bibliothecæ parochialis testamento suo prima jecit fundamenta Reverendus JOHANNES POMEROY, Archidiaconus Corcagiensis; omnibus dum vixit charus; mortuus ab omnibus defletus. Anno Domini, 1725."

The Archdeacon's relict became wife to Robert Carleton, Dean of Cork.

1724. November 3. Vacant. [V.B. D.R.]

1724. February 13. THOMAS RUSSELL, A.M., Archdeacon of Cork, and Rector of Ardnegihy, vacant by death of John Pomeroy. [D.R.] He took a second collation to this Archdeaconry and Ardnegihy on 23rd March, 1725. [D.R.]

On 26th April, 1730, Thomas Tuomy recants in St. Peter's Church; and on 5th Oct. 1734, Edward Gregg. In same year Thomas Burden, and in 1735 Daniel O'Leary, of Mill-street, recant, &c. [D.R.]

1732. May 22. Archdeacon Russell renews his lease of house, &c., near Dean's-court, from the Bishop, at 30*s*. per an. [D.R.]

Thomas Russell (eldest son of Lieutenant-Colonel John Russell, of Rutland, county Carlow, a kinsman of Peter Browne, Bishop of Cork), was born at Lisburn, and when only fourteen years old entered T.C.D. as Pensioner on 9th July, 1707.

From 1718 to 1719 he was P. Killanully; from 1719 to 1720, P. Kilbrittain; from 1720 to 1724, Precentor of Cork, and V. Athnowen; and from 1724 to 1745, Archdeacon of Cork, and R. Ardnegihy. He was also from 1718 to 1744, V. Cannaway; from 1719 to 1745, Precentor of Ross; and from 1732 to 1745, V. Athnowen. In 1725 he was made Vicar-General of Cork and Ross.

He married Philippa, dau. of Edward Wetenhall, M.D., of Cork, who was brother to Archdeacon John Wetenhall, and son of Bishop Edward Wetenhall.

In 1735, a Rev. Thomas Russell was licensed to the curacy of St. Peter's, and in 1747, Elisabeth Russell, of St. Peter's, was married to James Colthurst, esq. Perhaps these were children of the Archdeacon.

Mr. Russell published an edition of Bishop Browne's sermons in two volumes.

Bishop Browne bequeathed to Elisabeth Russell, sister to the Archdeacon, £3,000, which bequest, if she died without marriage or issue, was to revert to the library of St. Finbarry to purchase books.

1745. April 3. WILLIAM READER, A.B., Archdeacon, and R. St. Peter's, Dunbullog, Nohoval, Kilmonoge, and Dunisky, vacant by death of Russell. [D.R.]

William Reader was son of Enoch Reader, Dean of Kilmore, by Alice Jephson; and was grandson of Enoch Reader, Alderman and Lord Mayor of Dublin, who married Ann, dau. of Sir James Donelan, Lord Chief Justice of the Common Pleas.

William Reader was born in Dublin, in 1704, and when fifteen years old entered T.C.D. as Pensioner on 18th December, 1719, and was Scholar in 1722.

He was ordained Deacon at Cloyne on 23rd Sept. 1728. He was Vicar Choral of Ross from April to August in 1731. From 1732 to 1745 he was P. Cahirlag, and from 1745 to 1774 was Archdeacon of Cork. He held also from 1737 to 1741 the R. Ballymodan, and from 1741 to 1745 the V. Kinsale.

He died in July, 1774, and was buried in the cathedral of Cork.

1774. August 5. WILLIAM JEPHSON, A.M., Archdeacon, vacant by death of Reader. [D.R.] He took a second collation on 15th Dec. 1777. [D.R.] He was also Precentor of Ross, q. v.

1782. March 11. JOHN FORSAYETH, D.D., Archdeacon, R. St. Peter's, Dunbullog, Nohoval, Kilmonoge, Dunisky, and Ardnegihy, per ces. Jephson. [D.R.]

1782. Feb. 24. The Bishop consents to the memorial of Minister and churchwardens to rebuild St. Peter's on the old site.

John Forsayeth, son of Thomas Forsayeth, was born in Cork, in 1735, and when fourteen years old entered T.C.D. as a Pensioner on 5th July, 1749. He obtained a Fellowship in 1762.

He was ordained Deacon at Cloyne on 9th July, 1758, and Priest at Cork, on 26th August, 1759.

He was licensed to the curacy of St. Peter's, Cork, on 9th September, 1759. In 1782 he resigned his Fellowship for the college living of Rahy and Clondehorky, Raphoe, which he immediately exchanged for the Archdeaconry of Cork. He died on 17th April, 1785, and was buried at St. Anne's Churchyard, Dublin.

Archdeacon Forsayeth, in his will, dated in 1754, mentions his brothers, Samuel and Robert, and his nephews, Thomas, Robert, and John Forsayeth.

After bequeathing his own manuscripts and some of Archdeacon Reader's to his friends, Rev. Wm. Hales (the author of the Chronology), and Wm. Newcome (afterwards Primate), he desires certain of his books to be "sold in London, as in this kingdom books of this kind bear no price, I believe," continues the Archdeacon, "I may add books of divinity and church history, our Governors' long neglect of Irish clergymen having almost extinguished all zeal for the acquisition of learning among them."

The family of Archdeacon Forsayeth (or Forsayth, or Forsythe) is said to have come from Failzerton, Ayrshire, Scotland. Of the brothers of the Archdeacon, SAMUEL was father of Rev. Robert Forsayeth (author of "The History of the Life of our Lord and Saviour, compiled from the Holy Gospels, as harmonized by William Newcome, Bishop of Waterford," 8vo. Dublin, 1782), P. C. Nohoval, q. v.; and of Rev. John Forsayeth (R. Leighmoney, q. v.), who, by his wife, Ann Courtney, had issue seven children, of whom Thomas, born in 1798, is now Recorder of Cork, and John was in holy orders. The last-named John, was ordained Deacon on 20th May, and Priest on 19th Dec. 1830, at Cloyne. He was licensed to the curacy of Killowen on 19th Oct. 1830, and on 11th Feb. 1835, to that of St. Anne, Shandon. He died, *unmarried*, at the early age of thirty-eight, and was buried at St. Peter's, on 30th Nov. 1839.

Archdeacon Forsayeth's brother, ROBERT, was father of Thomas Forsayth, of Failzerton, whose only son, Thomas-Gifford, married, in 1863, Lucy-Harriette O'Toole.

1785. April 25. ROBERT AUSTEN, D.D., Archdeacon, and R. Ardnegihy. [F.F.]

"1788. This church wasfinished." [Inscription at St. Peter's.]

Robert Austen (son of Samuel Austen, of Cork, and of Ring, in county Cork, by Mary, dau. of Robert Atkins, esq., of Highfield, county Cork), was born in Cork, in 1723. and when sixteen years old entered T.C.D. on 9th July, 1739. He graduated A.B. in 1743, A.M. in 1747, and D.D. in 1774.

He was ordained, in Cork, Deacon on 20th May, and Priest on 19th August, 1750.

He was licensed to the curacy of Kilmichael on 22nd May, 1750, and to that of Holy Trinity on 24th December, 1758, and to the curacy of Kilnaglory on 14th June, 1764. From 1768 to 1774 he was Chancellor of Cork, and from 1774 to 1777, P. Lisclery; from 1777 to 1785, P. Kilnaglory, and from 1785 to 1792, Archdeacon of Cork.

He died on 10th November, 1792, leaving issue by his wife, Elisabeth, dau. of Rev. Wm. Ellis (P. Island, Ross, q. v.), three daughters, Mary, Judith, and Elisabeth, besides a son, Robert, Treasurer of Cloyne, q. v.

1793. January 15. JOHN WHETHAM, Archdeacon, and R. Ardnegihy. [F.F.]

John Whetham (second son of John Whetham, esq., of London, first Commissioner of Excise), was born on 12th April, 1733.

From 1791 to 1796 he was Dean of Lismore; and from 1793 to 1796 was also Archdeacon of Cork. From February to June, 1794, he was R. V. Scull; and from June, 1794, to 1795, was V. Brinny. From Dec. 1794, to 1796, he was also R. V. Callen, Coolaghmore, Tullaroan, Ballycallan, Killaloe, and Tullamain, in Ossory diocese.

He died at Clifton, near Bristol, on 1st May, 1796. He married, in 1766, Agatha, dau. of John Moore, esq., M.P., and had issue (besides a dau. Maria, wife of P. J. Miles, esq., of Leigh Court, Bristol) a son, Major-General John Whetham, for whom *vide* Burke's L. G. WHETHAM, of KIRKLINGTON HALL.

1796. June 1. ALEXANDER LAMILLIERE, LL.D., Archdeacon. [F.F.] On this appointment Ardnegihy is separated from the Archdeaconry.

Alexander Lamilliere (son of Cyrus Lamilliere, who, with his brother, Henry, entered T.C.D. in 1701, and who were natives of France, being sons of Florence La Milliere), was born in Dublin in 1723, and when seventeen years old entered T.C.D. as a Pensioner, on 9th July, 1740, and graduated A.B. in 1744, and A.M. in 1749.

From 1774 to 1782 he was Chancellor of Cork; from 1782 to 1796 Vicar of Holy Trinity; and from 1796 to 1800 Archdeacon of Cork.

He had a son, Alexander, who was ordained Priest on 1st August, 1790, for the Curacy of St. Nicholas, and who was buried at St. Nicholas on 23rd Nov. 1797. The Archdeacon died on 7th September, 1800, aged seventy-seven, and was buried (with his son) at St. Nicholas' church-yard, on 11th Sept. 1800. Henry, another son of the Archdeacon, was also buried in St. Nicholas' church-yard, on 2nd Oct. 1779.

1800. Sept. 20. WILLIAM THOMPSON, A.M., Archdeacon; certified to be worth £800 per annum. [D.R.]

1830. Protestant population, 2,507.

William Thompson, born 1766, became a Scholar T.C.D. in 1785.

In 1796, April 29, he was licensed to the Curacy of St. Finbarry; and in 1797 was Reader and Catechist in Cork cathedral.

In 1800 he was made Archdeacon of Cork. In 1814 he was one of the Commissaries chosen to execute the office of Vicar-General, vacant on Dr. Kenney's death; and in 1829, on 6th January, was appointed coadjutor of the Bishop of Cork.

He married, firstly, Ellen or Eleanor, dau. of Charles Ferguson, esq., and by her (who died in Cork, 29th June, 1803, aged twenty-one) had issue two sons, Edward-Pakenham (Rector of Myross, Ross, q. v.); and Charles-Ferguson, baptized at St. Peter's, Cork, on 20th March, 1802.

He married, secondly, Mary-Frances, dau. of Rev. John Chetwood, P. Cahirlag, and by her had issue, Frederick-Francis-Moore (born 1821), Richard-P., Thomas, Henry, John-Chetwood, and William (born 1814, now, 1863, R. Stoke Dry, Peterborough diocese); besides four daughters, Elisabeth-Clementina, Catherine, Mary-Frances, and Lucy, wife of Rev John Fitzgerald, of Nohoval, county Kerry.

The following inscriptions are taken from tombstones in St. Peter's church-yard, Cork :—

"Hic jacet Elionora Caroli Ferguson Filia, et Gulielmi Thompson, Archidiaconi Cork Uxor perdilecta. Obiit 29 Junii. Anno Ætatis 21. Anno Domini 1803. Heu."

"Sacred to the memory of the Venerable William Thompson, A.M., Archdeacon of Cork, and for thirty-three years Rector of this parish, who died June 19, 1833, aged 67. In grateful remembrance of the kindness of his heart, and the endearing courtesy of his manners, of his judicious attention to their parochial charities, and his mild consolation, administered in the true spirit of the Gospel, at the bed of sickness, of sorrow, and of penitence, the parishioners of St. Peter's parish have erected this tribute to the memory of their pious and respected pastor, and their affectionate and much esteemed friend."

1833. July 6. SAMUEL MOORE KYLE, A.M., Archdeacon. He read his assent and consent on 7th July, 1833. [D.R.]

1834. January 1. The school-house at Carrignavar was licensed for divine service.

1837. St. Peter's union, with cure, consisting of—1. St. Peter's rectory, half mile long by half mile broad; 2. Nohoval rectory; 3. Kilmanogue rectory; 4. Dunbulloge rectory, 6 miles long by 4 broad; 5. Dunisky rectory. Gross population of union, 12,501. Four Curates employed—two for St. Peter's parish, at stipends, to the senior, of £69 4*s.* 7½*d.* British, and to the junior, of £50 British, per annum; and two for the occasional duties of Dunbulloge and Dunisky parishes, at stipends, to the former, of £10 British, and to the latter of £5 British, per annum. The income is—from minister's money in St. Peter's parish, £200; tithe composition of Nohoval parish, £140; of Kilmanogue parish, £147 13*s.* 10*d.*; of Dunbulloge parish, £461 10*s.* 9*d.*; of Dunisky parish, £107. Surplice fees, £15. Rents of houses, £27 13*s.* 10¼*d.* Subject to visitation fees, 18*s.* Diocesan schoolmaster, £1 10*s.* No glebe-house. Incumbent resides in the city of Cork; and £80 a-year is considered a reasonable sum to be allowed in way of house-rent. The parochial church, situate in St. Peter's parish, capable of accommodating 1,500 persons, was built about forty years by means principally of subscriptions but at what cost unknown. No charge on the union in 1832 on account of the church. Divine service is celebrated thrice on the second Sunday in every month, and twice on all other Sundays, and on the principal festivals, besides a short service on all Wednesdays and Fridays. The sacrament is administered twice every month, and on the festivals. The benefices constituting this union are rectories. [Parl. Rep.]

1860. S. M. Kyle, Incumbent; Thomas B. Jones and S. O. Madden, Curates. The church of St. Peter's is pronounced by architects to be in a dangerous state. No glebe-house. Divine service twice on all Sundays and chief festivals, and once on all church holidays, &c. The sacrament is administered twice each month; average of communicants, 85; and at Christmas and Easter, average 226. 50 boys, 50 girls, and 55 infants (the average attendance being respectively 40, 44, and 55) are on the rolls of the schools, which are maintained by voluntary contributions and by Moses Deane's endowment. The Protestant population is about 1,100.

At Dunbullog or Carrignavar school-house there is divine service twice on all Sundays, and on Christmas Day and Good Friday. Sacrament four times in the year. 11 Protestant children (including 4 orphans) attend a Church Education school. The Protestant population, including the orphans and two Presbyterian families, amounts to 18. The churchwardens of St. Peter's act for this parish of Dunbollog, of which Mr. George Keybourne is Curate.

The gross value of the archdeaconry is £957 8*s*. 5*d*., arising from—minister's money, £282 11*s*. 3*d*.; tithe rent-charge of Dunbullog, £346 3*s*.; of Dunisky, £80 5*s*.; of Nohoval, £105; of Kilmonoge, £110 15*s*. 4*d*.; and from rents of houses, £32 13*s*. 10*d*. The necessary outgoings (exclusive of the expenses of collection, poor rates, schools, &c., &c.), are—£200 for stipends of three Curates (who have also the surplice fees, &c.); £75 for house rent; 18*s*. visitation fees; and £1 10*s*. for diocesan schoolmaster. The net annual value is, accordingly, but £680 0*s*. 5*d*., to which sum, however, must be added, one-fourth of the necessary disbursements, which is paid by the Ecclesiastical Commissioners, in addition to the minister's money.

S. M. Kyle (eldest son of Samuel Kyle, Bishop of Cork), was a Scholar of T.C.D. in 1819, and graduated A.B. in 1821, A.M. in 1824. He is also LL.D. of Dublin, and D.C.L. of Cambridge University.

He was ordained Deacon in 1824, and Priest on 30th October, 1825.

In 1824 he was licensed to the Curacy of Urglin, diocese of Leighlin.

From 1828 to 1831 he was Treasurer of Leighlin; from 1831 to 1833 R. Rathclaren; and from 1833 to the present time Archdeacon of Cork. He also held, in 1833, the P. Currograngemore, Ross, for a few months. From 1831 to the present time he has held also a Vicarage Choral in Cork.

In 1833 he was appointed a Surrogate; and in 1835 and 1836 was Commissary, in the absence of the Vicar-General.

He was made, on the 30th June, 1837, Vicar-General and Chancellor of Cork and Ross, for life; and in 1840 was also Vicar-General of Cloyne.

Archdeacon Kyle, for several years previous to the death of

his father, managed, with ability, the affairs of the united diocese. His judgment, as Vicar-General, in the case of Somerville *v.* Robinson, concerning "The Ministration of Private Baptism," was printed, and received the approval of some of the highest legal authorities both in England and Ireland.

He married, in 1833, Jane, eldest dau. of John Cotter, esq., of Ashton, county Cork, and by her had issue, besides a son, Samuel-Cotter, (born in 1834, Lieutenant, Royal Artillery) three daughters, Rebecca-Catherine (married in 1862 to Wyrly Birch, junior, esq., eldest son of George-Wyrly Birch, esq., of East Wretham, Norfolk), Annette-Margaret, and Catherine-Cotter.

TAXAX.

1591. "E. de Taxax vacat per resign' Avery olim incumbentis. Sequestr' p' Regina ex Scaccario." [MS. T.C.D. E. 3. 14.]

1613. Nov. 15. Richard Owen is admitted P. Donoghmore, Cloine, "cui prebendæ Epus univit P. de Kilnaglorie R. de Taxax et V. de Kinsale, nomine unius beneficii." Installed same day. [R.V. 1634.]

1615. Taxax (residens) Rector, Richardus Owen. Valor 5 li. Ecclesia et cancella in ruina. [R.V. R.I.A.]

1634. E. de Taxax Richs. Owen. Val. 14 li. per an. Galfridus Gallway miles patronus. Winsmore Curatus. [R.V. 1634.] For Owen, *vide* Kilnaglory.

1634. Oct. 11. John Johnson, Rector integer de Taxax. [F.F.] He was also V. Kinsale, q. v.

1639 to 1667. Jonas Stawell appears as Rector. [V.B. D.R.] He was also Archdeacon of Ross, &c., q. v.

1669 to 1681. Theodore Vesey appears. [V.B.] "Rectoria de Taxax vacat per mortem Jonæ Stawell clici. Theodorus Veasy habet curam animarum et emolumenta inde crescenda. Dom. Rex est patronus." [V.B. D.R. 1669.] In 1670 Rector de Taxax Theodore Veasey in presentatione Regis eo quod Gallway patronus est papista. [V.B. D.R.] Vesey was instituted to Taxax on 11th Dec., 1672, [F.F.] on letters patent of Dec. 6. [Lib. Mun.] He became, in 1676, P. Kilnaglory, q. v.

1682. Sept. 26. Thomas Meade, R. V. Rincurran and Taxax. [F.F.] He appears from 1682 to 1709. [V.B. D.R.] In 1693 he became P. Inskenny, q. v.

1709. June 7. George Synge is presented to the rectory of Taxax. [Lib. Mun.] He appears from 1709 to 1732. [V.B. D.R.]

G. Synge was son of Rev. George Synge, P. Kilbrogan. He was in 1706 R. V. Miros, Ross, in 1709 R. Taxax, and in 1718 V. Kilmacabee, &c., in Ross.

He married, firstly, in November, 1706, Margaret, dau. of Rev. Thomas Meade, P. Inskenny; and secondly, in October, 1720, Eliza Roberts, of Bridgetown, who was sister to Rev. Randol Roberts, Vicar Choral of Cork.

1733. July 3. PERCIVAL DAGGE, A.M., R. Taxax, per mortem Georgii Synge. [D.R.] On letters patent, dated 20th June, 1733. [Lib. Mun.] He appears 1733, Nov. 7. [V.B. D.R.]

Percival Dagge (son of John Dagg "generosi") was born in Cornwall, in England, and when twenty-eight years of age entered T.C.D. as Pensioner, on 17th Nov., 1714.

These two marriage bonds are all that I can find in Cork Records relative to Mr. Dagge:—"1723, Feb. 4, Percival Dagge, of Kinsale, Clk, with Serina Strike, of Kinsale;" and "1732, Dec. 14, Percival Dagge, of Kinsale, Clk., with Catherine Burscough, of Christchurch, Cork, spinster."

1734. July 9. JOHN JEPHSON, R. Taxax, per mortem P. Dagg. [D.R.] On letters patent, dated March 5, 1733/4. [Lib. Mun.] Jephson was Archdeacon of Cloyne, q. v.

From 1734 to 1829 Taxax was held with Rincurran, q. v.

1829. Nov. 3. HENRY HAMILTON BEAMISH, A.B., R. Taxax, vacant by death of Graves. Patron, the King. [D.R.]

1830. The Protestant population is not returned.

1837. Taxax: a rectory, with cure, containing 2,138A. 0R. 28P. Gross population, 515. No Curate employed. Tithe composition, £105, subject to visitation fees, 8s. 6*d*.; diocesan schoolmaster, 8s. No glebe-house. Incumbent is non-resident; he resides in London. No church. The benefice is a rectory. The Rector holds also the chaplaincy of Trinity Chapel, Conduit-street, London, and the cure of the Irish Episcopal Chapel, at St. Giles, London. [Parl. Rep.]

1860. H. H. Beamish, Rector; the Curate of Kinsale is Curate. No church. No glebe. No glebe-house. No service. No school. The Incumbent resides in London, and gives the income (£78 15s.) to pay a Curate in Kinsale. The Protestant population is four.

H. H. Beamish (son of Samuel Beamish, V. Kinsale, q. v.) was ordained Priest on 28th Feb., 1819, at Cork.

He was licensed to the curacy of Kinsale on 29th May, 1818. From 1826 to 1832 he was V. Kinsale, and from 1832 to 1863 was Incumbent of Trinity Chapel, Conduit-street, London, of which he is also Patron. He was reported to have resigned Taxax in 1863, on becoming Vicar of Old Cleeve, in the diocese of Bath and Wells.

It is expected that when this resignation is completed, the Privy Council will unite Taxax to Kinsale.

TEMPLEBRADY, DEANS.

1288. PHILIP is Dean. [Cod. Clar. 46.]

1291. "Jurisdicō Decani. Corcag. XXXs.—Eccia de Kullyn Vmr." [Tax. P. Nic.]

1302. In this year JOHN MACCARWILL, or O'CARROLL, Dean of Cork, was unanimously elected by the Chapter to the See of Cork, then vacant by the death of Bishop M'Donogh. The royal assent was given to this election on 12th June, and the Archbishop's confirmation was granted in July same year. In 1321 he became Bishop of Meath, and in 1327 Archbishop of Cashel. [Ware.]

1323 to 1326 DIONYSIUS appears as Dean. [MS. T.C.D. F. 4. 14.]

1328 to 1336. PHILIP ALBUS, or WHITE, appears as Dean. [MS. T.C.D. F. 4. 14.]

1337. G. is the initial of the Dean. [Placita. Com. Banci. Hib. and King's Collections, from the Rolls Office.]

1346. JO DE RUPE Decanus. [MS. T.C.D. F. 1. 18.] In 1347 John de Rupe, or Roche, Canon of the Cathedral of Cork, and a man descended of a noble family, was elected Bishop of Cork. He died 4th July, 1358. [Ware.]

1348. GERALD DE BARRY became Dean, in succession to John de Rupe. He was of the family of the Barrys, and in 1359 became Bishop of Cork. He died 4th January, 1393, and was buried in the Cathedral of Cork. [Ware, and MS. T.C.D. F. 4. 14.]

1370. WILLIAM BULL, B.C.L., appears as Dean. [MS. T.C.D. F. 4. 14.] He became Bishop of Ardfert, in 1379. [Ware.]

13—? JOHN WALSH appears as Dean. [MS. T.C.D. F. 4. 14.]

1404. MILO FITZJOHN appears as Dean. [Cod. Clar.] In 1418 he became Bishop of Cork. He died in 1430. [Ware.]

1496. JOHN HYERLACHY, Dean of Cork, witnesses a deed. [Sarsfield MSS.]

15—? THOMAS O'HEIRNAN, Dean of Cork, was the author of "Ad Jacobum Stanihurstum Epistolas plures," a work published about 1573. [Ware's Writers.]

1582. July 5. THOMAS LONG, utrius juris doctor, appears as Dean of Cork, and as one of the Vicars *spiritualitatis ecclesiæ Corkagen sede vacante.* [First Book of Cork Registry.] He died in 1607. [Rot. Pat. 5. Jac. I.]

1590. May 5. ROBERT GRAVE, A.M., was appointed Dean. [Cotton.] He received the royal license to hold this Deanery of Cork, the Precentorships of Christ Church, Dublin, and of Limerick, and the Prebend of Tullybracky, Limerick, on 17th July, 1600, when he became also Bishop of Ferns and Leighlin. [Rot. Pat.] He was drowned in October of that year in the bay of Dublin, while on his way to Wexford. [Ware.]

1591. August 9. "Decanus nullus. vacat et fructus sequestr. ex Scaccario p' primitiis Regineis. Regina patrona." [MS. T.C.D. E. 3. 14.] "E. de Cullin spectat ad Decanatum, Curatus nullus." [Ib.] "E. Sci Martini pertinet ad Decanatum." [Ib.] "Templebready vacat, Regina patrona, sequestrat." [Ib.]

1601. THOMAS RAM, M.A., is appointed Dean of Cork and of Ross.

Thomas Ram was born in 1564, at Windsor, in Berkshire, and was educated at Eton and at King's College, Cambridge. He came to Ireland as Chaplain to the Earl of Essex in 1599.

From 1600 to 1602 he was P. St. John's, Dublin, and a Vicar Choral of Christ Church, Dublin, and from 1600 to 1634 he was Precentor of Christ Church, Dublin. From 1601 to 1605 he was Dean of Cork and Ross. In 1602 he was P. St. Michan's, Dublin, and in 1604, R. Balrotherie, Dublin. From 1604 to 1625 he was Dean of Ferns. He was Bishop of Ferns and Leighlin from 1625 to 1634, and P. Fethard, Ferns, from 1629 to 1634. He died in Dublin on 24th November, 1634; and was buried at Gorey, county Wexford.

He married Joanna, the widow of Nicholas Devereux [Roll. Excheq.], and was founder of the family of Ram, of Ramsfort, county Wexford. The Bishop left four sons, Thomas, Dean of Ferns (who died without issue); Robert, Abel, and Henry; and four daughters. Abel Ram, of Ramsfort, county Wexford, esq., died in June, 1676, leaving two sons, Sir Abel Ram, knight, Lord Mayor of Dublin, and Andrew. Sir Abel left five sons, Abel, Stephen, George, Samuel, and Andrew. [U.O.]

1605. June 12. GEORGE LEE is appointed Dean by the Crown. Another patent is dated December 9. [Lib. Mun.] In 1593 he was elected Fellow T.C.D. He became R. Clonoe, Armagh, in 1603, and was also Archdeacon of Down, which he resigned on his appointment to the Deanery of Cork. [Dub. Univ. Cal. and Cotton.]

1615. Decanus. Residens. George Lee, A.M., minister et predicator, ibidem residens; valor. 24 li. Tenet etiam locum vicarii in ecclesia Cathedrali; val. 12 li. Homo dignus. Ecclesia Cathedralis in bene statu, bene reparata, ornata libris et omnibus necessariis. [R.V. R.I.A.]

1615. Kilcullie (als Bride als Templebready) Decanus Corcagiensis est Rector et Vicarius. Nullus curatus. The Dean is peremptorily admonished to provide a Curate. [Ib.]

1615. Cullen is the prebend of the Dean, who says that he serves the cure himself; but, inasmuch as the distance is too great for him to do so easily, he is ordered to provide another Curate. The church and chancel are in repair. [Ib.]

1615. E. Sci Martini spectat ad Decanatum et antea valuata est. Curatus RICHARDUS WHITE, minister legens. Ecclia et cancella in ruina. Decanus admonitus ad repãndum cancellam, Epus convenire parochianos ad repãndum Ecclia. [Ib.]

Lee died about 1628, when the Chapter of Cork elected as Dean, Thomas Wight (P. Kilnaglory, q. v.), which appointment was set aside by the Crown. [Chapter Book of Cork.]

1628. June 26. JOHN FITZGERALD, Chaplain to the Chancellor, is appointed Dean, [Lib. Mun.] per mortem Georgii Lee, on letters patent of 31st January, anno regni Caroli Regis 3°. Installatus, 13th Dec., 1628. [R.V. 1634.] Fitzgerald appears in 1639. [V.B. D.R.]

1634. "R. de Kilcully als Bride. Hosp. de Mora et Grany sunt Rectores. Valet 36 li. per an. Cormack McDonogh Carty impropriator. Nullus curatus. Vicaria ibm spectat ad Decanum Cork. Valet 18 li. per annum." "E. de Culline spectat ad Decanum." "E. Scti Martini spectat ad Decanum Cork." [R.V. 1634.]

1639. E. de Kilcully als Bride spectat ad Grany. Vicaria ibm spectat ad Decanum. Curatus ROBERTUS BECK. Ecclesia ruinata, desunt ornamenta, habent libros. [V.B.]

1639. Ecclia de Cullyn spect. ad decan. Ecclia bene. Curatus nullus. [V.B.] E. Templemartin : Curatus, WM. SARSFIELD, Rector Decanus. [V.B.]

John Fitzgerald was probably grandson of Edward Fitzgerald, Dean of Cloyne.

He was ordained Deacon on 25th Nov., 1623, and Priest on 15th March following, both by Lancelot, Abp. of Dublin.

From 1625 to 1633 he was Treasurer of Cashel, and from 1627 to 1641 P. Malahidart, Dublin. In 1626 he was P. Donomore, and V. Ballingarry, in Limerick, but resigned immediately. From 1628 to 1641 he was Dean of Cork, and from 1634 to 1641 P. Donoghmore, in Cloyne. On 9th December, 1625, James, Abp. of Armagh, gave Fitzgerald a faculty to hold with his Treasurership two other benefices. [R.V. 1634.]

Dean Fitzgerald married Catherine (6th dau. of Richard Boyle, Abp. of Tuam, 1638–1644) and had issue two sons, William, Dean of Cloyne, q. v., and John. The Dean died at Bristol, in 1641. [Lodge.]

1642. March 13. HENRY HALL is appointed Dean. [Lib. Mun.] He was born at Wells, in Somersetshire, and educated at Lincoln College, Oxon. He became Chaplain to James, MARQUIS of ORMONDE, Lord Lieutenant of Ireland from 1643 to 1649.

From 1642 to 1660 he was P. Malahidart, Dublin, and P. Blackrath, Ossory. From 1642 to 1645 he was Dean of Cork; from 1642 to 1647 P. St. Michael's, Dublin, and from 1645 to 1660 Precentor of Christchurch, Dublin. In January, 1660/1, he became Bishop of Killala; and dying on 23rd of July, 1663, was buried in his cathedral.

1644. May 1. EDWARD WORTH is appointed Dean. [Lib. Mun.]

Edward Worth was son of Rev. James Worth, of Newmarket,

county Cork, and P. Island, Ross, q. v., who was son of Jasper Worth of Tethrington, of Prestbury, in Cheshire. Jasper was thirteenth in descent of this ancient family, whose members had intermarried with the DOWNES, of Shrigley, VERNONS, of Hallington, DAVENPORTS, of Cornwall, WESTONS, of Madeley, &c. [*Vide* MSS. T.C.D., U.O., and Herald's Visitations of Cheshire.]

Edward Worth was ordained Priest, by the Archbishop of Dublin, at Tamlaght Church, on 20th June, 1641. In 1641 he was V. Kilmichael. From 1645 to 1661 he was Dean of Cork, and from 1661 to 1669 was Bishop of Killaloe.

Bishop Worth married Susannah, dau. of Dennis, and sister of Captain George Pepper, of Ballygart, county Meath, ancestor of that family; and by her had issue William, born at Cork in 1646, who was Baron of the Exchequer in Ireland; John, born at Cork in 1648, who was Dean of St. Patrick's, Dublin; Michael, who died in London; and Edward, M.D.; besides a daughter, Susannah, wife of Epinetus Crosse, esq., of the county Cork; whose daughter, Susannah Crosse, was wife to Rev. John Griffith, and was mother of the Countess of Castlecomer.

Bishop Worth proved himself a munificent benefactor to his native city, Cork, by founding and endowing the Blue Coat Hospital; the particulars of which good work may be seen in a book entitled "Pietas Corcagiana." 4to. 17—. He died at Hackney, near London, on August 2, 1669; and was buried in St. Mildred's Church, in Bread-street, London; *Dean* Hackett, of Cork, preaching his funeral sermon. [Peck's "Desiderata curiosa."] Beside the noble foundation of a hospital in Cork, mentioned by Ware, Bishop Worth bequeathed £100 to be laid out on the purchase of lands or houses to endow a hospital at the Dock of Kinsale. See a detailed account of his family, in Mason's History of St. Patrick's Cathedral. 4to. 1820, p. 205.

He has published—

1. A Sermon at the Funeral of Richard Boyle, Archbishop of Tuam. 4to. Cork, 1644.

2. Scripture Evidence for baptising the Children of Covenanters. 4to. Cork, 1653.

3. A Sermon at the Funeral of Chief Justice Pepys. 4to. Dublin, 1659.

The Bishop compiled, with great care and research, "An Accompt of all the Lands and other Profits belonging to the Bishop of Killalow, collected by me, Edv. Laon. 1667, soe farr as I could get information." Small 4to, pp. 159. [This curious manuscript is now in possession of the Rev. Dr. Todd, Fellow of T.C.D.]

1661. May 31. THOMAS HACKETT is appointed Dean of Cork, and R. V. Ringrone. [Lib. Mun.]

Thomas Hackett, an Englishman, was of Trinity College, Dublin. He was Chaplain in Ordinary to His Majesty.

From 10th August, 1660 to 1672, he was Vicar of Cheshunt, in Hertfordshire. [Clutterbuck's History of that county.] From 1661 to 1662 he was Dean of Cork, and R. V. Ringrone, and from 1672 to 1693 he was Bishop of Down and Connor.

He published—

1. A Sermon on 1 Corinth. xiv. 16, preached before the Convocation. 4to. Dublin, 1662.

2. A Sermon on Matt. vi. 19–22, preached at the Spittle. 4to. London, 1672.

1662. Oct. 9. ROGER BOYLE is appointed Dean. [Lib. Mun.] He was instituted on 2nd January, 1662/3. [F.F.]

Roger Boyle (younger brother of Richard, Bishop of Ferns) was, from 1660 to 1667, R. Carrigaline; and from 1662 to 1663 P. Lisclery, and Precentor of Ross. From 1662 to 1667 he was Dean of Cork. He was, from 1663 to 1667, Treasurer of Cloyne, and R. V. Glanbarrahan, Ross. From 1667 to 1672 he was Bishop of Down and Connor, and from 1672 to 1687 Bishop of Clogher. He died on 26th Nov., 1687, at Clones, where he was buried.

Roger Boyle published,

1. Inquisitio in Fidem Christianorum hujus Sæculi. 12° Corcagiæ, 1664. 8vo. Dublinii, 1681. A copy of the Cork edition is in Cashel Diocesan Library.

2. Summa Theologiæ Christianæ. 4to. Dublinii, 1681.

3. He was author also of a Common Place book, with abstract of Sir Kenelm Digby's Treatise on Bodies. N.B.—This work was never printed; it is in MS. in T.C.D. Library.

1667. Sept. 3. JOHN VESEY is appointed Dean. [Lib. Mun.] He was instituted on 4th Nov., 1667. [V.B. 1669. D.R.] On which day he was also admitted to R. Carrigaline, Treasurership of Cloyne, and R. Glanbarrahan, Ross. [F.F.] In 1669 Vicaria Templebready est membrum Decanatus. [V.B. 1669.] Rectoria Templemartin est particula Decanatus. [Ib.]

John Vesey, or Veasie, was son of Thomas Vesey, Minister at Coleraine under the Presbyterian party, and afterwards Archdeacon of Armagh. He was born at Coleraine, and was educated at Westminster and T.C.D.

He was Chaplain to the House of Commons in 1661.

From 1661 to 1667 he was R. Igtermurragh, Cloyne; from 1662 to 1663 Archdeacon of Armagh; from 1663 to 1668 P. Ballyhay, Cloyne; from 1663 to 1672 R. Shandrum, Cloyne; from 1666 to 1673 P. Kilpeacon, Limerick; from 1667 to 1668 P. Lisclery; from 1667 to 1672 Dean of Cork, Treasurer of Cloyne, R. Carrigaline, and R. Glanbarrahan, Ross; from 1672 to 1678 Bishop of Limerick, Ardfert, and Aghadoe; and from 1678 to 1716 Archbishop of Tuam and Bishop of Kilfenora. He was also, from 1677 to 1682 P. Killeedy, &c., Limerick; and from 1684 to 1716 Warden of Galway. He died 28th March, 1716, aged 79, and was buried at Hollymount.

He married, in June, 1662, Rebecca Wilson, of Cork House, Dublin.

He was ancestor of the Viscounts De Vesci, and of the Barons Fitzgerald and Vesey; for whom *vide* the peerages.

1672/3. Feb. 11. ARTHUR POMEROY, A.M., is presented to the Deanery of Cork, with several Rectories in Cork and other dioceses. [Lib. Mun.] He was instituted on 5th May, 1673, to Deanery of Cork and R. Carrigaline, Treasurership of Cloyne, and R. Glanbarrahan, in Ross; and R. Shandrum, in Cloyne. [F.F.] He was also, from 1673 to 1678, P. Kilpeacon, Limerick.

In 1687 Mr. Hugolinus Spencer, and in 1695 Mr. Sullevan, and in 1699 Mr. Nathanael Spencer, appear as Impropriators of Templebready, the vicarage being attached to the deanery. In 1699 "the Protestants (of Templebrady) go to Carrickaline." [V.B. 1699.] In 1699 there are no churchwardens nor parish clerk in Cullen, and the Protestants go to Carrickaline and Tracton. [Ib.] "The church of Cullen, in the road from Mr. Ogilby's house, is ruinous." [Downes' Tour.] Templemartin spectat ad Decanum. Mr. John Harrison, Curatus. "No church. Many dissenters, who go to the meeting at Bandon; the Protestants of the church go to Kilbrogan." [V.B. 1699.]

1706. Othowell Heayes, of Knocknegore, gentleman, by his will, dated 23rd June, 1705, and proved 6th July, 1706, left £5 to the poor of Templebrady parish, and £3 to the poor of Carrigaline. He also directed that "att my cost and charges" a stone wall should be built by his executors around the churchyard of Templebrady church.

Arthur Pomeroy was a scion of the house of Pomeroy, seated at Engeston, in Devonshire. He was educated at Westminster School, and was a Fellow of Trinity College, Cambridge, where he graduated B.A. in 1660, M.A. 1664, and D.D. 1676.

He came to Ireland in 1672 as Chaplain to the Earl of Essex, Lord Lieutenant of Ireland.

He married Elisabeth, second dau. of Sir John Osborne, of Ballintaylor, county Waterford, and had issue (besides a dau. Mary, wife of Richard, eldest son of Sir Richard Cox, bart.) two sons, John (Archdeacon of Cork, q. v.), whose son was the first VISCOUNT HARBERTON, and Richard, who died Sp. in 1732.

The Pomeroys seem to have settled in Cork before 1672. On 25th July, 1646, Richard Pomeroy and Margaret Wawker, both of Christchurch, Cork, were there married.

The Dean was summoned to Convocation in 1703. He gave

some communion plate to Cork Cathedral, and left £100 to the Bishop of Cork for a charity school at St. Finbarry's, &c. He died in 1709/10.

1709/10. February 17. ROWLAND DAVIES is appointed Dean. [Lib. Mun.] He succeeded also to the R. Carrigaline.

Rowland Davies was ordained Priest on 9th April, 1671, at Cork. From 1671 to 1675 he was P. Kilnaglory, and from 1673 to 1721 P. Inniscarra. He held from 1674 to 1676 the P. Inskenny, and five other livings in Cloyne. From 1676 to 1706 he was P. Lisclery; from 1678 to 1709 Dean of Ross; and from 1679 to 1707 R. Kilnagross and Templeomalus. He held, from 1681 to 1721, the Vicarage of Garrycloyne. From 1706 to 1709 he was Precentor of Cork; and from 1709 to 1721 was Dean of Cork. He held also, from 1710 to 1717, the Rectory of Carrigaline. He died on 11th December, 1721, and was buried at Cork Cathedral. He was 72 years old when he died.

The grandfather of Dean Rowland Davies was John Davies, of "the Bury in paroch. de Richard's Castle, in county Hereford," who married Elisabeth Sherman, of Ludlow; and died at Ludlow, Shropshire, circiter 1630, aged about 80, leaving issue a second son, Rowland Davies, esq., who was living at Bandon in 1643, and at Cork in 1683. This Mr. Rowland Davies married, on 6th April, 1643, Mary, dau. of —— ? Scudamore, and relict of Thomas Smith, esq., of Gill Abbey, Cork, and was father of the Dean, who "was borne uppon wensdaie the 6th of March, 1649, at eight of the clock at night."

When fifteen years of age Rowland was entered a Pensioner of T.C.D. on 27th Feb. 1665; and he graduated A.B. in 1671, A.M. in 1681, and LL.D. in 1706.

He married, in 1674, at Newmarket, Eliza, dau. of Captain Robert Stannard, by Martha, dau. of Sir Robert Travers, by Elisabeth, dau. of Richard Boyle, Archbishop of Tuam, and Lord Chancellor of Ireland. This Martha married, secondly, SIR RICHARD ALDWORTH, of Newmarket, and was ancestor of that family and of the LORDS DONERAILE.

The Dean had issue by his wife (who died 28th Feb. 1715, at Deanscourt, aged 50), Rev. Richard Davies, V. Durrus, q. v.; Rev. Boyle, P. Lisclery, q. v.; Simon (born 1686, died 1754, leaving issue, *inter alios*, Simon, R. Kilcolman, Cloyne, q. v.); Michael, Archdeacon of Cloyne, q. v.; besides other sons, who died young, and several daughters.

Dean Davies published—

1. "A Letter to a Friend concerning his Religion." London. Printed for Robert Clavell, and are to be sold by John North, bookseller in Dublin, 1692.

2. "The Truly Catholic and Old Religion, showing that the Established Church in Ireland is more truly a Member of the Catholick than the Church of Rome, and that all the ancient

Christians, especially in Great Britain and Ireland, were of her communion." Dublin. Printed by Samuel Fairbrother, bookseller, in Skinner-row, opposite the Tholsel; and are to be sold by George Bennett and John Redwood, booksellers, in Cork. 1716.

3. "Christian Loyalty." A sermon preached in the Cathedral of Cork on January, 1715. 4to. Dublin. 1716.

4. "The Right Use of Riches." A Sermon preached at St. Peter's, Cork, on 11th August, 1717, at the anniversary meeting of the poor children of the Green-coat Charity Schools. Published by request. Dublin. 1717.

5. "A Reply to a pretended Answer to a Book entitled," &c. This was a rejoinder to a book published at Antwerp in 1717 by Dr. O'Brien, a Roman Catholic clergyman, with the title of "Goliah beheaded with his own Sword." Dr. Timothy O'Brien had been Parish Priest of Castlelyons. Dr. Davies' reply was printed at Dublin. 4to. 1717.

6. Dean Davies published a second reply to another rejoinder. Dublin. 4to. 1720.

Dean Rowland Davies wrote also a diary of a very interesting nature, which was published by Mr. Richard Caulfield, of Cork, under the auspices of the Camden Society. It gives many details of family history, and is worthy of being again printed, as it is already scarce, and difficult to procure.

1721/2. March 8. Robert Carleton is appointed Dean of Cork. [Lib. Mun.] Installed March 31. [F.F.]

On 26th Nov. 1725, Carleton obtains a certificate for £341 4s. improvements and repairs on the deanery house. [D.R.]

1733. March 7. Samuel Hayles, A.B., was licensed to the Curacy of Templemartin. [D.R.]

Robert Carleton was second son of Christopher Carleton, esq., of Dublin.

He was, from 1709 to 1721, R. Shandrum, in Cloyne. He also held, from 1713 to 1714, the Vicarages of Ballyclogh and Castlemagner; from 1714 to 1716 the P. Killinemer; and from 1714 to 1721 the R. V. Mogeely; and from 1716 to 1721 the P. Glanworth, all in Cloyne. From 1721 to 1735 he was Dean of Cork, and also P. Inniscarra, V. Garrycloyne and Grenagh, in Cloyne.

He married, May, 1729, Elisabeth, relict of Rev. John Pomeroy, Archdeacon of Cork; but by her, who died 24th August, 1748, had no issue. The Dean's father, Christopher, who had an estate in Cumberland, called Woodside, was buried at St. Michan's, Dublin, on 4th January, 1703/4. [Davis.]

The Dean died in 1735.

1735/6. April 9. William Meade is appointed Dean. [Lib. Mun.]

He was admitted 9th June, 1736, and installed on the 10th June. [D.R.] On letters patent of May 3rd, 1736. [Lib. Mun.]

1739. April 30. William Meade memorials to improve the deanery house, "the kitchen being too small, and too near the parler, and the noise there made, and the smell of victualls drest, being very offensive," &c. The Bishop approves on 8th May, 1739, and on 6th Dec. 1746, a commission to examine issues, which returns on 24th December £20 2*s.* 8½*d.* as the value of Dean Meade's improvements, and finds the value of the deanery to be about £300 per annum. From this return it appears that in those days flagging cost in Cork 2*s.* 6*d.* per yard; tiling, 1*s.* 8*d.* per yard; nine-inch brickwork, 3*s.* 6*d.* per perch; glass, 8*d.* per foot; flooring, 30*s.* and roofing, 23*s.* per square; "windscoting" in front parlour, 4*s.* 6*d.* per yard; brick, 7*s.* per 1,000; lime, 1*s.* 6*d.* per barrel; slates, 3*s.* 9*d.* per 1,000; labourers, 6*d.* per day; and tradesmen, 1*s.* 6*d.* or 1*s.* 8*d.* per day. [D.R.]

1751. Samuel Hales, A.M., is licensed to be Curate of Templemartin. [D.R.]

William Meade was only son of Robert Meade (who was third son of Colonel William Meade, and brother to Sir John, and to Dominick Meade, Archdeacon of Cloyne, q. v.), by Frances, dau. and co-heir of Sir Peter Courthope, of the Little Island, Cork, by Catherine, dau. of Thomas Daunt, of Oulpten, in Gloucestershire.

He was born in Cork in 1686, and when sixteen years old became a Pensioner T.C.D. on 13th March, 1702. From 1709 to 1751 he was R. Ballymartle; from 1709 to 1752, R. Dunderrow; from 1720 to 1763, R. Garrivoe; from 1730 to 1763, R. Ringrone; and from 1736 to 1763, Dean of Cork.

He married in 1719 [M.B. Cork, 20th Feb.], Helena, dau. of Bryan Townsend, by Mary, dau. of Edward Synge, Bishop of Cork, Cloyne, and Ross. By her the Dean had issue four sons, John, R. Ballymartle, q. v.; Richard, Barrister-at-Law, born 1720, died 1769, unmarried; Robert, R. Dunderrow, q. v.; and William, R. Rincurran, q. v. The Dean's will was dated 29th Nov. 1762, and proved 31st May, 1764. He resigned the deanery in 1763.

1763. April 15. GEORGE CHINNERY, LL.D., is appointed Dean (*vice* Wm. Meade, resigned), on letters patent of June 2. He was instituted on 18th June. [Lib. Mun. and D.R.]

1763. October 14. George Chinnery, LL.D., Dean of Cork, states in a memorial to the Bishop, that Dean Carleton obtained a certificate of expenditure on improvements in deanery house and garden, in 1722 and 1723, for £341 4*s.*; and that Dean Meade paid of that sum, £227 9*s.* 4*d.*, being two-thirds; and that memorialist is chargeable with one-half of latter sum, £113 14*s.* 8*d.* He also states that Meade obtained a certificate for an outlay of £70 2*s.* 8½*d.*, in 1739, of which memorialist is to pay three-fourths, or £52 12*s.*; these two charges making a total of £166 6*s.* 8*d.* He states also that Meade suffered dilapidations to amount of £110, which memorialist retained from Meade's assigns, and he purposes to lay out £260 in addition to that £110. Chinnery, in 1763, Dec. 2, memorials to lay out in addition, £140, and in May, 1764, to spend a further sum of £350. In 1767, March 30, a commission to view issues, which returns on 18th September following, £1,066 6*s.* 9¼*d.* as the whole outlay of Chinnery, and finds the tithes of Templebready, Templemartin, and Cullen to be worth £390, the lands of Carrigdecanig to be let to Mr. Noblett Breton for £35, with an annual renewal fine of £17 10*s.*, other parts of same land let to Dominick Sarsfield, esq., at £12, and the deanery house and offices to be worth £60; in all £514 10*s.*, which is the true value of the deanery. Accordingly, on 12th October, 1767, the Bishop certifies for an outlay of £964 19*s.* 6½*d.*, in addition to £110 retained from Dean Meade; and decides that the Dean will be entitled to receive from his successor, £723 14*s.* 7½*d.*, being three-fourths of said charge, and also £35 1*s.* 4*d.*, being two-thirds of £52 12*s.*, paid to Meade's executors; total £758 15*s.* 11½*d.* Dean Chinnery did not charge for the carved work over the dining parlour chimney; nor for the urns on the front pier; nor for the chimney-piece and grate in drawing-room, dining parlour, or right-hand parlour; nor for brass locks or brass work of any kind. [D.R.]

George Chinnery (son of Rev. George Chinnery, R. Mallow, Cloyne, q. v., and brother to SIR BRODERICK CHINNERY, bart.), was born in county Cork, and when sixteen years old entered T.C.D. as Pensioner on 9th Nov. 1735. He was Scholar in 1738, and graduated A.M. in 1743, and LL.D. in 1751.

He was ordained Priest at Cloyne on 23rd Sept. 1745. From 1746 to 1779 he was R. Killeagh, Cloyne; from 1752 to 1779, P. Cahirultan, Cloyne; and from 1763 to 1779, Dean of Cork. He had been presented to R. Castleblakeney, Elphin, in 1761, and he resigned the office of Head Master of Middleton School, in 1775. From 1779 to 1780 he was Bishop of Killaloe, and from 1780 to August of same year he was Bishop of Cloyne.

He died 13th August, 1780, and was buried on the 15th, at Middleton grave-yard.

1779. January 21. JOHN ERSKINE, A.M., is appointed Dean of Cork. [Lib. Mun.] His patent was dated 24th Feb., and he was instituted March 31, 1779. [D.R.] In the same month he received the P. Cahirultan, and R. Killeagh, Cloyne, all which he retained until his death in 1795.

1779. Sept. 12. Templebrady Church was consecrated under the name of St. Matthew. It was built on the site of the old church, at the expense of the Board of First Fruits, the late Dean Chinnery and others. [D.R.]

1781. January 6. Dean Erskine applies for a commission of dilapidations, which returns that the deanery house is so rotten that it is best to pull it down and rebuild; that it would cost £1,087 3*s.* 6*d.* to rebuild, and that the old materials are value for only £183 10*s.* In this year the Bishop's certificate against Chinnery's executors is for £632 16*s.* dilapidations, which Dean Erskine is to stop out of £758 15*s.* 11*d.*, the amount of his charge for building in 1767.

1786. July 7. A commission issues to value Dean Erskine's new deanery house. They find he has spent £1,497 8*s.* 1½*d.*, and that £39 1*s.* 1½*d.* has been allowed for old materials, and that the tithes of Templebrady are worth £104 5*s.* 2*d.*; of Cullen, £159 17*s.* 9½*d.*; of Templemartin, £252 8*s.* 8*d.*; that 78 acres of land of Carrigdecanig are let at £35 rent, and £35 fines; 8 acres of same lands, at £12, with £2 5*s.* 6*d.* annual fine, and that the deanery house and gardens is worth £60; in all £660 17*s.* 1*d.* per annum. The Bishop, on 6th Oct. 1786, certifies for £1,453 15*s.* 7*d.* outlay; and that Erskine will be entitled to receive from his successor, £1,321 on foot of all charges.

Dean Erskine was author of an edition of the pamphlet of Dr. James Butler, Titular Archbishop of Cashel, written in reply to Bishop Woodward's Tract on the Church of Ireland, with severe critical notes. It appeared anonymously, under the signature R. R.

1796. January 7. THE HON. THOMAS ST. LAWRENCE is appointed Dean of Cork. [Lib. Mun.] His patent was dated 25th January, and he was instituted 10th Feb. [D.R.]

In 1802, the Dean spent £51 17*s.* 8*d.* in sinking a well at Deanscourt, and in 1805 he obtained a certificate of having expended £101 2*s.* 9*d.* on the deanery house, the deanery being worth more than £900 per an. [D.R.]

The Hon. Thomas St. Lawrence, second son of THOMAS, LORD HOWTH, was born, in 1755.

From 1789 to 1794 he was V. Galtrim and Cullmullen, Meath. He was also V. Timolin, Dublin. From 1794 to 1807 he was P. Yago, Dublin; from 1795 to 1806, V. Brinny; from 1796 to 1807, Dean of Cork; and from 1805 to 1807, P. Kilmacdonogh, and R. Mogeely, Cloyne.

From 1807 to 1831 he was Bishop of Cork and Ross. He died on 10th February, 1831, and was buried at the Cathedral, Cork.

He married Frances, eldest dau. and co-heir of Rev. Henry Coghlan, D.D., by whom he left issue, three sons, Thomas, P. Currograngemore, Ross, q. v.; Edward, Archdeacon of Ross, q. v.; Robert-Kingsborough, R. Murragh, and Treasurer of Ross, q. v.; and the following daughters, Emma (wife of Rev.

W. L. Beaufort, P. Cahirlag, q. v. ; Isabella, wife of John Leslie, Bishop of Elphin ; Letitia, wife of Rev. R. J. Rothe, R. Kilmichael, q. v. ; and Isabella, wife of Robert-Morgan Tighe, esq., of Mitchelstown, county Westmeath.

1807. Sept. 25. JOHN LESLIE, A.M., is appointed Dean of Cork. [Lib. Mun.] On letters patent of Oct. 5. Instituted 23rd Oct. [F.F.]

John Leslie was born in 1774, and was second son of Charles Powell Leslie, of Glasslough, and great grandson of the eminent divine, Dr. Charles Leslie.

From 1807 to 1812 he was Dean of Cork. In 1807, he was, from March to September, R. Fiddown, Ossory. From 1808 to 1812 he was R. Tynan, Armagh. From 1812 to 1819 he was Bishop of Dromore ; from 1819 to 1854 Bishop of Elphin ; and from 1841 to 1854 Bishop of Kilmore, and Ardagh, and Elphin. He died on 22nd Feb., 1854, at Kilmore, aged eighty-two. For his marriage and issue, *vide* Burke's L. G., article, LESLIE, of GLASSLOUGH, county Monaghan.

1812. May 1. JAMES SAURIN, A.M., is admitted Dean. [F.F.] His appointment was signed by the Prince Regent, on 5th Dec., 1811, and his patent was dated 12th Feb., 1812. [Lib. Mun.]

James Saurin, son of Rev. James Saurin, Vicar of Belfast, and grandson of Louis Saurin, Dean of Ardagh, was born 18th December, 1759. He was a Scholar of T.C.D. in 1777.

He was formerly Curate of St. Doulough's, Dublin, and was V. Rosenallis als Oregan, Kildare, in 1801.

From 1812 to 1813 he was Dean of Cork ; from 1813 to 1818, Archdeacon of Dublin; from 1818 to 1819, Dean of Derry; and from 1819 to 1842, Bishop of Dromore. He died at Kingstown, near Dublin, on 9th April, 1842.

1813. July 25. WILLIAM MAGEE was admitted Dean, on letters patent of July 1. [D.R. and Lib. Mun.]

On 21st July, 1814, a commission finds £104 13*s*. as dilapidations against Saurin. [D.R.]

William Magee (author of the celebrated work on the Atonement) was a Scholar of T.C.D. in 1784, Fellow 1788 to 1812, and Professor of Mathematics 1800 to 1813.

He was, from 1812 to 1813, R. Cappagh and Killileagh, Down ; from 1813 to 1819, Dean of Cork; from 1819 to 1822, Bishop of Raphoe ; and from 1822 to 1831, Archbishop of Dublin.

1820. March 25. ROBERT BURROWES, D.D., was instituted to the Deanery of Cork, on letters patent of 20th November, 1819. [D.R.] The appointment was signed by the Prince Regent, on 31st August, 1819. [Lib. Mun.]

1830. The Protestant population of Cullen parish is 22. For that of the other parishes composing this union, *vide* Templebrady, P. C., and Templemartin.

1837. Templebready Union : with cure, consisting of:—

1. Templebready rectory. 2. Templemartin rectory. 3. Cullen rectory. The union contains 6,382A. 3R. 32P. The occasional duties of Cullen parish, the gross population of which is 1,251, are discharged by the Curate of the adjoining parish, at a small annual stipend. The yearly income is, from tithe composition of Templebready parish, £160 7*s.* 2*d.*; of Templemartin parish, £500; of Cullen parish, £253 16*s.* 10*d.* 17A. 3R. 19P. of glebe in said parish, valued at £20, subject to visitation fees, 18*s.*; Diocesan schoolmaster, £1 10*s.* The rectory (otherwise the deanery) house, situate in the city of Cork, near the cathedral, built under the old Acts, but at what cost unknown, the whole of the expense having been discharged. Incumbent is resident two-thirds of the year on this benefice, and during the remainder of the year on his other benefice, in the county of Tyrone. Two churches in this union: one erected in Templebready, and the other in Templemartin parishes, in the perpetual cures established within these parishes, respectively, at a distance of 23 miles from each other. The benefices constituting this union are rectories. [Parl. Rep.]

Robert Burrowes (Scholar, T.C.D., in 1775, and Fellow from 1782 to 1796) was, in 1798, appointed Master of the Royal School of Enniskillen.

He was, from 1796 to 1798, Archdeacon of Ferns; from 1796 to 1807, R. Cappagh; from 1807 to 1841, R. Drumragh; and from 1819 to 1841, Dean of Cork.

He died, aged eighty-two, at his glebe-house, near Omagh, on 13th Sept., 1841, having had issue by his wife, Catherine Grierson, two sons, George, P. Currograngemore, Ross, q. v., and Samuel, who married Miss Jameson, and died Sp. The Dean had also three daughters, namely, Mrs. Tuke, Mrs. Elrington, and Sarah, wife of Rev. Samuel Rogers, R. V. Nathlash, Cloyne, q. v.

Dr. Burrowes was an accomplished scholar, and most eloquent preacher; a man of great talent, sparkling wit, and instructive conversation.

He is the author of the preface to the first volume of the Transactions of the Royal Irish Academy; and has left in print the following valuable Sermons:—

1. A Sermon before the Association for Discountenancing Vice. 8vo. Dublin, 1795. 2nd edition, ibid. 1815.

2. Advice, religious and political, delivered in four Sermons to a Congregation in the North of Ireland (preached during the years 1797 and 1798). 8vo. Dublin, 1801.

3. An Assize Sermon at Enniskillen, on March 23, 1806. 8vo. Dublin, 1806.

4. Sermons on the First Lessons of Sunday Mornings, from the first to the thirteenth Sunday after Trinity; with four others. 8vo. London, 1817.

5. A Sermon on the Coronation of King George IV. 8vo. Cork, 1821.

Dean Burrowes was also author of "A Letter to the Rev. Samuel Barber, on his Remarks on the Bishop of Cloyne's pamphlet on the Church of Ireland." 8vo. Dublin, 1787. Also, of Sermons on the Liturgy, and Sermons on the Apostles' Creed. [See an Obituary Notice of him in the "Irish Ecclesiastical Journal," vol. i. p. 255.]

1841. November 9. JAMES THOMAS O'BRIEN is appointed Dean. [Lib. Mun.] He was installed January 5, 1842. [D.R.] Besides this deanery he held the rectory of Arboe, Armagh, and the office of Archbishop King's Lecturer in Divinity, T.C.D.

J. T. O'Brien (son of Michael Bushe O'Brien, of New Ross, county Wexford) was, in 1813, a Scholar of T.C.D., and from 1820 to 1833 was a Fellow of that University.

From 1833 to 1842 he was Archbishop King's Lecturer in Divinity; from 1836 to 1837, R. Clondehorky, Raphoe; from 1837 to 1842, R. Arboe, Armagh; from 1841 to 1842, Dean of Cork; and from 1842 to present time he has been Bishop of Ossory, Ferns, and Leighlin.

1842. March 26. HORATIO TOWNSEND NEWMAN was installed Dean, on letters patent of 21st March. [D.R.]

On 18th April, 1843, Newman obtained a certificate of an outlay of £516 15*s.* 11*d.* on the deanery-house. [D.R.]

1860. The deanery-house is in good order. For an account of the parishes composing the corps of this deanery, *vide* Templebrady, P. C., Templemartin, P. C., and Cullen, P. C. The Dean has now no Incumbent duties in these parishes since their erection into separate perpetual cures. The tithes of Templebrady amount to £120 5*s.* 4*d.*; of Templemartin, to £375; of Cullen, to £145 7*s.* 7*d.* The total gross value of the deanery is £630 12*s.* 11*d.*

H. T. Newman (son of Adam Newman, of Dromore, county Cork, esq.) graduated A.B. in 1803, and M.A. in 1808.

He was ordained Deacon on 6th July, 1806, and Priest on 12th July, 1807, both at Cloyne.

On August 2, 1808, he was licensed to the curacy of St. Finbarry; from 1818 to 1842 he was P. Kilbrogan.

He published "A brief View of Ecclesiastical History from the earliest periods to the present time." 1844, and 12mo. 1856.

He married, on 10th Nov., 1817, Charlotte Elisabeth, third dau. of Rt. Hon. Denis Daly, of Dansandle, county Galway.

TEMPLEBRADY, P. C.

In 1813, April 1st, the Bishop issues a commission to value the glebe of Templebrady, and to report what lands would be convenient and sufficient to endow the Curate, Rev. Hugh Reynolds, with as much tithe as will, with the glebe, make up £60 per annum, as an endowment to erect Templebrady into a perpetual cure. The Commissioners, William Worth Newenham, of Coolmore, and Robert Warren, report, on May 14, that the glebe of Templebrady is worth £24 per annum, and that the town and lands of Hoddersfield would be suitable for the purpose of endowment. Accordingly, on 16th June, 1813, Templebrady is erected into a perpetual cure, and endowed with the entire glebe (12 acres) of Templebrady, and with the entire tithes, both great and small, of Hoddersfield, containing 1½ ploughlands, &c. [D.R.] This was done by virtue of the Act of Parliament, 11 and 12 Geo. III., chap. 16, and 13 and 14 Geo. III., chap. 27. [D.R.] The endowment was dated 30th June, 1813. [Lib. Mun.]

1813. June 16. HUGH REYNOLDS, the first Perpetual Curate of Templebrady, was licensed, on the nomination of the patron, the Dean of Cork. [D.R.]

1813. Oct. 22. Reynolds memorials for liberty to build a glebe-house on Templebrady glebe, on which there had never previously been a house. His estimate was £500; and in 1816, June 22, the Bishop certifies that Reynolds has duly expended that sum. [D.R.] Of this £500, £450 was a gift, and £50 a loan from the Board of First Fruits.

1823. JOHN JOHNSON appears as P. C. Templebrady. [Erck's Ecclesiastical Reg.] In Dec. 1829, he became P. Killanully, q. v.

1830. April 14. RICHARD LOANE CONNELL, A.B., Perpetual Curate. [D.R.]

1830. Protestant population, 101.

1832. Templebrady, a perpetual cure, with spiritual duties annexed, erected within the parish of the same name, appropriated to the deanery, 3 English miles long by 3 broad, containing 2,622 acres. Gross population, 1,789. No Curate assistant employed. Tithe composition, £39 12*s*. 10*d*. Augmentation allowance, payable by the Ecclesiastical Commissioners out of Boulter's fund, £23 2*s*. 12 acres of glebe, valued at 19*s*. per acre, £11 8*s*. Templebrady glebe-house, fit for residence, built under the new Acts in 1815, at the cost of £461 10*s*. 9½*d*. British, granted by the late Board of First Fruits, viz., £415 7*s*. 8¼*d*. in way of gift, and £46 3*s*. 1*d*. in that of loan; of which loan there remained £21 19*s*. 5*d*. chargeable on the benefice in 1832, repayable by annual instalments of £1 5*s*. 10*d*. Incumbent is constantly resident in the glebe-house. Templebrady church, capable of accommodating 140 persons, built about 80 years since, but at what cost, or from what funds unknown. No charge on the parish in 1832 on account of this church. Divine service is celebrated twice on Sundays in summer, and once in winter, and on the principal festivals. The sacrament is administered monthly, and on the festivals. The benefice, within which this perpetual cure has been established, is a rectory. [Parl. Rep.]

1833. William Cotter Williamson, A.B., P. C. Templebrady. He is now Precentor of Cloyne, q. v.

1837. William Tottenham Day, A.B., P. C. Templebrady. He is now R. Rathclaren, q. v.

1837. Dec. 12. A commission finds £17 9*s.* 11*d.* dilapidations against W. C. Williamson, late P. C. [D.R.]

1842. March 17. Samuel Sandiford, P. C. Templebrady. In 1856 he became R. V. Nathlash, Cloyne, q. v.

1856. Nov. —. George Whately, P. C. Templebrady.

On January 5, 1858, a commission finds £59 9*s.* 7*d.* as dilapidations against Sandiford. [D.R.] Whately resigned in 1859 or 1860, and accepted a Curacy in England.

1860. April 19. John Duncan Craig, A.M., P. C. Templebrady. [D.R.]

1860. A church and glebe-house; 12 acres of glebe in the Curate's use. Divine service twice on all Sundays, and on the usual holidays. Sacrament monthly, and at the principal festivals; average of communicants, 10. 33 children attend a Church Education school. The Protestant population is 169. The annual value is about £83, including land and augmentation, with residence. The Curate also holds the Chaplaincy of Camden Fort.

J. D. Craig (son of John Craig, esq., Horsehead, Cork), entered T.C.D. as Fellow Commoner in 1847, and graduated B.A. in 1851, and M.A. in 1855. He obtained a catechetical premium and first place at his divinity examination in T.C.D.

He was ordained Deacon by the Archbishop of Dublin in 1853, and Priest by the Bishop of Norwich in 1854.

He was successively Curate of St. John's, Dublin; Carrigaline, Cork; Killingley, Cork; Frankfield, Passage West, and Kinsale, before becoming P. C. of Templebrady.

He married, in 1860, Dorothea-Eliza (dau. of J. Sandys Bird, esq., of Kinsale, by whom, who died in 1863, he has issue a son, John.

Mr. Craig is author of "Scriptural Coincidences, or Traits of Truth." (Bagster and Sons). "The Crew of the Florence Barton." "The Cross in Sardinia." He has contributed largely to "The New Monthly Magazine," "Ainsworth's Magazine;" and also to "The Family Treasury of Sunday Reading," and "Chambers's Journal." He has written several tracts, and a "Hand-book to the Provençal Language," &c.

TEMPLEMARTIN, P. C.

1813. May 31. A commission issues to value the glebe of Templemartin, and to report what lands would supply sufficient tithes to make up, together with the glebe, £60 per annum for an endowment. On 12th June following, the commission reports the glebe to be worth £27 6*s.* per annum, and that the lands of Castleach, not including Mullaballane, are worth £32 14*s.* On 16th June, 1813, Templemartin was erected into a perpetual cure, under the 11 and 12 Geo. III., chap. 16, and endowed with the entire glebe, and also with great and small tithes of town and lands of Castleach, not including Mullaballane. [D.R.]

1813. June 16. FRANCIS CAREY SULLIVAN, P. C. Templemartin. [D.R.] He had been Stipendiary Curate from 1806.

1814. April 4. Sullivan memorials to build a glebe-house; and in June, 1815, obtains a certificate for an outlay of £508 17*s.* 3*d.* in building same. [D.R.]

1830. Protestant population, 233.

1837. Templemartin, a perpetual cure, with spiritual duties annexed, erected within the parish of that name, appropriated to the deanery, 3½ miles long by 2½ broad, containing 7,096 acres. Gross population, 2,730. No assistant Curate employed. Tithe composition, £19. Augmentation allowance, payable by Ecclesiastical Commissioners out of Boulter's fund, £30. 16 acres of glebe, valued at 15*s.* per acre, £12. Templemartin glebe-house, built under the new Acts in 1815, at a cost of £461 10*s.* 9¼*d.* British, whereof £415 7*s.* 8¼*d.* was granted as gift, and £46 3*s.* 1*d.* as loan by the late Board of First Fruits, of which loan there remained £17 3*s.* 5*d.* chargeable on the benefice in 1832, repayable by annual instalments of £1 4*s.* Incumbent resides in the glebe-house. Exclusive of the moneys aforesaid, Incumbent reports that he has expended about £92 6*s.* 1*d.* on improvements, without having any charge on his successor for the repayment of any portion thereof. One church, capable of accommodating 100 persons, built in 1797 by means of a gift of £461 10*s.* 9¼*d.* British, granted by the late Board of First Fruits. No charge on the parish in 1832 on account of this church. Divine service is celebrated once on Sundays, and on Christmas Day and Good Friday. The sacrament is administered monthly, and on the festivals. The benefice within which this cure has been established is a rectory. The Dean of Cork is patron. [Parl. Rep.]

F. C. Sullivan was a Scholar, T.C.D. in 1803.

He was ordained Deacon on 6th October, 1805, at Cork, and Priest at Cloyne on 6th July, 1806, for the Curacy of Templemartin.

1848. THOMAS BIGGS, P. C. Templemartin.

1849. April 14. Biggs obtains £138 dilapidations against his predecessor, Sullivan. [D.R.]

1860. One church. A glebe-house and 16 acres of land in Incumbent's use. Divine service once on all Sundays and usual holidays. Evening service also during summer. Sacrament monthly, and at festivals; average of communicants, 16. 11 children (in 1863) attend a Church Education school. The Protestant population is 132. The gross value of Templemartin (inclusive of land and augmentation), is about £72, with residence.

Thomas Biggs, LL.D., was Curate of Murragh from 1847 to 1848. He vacated Templemartin in 1861.

1861. THOMAS TOWNSEND, A.B., P. C. Templemartin, *vice* Biggs, resigned.

1862. June 17. Templemartin Church was re-opened for divine service after repairs. The Bishop preached.

Thomas Townsend was ordained Deacon in 1855. He was ordained Priest at Cork on 21st December, 1856.

TEMPLEMICHAEL DE DUAGH.

1591. "E. Scti michaelis de Dawghe D. LONG, idem Thesaurarius." [MS. T.C.D. E. 3. 14.] He was the Treasurer of Cork, q. v.

1615. "Sti Michaelis de Duagh (residens), JOHN HONICHURCH, Rector. Valor £6 13*s.* 4*d.*" He is also R. V. Leighmoney. [R.V. R.I.A.] He does not appear elsewhere.

1621. August 20. WILLIAM ROBINSON is admitted R. Sti. Michaelis de Duagh, and inducted 22nd August. [R.V. 1634.]

1634. St. Michael de Dowagh, William Robinson, Predicator, James Mellefont, Patronus. Val. 15 li. per an. [R.V. 1634.] Robinson appears as Rector in 1639, with the remark, "Ecclesia bene, deest baptisterium." [V.B. 1639. D.R.] Robinson appears as Curate of Ballinaboy in 1634 and 1639.

Robinson was ordained Deacon on 18th May, and Priest on 23rd May, 1619, both by John, "ffeneboren Epum." [MS. Consistorial Court, Dub.]

1666. MR. BUTLER appears in this year for Templemichael de Duagh at visitation. [V.B. D.R.] He was also P. Kilbrittain, q. v.

1667. June 29. JOHN MOORE, R. Templemichael de Duagh, per desertion of John Butler. [V.B. D.R. 1669.] He appears from 1667 to 1692. [V.B. D.R.] Moore was Archdeacon of Cloyne, q. v.

1693. May 24. FRANCIS MOORE, A.M., R. Templemichael de Duagh, per resignation of John Moore. [D.R.] Francis Moore was also R. Innishannon, q. v.

1698. September 6. JOHN MOORE, jun., A.B., R. Templemichael de Duagh, per resignation of Francis Moore. [D.R.] In 1699 John Moore, jun., became P. Kilbrittain, and in 1711 he was Treasurer of Cork, q. v.

1699. April 14. FRANCIS MOORE, A.M., R. Templemichael de Duagh. [F.F.] He was also R. Innishannon, q. v.

The people go to Innishonan. [V.B. 1699.]

1704. Nov. 3. MR. MICHAEL BUSTEAD appears in the Visitation Book, the name of Francis Moore being crossed out. Bustead appears 1704 to 1709. [V.B. D.R.]

Michael Bustead was ordained Priest at Cork on 31st May, 1702.

In 1704 he was Curate of Ballinaboy, &c. He was also V. Ballyfeard from 1711 (?) to 1751. He held this living from 1704 to 1715, when he resigned. He was from 1714 to 1751 a Vicar Choral of Lismore. He died on 17th Feb. 1751/2, aged seventy-nine. He was married, and his eldest son was Jephson Bustead.

The Rev. Michael Bustead, on 15th June, 1703, obtained a conveyance from the Trustees of forfeited estates of 183 acres in Knocklea; 224 in Ballingemanig; 22 in Knockacullin; and 60 in Kininеane, all in the barony of Kinalea, county Cork. [Reports of Public Records.]

1715 to 1746. MR. JOHN MOORE appears as R. Templemichael de Duagh. [V.B.] He was also Treasurer of Cork, q. v.

1746. July 24. CHARLES MOORE, A.M., R. Templemichael de Duagh, vacant by resignation of John Moore. [D.R.] He was also V. Innishannon, q. v.

1754. January 1. THOMAS BERMINGHAM, R. Templemichael de Duagh, vacant by death of Charles Moore. [D.R.]

Thomas Bermingham was, in 1751, Curate of Carrigrohane.

In 1744, January 19, he entered into bonds for marriage with Margaret Jackson, of St. Peter's, Cork. He left issue, at his death in 1768.

1768. January 16. JOHN KENNY, A.B., R. Templemichael de Duagh, vacant by death of Bermingham. [D.R.] In 1769 he became V. Durrus, and in 1796, P. Kilbrogan, q. v.

1769. March 16. THOMAS BROWNE, A.M., R. Templemichael. [F.F.] He was also P. Templebryan, Ross, q. v.

1807. Brown lives at Kinsale, and pays £10 for the occasional duties of this parish. He holds also Templebryan, in Ross. [Rep.] He resigned Templemichael on 10th July, 1811.

1812. January 11. ROBERT MEADE, A.M., R. Templemichael de Duagh. [D.R.] He was also R. Ballymoney, q. v.

In 1815 Robert Meade memorials to build at Templemichael; and in May, 1816, he obtains a certificate of expenditure for £900, of which sum £300 was a gift and £500 a loan from the Board of First Fruits. [D.R.]

1823. October 14. The tithe was certified at £266 per an., the average price of wheat for the seven years, ending 1st Nov. 1821, being £1 18*s.* 8*d.* per barrel. [D.R.] Robert Meade resigned in 1826. [F.F.]

1826. April 1. WILLIAM ROBERT MEADE, A.B., R. Templemichael de Duagh; certified under £300 in value. [D.R.] He resigned on 11th December, 1838, and became V. Kinsale, q. v.

1830. Protestant population, 58.

1837. Templemichael de Duagh: a rectory, with cure, 1¾ miles long by 1¼ broad, containing 2,027A. Gross population, 764. No Curate employed. Tithe composition, £230 15*s.* 4¾*d.*; 5A. 3R. 14P. of glebe, valued at 30*s.* per acre, £8 15*s.* 1½*d.*; subject to visitation fees, £1; diocesan schoolmaster, 12*s.* 6*d.* Templemichael de Duagh glebe-house, built under the new Acts in 1814, at the cost of £830 15*s.* 4½*d.* Brit., whereof £276 18*s.* 5½*d.* was granted in way of gift, and £461 10*s.* 9¼*d.* in that of loan, by the late Board of First Fruits, and the residue of £92 6*s.* 1¾*d.* was supplied out of the private funds of the builder, to whom the present Incumbent is next in succession; and having paid his predecessor the whole of the sum last-mentioned, he will be entitled to receive £69 4*s.* 7½*d.* from his successor on account thereof. Of the loan aforesaid, there remained £284 6*s.* 1*d.* chargeable on the benefice in 1832, repayable by annual instalments of £14. Incumbent resides entirely in the glebe-house. One church, capable of accommodating 100 persons, built in 1812, at the cost of £553 16*s.* 11*d.* Brit., granted in way of gift, by the late Board of First Fruits. No charge on the parish in 1832 on account of the church. Divine service is celebrated once on Sundays, and on the principal festivals. The sacrament is administered monthly, and on the festivals. The benefice is a rectory. [Parl. Rep.]

1839. January 16. NICHOLAS COLTHURST DUNSCOMBE, A.B., R. Templemichael de Duagh. [D.R.] In 1862 he became R. Macroom, Cloyne, q. v.

1854. January 19. JAMES GRANT, A.B., R. Templemichael de Duagh; certified net value, £170 8*s.* 3*d.* per an. [D.R.]

On May 18, 1854, Grant obtained, £124 10*s.* 3*d.* dilapidations against his predecessor. [D.R.]

1860. The church in order. The glebe-house in a state of decay. 6 acres of glebe in Rector's use. 6 children attend a Church Education school. The Protestant population is 18. The rentcharge is £173 1*s.* 6*d.* The land is worth £12. Total value, £185 1*s.* 6*d.* per annum, with residence.

James Grant was ordained Deacon on 18th March, 1820, and Priest on 14th April, 1822, both at Cloyne. On 15th July, 1824, he was licensed to the curacy of Monanimy. From 1842 to 1854 he was V. Templebodan.

He is married, and has issue.

TEMPLETRINE.

1591. "E. de Treyne sequestr. ex scaccario p' primitiis Regineis. MAURICIUS O'CONTYE, vicarius ibm." [MS. T.C.D. E. 3. 14.]

1615. "Templetrine (residens), HENRY HUSSEY, Rect. integ." He holds also the V. Ringrone, R. Kilgobban, a particle of Ballinadee, and the Particula of Gortnagrosse, which is also "parcella de Ballineddy." [R.V. R.I.A.]

1627. September 4. HELSHIAS HUSSY, Rector de Templetrine, inducted 26th September. [R.V. 1634.] He was Treasurer of Cork, q. v.

1634. E. de. Templetrine, Helshias Hussey. Val. 30 li. per an. James Karny, de Cork, merchant, est patronus. [R.V. 1634.] In 1639 Hussey is still Rector. "Ecclesia bene, deest omnia." [V.B. 1639. D.R.]

1666. January 9. THOMAS GOODMAN, R. Templetrine, per deprivationem Helkiæ Hussey, p' lett. pat. [V.B. 1669. D.R.] This institution was returned to F.F. as of 14th January. [F.F.] "In patronatu Regis eo quod Carney, patronus, est papista." [V.B. 1670.] Goodman appears 1666 to 1680. [V.B. D.R.] In 1675 he became also Precentor of Ross, q. v.

1681. August 3. GEORGE SYNGE, A.M., R. Templetrine. [F.F.] On letters patent of July 2, 1681. [Lib. Mun.] He appears 1681 to 1691. [V.B. D.R.] He was also P. Kilbrogan, q. v.

1682. "The church of Templetrine to be repaired." [County Cork Grand Jury Presentments.]

1692. October 18. EDWARD SYNGE, A.M., is presented to R. Templetrine [Lib. Mun.], per mortem Georgii Synge. [D.R.] Edward Synge was also P. Holy Trinity, q. v.

Once a fortnight divine service. Three or four families of Protestants. The church in repair. [V.B. 1699.]

1714. Dec. 9. PETER HEWITT, R. Templetrine. [Lib. Mun.] He appears 1715 to 1718. [V.B. D.R.] He was also Precentor of Cork, q. v.

1720. May 11. THOMAS GOODMAN, A.M., R. Templetrine, per mortem Petri Hewitt, ultimi incumbentis. [D.R.] On letters patent of April 29, 1719. [Lib. Mun.] Goodman appears 1720 to 1730, July 28. [V.B. D.R.]

Thomas Goodman, son of Thomas Goodman, was born in England, and when fifteen years old obtained Sizarship on 16th Feb. 1675, and Scholarship in 1681, in T.C.D.

He was ordained Priest on 23rd December, 1683, at Cloyne.

From 1683 to 1691 he was a Vicar Choral of Cork. In 1687, August 21, he was licensed to the curacy of Killaspugmullane, Cahirlag, Kilcully, and Dunbullog. From 1695 to 1731 he was Vicar Choral of Ross, and from 1719 to 1731 was Rector of Templetrine.

He married, in July, 1684, Martha Weldan, of St. Peter's parish, in Cork, spinster, and by her left issue an eldest son, Richard, and a younger son, Thomas.

His will was dated 24th August, 1730, and proved 28th April, 1731. In it he wishes to be buried in the south-west side of the steeple of the Cathedral Church of Ross, if he should die there, and leaves 8*s.* 8*d.* to the men that bear him to the grave.

1731. May 3. JOHN BLAIR, A.M., R. Templetrine, per mortem Thomæ Goodman. [D.R.] On letters patent of April 14, 1730/1. [Lib. Mun.] Blair appears from 1731 to 1743. [V.B. D.R.]

1744. May 28. JOHN KENNEY, A.M., R. Templetrine, vacant by death of Blair, and on the presentation of Francis Kearney, of Garrettstown, county Cork, esq. [D.R.] John Kenney was also, in 1751, P. Kilbrittain, q. v.

1769. May 29. EDWARD KENNEY, A.M., R. Templetrine, vacant by death of John Kenney, and on presentation of Francis Kearney, of Garrettstown. [D.R.] Edward Kenney was also P. Inskenny, q. v.

1813. March 1. Thomas Rochfort, of Garrettstown, grants the right of next presentation to Templetrine unto John Cuthbert, esq., and Lieut.-Col. Arthur Gibbins. [D.R.]

1818. June 20. JOHN ROGERSON COTTER, R. Templetrine, vacant by death of Kenney. [D.R.] On letters patent of May 13. In His Majesty's disposal, Thomas Rochfort being a Papist, and therefore incapacitated. [Lib. Mun.] Cotter in 1837 became R. V. Innishannon, q. v.

In 1821 Cotter memorials to build, and in 1823 the Bishop certified an outlay of £1,143 6*s.*; of which sum £825 was a loan from First Fruits, and £318 6*s.* was charged on his successor. [D.R.]

1830. Protestant population, 34.

1832. Templetrine: a rectory, with cure, 3½ miles long by 2 broad, containing 5,000A. Gross population, 2,180. No Curate employed. Tithe composition, £477; 28A. of glebe, valued at £26; subject to visitation fees, 8*s.*; diocesan schoolmaster, 14*s.* Templetrine glebe-house, built under the new Acts in 1822, at the cost of £1,107 13*s.* 10½*d.* Brit., whereof £92 6*s.* 1¾*d.* was granted in way of gift, and £761 10*s.* 9¼*d.* in that of loan, by the late Board of First Fruits; and the residue of £253 16*s.* 11¼*d.* was supplied out of the private funds of Incumbent, who will be entitled to receive the whole of the sum last-named from his successor. Of the loan aforesaid, there remained £517 16*s.* 11*d.* chargeable on the benefice in 1832, repayable by annual instalments of £30 9*s.* 2¾*d.* Incumbent is constantly resident in the glebe-house. Exclusive of the moneys aforesaid, Incumbent reports that he has expended £300 Brit. on the premises, without having any demand on his successor for the repayment of any part thereof. One church, capable of accommodating 180 persons, built in 1821, by means of a gift of £830 15*s.* 4½*d.* Brit., granted by the late Board of First Fruits. No charge on the parish in 1832 on account of the church. Divine service is celebrated twice on Sundays in summer, and once in winter, and on the principal festivals. The sacrament is administered monthly, and on the great festivals. The benefice is a rectory. [Parl. Rep.]

Cotter resigned 28th June, 1837.

1837. July 4. THOMAS MEADE, A.B., R. Templetrine, on the presentation of Thomas Cuthbert Kearney, esq., dated July 3. [D.R.]

Thomas Meade was eldest son of Rev. Richard Meade, R. V Innishannon, and was ordained Deacon on 21st December, 1797, and Priest on 23rd December, 1798, both at Cork.

He was licensed to the curacy of Innishannon on 5th July, 1799. From 1808 to 1837 was Rector of Innishannon, and from 1837 to his death on 14th March, 1838, was R. Templetrine.

He married, in 1808, Elisabeth, only child of Major John Campbell, of Innishannon; and had issue, John-Campbell, Richard-Thomas (in 1856 R. Templetrine); Thomas, Mary-de Courcey, Martha-Emma, and Frederica-Avice, besides three other children who died.

1838. Sept. 4. JOHN BEAVOR WEBB, A.B., R. Templetrine, vacant by death of Thomas Meade, and on the presentation of John Cuthbert Kearney, esq., dated August 30, 1838. [D.R.] J. B. Webb resigned 9th Dec. 1839, and became R. Dunderrow, q. v.

1840. January 9. JOHN STEWART, R. Templetrine, John Cuthbert Kearney, Patron. [D.R.]

John Stewart (third son of Henry Stewart, of the county Meath), was ordained Priest at Cork on 4th of June, 1809. In 1810 he was licensed to preach within the diocese of Cork and Ross. From 1832 to 1840 he was R. Killowen, and from 1840 to his death on 23rd April, 1852, was R. Templetrine.

He married Anne, dau. of Samuel Austen, esq., of Crookstown, county Cork; by whom he had seven children, of whom one is the Reverend William Stewart, Curate of Kilbrin.

1852. Sept. 2. ALEXANDER BEHN HALLOWELL, A.B., R. Templetrine, on the presentation of Thomas Cuthbert, of Kinsale; Abraham Thomas Forster, of Garrettstown, and Thomas Franks, esqrs., Trustees of the will of John Cuthbert Kearney. Date of presentation, 21st August, 1852. Net value, £344 4*s.* 6*d.* [D.R.] In 1856 Hallowell became P. Island, Ross, q. v.

On June 18, 1853, Hallowell obtains £80 4*s.* 8*d.* dilapidations against his predecessor. [D.R.]

1856. May 8. RICHARD THOMAS MEADE, R. Templetrine, on presentation, dated 5th May, 1856, of the Trustees of the will of John Cuthbert Kearney. £344 4*s.* 6*d.* net annual value. [D.R.] The appointment was conceded to the Bishop in this instance by the representatives of Thomas Rochfort, esq. [F.F.]

In 1859, Nov. 12. Meade obtained as dilapidations against Hallowell, two sums of £19 15*s.* 11*d.* and £10 0*s.* 10*d.* [D.R.]

1860. The church and glebe-house in good order. 28 acres of glebe in Rector's use. Divine service twice (during summer) on all Sundays in the church, and once in winter, and on the usual holidays. Evening service in the glebe-house in winter. Sacrament monthly; average of communicants, 18; and on festivals, average 46. 17 children attend a Church Education school. The Protestant population is 89. The rent-charge is £357 15*s.* The land is worth £24. Total value £381 15*s.* per annum, with residence.

R. T. Meade (second son of Rev. Thomas Meade, formerly Rector of this parish), was born in county Cork, and when eighteen years old became a Pensioner, T.C.D., on 4th Nov. 1833.

He was ordained Deacon in May, 1840, by the Bishop of Killaloe, and Priest in September of same year, by the Bishop of Limerick.

From 1840 to 1856 he was R. Killowen. In 1856 he was appointed P. Island, in Ross; but resigned that preferment, and became R. Templetrine.

He married, in 1843, Sarah, dau. of A. Lane, esq., of Bandon, by Elisabeth-Carleton, dau. of Nicholas Dunscombe, esq., of Mountdesart, near Cork. He has issue, Elisabeth-Thomasina, Gerald-De Courcey, Sarah-Avice, William-Dunscombe, Richard-Frederic, and John-Campbell.

TEMPLEUSQUE, OR GLANMIRE.

1291. "Eccia de Glynmaygyr VIImr." [Tax. P. Nic.]

1327. June 4. Mathew Sumery, Chaplain, enfeoffs Thomas fil. John de Sarsfield with the advowson and right of patronage of the Church of Glynmayr. [Sarsfield MSS.]

1420. July 10. Robert Mylys, Capellanus, enfeoffs William fil. Richī Sarsfield with the advowson and right of patronage of the Church of Glynmair. [Sarsfield MSS.]

1437. August 6. NICHOLAS COTTERELL, R. and V. St. Mary de Glanmire als Templeusque. Inducted by Archdeacon John Brasyl, according to Bishop Jordan's mandate of above date, and on the presentation of Richard Sarsfield. [Caulfield MSS.] I give the record, which is as follows:—"Jordanus Dei gracia Corke et Clonen Epus. Venerab. nro magro. Johi Brassyll Ecclæ Cork Archidiac. Saltm. nos ad rect. et vicar. Ecclie btæ Mariæ de Glanmayre ad presens vacant. ed ad presentationem Ricardi Sarsfield spectantem. Dilect. nobis in Christo Nicholaum Cotterell capellanum admissimus, &c. Dat. apud Cork die sexto Augusti anno Dni millimo. quad. tricessio septimo."

1569. April 25. "Dominus Richūs Barrett de Cork, Presbyter, et Geraldus Miagh," are appointed trustees of the manor, &c., and advowson of Glanmayre. [Sarsfield MSS.]

15—? JOHN BARRY, Rector of Glanmire.

1582. November 7. MAURICIUS DERMODY, Presbyter, is presented to the rectory of the B. V. M. de Glanmeyre, now vacant by death of John Barry, the last Incumbent, by Thomas Sarsfield, the true and undoubted Patron of the entire rectory of B. V. Mary de Glanmeyre. [Sarsfield MSS.]

1591. "E. Templeusky als Claymmoyre Mauricius McDermott incūbens et Rector de murmullane. Amovend: de marmullane. Suspens: postea p. plur." [MS. T.C.D. E. 3. 14.]

1593. March 22. WILLIAM FELDE, Parson of Christchurch, is presented to the rectory of Glanmire on the death of McDermody. [Sarsfield MSS.] I give at length a transcript of the document concerning Field and McDermody:—

"The copie of my p'sentacon to Tampell-losky by Glanmeyr, in April, 1594, with the copie of my lre. to my l. byshop touching the same, the xxij of March, 1593.

"My dutie to yo'r good lp. alwey remembred, understanding that yo'r lp. was to dep'te herehenst before Sonday towards Rosse, I thought it my p'te, having a lytle helth left, sicknes might not p'vnt me to do the same hereafter, before yo'r going, to write and seale my p'ntacon of Temple-losky w'ch I send yo'r lp. here inclosed, w'th a Blank therein to nōiate and appoint whome yo'r lp. shall think mete, assuring yo'r lp. yt if it were a better request, myne abilitie striving thereunto, it shold be at yo'r lps. dyspicon, but in truth I have writen syth the last Incumbent's death to a kinsman of myne in Lymrke, named Richard Sarsfeld, an Englishman borne, who hath not taken of orders, that if it please him getting yo'r lps. good will, I wold willingly bestow that pore living upon him for his better maintenance, syth w'ch tyme I understand from Mr. Philip ffeld that my said kinsman will not dep'te Lymke and prayed me to p'sent thereunto Mr. Wm. ffeld, p'son of Christe church, who is my kinsman and frend, of whom or any other discrete man yo'r lp. shall appoint I shall very well lyke of. And so referring the same to yo'r lps. determynacon and good discretion w'h my dutifull cōemdacon I betake yo'r to thalmightie yo'r lp. all happines who granteth helth both of body and soule to his glory, from my chamber in Cork, this xxij of M'rch, 1593.

"Yo'r lps. to comd. alwey,

"Thomas Sarsfeld.

"To the Reverend Father in God, my verey good l. the l. byshop of Cork.

"(Endorsed.) Revendo in Xto Patri ac] Dno Guilbelmo

Corkagen Epo, &c., the presentation of Wm. ffelde, on death of Maurice McDermody, to the rectory of the church of the B. V. de Glenmyre."

Feld, in 1591, was P. Holy Trinity, q. v.

1615. Templeusque als Glanmire ROBERT TRAVERS, diaconus, Rector. Valor 8 li. per an. Curatus residens JOHN GOLD, minister legens. Ecclesia ruinosa, cancella in ruinis. [R.V. R.I.A.]

Robert Travers does not appear elsewhere.

I am inclined to think that this Robert Travers is the same person who was afterwards Sir Robert Travers. I give an extract from a letter of the late John Moore Travers, esq., of Clifton, Cork, which concerns the Travers' pedigree. It is to be noticed that Joseph Travers (Chancellor of Cloyne, q. v.) is omitted by Mr. Travers. This extract is from Craik's "Spenser and his Poetry." Vol. ii., page 250. London: Knight & Co. 1845.

"The family of Travers were settled, in the reign of Edward I., at Natesby, in Lancashire, which estate they held in direct succession from father to son till the reign of Philip and Mary, when it descended to Brian Travers, who sold it (or rather mortgaged it) to George Strickland, who sold it to a person of the name of Leyburne. This Brian Travers afterwards settled at Pill, in the neighbourhood of Bristol, having inherited the estate of Pill in right of his wife. He had a son named John Travers, who came to Ireland when Lord Grey de Wilton came over as Lord Lieutenant, and he was the first of the family of Travers that settled in Ireland. This John Travers married Sarah Spenser, the sister of Edmund Spenser, the poet, who granted to him as a marriage portion with his sister, the townlands of Ardenbane and Knocknacaple, in Roches country, in the county of Cork, which was part of 3,028 acres of land, part of the forfeited estate of the Earl of Desmond, granted by Queen Elizabeth to the said Edmund Spenser, in which grant Kilcolman Castle and Lake were comprised. There seems to have been some doubt as to the power of Edmund Spenser to convey away this land to Travers, and, therefore, he passed his bond to Travers for a sum of money by way of guarantee of the title. These lands appear to have been held by the second son of John Travers, but they have not continued in his family. I know not in what way, or by whom they were parted with, nor whether either the grant or the bond be in existence; but neither of them is in the possession of any of the family.

"The above-named John Travers, and Sarah Spenser, his wife, had two sons, viz., Robert Travers, the eldest, afterwards SIR ROBERT TRAVERS, who married Elizabeth, the daughter of the Primate Boyle (ancestor of the EARLS of CORK and ORRERY and the EARLS of SHANNON), and was Judge-Advocate in Ireland, and Vicar-General of Cork. Sir Robert inherited and purchased several estates in the county of Cork, particularly in the baronies of Ibane and Barryroe, and his principal seat, called Ballinamona, near Courtmacsherry, was situated in these baronies, the estates in which have ever since continued in his family, and are now in my possession, as the lineal descendant of Sir Robert. Sir Robert was killed at the battle of Knocknaness, in the county of Cork, in the rebellion of 1641.

"The second son of John Travers and Sarah Spenser was Zachary Travers. I do not know whom he married; however, he left two sons, viz., Walter, who was the second Provost of Trinity College, Dublin (having succeeded Adam Loftus, who was the first Provost), and John, who having the command of a troop of dragoons, under Lord Broghill, was killed in an ambuscade, in the rebellion of Ireland, January, 1642. He left no issue, nor did the Provost, Walter, leave any. The estates of Zachary, which had descended to Walter, he devised to John Travers, the second son of Sir Robert Travers, who was his first cousin; and these estates, which were considerable, thus descended to John Travers, of Garrycloyne, now residing at Birchhill, in the county of Cork.

"Sir Robert Travers left two sons, Richard and John; and two daughters—Margaret, who married Sir Richard Aldworth, the ancestor of the present Lord Doneraile; and Elizabeth, who married Sir John Meade, the ancestor of the present Earl of Clanwilliam. Richard Travers, the eldest son of Sir Robert, who was my great-great-grandfather, married Ellen Stawell. The children of Sir Robert being very young when he was killed, many valuable documents and records of the family were lost, and the title-deeds only were preserved. Richard Travers had five sons. The eldest, Robert, married Hester Hodder, and had Boyle Travers, my grandfather, who married Anna-Maria Moore. Boyle Travers left two sons, John Moore Travers, who died without issue male; and Robert Travers, my father, to whom the estates in Ibane and Barryroe descended, with the family seat of Ballinamona, now in my possession. Robert Travers left three sons, viz., myself, Boyle Travers, a General in her Majesty's service; and Thomas Otho Travers, a Captain in the service of the East India Company, who died July, 1844, at his seat of Leemount, in the county of Cork.

"We have to add that Mr. Travers's only child is the lady of SIR WILLIAM ST. LAWRENCE CLARKE, of Gloucester-place, Portman-square, London."

16—? JAMES JEFFRAY. R. Templeusque.
He does not appear elsewhere.

1623. Sept. 5. WILLIAM DORNEY, clericus, is presented by David, Vicecomes Buttevant, the guardian of Thomas Sarsfield, to the rectory of Glanmeyr, vacant by the free resignation of James

Jeffray, "clericus." [Sarsfield MSS.] In 1615 Dorney was V. Clondulane and Leitrim, in Cloyne.

1632/3. April 8. THOMAS DAVIES is presented by Thomas Sarsfield to the rectory of the Church of the B. V. M. de Glanmire als Templeusque "vacant. per mortem Willmi. Dorney ultimi incumbentis." [Sarsfield MSS.] On 4th Oct., 1633, Thomas Davies, P. Inskenny, R. Kilnemartery, and V. Aglish, is instituted to R. de Glanmoire als Templeusky. 1634. "E. de Templeusky, Thomas Davies, R. et V. Valent 16 li. per an. Thomas Sarsfield de Cork, generosus, est patronus. [R.V. 1634.]

Davies was also P. Inskenny, q. v.

1639. "E. de Templeusque WILLIAM SKERSFIELD—bene, desunt ornamenta et libri." [V.B. 1639. D.R.]

1666. SAMUEL BONNER appears as R. Templeusky "ægrotat." [V.B. D.R.]

1667. Vacant by death of SAMUEL BONNER. [V.B. D.R.]

1668. JOHN BAYLEY appears as Rector. [V.B. D.R.] He was instituted July 11, 1669, to R. Templeusque, vacant. per mortem Samuelis Bonner. [V.B. 1669. D.R.] Bayley was admitted on the same day to P. St. Michaels, Rectoriam integram de Templeusque, R. Kilcoan, and R. V. Insula parva. [F.F.] In 1670 and 1671 Templeusky is said to be in the King's patronage. [V.B. D.R.]

For Bayley, *vide* St. Michael's.

1697. June 17. VALENTINE FRENCH, P. St. Michaels, R. Templeusky, Kilcoan, Insulæ parvæ, et Kilroan per mortem John Bayley. [D.R.] In 1717 French became Dean of Ross, q. v.

1699. No Protestants in Templeusky parish, except Mr. Hugh Harding, and Mr. Clark, who go to Rathcony. [V.B. 1699.]

"Oct. 1. 1700. I saw Templeusky Church, the walls of which were built with stone and clay. A great part of the walls is down. It stands about 2 miles distant from Rathcony to the north of Rathcony, near the Dublin road. From this church we saw St. Michael's Church (ruinous) at about a mile distance towards the west. About a mile beyond St. Michael's are the ruins of the church of Dunbullog. This ruinous church is seen from Templeusky church-yard. Templeusky church-yard is fenc't with a ditch. Templeusky Church is on the left hand of the road from Corke to Rathcormack, about half a mile beyond Glanmire bridge. There have been no churchwardens in this, nor in the other parishes united under Mr. French, for above 20 years last past. This parish was almost all the estate of Mr. Sarsfield, of Sarsfield-court, who forfeited it in the last rebellion. It was granted to the Lord Romney. Mr. Hugh Harding, at Sarsfield-court; Clark, Protestant; and Cahil, a Papist, and Lehy, Papist, live in this parish. If there was a church at Killvillane, or if Templeusky Church was in repair, there would be about 50 persons at a congregation. In these and the adjoining parishes there are at least 10 Papists to 1 Protestant. Several of the inhabitants of Mr. French's union are desirous to have the church of Killvillane rebuilt, but Templeusky seems to stand nearer the centre. This parish is an entire rectory, worth about £40 per an. to the Incumbent. Cornelius Curtine is Popish Priest of this parish and Kilroan als Ballideloughy and Racony. He has been many years in these parishes. The people of this parish go to Racony Church. No glebe in this parish." [Downes' Tour.]

In 1704 French resigned the P. St. Michael's, and took that of Killaspugmullane, with which Prebend Templeusky was held in union until 1842, when Templeusky and Ballydelohar, *alias* Kilroan, were severed from the P. Killaspugmullane, and formed into a benefice, called Ballydelohar, q. v.

TRACTON.

Under Tracton are given notices of other impropriate parishes, viz., Barnahely, Clontead, Kilmoney, Kinure, Kilpatrick, Krivir, and Rosbeg als Bracknane als Templebracknany.

1291. "Eccia de Pollakely VImr." "Eccia de Crewdiry IIImr." "Eccia de Clonced VIImr." [Tax. P. Nic.]

1591. "E. de Clonteide spectat ad Ab. de Tracton. DONOGH O'CAGHAN, Curatus." "E. de Krivir et E. de Clonteide spectant ad Ab. de Tracton. Donogh o Caghan, Curatus." "E de Pollaplick. Abb. de Tracton Rector, etiam vicar. p' usurpacõem." "E. de Bernehely spectat ad ab. de Antro. Regina. Edmundus m'breen, Curatus." "E. de Kilmoone similiter." "R. de Rosbeg spectat ad ab scẽ Catherine Waterford, Vic ibm, cum Shanballye pticula, Thomas Wood." In another part, "Rector sci brachany de Rossbege—Thomas Wood." [MS. T.C.D. E. 3. 14.]

1615. Clontead. Rectoria impropriata. Spectat ad Abb. de Tracton. Thomas Dant firmarius. The church and chancel almost in ruins. Val. 8 li. No Curate. No service. The vicarage is vacant, and usurped by the possessors of the Rectory, although it appears from the Bishop's records that the vicarage is endowed. [R.V. R.I.A.]

"Knever Rector Abbas de Tracton. Thomas Dant firmarius. Ecclia et cancella ruinantur; nullus curatus. Vicaria vacat et usurpatur p' firmarium Rectoriæ etsi rotuli Episcopi testantur esse ibm. vicariam indotatam."

"Poliplick als Ballyfiard. Rector Abb. de Tracton, firmarius Thomas Dant. Ecclia repata. Cancella ruinata. Curatus nullus. Vicaria vacat et usurpatur et si in Rotulis Episcopi recordatur pro vicaria."

"Barnahely spectat ad Gille abby. Ecclia et cancella ruinantur. Curatus nullus. Vicaria vacat et usurpatur. Apparet per rotulos quod est vicaria tamen usurpatur per possessores Rectoriæ."

"Rosbeg als Bracknan. Rex est Rector. Vicarius JOHANNES GOLD, minister legens: p'ticula de Kilmighill. Nulla ecclesia. Nullus curatus." [R.V. R.I.A.]

1634. "E. de Clonteid spectat ad Abb. de Tracton. Valet 20 li. per annum. Comes Cork firmarius. ROBERTUS BECK, curatus, habet tantum 15*s*. per annum p' inservicione curæ." [R.V. 1634.]

1634. "E. de Knever spectat ad Abb. de Tracton. Comes Corke firmarius. Val. 15 li. per annum. BECK, curatus, habet 15*s*. per an. pro inservicione curæ." [R.V. 1634.]

1634. "E. de Pollyplicke als Beaffoile spectat ad Abb. de Tracton. Comes Corke impropriator. Valet 20 li. per annum. ROBERTUS BECK, curatus, habet tantum 20*s*. per an. pro inservicione curæ." [R.V. 1634.]

1634. "E. de Barnehely spectat ad Abb. de Tracton. Valet 20*s*. per an. ROBERTUS BECK est Curatus. Comes Corke possidet." [R.V. 1634.]

1634. "R. de Brecknane. Rex est Rector. Vicecomes Kilmallock tenet hanc rectoriam. Valet 40*s*. per annum. Nullus curatus. Vicaria ibm. spectat ad mensam Epi. Valet 40*s*. per annum." [R.V. 1634.]

1639. "Rector de Tracton. Vicecomes de Kilmallock. Vicarius ROBERT BECK. Ecclesia ruinata." [V.B. 1639. D.R.] Beck was also V. Brackynane, and Curate of Barnehealy and Kilmorey.

1639. "E. de Clontyde spect ad Tracton. Ecclia bene. Curatus JOHN FULHAM." [V.B. D.R.]

1639. "E. de Pollyplicke ad Tracton. Ecclesia ruinata et desunt omnia. JOHN STUKELY, Curatus." [V.B. 1639.]

1639. Beck is still Curate of Barnahely. "Ecclesia bene, desunt ornamenta." [Ib.]

1639. "Brackynane: Rector est Vicecomes Kilmallock. Vicarius ROBERTUS BECK. Ecclesia ruinata." [V.B. D.R.]

1666. HUGO SCAMPE, A.M., was Curate of Tracton, Barnahealy, and Kilpatrick. [V.B. D.R.] Scampe was V. Aghadowne, Ross, q. v.

1668. In a V.B. of this year Bishop Synge enters this memorandum—"to speak to my Lord Shannon that the cures of Tracton, Barnahely, Kilmurry, &c., may be better supplied." [D.R.]

1669. In this year "Dominus Franciscus Boyle Vicecomes de Shannon" appears as Impropriator of Ballinaboy, Kilmoney, Barnahely, Kilpatrick, Tracton, Ballyfiard, Pollyplicke, Clontide, and Kinnure. Nulli vicarii indotati. JOHN HARRISON, Clicus, Curatus. [V.B. 1669.]

Harrison is Curate in 1670. [V.B. D.R.]

1680. The communion cup bears this legend—"Tracton Abby Church, the gift of Mrs. Jane Daunt, widow, Sept. 10, 1680."

1687. Mr. THOMAS DENT appears as Curate of Tracton, Barnehely, Kilmorey, &c. He was also P. Kilnaglory, q. v. [V.B. D.R.] From 1687 to 1692 the entry for Pollyplicke is "vicaria vacat. Viscount Shannon, Impropriator." [V.B.]

1688. Mr. BARRY LOVE appears as Curate of Tracton, Barnahely, Kilmorey, &c. [V.B.]

1692. JAMES WADE appears as Curate of Tracton, Barnahealy, Kilmorey, &c. [V.B.]

1693. May 12. ALEXANDER O'GILBY is admitted Curate of Tracton, Ballinaboy, Barnahealy, Kilmoney, Kilpatrick justa Tracton, Ballyfiard, Pollyplicke, Clontead, and Kinnure. [D.R.]

In 1699, at Barnahealy, it is remarked "the Protestants go to Carrigoline." [V.B. D.R.]

From 1694 to 1699 the vicarage of Pollyplicke is marked "vacat" in the visitation books. [D.R.]

In 1699 it is remarked, concerning Clontead, that the Curate of Ballinaboy is Curate of Clontead, and that "the Protestants go to Kinsale." [V.B. 1699.]

"1699. Tracton Church in good repair; only some of the timber of the roof sinks. Seats, a pulpit, cushion, font, a silver chalice, and pewter flagon; no bell. The sacrament administered three times in Tracton yearly. The church-yard partly fenc't with a wall, partly with a ditch. Betwixt 40 or 50 were confirmed at Tracton Church, Oct. 18, 1699." [Downes' Tour.]

1703. The paten now (1862) in use is inscribed, "For the use of the Church of Tracton, 1703."

1743. ACHILLES DAUNT was licensed Curate (on the nomination of Hon. Mrs. Grace Boyle) of Tracton, Barnahealy, Kilpatrick, Pollyplicke, Kilmonoge, Clontead, and Kinure, at a stipend of £30. [D.R.]

In 1755, March 18, the Bishop unites "the parishes or impropriate rectories of Kilmoney, Kilpatrick, near Tracton, Pollyplicke, otherwise Bialofile, Clontead, and Kinure, to or with the parish or impropriate rectory of Tracton," because of their nearness to each other, and because the parishioners of Tracton alone are not able to keep their parish church in repair. The Rev. Achilles Daunt is now Curate, on the nomination of Grace, Countess of Middlesex, Impropriatrix of said parishes. [D.R.]

Daunt died in 1784. He was R. V. Kilcully, q. v.

1784. Nov. 16. ROBERT FORSAYETH, A.B., was licensed to be Curate, on the nomination of the Earl of Shannon, at £30 per an. [D.R.] He was also Curate of Nohoval, q. v.

1785. The parish registry commences.

1791. Oct. 28. ROBERT MEADE, A.B., was licensed to be Curate on Lord Shannon's nomination, at £30. [D.R.] He was afterwards R. Ballymoney, q. v.

1809. January 5. WILLIAM ALLEYNE EVANSON, A.B., was licensed to be Curate on Lord Shannon's nomination, at £25. [D.R.]

In 1809 the First Fruit Commission agreed with Lord Shannon to give £50 yearly to each of two Curates, one for Ballinhassig, the other for Tracton, on condition that his Lordship should divide the stipend hitherto paid to one Curate, who officiated at Ballinhassig, the service at Tracton being celebrated on alternate Sundays by a clergyman resident in Cork. At this time the Board of First Fruits pay £450 as a fine for a lease of 24 acres of land for ever, at a rent of £29 5*s.* 6*d.*, for ever. The same Board also grant £450, and lend £50 to build a glebe-house. [D.R.] In 1812 the Rev. W. A. Evanson memorials to build; and in 1814, Aug. 24, the Bishop certifies an expenditure of £636 19*s.* 0¼*d.* [D.R.]

In October, 1817, Mr. Evanson leaves Tracton, and he then receives an address and a piece of plate from his parishioners, in acknowledgment of his services for nine years in Tracton as their Minister. [Cork Intelligencer.]

W. A. Evanson was eldest son of Alderman Charles Evanson, of Cork. In 1803 he was a Scholar, T.C.D. He was ordained Deacon, on 20th November, 1808, and Priest, on 24th Sept., 1809, both at Cork.

He married, on 23rd January, 1811, Lyndon, only dau. of Robert MacDonnell, esq., of Seafort, county Cork, and had issue.

1817. RICHARD BOSTON appears as Curate, on nomination of the Earl of Shannon. [Erck.]

Boston was ordained Deacon, at Cloyne, on 30th Nov., 1811, and Priest, at Cork, on 4th April, 1813. He held Tracton from 1817 to 1828.

1828. Feb. 9. WILLIAM ROBINSON TOWNSEND, A.B., was licensed to be Curate, on the nomination of Henry, Earl of Shannon, at £25 per an. [D.R.] He is now R. Aghadda, Cloyne, q. v.

1828. Oct. 8. JOHN DENIS PENROSE, A.B., P. C. Tracton. [D.R.] In 1851 he became R. Magourney, als Kilcoleman, Cloyne, q. v.

1830. Protestant population of Tracton, 52; of Kilpatrick, 36; of Kilmoney, 26; of Ballifoyle, 41; of Kinure, 64; of Clontead, 31. Total Protestant population of union is 250.

1832. Tracton Union: a perpetual cure, with spiritu· duties annexed, consisting of—1. Tracton parish; 2. Kilpatrick parish; 3. Kilmoney parish; 4. Ballifoyle parish; 5. Kinnure parish; 6. Clontead parish. The union is 11 miles long by 7 broad, containing 27,809A. 1R. 24P. Gross population, 8,419. No Curate assistant employed. Stipend payable by the patron,

£25. Augmentation allowance, payable by Ecclesiastical Commissioners out of Boulter's fund, £46 3s. 1d. Tracton glebe-house built in 1814, under the new Acts, at the cost of £461 10s. 9½d. Brit., whereof £415 7s. 8½d. was granted as gift, and £46 3s. 1d. as loan, by the late Board of First Fruits; of which loan there remained £22 6s. 9d. chargeable on the benefice in 1832, repayable by annual instalments of £1 4s. Incumbent is resident in the benefice in Kilmoney parish, but not in the glebe-house, which, with 24A. 2R. 38P. of land, he states he had succeeded in getting rid of, in consequence of the exorbitant rent paid for the ground, the dilapidated state of the house, and its remoteness from the church, being three miles distant therefrom. One church, situate in Tracton parish, capable of accommodating 200 persons, built in 1819, at the cost of £293 1s. 6½d. Brit., granted in way of loan by the late Board of First Fruits, of which loan there remained £477 5s. 11d. chargeable on the union in 1832, repayable by annual instalments of £28 1s. 3d. Divine service is performed once on all Sundays, and on the festivals. The sacrament is administered monthly. The tithes of the parishes forming this union are impropriate, and belong to the Earl Shannon, and are compounded as follows: Those of Tracton, for £403 10s.; of Kilpatrick, for £120; of Kilmoney, for £100; of Ballifoyle, for £109 4s. 6d.; of Kinnure, for £86 8s. 11d., and those of Clontead, for £73 17s. [Parl. Rep.]

1834. August 20. John Conolly, A.B., was licensed to be Curate, on the nomination of Henry, Earl of Shannon. [D.R.] He is now V. Holy Trinity, q. v.

1848. John Lovel Robinson was appointed Curate. He is now Treasurer of Cloyne, q. v.

1850. October 7. John Pickering Phair is admitted Curate. [D.R.] He is now Incumbent of Buttevant, Cloyne, q. v.

1860. The church is about to be rebuilt. No glebe-house or glebe. Divine service twice in summer, and once in winter, and on the usual holidays. Sacrament monthly, average of communicants, 14; and on festivals, average, 27. 54 children attend the school, which is under the National Board of Education. The Protestant population is 187. The stipend payable by the Impropriator is £25. The augmentations are £74. Total income, £97, without residence. The Countess of Carnwath is Patron.

1861. Robert Peter Foley is admitted Curate.

R. P. Foley (son of Robert Yarde Foley, esq., of Kinsale, by Susan, dau. of Edward Green, esq., of Youghal) was educated at Kinsale Endowed School, and graduated A.B., T.C.D., on 4th March, 1851. He obtained a first-class divinity testimonium.

He was ordained Deacon, at Dublin, on 6th June, 1852; and Priest, at Cork, on 22nd May, 1853.

In 1852 he was Curate of Donoghmore, and in 1853 of Aghinagh, in Cloyne. On 23rd of April, 1854 he was appointed to the curacy of St. Mary, Shandon, Cork.

He married, in 1855, Amelia, dau. of Captain Bagshot, R.N., and has issue.

END OF FIRST VOLUME.

CPSIA information can be obtained
at www.ICGtesting.com
Printed in the USA
LVHW101648140522
718424LV00010B/100

9 783375 006259